David Gemmell is a full-time w̲ e
previous novels have placed him ̲ ̲ ̲ ̲ ̲ ̲ ̲ ̲ ̲ ̲ ̲ ̲ ̲ ̲ ̲ ̲ ̲ ̲ fantasy
field; now joined by the epic first volume of *Lion of Macedon*, they
are the Drenai novels, the Sipstrassi novels and *Knights of Dark
Renown*.

DRENAI TALES

Waylander
Druss the Legend
Legend
The King Beyond the Gate

David Gemmell

CENTURY
A LEGEND BOOK
LONDON SYDNEY AUCKLAND JOHANNESBURG

First published in Great Britain in 1991 by Legend,
an imprint of Random Century Group
20 Vauxhall Bridge Road
London SW1V 2SA

Century Hutchinson South Africa (Pty) Ltd
PO Box 337, Bergvlei 2012
South Africa

Random Century Australia Pty Ltd
20 Alfred St, Milsons Point, Sydney, NSW 2061
Australia

Random Century New Zealand Ltd
PO Box 40–086, Glenfield, Auckland 10
New Zealand

The catalogue data for this book is available from the
British Library

ISBN 0 7126 4629 9

Phototypeset by Input Typesetting Ltd, London
Printed and bound in Great Britain by
Mackays of Chatham PLC, Chatham, Kent

Contents

Introduction

In July of 1977, on a Thursday, the first of the Drenai tales was born from fear. It surfaced from the uncharted oceans of the subconscious fully formed, constructed around the giant frame of an axeman named Druss.

The day is an easy one to remember. A specialist had told me I might have cancer. My symptoms suggested it as a strong possibility and the doctors had ruled out infection. The odds, said the specialist, were that I had an 'internal wart' or a tumour.

'How do you define wart?' I asked him.

He seemed uncomfortable. 'Well,' he said, softly, 'it's a kind of growth.'

'A tumour?'

'I don't want you to be unduly worried, Mr Gemmell . . .'

I walked from the hospital in a state of shock. Cancer? I was twenty-nine years old and enjoying a career in provincial journalism in the seaside town of Hastings. Life was good. And now it might be over.

Not a day you're likely to forget.

Back home, my wife Val was very supportive. There were two weeks to wait for the test results and, since I was on sick leave, she suggested I did something to take my mind off my problems.

I took out an old Olympia portable typewriter and placed it on the kitchen table.

And Druss the Legend came to life. With him came a fortress, and a small army – the Drenai army. And with them a history, a land, a world peopled by heroes. Not the heroes of fantasy, mightily muscled and invulnerable, but ordinary heroes, men without special skills or talents. They were not, in the main, magnificent swordsmen or lancers, yet, in their ill-fitting helms and breastplates, they took their places on the walls of Dros Delnoch to defy the mightiest army the world had ever seen.

I fell in love with the Drenai. For two solid weeks I wrote from 7 a.m. to dusk. At the end I had a fast-paced action novel of 50,000 words – and the cancer tests were negative.

Three years later, still a journalist in Hastings, I showed the manuscript to Stella Graham, a friend and colleague on the *Hastings Observer*. She advised me to rework it, building the story and extending it.

By the summer of 1982 *Legend* was completed, and bought by Century.

It is – and will always remain – my favourite book. The fears of the defenders were my fears, their hopes my hopes.

Soon after its publication in April 1984 the fan letters began. When is the next Drenai tale? Will there be a new Druss story? What happened next?

In 1985 Century published the sequel, *The King Beyond the Gate*. The story had moved on a hundred years or so and the Drenai were suffering under the rule of a mad emperor. The book increased interest in the Drenai and *Legend* was reprinted. It has remained in print ever since.

By 1986 the third of the Drenai stories was ready. *Waylander* pre-dated the story of *Legend* by more than a century and completed the first Drenai trilogy. It dealt with the quest of a lone warrior, Waylander the Slayer, and his journey to redemption in a war-torn land.

By now letters from readers were coming in from all over the world – New Zealand, Australia, the United States, Germany, Africa. The writers were enthusiastic, but the requests remained much the same: give us more.

There will be – God willing – more Drenai novels, but this omnibus edition contains an all-new 15,000-word story, *Druss the Legend*, and brings together the first three books of the Drenai saga for the first time under one cover.

No author can tell you where his stories come from, or how his characters are formed. All I can say is that the books of the Drenai were not cynically written, not attempts to become rich and famous. They were – and are – works of the heart.

The philosophy is not complicated. It is based around the simple premise that evil thrives when good men do nothing.

The Drenai world has its compromisers and its cowards. But they do not take centre stage. That is reserved for the heroes, the men and women who stand their ground, whatever the odds.

Welcome to that world.

David A. Gemmell
Hastings 1990

DRENAI TALES

WAYLANDER

This book is dedicated with love to Denis and Audrey Ballard, my parents-in-law, for the friendship of two decades.

And to their daughter Valerie, who changed my world on December 22 1965.

Acknowledgements

My thanks go to my agent Leslie Flood, whose support carried me through the lean years; my local editor, Ross Lempriere, without whom Waylander would not have stalked the dark woods; Stella Graham, the finest of proof-readers, and Liza Reeves, Jean Maund, Shane Jarvis, Jonathan Poore, Stewart Dunn, Julia Laidlaw and Tom Taylor.

Special thanks to Robert Breare for the fun of it all, and for holding the fortress against the odds.

Prologue

The monster watched from the shadows as the armed men, torches aloft, entered the darkness of the mountain. He backed away as they advanced, keeping his huge bulk from the glare.

The men made their way to a rough-hewn chamber and placed the torches in rusty iron brackets on the granite walls.

At the centre of the twenty-strong group was a figure in armour of bronze, which caught the torchlight and seemed to blaze like fashioned flames. He removed his winged helm and two retainers erected a wooden skeleton frame. The warrior placed the helm atop the frame and unbuckled his breastplate. He was past middle age, but still strong – his hair thinning, his eyes squinting in the flickering light. He passed the armoured breastplate to a retainer who laid it on the frame, rebuckling the straps.

'Are you sure of this plan, my lord?' asked an elderly figure, slender and blue-robed.

'As sure as I am of anything, Derian. The dream has been with me now for a year and I believe in it.'

'But the Armour means so much to the Drenai.'

'That is why it is here.'

'Could you not – even now – reconsider? Niallad is a young man and he could wait at least two more years. You are still strong, my lord.'

'My eyes are failing, Derian. Soon I shall be blind. You think that a good trait in a King renowned for his skill in war?'

'I do not wish to lose you, my lord,' said Derian. 'It may be that I am speaking out of turn, but your son . . .'

'I know of his weaknesses,' snapped the King, 'as I know his future. We are facing the end of all we have fought for. Not now . . . not in five years. But soon will come the days of blood and then the Drenai must have some hope. This Armour is that hope.'

'But, my lord, it is not magical. *You* were magical. This is merely metal which you chose to wear. It could have been silver, or gold, or leather. It is Orien the King who has built the Drenai. And now you will leave us.'

The King, dressed now in a brown tunic of doeskin, placed his hands on the statesman's shoulders.

'I have been much troubled these past few years, but always I have been guided by your good counsel. I trust you, Derian, and I know you will look to Niallad and guide him where you can. But in the days of blood he will be beyond your advice. My vision is black indeed: I see a terrible army falling upon the Drenai people; I see our forces sundered and in hiding – and I see this Armour shining like a torch, drawing men to it, giving them faith.'

5

'And do you see victory, my lord?'

'I see victory for some. Death for others.'

'But what if your vision is not true? What if it is merely a deceit fashioned by the Spirit of Chaos?'

'Look to the Armour, Derian,' said Orien, leading him forward.

It glinted in the torchlight still, but now had gained an ethereal quality which puzzled the eye. 'Reach out and touch it,' ordered the King. When Derian did so, his hand passed through the image and he recoiled as if stung.

'What have you done?'

'I have done nothing, but it is the first promise of the dream. Only the Chosen One can claim the Armour.'

'There may be some who can undo the spell and steal the Armour?'

'Indeed there may, Derian. But look beyond the torchlight.'

The statesman turned to see scores of eyes blinking at him from the darkness. He stepped back. 'Gods! What are they?'

'Once they were human, it is said. But the tribes who live in this area talk of a stream that runs black in the summer. Water from this stream is all there is, but when drunk by pregnant women it becomes a rare poison which deforms the child in the womb. The Nadir leave the babes on the mountain to die . . . obviously not all have done so.'

Derian tugged a torch from its bracket and advanced on the doorway, but the King stopped him.

'Don't look, my friend, it would haunt you to your dying day. But be assured they are ferocious in the extreme. It would need a great force to come here, and if any but the Chosen One attempts to remove the Armour he will be torn to pieces by the beasts who dwell in the darkness.'

'And what will you do now, my lord?'

'I will say farewell.'

'Where will you go?'

'Where no one will know me as a king.'

There were tears in Derian's eyes as he dropped to his knees before Orien, but the King pulled him to his feet.

'Put aside rank, old friend. Let us part as comrades.'

The two men embraced.

1

They had begun to torture the priest when the stranger stepped from the shadows of the trees.

'You stole my horse,' he said quietly. The five men spun round. Beyond them the young priest sagged against the ropes which held him, raising his head to squint through swollen eyes at the newcomer. The man was tall and broad-shouldered and a black leather cloak was drawn about him.

'Where is my horse?' he asked.

'Who is to say? A horse is a horse and the owner is the man who rides him,' answered Dectas. When the stranger first spoke Dectas had felt the thrill of fear course through him, expecting to find several men armed and ready. But now, as he scanned the trees in the gathering dusk, he knew the man was alone. Alone and mad. The priest had proved but sorry sport, gritting his teeth against the pain and offering neither curse nor plea. But this one would sing his song of pain long into the night.

'Fetch the horse,' said the man, a note of boredom in his deep voice.

'Take him!' ordered Dectas and swords sang into the air as the five men attacked. Swiftly the newcomer swept his cloak over one shoulder and lifted his right arm. A black bolt tore into the chest of the nearest man, a second entered the belly of a burly warrior with upraised sword. The stranger dropped the small double crossbow and lightly leapt back. One of his attackers was dead and a second knelt clutching the bolt in his belly.

The newcomer loosened the thong which held his cloak, allowing it to fall to the ground behind him. From twin sheaths he produced two black-bladed knives.

'Fetch the horse!' he ordered.

The remaining two hesitated, glancing to Dectas for guidance. Black blades hissed through the air and both men dropped without a sound.

Dectas was alone.

'You can have the horse,' he said, biting his lip and backing towards the trees. The man shook his head.

'Too late,' he answered softly.

Dectas turned and sprinted for the trees, but a sharp blow in the back caused him to lose balance and his face ploughed the soft earth. Pushing his hands beneath him, he struggled to rise. Had the newcomer thrown a rock, he wondered? Weakness flowed through him and he slumped to the ground . . . the earth was soft as a feather-bed and sweet-smelling like lavender. His leg twitched.

The newcomer recovered his cloak and brushed the dirt from its folds before fastening the thongs at the shoulder. Then he recovered his three knives, wiping them clean on the clothes of the dead. Lastly he collected his bolts, despatching the wounded man with a swift knife-cut across the throat. He picked up his crossbow and checked the mechanism for dirt before clipping it to his broad black belt. Without a backward glance he strode to the horses.

'Wait!' called the priest. 'Release me. *Please!*'

The man turned. 'Why?' he asked.

The question was so casually put that the priest found himself momentarily unable to phrase an answer.

'I will die if you leave me here,' he said, at last.

'Not good enough,' said the man, shrugging. He walked to the horses, finding that his own mount and saddlebags were as he had left them. Satisfied, he untied his horse and walked back to the clearing.

For several moments he stared at the priest, then he cursed softly and cut him free. The man sagged forward into his arms. He had been badly beaten and his chest had been repeatedly cut; the flesh hung in narrow strips and his blue robes were stained with blood. The warrior rolled the priest to his back, ripping open the robes, then walked to his horse and returned with a leather canteen. Twisting the cap he poured water on the wounds. The priest writhed but made no sound. Expertly the warrior smoothed the strips of skin back into place.

'Lie still for a moment,' he ordered. Taking needle and thread from a small saddlebag, he neatly stitched the flaps. 'I need a fire,' he said. 'I can't see a damned thing!'

The fire once lit, the priest watched as the warrior went about his work. The man's eyes were narrowed in concentration, but the priest noted that they were extraordinarily dark, deep sable-brown with flashing gold flecks. The warrior was unshaven, and the beard around his chin was speckled with grey.

Then the priest slept . . .

When he awoke, he groaned as the pain from his beating roared back at him like a snarling dog. He sat up, wincing as the stitches in his chest pulled tight. His robes were gone and beside him lay clothes obviously taken from the dead men, for brown blood stained the jerkin which lay beside them.

The warrior was packing his saddlebags and tying his blanket to his saddle.

'Where are my robes?' demanded the priest.

'I burned them.'

'How dare you! Those were sacred garments.'

'They were merely blue cotton. And you can get more in any town or village.' The warrior returned to the priest and squatted beside him. 'I spent two hours patching your soft body, priest. It would please me if you allowed it to live for a few days before hurling yourself on the fires of martyrdom. All across the country your brethren are burning, or hanged, or dismembered. And all because they don't have the courage to remove those damned robes.'

'We will not hide,' said the priest defiantly.

'Then you will die.'

'Is that so terrible?'

'I don't know, priest, you tell me. You were close to it last evening.'

'But you came.'

'Looking for my horse. Don't read too much into it.'

'And a horse is worth more than a man in today's market?'

'It always was, priest.'

'Not to me.'

'So if I had been tied to the tree, you would have rescued me?'

'I would have tried.'

'And we would both have been dead. As it is, you are alive and, more importantly, I have my horse.'

'I will find more robes.'

'I don't doubt that you will. And now I must go. If you wish to ride with me, you are welcome.'

'I don't think that I do.'

The man shrugged and rose. 'In that case, farewell.'

'Wait!' said the priest, forcing himself to his feet. 'I did not wish to sound ungrateful and I thank you most sincerely for your help. It is just that were I to be with you, it would put you in danger.'

'That's very thoughtful of you,' answered the man. 'As you wish, then.'

He walked to his horse, tightened the saddle cinch and climbed into the saddle, sweeping out his cloak behind him.

'I am Dardalion,' called the priest.

The warrior leaned forward on the pommel of his saddle.

'And I am Waylander,' he said. The priest jerked as if struck. 'I see you have heard of me.'

'I have heard nothing that is good,' replied Dardalion.

'Then you have heard only what is true. Farewell.'

'Wait! I will travel with you.'

Waylander drew back on the reins. 'What about the danger?' he asked.

'Only the Vagrian conquerors want me dead, but at least I have some friends – which is more than can be said for Waylander the Slayer. Half the world would pay to spit on your grave.'

'It is always comforting to be appreciated,' said Waylander. 'Now, Dardalion – if you are coming, put on those clothes and then we must be away.'

Dardalion knelt by the clothes and reached for a woollen shirt, but as his fingers touched it he recoiled and the colour drained from his face.

Waylander slid from his saddle and approached the priest. 'Do your wounds trouble you?' he asked.

Dardalion shook his head, and when he looked up Waylander was surprised to see tears in his eyes. It shocked the warrior, for he had watched this man suffer torture without showing pain. Now he wept like a child, yet there was nothing to torment him.

Dardalion took a shuddering breath. 'I cannot wear these clothes.'

'There are no lice, and I have scraped away most of the blood.'

'They carry memories, Waylander . . . horrible memories . . . rape, murder, foulness indescribable. I am sullied even by touching them and I cannot wear them.'

'You are a mystic, then?'

9

'Yes. A mystic.' Dardalion sat back upon the blanket, shivering in the morning sunshine. Waylander scratched his chin and returned to his horse, where he removed a spare shirt, leggings and a pair of moccasins from his saddlebag.

'These are clean, priest. But the memories they carry may be no less painful for you,' he said, tossing the clothes before Dardalion. Hesitantly the young priest reached for the woollen shirt. As he touched the garment he felt no evil, only a wave of emotional pain that transcended anguish. He closed his eyes and calmed his mind, then he looked up and smiled.

'Thank you, Waylander. These I can wear.'

Their eyes met and the warrior smiled wryly. 'Now you know all my secrets, I suppose?'

'No. Only your pain.'

'Pain is relative,' said Waylander.

Throughout the morning they rode through hills and valleys torn by the horns of war. To the east pillars of smoke spiralled to join the clouds. Cities were burning, souls departing to the Void. Around them in the woods and fields were scattered corpses, many now stripped of their armour and weapons, while overhead crows banked in black-winged hordes, their greedy eyes scanning the now fertile earth below. The harvest of death was ripening.

Burnt-out villages met the riders' eyes in every vale and Dardalion's face took on a haunted look. Waylander ignored the evidence of war but he rode warily, constantly stopping to study the back-trails and scanning the distant hills to the south.

'Are you being followed?' asked Dardalion.

'Always,' answered the warrior grimly.

Dardalion had last ridden a horse five years before when he left his father's cliff-top villa for the five-mile ride to the temple at Sardia. Now, with the pain of his wounds increasing and his legs chafing against the mare's flanks, he fought against the rising agony. Forcing his mind to concentrate, Dardalion focused his gaze on the warrior riding ahead; noting the easy way he sat his saddle and the fact that he held the reins with his left hand, his right never straying far from the broad black belt hung with weapons of death. For a while, as the road widened, they rode side by side and the priest studied the warrior's face. It was strong-boned and even handsome after a fashion, but the mouth was a grim line and the eyes hard and piercing. Beneath his cloak the warrior wore a chain-mail shoulder-guard over a leather vest which bore many gashes and dents and carefully repaired tears.

'You have lived long in the ways of war?' asked Dardalion.

'Too long,' answered Waylander, stopping once more to study the trail.

'You mentioned the deaths of the priests and you said they died because they lacked the courage to remove their robes. What did you mean?'

'Was it not obvious?'

'It would seem to be the highest courage to die for one's beliefs,' said Dardalion.

Waylander laughed. 'Courage? It takes no courage to die. But living takes nerve.'

'You are a strange man. Do you not fear death?'

'I fear everything, priest – everything that walks, crawls or flies. But save your talk for the camp-fire. I need to think.' Touching his booted heels to his horse's flanks, he moved ahead into a small wood where, finding a clearing in a secluded hollow by a gently flowing stream, he dismounted and loosened the saddle cinch. The horse was anxious to drink, but Waylander walked him round slowly, allowing him to cool after the long ride before taking him to the stream. Then he removed the saddle and fed the beast with oats and grain from a sack tied to the pommel. With the horses tethered Waylander set a small fire by a ring of boulders and spread his blanket beside it. Following a meal of cold meat – which Dardalion refused – and some dried apples, Waylander looked to his weapons. Three knives hung from his belt and these he sharpened with a small whetstone. The half-sized double crossbow he dismantled and cleaned.

'An interesting weapon,' observed Dardalion.

'Yes, made for me in Ventria. It can be very useful; it looses two bolts and is deadly up to twenty feet.'

'Then you need to be close to your victim.'

Waylander's sombre eyes locked on to Dardalion's gaze. 'Do not seek to judge me, priest.'

'It was merely an observation. How did you come to lose your horse?'

'I was with a woman.'

'I see.'

Waylander grinned. 'Gods, it always looks ridiculous when a young man assumes a pompous expression! Have you never had a woman?'

'No. Nor have I eaten meat these last five years. Nor tasted spirits.'

'A dull life but a happy one,' observed the warrior.

'Neither has my life been dull. There is more to living than sating bodily appetites.'

'Of that I am sure. Still, it does no harm to sate them now and again.'

Dardalion said nothing. What purpose would it serve to explain to a warrior the harmony of a life spent building the strength of the spirit? The joys of soaring high upon the solar breezes weightless and free, journeying to distant suns and seeing the birth of new stars? Or the effortless leaps through the misty corridors of time?

'What are you thinking?' asked Waylander.

'I was wondering why you burned my robes,' said Dardalion, suddenly aware that the question had been nagging at him throughout the long day.

'I did it on a whim, there is nothing more to it. I have been long without company and I yearned for it.'

Dardalion nodded and added two sticks to the fire.

'Is that all?' asked the warrior. 'No more questions?'

'Are you disappointed?'

'I suppose that I am,' admitted Waylander. 'I wonder why?'

'Shall I tell you?'

11

'No, I like mysteries. What will you do now?'

'I shall find others of my order and return to my duties.'

'In other words you will die.'

'Perhaps.'

'It makes no sense to me,' said Waylander, 'but then life itself makes no sense. So it becomes reasonable.'

'Did life ever make sense to you, Waylander?'

'Yes. A long time ago before I learned about eagles.'

'I do not understand you.'

'That pleases me,' said the warrior, pillowing his head on his saddle and closing his eyes.

'Please explain,' urged Dardalion. Waylander rolled to his back and opened his eyes, staring out beyond the stars.

'Once I loved life and the sun was a golden joy. But joy is sometimes short-lived, priest. And when it dies a man will seek inside himself and ask: Why? Why is hate so much stronger than love? Why do the wicked reap such rich rewards? Why does strength and speed count for more than morality and kindness? And then the man realises . . . there are no answers. None. And for the sake of his sanity the man must change perceptions. Once I was a lamb, playing in a green field. Then the wolves came. Now I am an eagle and I fly in a different universe.'

'And now you kill the lambs,' whispered Dardalion.

Waylander chuckled and turned over.

'No, priest. No one pays for lambs.'

2

The mercenaries rode off, leaving the dead behind them. Seventeen bodies littered the roadside; eight men, four women and five children. The men and the children had died swiftly. Of the five carts which the refugees had been hauling, four were burning fiercely and the fifth smouldered quietly. As the killers crested the hills to the south a young red-haired woman pushed herself clear of the screen of bushes by the road and led three children to the smouldering cart.

'Put out the fire, Culas,' she told the oldest boy. He stood staring at the corpses, his wide blue eyes blank with shock and terror. 'The fire, Culas. Help the others put out the fire.' But he saw the body of Sheera and groaned.

'Grandmother . . .' muttered Culas, stepping forward on shaking legs. Then the young woman ran to him, taking him in her arms and burying his head against her shoulder.

'She is dead and she can feel no pain. Come with me and put out the fire.' She led him to the cart and handed him a blanket. The two younger children – twin girls of seven – stood hand in hand, their backs turned to the dead.

'Come now, children. Help your brother. And then we'll be going.'

'Where can we go, Danyal?' asked Krylla.

'North. The general Egel is in the north, they say, with a great army. We'll go there.'

'I don't like soldiers,' said Miriel.

'Help your brother. Quickly, now!'

Danyal turned away from them, shielding them from her tears. Vile, vile world! Three months back, when the war had begun, word had reached the village that the Hounds of Chaos were marching on Drenan. The men had laughed at the news, confident of speedy victory.

Not so the women, who instinctively knew that any army revelling in the title Hounds of Chaos would be bitter foes. But how bitter few had realised. Subjugation Danyal could understand – what woman could not? But the Hounds brought more than this; they brought wholesale death and terror, torture, mutilation and horror beyond belief.

Source priests were hunted down and slain, their order outlawed by the new masters. And yet the Source priests offered no resistance to any government, preaching only peace, harmony and respect for authority. What threat did they pose?

Farming communities were burnt out and destroyed. So who would gather the crops in the Fall?

Rape, pillage and murder without end. It was incomprehensibly savage and beyond Danyal's ability to understand. Three times now she had been raped. Once by six soldiers – that they had not killed her was testimony to her skills as an actress, for she had feigned enjoyment and on each occasion they had let her leave, bruised and humiliated but always smiling. Some instinct had told her that today would be different and when the riders first appeared she had gathered the children and fled to the bushes. The riders were not seeking rape, only plunder and wanton destruction.

Twenty armed men who stopped to butcher a group of refugees.

'The fire is out, Danyal,' called the boy Culas. Danyal climbed into the cart, sorting out blankets and provisions left by the raiders as being too humble for booty. With lengths of hide she tied three blankets into rucksacks for the children, then gathered up leather canteens of water which she hung over her shoulder.

'We must go,' she said, and led the trio off towards the north.

They had not moved far when the sound of horses' hooves came drumming to their ears and Danyal panicked, for they were on open ground. The two girls began to cry, but young Culas produced a long-bladed dagger from a sheath hidden in his blanket roll.

'Give me that!' yelled Danyal, snatching the blade and hurling it far away from the road while Culas watched in horror. 'It will avail us nothing. Listen to me. Whatever they do to me, you just sit quietly. You understand? Do not shout or scream. You promise?'

Two riders rounded the bend in the road. The first was a dark-haired warrior of a type she was coming to know too well; his face was hard, his eyes harder. The second was a surprise, for he was slender and ascetic, fine-boned and seemingly gentle of countenance. Danyal tossed her long red hair over her shoulder and smoothed the folds of her green tunic as they approached, forcing a smile of welcome to her lips.

'You were with the refugees?' asked the warrior.

'No. We just passed that way.'

The young one with the gentle face stepped carefully from the saddle, wincing as if in pain. He approached Danyal and held out his hands.

'You need not lie to us, sister, we are not of that ilk. I am sorry for your pain.'

'You are a priest?'

'Yes.' He turned to the children. 'Come to me, come to Dardalion,' he said, kneeling and opening his arms. Amazingly they responded, the little girls first. His slender arms touched all three. 'You are safe for a little while,' he said. 'I bring you no more than that.'

'They killed grandmother,' said the boy.

'I know, Culas. But you and Krylla and Miriel are still alive. You have run a long way. And now we will help you. We will take you to Gan Egel in the north.'

His voice was soft and persuasive, the sentences short, simple and easily understood. Danyal stood by, transfixed at the power he exerted over them. And she did not doubt him, but her eyes were drawn to the dark-haired warrior who still sat his mount.

'You are not a priest,' she said.

'No. And you are not a whore.'

'How would you know?'

'I spend my life around whores,' he answered. Lifting his leg over the pommel of his saddle he slid to the ground and approached her. He smelt of stale sweat and horseflesh and close up he was as terrifying as any of the raiders she had known. Yet strangely she viewed the terror from a distance as if she were watching a play, knowing that the villain is terrible but comforted by the thought that he cannot leave the stage. The power in him encompassed her without threat.

'You hid in the bushes,' he said. 'Wise. Very wise.'

'You were watching?'

'No. I read the tracks. We hid from the same raiders an hour back. Mercenaries – not true Hounds.'

'*True* Hounds? What more do they need to do to serve their apprenticeship?'

'They were sloppy – they left you alive. You would not escape the Hounds so easily.'

'How is it,' asked Danyal, 'that a man like you travels with a priest of the Source?'

'A man like me? How swiftly you judge, woman,' he answered equably. 'Perhaps I should have shaved.'

She turned from him as Dardalion approached.

'We must find a place to camp,' said the priest. 'The children need sleep.'

'It is only three hours after noon,' said Waylander.

'They need a special kind of sleep,' said Dardalion. 'Trust me. Can you find a place?'

'Walk with me aways,' said the warrior, moving some thirty feet down the trail. Dardalion joined him. 'What is the matter with you? We cannot saddle ourselves with them. We have two horses and the Hounds are everywhere. And where they are not, there are mercenaries.'

'I cannot leave them. But you are right – you go.'

'What have you done to me, priest?' snapped the warrior.

'I? Nothing.'

'Have you put a spell on me? Answer me!'

'I know no spells. You are free to do as you please, obey whatever whims you care to.'

'I don't like children. And I don't like women I can't pay for.'

'We must find a resting place where I can ease their torment. Will you do that before you go?'

'Go? Where should I go?'

'I thought you wanted to leave, to be free of us.'

'I cannot be free. Gods, if I thought you had put a spell on me I would kill you. I swear it!'

'But I have not,' said Dardalion. 'Nor would I if I could.'

Muttering dark curses under his breath, Waylander walked back to Danyal and the children. As he approached the girls clutched Danyal's skirt, their eyes wide with fear.

He waited by his horse until Dardalion was with the children. 'Anyone want to ride with me?' he asked. There was no answer and he chuckled, 'I thought not. Follow me into the trees yonder. I will find a place.'

Later, as Dardalion sat with the children telling them wondrous tales of elder magic, his voice softly hypnotic, Waylander lay by the fire watching the woman.

'You want me?' she asked suddenly, breaking his concentration.

'How much?' he asked.

'For you, nothing.'

'Then I don't want you. Your eyes don't lie as well as your mouth.'

'What does that mean?'

'It means you loathe me. I don't mind that; I've slept with women aplenty who've loathed me.'

'I don't doubt it.'

'Honesty at last?'

'I don't want any harm to come to the children.'

'You think I would harm them?'

'If you could.'

'You misjudge me, woman.'

'And you underestimate my intelligence. Did you not seek to stop the priest from aiding us? Well?'

'Yes, but . . .'

'There are no buts. Without aid our chance of survival is next to nothing. You don't call that harm?'

'Woman, you have a tongue like a whip. I owe you nothing and you have no right to criticise me.'

'I don't criticise you. That would suggest I cared enough to improve you. I despise you and all your loathsome brethren. Leave me alone, damn you!'

Dardalion sat with the children until the last was asleep, then he placed his hand on each brow in turn and whispered the Prayer of Peace. The two girls lay with arms entwined under a single blanket, while Culas was stretched out beside them with his head pillowed on his arm. The priest concluded his prayer and sat back exhausted. Somehow it was hard to concentrate while wearing Waylander's clothes. The blurred images of pain and tragedy had softened now, but still they kept Dardalion from the uppermost pathways of the Road to the Source.

A distant scream pulled him to the present. Somewhere out in the darkness another soul was suffering.

Dardalion shivered and moved to the fireside where the young woman Danyal was sitting alone. Waylander was gone.

'I insulted him,' said Danyal as the priest sat opposite her. 'He is so cold. So hard. So fitted to the times.'

'Yes, he is,' agreed Dardalion, 'but he is also the man who can lead us to safety.'

'I know. Do you think he will come back?'

'I think so. Where are you from?'

Danyal shrugged. 'Here and there. I was born in Drenan.'

'A pleasant city with many libraries.'

'Yes.'

'Tell me about your days as an actress,' said Dardalion.

'How did you . . . oh yes, there are no secrets from the Source.'

'Nothing so magical, Danyal. The children told me; they said you once performed the Spirit of Circea before King Niallad.'

'I played the sixth daughter and had three lines,' she said, smiling. 'But it was an experience to remember. They say the King is dead, slain by traitors.'

'So I have heard,' said Dardalion. 'Still, let us not concentrate on such things. The night is clear, the stars are beautiful, the children sleep dreaming sweet dreams. Tomorrow we will worry about death and despair.'

'I cannot stop from thinking about it,' she said. 'Fate is cruel. At any moment raiders may run from the trees and the terror will begin again. You know it is two hundred miles to the Delnoch range where Egel trains his army?'

'I know.'

'Will you fight for us? Or will you stand by and let them kill us?'

'I do not fight, Danyal. But I will stand with you.'

'But your friend will fight?'

'Yes. It is all he knows.'

'He is a killer,' said Danyal, lifting her blanket around her shoulders. 'He is no different from the mercenaries or the Vagrians. And yet I hope he comes back – is that not strange?'

'Try to sleep,' urged Dardalion. 'And I will see that your dreams are untroubled.'

'That would be nice – and of a magic I could warm to.'

She lay by the fire and closed her eyes. Dardalion breathed deeply and entered once more into concentration, summoning the Prayer of Peace and projecting it silently to shroud her body. Her breathing deepened. Dardalion released the chains of his spirit and soared into the night sky, twisting over and over in the bright moonlight, leaving his body hunched by the fire.

Free!

Alone with the Void.

Stopping his upward spiral with an effort, he scanned the earth below for sign of Waylander.

Far to the south-east the burning cities illuminated the night sky in a jagged crimson arc, while to the north and west watch-fires burned, their regular setting identifying them as Vagrian sentry fires. To the south a single blaze twinkled in a small wood and, curious, Dardalion swooped towards it.

Six men slept around the fire while a seventh sat upon a rock spooning mouthfuls of stew from a copper pot. Dardalion hovered above them, an edge of fear seeping into him. He sensed great evil and prepared to depart.

Suddenly the seated man glanced up at him and grinned.

'We will find you, priest,' he whispered.

Dardalion did not move. The man placed the copper pot by his feet

17

and closed his eyes . . . and Dardalion was no longer alone. Hovering beside him was an armed warrior, bearing shield and black sword. The young priest darted for the skies, but the warrior spirit was faster, touching him lightly on the back as he passed. Pain lanced Dardalion and he cried out.

The warrior hovered before him, grinning.

'I will not kill you *yet*, priest. I want Waylander. Give him to me and you can live.'

'Who are you?' whispered Dardalion, fighting for time.

'My name would mean nothing to you. But I am of the Brotherhood and my task is set. Waylander must die.'

'The Brotherhood? You are a priest?'

'Priest? In a way you would never understand, you pious pig! Strength, guile, cunning, terror – these are the things I worship, for they bring power. True power.'

'You serve the Darkness then?' said Dardalion.

'Darkness or Light . . . word tricks of confusion. I serve the Prince of Lies, the Creator of Chaos.'

'Why do you hunt Waylander? He is not a mystic.'

'He killed the wrong man, though doubtless the death was well-deserved. And now it is decreed that *he* must die. Will you deliver him to me?'

'I cannot.'

'Go your way then, worm. Your passivity offends me. I shall kill you tomorrow – just after dark. I will seek out your spirit wherever it hides and I will destroy it.'

'Why? What will you gain?'

'Only pleasure,' answered the warrior. 'But that is enough.'

'Then I will await you.'

'Of course you will. Your kind like to suffer – it makes you holy.'

Waylander was angry, which surprised him, leaving him uneasy and ridiculously resentful. He rode his horse to a wooded hill and dismounted. How can you resent the truth, he asked himself?

And yet it hurt to be bracketed with the likes of mercenaries who raped and plundered the innocent, for despite his awesome reputation as a bringer of death he had never killed a woman or a child. Neither had he ever raped nor humiliated anyone. So why did the woman make him feel so sullied? Why did he now see himself in such dark light?

The priest.

The damned priest!

Waylander had lived the last twenty years in the shadows, but Dardalion was like a lantern illuminating the dark corners of his soul.

He sat down on the grass. The night was cool and clear, the air sweet.

Twenty years. Vanished into the vacuum of memory. Twenty years without anger as Waylander clung like a leech to the ungiving rock of life.

But what now?

18

'You are going to die, you fool,' he said aloud. 'The priest will kill you with his purity.'

Was that it? Was that the spell he feared so much?

For twenty years Waylander had ridden the mountains and plains of the civilised nations, the Steppes and outlands of the Nadir savages and the far deserts of the nomads. In that time he had allowed himself no friends. No one had touched him. Like a mobile fortress, deep-walled and safe, Waylander had ghosted through life as alone as a man could be.

Why had he rescued the priest? The question tormented him. His fortress had crumbled and his defences fallen apart like wet parchment.

Instinct told him to mount up and leave the little group – and he trusted his instincts, for they were honed by the danger his occupation aroused. Mobility and speed had kept him alive; he could strike like a snake and be gone before the dawn.

Waylander the Slayer, a prince among assassins. Only by chance could he ever be captured, for he had no home – only a random list of contacts who held contracts for him in a score of cities. In the deepest darkness he would appear, claim his contracts or his fees and then depart before the dawn. Always hunted and hated, the Slayer moved among shadows, haunting the dark places.

Even now he knew his pursuers were close. Now, more than ever, he needed to vanish into the outlands or across the sea to Ventria and the eastern kingdoms.

'You fool,' he whispered. 'Do you want to die?'

Yet the priest held him with his uncast spell.

'You have clipped the eagle's wings, Dardalion,' he said softly.

There had been a flower-garden at the farm, bright with hyacinths and tulips and ageing daffodils. His son had looked so peaceful lying there and the blood had not seemed out of place among the blooms. The pain tore into him; memories jagged like broken glass. Tanya had been tied to the bed and then gutted like a fish. The two girls . . . babes . . .

Waylander wept for the lost years . . .

He returned to the camp-site in the hour before dawn and found them all sleeping. He shook his head at their stupidity and stirred the fire to life, preparing a meal of hot oats in a copper pan. Dardalion was the first to wake; he smiled a greeting and stretched.

'I am glad you came back,' he said, moving to the fire.

'We will need to find some food,' said Waylander, 'for our supplies are low. I doubt we'll find a village unburned, so it means hunting meat. You may have to forget your principles, priest, if you don't want to collapse from hunger.'

'May I speak with you?' asked Dardalion.

'An odd request. I thought we were speaking?'

Dardalion moved away from the fire and Waylander sighed and removed the copper pot from the heat before joining him.

'Why so downcast? Are you regretting saddling us with the woman and her get?'

'No. I . . . I need to ask a favour of you. I have no right . . .'

19

'Out with it, man. What is wrong with you.'

'Will you see them safely to Egel?'

'I thought that was the plan. Are you all right, Dardalion?'

'Yes . . . No . . . I am going to die, you see.' Dardalion turned away from him and walked up the slope to the crest of the hollow. Waylander followed. Once there Dardalion told him of his spirit meeting with the hunter and the other listened in silence. The ways of mystics were closed to him, but he knew of their powers and doubted not that Dardalion was speaking the literal truth. He was not surprised that the hunters were on his heels. After all, he had killed one of their number.

'So you see,' concluded the priest, 'once I am gone I was hoping you would still guide Danyal and the children to safety.'

'Are you so well trained in defeat, Dardalion?'

'I cannot kill – and that is the only way to stop him.'

'Where was their camp?'

'To the south. But you cannot go there – there are seven of them.'

'But only one, you think, with the Power?'

'As far as I could tell; he said he would kill me just after dark. Please don't go, Waylander. I do not wish to be the cause of anyone's death.'

'These men are hunting me, priest, and I don't have many choices. If I promise to stay with the woman, then they will find me anyway. Better that I find them and fight on my terms. Today you must stay here. Wait for me. If I do not return by morning, set off for the north.'

Waylander gathered his saddlebags and gear and rode away to the south just as the dawn was breaking. Swinging in the saddle he called out, 'And kill the fire – the smoke can be seen for miles. Don't light it again until dusk.'

Dardalion stared gloomily after him.

'Where is he going?' asked Danyal, coming to stand beside the priest.

'He is going to save my life,' said Dardalion, and once more he told the story of his spirit travels. The woman seemed to understand and he saw the pity in her eyes. He realised in that moment that he was engaged in confession and knew that he had compromised himself badly. In telling Waylander he had forced the man to fight for him.

'Don't blame yourself,' said Danyal.

'I should have said nothing.'

'Would that not have doomed us all? He had to know they were hunting him.'

'I told him so that he would save me.'

'I don't doubt it. But he had to know. You had to tell him.'

'Yes. But there was only selfishness in my mind.'

'You are a man, Dardalion, as well as a priest. You are too hard on yourself. How old are you?'

'Twenty-five. And you?'

'Twenty. How long have you been a priest?'

'Five years. I was trained as an architect by my father, but my heart was never in it. Always I wanted to serve the Source. And as a child I would often have visions. My parents were embarrassed by them.' Dardalion grinned suddenly and shook his head. 'My father was convinced I was possessed and when I was eight he took me to the Source temple at Sardia to have me exorcised. He was furious when they told him I was merely gifted! From then on I attended the temple school. I should have become an acolyte at fifteen, but father insisted I stay at home and learn about business. By the time I had talked him round, I was twenty.'

'Is your father still alive?'

'I don't know. The Vagrians burned Sardia and murdered the priests. I assume they did the same with neighbouring townsfolk.'

'How did you escape?'

'I was not there for the horror; the Abbot sent me to Skoda with messages for the Mountain Monastery, but when I arrived that also was burning. I was on my way back when I was captured, then Waylander rescued me.'

'He does not seem like a man who would bother to rescue anyone.'

Dardalion chuckled. 'Well, no. He was actually recovering his horse which the mercenaries had stolen and I was, somewhat ignominiously, part of the package.'

Dardalion laughed once more, then took Danyal by the hand. 'My thanks to you, sister.'

'For what?'

'For taking the time to lead me away from the paths of self-pity. I'm sorry I burdened you.'

'It was no burden. You are a kind man and you are helping us.'

'You are very wise and I am glad we met,' said Dardalion, kissing her hand. 'Come, let us wake the children.'

Throughout the day Dardalion and Danyal played with the children in the woods. The priest told them stories while Danyal led them on a treasure hunt, collecting flowers and threading garlands. The sun shone for most of the morning, but the sky darkened in mid-afternoon and rain drove the group back to the camp-site to shelter beneath a spreading pine. Here they ate the last of the bread and some dried fruit left by Waylander.

'It's getting dark,' said Danyal. 'Do you think it's safe to light the fire?'

Dardalion did not reply. His eyes were fixed on the seven men advancing through the trees, swords in hand.

3

Wearily Dardalion pushed himself to his feet. The stitches pulled tight against the skin of his chest and the bruises around his ribs made him wince. Even were he a warrior, he could not have stood alone against even one of the men walking slowly towards him.

Leading them was the man who had filled him with fear the night before, smiling as he approached. Behind him, advancing in a half-circle, were six soldiers with their long blue cloaks fastened over black breast-plates. Their helms covered their faces and only their eyes were visible through rectangular slits in the metal.

Behind Dardalion Danyal had turned away from the warriors and put her arms around the children, pulling them in close to her so that, at the very least, they would be spared the terror of the kill.

The priest felt a terrible hopelessness seep into him. Only days before, he had been willing to bear torture – torture and death. But now he could feel the children's fear, and he wished he had a sword or bow to defend them.

The advancing line stopped and the lead warrior swung away from Dardalion, staring across the hollow. Dardalion looked back.

There in the fading red glow of dusk stood Waylander, his cloak drawn close about him. The sun was setting behind him and the warrior was silhouetted against the blood-red sky – a still figure, yet so powerful that he laid a spell upon the scene. His leather cloak glistened in the dying light and Dardalion's heart leapt at the sight of him. He had seen this drama played out once before and knew that beneath his cloak Waylander carried the murderous crossbow, strung and ready.

But even as hope flared, so it died. For where before there had been five unsuspecting mercenaries, here there were seven warriors in full armour. Trained killers. The Vagrian Hounds of Chaos.

Waylander could not stand against such as these.

In those first frozen moments Dardalion found himself wondering just why the warrior had come back on such a hopeless mission. Waylander had no cause to give his life for any of them – he had no beliefs, no strongly-held convictions.

But there he stood, like a forest statue.

The silence was unnerving, more so for the Vagrians than for Dardalion. The warriors knew that in scant seconds lives would be lost, death would strike in the clearing and blood seep through the soft loam. For they were men of war who walked with death as a constant companion, holding him at bay with skill or with rage, quelling their fears in blood-lust. But here they were caught cold . . . and each felt alone.

The dark priest of the Brotherhood licked his lips, his sword heavy in his hand. He knew that the odds favoured his force, knew with certainty that Waylander would die if he gave the word to attack. But the double-edged knowledge held a second certainty . . . that the moment he spoke, he would die.

Danyal could stand the suspense no longer and, twisting round, she saw Waylander. Her movement caused Miriel to open her eyes and the first thing the child saw were the warriors in their helms.

She screamed.

The spell broke . . .

Waylander's cloak flickered and the dark priest of the Brotherhood pitched backwards with a black bolt through one eye. For several seconds he writhed and then was still.

The six warriors stood their ground, then the man in the centre slowly sheathed his sword and the others followed suit. With infinite care they backed away into the gathering darkness of the trees.

Waylander did not move.

'Fetch the horses,' he said quietly, 'and gather the blankets.'

An hour later they were camped on high ground in a shallow cave; the children were sleeping and Danyal lay awake beside them as Dardalion and the warrior sat together under the stars.

After a while Dardalion came into the cave and stirred the small fire to life. The smoke drifted up through a crack in the roof of the cave, but still their small shelter smelt of burning pine. It was a comforting scent. The priest moved to where Danyal lay and, seeing she was awake, sat beside her.

'Are you well?' he asked.

'I feel strange,' she admitted. 'I was so prepared for death that all fear left me. Yet I am alive. Why did he come back?'

'I do not know. He does not know.'

'Why did they go away?'

Dardalion leaned his back against the cave wall, stretching his legs towards the fire.

'I am not sure. I have given much thought to it and I think perhaps it is the nature of soldiers. They are trained to fight and kill upon a given order – to obey unquestioningly. They do not act as individuals. And when a battle comes it is usually clear-cut: there is a city which must be captured or a force which must be overcome. The order is given, excitement grows – dulling fear – and they attack in a mass, drawing strength from the mob around them.

'But today there was no order and Waylander, in remaining still, gave them no cause to fire their blood.'

'But Waylander could not have known they would run away,' she insisted.

'No. He didn't care.'

'I don't understand.'

'In truth I am not sure that I do. But I sensed it during those moments. He didn't care . . . and they knew it. But they cared, they cared very much. They didn't want to die and they were not charged up to fight.'

'But they could have killed him . . . killed us all.'

'*Could* have, yes. But they didn't – and for that I am thankful. Go to sleep, sister. We have won another night.'

Outside Waylander watched the stars. He was still numbed from the encounter and ran the memories through time and again.

He had found their camp deserted and had followed them, a growing fear eating at him. Dismounting below the woods, he had made his way to the clearing, only to see the Hounds advancing. He had strung his crossbow, and then stopped. To advance was to die and every instinct screamed at him to go back.

Yet he had advanced, throwing aside years of caution, to give away his life for a nonsense.

Why in the name of Hell had they walked away?

No matter how many times he considered it, an answer always eluded him.

A movement to his left jerked him from his reverie and he turned to see one of the the children walking from the cave. She looked neither to right nor left. Waylander went to her and touched her lightly on the arm, but she moved on, unaware of him. Stooping, he lifted her. Her eyes were closed and her head drooped to his shoulder. She was very light in his arms as he walked back to the cave, ready to lay her beside her sister. But then he stopped in the cave mouth and sat with his back against the wall, drawing her close with his cloak about her.

For several hours he stayed quietly, feeling the warmth of her breath against his neck. Twice she woke, then snuggled down once more. As dawn lightened the sky he took her back into the cave and laid her beside her sister.

Then he returned to the cave mouth . . .

Alone.

Danyal's scream snatched Waylander from sleep, his heart pounding. Rolling to his feet with knife in hand he ran into the cave to find the woman kneeling beside Dardalion's still form. Waylander dropped to his knees and lifted the priest's wrist. The man was dead.

'How?' whispered Danyal.

'Damn you, priest!' shouted Waylander. Dardalion's face was white and waxen, his skin cold to the touch. 'He must have had a weak heart,' said Waylander bitterly.

'He was fighting the man,' said Miriel. Waylander turned to the child, who was sitting at the back of the cave holding hands with her sister.

'Fighting?' he asked. 'Who was he fighting?' But Miriel looked away.

'Come along, Miriel,' urged Danyal. 'Who was he fighting?'

'The man with the arrow in his eye,' she said.

Danyal turned to Waylander. 'It was just a dream; it means nothing. What are we to do?'

Waylander did not reply. Throughout the questioning of the child he had held on to Dardalion's wrist and now he felt the weakest of pulses.

'He is not dead,' he whispered, 'Go and talk to the child. Find out about the dream – quickly, now!'

24

For some minutes Danyal sat quietly with the girl, then she returned. 'She says that the man you killed took hold of her and made her cry. Then the priest came and the man shouted at him; he had a sword and was trying to kill the priest. And they were flying – higher than the stars. That is all there is.'

'He feared this man,' said Waylander, 'believing he had demonic powers. If he was right, then maybe death did not stop him. Perhaps even now he is being hunted.'

'Can he survive?'

'How?' snapped Waylander. 'The man won't fight.' Danyal leaned forward, placing her hand on Waylander's arm. The muscles were tensed and quivering. 'Take your hand from me, woman, or I'll cut it off at the wrist. No one touches me!' Danyal jerked back with green eyes ablaze, but she mastered her anger and moved back to the children.

'Damn you all!' hissed Waylander. He took a deep breath, quelling the fury boiling inside him. Danyal and the children sat quietly, watching him intently. Danyal knew what was tormenting him: the priest was in danger and the warrior, for all his deadly skill, was powerless. A battle was taking place in another world and Waylander was a useless bystander.

'How could you be so stupid, Dardalion?' whispered the warrior. 'All life fights to survive. You say the Source made the world? Then he created the tiger and the deer, the eagle and the lamb. You think he made the eagle to eat grass?'

For some minutes he lapsed into silence, remembering the priest as he had knelt naked by the robbers' clothes.

'I cannot wear these, Waylander . . .'

He transferred his grip from the priest's arm to his hand and as their fingers touched, there came an almost imperceptible movement. Waylander's eyes narrowed. As he gripped the priest's hand more firmly, Dardalion's arm jerked spasmodically and his face twisted in pain.

'What is happening to you, priest? Where in Hell's name are you?'

At the name of Hell Dardalion jerked again, and moaned softly.

'Wherever he is, he is suffering,' said Danyal, moving forward to kneel beside the priest.

'It was when our hands touched,' said Waylander. 'Fetch the crossbow, woman – there, by the cave mouth.' Danyal moved to the weapon and carried it to Waylander. 'Put it in his right hand and close his fingers about it.' Danyal opened Dardalion's hand, and curled his fingers around the ebony hilt. The priest screamed; his fingers jerked open and the crossbow clattered to the ground. 'Hold his fingers around it.'

'But it is causing him pain. Why are you doing this?'

'Pain is life, Danyal. We must get him back into his body – you understand? The corpse-spirit cannot touch him there. We must draw him back.'

'But he is a priest, a man of purity.'

'So?'

'You will sully his soul.'

Waylander laughed. 'I may not be a mystic, but I do believe in souls. What you are holding is merely wood and metal. Dardalion will be stung

25

by it, but I do not believe his soul is so fragile that it will kill him. But his enemy will – so you decide!'

'I believe that I hate you,' said Danyal, opening Dardalion's hand and forcing him to grip the ebony handle once more. The priest twisted and screamed. Waylander pulled a knife from his belt and sliced a cut across the flesh of his forearm. Blood oozed and then gushed from the wound. As Waylander held his arm over Dardalion's face, blood spattered to his skin, flowed over his closed eyes and down – coursing over his lips and into his throat.

A last terrible scream ripped from the priest and his eyes snapped open. Then he smiled, and his eyes closed again. A deep shuddering breath swelled his lungs and he slept. Waylander checked his pulse – it was strong and even.

'Sweet Lord of Light!' said Danyal. '*Why?* Why the blood?'

'According to the Source no priest shall taste blood, for it carries the soul,' explained Waylander softly. 'The weapon was not enough, but the blood brought him back.'

'I don't understand you. And I do not wish to,' she said.

'He is alive, woman. What more do you want?'

'From you, nothing.'

Waylander smiled and pushed himself to his feet. Taking a small canvas sack from his saddlebag, he removed a length of linen bandage and clumsily wound it around the shallow cut in his arm.

'Would you mind tying a knot in this?' he asked her.

'I'm afraid not,' she answered. 'It would mean touching you and I do not want my hand cut off at the wrist!'

'I am sorry for that. It should not have been said.'

Without waiting for a reply, Waylander left the cave, tucking the bandage under its own folds as he went.

The day was bright and cool, the mountain breezes sharp with the snow of the Skoda peaks as Waylander walked to the crest of a nearby hill and gazed into the blue distance. The Delnoch mountains were still too far off to be seen by the naked eye.

For the next three or four days the trail would be easy, moving from wood to forest to wood, with only short stretches of open ground. But thereafter the Sentran Plain would lie before them, flat and formless.

To cross that emptiness unobserved would take more luck than a man had any right to ask. Six people and two horses! At the pace they must travel they would be on the Plain for nigh a week – a week without fires or hot food. Waylander scanned the possible trails to the north-east, towards Purdol, the City by the Sea. It was said that a Vagrian fleet had berthed at the harbour mouth, landing an army to besiege the citadel. If that were true – and Waylander thought it likely – then Vagrian outriders would be scouring the countryside for food and supplies. To the north-west was Vagria itself and the citadel of Segril, but from here troops were pouring into the Drenai lands. The Sentran Plain was due north, and beyond it Skultik forest and the mountains said to be the last Drenai stronghold west of Purdol.

But did Egel still hold Skultik?

Could anyone hold together the remnants of a defeated army against the Hounds of Chaos? Waylander doubted it . . . yet beyond the doubts there was a spark of hope. Egel was the most able Drenai general of the age, unspectacular but sound – a stern disciplinarian, unlike the courtiers King Niallad normally placed in charge of his troops. Egel was a northerner, uncultured and at times uncouth, but a man of charisma and strength. Waylander had seen him once during a parade in Drenan and the man had stood out like a boar amongst gazelle.

Now the boar had gone to ground in Skultik.

Waylander hoped he could hold, at least until he delivered the woman and the children.

If he *could* deliver them.

Waylander killed a small deer during the afternoon. Hanging the carcass from a nearby tree, he cut prime sections and then carried the meat back to the cave. It was growing dark when he arrived and the priest still slept. Danyal set the fire while Waylander rigged a rough spit to roast the venison. The children sat close to the fire, watching the drops of fat splash into the flames – their stomachs tight, their eyes greedy.

Lifting the meat from the spit, Waylander laid it to rest on a flat rock to cool; then he sliced sections for the children and lastly Danyal.

'It is a little tough,' complained the woman.

'The deer saw me just as I loosed the shaft,' said Waylander. 'Its muscles were bunched to run.'

'It tastes good all the same,' she admitted.

'Why is Dardalion still asleep?' asked Miriel, smiling at Waylander and tipping her head to one side so that her long fair hair fell across her face.

'He was very tired,' answered the warrior, 'after his tussle with the man you saw.'

'He cut him into little bits,' said the child.

'Yes, I'm sure he did,' said Danyal. 'But children shouldn't make up stories – especially nasty stories. You'll frighten your sister.'

'We saw him,' said Krylla and Miriel nodded agreement. 'When you were sitting with Dardalion, we closed our eyes and watched. He was all silver and he had a shining sword – he chased the bad man and cut him into little bits. And he was laughing!'

'What can you see when you close your eyes?' asked Waylander.

'Where?' asked Miriel.

'Outside the cave,' said the warrior softly.

Miriel closed her eyes. 'There's nothing out there,' she said, her eyes still closed.

'Go further down the trail, near the big oak. Now what do you see?'

'Nothing. Trees. A little stream. Oh!'

'What is it?' asked Waylander.

'Two wolves. They're jumping by a tree – like they're dancing.'

'Go closer.'

'The wolves will get me,' Miriel protested.

27

'No, they won't – not with me here. They won't see you. Go closer.'

'They are jumping after a poor little deer that's in the tree; he's hanging there.'

'Good. Come back now, and open your eyes.'

Miriel looked up and yawned. 'I'm tired,' she said.

'Yes,' said Waylander softly. 'But tell me first – like a bedtime story – about Dardalion and the other man.'

'You tell him, Krylla. You're better at telling stories.'

'Well,' said Krylla, leaning forward, 'the nasty man with the arrow in his eye caught hold of Miriel and me. He was hurting us. Then Dardalion came and the man let us go. And a big sword appeared in the man's hand. And we ran away, didn't we, Miriel? We went and slept in your lap, Waylander. And we were safe there. But Dardalion was being cut a lot and he was flying very fast. And we couldn't catch up. But we saw him again, when you and Danyal were holding him. He seemed to grow very tall, and silver armour covered him up, and his robes caught fire and burned away. Then he had a sword and he was laughing. The other man's sword was black – and it broke, didn't it, Miriel?'

'Then he fell on his knees and began to weep. And Dardalion cut off his arms and legs and he just disappeared. After that Dardalion laughed even more. Then he disappeared and came home to where his body lives. And we are all right now.'

'Yes, we are all right now,' agreed Waylander. 'I think it is time to sleep now. Are you tired, Culas?' The boy nodded glumly.

'What is wrong, boy?'

'Nothing.'

'Come, tell me.'

'No.'

'He's angry because he cannot fly with us,' said Miriel, giggling.

'No, I'm not,' snapped Culas. 'Anyway, you are making it up.'

'Listen, Culas,' said Waylander, 'I can't fly either and it doesn't worry me. Now let's stop the arguing and sleep. Tomorrow will be a long day.'

With the children huddled together by the far wall, Danyal moved alongside Waylander.

'Were they speaking the truth, do you think?' she asked.

'Yes, for Miriel saw where I hid the deer.'

'Then Dardalion did kill his enemy?'

'It would appear so.'

'It makes me feel uneasy – I don't know why.'

'It was a spirit of evil. What else would you expect a priest to do? Bless it?'

'Why are you always so unpleasant, Waylander?'

'Because I choose to be.'

'In that case, I don't suppose you have many friends.'

'I don't have *any* friends.'

'Does that make you lonely?'

'No. It keeps me alive.'

'And what a life it must be for you, full of fun and laughter!' she mocked. 'I'm surprised you're not a poet.'

'Why so angry?' he asked. 'Why should it affect you?'

'Because you are part of our lives. Because for as long as we live, you will remain in our memories. Speaking for myself, I would have preferred another saviour.'

'Yes, I have seen the arena-plays,' said Waylander. 'The hero has golden hair and a white cloak. Well, I am not a hero, woman – I am a man trapped in the priest's web. You think he has been sullied? Well, so have I. The difference is that he needed my darkness to survive. But his Light will destroy me.'

'Will you two never stop rowing?' asked Dardalion, sitting up and stretching his arms.

Danyal ran to his side. 'How do you feel?'

'Ravenous!' He threw aside the blanket and moved to the fire, casually spearing two strips of venison with the spit. Laying it in place, he added fuel to the dwindling blaze.

Waylander said nothing, but sadness settled on him like a dark cloak.

4

Waylander woke first and made his way from the cave. Stripping off his shirt and leggings, he stepped into the icy steam and lay flat on his back, allowing the water to flow over him. The stream was mere inches deep, running over rounded rocks, but the force of the flow was strong and he felt himself gently sliding down the sloping stream-bed. Rolling over, he splashed his face and beard and stood up before clambering from the water, where he sat on the grass waiting for the dawn breezes to dry his skin.

'You look like a three-day-dead fish,' said Danyal.

'And you're beginning to smell like one,' he responded, grinning. 'Go on, wash yourself!'

For a moment she looked at him closely, then she shrugged and removed the green woollen tunic dress. Waylander leaned back and watched her. Her waist was slim, her hips smooth, her skin . . .

He turned away to watch a red squirrel leaping in the branches nearby, then stood and stretched. Near the stream was a thick screen of bushes, and within it a small clump of lemon balm. Pulling free a handful of the shield-shaped leaves, he carried them back to where Danyal sat.

'Here, crush these in your hand and wipe them on your skin.'

'Thank you,' she said, reaching up.

Suddenly aware of his nakedness, Waylander found his clothes and dressed. He wished he still had a spare shirt, but the priest wore it and he was uncomfortably aware of the dust in his own.

Once dressed, Waylander returned to the cave and looped his chain-mail shoulder-guard in place over his black leather jerkin. Taking his boots, he removed the two spare knives and sharpened them with his whetstone before replacing them carefully in the sheaths stitched inside each boot.

Dardalion watched him, noting the care with which he handled his weapons.

'Could you spare me a knife?' he asked.

'Of course. Heavy or light?'

'Heavy.'

Waylander picked up his belt and pulled clear a dark sheath complete with ebony-handled blade. 'This should suffice. The blade is keen enough to shave with and double-edged.'

Dardalion threaded his narrow belt through the sheath and settled it in place against his right hip.

'Are you left-handed?' asked Waylander.

'No.'

'Then angle it on your left hip. That way, when you pull it clear the blade will face your enemy.'

'Thank you.'

Waylander buckled his own belt in place, then rubbed his chin. 'You worry me, priest,' he said.

'Why?'

'Yesterday you would have walked around a crawling bug. Now you are ready to kill a man. Was your faith so weak?'

'My faith remains, Waylander. But now I see things a little more clearly. You gave me that with your blood.'

'I wonder. Was it a gift – or a theft? I feel I have robbed you of something precious.'

'If you have, then be assured I do not miss it.'

'Time will tell, priest.'

'Call me Dardalion. You know that is my name.'

'Is "priest" no longer good enough for you?'

'Not at all. Would you prefer it if I called you "assassin"?'

'Call me what you like. Nothing you say will affect the way I perceive myself.'

'Have I offended you?' asked Dardalion.

'No.'

'You have not asked me about my duel with the enemy.'

'No, I have not.'

'Is it because you do not care?'

'No, Dardalion. I don't know why, but I *do* care. My reasons are far more simple. I deal in death, my friend – death which is final. You are here, therefore you killed him and he is no longer of interest to me. It disturbs me that you cut away his arms and legs, but I shall get over that, as I shall get over you once you are safely with Egel.'

'I had hoped we could be friends.'

'I have no friends. I wish for none.'

'Was it always so?'

'Always is a long time. I had friends before I became Waylander. But that was another universe, priest.'

'Tell me.'

'I see no reason why I should,' replied Waylander. 'Wake the children. We have a long day before us.'

Waylander strolled from the cave to where he had picketed the horses, then saddled them and rode his own gelding to the spot where he had hung the deer. Taking a canvas bag, he cut several strips from the carcass and packed them away for the evening meal. Then he pulled the remains from the tree to lie on the grass for the wolves.

'Did you have friends, little doe?' he asked, staring at the blank grey eyes.

He turned his horse towards the cave, remembered the days of camaraderie at Dros Purdol. As a young officer he had excelled, though why he had no idea; he had always disliked authority, but had relished the discipline.

He and Gellan had been closer than brothers, always together whether on patrol or whoring. Gellan had been a witty companion and only in the

31

Silver Sword tourney had they ever found themselves as opponents. Gellan always won, but then the man was inhumanly swift. They had parted when Waylander met Tanya – a merchant's daughter from Medrax Ford, a small town to the south of Skeln Pass. Waylander was in love before he knew it and had resigned his commission for life on the farm.

Gellan had been heartbroken. 'Still,' he had said on that last day, 'I expect I won't be long following you. Army life will be dreadfully dull!'

Waylander wondered if Gellan had done so. Was he a farmer somewhere? Or a merchant? Or was he dead in one of the many lost battles fought by the Drenai?

If the latter, Waylander guessed that a neat pile of corpses would surround his body, for his blade moved faster than a serpent's tongue.

'I should have stayed, Gellan,' he said. 'I really should.'

Gellan was hot and tired, sweat sliding down the back of his neck under the chain-mail shoulder-guard and causing his spine to itch unbearably. He removed his black helm and ran his fingers through his hair. There was no breeze and he cursed softly.

Forty miles from Skultik and the relative security of Egel's camp – and the horses were tired, the men weary and dispirited. Gellan raised his right arm with fist clenched, giving the signal to 'Walk Horses'. Behind him the fifty riders dismounted; there was no conversation.

Sarvaj rode his mount alongside Gellan and the two men dismounted together. Gellan hooked his helm over the pommel of his saddle and pulled a linen cloth from his belt. Wiping the sweat from his face, he turned to Sarvaj.

'I don't think we'll find a village standing,' he said. Sarvaj nodded but did not reply. He had served under Gellan for half a year, and knew by now when the officer's comments were rhetorical.

They walked side by side for half an hour, then Gellan signalled for a rest stop and the men sat down beside their horses.

'Morale is low,' said Gellan and Sarvaj nodded. Gellan unclipped his red cloak, laying it over his saddle. Pushing his hands into the small of his back he stretched and groaned. Like most tall men, he found long hours in the saddle irksome and was plagued by continual backache.

'I stayed too long, Sarjav. I should have quit last year. Forty-one is too old for a Legion officer.'

'Dun Esterik is fifty-one,' Sarvaj commented.

Gellan grinned. 'If I had quit, you would have taken over.'

'And what a fine time to do so, with the army crushed and the Legion skulking in the woods. No thank you!'

They had stopped in a small grove of elm and Gellan wandered off to sit alone. Sarvaj watched him go and then removed his helm; his dark brown hair was thinning badly and his scalp shone with sweat. Self-consciously he swept his hair back over the bald patches and replaced the helm. Fifteen years younger than Gellan, yet here he was looking like an old man. Then he grinned at his vanity and pulled the helm clear.

He was a stocky man – ungainly when not in the saddle – and one of the few career soldiers left in the Legion following the savage reductions of the previous autumn, when King Niallad had ordered a new militia programme. Ten thousand soldiers had been dismissed and only Gellan's determination had saved Sarvaj.

Now Niallad was dead and the Drenai all but conquered.

Sarvaj had shed no tears for the King, for the man was a fool . . . worse than a fool!

'Off on his walks again?' said a voice and Sarvaj glanced up. Jonat sat down on the grass and stretched his long bony frame to full length, lying back with his head on his hands.

'He needs to think,' said Sarvaj.

'Yes. He needs to think about how to get us through the Nadir lands. I am sick of Skultik.'

'We are all sick of Skultik, but I don't see that riding north would help. It would merely mean fighting the Nadir tribes instead of the Vagrians.'

'At least we'd have a chance there. Here we have none.' Jonat scratched his thin black beard. 'If they'd damn well listened to us last year, we would not be in this mess.'

'But they didn't,' said Sarvaj wearily.

'Pox-ridden courtiers! In some ways the Hounds did us a favour by butchering the whoresons.'

'Don't say that to Gellan – he lost a lot of friends in Skoda and Drenan.'

'We all lost friends,' snapped Jonat, 'and we'll lose a lot more. How long is Egel going to keep us cooped up in that damned forest?'

'I don't know, Jonat. Gellan doesn't know and I doubt if Egel himself knows.'

'We ought to strike north, through Gulgothir, and make for the eastern ports. I wouldn't mind settling down in Ventria. Always hot, plenty of women. We could hire out as mercenaries.'

'Yes,' said Sarvaj, too weary to argue. He failed to understand why Gellan had promoted Jonat to command of a Quarter – the man was full of bile and bitterness.

But – and this was so galling – he was right. When Niallad's militia plan had first been put forward, the men in the Legion had bitterly opposed it. All the evidence indicated that the Vagrians were preparing for invasion. But Niallad claimed that the Vagrians themselves feared an attack from a strong Drenai army, and that his gesture would promote a lasting peace and a growth in trade.

'They should have roasted the bastard over a hot fire,' said Jonat.

'Who?' asked Sarvaj.

'The King, Gods rot his soul! The word is that he was killed by an assassin. They should have taken him in chains through the empire so that he could see the results of his stupidity.'

'He did what he thought was best,' said Sarvaj. 'He had the best motives.'

'Oh yes,' mocked Jonat. 'The best motives! He wanted to save money. *Our* money! If one good thing has come out of this war, it is that the noble class is gone for good.'

33

'Perhaps. But then Gellan is a nobleman.'

'Yes?'

'You don't hate him, do you?'

'He's no better than the rest.'

'I thought you liked him.'

'I suppose he's not a bad officer. Too soft. But underneath he still looks down on us.'

'I've never noticed it,' said Sarvaj.

'You don't look hard enough,' responded Jonat.

A horseman galloped into the grove and the men lurched to their feet with hands on sword-hilts. It was the scout, Kapra.

Gellan walked from the trees as the man dismounted. 'Anything to the east?' he asked.

'Three gutted villages, sir. A few refugees. I saw a column of Vagrian infantry – maybe two thousand. They made camp near Ostry, by the river.'

'No sign of cavalry?'

'No, sir.'

'Jonat!' called Gellan.

'Yes, sir.'

'The infantry will be expecting supplies. Take two men and scout to the east – when you see the wagons, get back here as fast as you can.'

'Yes, sir.'

'Kapra, get yourself some food and then take a fresh mount and move out with Jonat. We will wait here for you.'

Sarvaj smiled. The difference in Gellan was startling now that the prospect of action loomed – his eyes were bright and alive and his voice curt and authoritative. Gone was the habitual stoop and the casually distant manner.

Egel had sent them out to find supplies to feed his beleaguered force, and so far they had been riding for three days without success. Villages had been wantonly destroyed and food stores taken or burnt. Cattle had been driven off and sheep poisoned in their fields.

'Sarvaj!'

'Sir?'

'Get the horses picketed and separate the men into five groups. There's a hollow past the thicket there and room for three fires – but none to be lit until the north star is clear and bright. You understand?'

'Yes, sir.'

'Four men to stand watch, change every four hours. You pick the places.'

'Yes, sir.'

Gellan smoothed his dark moustache and grinned boyishly.

'Let them be carrying salt beef,' he said. 'Pray for salt beef, Sarvaj!'

'And a small escort. It might be worth praying for a Ten.'

The smile faded from Gellan's face. 'Unlikely. They'll have at least a Quarter, maybe more. And then there will be the cartsmen. Still, cross

34

that river when we reach it. When the men are resting, organise a sabre check; I want no blunted weapons when we ride.'

'Yes, sir. Why don't you get some rest?'

'I'm fine.'

'It wouldn't do any harm,' Sarvaj urged.

'You're fussing round me like an old woman. And don't think I don't appreciate it – but I am all right now, I promise.' Gellan smiled to hide the lie, but it did not fool Sarvaj.

The men were glad of the rest and without Jonat the mood lightened. Sarvaj and Gellan sat apart from the troop, chatting lightly about the past. Careful to avoid bringing up subjects which would remind Gellan of his wife and children, Sarvaj talked mainly of regimental memories.

'Do you mind if I ask you a question?' he said suddenly.

'Why should I?' answered Gellan.

'Why did you promote Jonat?'

'Because he's talented – he just doesn't realise it yet.'

'He doesn't like you.'

'That doesn't matter. Watch him – he'll do well.'

'He brings the men down, lessens morale.'

'I know. Be patient.'

'He's pushing for us to run north – to break out of Skultik.'

'Stop worrying about it, Sarvaj. Trust me.'

I trust you, thought Sarvaj. I trust you to be the finest swordsman in the Legion, to be a caring and careful officer and to be a firm friend. But Jonat? Jonat was a snake and Gellan was too trusting to see it. Given the time, Jonat would start a mutiny which would spread like a prairie fire through the dispirited ranks of Egel's army.

That night, as Gellan lay under his cloak away from the fire, he fell into a deep sleep and the dreams returned. He woke with a start and the tears flowed, though he swallowed the sobs that ached to be loose. As he stood up and wandered away from camp, Sarvaj turned over and opened his eyes.

'Damn!' he whispered.

Towards dawn, Sarvaj arose and checked the sentries. This was the worst time of the night for concentration, and often a man who could stand a shift from dusk until midnight would find it impossible on another night to stay awake from midnight to dawn. Sarvaj had no idea what caused this phenomenon, but he knew what cured it; a man found sleeping on duty was lashed twenty times, and for a second offence the sentence was death. Sarvaj had no wish to see his men hung, so he made a name for himself as a nightwalker.

On this night, as he crept soundlessly through the wood, he found all four men alert and watchful. Pleased, he made his way back to his blankets where he found Gellan waiting for him. The officer looked tired, but his eyes were bright.

'You haven't slept,' said Sarvaj.

'No, I was thinking about the convoy. What we can't steal, we must

35

destroy; the Vagrians must be taught to suffer. I don't understand the way they are conducting this war. If they left the farming villages alone there would always be sufficient supplies, but by raping and killing and burning they are making the land a wilderness. And it will turn on them. Come winter they will be on short rations and then, by all the Gods, we'll hit them.'

'How many wagons do you think there'll be?'

'For a force of two thousand? No fewer than twenty-five.'

'So,' said Sarvaj, 'if we take the convoy without loss we'll have around twenty escort riders, and three days in the open back to Skultik. That's asking for a lot of luck.'

'We are entitled to a little, my friend,' replied Gellan.

'Entitlement means nothing. I've lost at dice ten days in a row!'

'And on the eleventh?'

'I lose again. You know I never win at dice.'

'I know you never pay your debts,' said Gellan. 'You still owe me three silver pieces. Get the men together – Jonat should be back soon.'

But it was mid-morning before Jonat and the others cantered into the clearing. Gellan strode to meet them as Jonat lifted his leg over the pommel and slid to the ground.

'What news?' he asked.

'You were right, sir – there's a convoy three hours to the east. Twenty-seven wagons. But there are fifty mounted guards and two outriding scouts.'

'Were you seen?'

'I do not believe so,' replied Jonat stiffly.

'Tell me of the ground.'

'There's only one spot to take them, but it's close to Ostry and the infantry. However, the trail winds between two wooded hills; there's plenty of cover on both sides and the wagons will move slowly, for the track is muddy and steep.'

'How soon can we be there and in place?'

'Two hours. But that will leave it very tight, sir. We might even arrive as the wagons enter the trees on the far side.'

'That's *too* damned tight,' said Sarvaj, 'especially since they have scouts out.'

The risks were too great, Gellan knew, yet Egel needed supplies desperately. What was worse, there was no time to plan, to think.

'Mount up!' he shouted.

As the troop thundered to the east, Gellan was cursing his shortcomings. What was needed before setting out was a powerful short speech to the men, something to fire their blood. But he had never been good with groups and knew the men felt him to be a cold, distant leader. Now he was uncomfortably aware that he was leading some of them – perhaps all – to their deaths on a harebrained attack best left to reckless, colourful men like Karnak or Dundas. How the men worshipped them – young, dashing and totally fearless, they led their Centuries against the Vagrians time and again, cutting and running, letting the enemy know there was still some fight in the Drenai.

They had little time for veterans like Gellan. Perhaps rightly so, he considered, as the wind tore at his face.

I should have retired, he thought. He had made up his mind to quit this autumn, but there was no quiet retirement for a Drenai officer now.

They reached the wood in under two hours and Gellan called a swift meeting with his under-officers. Two of his best bowmen were dispatched to deal with the advance scouts, and then he split his force to left and right of the track. He himself took command of the right-hand slope, giving Jonat the left, ignoring Sarvaj's disapproving glare.

With the orders given, the men settled down to wait and Gellan bit his lip, his mind racing round in infuriating circles as he struggled to find a flaw in his plan – a flaw he felt certain was there for all to see.

On the left-hand slope Jonat crouched behind a thick bush, rubbing at his neck to ease the tension. On either side his men waited, bows ready and arrows notched.

He wished Gellan had given this command to Sarvaj; he felt ill at ease with the responsibility.

'Why don't they come?' hissed a man to his left.

'Keep calm,' Jonat heard himself say. 'They'll come. And when they do, we'll kill them. *All* of them! We'll teach them what it means to invade Drenai lands.'

He grinned at the soldier and as the man grinned back, Jonat felt the tension ease from him. Gellan's plan was a good one, but then Jonat would expect little else from such an ice-man. To hear him talk you would think that it was just another manoeuvre, but then Gellan was one of the warrior class, damn him! Not the son of a farm labourer best known for his ability to dance while drunk. Anger flared, but Jonat quelled it as the first creaking sounds of the wagons drifted up to him.

'Steady now!' he whispered. 'No one lets fly before the order. Pass the word along – I'll flay the man alive who disobeys!'

The wagons were led by six horsemen, their black horned helms down, swords in their hands. Behind them trundled the heavy wagons and carts, twenty-two horsemen filing along both sides of the track.

Slowly they came on and as the lead horsemen passed Jonat's position he notched an arrow to his bow, waiting, waiting . . .

'Now!' he yelled as the last wagons began the incline.

Black shafts flashed from the trees on both sides. Horses reared screaming and pandemonium came to the woods. One horseman tipped over the back of his horse, two arrows appearing in his chest. Another pitched forward as a shaft sliced his throat.

Cartsmen dived for cover below the wagons as the massacre continued. Three horsemen galloped west, ducking low over their horses' necks. One was brought down when an arrow hammered into his mount's neck; as he scrambled to his feet, three shafts plunged into his back. The other two broke clear over the hill-top and straightened in their saddles . . .

Only to find themselves galloping towards Sarvaj and ten bowmen.

37

Arrows peppered them and both horses fell dying, pitching their riders to the ground. Sarvaj and his men ran forward, killing the riders before they could rise.

In the woods Jonat led his men on a reckless charge to the wagons. Several of the cartsmen crawled out to meet them with hands raised, but the Drenai were in no mood for prisoners and they were despatched without mercy.

Within three minutes of the onset of the encounter, all the Vagrians were dead.

Gellan walked slowly down to the wagons. Six of the oxen used to pull the lead wagon were down and he ordered them cut clear. The action had gone better than he could have hoped for: seventy Vagrians dead and not one of his men wounded.

But now came the hard part – he had to get the wagons to Skultik.

'Good work, Jonat!' he said. 'Your timing was excellent.'

'Thank you, sir.'

'Strip the cloaks and helms from the dead – and get the bodies hidden in the woods.'

'Yes, sir.'

'We're going to be Vagrians for a little while.'

'It's a long way to Skultik,' said Jonat.

'We'll get there,' answered Gellan.

5

Waylander paused at the foot of a grass-covered hill and lifted Culas and Miriel from the saddle. The trees were thinning now and once over the crest the group would be on open ground. Waylander was tired; his limbs felt heavy and his eyes ached. A strong man, he was unused to this physical weariness and at a loss to understand it. Dardalion halted beside him and Danyal lowered Krylla into the priest's arms.

'Why are we stopping?' asked Danyal. Dardalion shrugged.

Waylander walked to the top of the hill and lay on his belly scanning the plain beyond. In the far distance a column of wagons was heading north, escorted by Vagrian cavalry. Waylander chewed at his lip and frowned.

Heading north?

Towards Egel?

This could only mean that Egel had been forced out of Skultik, or had made a run for Purdol. If either was the case, then there was little point in taking the children to the forest. But where else could they go? Waylander returned his gaze to the plain itself: thousands of square miles of flat, unending grassland, dotted with occasional trees and ground-hugging hedgerows. And yet the land was deceptive, he knew. What looked like flatlands hid scores of gullies and hollows, random dips and curves in the earth. The entire Vagrian army could be camped within the range of his sight and yet be hidden from him. He glanced back and saw the two little girls gathering bluebells. The sound of laughter echoed on the hillside. Waylander cursed softly. Moving back carefully from the crest he stood up and turned towards the group.

As he walked down the hill four men moved out of the trees.

Waylander's eyes narrowed, but he walked on. Dardalion had not seen the men and was talking to the boy, Culas.

The men spread out as Waylander approached. All four were bearded, their faces grim. Each wore a longsword and two of them carried bows. Waylander's crossbow was clipped to his belt, but it was useless, for the metal arms were snapped shut.

Dardalion turned as Waylander walked past him, and saw the newcomers. The sisters ceased their flower-gathering and ran to Danyal, Culas moving alongside them as Dardalion went to stand just behind Waylander.

'Nice horses,' said the man at the centre of the group. He was taller than the others and wore a green cloak of homespun wool.

Waylander said nothing and Dardalion could feel the tension rising. He wiped his palm on his shirt and hooked his thumb in his belt close to the hilt of the knife. The green-cloaked newcomer observed the movement and smiled, his blue eyes flickering back to Waylander.

'You don't offer much in the way of greetings, my friend,' he said.

Waylander smiled. 'Did you come here to die?' he asked softly.

'Why this talk of dying? We are all Drenai here.' The man was uncomfortable now. 'My name is Baloc and these are my brothers Lak, Dujat and Meloc – he's the youngest. We're not here to cause you harm.'

'It would not matter if you were,' said Waylander. 'Tell your brothers to sit down and be comfortable.'

'I do not like your manner,' said Baloc, stiffening. He edged back a step and the brothers fanned out to form a semi-circle around Waylander and the priest.

'Your likes and dislikes are immaterial to me,' said Waylander. 'And if your brother makes one more move to the right, I'll kill him.'

The man stopped instantly and Baloc licked his lips. 'You are big on threats for a man with no sword.'

'That should tell you something,' said Waylander. 'But then you look like a stupid man, so I will spell it out for you. I don't need a sword to deal with scum like you. No, don't say a word – just listen! Today I am in a good mood. You understand? Had you arrived yesterday I would probably have killed you without all this conversation. But today I feel expansive. The sun is shining and all is well. So take your brothers and go back the way you came.'

Baloc stared into Waylander's eyes, unsure and aware of a growing unease. Two men against four and not a sword in sight. Two horses and a woman as the prize. Yet still he was unsure.

The man was so confident, so calm. Not an ounce of tension showed in his stance or his manner . . . and his eyes were cold as tombstones.

Baloc grinned suddenly and spread his arms. 'All this talk of death and killing . . . Is there not enough trouble in the world? All right, we'll leave.' As he backed away, watching Waylander, his brothers joined him and all the men disappeared back into the trees.

'Run,' said Waylander.

'What?' asked Dardalion. But the dark-haired warrior was already sprinting towards the horses, pulling his crossbow clear and snapping the hinges open.

'Lie down!' he yelled and Danyal hurled herself to the ground, dragging the sisters with her.

Black-shafted arrows hissed from the trees. One flashed by Dardalion's head and he dived for the grass; a second missed Waylander by inches. Snapping two bolts into place and stretching the bow-arms tight, he ran for the trees, zig-zagging and ducking. Arrows flew perilously close. One hissed above Dardalion; he heard a choking cry and rolled over. The boy, Culas, had remained standing but now he knelt in pain, his small hands clutching a shaft buried in his belly.

Anger roared through Dardalion and with knife in hand he followed Waylander. As he went, a scream came from the forest . . . then another. Dardalion entered the trees at a run and saw two of the men down while Waylander, a knife in each hand, faced the other pair. Baloc ran forward, his sword flashing towards Waylander's neck, but Waylander ducked under the sweeping blade and rammed his right-hand knife into the man's groin. Baloc doubled over and fell, dragging Waylander with him. As the last robber ran forward with sword raised, Dardalion's arm came up and swept down. The black blade thudded home in the robber's throat and he toppled backwards to writhe on the dark earth. Waylander wrenched his knife clear of Baloc and then, grabbing the man's hair, pulled his head back.

'There are some who never learn,' he said, opening the man's jugular.

Standing, he moved to the writhing man downed by Dardalion and, tearing the knife clear, wiped the blade on the man's jerkin before returning it to the priest. Recovering his two bolts from the other bodies, he cleaned his crossbow and pressed the bow-arms back into place alongside the handle.

'Well thrown!' he said.

'They've killed the boy,' Dardalion told him.

'Blame me,' said Waylander bitterly. 'I should have killed them instantly.'

'They may have meant no harm,' said Dardalion.

'Collect two swords and scabbards and one of the bows,' asked Waylander. 'I'll see to the boy.'

Leaving Dardalion in the woods, he walked slowly back to the horses. The sisters were sitting together, silent in shock; Danyal was crying as Culas lay with his head in her lap, his eyes open and his hands still clutching the arrow.

Waylander knelt by his side. 'Is there much pain?'

The boy nodded. He bit his lip and tears flowed. 'I'm going to die! I know I am.'

'Of course you are not,' said Danyal fiercely. 'We'll just rest for a little while, then we'll take the arrow out for you.'

Culas let go of the arrow and lifted his hand; it was drenched in blood. 'I can't feel my legs,' he wailed. Waylander reached out and took the boy's hand.

'Listen to me, Culas. There is nothing to frighten you. In a little while you will go to sleep, that's all. Just a deep sleep . . . there will be no pain.'

'It hurts now,' said Culas. 'It's like fire.'

As Waylander gazed down on the young face, distorted now by agony, he saw again his son lying among the flowers.

'Close your eyes, Culas, and listen to my voice. A long time ago I had a farm. A lovely farm, and there was a white pony that could run like the wind . . .' And as he spoke Waylander drew his knife and touched it to Culas' thigh. The boy did not react. Waylander carried on speaking in a low, gentle voice and turned the knifepoint into Culas' groin, slicing the artery at the top of the thigh. Blood gushed from the wound and still Waylander's voice continued as Culas' face grew pale and a blue tinge appeared on his eyelids.

'Sleep softly,' whispered Waylander and the boy's head sagged sideways. Danyal blinked and looked up, seeing the knife in Waylander's hand. Her arm lashed out, catching him on the side of the head.

'You swine, you despicable swine! You killed him!'

'Yes,' he said. He stood up and touched his lip. Blood was seeping from a split at the edge of his mouth where her fist had caught him.

'Why? Why did you do it?'

'I enjoy killing boys,' he said sardonically and walked to his horse. Dardalion joined him; the priest was now wearing Baloc's longsword.

'What happened?' he asked, passing a second sword and belt to Waylander.

'I killed the boy . . . he would have lingered in pain for days. Gods, priest, I wish I had never met you! Get the children mounted and head north – I'm going to scout around for a while.'

He rode for an hour, alert and watchful, until he found a shallow dip in the land. Riding down into it, he located a camp-site near a broken tree and dismounted. After feeding his horse the last of the grain, he sat down on the stump of the tree, where he stayed without moving for another hour until the light began to fade, then he walked up the slope and stood waiting for Dardalion.

The group arrived just as the sun slid behind the western mountains. Waylander led them to the camp-site and lifted the sisters from the saddle.

'There's a man coming to see you, Waylander,' said Krylla, curling her arms around his neck.

'How do you know?'

'He told me; he said he would join us for supper.'

'When did you see him?'

'A little while ago. I was nearly asleep and Danyal was holding me and I must have drifted. The man said he would see you tonight.'

'Was he a nice man?' asked Waylander.

'His eyes were on fire,' said Krylla.

Waylander lit a small fire in a circle of stones, then walked out on to the plain to see if the glare could be spotted. Satisfied that the camp-site was hidden, he made his way slowly through the long grass towards the hollow.

A cloud drifted across the moon and the plain was plunged into darkness. Waylander froze. A whisper of movement to his right saw him drop to the ground, knife in hand.

'Get up, my son,' came a voice from beside him.

Waylander rolled left and came up on one knee, knife extended. 'You will not need your weapon. I am alone and very old.'

Waylander eased his way back along the trail and edged to the right.

'You are a cautious man,' said the voice. 'Very well, I will go on and meet you by your fire.'

The cloud passed and silver light bathed the plain. Waylander straightened. He was alone. Swiftly he scouted the area. Nothing. He returned to the fire.

Sitting beside it with hands outstretched to the warmth was an old man. Krylla and Miriel were sitting beside him, Dardalion and Danyal opposite.

Waylander approached cautiously and the man did not look up. He was bald and beardless and the skin of his face hung in slender folds. Way-

42

lander guessed from the width of his shoulders that he had once been very strong. Now he was skeletal and his eyelids were flat against the sockets.

A blind man!

'Why doesn't your face fit?' said Miriel.

'It did once,' said the old man. 'I was considered handsome in my youth, when my hair was golden and my eyes emerald green.'

'You look awful now,' said Krylla.

'I am sure that I do! Thankfully I can no longer see myself and therefore am spared great disappointment. Ah, the Wanderer returns,' said the old man, tilting his head.

'Who are you?' asked Waylander.

'A traveller like yourself.'

'You travel alone?'

'Yes . . . but not as alone as you.'

'Are you the mystic who spoke to Krylla?'

'I had that honour – and a delightful child she is. Very gifted for one so young. She tells me that you are a saviour, a great hero.'

'She sees with the eye of a child. All is not always as it seems,' said Waylander.

'Children see many things we no longer see. If we did, would we wage war so terribly?'

'Are you a priest, man? I've had my damned fill of priests,' snapped Waylander.

'No. I am merely a student of life. I would like to have been a priest, but I fear my appetites always had the better of me. I could never resist a pretty face or a fine wine. Now that I am old I wish for other delights, but even these are now denied me.'

'How did you find us?'

'Krylla showed me the way.'

'And I suppose you would like to travel with us?'

The man smiled. 'Would that I could! No, I shall bide with you tonight, and then I must embark on another journey.'

'We do not have much food,' said Waylander.

'But you are welcome to what we have,' said Dardalion, moving to sit beside the old man.

'I am not hungry, but thank you. You are the priest?'

'Yes.'

The old man reached out and touched the hilt of Dardalion's dagger. 'An unusual object for a priest to carry?'

'These are unusual days,' answered Dardalion, his face flushing.

'They must be.' He turned his head towards Waylander. 'I cannot see you, but I feel your power. And also your anger. Are you angry with me?'

'Not yet,' said Waylander, 'but I am wondering when you will arrive at the point of your visit.'

'You think I have some ulterior motive?'

'Not at all,' said Waylander drily. 'A blind man invites himself to supper through the mystic talents of a frightened child and finds our fire in the middle of a veritable wilderness. What could be more natural? Who are you and what do you want?'

'Do you always have to be so loathsome?' said Danyal. 'I don't care who he is, he's welcome. Or perhaps you'd like to kill him? After all, you haven't killed anyone for a couple of hours.'

'Gods, woman, your prattle turns my stomach,' snarled the warrior. 'What do you want from me? So the boy died. That's what happens in wars . . . people *die*. And before you let fly with your viper responses, remind yourself of this: when I shouted to get down I see *you* managed to save yourself. Perhaps if you had thought about the boy, he wouldn't have had an arrow in his guts.'

'That's not fair!' she shouted.

'Life is like that.' He swept up his blankets and walked away from the group, his heart pounding as rage threatened to engulf him. He strode to the top of the rise and stared out over the plain. Somewhere out there were riders hunting him. They could not allow him to live. For if they failed in their quest their own lives would be forfeit. And here was Waylander trapped by a priest and a woman – caught like a monkey in a net while the lions moved in.

Folly. Sheer folly.

He should never have accepted a contract from that Vagrian serpent, Kaem. The man's name was a byword for treachery: Kaem the Cruel, Kaem the Killer of Nations – the web-weaver at the centre of the Vagrian army.

All of Waylander's instincts had screamed at him to spurn Kaem's contract, but he had ignored them. Now the Vagrian general would have sent out groups of assassins in every direction; they would know he had not headed south or west, and the ports to the east would be closed to him. Only the north beckoned – and the killers would be watching all paths to Skultik.

Waylander cursed softly. Kaem had offered 24,000 gold pieces for the contract and, as a gesture of faith, had lodged half of the amount in Waylander's name with Cheros, the main banker in Gulgothir. Waylander had completed the contract with his customary skill, though his memory burned with the shame of it. Seeing again the arrow in flight, he squeezed shut his eyes . . .

The night was cool, the stars gleaming like spear-points. Waylander stretched, forcing his mind to the present, but his victim's face returned again and again . . . a gentle face, haunted by failure . . . soft eyes and a kind smile. He had been stooping to pick a flower when Waylander's bolt pierced his back . . .

'No!' shouted Waylander, sitting upright, his hand lashing out as if to drive the memory from him. Think of something else . . . anything else!

After the kill he had slipped away to the east, for the journey to Vagria and the promise of Kaem's gold. While on the road he met a merchant travelling from the north who told him in conversation of the death of

Cheros the Banker. Three assassins had killed him at his home and made off with a fortune in gold and gems.

Waylander had known then that he was betrayed, but some instinct – some inner compulsion – drove him on. He had arrived at Kaem's palace and scaled a high garden wall. Once inside, he killed two guard dogs and entered the main building. Locating Kaem's room had posed a problem, but he woke a serving girl and forced her at knifepoint to lead him to the general's bedchamber. Kaem was asleep in his apartments on the third floor of the palace. Waylander struck the girl on the neck, catching her as she fell and lowering her to a white fur rug on the floor. Then he went to the bed and touched his knife to Kaem's throat. The general's eyes flared open.

'Could you have not come at a more reasonable hour?' he had asked smoothly.

Waylander's knife pressed forward a fraction of an inch and blood seeped from the cut as Kaem stared into the dark eyes above him.

'I see you have heard about Cheros. I hope you don't think it was my doing.' The knife pressed deeper and this time Kaem winced.

'I know it was your doing,' hissed Waylander.

'Can we talk about it?'

'We can talk about 24,000 gold pieces.'

'Of course.'

Suddenly Kaem twisted and his arm lashed out to knock Waylander from the bed. The speed of the attack stunned the assassin and he rolled to his feet to find himself facing the wiry general who had now clambered from the bed and pulled a sword from the scabbard hanging on the bedpost.

'You're getting old, Waylander,' said Kaem.

The door burst open and a young man ran in, carrying a bow with arrow notched to the string.

Waylander's arm shot forward and the young man collapsed with a black-bladed knife in his throat. Waylander ran to the door, hurdling the corpse.

'You'll die for that!' screamed Kaem. 'You hear me? You will *die!*'

The sound of sobbing followed Waylander as he ran down the wide stairs, for the dead man was Kaem's only son . . .

And now the hunters were searching for his killer.

Wrapped in his blankets with his back against a jutting rock, Waylander heard the old man approach, the coarse cloth of his robes whispering against the long grass.

'May I join you?'

'Why not?'

'It is a glorious night, is it not?'

'How does a blind man define glorious?'

'The air is fresh and cool and the silence a mask – a cloak which hides so much life. To the right there, a hare is sitting, wondering why two men are so close to his burrow. Away to the left is a red fox – a vixen by the smell – and she is hunting the hare. And overhead the bats are out, enjoying the night as am I.'

'It's too bright for my liking,' said Waylander.

'It is always hard to be hunted.'

'I had a feeling you knew.'

'Knew what? The feeling of being hunted, or the fact that the Dark Brotherhood are seeking you?'

'Either. Both. It does not matter.'

'You were right, Waylander. I was seeking you and there is an ulterior motive. So shall we stop fencing?'

'As you wish.'

'I have a message for you.'

'From whom?'

'That is not part of my brief. And also it would take more time than I have to explain it to you. Let me say only that you have been given a chance to redeem yourself.'

'Nice of you. However, there is nothing to redeem.'

'If you say so. I do not wish to argue. Soon you will reach the camp of Egel where you will find an army in disarray: a force doomed to ultimate defeat. You can aid them.'

'Are your wits addled, old man? Nothing can save Egel.'

'I did not say "save". I said "aid".'

'What is the purpose of aiding a dead man?'

'What was the purpose in saving the priest?'

'It was a whim, damn you! And it will be a long time before I allow myself another such.'

'Why are you angry?'

Waylander chuckled, but there was no humour in the sound.

'You know what has happened to you?' asked the old man. 'You have been touched by the Source and those are the chains you rail against. Once you were a fine man and knew love. But love died, and since no man lives in a vacuum you filled yourself not with hate but with emptiness. You have not been alive these past twenty years – you have been a walking corpse. Saving the priest was your first decent deed in two decades.'

'So you came to preach?'

'No, I am preaching in spite of myself. I cannot explain the Source to you. The Source is about foolishness, splendid foolishness; it is about purity and joy. But against the wisdom of the world it fails, because the Source knows nothing of greed, lust, deceit, hate, nor evil of any kind. Yet it always triumphs. For the Source always gives something for nothing: good for evil, love for hate.'

'Sophistry. A small boy died yesterday – he hated no one, but an evil whoreson cut him down. All over this land good, decent people are dying in their thousands. Don't tell me about triumphs. Triumphs are built on the blood of innocence.'

'You see? I speak foolishness. But in meeting you I know what triumph means. I understand one more fragment.'

'I am pleased for you,' mocked Waylander, despising himself as he spoke.

'Let me explain,' said the old man softly. 'I had a son – not a dazzling boy, not the brightest of men. But he cared about many things. He had a dog that was injured in a fight with a wolf and we should have killed the dog, for it was grievously hurt. But my son would not allow it; he stitched the wounds himself and sat with the hound for five days and nights, willing it to live. But it died. And he was heartbroken, for life was precious to him. When he became a man I passed on everything I had to him. He became a steward, and I left on my travels. My son never forgot the dog and it coloured everything he did . . .'

'Is there a point to this tale?'

'That depends on you, for you enter the tale at this juncture. My son saw that everything I had left him to care for was in peril, and he tried desperately to save it. But he was too soft, and raiders came to my lands and slew my people. Then my son learnt the error of his ways and became truly a man, for he now knew that life often brings hard decisions. So he gathered his generals and worked on a plan to free his people. And then an assassin slew him. His life was ended . . . and as he died all he could see was a failure, and a terrible despair went out from him that touched me a thousand leagues away.

'A terrible rage filled me and I thought to kill you. I could, even now. But then the Source touched me. And I am now here merely to talk.'

'You son was King Niallad?'

'Yes. I am Orien of the Two Blades. Or, more exactly, I was Orien once.'

'I am sorry for your son. But it is what I do.'

'You speak of the death of innocents. Perhaps – had my son lived – many of those innocents would also have lived.'

'I know. And I regret it . . . but I can't change it.'

'It is not important,' said Orien. 'But *you* are important. The Source has chosen you, but the choice is yours.'

'Chosen me for what? My only talent is hardly one your Source would admire.'

'It is not your only talent. You know of my early life?'

'I know you were a great warrior, never beaten in battle.'

'Have you seen the statue of me in Drenan?'

'Yes. The Armour of Bronze.'

'Indeed. The Armour. Many would like to know its whereabouts and the Brotherhood seek it, for it threatens the Vagrian empire.'

'Is it magic then?'

'No – at least, not in the sense that you mean. It was made long ago by the great Axellian. Superb workmanship and the two swords are of a metal beyond compare – a silver steel that never dulls. With that Armour Egel has a chance – no more than that.'

'But you said it carries no magic?'

'The magic is in the minds of men. When Egel wears that Armour it will be as if Orien has returned. And Orien was never beaten. Men will flock to Egel and he will grow – he is the best of them, an iron man of indomitable will.'

'And you want me to fetch this Armour?'

'Yes.'

'I take it there is some danger involved?'

'I think that is a fair assessment.'

'But the Source will be with me?'

'Perhaps. Perhaps not.'

'I thought you said I was chosen for this task. What is the point of having aid from a God without power?'

'A good question, Waylander. I hope you learn the answer.'

'Where is the Armour?'

'I hid it in a deep cave high up the side of a tall mountain.'

'Somehow that doesn't surprise me. Where?'

'Do you know the Nadir Steppes?'

'I am not going to like this.'

'I take it that you do. Well, two hundred miles west of Gulgothir is a range of mountains . . .'

'The Mountains of the Moon.'

'Exactly. At the centre of the range is Raboas . . .'

'The Sacred Giant.'

'Yes,' said Orien, grinning. 'And that's where it is.'

'That is insane. No Drenai has ever penetrated that far into Nadir lands.'

'I did.'

'Why? What purpose could you have had?'

'I wondered that at the time. Put it down to a whim, Waylander; you know about whims. Will you fetch the Armour?'

'Tell me, Orien, how much of a mystic are you?'

'What do you mean?'

'Can you see the future?'

'In part,' admitted Orien.

'What are my chances of success?'

'That depends on who accompanies you.'

'Then let's say that the Source chooses the right company.'

The old man rubbed his ruined sockets and leaned back.

'You have no chance,' he admitted.

'That's what I thought.'

'But that is no reason to refuse.'

'You are asking me to ride a thousand miles through hostile lands swarming with savages. You tell me that the Brotherhood are also seeking the Armour? Do they know it is in Nadir lands?'

'They know.'

'So they will be hunting me also?'

'They are already hunting you.'

'Agreed. But they don't know where I'm going. If I set off on this quest of yours, they'll soon find out.'

'True.'

48

'So . . . there will be Nadir warriors, warrior wizards and Vagrian troops. And if I get through those I have to scale the Sacred Giant, the holiest place on the Steppes, and risk myself in the bowels of a dark mountain. Then I merely have to ride out again, burdened down with half a ton of armour.'

'Eighty pounds.'

'Whatever!'

'There are also the werebeasts who live in the caves of Raboas. They don't like fire.'

'That's comforting,' said Waylander.

'So will you go?'

'I am beginning to understand your comments concerning foolishness,' said the warrior. 'But yes, I will go.'

'Why?' asked Orien.

'Does there have to be a reason?'

'No. But I am curious.'

'Then let us say it's in memory of a dog that should not have died.'

6

Dardalion closed his eyes. Danyal was asleep beside the sisters and the young priest released his spirit to the Void. The moon was an eldritch lantern and silver light bathed the vast Sentran Plain, while the forest of Skultik spread like a stain from the Delnoch mountains.

Dardalion hovered below the clouds, his mind free of doubts and cares. Normally when he soared he found himself clothed in shimmering robes of pale blue. But now he was naked and, try as he might, no robes appeared. He didn't care. In the blink of an astral eye he was garbed in silver armour, a white cloak flowing from his shoulders. By his side hung two silver swords and as he drew them exhilaration flooded him. Far to the west, the camp-fires of a Vagrian army blazed like fallen stars. Dardalion sheathed his swords and flew towards them. More than ten thousand men were camped in the foothills of the Skoda mountains. Eight hundred tents lined the area in ranks of four and a wooden corral had been hastily erected for two thousand horses. Cattle grazed on the mountainside and a sheep-pen had been built beside a fast-moving stream.

Dardalion moved south over rivers and plains, hills and forests. A second Vagrian force was camped outside Drenan – no fewer than thirty thousand men and twenty thousand horses. The city gates of oak and bronze had been sundered, and no citizens could be seen within its walls. To the east of the city a vast trench had been carved from the earth and Dardalion swooped towards it – then veered away, repulsed. The trench was filled with bodies. Two hundred yards in length and six yards wide, the enormous grave housed more than a thousand corpses. Not one wore the armour of a soldier. Steeling himself, Dardalion returned to the trench.

It was over ten feet deep.

Returning to the night sky, the priest headed east where a Vagrian army was waiting on the borders of Lentria. The Lentrian force, only two thousand strong, was camped within a mile, waiting grimly for the invasion. North travelled Dardalion, following the line of the sea until he reached the eastern valleys and finally the sea citadel of Purdol. By torchlight the battle for Purdol was still being waged. The Drenai fleet was sunk in the harbour mouth and the Vagrian army camped in the area of the docks. The fortress of Purdol, manned by six thousand Drenai warriors, was holding back a Vagrian force of more than forty thousand led by Kaem, the Prince of War.

Here, for the first time, the Vagrians were facing a setback.

With no siege engines they could not storm the thirty-foot walls, and were relying on ladders and ropes. They were dying in their hundreds.

Dardalion soared to the west until he reached Skultik, the forest of dark legend. It was immense, thousands of square miles of trees, clearings, hills and valleys. Three towns – one verging on city status – had been

50

built within the forest: Tonis, Preafa and Skarta. To the last of these flew Dardalion.

Here Egel was camped with four thousand Legion warriors. As Dardalion neared the clearing he felt the presence of another mind and his swords flashed into his hands. Before him hovered a slender man in the blue robes of the Source priest.

'Do not pass me,' said the man quietly.

'If you say not, brother,' answered Dardalion.

'Who are you that calls me brother?'

'I am a priest, even as you.'

'A priest of what?'

'Of the Source.'

'A priest with swords? I think not. If you must slay me, do so.'

'I am not here to slay you. I am as I claim.'

'Then you were a priest?'

'I *am* a priest!'

'I sense death upon you. You have killed.'

'Yes. An evil man.'

'Who are you to judge?'

'I did not judge him – his own deeds did that for him. Why are you here?'

'We are watching.'

'We?'

'My brothers and I. We tell the Lord Egel when the enemy is approaching.'

'How many brothers are here?'

'Almost two hundred. There were three hundred and seven of us at the start. One hundred and twelve have joined the Source.'

'Murdered?'

'Yes,' said the man sadly. 'Murdered. The Dark Brotherhood destroyed them. We try to be careful as we soar, for they are swift and merciless.'

'One tried to kill me,' said Dardalion, 'and I learned to fight.'

'Each man chooses his own path.'

'You do not approve?'

'It is not for me to approve or disapprove. I do not judge you. How can I?'

'You thought I was of the Brotherhood?'

'Yes. For you carry a sword.'

'And yet you stood before me. You have great courage.'

'It is no hardship for me to be sent to join my God.'

'What is your name?'

'Clophas. And you?'

'Dardalion.'

'May the Source bless you, Dardalion. But I think you should leave now. As the moon reaches its height, the Brotherhood take to the sky.'

'Then I shall wait with you.'

'I do not desire your company.'

'You have no choice.'

'So be it.'

They waited in silence as the moon climbed higher. Clophas refused to speak and Dardalion took to studying the forest below. Egel had camped his army outside the southern wall of Skarta and the priest could see scouts patrolling the edge of the trees. It would be no easy task for the Vagrians to conquer the Earl of the North, for few were the sites for pitched battles within Skultik. On the other hand were they to attack the towns Egel would be left with an army intact, but no one to defend. Egel himself was faced with similar problems. Staying where he was guaranteed short term safety, but could not win him the war. Leaving Skultik was suicidal for he had not the resources to conquer one Vagrian army. To stay was to lose, to leave was to die.

And while the problems mounted, the lands of the Drenai were becoming the charnel house of the continent.

Dardalion found the thought depressing in the extreme, and was about to return to his body when he heard the soul scream from Clophas.

He glanced round to see that the priest had gone and five black-armoured warriors floated below him, dark swords in their hands.

Furious, Dardalion drew his swords and attacked. The five warriors did not see him until he was upon them, and two vanished into oblivion as his silver blades pierced their astral bodies. Then as the remaining three rushed him, he parried a thrust with his left-hand blade and blocked a sweeping cut with his right. His fury gave him lightning speed and his eyes blazed as he fought. Twisting his right wrist, he slid his sword under one warrior's guard, the blade piercing the man's throat. The warrior vanished. The last two pulled back from the fight and sped west, but Dardalion flew after them, catching the first just above the Skoda mountain range and killing him with a savage cut. The sole survivor returned to the sanctuary of his body with but a second to spare . . .

His eyes jerked open and he screamed. Soldiers ran to his tent and he lurched to his feet. Sprawled on the ground beside him lay his four companions, rigid in death.

'What in Hell's name is happening here?' demanded an officer, pushing men aside as he entered the tent. He gazed down at the corpses, then up at the survivor.

'The priests have learned to fight,' muttered the warrior, his breath coming in short gasps and his heart pounding.

'You are telling me that these men were killed by Source priests? It is inconceivable.'

'One priest,' said the man.

The officer waved the soldiers away and they were glad to depart. Hardened as they were to death and destruction, the Vagrian troops wanted no part of the Dark Brotherhood.

The officer sat down on a canvas-backed chair. 'You look as if you have seen a ghost, Pulis, my friend.'

'No jests, please,' said Pulis. 'The man almost killed me.'

'Well, you've killed enough of his friends these past months.'

'That is true. But nevertheless it is unsettling.'

'I know. What is the world coming to when Source priests stoop to defending themselves?'

The warrior glared at the young officer, but said nothing.

Pulis was no coward – he had proved that a score of times – but the silver priest had frightened him. Like most warriors of the Brotherhood he was not a true mystic, relying on the power of the Leaf to free him from his body. But even so, with his powers enhanced, he had experienced visions . . . flashes . . . of a premonitory nature. It had been so with the priest.

Pulis had felt a terrible danger emanating from the silver warrior – not just personal danger, but a timeless threat which would attack his cause from now until the end of time. Yet it was so nebulous, more an emotional reaction than a vision. Although he had seen something . . . what was it? He searched his memory.

That was it! A runic number hanging in the sky, bathed in flames.

A number. Meaning what? Days? Months? Centuries?

'Thirty,' he said aloud.

'What?' replied the officer. 'The Thirty?'

A cold chill hit Pulis, like a demon crossing his grave.

Dawn found Waylander alone as he opened his eyes and yawned. Strange, he thought, for he could not remember falling asleep. But he did remember his promise to Orien and he shook his head, puzzled. He glanced round, but the old man had gone.

He rubbed his chin, scratching at the skin below his beard.

The Armour of Orien.

Such a grand nonsense.

'This quest will kill you,' he whispered.

Taking a knife from his belt he honed it for several minutes, then shaved with care. His skin was raw under the blade, but the morning breeze felt good on his face.

Dardalion emerged from the hollow and sat beside him. Waylander nodded, but did not speak. The priest looked tired, his eyes set deep in his face; he was thinner now, thought Waylander, and subtly changed.

'The old man is dead,' said Dardalion. 'You should have spoken to him.'

'I did,' said Waylander.

'No, I mean *really* speak. Those few words at the fire were nothing. Do you know who he was?'

'Orien,' said Waylander. The look of surprise on Dardalion's face was comical.

'You recognised him?'

'No. He came to me last night.'

'He had great power,' said Dardalion softly. 'For he died without leaving the fire. He told us many tales of his life, then he lay back and slept. I was beside him and he died in his sleep.'

'You were mistaken,' said Waylander.

'I think not. What did you speak about?'

'He asked me to fetch something for him. I said that I would.'

'What was it?'

'No business of yours, priest.'

'It is too late to turn me away, warrior. When you saved my life, you opened your soul to me. When your blood was in my throat, I knew your life and every instant of your being flooded me. I look in a mirror now and I see you.'

'You are looking in the wrong mirrors.'

'Tell me of Dakeyras,' said Dardalion.

'Dakeyras is dead,' snapped Waylander. 'But you have made your point, Dardalion. I saved your life. Twice! You owe me the right to my solitude.'

'To allow you to return to the man you were? I do not think so. Look at yourself. Half your life has been wasted. You suffered great tragedy – and it broke you. You wanted to die, but instead you killed only part of yourself. Poor Dakeyras, lost for two decades while Waylander strode the world, slaying for gold he would never spend. All those souls sent to the Void. And for what? To lessen a pain you could not touch.'

'How dare you preach to me!' said Waylander. 'You talk of mirrors? Tell me what you have become since killing two men.'

'Six men. And there will be more,' said Dardalion. 'Yes, that is why I understand you. I may be wrong in all that I do, but I will stand before my God and I will say that I did what I felt was right – that I defended the weak against the evil strong. You taught me that. Not Waylander the man who kills for money, but Dakeyras, the man who saved the priest.'

'I do not want to talk any more,' said Waylander, staring away.

'Did Orien know that you killed his son?'

The assassin swung back. 'Yes, he knew. It was my foulest deed. But I will pay for it, priest. Orien saw to that. You know, I used to think that hatred was the most powerful force on earth. And yet last night I learned something bitter. He forgave me . . . and that is worse than hot irons on my flesh. You understand?'

'I think I do.'

'So now I will die for him, and that will settle my debts.'

'Your death will settle nothing. What did he ask you to do?'

'To fetch his Armour.'

'From Raboas, the Sacred Giant.'

'He told you?'

'Yes. He also told me that a man named Kaem would be hunting the same treasure.'

'Kaem hunts me. But he would be wise not to find me.'

Kaem's dreams were troubled. The Vagrian general had commandeered a fine house overlooking the Purdol harbour, and guards patrolled the gardens, while his two most trusted soldiers stood outside his door. The window was barred and the heat within the small room oppressive.

He came awake with a jerk and sat up scrabbling for his sword. The door opened and Dalnor ran inside, blade in hand.

'What is it, my lord?'

'It is nothing. A dream. Did I call out?'

'Yes, my lord. Shall I stay with you?'

'No.' Kaem took a linen towel from the chair beside the bed and wiped the sweat from his face and head. 'Damn you, Waylander,' he whispered.

'My lord?'

'Nothing. Leave me.' Kaem swung his legs from the bed and walked to the window. He was a thin man and totally hairless, his wrinkled skin giving him the appearance of a beached turtle robbed of his shell. Many thought him a comical figure on first sight, but most came to see him as he was: the finest strategist of the age, the man dubbed the Prince of War. His soldiers respected him, though not with the adoration reserved for some other and more charismatic generals. But that suited him, for he was uncomfortable with emotions and found such displays among the men childlike and foolish. What he wanted was obedience from his officers and courage from his men. He expected both. He *demanded* both.

Now his own courage was being tested. Waylander had killed his son and he had sworn to see him dead. But Waylander was a skilled hunter, and Kaem felt sure that one dark night he would once more wake to feel a knife at his throat.

Or worse . . . he might not wake at all. The Brotherhood were hunting the assassin, but first reports were not encouraging. A tracker dead, and talk now amongst the Brotherhood of a mystic warrior priest who travelled with the assassin.

Kaem, for all his strategic skills, was a cautious man. As long as Waylander lived he was a threat to Kaem's plans. Such grand plans – that when this conquest was complete he would rule an area greater than Vagria itself. Lentria, Drenai, and the Sathuli lands to the north – sixteen ports, twelve major cities and the spice routes to the east.

Then the civil war could begin, and Kaem would risk his strength against the failing guile of the Emperor. Kaem wandered to the bronze mirror on the far wall and gazed at his reflection. The crown would look out of place upon his bony head, but then he would not have to wear it often.

He returned to his bed, calmer now. And slept.

He found himself on a dark mountain, under strange stars, his mind dazed and confused. Before him was an old man in ragged brown robes. His eyes were closed as he spoke:

'Welcome, general. Do you seek the Armour?'

'Armour?' asked Kaem. 'What armour?'

'The Armour of Bronze. Orien's Armour.'

'He hid it,' said Kaem. 'No man knows where.'

'I know.'

Kaem sat down opposite the old man. Like all students of modern history, he had heard of this Armour. Some claimed it had magical properties which ensured victory to the wearer, but these were simple souls, or saga-poets. Kaem had long studied the process of war and knew that Orien was merely a master strategist. And yet the Armour was a symbol and a powerful one.

'Where is it?' he asked.

The old man did not open his eyes. 'How badly do you desire it?'

'I would like it,' said Kaem, 'but it is not important.'

'How do you define importance?'

'I will win with it, or without it.'

'Are you so sure, general? Purdol resists you and Egel has an army within Skultik.'

'Purdol is mine. It may take a month, but it will fall. And Egel is trapped – he cannot harm me.'

'He can if he has the Armour.'

'How so? Is it magic, then?'

'No, it is merely metal. But it is a symbol and the Drenai will flock to the man who wears it. Even your own soldiers know of its supposed properties and their morale will suffer. You know this is true.'

'Very well,' said Kaem. 'I accept that it could harm me. Where is it?'

'In the lands of the Nadir.'

'That covers a wide area, old man.'

'It is hidden in the heart of the Mountains of the Moon.'

'Why do you tell me this? Who are you?'

'I am a dreamer within a dream – your dream, Kaem. My words are true, and your hopes rest on how you interpret them.'

'How will I find the Armour?'

'Follow the man who seeks it.'

'Who is this man?'

'Whom do you fear most in the world of flesh?'

'Waylander?'

'The same.'

'Why would he seek the Armour? He has no interest in this war.'

'He killed the King for you, Kaem. And yet you hunt him. The Drenai would kill him if they knew and the Vagrians will kill him if they find him. Perhaps he seeks to bargain.'

'How does he know its whereabouts?'

'I told him.'

'Why? What game is this?'

'A game of death, Kaem.'

The old man's eyes opened and Kaem screamed as tongues of fire flashed about him.

And he woke.

For three nights Kaem's dreams were haunted by visions of bronze armour and two fabulous swords. Once he saw the Armour floating above Skultik forest, shining like a second sun. Then it dropped, so slowly, towards the trees and he saw Egel's army bathed in its light. The army grew in number as the trees themselves became men – a vast, invincible force.

On the second night he saw Waylander coming through the trees bearing one of those terrible swords, and then he realised that the assassin was stalking him. He had run, but his legs were weak and heavy and he had watched in horror as Waylander slowly dismembered him.

On the third night he saw himself clad in the Armour of Orien, mounting the marble steps to Vagria's throne. The cheering of the crowds filled him with joy, and when he looked into the eyes of his new subjects he saw adoration.

On the morning of the fourth day, he found his mind wandering as he listened to the reports from his junior generals.

Kaem forced himself to concentrate through the seemingly endless series of small problems which affect an army at war. Supplies were slow from the west, since wagons had proved more scarce than expected; new wagons were under construction. Six hundred horses had been slaughtered near Drenan after a small number had been found coughing blood; it was thought that the disease had been checked. Some breakdown in discipline among the men had been severely dealt with, but it had to be remembered that they were now on short rations.

'What about the Lentrians?' asked Kaem.

Xertes, a young officer distantly related to the Emperor, stepped forward. 'They repulsed our first attack, my lord. But we have now pushed them back.'

'You promised me that with an army of ten thousand you could take Lentria within a week.'

'The men lacked courage,' said Xertes.

'That has never been a Vagrian weakness. What they lacked was leadership.'

'Not from me,' said Xertes fiercely. 'I ordered Misalas to take the high ground on their right flank so that I could push forward with a wedge through their centre. But he failed – it was not my fault.'

'Misalas is light cavalry – leather breastplates and sabres. The enemy right flank was dug in and the hill covered with trees. How in the name of the Spirit did you expect light cavalry to take that position? They were cut to pieces by archers.'

'I will not be humiliated in this way,' shouted Xertes. 'I will write to my uncle.'

'Noble birth does not exclude you from responsibilities,' stated Kaem. 'You made many promises and have fulfilled not one. Pushed back, you say? My understanding is that the Lentrians gave you a bloody nose and then repositioned themselves ready to give you another. I told you to move into Lentria at speed, giving them no time to dig in. What did you do? You camped on their borders and had your scouts examine the land, making it clear to a blind man where you planned to attack. You have cost me two thousand men.'

'That is not fair!'

'Be silent, you worm! You are dismissed from my service. Go home, boy!'

The colour faded from Xertes' face and his hand moved close to his ornate dagger.

Kaem smiled . . .

Xertes froze, bowed swiftly and marched stiff-legged from the room.

Kaem looked around the group: ten officers rigidly at attention, not one set of eyes meeting his own.

'Dismissed,' he said and when they had gone he summoned Dalnor to him. The young officer entered and Kaem offered him a chair.

'Xertes is going home,' said Kaem.

'I heard, my lord.'

'It is a dangerous journey . . . much could happen.'

'Indeed, my lord.'

'The assassin Waylander, for example?'

'Yes, my lord.'

'The Emperor would be appalled if such a man were to kill someone of royal Vagrian blood.'

'He would indeed, my lord. He would use all his resources to have him tracked down and killed.'

'Then we must ensure that nothing untoward happens to young Xertes. See that he has an escort.'

'I will, my lord.'

'And Dalnor . . .'

'Yes, my lord.'

'Waylander uses a small crossbow with bolts of black iron.'

7

The old fort had only three good walls, each twenty feet high, the fourth having been partly stripped by villagers using the stones for foundations. Now the village was deserted and the fort stood like a crippled guard over the remains. The Keep – such as it was – was damp and cold, part of the roof having fallen in some years before, and there was some evidence that the central chamber had been used as a cattle store, the stench remaining long after the animals had been moved.

Gellan had the carts moved into place against the exposed fourth wall, providing a barrier of sorts against Vagrian attack. And the rain pounded down, lashing the stone of the ancient battlements and making them glisten like marble.

Lightning blazed across the night sky and thunder rumbled in the east as Gellan drew his cloak about him and stared to the north. Sarvaj climbed the creaking, rotted steps to the battlements and moved alongside the officer.

'I hope you are right,' he said, but Gellan did not respond. His despair was almost complete.

On the first day he had been convinced the Vagrians would find them. On the second his worries had grown. On the third he had allowed himself some hope that they would arrive in Skultik to a fanfare of triumph.

Then the rain had struck, bogging down the wagons in a sea of mud. At that point he should have destroyed the supplies and made a run for the forest – he knew that now. But he had dithered too long, and the Vagrians had circled ahead of him.

There had been time to cut and run – as Jonat pointed out – but by then Gellan had become obsessed with bringing the supplies to Egel.

He had hoped there would be fewer than two hundred Vagrians opposing him and had turned the wagons west to the ruined fort at Masin. Fifty men could hold the fort for perhaps three days against a force of two hundred. In the meantime he had sent three riders to Skultik requesting urgent aid.

But Gellan's luck was running true to form. His scouts reported that the force opposing him was five hundred and the chances were they would be overrun on the first assault.

The scouts had been sent to Egel and no one at the fort knew of the enemy strength. Gellan felt like a traitor for not informing Sarvaj, but morale was a delicate beast at best.

'We can hold,' said Gellan at last, 'even if they have more men than we think.'

'The western wall is rotten. I think an angry child could push it in,' said Sarvaj. 'The wagons don't make much of a barrier.'

'They'll do.'

'So you think two hundred?'

'Maybe three,' admitted Gellan.

'I hope not.'

'Remember the manual, Sarvaj – and I quote, "Good fortifications can be held against an enemy ten times the strength of the defending force." '

'I don't like to argue with a superior officer, but didn't the manual say "five times"?'

'We'll check it when we reach Skultik.'

'Jonat is complaining again. But the men are glad to be under cover; they have a fire going in the Keep. Why don't you go inside for a while?'

'You're getting concerned about my old bones?'

'I think you should rest. Tomorrow could get a little tense.'

'Yes, you are right. Keep the sentries alert, Sarvaj.'

'I'll do my best.'

Gellan walked to the steps, then returned. 'There are over five hundred Vagrians,' he said.

'I guessed that,' said Sarvaj. 'Get some sleep. And watch out for those steps – I say a prayer every time I mount them!'

Gellan made his way gingerly down the steps and across the cobbled courtyard to the Keep. The hinges of the gates had rusted through, but the soldiers had wedged the doors in place. Gellan squeezed through and made his way to the huge hearth. The fire was welcome and he warmed his hands against the blaze. The men had fallen silent as he entered, then one of them – Vanek – approached him.

'We lit a fire for you, sir. In the eastern room. There's a pallet bed if you wanted to catch some sleep.'

'Thank you, Vanek. Jonat, will you join me for a moment?'

The tall, bony Jonat pushed himself to his feet and followed the officer. Sarvaj had been complaining again, he guessed, preparing his arguments. Once inside the small room, Gellan removed his cloak and breastplate and stood before the crackling fire.

'You know why I promoted you?' Gellan asked.

'Because you thought I could handle it?' ventured Jonat.

'More than that. I knew you could. I trust you, Jonat.'

'Thank you, sir,' said Jonat uneasily.

'So let me tell you – and I want you to keep it to yourself for tonight – that there are at least five hundred Vagrians ranged against us.'

'We'll never hold.'

'I hope that we will, for Egel needs these supplies. Three days is all it will take. I want you to hold the western wall. Pick twenty men – the best archers, the finest swordsmen – but hold it!'

'We should have cut and run; we still could.'

'Egel has four thousand men and they are short of equipment, food and medicines; the people of Skarta are going hungry to supply them. But it cannot go on. I checked the wagons tonight. You know there are over twenty thousand shafts, spare bows, swords and spears; also salt meats, dried fruits and more than one hundred thousand silver pieces.'

'One hundred . . . it's their pay!'

'Exactly. But with it Egel can open trade links even with the Nadir.'

'No wonder they sent five hundred men to recover it. I'm surprised they didn't send a thousand.'

'We'll make them wish they had,' said Gellan. 'Can you hold the western wall with twenty men?'

'I can give it a try.'

'That's all I ask.'

After Jonat had gone Gellan lay back on the pallet bed. It smelt of dust and decay, but it felt finer than a silk-covered four-poster.

Gellan fell asleep two hours before dawn. His last waking thought was of the children, on the day he had taken them to play in the mountains.

If only he had known it was their last day together, he would have made it so different for them. He would have hugged them and told them he loved them . . .

The storm passed during the night and the dawn sky was clear of cloud, a brilliant spring blue. Gellan was awoken within the hour when riders were seen to the east. He dressed swiftly and shaved, then made his way to the wall.

Two horses could be seen in the distance, moving slowly and heavily laden. As they neared, Gellan saw that one horse carried a man and a woman, while the second bore a man and two children.

When they approached he waved them round to the ruined gates of the western wall and ordered the wagons pulled back so as to allow the horses to enter.

'Go and question them,' he ordered Sarvaj.

The young soldier descended to the courtyard as the group were dismounting, and was drawn instantly to the man in the black leather cloak. He was a tall man with dark, grey-streaked hair, and eyes so deep a brown there appeared to be no trace of pupils. His face was set and grim and he moved with care, always balanced. In his hand he held a small black crossbow, and several knives hung on his broad black belt.

'Good morning,' said Sarvaj. 'Have you travelled far?'

'Far enough,' answered the man, turning his gaze to the wagons being pulled back in place.

'It might be safer for you to move on.'

'No,' said the man quietly. 'Vagrian outriders are everywhere.'

'They are hunting us,' said Sarvaj. The man nodded and moved towards the battlements, while Sarvaj turned to the other man standing with a young woman and the two children.

'Welcome to Masin,' he said, extending his hand which Dardalion shook warmly. Sarvaj bowed to Danyal, then squatted down before the children. 'My name is Sarvaj,' he told them, removing his plumed helm. Frightened, the sisters hugged Danyal's skirt and turned their heads away.

'I've always been good with children,' he said, with a wry smile.

'They have suffered a great deal,' said Danyal, 'but they will be better in a little while. Do you have any food?'

'How remiss of me. Come this way.'

He took them into the Keep where the cook was preparing breakfast of hot oats and cold pork and they sat at the makeshift table. The cook served them with plates of oats, but the children, after one taste, pushed the dishes away.

'It's horrible,' said Miriel.

One of the men sitting nearby came to the table.

'What's wrong with it, princess?'

'It's sour,' she said.

'You have some sugar hidden in your hair. Why don't you sweeten it?'

'I haven't any sugar,' she said. The man leaned forward, ruffled her hair and then opened his hand to show a tiny leather sack sitting on his palm. He unfastened it and poured some sugar on the oats.

'Is there sugar in *my* hair?' asked Krylla eagerly.

'No, princess, but I'm sure your sister would not mind you sharing hers.' He added the rest of his small store to Krylla's plate and the sisters began to eat.

'Thank you,' said Danyal.

'A pleasure, my lady. I am Vanek.'

'You are a kind man.'

'I like children,' he said, then moved back to his table. Danyal noticed that he walked with a slight limp.

'A horse fell on him about two years ago,' said Sarvaj. 'Crushed his foot. He's a good man.'

'Do you have spare weapons here?' asked Dardalion.

'We captured some Vagrian supplies. There are swords, bows and breastplates.'

'Must you fight, Dardalion?' asked Danyal.

Reading the concern in her voice, Sarvaj switched his gaze to the young man. He looked strong enough, though his face was gentle – more of a scholar than a warrior, thought Sarvaj; he reached out and took Danyal's hand, saying nothing.

'You don't have to fight, sir,' said Sarvaj. 'It's not obligatory.'

'Thank you, but I have chosen my path. Would you help me choose a weapon? I am not skilled in such matters.'

'Of course. Tell me about your friend.'

'What would you like to hear?' asked Dardalion.

Sarvaj grinned. 'He seems more of a loner,' he said lamely. 'Not someone I would expect to see in the company of a woman and children.'

'He saved our lives,' said Dardalion, 'and that speaks more highly of him than his looks.'

'Indeed it does,' admitted Sarvaj. 'What is his name?'

'Dakeyras,' said Dardalion swiftly. Sarvaj caught the look on Danyal's face and did not press the matter; there were far more important issues at stake than a change of name. It was likely that Dakeyras was an outlaw, which six months ago would have meant something. Now it was immaterial.

'He spoke of Vagrian outriders. Did you see them?'

'There are just under five hundred soldiers,' said Dardalion. 'They were camped in a gully to the north-east.'

'Were?'

'They moved out an hour before dawn, seeking sign of your wagons.'

'You know a great deal about their movements.'

'I am a mystic, once a priest of the Source.'

'And you want weapons?'

'I have experienced a change of perspective, Sarvaj.'

'Can you see where the Vagrians are now?'

Dardalion closed his eyes, resting his head on his elbows. Seconds later he opened them again.

'They have found the tracks where you cut to the west. Now they are moving this way.'

'What regiment are they?'

'I have no idea.'

'Describe their armour.'

'Blue cloaks, black breastplates and helms that cover their faces.'

'Are the visors clear or embossed?'

'On the forehead is an image of a snarling wolf.'

'Thank you, Dardalion. Excuse me.' Sarvaj rose from the table and returned to the battlements, where Gellan was supervising the distribution of arrows to the men: quivers of fifty shafts allocated to each archer.

Sarvaj removed his helm and ran his fingers through his thinning hair.

'You trust this man?' asked Gellan, after Sarvaj had given him the news.

'I would say that he is honest. I could be wrong.'

'We will know within the hour.'

'Yes. But if he's right we are up against the Hounds.'

'They are men, Sarvaj; there's nothing supernatural about them.'

'It is not the supernatural that worries me,' said the soldier. 'It is the fact that they always win.'

Waylander unsaddled his horse, stowing his saddlebags inside the Keep. Then he took his weapons to the decaying battlements of the western wall. Six throwing knives and two quivers of bolts for his crossbow he left leaning against the ramparts. Then he saw Dardalion and Sarvaj standing at a wagon below the eastern wall; here the wagons had been drawn in a line to create a pen for the oxen.

Waylander strolled across the courtyard. Dardalion had put aside the sword and scabbard he had taken from the dead robber and had selected a sabre of blue steel. The broadsword had been too heavy for the slender priest. Sarvaj produced a breastplate from under the tarpaulin. It was wrapped in oilskin, and when he brought it out into the sunshine it shone like silver.

'A Vagrian officer of the Blue Riders,' said Sarvaj. 'Made to order. Try it on.' Delving deeper into the depths of the wagon, he pulled clear a large parcel. Ripping it open he discovered a white cloak, trimmed with leather.

'You'll stand out like a dove among crows,' said Waylander, but Darda-lion merely grinned and swept the cloak over his shoulders. Shaking his head, Waylander climbed on to the wagon where he selected two short swords of blue steel in matching black scabbards; these he threaded to his belt. The edges were dulled and he moved away to the battlements to hone them.

When Dardalion joined him Waylander blinked in mock disbelief. A white horse-hair plumed helmet was buckled at the chin, and the leather-trimmed cloak lay over a shimmering breastplate embossed with a flying eagle. A leather kilt, studded with silver, protected Dardalion's thighs, while silver greaves were buckled to his calves. By his side hung a cavalry sabre, and on his left hip a long, curved knife sat in a jewelled scabbard.

'You look ridiculous,' said Waylander.

'Most probably. But will it serve?'

'It will serve to draw the Vagrians to you like flies to a cowpat.'

'I do feel rather foolish.'

'Then take it off and find yourself something less garish.'

'No. I can't explain why, but this is right.'

'Then keep away from me, priest. I want to stay alive!'

'Will you not get yourself some armour?'

'I have my mailshirt. I don't intend to stand in one place long enough to be cut.'

'I would appreciate some advice on swordsmanship,' said Dardalion.

'Gods of Mercy!' snapped Waylander. 'It takes years to learn and you have an hour, maybe two. There's nothing I can teach you – just remember throat and groin. Protect your own, slice theirs!'

'By the way, I told Sarvaj – the soldier who greeted us – that your name was Dakeyras.'

'It does not matter. But thank you anyway.'

'I am sorry that saving me has brought you to this,' said Dardalion.

'*I* brought myself to this; don't blame yourself. Just try to stay alive, priest.'

'I am in the hands of the Source.'

'Whatever. Keep the sun to your back – that way you'll blind them with your magnificence! And get yourself a canteen of water – you'll find war dries the throat.'

'Yes, I'll do that now. I . . .'

'No more speeches, Dardalion. Fetch yourself some water and position yourself down there by the wagons. That is where the action will be.'

'I feel I ought to say something. I owe you my life . . . But the words are all trapped inside me.'

'You need say nothing. You are a good man, priest – and I am glad I saved you. Now, for pity's sake, go away!'

Dardalion returned to the courtyard and Waylander strung his cross-bow, testing the strings for tension. Satisfied, he laid it gently on the stone rampart. Then, taking a short length of rawhide, he tied back his hair at the nape of the neck.

A young, bearded soldier approached. 'Good morning, sir. My name is Jonat. This is my section.'

'Dakeyras,' said Waylander, extending his hand.

'Your friend looks dressed for a royal banquet.'

'It was the best he could find. But he'll stand firm.'

'I am sure that he will. Do you intend to stay up here?'

'That is what I had in mind,' said Waylander drily.

'It is just that this is the best spot to cover the gap and I would prefer to place one of my archers here.'

'I can understand that,' said Waylander, picking up his crossbow and drawing back the upper string. Snapping a bolt in place, he glanced down at the wagon blocking the ruined gate; the wagon tongue had been pushed up, making a cross with the oxen bar. Waylander pulled back the lower string, slipping a bolt into position.

'How wide would you say the bar is?' asked Waylander.

'Narrow enough to make a difficult target,' agreed Jonat.

Waylander's arm came up and a black bolt flashed through the air to punch its way through the right-hand bar. A second bolt thudded into the left side.

'Interesting,' commented Jonat. 'May I try it?'

Waylander handed him the weapon and Jonat turned it over in his hands. It was beautifully constructed. Loading only one arrow, Jonat sighted on the centre tongue and let fly. The arrow glanced from the wood and hit the cobblestones of the courtyard, sending a shower of sparks into the air.

'Nice weapon,' said Jonat. 'I would love to practise with it.'

'If anything happens to me, you can have it,' said Waylander.

Jonat nodded. 'You'll be staying here, then?'

'I think so.'

Suddenly from the eastern wall came a shout of warning and Jonat ran to the battlement steps, joining the stream of men rushing to see the enemy. Waylander settled back against the ramparts; he had seen armies before. He took a swig from his canteen and swished the warm water around his mouth before swallowing it.

On the eastern wall Gellan and Sarvaj were joined by Jonat.

Out on the plain some six hundred Vagrian horsemen came into view and two scouts rode from the enemy ranks, galloping their horses to the western wall. Then they returned. For several minutes nothing happened as the Vagrian officers dismounted and sat together at the centre; then one rose and remounted.

'Talk time,' muttered Sarvaj.

The officer rode to the eastern wall, his hand raised. Lifting his helm from his head, he called out: 'I am Ragic. I speak for the Earl Ceoris. Who speaks for the Drenai?'

'I do,' shouted Gellan.

'Your name?'

'It is no business of yours. What do you have to say?'

65

'As you can see, you are vastly outnumbered. The Earl Ceoris offers you the opportunity to surrender.'

'On what conditions?'

'Once your weapons have been surrendered, you will be free to go.'

'Very generous!'

'Then you agree?'

'I have heard of the Earl Ceoris. It is said that his word is given as lightly as the promise of a Lentrian whore. The man has no honour.'

'Then you refuse?'

'I don't deal with jackals,' said Gellan.

'That is a decision you will live to rue,' shouted the herald, pulling on the reins and spurring his horse back to the enemy line.

'I think he is probably right about that,' muttered Jonat.

'Ready the men,' said Gellan. 'The Vagrians have no ropes or siege equipment and that means they must attack the breach. Sarvaj!'

'Sir.'

'Leave only five men per wall. The rest to go with Jonat. Do it now!'

Sarvaj saluted and moved from the battlements. Jonat followed him.

'We should have cut and run,' said Jonat.

'Give your mouth a rest,' snapped Sarvaj.

The Vagrians heeled their horses to the right and cantered round to face the western wall, then advanced until they were just beyond bowshot. Dismounting, the men thrust their lances into the earth and tied their mounts to them; then lifting shields and drawing swords, they advanced slowly.

Dardalion watched them come and licked his lips. His hands were sweating and he wiped them on his cloak. Jonat grinned at him. 'Handsome whoresons, aren't they?'

Dardalion nodded. The men around him were tense and the priest realised he was not alone in his fear. Even Jonat's eyes were burning more brightly and his face was set. Dardalion glanced up to where Waylander sat with his back to the wall, setting out crossbow bolts before him. He alone was not watching the advancing soldiers. A man to the right loosed a shaft that sailed towards the Vagrians; an enemy soldier lifted his shield and the arrow glanced from it.

'Hold until I order it!' bellowed Jonat.

With a sudden roar the Vagrians charged. Dardalion swallowed hard and drew his swords.

With the enemy a bare thirty feet from the breach Jonat bellowed, 'Now!' Shafts hammered into the advancing line, but most were turned aside by the brass-rimmed round shields. Others glanced from black helms, but several of the enemy fell as the barbed shafts cut into unprotected necks.

A second volley sliced home as the Vagrians gained the breach. And this time more than a dozen warriors fell back. Then they were at the wagons. A burly soldier clambered over the wooden frame with sword raised, but Waylander's bolt punched through his helm above his right ear and he fell without a sound. A second bolt skewered the neck of the soldier behind him.

Jonat had placed his defenders well. A dozen knelt on the northern battlements loosing shaft after shaft into the enemy as they struggled to clear the wagons, while twenty more archers stood in the courtyard picking off the enemy with ease. The bodies mounted, but still the Vagrians pushed on.

Waylander heard a scrabbling noise behind him and swung round to see a hand grasp the ramparts as a Vagrian soldier pulled himself over the wall. Another followed . . . and another. Waylander cocked his bow and fired and the first soldier pitched backwards and rolled from the battlements. The second took a bolt through the shoulder, but ran on, screaming his hatred. The assassin dropped his bow and dragged his sword from its scabbard, blocking a downward cut; then he kicked out to catch the man in the groin. As the soldier staggered Waylander hammered a blow to his neck and with blood gushing from the wound, the man toppled to the courtyard below.

Waylander dropped to his knees as another warrior aimed a vicious blow to his head. He stabbed upwards, feeling the blade sink into the man's groin. Waylander kicked him from the battlements and faced another soldier, but the man suddenly pitched forward with an arrow jutting from the back of his neck. A Drenai soldier stepped from the doorway of the tower, bow in hand; he grinned at Waylander and limped forward.

Below, four Vagrians finally burst through the crossfire and leapt into the courtyard. Jonat killed the first with a reverse cut to the neck. Dardalion ran forward, heart pounding, and thrust his sword at an enemy warrior. The man brushed the blade aside and crashed his shield into the priest. Dardalion fell back, tripping on the cobbles. The Vagrian lashed out and the priest rolled clear as the blade clanged against the stones. Pushing himself to his feet, Dardalion drew his second sword and faced the warrior. The man advanced, his sword stabbing towards Dardalion's groin. The priest parried the blade with his right-hand sword, stepped forward and thrust his left-hand blade into the man's throat; blood bubbled from under the black helm and he fell to his knees.

'Look out!' yelled Waylander, but Dardalion's sword came up too late and a second Vagrian soldier ran forward crashing a blow to his head. The blade glanced from the silver helm and thundered to his shoulder. Dazed, he stumbled back and the Vagrian moved in for the kill.

Jonat despatched another man, then swung to see Dardalion in trouble. He ran forward and leapt feet-first at the attacker, catapulting him from his feet. Jonat scrambled up and threw himself on the man's back; then, drawing a slender dagger, he tore the man's helm clear and cut his throat.

A single bugle blast pierced the battle clamour and the Vagrians pulled back out of bowshot.

'Clear away the bodies!' shouted Jonat.

Waylander retrieved his crossbow and counted the remaining bolts.

Twelve. He climbed down to the courtyard and began searching the bodies, reclaiming fifteen bolts that were usable.

Dardalion sat with his back to the northern wall, dizzy and unable to stand. Waylander strolled over and knelt by his side.

'Drink,' he said.

Dardalion weakly pushed the canteen away. 'I feel sick.'

'You cannot sit there, priest; they'll be back within minutes. Get yourself to the Keep.'

Dardalion pulled his legs under him and struggled to rise. Waylander pulled him upright.

'Can you stand?'

'No.'

'Lean on me, then.'

'I did not perform too well, Waylander.'

'You killed your first man in combat. It is a start.'

Together they made their way to the Keep and Waylander laid the priest down on a bench table. Danyal ran forward, her face white with shock.

'He's not dead, merely dazed,' said Waylander. Ignoring him she moved to Dardalion, pulling his helm clear and examining the shallow cut to his head where the helm had dented.

A bugle blast echoed over the plain.

Waylander cursed softly and made for the door.

8

To free himself from pain and dizziness Dardalion released his spirit and soared, passing through the walls of the Keep and out into the bright midday sunshine.

The battle below raged on. Waylander, back on the battlements, took aim carefully and loosed bolt after bolt into the oncoming Vagrians. Jonat, full of near-maniacal energy, gathered to him twenty warriors and rushed the Vagrians who had cleared the wagons. On the battlements to left and right, Drenai archers picked their targets with care. On the eastern wall the enemy had gained a foothold by climbing the pitted outer ramparts. Here three men fought hard to hold the tide and Dardalion floated towards them.

At the centre of the three stood a middle-aged officer whose swordplay was exquisite. Not for him the wild hacking, the fanatic attack; he fought with subtle grace and style, his sword flickering into play and scarcely seeming to touch his opponents. But down they went, choking on their own blood. His face was calm, even serene, thought Dardalion, and his concentration intense.

Through his spirit eyes the priest could see the flickering auras that marked the mood of each man. Bright red pulsed the colours on all but two of the combatants.

The officer glowed with the blue of harmony, and Waylander with the purple of controlled fury.

More Vagrians cleared the battlements of the eastern wall, while Jonat and his men were being forced back from the breach on the western wall. Waylander, his bolts exhausted, drew his sword and leapt from the ramparts to the wagon below, crashing into several Vagrian soldiers and bowling them from their feet. He came up swinging his sword, killing two before they could recover their balance. A third died even as he swung his sword into play. Waylander blocked the cut and tore open the man's throat with a downward sweep.

Back in the Keep, Danyal took the sisters up the winding stair to the tower and then sat them with their backs to the ramparts. From here the sound of battle was muted, and she took the sisters in her arms.

'You are very frightened, Danyal,' said Krylla.

'Yes, I am. You'll have to look after me,' answered Danyal.

'Will they kill us?' asked Miriel.

'No . . . I don't know, little one.'

'Waylander will save us; he always does,' stated Krylla.

Danyal closed her eyes and Waylander's face filled her mind: the dark eyes, deep-set under fine brows, the angular face and square chin, the wide mouth with the faintly mocking half-smile.

The scream of a dying man echoed above the clamour of the battle.

Danyal released the children and stood leaning out over the crenellated wall.

Waylander stood with a little knot of men trying to fight their way back to the Keep, but they were almost surrounded. She could look no more and slumped down beside the girls.

Inside the Keep Dardalion roused himself and groped for his swords. He felt less groggy now, awareness of imminent death overriding the pain. He moved to the doors and hauled them open. Outside the sun was so bright it brought tears to his eyes; blinking, he saw four men rush towards him.

Fear swamped him, but instead of forcing it back, he released it, hurling it with terrible power at the four soldiers. The mind blast staggered them. One fell clutching at his heart and died within seconds; another dropped his sword and ran screaming towards the breach. The remaining two – stronger men than most – merely backed away.

Dardalion advanced on the main group, eyes wide and startlingly blue, pupils almost invisible. Growing in strength, he hurled his fear into the blue-cloaked mass of attackers. Men screamed as it hit them and panic swept through the Vagrians like a plague. They swung round, ignoring the swords of the Drenai and faced the silver warrior advancing on them. A man at the front dropped to his knees, shaking uncontrollably, then he pitched forward unconscious.

Later, under the most intensive questioning, not one Vagrian soldier could describe the terror he had felt, nor the awful menace that produced it . . . though most could recall the silver warrior who shone like white fire and whose eyes radiated death and despair.

The Vagrians broke and ran, dropping their weapons behind them.

The Drenai watched in awe as Dardalion followed them to the breach, his swords in his hands.

'Gods of Light,' whispered Jonat. 'Is he a sorcerer?'

'It looks that way,' said Waylander.

The men broke ranks and ran to the priest, pounding him on the back. He staggered and almost fell, but two of the warriors hoisted him to their shoulders and he was carried back to the Keep. Waylander smiled and shook his head.

'Dak?' said a voice. 'Is it you?' And Waylander swung round to face Gellan. The officer looked older, his hair was thinning and his eyes were tired.

'Yes, it is me. How are you, Gellan?'

'You haven't changed a jot.'

'Nor you.'

'What have you been doing with yourself?'

'I've travelled a fair deal. I see you stayed with the Legion – I thought you wanted to be married and gone.'

'I married and stayed,' said Gellan and Waylander read the pain in the man's face, though Gellan fought to disguise it. 'It is good to see you. We will talk later, there is much to do.'

Gellan left him then, but the man who had first spoken to Waylander remained.

'You are old friends?' asked Sarvaj.

'What? Yes.'

'How long since you've seen him?'

'Twenty years.'

'His children died in the plague at Skoda and his wife killed herself soon after.'

'Thank you for telling me.'

'He's a good officer.'

'He always was, better than he knew.'

'He was going to retire this year – he had bought a farm near Drenan.'

Waylander watched Gellan directing the men to aid the wounded and clear away the bodies of the slain. Others he sent to the battlements to watch for the Vagrians.

Leaving Sarvaj in mid-sentence, Waylander strolled back to the western wall ramparts to collect his crossbow. He found a Drenai warrior sitting beside it – the man who had saved him earlier with a well-timed arrow. In no mood for conversation, Waylander stepped past him and picked up the weapon.

'Drink?' asked the man, offering Waylander a canteen.

'No.'

'It's not water,' said the soldier, grinning.

Waylander sipped it and his eyes bulged.

'They call it Lentrian Fire,' commented Vanek.

'I can see why!'

'It makes for sweet dreams,' said Vanek, stretching out and resting his head on his arms. 'Wake me if they come back, will you?'

The Vagrians had retired out of bowshot and were massed together listening to their general. Waylander could not hear his words, but the gestures spoke most powerfully. He sat on a tall grey horse, his white cloak billowing in the afternoon breeze; his fist was being waved about extravagantly, and the men were cowed. Waylander scratched his chin and took a long swallow of Lentrian Fire.

What spell had the priest cast, he wondered, that could so demoralise such excellent fighting men? He glanced at the sky and raised the canteen to the clouds.

'Maybe you have some power after all,' he acknowledged.

He drank deeply and sat down abruptly, his head spinning. Then with great care he replaced the stopper in the canteen and laid it at his side.

Stupid, he told himself. The Vagrians would be back. He chuckled. Let Dardalion handle them! He took a deep breath and leaned his head against the cold stone. The sky was bright and clear, but dark shapes wheeled and dived over the fort.

'You can smell the death, can you?' said Waylander, and the raucous cries of the crows floated back to him on the wind. Waylander shivered. He had seen these birds feast before, tearing eyes from sockets and

71

squabbling over juicy morsels from still-warm corpses. He transferred his gaze to the courtyard.

Men were working to clear away the bodies. The Vagrians were dumped outside the breach, while the Drenai dead were laid side by side against the northern wall with their cloaks over their faces. Twenty-two bodies were laid out. Waylander counted the remaining men. Only nineteen were in view – not enough to hold the fort against another charge. A shadow fell across him and he glanced up to see Jonat carrying a small bundle of his bolts.

'I thought you might need these,' said the under-officer. Waylander accepted them with a lopsided grin.

'Drink?' he asked.

'No. Thank you.'

'It's not water,' said Waylander.

'I know, I recognised Vanek's canteen! Dun Gellan would like to see you.'

'He knows where I am.'

Jonat squatted down and smiled grimly. 'I like you, Dakeyras. It would be unseemly if I had three men drag you into the Keep – unseemly and ridiculous.'

'True. Help me up.'

Waylander's legs were unsteady, but with an effort he walked alongside Jonat, through the main hall to a small room at the rear. Gellan was sitting on a pallet bed with quill in hand, completing his reports.

Jonat saluted and backed out of the door, pulling it closed behind him. For want of a better place, Waylander sat on the floor with his back to the wall.

'I was wrong,' said Gellan. 'You have changed.'

'We all change. It's part of the process of dying.'

'I think you know what I mean.'

'You tell me – it's your fort.'

'You're cold, Dak. We were friends once. Brothers. Yet out there you greeted me like a one-time acquaintance.'

'So?'

'So tell me what's happened to you.'

'If I want confession, I can find a temple. And besides, you have more important problems to consider. Like an army waiting to destroy you.'

'Very well,' said Gellan sadly, 'we might forget our past friendship. Tell me of your friend. What vast powers does he have – and from where does he come by them?'

'Damned if I know,' said Waylander. 'He is a Source priest. I stopped some men from torturing him to death, since when he has been a positive burden to me. But I have not seen any evidence of powers before today.'

'He could be valuable to us.'

'He certainly could. Why don't you talk to him?'

'I shall. Will you be coming to Skultik?'

'Probably. If we survive.'

'Yes, if we survive. Well, if you do, do not carry that crossbow.'

'It is a good weapon,' said Waylander.

'Yes, and very unusual. All officers have been told to watch for a man bearing such a weapon; it is said he killed the King.'

Waylander said nothing, but his dark eyes met Gellan's gaze and the assassin looked away. Gellan nodded. 'Go now, Dakeyras. I wish to speak to your friend.'

'Everything is not always as it seems,' said Waylander.

'I do not want to hear it. Go now.'

As Waylander left, the door opened and Dardalion entered. Gellan stood to receive him, offering his hand. The priest shook it. The clasp was firm, but not strong, thought Gellan.

'Sit down,' said Gellan, offering Dardalion the bed. 'Tell me about your friend.'

'Dakeyras or Danyal?'

'Dakeyras.'

'He rescued me . . . all of us. He has proved a fine friend.'

'Have you always known him as Dakeyras?'

'Of what concern is that to you, sir?'

'Then you did know him by another name?'

'I shall not divulge it to you.'

'I have already spoken to the children,' said Gellan.

'Then you do not need me to corroborate.'

'No. I knew Dakeyras once – or thought I did. A man of honour.'

'He has shown himself to be such a man over the last few days,' said Dardalion. 'Let that suffice.'

Gellan smiled and nodded. 'Perhaps. Tell me about yourself and the dread powers you showed today.'

'There is little I can tell you. I am . . . was . . . a priest of the Source. I have some powers of Travel and communication.'

'But what made the enemy run?'

'Fear,' said Dardalion simply.

'Of what?'

'Merely fear. My fear hurled into their minds.'

'Make me feel fear,' said Gellan.

'Why?'

'So that I may understand.'

'But I feel no fear at this time. I have nothing to use.'

'Will the enemy return? Can you tell me that?'

'I do not think that they will. There is a man among them – his name is Ceoris – who is urging them to attack, but they are afraid. Given time he will convince them, but within the hour your reinforcements will be here.'

'Who is coming?'

'A large man named Karnak. He has four hundred riders with him.'

'That is good news indeed. You are a useful man to know, Dardalion. What are your plans?'

'Plans? I have no plans. I have not thought . . .'

'We have priests in Skultik – more than two hundred. But they won't fight like you do – if they did, the Drenai could gain much. Using your powers, magnified a hundredfold, we could set entire Vagrian armies fleeing before us.'

'Yes,' said Dardalion wearily, 'but that is not the way of the Source. I became what I am from weakness. Were I as strong as so many of my brother priests I would have resisted – even as they do – such abuses of power. I cannot ask them to become what they loathe. The true power of the Source has always lain in the absence of power. Can you understand that?'

'I am not sure that I can.'

'It is like holding a spear to the chest of an enemy, then laying it aside. Even as he kills you – if such he does – he knows that he does not do it by his strength, but by your choice.'

'But – to continue with your analogy – you are still dead, yes?'

'Death is not important. You see, the Source priests believe that for life to exist there must be harmony created by balance. For every man who lives to steal or kill, there must be another who lives to give and save. Tidal love was the name they gave it at my temple; my Abbot used to teach it often. In a merchant's shop, the merchant gives you too many coins in change. You keep the coins, marvelling at your good fortune. But when you have gone he realises his mistake and is angry, both with himself and with you. So the next man who comes into the shop he cheats, to gain back his money. This man in turn realises later and he is angry, and perhaps takes out his anger on someone else. So the tide goes out, each wave affecting more and more people.

'The Source teaches us to do only kind deeds – to be honest and loving, giving good for evil, to bring the tide back in.'

'All very noble,' said Gellan, 'but wondrously impractical. When a wolf raids the fold, you don't make it go away by feeding it lambs! However, this is not the time for theological debate. And you have already proved where your feelings lie.'

'May I ask you something, Dun Gellan?'

'Of course.'

'I watched you fight today, and you were unlike any other warrior. You were calm and at peace. Amid the slaughter and the fear you alone remained calm. How was it done?'

'I had nothing to lose,' said Gellan.

'You had your life.'

'Ah yes, my life. Was there anything else you wished to know?'

'No, but if you will forgive me, let me say this: all children are creatures of joy, and all people are capable of love. You feel you lost everything, but there was a time before your joy when your children did not exist and your wife was unknown to you. Could it not be that there is a woman somewhere who will fill your life with love, and bear you children to bring you joy?'

'Go away, priest,' said Gellan gently.

Waylander returned to the wall and watched the enemy. Their leader had finished his speech and the men were sitting, staring sullenly towards the fort. Waylander rubbed his eyes. He knew how they felt. This morning they had been confident of their skills, arrogant and proud. Now they were demoralised by the realisation of defeat.

His own thoughts echoed their despair. A week ago he had been Waylander the Slayer, secure in his talents and unaware of any guilt.

Now he felt more lonely than at any time in his life. How strange that loneliness should lay him low while he was surrounded by people, he thought. He had never sensed this emotion while living alone in the mountains or the forests. His conversation with Gellan had hurt him deeply and he had withdrawn, as ever, into flippancy. Of all the people who thronged his memories, Gellan alone he regarded with affection.

But what could he have said to him? Well, Gellan my friend, I see you stayed with the army. Me? Oh, I became an assassin. I'll kill anyone for money – I even killed your King. It was so easy; I shot him in the back while he walked in his garden.

Or perhaps he could have mentioned the murder of his family. Would Gellan have understood his despair and what it did to him? Why should he? Had he not lost his own?

It was the damned priest. He should have left him tied to the tree. The priest had power: when he had touched the clothes of the robbers he had sensed their evil through the cloth. Waylander had turned him into a killer by staining his purity. But was such power double-edged? Had the priest returned the unholy gift by touching Waylander with goodness? Waylander smiled.

A Vagrian rider galloped from the north and dragged his mount to a halt before the general. Within minutes the Vagrians were mounted and heading east.

Waylander shook his head and loosened the strings of his crossbow. Drenai soldiers ran to the walls to watch the enemy depart and a ragged cheer went up. Waylander sat down. Vanek yawned and stretched.

'What's happening?' he asked, sitting up and yawning once more.

'The Vagrians have gone.'

'That's good. Gods, I'm hungry.'

'Do you always sleep in the middle of a battle?'

'I don't know, this is the first battle I've been in – unless you count when we captured the wagons, which was more of a massacre. I'll let you know when I've been in a few more. Did you finish my canteen?'

Waylander threw him the half-empty canteen, then rose and wandered to the Keep. A barrel of apples had been opened by the cook and Waylander took two and ate them before making his way to the winding stair and the tower, emerging into the sunlight to see Danyal leaning on the rampart and staring north.

'It's over,' said Waylander. 'You are safe now.'

She turned and smiled. 'For the while.'

'That is all anyone can ask.'

'Stay and talk,' she said. He looked at her, seeing the sunlight glinting from her red-gold hair.

'I have nothing to say.'

'I feared for you in the fighting. I didn't want you to die,' she said hurriedly, as he stepped into the shadows of the doorway. He stopped then, standing with his back to her for several seconds, then he turned.

'I am sorry about the boy,' he said softly. 'But the wound was grievous and he would have been in great pain for hours, perhaps days.'

'I know.'

'I do not enjoy killing boys. I don't know why I said it. I am not good with words . . . with people.' He wandered to the ramparts and gazed down on the soldiers harnessing the oxen to the wagons and preparing for the long ride to Skultik. Gellan was at the centre of the operation, flanked by Sarvaj and Jonat. 'I used to be an officer. I used to be many things. A husband. A father. He looked so peaceful lying there among the flowers. As if he was asleep in the sunshine. Only the day before I had taught him to ride his pony over the short jumps. I went out hunting . . . he wanted to come with me.' Waylander stared down at the grey stone. 'He was seven years old. They killed him anyway. There were nineteen of them – renegades and deserters.'

He felt her hands on his shoulders and turned into her arms. Danyal had not understood much of what he said, but she read the anguish in his words. He sat back on the ramparts, pulling her to him, his face against hers, and she felt his tears upon her cheeks.

'He looked so peaceful,' said Waylander.

'Like Culas,' whispered Danyal.

'Yes. I found them all – it took years. There was a price on their heads and I used each bounty to finance my search for the others. When I caught the last, I wanted him to know why he was going to die. And when I told him who I was, he couldn't remember the killings. He died not knowing.'

'How did you feel?'

'Empty. Lost.'

'How do you feel now?'

'I don't know. It is not something I want to think about.'

Her hands came up and cupped his face, turning it towards her own. Tilting her head she kissed him, first on the cheek, then on the mouth. Then she moved back, pulling him to his feet.

'You gave us life, Dakeyras, the children and me. We will always love you for that.'

Before he could answer, another cheer went up from the walls below.

Karnak had arrived with four hundred riders.

9

Gellan ordered the wagons pulled back from the breach and Karnak rode into the fort with ten of his officers. He was a huge man, running to fat, who looked older than his thirty-two years. He dismounted beside Gellan and grinned.

'Gods, man, you're a wonder!' he said. Swinging round, he unfastened his green cloak and draped it over his saddle. 'Gather round, you men,' he shouted. 'I want to see the heroes of Masin. That means you too, Vanek,' he called. 'And you, Parac!'

The twenty-five survivors came forward, grinning sheepishly. Many of them were wounded, but they bore themselves proudly before the charismatic general.

'Gods, I'm proud of you all! You've seen off a crack force of some of the best the Vagrians can offer. What's more, you've taken enough supplies to keep us for a month. But even better than that, you've shown what Drenai courage can do. Your deeds here will shine like a torch to the Drenai people – and I can promise you that this is only the beginning. At the moment we may be down, but we're not finished – not while we have men like you. We'll take this war to the enemy and make them suffer. You have my word on it. Now let's get to Skultik and I'll really show you how to celebrate.' He moved to Gellan, throwing a brawny arm over the officer's shoulder.

'Now where's this sorcerer of yours?'

'He is in the Keep, sir. How do you know of him?'

'That's why we're here, man. He contacted one of our priests last night and told us of your plight. Damn it all, this could be a turning point for us.'

'I hope so, sir.'

'You did wonderfully well, Gellan.'

'I lost almost half my men, sir. I should have abandoned the wagons two days ago.'

'Nonsense, man! Had we not arrived in time and you had all been killed, I would have agreed with you. But the victory was worth the risk. I've got to be honest – I didn't expect it of you. Not that I doubt your courage, but you are a cautious man.'

'You use "cautious" as an insult, sir.'

'Maybe I do. But these are desperate times and they call for the odd risk. Caution won't send the Vagrians packing. And make no mistake, Gellan, what I said to the men was not mere rhetoric. We *will* win. Do you believe that?'

'It is very hard not to believe what you say, general. The men think that if you wanted the sky green instead of blue, you would climb a mountain and paint it as it passed.'

'And what do you think?'

'I am ashamed to admit that I agree with them.'

'The men need leaders, Gellan. Men with fire in their bellies. When morale goes, there can be no victory. Remember that.'

'I am aware of it, sir. But I am not good with speeches.'

'Don't worry about that, I'll handle the speeches. You've done fine work today and I'm proud of you. You know Purdol is still holding?'

'I am glad to hear it, sir.'

'I'm going there tomorrow.'

'But it's surrounded.'

'I know, but it's important that the fortress holds. It ties down the bulk of the Vagrian force.'

'With respect, sir, it is far more important that you stay free. It is said they have put a price of 10,000 gold pieces on your head – almost as much as they've offered for Egel himself.'

'Have you forgotten so swiftly what I just said about risks?'

'But if they realise you are in Purdol, they will redouble their efforts to take it and bring in more troops.'

'Precisely!'

'I am sorry, sir, but I think it's insane.'

'That's where you and I differ, Gellan. You don't see things on the grand scale. Look at me! I'm too big to sit a horse with any confidence and I am no cavalry general – give me a fortress to hold and I'm in my element. But Egel is a strategist and a fine, wily campaigner. They don't need me in Skultik. But if I can get into Purdol the Vagrians will mass troops there, giving Egel a chance to break from the forest.'

'I see the logic and I don't want to sound like a sycophant, but we *need* you. If you are captured or killed, the Drenai cause will be close to lost.'

'Nice of you to say so. But the plan is set. How do you fancy coming with me?'

'I wouldn't miss it for the world,' said Gellan, grinning.

'That's my man,' said Karnak. 'Now where is this sorcerer?'

Gellan took the general into the Keep where Dardalion sat with the children.

'That is the sorcerer?' asked Karnak, staring at the young man in the silver armour.

'I am afraid so,' replied Gellan.

Dardalion turned as they entered and stood, bowing to the general.

'You are Dardalion?'

'I am.'

'I am Karnak.'

'I know, general. You are most welcome.'

'You are the most unlikely sorcerer I ever met.'

'I am hardly a sorcerer; I cast no spells.'

'You certainly cast one over the Vagrians – you saved the fort and every man in it. Will you ride with me?'

'I should be honoured.'

Karnak smiled at the children, but they hid behind Dardalion. 'You

78

know, I believe the tide is turning,' said Karnak. 'If I can but avoid the soldiers around Purdol and the cursed Dark Brotherhood, I think we might just be ready to deliver a few death blows to the Vagrian hopes.'

'The Dark Brotherhood are hunting you?' asked Dardalion.

'They have been for months. And added to that, it is said that Waylander the Slayer has been hired to kill me.'

'That is most unlikely,' said Dardalion.

'Really? You are a prophet also?'

'No . . . yes . . . it is not Waylander's way.'

'You know him?' asked Karnak.

'Yes, he knows him,' said Waylander, moving into sight on the stairway with his crossbow in hand.

Karnak turned slowly and Gellan moved in front of him.

'I am Waylander, and if I wanted you dead you would *be* dead. So now all you have to worry about is the Brotherhood.'

'You think I should believe you?'

'It would be a wise move in the circumstances.'

'I have four hundred men within call.'

'But they are not here now, general.'

'That is true,' Karnak agreed. 'So you are not here to kill me?'

'No. I have other business.'

'Does it affect the Drenai cause?'

'And if it does?' asked Waylander.

'Then I will walk over to you and break your neck,' said Karnak.

'Luckily it should help your cause,' said Waylander. 'I have been asked to supply Egel with a new suit of Armour!'

They rode warily, a dozen scouts ringing the main party and the warrior general at the centre of the force shielded by six riders. Dardalion rode on his left and Gellan on the right. Behind them came the wagons, each pulled by six oxen.

Danyal and the children rode in the lead wagon alongside the warrior Vanek. She found him to be an amusing companion. At one point, as the two lead oxen pulled in opposite directions, Vanek said, straight faced: 'Highly trained, these animals – obey my every command. I'm making them do this.'

Behind the wagons rode the rearguard of a hundred men led by Dundas, Karnak's aide: a young man with fair hair and a friendly, open face. Beside him rode Waylander, in no doubt that he was a virtual prisoner; four riders sat their mounts close to him, hands on sword-hilts.

Waylander hid his annoyance and allowed his mind to wander as his eyes soaked in the green beauty of the Sentran Plain where it merged with the grey-blue mountains of the north. After all, what did it matter if they killed him? Had he not murdered their king? And what was so special about life that he should desire to extend his span?

None of it mattered, he realised, as the mountains loomed ever more close. How much death had these peaks seen? Who would care about this petty war in a thousand years?

'You are an undemanding companion,' remarked Dundas, lifting his helm and running his fingers through his hair.

Waylander did not reply. Swinging his horse's head to the left, he made to canter forward but his way was blocked by a rider.

'The general thinks we should hold formation while in dangerous territory,' said Dundas smoothly. 'You don't object?'

'And if I do?'

'It will not be for long, I assure you.'

As the day wore on, Dundas tired of attempting conversation with the dark-haired warrior. He didn't know why Karnak wanted him guarded and, in truth, he didn't care. But then that was Karnak's way – to explain only what was necessary and expect his orders to be carried out to the letter. At times it made him an extraordinarily aggravating man to serve under.

'What is he like?' asked Waylander suddenly.

'I am sorry, my mind was wandering,' said Dundas. 'What did you say?'

'The general – what is he like?'

'Why do you want to know?'

'Curiosity. I understand he was a First Dun officer in charge of a hill fort. Now he is a general.'

'You have not heard of Hargate and the siege?'

'No.'

'I should really let the general tell it. There are so many wonderful embellishments to the tale now that it would not surprise me to hear that dragons have been introduced. But still . . . would you like to hear it?'

'Were you there?'

'Yes.'

'Good. I prefer first-hand accounts.'

'Well, as you say, Karnak was First Dun at Hargate. The fort is not large – probably twice the size of Masin, and there is . . . was . . . a small town outside the keep. Karnak had six hundred men under his command. The Vagrians poured into Skoda and surrounded Hargate, demanding our surrender. We refused and held off their attacks for the first day, then watched as they made their night camp. We had lost sixty men during the day, but we were holding well and the Vagrians believed they had us all in their net.'

'How many of them were there?' asked Waylander.

'We estimated eight thousand. Anyway, Karnak had sent scouts to watch for the Vagrians – he never trusted their promises of peace – so we had advance warning of their attack. Do you know Hargate . . . ?' Waylander nodded. 'Then you know there is a small wood about a mile to the east. Karnak had taken three hundred men there during the previous night. Now, as the Vagrians slept in their camp he descended on them in the darkest hours of the night, firing their tents and stampeding their horses. Our warriors made enough noise to be mistaken for a whole Drenai army, and we opened the gates and led an attack from the front. The Vagrians pulled back to re-form, but by dawn we were away to Skultik. We must have slain more than eight hundred of them.'

'Clever,' said Waylander, 'but hardly a victory.'

'What do you mean? We were outnumbered more than ten to one.'

'Exactly. When you first received news of the invasion, you could have pulled back. What point was there in fighting at all?'

'Have you no sense of honour? We gave them a bloody nose – we let them know the Drenai can fight as well as they run.'

'But still they took the fort.'

'I do not understand you, Dakeyras . . . or whatever your name is. If running means so much to you, why did you go to Masin and help Gellan and his men?'

'It was the only safe place. Or rather the safest I could find.'

'Well, you will be safe enough in Skultik. The Vagrians dare not invade.'

'I hope the Vagrians know that.'

'What does that mean?' snapped the young officer.

'Nothing at all. Tell me about Egel?'

'Why? So that you can mock *his* achievements?'

'You are young and full of fire, and you see mockery where none exists. It is not blasphemy to question a military decision. It could be, as you say, that Karnak's decision to give a bloody nose to the Vagrians was a good one; it would lift morale, for example. But it strikes me that it was a risky venture which could have whiplashed against him. What if the enemy had scouted the woods? He would have been forced to run, leaving you and three hundred men trapped.'

'But they did not.'

'Exactly – and now he is a hero. I have known many heroes. Mostly other men die to build their legends.'

'I would be proud to die for Karnak – he is a great man. And beware of insulting him, unless you wish to cross swords with any man within earshot.'

'I think your message is clear, Dundas. He is revered.'

'And rightly so. He does not send his men into danger without risking himself. He is always in the thick of the fighting.'

'Very wise,' observed Waylander.

'Even now he plans to ride to the aid of Purdol. Is that the act of a vainglorious man?'

'Purdol? It is surrounded.'

Dundas bit his lip and turned away momentarily, his face reddening. 'I would be obliged if you did not repeat that. I should not have said it.'

'I am not known for being loose-tongued,' said Waylander. 'It is forgotten.'

'Thank you, I am grateful. It is just that I was angry. He is a very great man.'

'I am sure that he is. And now that we trust each other, I am sure you will not object to my riding forward to speak with my companions?'

Dundas' face was a picture of confusion, but a resigned expression settled over his features. 'Of course not. I need to feel the wind in my face also. I will ride with you.'

The two men spurred their horses into a canter and Waylander rode to the centre of the column. Karnak swung in the saddle as he approached, followed by the young officer.

'Welcome to our group, Waylander,' said the general, grinning. 'You've just missed the tale of Hargate.'

'No, I did not. Dundas spoke of it. But were there dragons in your account?'

'Not yet, but I'm working on it,' replied Karnak. 'Come ride beside me. I understand you and Gellan are old friends?'

'We knew one another once,' said Gellan, 'but not very well.'

'No matter,' said Karnak. 'Tell me, Waylander, why do the Brotherhood hunt you?'

'I killed Kaem's son.'

'Why?'

'His father owed me money.'

'God, you sicken me!' snapped Gellan. 'Excuse me, general, but I need to ride awhile and stretch my back.' Karnak nodded and Gellan pulled his horse from the group.

'You're a strange man,' said Karnak.

Waylander smiled coldly. 'So are you, general. What are you seeking?'

'Victory. What else is there?'

'Immortality?'

Karnak smiled. 'Do not misread me, Waylander – I am no man's fool. I am vain. I am conceited. My strength is that I *know* what I am. I am the finest general you will ever know, and the greatest warrior of the age. Yes, I want immortality. And I will not be remembered as a gallant loser. Count on it.'

Although they pushed on through most of the night, a sudden storm bogged down the wagons and Karnak called a halt. Tarpaulins were hastily erected against the sides of the wagons to create makeshift tents and men huddled there together against the lashing rain.

Karnak kept Waylander close to him, but the assassin could not fail to notice the presence of two armed men who watched him constantly. Nor did he miss the venomous glance Karnak hurled at Dundas as the young officer returned to his men. Yet for all that the general remained, on the surface, in good humour. Sitting below the crude tent, his clothes wet and clinging to his body, Karnak ought – Waylander considered – to cut a ridiculous figure. The man was overweight and outlandishly garbed in clothes of green, blue and yellow. And yet he was still impressive.

'What are you thinking?' asked Karnak, drawing his cloak about his shoulders.

'I am wondering what on earth possesses you to dress like that,' said Waylander, grinning. 'Blue shirt, green cloak, yellow leggings! It seems that you dressed in stages while drunk.'

'I am not shaped for fashionable garments,' admitted Karnak. 'I dress for comfort. Now tell me about this Armour of Egel's.'

'An old man asked me to fetch it for him and I said that I would. There is no mystery to it.'

'How splendidly you understate your mission. The old man was Orien, while the Armour is legend and hidden in the lands of the Nadir.'

'Dardalion told you. Well then, there is no need for you to question me further. You know all there is to know.'

'I do not know why you chose to go. What does it profit you?'

'That is my business.'

'Indeed. But the Armour means a great deal to the Drenai and that *is* my concern.'

'You have come a long way in a short time, general. It is hardly the concern of a First Dun at a run-down fort.'

'Understand me, Waylander. I am a genial man with a heart of gold . . . when people humour me. Now, I like you and I am trying to forget that a man dressed in black and carrying a small crossbow killed King Niallad. Such a man would receive swift sentencing.'

'Why do you need to know?'

Karnak leaned back, his pale eyes locking to Waylander's gaze. 'I could use the Armour, it would help me.'

'It would not fit you, general.'

'It can be altered.'

'But it is promised to Egel.'

'He does not even know of it.'

'You are a man full of surprises, Karnak. Here you sit on the edge of defeat and already you plan your brilliant future. What is it to be? King Karnak? That has a ring to it. Earl Karnak, perhaps?'

'I am not looking that far ahead, Waylander. I trust my judgements. Egel is a fine warrior and a good general. Cautious, yes, but there is steel in the man. Given certain advantages, he could swing this war.'

'The Armour would be just such an advantage,' commented Waylander.

'Indeed it would. But it could be put to better use elsewhere.'

'Where?'

'Purdol,' said Karnak, leaning forward and watching Waylander intently.

'The fortress is already surrounded.'

'There is a way in.'

'What do you have in mind?'

'I will send twenty of my best men with you to fetch the Armour. You will bring it to Purdol – to me.'

'And you will stand on the battlements in Orien's Armour of Bronze and carve yourself a role in the history of the Drenai people.'

'Yes. What do you say?'

'I say forget it. Orien asked a favour of me and I said that I would attempt it. I may not be a great man, Karnak, but when I speak you can rely on my word. If it is humanly possible to retrieve the Armour, I will do so . . . and deliver it to Egel in Skultik, or wherever he may be. Does that answer the question?'

'You realise I am holding your life in the palm of my hand?'

'I do not care, general. That is the simple beauty of this quest. I do not care if it is successful – and I care even less about threats to my life. I have nothing to live for, my blood runs in no living thing. Can you understand that?'

'So I cannot tempt you with riches or with threats?'

'That is true. It makes a nonsense of my reputation, does it not?'

'Is there anything I can do to help you with your quest?'

'That is a somewhat abrupt change of stance, general.'

'I am a realist. I know when to walk away. If I cannot have the Armour, then Egel is the next best thing for the Drenai. So ask. Anything you require?'

'I require nothing. I have funds enough in Skarta.'

'But surely you cannot intend to go alone?'

'Ideally I would like to take an army – but short of that, one man has more chance of success.'

'What of Dardalion?'

'His destiny lies elsewhere. He can, and will, prove useful to you.'

'How soon do you plan to leave?'

'Soon.'

'Still you do not trust me?'

'I trust no one, general. Trust implies need, need implies caring.'

'And you care for nothing? Not even the woman and the children?'

'I care for nothing.'

'I read men as other men read tracks. You are an open book to me, Waylander, and I think you are lying – as you lied when I asked about Kaem's son. But we will let it lie; it matters not a whit, except to you. I will let you sleep now.'

The huge general pushed himself to his feet and stepped out into the night. The rain had stopped. Karnak stretched his back and moved off along the column, flanked by his two bodyguards.

'What do you make of him, Ris?' he asked the taller of the two.

'I don't know, general. They say he fought well at Masin. He's steady. Cool.'

'But would you trust him?'

'I think I would. I would certainly sooner trust him than fight him.'

'Well said.'

'I do have a question, sir, if I may?'

'Gods, man, you don't have to ask. Go ahead.'

'All that about the Armour. What would you do with it?'

'I would have sent it to Egel.'

'I do not understand. That is where he plans to take it.'

'All life is a riddle, my friend,' said Karnak.

10

The town of Skarta sprawled across a clearing between two hills in the south-west of Skultik. There were no walls around it, though hastily constructed defences were in evidence – loosely packed barriers of local rock built behind deep ditches. Soldiers were at work everywhere, increasing the height of the barricades or filling in the outfacing windows of perimeter homes.

But all work ceased as Karnak, now at the head of the column, led the wagons into the town.

'Welcome back, general!' shouted one man, sitting back on the wall he was building.

'Meat tonight. How does that sound?' yelled Karnak.

Back at the rear of the column Waylander rode with Dardalion.

'Another great Karnak victory,' observed Waylander. 'See how the crowds flock to him! You would think he defended Masin himself. Where is Gellan in this moment of triumph?'

'Why do you not like him?' asked Dardalion.

'I do not dislike him. But he is a poseur.'

'Do you not think he needs to be? He has a demoralised army – a force in need of heroes.'

'Perhaps.' Waylander cast his eyes over the defences. They were well planned, the ditches deep enough to prevent a force of horsemen from charging the town and the walls strategically placed to allow archers to inflict heavy losses on an attacking army. But they were useless in any long-term encounter, for they were neither high nor strong. Nor were they linked. It was not possible to turn Skarta into a fortress, and Waylander guessed the defences were more for the town's morale than for any genuine attempt to fight the Vagrians.

Once through the outer defences, the wagons pulled into the centre of Skultik. The buildings were mainly of white stone, hewn from the Delnoch mountains to the north. Mostly single-storey dwellings, the town was built around an old fort villa at the centre which now was the Hall of Council and Egel's headquarters.

Waylander reined in his horse as the column entered.

'I will find you later,' he called to Dardalion, then rode to the eastern quarter. Since his meeting with Karnak he was no longer guarded, but he still proceeded cautiously, checking several times to see if he was being followed. The houses were poorer here, the walls painted white to imitate the grand granite and marble homes of the northern quarter, but the stone was inferior quality.

Waylander rode to an inn near the Street of Weavers and left his mount in a stable at the rear. The inn was crowded, the air thick with the smell of stale sweat and cheap beer. He pushed his way through to the long wooden bar, his eyes raking the crowd; the barman lifted a pewter mug as he saw him approach.

'Ale?' he asked.

Waylander nodded. 'I am looking for Durmast,' he said.

'Many people look for Durmast. He must be a popular man.'

'He's a pig. But I need to find him.'

'Owe you money, does he?' The barman grinned, showing stained and broken teeth.

'I am ashamed to admit that he's a friend of mine.'

'Then you ought to know where he is.'

'Is he in that much trouble?'

The barman grinned again and filled Waylander's jug with frothing ale. 'If you are seeking him, you'll find him. Enjoy your drink.'

'How much?'

'Money's not worth that much here, friend. So we are giving it away.'

Waylander drank deeply. 'Tasting like this, you ought to pay people for drinking it!' The barman moved away and Waylander settled his arms on the bar and waited. After several minutes, a thin, hatchet-faced young man tapped his arm.

'Follow me,' he said.

They moved through the crowd to a narrow door at the back of the inn, which opened on to a small courtyard and a series of alleys. The man's slight figure jogged ahead, cutting left and right through the maze until at last he stopped at a wide door studded with brass. There he knocked three times, waited, then twice more and the door was opened by a woman wearing a long green dress. Wearily she led them to a room at the back of the house and the young man knocked again. Then he grinned at Waylander and moved away.

Waylander placed his hand on the door-latch, then stopped. Moving to one side with his back against the wall, he flicked the latch and pushed the door open. A crossbow shaft hammered into the wall opposite, sending a shower of sparks across the corridor.

'Is that any way to greet an old friend?' asked Waylander.

'A man has to be careful among friends,' came the reply.

'You owe me money, you reprobate!'

'Come in and collect it.'

Waylander moved away from the door to the other side of the corridor. Taking two running steps, he hurled himself head-first into the room, rolling forward to his feet with knife in hand as he hit the floor.

'Game is over and you are dead!' came the voice, this time from the doorway. Waylander turned slowly. Standing behind the door was a huge bear of a man holding a black crossbow, the bolt aimed at Waylander's stomach.

'You are getting old and slow, Waylander,' commented Durmast. Lifting the bolt from the weapon, he snapped the string forward and placed the crossbow against the wall. Waylander shook his head and sheathed his knife. Then the big man moved across the room and lifted him from his feet in a bone-crushing bear hug. He planted a kiss on Waylander's forehead before releasing him.

'You stink of onions,' said Waylander.

Durmast grinned and lowered his huge frame into a leather chair. The man was even bigger than the assassin remembered, and his brown beard was shaggy and unkempt. He was dressed as always in a mixture of green and brown homespun wool which gave him the appearance of a human tree: a thing created from sorcery. Durmast was just under seven feet tall and weighed more than three large men. Waylander had known him for eleven years and, in as much as he trusted any living man, he trusted the giant.

'Well, get to the point,' said Durmast. 'Who are you hunting?'

'No one.'

'Then who is hunting you?'

'Just about everyone. But mainly the Brotherhood.'

'You pick your enemies well, my friend. Here, read this.' Durmast delved into an untidy mass of parchment scrolls and came up with a tightly rolled package, sealed with a black circle of wax. The seal was broken. Waylander took the scroll and read it swiftly.

'Five thousand gold pieces? It makes me valuable.'

'Only dead,' said Durmast.

'Hence the crossbow greeting.'

'Professional pride. If times get tough I can always rely on you – and the price on your wolf's head.'

'I need your help,' said Waylander, pulling up a seat opposite the giant.

'Helping you will prove costly.'

'You know I can pay. You already owe me six thousand in silver.'

'Then that is the price.'

'You don't know yet what aid I need.'

'True – but that is the price anyway.'

'And if I refuse?'

The smile faded from the giant's face. 'Then I will collect the Brotherhood's bounty on you.'

'You drive a hard bargain.'

'No harder than the one you forced me to on that Ventrian mountainside when my leg was broken. Six thousand for a splint and a horse?'

'There were enemies close by,' said Waylander. 'Was your life worth so little?'

'Another man would have rescued me out of friendship.'

'But then men like us have no friends, Durmast.'

'So do you agree the price?'

'Yes.'

'Fine. What do you need?'

'I need someone to guide me to Raboas, the Sacred Giant.'

'Why? You know where it is.'

'I want to get back alive – and I shall be bringing something with me.'

'You intend to steal Nadir treasure from their holiest place? You don't need a guide, you need an army! Ask the Vagrians – they just might be strong enough. But I doubt it.'

'I need someone who knows the Nadir and is welcome in their camps. What I am seeking is not a Nadir treasure; it belongs to the Drenai. But I will not lie to you, Durmast, there is great danger. The Brotherhood will be on my train and they seek the same goal.'

'Valuable, is it?'

'It is worth more than a king's ransom.'

'And what percentage do you offer me?'

'Half of what I am receiving.'

'That's fair. What are you getting?'

'Nothing at all.'

'Are you telling me that this is something you promised to do for your sick mother on her deathbed?'

'No. I promised an old blind man on his.'

'I don't believe a word of this. You never did anything for nothing in your life. Gods, man, I saved you twice at cost to myself, yet when I was in trouble you charged me silver. Now you tell me you have become an altruist? Do not make me angry, Waylander. You would not like me angry.'

Waylander shrugged. 'I am surprising myself. There is little more I can tell you.'

'But there is. Tell me about the old man.'

Waylander leaned back. What could he tell him? In what way could he lay out the story so that Durmast would understand what had happened to him? No way at all. The giant was a killer, merciless and amoral – even as Waylander had been but a few short days before. How could he understand the shame the old man had inspired in Waylander? He took a deep breath and launched into the tale, allowing no embellishments. Durmast listened in silence, no flicker of expression on his wide features, no glint of emotion in his green eyes. At the conclusion Waylander spread his arms and lapsed into silence.

'The Drenai would pay all that they have to get the Armour?' asked Durmast.

'Yes.'

'And the Vagrians would pay more?'

'Indeed they would.'

'And you are going to do it for nothing?'

'With your help.'

'When do you plan to leave?'

'Tomorrow.'

'You know the grove of oaks to the north?'

'Yes.'

'I'll meet you there and we'll go out over the Delnoch Pass.'

'What about the money?' asked Waylander softly.

'Six thousand, you said. It wipes the slate clean.'

Waylander nodded thoughtfully. 'I had expected you to ask for more, considering the size of the task.'

'Life is full of surprises, Waylander.'

After the assassin had gone, Durmast called the hatchet-faced young man into the room.

'Did you hear all that?' he asked.

'Yes. Is he mad?'

'No, he's merely gone soft. It happens, Sorak. But do not underestimate him. He is one of the finest warriors I have ever seen and will prove a hard man to kill.'

'Why do we not just kill him for the bounty?'

'Because I want that Armour *and* the bounty.'

'So much for friendship,' said Sorak, grinning.

'You heard the man. People like us have no friends.'

Danyal took the children to a tiny schoolhouse behind the Hall of Council. It was run by three Source priests and there were more than forty children housed there, orphans of the war. A further three hundred had been billeted with the townspeople of Skarta. Krylla and Miriel seemed content enough to be left there and waved happily from the play area as Danyal walked away beside an elderly priest.

'Tell me, sister,' he asked as they halted by the wrought-iron gate, 'what do you know of Dardalion?'

'He is a priest like yourself,' she answered.

'But a priest who kills,' he said sadly.

'I cannot help you. He did what he felt was necessary to save lives – there is no evil in him.'

'There is evil in all of us, sister, and the mark of a man is how he defies the evil within. Our young men talk much of Dardalion and I fear he poses a terrible threat to our Order.'

'Or perhaps he will help to save it,' she ventured.

'If we need saving by men, then all we believe is nonsense. For if Man is ultimately more powerful than God, what need have we to worship a deity at all? But I do not wish to burden you with our problems. May the Source bless you, sister.'

She left him and wandered through the white-walled streets. Her dress was filthy and torn and she felt like a beggar under the stares of the townsfolk. A short fat man approached her, offering money, but she dismissed him with an angry glare. Then a woman touched her arm as she passed.

'Did you just come in, my dear?' she asked.

'Yes.'

'Was there a man named Vanek with your party?'

'Yes, a soldier with a limp.'

The woman looked relieved. She was plump, and once must have been pretty, but now her face was lined and she had lost several teeth on the right side of her face which gave her a lopsided appearance.

'My name is Tacia. There is a bath-house next to my home and you are welcome to use it.'

The bath-house was deserted and the main bath empty, but several tubs remained in the side rooms. Tacia helped Danyal to fill a copper tub with buckets of water from a well at the rear of the bath-house, then sat down as she removed her dress and lowered herself into the cold water.

'They do not heat the water any more,' said Tacia. 'Not since the council man left. He owned the House; he went to Drenan.'

'It is fine,' said Danyal. 'Is there any soap?'

Tacia left her and returned some minutes later carrying soap, towels and a skirt and tunic top.

'It will be too large for you, but I can soon alter it,' she said.

'Are you Vanek's wife?'

'I was,' she said, 'but he lives now with a young girl from the southern quarter.'

'I am sorry.'

'Never wed a soldier – isn't that what they say? The children miss him; he is very good with children.'

'Were you married long?'

'Twelve years.'

'Maybe you'll get back together,' said Danyal.

'Maybe – if my teeth grow again and the years fall away from my face! Have you anywhere to stay?'

'No.'

'You are welcome to share our house. It isn't much, but it is comfortable – if you don't mind children.'

'Thank you, Tacia, but I am not sure I am staying in Skarta.'

'Where else is there to go? Purdol is ready to fall, I hear, despite the promises from Karnak and Egel. They must think we are stupid. No one is going to resist the Vagrians for long . . . look how swiftly they have conquered the country.'

Danyal said nothing, knowing she had no antidote to the woman's despair.

'Do you have a man?' asked Tacia.

Danyal thought instantly of Waylander, then shook her head.

'You are lucky,' said the woman. '*We* fall in love with men, *they* fall in love with soft skin and bright eyes. I really loved him, you know. I would not have minded had he slept with her now and again. But why did he have to leave me for her?'

'I am sorry. I do not know what to say.'

'No. You'll know one day though, when that pretty red hair of yours streaks with grey and your skin gets hard. I wish I was young again. I wish I had pretty red hair and did not know how to answer an old woman.'

'You are not old.'

Tacia stood and laid the clothes on the chair. 'When you are ready, come next door. I have some supper prepared – vegetables only, I'm afraid, but we still have some spices to give it flavour.'

Danyal watched the woman leave, then poured soap into her hair and scrubbed away the dirt and grease. At last she stood and dried herself before a bronzed mirror at the far end of the room.

Somehow the sight of her beauty failed to lift her as it usually did.

Dardalion wandered to the outskirts of the town, crossing a curved stone bridge over a narrow stream. The trees were thinner here – elm and birch, slender and graceful compared with the giant oaks of the forest. Flowers bloomed by the stream, bluebells seeming to float above the ground like a sapphire mist. There was tranquillity here, thought Dardalion. Harmony.

The tents of the priests were spread in a meadow in an orderly circle. Nearby was a fresh graveyard, the mounds carpeted with flowers.

Uncomfortable in his armour, Dardalion walked into the meadow and watched the eyes of the priests turn towards him. A mixture of emotions stuck him forcefully: anguish, pain, disappointment, elation, pride, despair. He absorbed them, as he absorbed the mind-faces of those who projected the feelings, and he responded with love born of sorrow.

As he came near the priests gathered around him silently, leaving a path to the tent at the centre of the circle. When he approached an elderly man stepped from the tent and bowed deeply. Dardalion fell to his knees before the Abbot and bowed his head.

'Welcome, brother Dardalion,' said the old man softly.

'Thank you, Father Abbot.'

'Will you remove the garments of war and rejoin your brethren?'

'It is with regret that I must refuse.'

'Then you are no longer a priest and should not kneel before me. Stand as a man, freed of your vows.'

'I do not wish to be free of my vows.'

'The eagle does not pull a plough, Dardalion, and the Source accepts no half-way heroes.'

The old man reached down and gently pulled Dardalion to his feet. The young warrior priest looked into his eyes, seeking righteous anger but finding only sadness. The Abbot was very old, his face webbed with the weight of his life. Yet his eyes were bright, alive with intelligence.

'I do not wish to be free. I wish to follow a different path to the Source.'

'All paths lead to the Source, whether for judgement or joy.'

'Do not play word games with me, Father Abbot. I am no child. But I have seen great evil in the land and I will not sit by and watch it triumph.'

'Who is to say where triumph lies? What is life but a search for God? A battleground, a cesspit, a paradise? I see the pain you see and it saddens me. And where I find pain I bring comfort, and where I find sorrow I bring promises of future joy. I exist to heal, Dardalion. There is no victory in the sword.'

Dardalion drew himself upright and glanced about him, feeling the weight of the unasked questions. All eyes were on him and he sighed and closed his eyes, praying for guidance. But his prayer was unanswered, and he felt no lifting of the burden upon him.

'I brought two children to Skarta – bright, lively youngsters with rare talents. And I have seen the deaths of evil men, and know that through their deaths other innocents will know life. And I have prayed constantly about my path, and my deeds, and my future. It seems to me, Father Abbot, that the Source requires balance in the world. Hunters and hunted.

The weakest calf in the herd is the one to be caught by wolves. Therefore the bloodlines remain strong in the herd. But too many wolves will destroy the herd, so the huntsmen track the wolves, catching the weakest and oldest.

'How many examples do we need to show that the Source is a God of equity? Why create the eagle and the wolf, the locust and the scorpion? At every turn there is balance. Yet when we see the evil of the Brotherhood at work, and the worshippers of Chaos stain the land, we sit in our tents and ponder the mysteries of the stars. Where is the balance there, Father Abbot?'

'We seek to teach the world that our values are those to be followed. But if all followed us in celibacy, where would the world be? Mankind would cease.'

'And there would be no more war,' said the Abbot. 'No more greed, lust, despair and sorrow.'

'Yes. And no love, joy, or contentment.'

'Are you content, Dardalion?'

'No. I am heartsick and lost.'

'And were you content as a priest?'

'Yes. Sublimely so.'

'And does not that show where the error lies in your thinking?'

'It does not – rather it exposes the selfishness of my soul. We seek to be altruistic, for we yearn to be blessed by the Source. But then it is not altruism, nor love, that guides us, but self-interest. We do not spread the message of love for love's sake, but for our own futures as priests of the Source. You bring comfort to those in pain? How? How can you under-stand their pain? We are all cerebral men, living apart from the world of reality. Even our deaths are a moral disgrace, for we welcome them as chariot rides to paradise. Where is the sacrifice? The enemy brings us what we desire and we accept death from him as a gift. A gift of Chaos – a stained, bloody, vile gratuity from the Devil himself.'

'You speak as one who has been stained by Chaos. All that you say is plausible, yet that is the strength of the Chaos Spirit. That is why he was called the Morning Star and is now the Prince of Lies. The gullible devour his promises as he devours them. I have looked inside you, Dardalion, and I find no evil. But your very purity was your downfall, when you allowed yourself to travel with the assassin Waylander. You were too confident in your purity, and the evil of the man overcame you.'

'I do not see him as evil,' said Dardalion. 'Amoral, cruel, but not evil. You are right, though, when you say he affected me. But purity is not a cloak which can be stained in a storm. He merely made me question values I had accepted.'

'Nonsense!' snapped the Abbot. 'He fed you his blood and therefore his soul. And you became one with him, even as he now struggles against the stain you have placed on his evil. You are joined, Dardalion, like symbiotic twins. He struggles to do good, while you struggle to commit evil. Can you not see it? If we listen to you, then our Order is finished, our discipline gone to the winds of the desert. What you ask is selfishness, for you seek safety among the numbers of the Source priests. If we accept you, then we lessen your doubt. We will not accept you.'

'You speak of selfishness, Father Abbot. Then let me ask you this: if our lives as priests teach us to abhor selfishness, why do we allow the Brotherhood to kill us? For if unselfishness means giving up that which we desire in order to help others, then surely fighting the Brotherhood would achieve it? We do not want to fight, we want to die, therefore when we fight we are being unselfish and helping the innocents who would otherwise be slain.'

'Go away, Dardalion, you are tainted beyond my humble counsel.'

'I will fight them alone,' said Dardalion bowing stiffly.

As he turned, the priests moved back to allow him a path, and he walked it without turning his head to see their faces, his mind closed to their emotions.

Clearing their ranks, he crossed the stone bridge and paused to stare at the stream. He no longer felt uncomfortable in the armour, and the burden was gone from his soul. The sound of footsteps caused him to turn and he saw a group of priests crossing the bridge, all of them young. The first to come was a short, stocky man with bright blue eyes and close-cropped blond hair.

'We wish to speak with you, brother,' he said. Dardalion nodded, and they formed a half-circle around him and sat down on the grass. 'My name is Astila,' said the blond priest, 'and these of my brethren have been waiting for you. Do you object to communing with us?'

'For what purpose?'

'We wish to know of your life, and the change you have undergone. We will best understand that by sharing your memories.'

'And what of the stain to your purity?'

'There are enough of us to withstand it, if such it be.'

'Then I agree.'

The group bowed their heads and closed their eyes. Dardalion shuddered as the priests flowed into his mind and he merged into the oblivion of their mass. A kaleidoscope of memories flickered and flashed. Childhood, joy and torment. Study and dreams. The mad rush of images slowed as the mercenaries tied him to the tree and went to work with their knives, and the pain returned. Then . . .

Waylander. The rescue. The cave. The blood. The savage joy of battle and death. The walls of Masin. But through it all the constant prayers for guidance. All unanswered. Nausea swept through him as the priests returned to their bodies.

He opened his eyes and almost fell, but sucking in air, he steadied himself.

'Well?' he asked. 'What did you find?'

'You were stained,' said Astila, 'in the first moments when Waylander's blood touched you. That is why you cut your opponent to pieces. But since then you have struggled – as the Abbot pointed out – to restrain the evil.'

'But you think I am wrong?'

'Yes. And yet I will join you. We will all join you.'

'Why?'

'Because we are weak, even as you are weak. Poor priests we have been, despite our struggles. I am prepared to be judged by the Source for all my deeds, and if His judgement says eternal death then so be it. But I am tired of watching my brothers slain. I am sickened by the deaths of the children of the Drenai, and I am ready to destroy the Brotherhood.'

'Then why have you not done so before now?'

'That is not an easy question to answer. I can only speak for myself, but I feared that I might become as one with the Brotherhood. For my hatred was growing – I did not know if a man could retain any purity, any sense of God. You have, so I will follow you.'

'We were waiting for a leader,' said another man.

'And you have found one. How many are we?'

'With you, thirty.'

'Thirty,' said Dardalion. 'It is a beginning.'

11

Waylander dismissed the two female servants and rose from the bath, brushing flower petals from his body. Wrapping a towel around his waist, he walked to a full-length mirror and shaved slowly. His shoulder ached, the muscles were tense and knotted from the battle at Masin, and an ugly bruise was flowering along his ribs. He pressed it lightly and winced. Ten years ago such a bruise would have long since vanished; ten years before that, no bruise would have flowered at all.

Time was a greater enemy than any he had faced.

He stared into his own dark brown eyes, then scanned the fine lines of his face and the grey hair fighting for dominance at his temples. His gaze flickered down. The body was still strong, but the muscles were looking stretched and thin, he thought. Not many years left for a man in his occupation.

Waylander poured himself some wine and sipped it, holding it on his tongue and enjoying the sharp, almost bitter flavour.

The door slid open and Cudin entered; he was short and fat, sweat shining on his face. Waylander nodded a greeting. The merchant was followed by a young girl carrying clothing. She laid it on a gilded chair and left the room with eyes downcast, while Cudin hovered, rubbing his hands nervously.

'Everything as you requested, my dear fellow?'

'I will also need a thousand in silver.'

'Of course.'

'Have my investments gone well?'

'Well, these are hard times. But I think you will find the interest has been substantial. I have lodged the greater part of the eight thousand in Ventria, for the spice trade, so the war should not affect it. You may collect it at Isbas, at the bank of Tyra.'

'Why so nervous, Cudin?'

'Nervous? Not I – it is the heat.' The fat man licked his lips and tried to smile, but he was not successful.

'Someone has been looking for me, yes?'

'No . . . yes. But I told them nothing.'

'Of course not; you *know* nothing of my movements. But I shall tell you what you promised them – you said that you would let them know if ever I called on you. And you told them about the bank at Tyra.'

'No,' whispered Cudin.

'Do not be afraid, merchant, I do not blame you. You are not a friend and there is no reason to risk yourself for me; I would not expect it. Indeed, I would think you a fool if you did. Have you informed them yet of my arrival?'

The merchant sat down beside the pile of clothing. His flesh seemed to sag as if the muscles of his face had suddenly ceased to function.

'Yes, I sent a messenger into Skultik. What can I say?'

'Who came to you?'

'Cadoras the Stalker. Gods, Waylander, he has the eyes of Hell. I was terrified.'

'How many men did he have with him?'

'I do not know. I remember he said "they" would be camped at the Opal Creek.'

'How long ago was this?'

'Five days. He knew you were coming.'

'Have you seen him since?'

'Yes. He was in a tavern, drinking with the giant outlaw – the one who looks like a bear. You know him?'

'I know him. Thank you, Cudin.'

'You will not kill me?'

'No. But had you not admitted it to me . . .'

'I understand. Thank you.'

'There is nothing to thank me for . . . Now on another matter – there are two children recently brought to Skarta, now lodged with the Source priests. Their names are Krylla and Miriel. You will see they are looked after? There is also a woman, Danyal; she too will have need of money. For this service you will keep the interest from my investments. You understand?'

'Yes. Krylla, Miriel, Danyal. I understand.'

'I came to you, Cudin, because of your reputation for honest dealings. Do not fail me.'

The merchant backed from the room and Waylander moved to the clothing. A fresh linen shirt lay at the top of the pile and he lifted it to his face; it smelled of roses. Slipping it on, he tied the cuffs. Next was a pair of black troos in thick cotton, and then a woollen-backed leather jerkin and a pair of thigh-length black riding boots. Moving to the window, he hefted his mailshirt and placed it over his shoulders. The rings were freshly greased, the metal cold to his body. He dressed swiftly, buckling on his knife-belt and sword. His crossbow lay on the broad bed with a fresh quiver of fifty bolts; he clipped both to his belt and left the room.

Outside in the hall the girl waited and Waylander gave her four silver pieces. She smiled and moved away, but he called her back when he saw the bruise on her upper arm.

'I am sorry for being rough on you,' he said.

'Some men are worse,' she replied. 'You didn't know you were doing it.'

'No. I did not.' He gave her another silver piece.

'You cried in your sleep,' she said softly.

'I am sorry if it wakened you. Tell me, does Hewla still live in Skarta?'

'She has a cabin north of the town.' The girl was frightened, but she gave Waylander directions and he left the merchant's house, saddled his horse and rode north.

The cabin was badly built; the unseasoned wood was beginning to warp and mud had been pushed into the cracks. The main door was poorly fitted and a curtain had been hung behind it so as to cut down the draughts. Waylander dismounted, tethered his horse to a stout bush and knocked on the door. There was no answer and he moved inside warily.

Hewla was sitting at a pine table staring into a copper dish filled to the brim with water. She was old and almost bald, and even more skeletal than the last time Waylander had visited her two years before.

'Welcome, Dark One,' she said, grinning. Her teeth were white and even, strangely out of place amidst the ruin of her face.

'You have come down in the world, Hewla.'

'All life is a pendulum. I shall return,' she answered. 'Help yourself to wine – or there is water if you prefer.'

'Wine will be fine,' he said, filling a clay goblet from a stone carafe and sitting opposite her.

'Two years ago,' he said softly, 'you warned me against Kaem. You spoke of the death of princes, and of a priest with a sword of fire. It was pretty, poetic and meaningless. Now it has meaning . . . and I wish to know more.'

'You do not believe in pre-destiny, Waylander. I cannot help you.'

'I am not a fatalist, Hewla.'

'There is a war being waged.'

'You surprise me.' His tone was ironic.

'Close your mouth, boy!' she snapped. 'You learn nothing while your lips flap.'

'I apologise. Please go on.'

'The war is on another plane, between forces whose very nature we do not understand. Some men would call these forces Good and Evil, others refer to them as Nature and Chaos. Still others believe the power is of one Source that wars on itself. But whatever the truth, the war is real. I myself tend towards the simplistic: good and evil. In this struggle there are only small triumphs and no final victory. You are now a part of this war – a mercenary who has changed sides at a crucial time.'

'Tell me of my quest,' said Waylander.

'I see the global view does not excite your interest. Very well. You have allied yourself with Durmast, a brave decision. He is a killer without conscience and in his time has slain men, women and babes. He is without morality, neither evil nor good – and he will betray you, for he has no understanding of true friendship. You are hunted by Cadoras, the Scarred One, the Stalker, and he is deadly for, like you, he has never been bested with the sword or the bow. The Dark Brotherhood seek you, for they desire Orien's Armour and your death, and the Ventrian emperor has ordered a team of assassins against you for killing his nephew.'

'I did not kill him,' said Waylander.

'No. The deed was arranged by Kaem.'

'Go on.'

Hewla gazed into the bowl of water. 'Death is being drawn to you from

97

every side. You are trapped at the centre of a web of fate and the spiders are closing in.'

'But will I succeed?'

'It depends on your definition of success.'

'No riddles, Hewla. I have no time.'

'That is true. Very well then, let me explain about prophecy. Much depends on interpretation, nothing is clear-cut. If you were to take your knife and hurl it into the forest, what chance would you have of hitting the fox that killed my chickens?'

'None at all.'

'That is not strictly true. The law of probability says you *might* kill it. And that is the size of your task.'

'Why me, Hewla?'

'Now that is a question I have heard before. If I could lose a year for every time it has been asked, I would be sitting before you as a virgin beauty. But it was honestly asked and I will answer it. You are nothing in this game but a catalyst. Through your actions a new force has been birthed in the world. This was born the moment you saved the priest. It is invulnerable and immortal and will ride through the centuries until the end of time. But no one will remember you for it, Waylander. You will fade into the dust of history.'

'I care nothing for that. But you have not answered my question.'

'True. Why you? Because you alone have the chance, slim as it is, to change the course of this nation's history.'

'And if I refuse?'

'A pointless question – you will not.'

'Why so sure?'

'Honour, Waylander. You are cursed with it.'

'Do you not mean blessed?'

'Not in your case. It will kill you.'

'Strange. I thought I would live for ever.'

He stood to leave, but the old woman raised her hand.

'I can give you one warning: beware the love of life. Your strength is that you care not about death. The powers of Chaos are many and not all of them involve pain and sharp blades.'

'I do not understand you.'

'Love, Waylander. Beware of love. I see a red-haired woman who could bring you grief.'

'I shall not see her again, Hewla.'

'Maybe,' grunted the old woman.

As Waylander stepped from the cabin, a shadow flickered to his left and he dived forward as a sword blade whistled over his head. Hitting the ground on his shoulder, he rolled to his knees, his knife flashing through the air to take his attacker under the chin. The wounded man sank to his knees, tearing the blade loose, blood gushing from his throat as he toppled forward. Waylander swung round, scanning the trees, then rose and walked to the corpse. He had never seen the man before.

He cleaned his knife and sheathed it as Hewla stepped into the doorway.

'You are a dangerous man to know,' she said, grinning.

His dark eyes fixed on her wrinkled face. 'You knew he was here, you crone.'

'Yes. Good luck on your quest, Waylander! Walk warily.'

Waylander rode east through the darkest section of the forest, his crossbow primed and his dark eyes scanning the undergrowth for movement. Above him the branches interlaced and shafts of sunlight splayed the trees. After an hour he turned north, the tension growing within him causing his neck to ache.

Cadoras was not a man to be taken lightly. His was a name spoken in whispers in the darkest alleyways of forbidden cities: Cadoras the Stalker, the Dream Ender. It was said that none could match him for cunning and few for cruelty, but Waylander dismissed the more wild stories, for he knew how legend could add colour to the whitest of deeds.

For he, of all men, could understand Cadoras.

Waylander the Slayer, the Soul Stealer, the Chaos Blade.

Saga-poets sang dark songs about the wandering assassin, the stranger, the Waylander, choosing always to finish their tale-telling with Waylander's exploits as the fires guttered low and the tavern dwellers prepared for a walk home in the dark. Waylander had sat unnoticed in more than one inn while they entertained the crowds with his infamy. They would begin their performances with stories of golden heroes, beautiful princesses, courageous tales of shadow-haunted castles and silver knights. But as the hours passed they introduced an edge of fear, a taste of terror, and men would walk out into darkened streets with fearful eyes which searched the shadows for Cadoras the Stalker, or for Waylander.

How the poets would dance with glee when they heard that Cadoras had been paid to stalk the Slayer!

Waylander turned west along the line of the Delnoch mountains until he entered a large clearing where some thirty wagons were waiting. Men, women and children sat at breakfast fires while the giant Durmast walked among the groups collecting his payments.

Once out of the trees, Waylander relaxed and cantered into the campsite. He removed the bolts from the crossbow and loosed the strings; clipping the weapon to his belt, he slid from the saddle. Durmast – two leather saddlebags drooped over one huge shoulder – spotted him and waved. Moving to a nearby wagon, he heaved the bags inside and wandered back to Waylander.

'Welcome,' he said, grinning. 'This war is making for good business.'

'Refugees?' queried Waylander.

'Yes, heading for Gulgothir. With all their worldly possessions.'

'Why do they trust you?'

'Just stupidity,' said Durmast, his grin widening. 'A man could get rich very quickly!'

'I don't doubt it. When do we leave?'

'We were only waiting for you, my friend. Gulgothir in six days, then the river east and north. Say three weeks. Then Raboas and your Armour. Sounds easy, does it not?'

'As easy as milking a snake. Have you heard that Cadoras is in Skultik?'

Durmast's eyes opened wide in mock surprise. 'No!'

'He is hunting me, so I am told.'

'Let us hope he does not find you.'

'For his sake,' said Waylander. 'How many men do you have?'

'Twenty. Good men. Tough.'

'Good men?'

'Well no, scum as a matter of fact. But they can fight. Would you like to meet some of them?'

'No, I have just eaten. How many people are you taking?'

'One hundred and sixty. Some nice-looking women among them, Waylander. It should be a pleasant few days.'

Waylander nodded and glanced around the camp. Runners all of them, yet he felt pity for the families forced to trust a man like Durmast. Most of them would escape with their lives, but they would arrive in Gulgothir as paupers.

He transferred his gaze to the tree-lined hills to the south. A flash of light caught his eye and for some time he stared at the distant slopes.

'What is it?' asked Durmast.

'Perhaps nothing. Perhaps sunlight on a piece of quartz.'

'But you think it is Cadoras?'

'Who knows?' said Waylander, leading his horse away from the wagons and settling down in the shade of a spreading pine.

High in the hills, Cadoras replaced the long glass in its leather container and sat back on a fallen tree. He was a tall, thin man, black-haired and angular. A scar ran from his forehead to his chin, cutting across his lips and giving him a mocking devil's smile. The eyes were cloudy grey and cold as winter mist. He wore a black mailshirt, dark leggings and riding boots, and by his hips hung two short swords.

Cadoras waited for an hour, watching the wagons hitched to oxen and then assembled into a north-pointing line. Durmast rode to the head of the column and led the way towards the mountains and the Delnoch Pass. Waylander rode at the rear.

A sound from behind him caused Cadoras to turn sharply. A young man emerged from the bushes, blinking in surprise as he saw the knife in Cadoras' raised hand.

'He didn't come,' said the man. 'We waited where you said, but he didn't come.'

'He came – but he circled you.'

'Vulvin is missing. I sent Macas to find him.'

'He will find him dead,' said Cadoras.

'How can you be sure?'

'Because I wanted him dead,' said Cadoras, walking away and staring after the wagons. Gods, why did they give him such fools? Bureaucrats! Of course Vulvin was dead. He had been ordered to watch the cabin of

Hewla, but on no account to tackle Waylander. Why not? he had asked, he is only a man. Cadoras had known the fool would do something foolish, but then Vulvin was no loss.

An hour later Macas returned – short and burly, with a petulant mouth and a permanently surly manner. He moved to Cadoras, ignoring the younger man.

'Dead,' he said simply.

'Did you kill the old woman?'

'No. She had two wolves with her – they were eating Vulvin.'

'And you did not want to disturb their lunch?'

'No, Cadoras, I did not want to die.'

'Very wise. Hewla would have struck you dead in an instant; she has rare powers. By the way, there were no wolves.'

'But I saw them . . .'

'You saw what she wanted you to see. Did you ask her how Vulvin died?'

'I did not have to. She said it was pointless sending jackals after a lion – told me to tell you that.'

'She is right. But you jackals were part of the contract. Mount up.'

'You do not like us, do you?' asked Macas.

'Like you, little man? What is to like? Now mount up.'

Cadoras walked to his horse and swung smoothly into the saddle. The wagons were out of sight now and he eased his mount out on to the slope, sitting back in the saddle and keeping the beast's head up.

'Don't make it too easy, Waylander,' he whispered. 'Do not disappoint me.'

12

When Karnak entered the council chamber, the twenty officers stood and saluted. Waving them to their seats, the general moved to the head of the table and removed his cloak, draping it over the chair behind him.

'Purdol is ready to fall,' he declared, his blue eyes scanning the grim faces around the table. 'Gan Degas is old, tired and ready to crack. There are no Source priests at Purdol and the Gan has received no news for more than a month. He believes he is alone.'

Karnak waited, allowing the news to sink in and gauging the rising tension. He watched Gellan, noting the sustained absence of emotion. Not so young Sarvaj, who had leaned back with disappointment etched into his features. Jonat was whispering to Gellan, and Karnak knew what he was saying; he was harping on past mistakes. Young Dundas waited expectantly, his belief in Karnak total. The general glanced around the table. He knew every man present, their weaknesses and their strengths – the officers prone to melancholy and those whose reckless courage was more dangerous than cowardice.

'I am going to Purdol,' he said, judging the moment. A gasp went up from the men and he lifted his hand for silence. 'There are three armies ranged against us, with Purdol taking the lion's share. If the fortress falls it will release 40,000 men to invade Skultik. We cannot stand against such a force. So I am going there.'

'You will never get in,' said one officer, a bearded Legion warrior named Emden. 'The gates are sealed.'

'There is another way,' said Karnak. 'Over the mountains.'

'Sathuli lands,' muttered Jonat. 'I've been there. Treacherous passes, ice-covered ledges – it is impassable.'

'No,' said Dundas, rising to his feet. 'Not impassable – we have more than fifty men working to clear the way.'

'But the mountains do not lead into the fortress,' protested Gellan. 'There is a sheer cliff rising from the back of Purdol. It would be impossible to climb down.'

'We are not going over the mountain,' said Karnak. 'We are going *through* it. There is a deep honeycomb of caves and tunnels and one tunnel leads through to the dungeons below the main Keep; at the moment it is blocked, but we will clear it. Jonat is right: the way is difficult and there will be no room for horses. I intend to take a thousand men, each bearing sixty pounds of supplies. Then we will hold until Egel breaks out of Skultik . . .'

'But what if he doesn't?' demanded Jonat.

'Then we retreat through the mountains and disperse into small raiding groups.'

Sarvaj raised his hand. 'One question only, general. According to the fortress specifications, Purdol should be manned by 10,000 men. Even if we get through, we will only raise the defenders to a sixty-per-cent complement. Can we thus hold?'

'Only architects and bureaucrats work in numbers, Sarvaj. The first wall at Purdol has already fallen, which means that the harbour and the docks are already held by the Vagrians and allowing them to ship in supplies and troops. The second wall has only two gates and they are holding firm. The third wall has but one gate – and after that there is the Keep. A strong force could hold Purdol for at least three months; we will not need more than that.'

Gellan cleared his throat. 'Have we any idea,' he said, 'as to losses at Purdol?'

Karnak nodded. 'Eight hundred men. Six hundred dead, the rest too badly wounded to fight.'

'And what of Skarta?' asked Jonat. 'There are Drenai families here depending on us for protection.'

Karnak rubbed at his eyes and let the silence grow. This was the question he had feared.

'There is a time for hard decisions, and we have reached it. Our presence here may give the people hope, but it is false hope. Skarta is indefensible. Egel knows it, I know it – and that is why he raids the west, to keep the Vagrians on the move, to disconcert them and hopefully to prevent a large-scale invasion here. But we are pinning down troops desperately needed elsewhere. We will leave a token force of some 200 men . . . but that is all.'

'The people will be wiped out,' said Jonat, rising to his feet, his face flushed and angry.

'They will be wiped out anyway,' stated Karnak, 'should the Vagrians attack. At the moment the enemy waits for Purdol to fall and they won't risk entering the forest. Holding Purdol is the best chance for Skarta and the other Skultik towns. Egel will be left with just under 4,000 men, but there are others coming in from the mountains of Skoda. We must win him time.

'I know what you are thinking: that it is madness. I agree with you! But the Vagrians have all the advantages. Every major port is in their hands. The Lentrian army is being pushed back. Drenan has fallen and the routes to Mashrapur are closed. Purdol alone holds against them. If it falls before Egel breaks clear, we are finished and the Drenai will be wiped out. The Vagrian farmers are being offered choice Drenai lands, merchants are planning for the day when all of our lands will be part of Greater Vagria. We are doomed people unless we take our fate in our hands and risk everything.

'Quite simply, my friends, there is no more room for manoeuvre. Bereft of choices, we must hold the tiger by the throat and hope that he weakens before we tire. Tomorrow we ride for Purdol.'

Deep down Gellan knew the venture was perilous, moreover a tiny spark of doubt told him that Karnak's real reason for wanting to aid

Purdol owed more to personal ambition than to strategic sanity. And yet . . .

Was it not better to follow a charismatic leader to the gates of Hell, rather than a mediocre general to a dull defeat?

The meeting ended at dusk and Gellan wandered to his tiny room to pack his few possessions into canvas and leather saddlebags. There were three shirts, two sets of woollen leggings, a battered leather-covered hand-written Legion manual, a jewelled dagger and an oval wooden painting of a blonde woman and two young children. He sat down on the bed, removed his helmet and studied the portrait. When it had been presented to him he had disliked it, feeling it failed to capture the reality of their smiles, the joy of their lives. Now he saw it as a work of rare genius. Carefully he wrapped the painting in oilskin and placed it in a saddlebag between the shirts. Lifting the dagger, he slid it from its scabbard; he had won it two years before when he became the first man to win the Silver Sword six times.

His children had been so proud of him at the banquet. Dressed in their best clothes, they had sat like tiny adults, their eyes wide and their smiles huge. And Karys had spilt not one drop of soup on her white dress, a fact she pointed out to him all evening. But his wife, Ania, had not attended the banquet; the noise, she had said, would only make her head ache.

Now they were dead, their souls lost to the Void. It had been hard when the children died, bitter hard. And Gellan had retreated into himself, having nothing left with which to comfort Ania. Alone she had been unable to cope and eighteen days after the tragedy she had hung herself with a silken scarf . . . Gellan had found the body. Plague had claimed his children. Suicide took his wife.

Now all he had was the Legion.

And tomorrow it would head for Purdol and the gates of Hell.

Dardalion waited silently for his visitor. An hour ago the Drenai general Karnak had arrived at the meadow, and had sat outlining his plan to aid Purdol. He had asked if Dardalion could help him, by keeping at bay the spirits of the Dark Brotherhood.

'It is vital we arrive unnoticed,' said Karnak. 'If there is the merest whisper of my movements, the Vagrians will be waiting for us.'

'I will do what I can, Lord Karnak.'

'Do better than that, Dardalion. Kill the whoresons.'

After he had gone, Dardalion knelt on the grass before his tent and bowed his head in prayer. He had stayed thus for more than an hour when the Abbot came and knelt before him.

Dardalion sensed his presence and opened his eyes. The old man looked tired, his eyes red-rimmed and sorrowful.

'Welcome, Lord Abbot,' said Dardalion.

'What have you done?' asked the old man.

'My Lord, I am sorry for the pain you feel, but I can only do what I feel is right.'

'You have sundered my brotherhood. Twenty-nine priests are now preparing for war and death. It *cannot* be right.'

'If it is wrong, we will pay for it, for the Source is righteous and will suffer no evil.'

'Dardalion, I came to plead with you. Leave this place, find a far monastery in another land and return to your studies. The Source will show you the path.'

'He has shown me the path, my lord.'

The old man bowed his head and tears fell to the grass.

'I am powerless, then, against you?'

'Yes, my lord. Whereas I am not against you at all.'

'You are now a leader, chosen by those who would follow you. What title will you carry, Dardalion. The Abbot of Death?'

'No, I am not an abbot. We will fight without hate and we will find no joy in the battle. And when it is won – or lost – we will return to what we were.'

'Can you not see the folly in your words? You will fight evil on its own ground, with its own weapons. You will defeat it. But will that end the war? It may stop the Brotherhood, but there are other brotherhoods and other evils. Evil does not die, Dardalion. It is a weed in the garden of life. Cut it, burn it, uproot it, yet will it return the stronger. This path of yours has no ending – the war merely changes.'

Dardalion said nothing, the truth of the Abbot's words hammering home to him.

'In this you are right, my lord. I see that. And I see also that you are correct when you name me "Abbot". We cannot merely become Soul Warriors. There must be order and our mission must be finite. I will consider your words carefully.'

'But you will not change your immediate course?'

'It is set. What I have done, I have done in faith and I will not go back on it, any more than you will break your own faith.'

'Why not, Dardalion? You have already broken faith once. You took an oath that all human life – all life, indeed – would be sacred to you. Now you have slain several men and have eaten meat. Why should one more act of "faith" concern you?'

'I cannot argue with that, my lord,' said Dardalion. 'The truth of it grieves me.'

The Abbot pushed himself to his feet. 'I hope that history does not recall you and your Thirty, Dardalion, though I fear that it will. Men are always impressed by acts of violence. Build your legend carefully, lest it destroy all we stand for.'

The Abbot walked away into the darkening dusk where Astila and the other priests waited in silence. They bowed as he passed, but he ignored them.

The priests gathered in a ring around Dardalion and waited while he concluded his prayers. Then he looked up.

'Welcome, my friends. Tonight we must aid Lord Karnak, but above this we must learn about ourselves. There is more than a chance that the path we follow is the road to perdition, for it may be that everything we do is against the will of the Source. So we must hold in our hearts the strength of our faith and the belief in our cause. Tonight some of us may die. Let us not travel to the Source with hate in us. We will begin now by joining in prayer. We will pray for our enemies, and we will forgive them in our hearts.'

'How can we forgive them and then slay them?' asked a young priest.

'If we do not forgive, then hate will flower. But think on this: if you had a dog that became rabid, you would slay it with regret. You would not hate it. That is what I ask. Let us pray.'

As darkness closed in around them they concluded their communion, and their spirits rose into the night sky.

Dardalion glanced about him. All the priests were clothed in silver armour, shining shields upon their arms and swords of fire in their hands. The stars shone like gems in a blaze, and the mountains of the moon cast sharp shadows as The Thirty waited for the Brotherhood. All was silence.

Dardalion could feel the tension among the priests, for their minds were still linked. Doubts and uncertainties flickered and faded. The night was clear and calm, the forest below them bathed in silver light.

The hours stretched on, impossibly long, and fear ebbed and flowed among the priests to touch each of them with icy fingers.

The night grew more menacing and to the west sombre clouds gathered, staining the moonlight.

'They are coming!' pulsed Astila. 'I can sense it.'

'Be calm,' urged Dardalion.

The dark clouds drew nearer and Dardalion's sword flickered into his hand, the blade burning with white fire.

The clouds loomed and disgorged black-cloaked warriors who swept down on a wave of hatred that engulfed The Thirty. The dark emotion closed over Dardalion, but he shook himself free and soared to meet the attackers. His blade cut and sliced into their mass and his shield rang with returned blows. The Thirty flew to his aid and the battle was joined.

There were more than fifty black warriors, but they could not match the silver-armoured priests and their fiery swords, and they fell back towards the clouds. The Thirty gave chase.

Suddenly Astila screamed a mind warning and Dardalion, about to enter the clouds, veered away.

The cloud bunched in on itself – forming a bloated body, scaled and dark. Huge wings unfurled and a gaping red maw opened at the front of the beast. The Brotherhood were absorbed into its mass and it grew yet more solid.

'Back!' pulsed Dardalion, and The Thirty fled over the forest.

The beast pursued them and Dardalion halted in his flight, his mind racing. Somehow the combined forces of the Brotherhood had created this thing. Was it real? Instinctively he knew that it was.

'To me!' he pulsed. The Thirty gathered around him. 'One warrior. One mind. One mission,' he intoned, and The Thirty merged. Dardalion was swamped and his mind swam as his power multiplied.

Where there had been Thirty, now there was One whose eyes blazed with fire and whose sword was jagged like frozen lightning.

With a roar of rage, the One hurled himself at the beast. The creature reared and taloned arms raked out at the warrior, but the One hammered his lightning blade across its body, severing one limb at a stroke. The beast bellowed in pain and with jaws opened wide it plunged towards its attacker. The One looked up into the giant maw, seeing row upon row of teeth, shaped like the dark swords of the Brotherhood. Hefting his blade, he threw it like a thunderbolt into the cavern of the mouth. As the weapon speared home the One created another and another, hurling them deep into the monster. The beast drew back, its form shifting and changing as the lightning blades lanced its body.

Small dark shapes fled from its mass and it shrank. Then the One spread his hands and flew like an arrow into the heart of the cloud, tearing at the astral flesh. His mind was full of screams and pain as the Brotherhood died one by one. When the cloud broke up and the surviving warriors fled for the safety of their bodies, the One hurled bolts of light at them as they went, then hovered under the stars, seeing them for the first time.

How beautiful, he thought. His far-seeing eyes scanned the planets, the shifting of colours, the swirling of distant clouds over dried-out oceans, and far off he spied a comet arcing through the galaxy. So much to see.

Within the One, Dardalion struggled for identity; his name was a lost thing to him and he fell asleep in the mass. Astila fought on, his thoughts things of mist ebbing and flowing. One. The One. More than One. Numbers. A wave of joy suffused him as he fought, and his vision was blanked by the sight of a meteor shower exploding in rainbow colours through the atmosphere. The One was mightily pleased with the display.

Astila clung to his task. Numbers. A number. No . . . not One. Slowly he forced himself to count, searching what was left of his memory for thoughts that were his alone. Then a name struck him. Dardalion. Was it *his* name? No. Another. He called out weakly, but there was no response. A number.

Thirty. That was the number of power. *Thirty*. The One shivered and Astila burst clear.

'Who are you?' asked the One.

'Astila.'

'Why have you withdrawn from me? We are One.'

'I seek Dardalion within you.'

'Dardalion?' said the One, and deep within him the young priest stirred to life. One by one Astila called the names of The Thirty and the priests came to themselves, drawing away confused and uncertain.

Dawn was near when Astila led the group home.

Once more in their bodies, they slept for several hours.

Dardalion was the first to wake. He roused the others and called Astila to him.

'Last night you saved us,' said Dardalion. 'You have a gift for seeing through deceptions.'

107

'But you created the One,' said Astila. 'Without that we would not have survived.'

'We almost did not survive. The One was as great a danger to us as the Cloudbeast and you saved us a second time. Yesterday the Abbot gave me a warning and I said I would think on his words. We need form, Astila . . . discipline. I shall be the Abbot of The Thirty. But you must have a senior part. I shall be the Voice and you will be the Eyes. Together we will find the path to the will of the Source.'

13

Waylander leaned back in the saddle and stared out over the Delnoch Pass to the Nadir plains beyond. Behind him the wagons had bunched for the night, ready for the perilous descent tomorrow. The pass sloped down for over a mile in a series of treacherous scree-covered ledges, and it took a brave man to drive a wagon over the narrow winding trail. Most of the refugees had paid Durmast's men handsome sums to take over the reins for the descent, while they walked behind in comparative safety.

A cool breeze was blowing from the north and Waylander allowed himself to relax. There had been no sign of Cadoras or of the Brotherhood, and he had checked the back trails with care. Suddenly he grinned. It was said of Cadoras that when you saw him there was danger – that when you did not see him, there was death. Waylander slid from his horse's back and led the animal to the picket ropes. Stripping off the saddle, he rubbed the horse down, fed it with grain and moved into the centre of the camp where the fires crackled under iron cooking-pots.

Durmast was sitting with a group of travellers, regaling them with tales of Gulgothir. In the red firelight his face was less brutal and his smile warm and friendly. Children sat around him, gazing in awe at the giant and relishing his outrageous stories. It was hard to believe that these people were fleeing from a terrible war; that many of them had lost friends, brothers and sons. Their relief at the prospect of escape was showing itself in over-loud laughter and jests. Waylander transferred his gaze to Durmast's men, sitting in a group apart from the others. Hard men, Durmast had said, and Waylander knew their type. They were not hard, they were murderous. In days of peace and plenty, the worthy townsfolk who now laughed and sang would bolt their doors against such as these; you could not have paid them enough to travel with Durmast. Now they laughed like children, unable to see that their danger was just as great.

Waylander turned to fetch his blankets – and froze. Standing not ten feet away from him, facing a fire, was Danyal. The firelight danced in her red-gold hair, and she was wearing a new dress tunic of wool embroidered and edged with gold thread. Waylander swallowed hard and took a deep breath. Then she lifted a hand to her hair and turned, seeing him for the first time. Her smile was genuine and he hated her for it.

'So you notice me at last,' she said, moving towards him.

'I thought you were staying in Skarta with the children?'

'I left them with the Source priests. I am tired of war, Waylander. I want to go somewhere where I can sleep at night without fearing tomorrow.'

'There is no such place,' he said bitterly. 'Come, walk with me.'

'I am preparing some food.'

'Later,' he said, walking away towards the pass. She followed him to a grassy knoll where they sat on jutting boulders. 'Do you know who is leading this caravan?'

'Yes,' she answered. 'A man called Durmast.'

'He is a killer.'

'So are you.'

'You don't understand. You are in more danger here than back in Skultik.'

'But you are here.'

'What has that to do with it? Durmast and I understand one another. I need him to help me find the Armour; he knows the Nadir, and I might not get through without him.'

'Will you allow him to harm us?'

'*Allow*, woman? What on earth do you think I could do to stop him? He has twenty men. Damn you, Danyal, why are you dogging my footsteps?'

'How dare you?' she stormed. 'I didn't know you were travelling with us. Your conceit is colossal.'

'That's not what I meant,' he said defensively. 'It just seems that whenever I turn round you are there.'

'How depressing for you!'

'For pity's sake, woman – can you not hold back from jumping down my throat? I do not want to fight with you.'

'In that case, let me say that you have a regrettable line in small talk.'

For a while they sat in silence, watching the moon traverse the Delnoch Pass.

'I am not going to live very long, Danyal,' he said at last. 'Maybe three weeks, maybe less. I would very much like to end my life successfully . . .'

'Just the sort of stupid remark I would expect from a man! Who is going to care if you find that Armour of yours? It is not magic, it is just metal. And not even precious metal.'

'*I* will care.'

'Why?'

'What sort of question is that?'

'Stalling for time, Waylander?'

'No, I meant it. You think men stupid when they lust after glory? So do I. But this is not about glory – it concerns honour. I have lived in shame for many years and I fell to a level I would not have believed possible. I killed a good man . . . ended his life for money. I cannot undo that act. But I can atone. I do believe in Gods who care about humans. I do not seek forgiveness from some higher authority. I want to forgive myself. I want to find the Armour for Egel and the Drenai and fulfil a promise I made Orien.'

'You do not have to die to do that,' she said softly, placing her hand gently on his.

'No, I don't – and would prefer to live. But I am a hunted man. Cadoras hunts me. The Brotherhood seek me. And Durmast will sell me when the time is right.'

'Then why stay here like a tethered goat? Strike out on your own.'

'No. I need Durmast for the first part of my journey. I have an advantage! I know my enemies and I have no one to rely on.'

'That makes no sense.'

'Only because you are a woman and cannot understand the simplicity of the words. I am alone, so there is no one to let me down. When I run – if I run – I carry no baggage. I am self-sufficient and very, very deadly.'

'Which brings us to our first point,' said Danyal. 'You are trying to tell me that I am baggage to weigh you down.'

'Yes, Durmast must not realise that we know one another, else he will use you against me.'

'It is too late for that,' said Danyal, looking away. 'I wondered why he changed his mind about allowing me to ride with the wagons when I had no money. But I thought it was my body he desired.'

'Explain,' said Waylander wearily.

'A woman I met directed me to Durmast, but he told me that with no money I was useless to him. Then he asked where I was from, as he had not seen me before in Skarta, and I told him that I came in with you. Then he changed and asked me all about you, after which he said I could come.'

'You are leaving something out.'

'Yes. I told him I loved you.'

'Why? Why would you do that?'

'Because it's true!' she snapped.

'And he asked you whether I felt the same?'

'Yes. I told him no.'

'But he did not believe you.'

'How do you know?'

'Because you are here.' Waylander lapsed into silence, remembering Hewla's words about the red-headed woman and Orien's enigmatic warning concerning companions. What was it the old man had said?

That success or failure would depend on Waylander's companions. Or rather on whom he chose to accompany him.

'What are you thinking?' she asked, seeing him smile, and the tension fade from his face.

'I was thinking that I am glad you are here. It is very selfish of me. I will die, Danyal. I am a realist and the odds are too great. But knowing you will be with me, for a few days at least, gives me pleasure.'

'Even though Durmast will use me against you?'

'Even so.'

'Do you have a small copper coin?' she asked.

He fished in his money-sack, producing a tiny coin carrying the head of Niallad which he handed to her.

'What do you want it for?'

'You once said you never took a woman you had not paid for. Now you have paid.'

Leaning over, she kissed him softly and his arms moved round her waist, pulling her in to him.

Hidden in the trees, Durmast watched the lovers move to the grass beside the boulders. The big man shook his head and smiled.

The dawn broke bright and clear, but dark clouds loomed in the north and Durmast cursed loudly.

'Rain,' he spat. 'That's all we damned well need!'

The first of the wagons was led to the crest of the Pass. Pulled by six oxen, it was some twenty feet long and heavily laden with boxes and crates. The driver licked his lips, his eyes narrowing as he gauged the dangers of the trail. Then he cracked his whip over the head of the lead oxen and the wagon lurched forward. Waylander walked behind, with Durmast and seven of his men. The first two hundred yards were steep, though relatively simple to travel for the path was wide and firm. But then it narrowed and dipped to the right. The driver hauled back on the reins and jammed the wheel-brake tight against the rim, but the wagon slid slowly sideways towards the yawning drop on the left.

'Ropes!' bellowed Durmast and the men ran forward to hook inch-thick hemp ropes about the axles. The wagon stopped its slide. Waylander, Durmast and the others took up the two ropes and gathered in the slack.

'Now!' called Durmast and the wagoner gently released the brake. The wagon inched forward, slithering to a stop some twenty paces on. The trail was angled here, and the weight of the wagon caused it to pull towards the edge. But the men on the ropes were strong, and well-used to the perils of the Delnoch Pass.

For over an hour they toiled, until at last the wagon came to level ground.

Far behind them a second wagon was making the descent, with seven more of Durmast's men hauling on ropes. The giant sat back and grinned as he watched them strain.

'They earn their money when they work with me,' he said.

Waylander nodded, too weary to speak. 'You've gone soft, Waylander. A little gentle exercise and you're sweating like a pig in heat!'

'Pulling wagons is not my usual occupation,' said Waylander.

'Did you sleep well?' asked Durmast.

'Yes.'

'Alone?'

'What sort of question is that from a man who hid in the bushes and watched?'

Durmast chuckled and scratched his beard. 'You don't miss much, my friend. Soft you may be, but your eyes have lost nothing in sharpness.'

'Thank you for allowing her to come,' said Waylander. 'It will make the first few days of the journey more pleasurable.'

'The least I could do for an old friend. Are you taken with her?'

'She loves me,' replied Waylander with a grin.

'And you?'

'I shall say farewell at Gulgothir – with regret.'

'Then you are fond of her?'

'Durmast, you watched us last night. Did you see what happened before we made love?'

'I saw you pass her something.'

'You saw me give her money. *Love?* You tell me.'

Durmast leaned back, closing his eyes against the morning sun.

'You ever wished you had settled down? Raised a family?'

'I did once, they died,' said Waylander.

'Me too. Only mine didn't die – she ran off with a Ventrian trader and took my sons with her.'

'I am surprised you didn't go after her.'

Durmast sat up and stretched his back. 'I did, Waylander,' he said.

'And?'

'I gutted the trader.'

'And your wife?'

'She became a whore in the dockside taverns.'

'What a fine pair we make! I pay for my pleasures because I will never again risk love, while you are haunted by love's betrayal.'

'Who says I am haunted?' demanded the giant.

'I do. And don't let yourself get too angry, my friend, for soft though I may be you cannot handle me.'

For several seconds Durmast's angry glare remained, then it faded from his eyes and he smiled. 'At least some of the old Waylander remains,' he said. 'Come, it's time for the long climb and another wagon.'

Throughout the day the men toiled and by dusk all the wagons were safely at the foot of the pass. Waylander had rested through the afternoon, his instincts warning him that he would need all his strength over the next few days.

The rain passed them by and by nightfall the camp-fires were blazing and the smell of cooking meat hung in the air. Waylander made his way to the wagon of the baker, Caymal, who had allowed Danyal to ride with him and his family. On his arrival he found Caymal nursing a bruised eye, his wife Lyda, beside him.

'Where is Danyal?' asked Waylander.

Caymal shrugged. His wife, a lean dark-haired woman in her late thirties, looked up.

'You animals!' she hissed.

'Where is she?'

'Wait your turn,' said Lyda, her lip trembling.

'Listen to me, woman – I am a friend of Danyal's. Now where is she?'

'A man took her. She didn't want to go and my husband tried to stop him but he hit Caymal with a club.'

'Which way?'

The woman pointed to a small grove of trees. Waylander lifted a rope from the back of the wagon, coiled it over his shoulder and loped off in that direction. The moon shone bright in a clear sky and he slowed his pace as he neared the grove, closing his eyes and focusing his hearing.

There! To the left was the sound of coarse cloth against tree bark. And to the right, a muffled cry. Angling towards the left Waylander moved slowly forward, bursting into a sprint just as he reached the trees.

A knife flashed past his head and he hit the ground on one shoulder and rolled. A dark shadow detached itself from the trees, moonlight shining from a curved sword. Waylander rolled to his feet and leapt, his right foot crashed into the man's head and then – as the stranger staggered – Waylander spun on his heel, his right elbow exploding against the man's ear. He fell without a sound. Waylander crept to the right. There in a shallow hollow lay Danyal, her dress ripped open, her legs spread. A man was kneeling over her as Waylander slid the rope from his shoulder and opened the noose.

Moving forward silently he came up behind the man, slipping the noose over his head and jerking it tight. He fell back, scrabbling at the noose, but Waylander pulled him from his feet and dragged him across the hollow to a tall elm. Swiftly he hurled the rope over a branch some ten feet from the ground and hauled the struggling man to his feet. The attacker's eyes were bulging and his face above the dark beard was purple.

Waylander had never seen him before.

Then a whisper of movement from behind caused him to drop the rope and dive to his right. An arrow hissed past him to thud into the bearded attacker. The man grunted and his knees gave way. Waylander bunched his legs under him and came up running, cutting left and right to hinder the aim of the hidden assassin. Once into the trees he dropped low and began to crawl through the bushes, circling the hollow.

The sound of horse's hooves caused him to curse and he straightened, slipping his dagger into his sheath. Returning to the clearing he found Danyal unconscious. Across her naked breasts someone had laid a goose-feathered arrow. Waylander snapped it in half.

Cadoras!

Lifting Danyal, he walked back to the wagons, where he left her with the baker's wife and returned to the grove. The first man who had attacked him lay where he had fallen; Waylander had hoped to question him, but his throat had been cut. Swiftly he searched the body, but there was nothing to identify him. The second man had three gold coins in a belt pouch. Waylander took the coins back to the camp and gave them to Lyda.

'Hide them about your person,' he told her.

She nodded and lifted the canvas flap, allowing Waylander to climb into the wagon.

Danyal was awake, her lip swollen and a bruise on her cheek. Caymal sat beside her. The wagon was cramped and the baker's two young children were sleeping beside Danyal.

'Thank you,' she said, forcing a smile.

'They will not trouble you again.'

Caymal eased himself past Waylander and climbed out over the tailboard. Waylander moved up to sit beside Danyal.

'Are you hurt?' he asked.

'No. Not much anyway. Did you kill them?'

'Yes.'

'How is it you can do these things?'

'Practice,' he said.

'No, that's not what I meant. Caymal tried to stop the man . . . and Caymal is strong, but he was brushed aside like a child.'

'It is all about fear, Danyal. Do you want to rest now?'

'No, I want some air. Let's walk somewhere.'

He helped her from the wagon and they walked to the cliff face and sat on the rocks.

'Tell me about fear,' she said.

He walked away from her and stooped to lift a pebble.

'Catch this,' he said, flicking the stone towards her. Her hand snaked out and she caught the pebble deftly. 'That was easy, was it not?'

'Yes,' she admitted.

'Now if I had Krylla and Miriel here, and two men had knives at their throats and you were told that if you missed the pebble they would die, would it still be easy to catch? Think of those times in your life when you were nervous, and your movements became disjointed.

'Fear makes fools of us all. So too does anger, rage and excitement. And then we move too fast and there is no control. You follow me?'

'I think so. When I had to give my first performance before the King in Drenan, I froze. All I had to do was walk across the stage, but my legs felt as if they were carved from wood.'

'That is it. Exactly! The onset of fear makes the simplest of actions complex and difficult. No more so than when we fight . . . and I can fight better than most because I can bring all my concentration to bear on the small things. The pebble remains a pebble, no matter what hangs upon success or failure.'

'Can you teach me?'

'I don't have time.'

'You are not obeying your own maxim. This is a small thing. Forget the quest and concentrate on me, Waylander – I need to learn.'

'How to fight?'

'No – how to conquer fear. Then you can teach me to fight.'

'Very well. Start by telling me what is death?'

'An ending.'

'Make it worse.'

'Maggots and grey rotting flesh?'

'Good. And where are you?'

'Gone. Finished.'

'Do you feel anything?'

'No . . . perhaps. If there is a paradise.'

'Forget paradise.'

'Then I feel nothing. I am no longer alive.'

'This death, can you avoid it?'

'Of course not.'

'But you can delay it?'

'Yes.'

'And what will that give you?'

'The prospect of more happiness.'

'But at worst?'

'The prospect of more pain,' she said. 'Old age, wrinkles, decay.'

'Which is worse? Death or decay?'

'I am young. At the moment I fear both.'

'To conquer fear, you must realise that there is no escape from what you dread. You must absorb it. Live with it. Taste it. Understand it. Overcome it.'

'I understand that,' she said.

'Good. What do you fear most at this moment?'

'I fear losing you.'

He moved away from her and lifted a pebble. Clouds partly obscured the moonlight and she strained to see his hand.

'I am going to throw this to you,' he said. 'If you catch it, you stay – if you miss it, you return to Skarta.'

'No, that's not fair! The light is poor.'

'Life is not fair, Danyal. If you do not agree, I shall ride away from the wagons alone.'

'Then I agree.'

Without another word he flicked the stone towards her – a bad throw, moving fast and to her left. Her hand flashed out and the pebble bounced against her palm, but she caught it at the second attempt. Relief swept through her and her eyes were triumphant.

'Why so pleased?' he asked.

'I won!'

'No. Tell me what you did.'

'I conquered my fear?'

'No.'

'Well, what then? I don't understand you.'

'But you must, if you wish to learn.'

Suddenly she smiled. 'I understand the mystery, Waylander.'

'Then tell me what you did.'

'I caught a pebble in the moonlight.'

During the first three days of travel Danyal's progress astonished Waylander. He had known she was strong and supple and quick-witted but, as he discovered, her reflexes were staggeringly swift and her ability to assimilate instructions defied belief.

'You forget,' she told him, 'I performed on the stages of Drenan. I have been trained to dance and to juggle, and I spent three months with a group of acrobats.'

Every morning they rode away from the wagons out on to the undulating terrain of the Steppes. On the first day he taught her to throw a knife; the ease with which she adapted to the skill caused him to re-think his training methods. He had planned to humour her at first, but now he pushed her in earnest. Her juggling skills gave her a sense of balance which was truly extraordinary. His knives were of different weights and lengths, but in her hands they performed equally. She merely hefted the blade in her fingers, judging the weight, and then let fly at the target. Of her first five throws, only one failed to thud home into the lightning-blasted tree.

Waylander found a rock with high chalk content and outlined the figure of a man on the tree bole. Handing Danyal a knife he turned her round, facing away from the tree.

'Without pause I want you to turn and throw, aiming for the neck,' he said. Spinning on her heel, her arm flashed forward and the knife hammered into the tree just above the right shoulder of the chalk figure.

'Damn!' she said. Waylander smiled and retrieved the knife.

'I said turn, not spin. You were still moving to your left when you threw – and that carried your arm past the target. But, nevertheless, it was a fine effort.'

On the second day he borrowed a bow and quiver of arrows. She was less skilled with this weapon, but her eye was good. For some time Waylander watched her, then he bade her remove her shirt. Taking it by the sleeves, he moved behind her and tied it tightly around her, flattening her breasts against her ribs.

'That is not very comfortable,' she protested.

'I know. But you are bending your back as you pull, to avoid the string catching your body – that affects your aim.'

But the idea was not a success and Waylander moved on to the sword. One of Durmast's men had sold him a slender sabre with an ivory hilt and a filigreed fist-shield. The weapon was well-balanced and light enough to allow Danyal's greater speed to offset her lack of strength.

'Always remember,' he told her as they sat together after an hour of work, 'that most swords are used as hacking weapons. Your enemy, in the main, will be right-handed. He will lift his sword over his right shoulder and sweep it down from right to left, aiming at your head. But the shortest distance between two points is a straight line. So thrust! Use the point of the sword. Nine times out of ten you will kill your opponent. Most men are untrained, they hack and slash in a frenzy and are easy to despatch.' Taking up two sticks he had whittled to resemble swords, he handed one to Danyal. 'Come, I will play the part of your opponent.'

On the fourth day he began to teach her the principles of unarmed combat.

'Hammer this thought into your mind: Think! Harness your emotions and act on the instincts this training will inspire. Rage is useless, so do not lash out. *Think!* Your weapons are fists, fingers, feet, elbows, and head. Your targets are eyes, throat, belly and groin. These are the areas in which a well-timed blow will disable an enemy – you have one great advantage in this kind of combat: you are a woman. Your enemies will expect, fear, terror . . . and ultimately surrender. If you stay cool you will survive – and they will die.'

On the afternoon of the fifth day, as Waylander and Danyal rode back towards the wagons a group of Nadir warriors galloped into sight whooping and cheering. Waylander reined in his horse as they approached. There were some two hundred riders and they were heavily laden with blankets, trade goods and saddlebags bulging with coins and jewels. Danyal had never seen Nadir tribesmen, but she knew of their reputation as ferocious killers. Squat and powerful men they were, with slanted eyes and flat faces; many wore lacquered breastplates and fur-trimmed helms; most carried two swords and an assortment of knives.

The Nadir pulled up, spreading across the trail. Meanwhile Waylander sat quietly, trying to pick out the leader.

After several tense seconds a middle-aged warrior rode from the group; his eyes were dark and malicious, his smile cruel. The eyes flickered to Danyal and Waylander read his thought.

'Who are you?' asked the leader, leaning forward on the pommel of his saddle.

'I ride with Ice-eyes,' said Waylander, using the Nadir form of Durmast's name.

'You say.'

'Who is there to doubt me?'

The dark eyes fixed on Waylander and the Nadir nodded.

'We have come from Ice-eyes' wagons. Many gifts. You have gifts?'

'Only one,' said Waylander.

'Then give it to me.'

'I already have. I gave you the gift of life.'

'Who are you to give what I already possess?'

'I am the Soul Stealer.'

The Nadir showed no emotion. 'You ride with Ice-eyes?'

'Yes. We are brothers.'

'Of the blood?'

'No. Of the blade.'

'Ride in peace on this day,' said the Nadir. 'But remember – there will be other days.'

Lifting his arm, the Nadir leader waved on his men and the group thundered past the two riders.

'What was that all about?' asked Danyal.

'He did not want to die,' said Waylander. 'There is a lesson there, if you care to consider it.'

'I have had enough lessons for one day. What did he mean – many gifts?'

Waylander shrugged. 'Durmast betrayed the wagon folk. He took their money to lead them to Gulgothir, but he already had a deal with the Nadir. So the Nadir rob the wagons and Durmast takes a percentage. At the moment they still have their wagons, but the Nadir will come again before Gulgothir and take even those. The people who survive will arrive in Gulgothir as paupers.'

'That is despicable.'

'No. It is the way of the world. Only the weak run . . . now they must pay for their weakness.'

'Are you really that callous?'

'I am afraid so, Danyal.'

'That is a shame.'

'I agree with you.'

'You are an infuriating man!'

'And you are a very special woman – but let us think about that this evening. For now, answer me the question of the Nadir rider: Why did he let us live?'

Danyal smiled. 'Because you isolated him from his men and threatened him as an individual. Gods, will these lessons never cease?'

'All too soon,' said Waylander.

14

Danyal and Waylander made love in a sheltered hollow away from the wagons, and the experience shook Waylander. He could not recall the moment of penetration, nor any sense of passion. He had been filled with a desire to be closer to Danyal, to somehow absorb her body into his own – or perhaps lose his own within hers. And for the first time in many years he had ceased to be aware of movement around him. He had been lost within the lovemaking.

Now alone, fear tugged at him.

What if Cadoras had crept upon them?

What if the Nadir had returned?

What if the Brotherhood . . . ?

What if?

Hewla was right. Love was a greater enemy at this time.

'You are getting old,' he told himself. 'Old and tired.'

He knew he was no longer as swift or as strong and the silver hairs were multiplying. Somewhere out in the vast blackness of the world was a young killer more swift, more deadly than the legendary Waylander. Was it Cadoras? Or one of the Brotherhood?

The moment of drama with the Nadir had been telling. Waylander had survived it on experience and bluff, for with Danyal beside him he had not wanted to die. His greatest strength had always been his lack of fear but now – when he needed all his talents – the fear was returning.

He rubbed at his eyes, aware of the need for sleep yet reluctant to give in. Sleep is the brother of Death, said the song. But it is gentle and kind. Weariness eased its warmth into his muscles, and the rock against which he sat seemed soft and welcoming. Too tired to pull his blankets over himself, he laid his head back on the rock and slept. As he fell into darkness he saw the face of Dardalion; the priest was calling to him, but he could not hear the words.

Durmast was sleeping beneath the lead wagon when the dream came to him. He saw a man in silver armour: a handsome young man, clean-cut and strong. Durmast was dreaming of a woman with hair of shining chestnut brown – and of a child, sturdy and strong. He pushed away the image of the warrior, but it returned again and again.

'What do you want?' shouted the giant, as the woman and the child shimmered and disappeared. 'Leave me!'

'Your profits are dust unless you wake,' said the warrior.

'Wake? I am awake.'

'You are dreaming. You are Durmast and you lead the wagons to Gulgothir.'

'Wagons?'

'Wake up, man! The hunters of the night are upon you!'

The giant groaned and rolled over; he sat up, rapping his head sharply against the base of the wagon, and cursed loudly. Rolling clear, he straightened – the dream had gone, but a lingering doubt remained.

Taking up a short double-headed axe, he moved towards the west.

Danyal awoke with a start. The dream had been powerful and in it Dardalion had urged her to seek Waylander. Easing herself past the sleeping baker and his family, she slid the sabre clear of its scabbard and leapt forward from the tailboard.

Durmast swung round as she appeared beside him.

'Don't do that!' he snapped. 'I might have taken your head off.'

Then he noticed the sword. 'Where do you think you are going with that?'

'I had a dream,' answered Danyal lamely.

'Stay close to me,' he ordered, moving away from the wagons.

The night was clear, but clouds drifted across the moon and Durmast spat out an oath as he strained to see into the darkness. A hint of movement to the left! His arm swept out, knocking Danyal from her feet. Arrows hissed by him as he dived for the ground. Then a dark shadow lunged at him and the axe swept up to cleave into the man's side, smashing his ribs to shards before exiting in a bloody swathe. Danyal rolled to her feet as the clouds suddenly cleared to show two men in black armour running towards her with swords raised. She dived forward, rolling on her shoulder, and the men cannoned into her and fell headlong into the dust. Danyal came up fast, spearing the point of the sabre into the back of one man's neck; the second man swung round and lunged at her, but Durmast's axe buried itself in his back. His eyes opened wide, but he was dead before a scream could sound.

'Waylander!' bellowed Durmast as more black shapes came from the darkness.

At the boulder Waylander stirred, his eyes drifting open but his body heavy with deep sleep. Above him a man crouched, a wickedly curved blade in his hand.

'Now you die,' said the man and Waylander was powerless to stop him. But suddenly the man froze and his jaw dropped. Sleep fell from the assassin and his hand whipped out to punch his assailant from his feet. As he fell, Waylander saw that a long goose-feathered shaft had pierced the base of his skull.

Rolling to his left, Waylander lunged upright with knives in his hands as a dark figure leapt at him. He blocked the downward sweep of the sword, catching it on the hilt-guard of his left-hand knife. Dropping his shoulder, he stabbed his attacker low in the groin; the man twisted as he fell, tearing the knife from Waylander's hand.

The clouds closed in once more and Waylander threw himself to the ground, rolled several yards and lay still.

There was no movement around him.

For several minutes he strained to hear, closing his eyes and calming his mind.

Satisfied that his attackers had fled, he slowly raised himself to his feet. The clouds cleared . . .

Waylander spun on his heel, his hand whipping out. The black-bladed knife thudded into the shoulder of a kneeling archer. Waylander ran forward as the man lunged to his feet, but his opponent side-stepped and ran off into the darkness.

Weaponless, Waylander dropped to one knee and waited.

A scream sounded from the direction the wounded man had taken. Then a voice drifted to the kneeling assassin:

'You had best be more careful, Waylander.' A dark object sailed into the air to land with a thud beside him. It was his knife.

'Why did you save me?'

'Because you are mine,' replied Cadoras.

'I will be ready.'

'I hope so.'

Durmast and Danyal ran to him.

'Who were you speaking to?' asked the giant.

'Cadoras. But it doesn't matter – let's go back to the wagons.'

Together the trio moved back into the relative sanctuary of the camp, where Durmast stoked a dying fire to life and then cleaned the blood from his axe.

'That is some woman you have there,' he said. 'She killed three of the swine! And you had me thinking she was a casual bedmate! You are a subtle devil, Waylander.'

'They were Brotherhood warriors,' said the assassin, 'and they used some kind of sorcery to push me into sleep. I should have guessed.'

'Dardalion saved you,' said Danyal. 'He came to me in a dream.'

'A silver warrior with fair hair?' asked Durmast.

Danyal nodded.

'He came to me also. You have powerful friends – a she-devil and a sorcerer.'

'And a giant with a battleaxe,' said Danyal.

'Do not confuse business with friendship,' muttered Durmast. 'And now, if you'll excuse me, I have some sleep to catch up on.'

The old man gazed with weary eyes at the Vagrian warriors seated before him in what had once been the Palace of Purdol. Their faces shone with the arrogance born of victory, and he knew only too well how he appeared to them: old, tired and weak.

Gan Degas removed his helm and laid it on the table.

Stone-faced, Kaem sat opposite him.

'I take it you are ready to surrender,' said Kaem.

'Yes. If certain conditions are met.'

'Name them.'

'My men are not to be harmed – they are to be released to return to their homes.'

'Agreed . . . once they have laid down their weapons and the fortress is ours.'

'Many citizens fled to the fortress; they also must be allowed to go free and reclaim the homes your men took from them.'

'Petty bureaucracy,' said Kaem. 'It will cause us no problems.'

'What guarantees of faith can you give me?' asked Degas.

Kaem smiled. 'What guarantees can any man give? You have my word – that should be enough between generals. If it is not, you have only to keep the gates barred and fight on.'

Degas dropped his eyes. 'Very well. I have your word, then?'

'Of course, Degas.'

'The gates will be opened at dawn.'

The old warrior pushed himself to his feet and turned to leave.

'Do not forget your helm,' mocked Kaem.

Laughter echoed in the corridor as Degas was led from the hall, flanked by two men in black cloaks. Out in the night air he walked along the docks and up towards the eastern gate. There a rope was lowered from the gate tower; Degas looped his wrist around it and was hauled up into the fortress.

Back at the palace, Kaem silenced his officers and turned to Dalnor.

'There are some four thousand men in the fortress. Killing them all will take some planning – I don't want a mountain of rotting corpses spreading plague and disease. I suggest you split the prisoners into twenty groups, then take them down to the harbour group by group. There are a score of empty warehouses. Kill them and cart their bodies into the discharged grain ships. Then they can be dumped at sea.'

'Yes, my lord. It will take some time.'

'We *have* time. We will leave a thousand men to man the fortress and push west into Skultik. The war is almost over, Dalnor.'

'Indeed it is – thanks to you, my lord.'

Kaem swung round to a dark-bearded officer on his right.

'What news of Waylander?'

'He still lives, Lord Kaem. Last night he and his friends fought off an attack by my Brothers. But more are on their way.'

'I must have the Armour.'

'You will have it, my lord. The Emperor has commissioned the assassin Cadoras to hunt Waylander. And twenty of my Brothers are closing in. Added to this, we have received word from the robber Durmast; he asks 20,000 silver pieces for the Armour.'

'Of course you agreed?'

'No, my lord, we beat him down to 15,000. He would have been suspicious had we met his original request without argument. Now we have his trust.'

'Be careful of Durmast,' warned Kaem. 'He is like a rogue lion – he will turn on anyone.'

'Several of his men are in our employ, my lord; we have anticipated all eventualities. The Armour is ours. Waylander is ours – just as the Drenai are ours.'

'Beware of over-confidence, Nemodes. Do not count the lion's teeth until you see flies on his tongue.'

'But surely, my lord, the issue is no longer in doubt?'

'I had a horse once, the fastest beast I ever owned. It could not lose and I wagered a fortune on it. But a bee stung it in the eye just before the start. The issue is always in doubt.'

'Yet you said the war was almost over,' protested Nemodes.

'So it is. And until it is, we will remain wary.'

'Yes, my lord.'

'There are three men who must die. Karnak is one. Egel is the second. But most of all I want to see Waylander's head on a lance.'

'Why Karnak?' asked Dalnor. 'One battle is not sufficient to judge him dangerous.'

'Because he is reckless and ambitious. We cannot plan for him,' answered Kaem.

'There are some men who are good swordsmen, archers or strategists. There are others, seemingly gifted by the Gods, who are masters of all they touch. Karnak is one of these – I cannot read him and that disturbs me.'

'He is said to be in Skarta, serving under Egel,' said Dalnor. 'We will have him soon.'

'Perhaps,' said Kaem doubtfully.

Kaem fought to control his tension as he stood at the head of the Second Legion in the shadow of the eastern gate. Dawn was now minutes old, but still there was no movement from beyond the gates. He was acutely aware of the hostile stares from the archers on the battlements of the gate tower as he stood in full red and bronze battle gear with the sweat trickling between his shoulder-blades.

Dalnor stood behind him, flanked by swordsmen: dark-eyed warriors of the First Elite, the most deadly fighting men of the Second Legion of the Hounds of Chaos.

The sound of tightening ropes and the groaning of rusty ratchets ended Kaem's tension – beyond the gates of oak and iron, the huge bronze reinforced bar was being lifted. Minutes passed and then the gates creaked open. A swelling sense of triumph grew within Kaem, but he swallowed it back, angry at the power of his emotions.

Behind him men began shuffling their feet, anxious to end the long siege and enter the hated fortress.

The gates widened.

Kaem walked into the shadows of the portcullis and out into the bright sunlight of the courtyard . . .

And there stopped so suddenly that Dalnor walked into him knocking him forward; his helmet tipped over his eyes and he straightened it. The courtyard was ringed with fighting men, swords drawn. At the centre, leaning on a double-headed battleaxe, stood a huge warrior, barbarously ill-clad. The man handed the axe to a companion and strolled forward.

'Who is that fat clown?' whispered Dalnor.

'Be silent!' ordered Kaem, his brain working at furious pace.

'Welcome to Dros Purdol,' said the man, smiling.

'Who are you, and where is Gan Degas?'

'The Gan is resting. He asked me to discuss your surrender.'

'What nonsense is this?'

'Nonsense, my dear general? What can you mean?'

'Gan Degas agreed to surrender to me today after his conditions were met.' Kaem licked his lips nervously as the huge warrior grinned down at him.

'Ah, the conditions,' he said. 'I think there was a misunderstanding. When Gan Degas asked for safety for his men, he didn't quite mean taking them in groups of twenty to the warehouse dock and killing them.' The man's eyes narrowed and the humour vanished from his smile. 'I opened the gates to you, Kaem, so that you could see me. Know me . . . Understand me. There will be no surrender. I have brought with me three thousand men,' lied Karnak, 'and I command this fortress.'

'Who are you?'

'Karnak. Bear the name in mind, Vagrian, for it will be the death of you.'

'You make loud noises, Karnak, but few men fear a yapping dog.'

'True, but you fear me, little man,' said Karnak equably. 'Now – you have twenty seconds to clear your men from the gate. After that the air will be thick with arrows and death. *Go!*'

Kaem turned on his heel to find himself staring at several hundred warriors – the cream of his force – and the full humiliation struck him like a blow. He was inside the fortress with the gates open, yet he could not order the attack, for every archer had his bow bent and the shaft aimed at himself. And to save himself – and save himself he must – he had to order them to withdraw. His stock would sink among the men and morale would be severely dented.

He swung back, his face purple with fury. 'Enjoy your moment, Drenai! There will be few such highlights from now on.'

'Fifteen seconds,' said Karnak.

'Back!' shouted Kaem. 'Back through the gates.'

The sound of mocking laughter followed the Vagrian general as he shouldered his way through his troops.

'Close the gates,' yelled Karnak, 'and then get ready for the whoresons!'

Gellan moved alongside Karnak. 'What did you mean about warehouses and killing?'

'Dardalion told me that was the plan. Kaem had promised Degas that the men would be unharmed; it was a foul lie and exactly what you would expect from Kaem, but Degas was too weary to see it.'

'Speaking of weariness,' said Gellan, 'having spent more than ten hours burrowing through rock below the dungeons, I am feeling a little weary myself.'

Karnak thumped him hard between the shoulder-blades. 'Your men worked well, Gellan. The Gods only know what would have happened had we arrived an hour later. Still, it is good to know we are riding a lucky horse, eh?'

'Lucky, general? We have burrowed our way into a besieged fortress

125

and have angered the most powerful general on the continent. Tell me what's lucky.'

Karnak chuckled. 'He *was* the most powerful general on the continent, but he suffered today. He was humiliated. That won't help him; it will open a little tear in his cloak of invincibility.'

Jonat stalked the wall shouting at the fifty men under his command. They had been disgraced that morning, breaking in panic as the Vagrians cleared the wall beside the gate tower. With ten swordsmen, Jonat had rushed in to plug the gap and by some miracle the rangy, black-bearded Legion rider had escaped injury though six of his comrades had died beside him. Karnak had seen the danger and run to Jonat's aid, swinging a huge double-headed battleaxe, followed by a hundred fighting men. The battle by the gate tower was brief and bloody, and by the end of it the men of Jonat's section had returned to the fighting.

Now, with dusk upon them and the sun sinking in fire, Jonat lashed them with his tongue. Beyond his anger the tall warrior knew the cause of their panic, even understood it. Half the men were Legion warriors, half were conscripted farmers and merchants. The warriors did not trust the farmers to stand firm, while the farmers felt out of their depth and lost within the mad hell of slashing swords and frenzied screams.

What was worse, it had been the warriors who had broken.

'Look around you,' shouted Jonat, aware that other soldiers were watching the scene. 'What do you see? A fortress of stone? It is not as it appears – it is a castle built of sand and the Vagrians lash at it like an angry sea. It stands only so long as the sand binds together. You understand that, you dolts? Today you fled in terror and the Vagrians breached the wall. Had it not been retaken swiftly they would have flowed into the courtyard behind the gates and the fortress would have become a giant tomb.

'Can you not get it through your heads that there is nowhere to run? We fight or we die.

'Six men died beside me today. Good men – better men than you. You think of them tomorrow when you want to run.'

One of the men, a young merchant, hawked and spat. 'I did not ask to be here,' he said bitterly.

'Did you say something, rabbit?' hissed Jonat.

'You heard me.'

'Yes, I heard you. And I watched you today, sprinting away from the wall like your backside was on fire.'

'I was trying to catch up with your Legion soldiers,' snapped the man. 'They were leading the retreat.' An angry murmur greeted his words, but this fell to silence as a tall man moved along the battlements. He placed his hand on Jonat's shoulder and smiled apologetically.

'May I say a few words, Jonat?'

'Of course, sir.'

The officer squatted down amongst the men and removed his helm. His eyes were grey-blue and showed the weariness of six days and nights of

126

bitter struggle. He rubbed at them wearily, then looked up at the young merchant.

'What is your name, my friend?'

'Andric,' replied the man suspiciously.

'I am Gellan. What Jonat said about a castle of sand was a truth to remember and was well put. Each one of you here is vital. Panic is a plague which can turn a battle, but so is courage. When Jonat led that suicidal counter-charge with only ten men, you all responded. You came back – I think you are the stronger for it. Beyond these walls is an enemy of true malevolence, who has butchered his way across Drenai lands slaying men, women and children. He is like a rabid animal. But he stops here, for Dros Purdol is the leash around the mad dog's neck and Egel will be the lance that destroys him. Now I am not one for speeches, as Jonat here will testify, but I would like us all to be brothers here, for we are all Drenai and, in reality, we are the last hope of the Drenai race. If we cannot stand together on these walls, then we do not deserve to survive.

'Now look around you and if you see a face you do not recognise, ask a name. You have a few hours before the next attack. Use them to get to know your brothers.'

Gellan pushed himself to his feet, replaced his helm and moved away into the gathering darkness, taking Jonat with him.

'That there is a gentleman,' said Vanek, leaning his back to the wall and loosening the chin-strap of his helm. One of the ten to fight beside Jonat, he too had come through without a scratch, though his helm had been dented in two places and now sat awkwardly on his head. 'You listen to what he said – you take it in like it was written on tablets of stone. For those of you "brothers" who don't know me – my name is Vanek. Now I am a lucky bastard and anyone who feels like living ought to stay close to me. Anyone who feels like running tomorrow can run in my direction, because I am not going through those two speeches again.'

'You think we can really hold this place, Vanek?' asked Andric, moving over to sit beside him. 'All day ships have been arriving, bringing more Vagrians, and now they're building a siege tower.'

'I suppose it keeps them busy,' answered Vanek. 'As for the men, where do you think they are coming from? The more we face here, the less there are of them elsewhere. In short, brother Andric, we are bringing them together like pus in a boil. You think Karnak would have come here if he thought we could lose? The man's a political whoreson. Purdol is a stepping-stone to glory.'

'That's a little unfair,' said a lantern-jawed soldier with deep-set eyes.

'Maybe it is, brother Dagon, but I speak as I see. Do not misunderstand me – I respect the man, I'd even vote for him. But he's not like us; he has the mark of greatness on him and he put it there himself, if you understand me.'

'I don't,' said Dagon. 'As far as I can see he's a great warrior and he's fighting for the Drenai same as me.'

'Then let's leave it at that,' said Vanek, smiling. 'We both agree he's a great warrior, and brothers like us shouldn't quarrel.'

Above them in the gate tower Karnak, Dundas and Gellan sat under the new stars and listened to the conversation. Karnak was grinning broadly as he signalled Gellan to the other side of the ramparts where their talk could not be overheard.

'Intelligent man, that Vanek,' said Karnak softly, his eyes locked on Gellan's face.

Gellan grinned. 'Yes, he is, sir. Except for women!'

'There isn't a man alive who knows how to deal with women,' said Karnak. 'I should know – I have been married three times and never learned a damned thing.'

'Does Vanek worry you, sir?'

Karnak's eyes narrowed, but there was a glint of humour in them. 'And if he does?'

'If he did, you wouldn't be a man I follow.'

'Well put. I like a man who stands by his own. Do you share his views?'

'Of course, but then so do you. There are no saga-poet heroes. Each man has his own reason for being prepared to die, and most of the reasons are selfish – like protecting wife, home or self. You have bigger dreams than most men, general; there's no harm in that.'

'I am glad you think so,' said Karnak, an edge of sarcasm in his voice.

'When you do not want to hear the truth, sir, let me know. I can lie as glibly as any man.'

'The truth is a dangerous weapon, Gellan. For some it is like sweet wine, for others it is poison, yet it remains the same. Go and get some sleep – you look exhausted, man.'

'What was all that about?' asked Dundas as Gellan moved into the torch-lit stairwell.

Karnak shrugged and walked to the ramparts, gazing out over the camp-fires of the Vagrian army around the harbour. Two ships were gliding on a jet-black sea towards the dock, their decks lined with men.

'Gellan worries me,' said Karnak.

'In what way? He's a good officer – you've said that yourself.'

'He gets too close to his men. He thinks he is a cynic, but in fact he's a romantic – searching for heroes in a world that has no use for them. What makes a man like that?'

'Most men think you are a hero, sir.'

'But Gellan does not want a pretend hero, Dundas. What was it Vanek called me? A political whoreson? Is it a crime to want a strong land, where savage armies cannot enter?'

'No, sir, but then you are not a pretend hero. You are a hero who pretends to be otherwise.'

But Karnak appeared not to have heard. He was staring out over the harbour as three more ships ghosted in towards the jetty.

Dardalion touched the wounded soldier's forehead and the man's eyes closed, the lines of pain disappearing from his face. He was young and

128

had not yet found need of a razor. Yet his right arm was hanging from a thread of muscle and his torn stomach was held in place by a broad leather belt.

'There is no hope for this one,' Astila's mind pulsed.

'I know,' answered Dardalion. 'He sleeps now . . . the sleep of death.'

The makeshift hospital was packed with beds, pallets and stretchers. Several women moved among the injured men – changing bandages, mopping brows, talking to the wounded in soft compassionate voices. Karnak had asked the women to help and their presence aided the men beyond even the skill of the surgeons, for no man likes to appear weak before a woman and so the injured gritted their teeth and made light of their wounds.

The chief surgeon – a spare slight man named Evris – approached Dardalion. The two had struck up an instant friendship and the surgeon had been overwhelmingly relieved when the priests augmented his tiny force.

'We need more room,' said Evris, wiping his sweating brow with a bloody cloth.

'It is too hot in here,' said Dardalion. 'I can smell disease in the air.'

'What you can smell is the corpses below. Gan Degas had nowhere to bury them.'

'Then they must be burnt.'

'I agree, but think of the effect on morale. To see your friends cut down is one thing, to see them tossed on a raging fire is another.'

'I'll talk to Karnak.'

'Have you seen anything of Gan Degas?' asked Evris.

'No. Not for several days in fact.'

'He's a proud man.'

'Most warriors are. Without that pride there would be no wars.'

'Karnak used hard words on him – called him a coward and a defeatist. Neither was true. A braver, stronger man never lived. He was trying to do what was best for his men and had he known Egel still fought, he would never have thought of surrender.'

'What do you want from me, Evris?'

'Talk to Karnak – persuade him to apologise, to spare the old man's feelings. It would cost Karnak nothing, but it would save Degas from despair.'

'You are a good man, surgeon, to think of such a thing when you are exhausted from your labours among the wounded. I will do as you bid.'

'And then get some sleep. You look ten years older than when you arrived six days ago.'

'That is because we work during the day and we guard the fortress by night. But you are right again. It is arrogant of me to believe I can go on like this for ever. I will rest soon, I promise you.'

Dardalion walked from the ward to a small side-room and stripped off his bloodied apron. He washed swiftly, pouring fresh water from a wooden bucket into an enamelled bowl; then he dressed. He started to buckle on his breastplate, but the weight bore him down and he left his armour on the narrow pallet bed and wandered along the cool corridor. As he reached the open doors to the courtyard the sounds of battle rushed upon him – clashing swords and bestial screams, shouted orders and the anguished wails of the dying.

Slowly he climbed the worn stone steps into the Keep, leaving the dread clamour behind him. Degas' rooms were at the top of the Keep and there Dardalion tapped at the door and waited, but there was no answer. He opened the door and stepped inside. The main room was neat and spart-anly furnished with a carved wooden table and seven chairs. Rugs were laid before a wide hearth and a cabinet stood by the window. Dardalion sighed deeply and strode to the cabinet. Inside were campaign medals ranging over forty years, and some mementoes – a carved shield presented to Dun Degas to celebrate a cavalry charge, a dagger of solid gold, a long silver sabre with the words FOR THE ONE etched in acid on the blade.

Dardalion sat down and opened the cabinet. On the bottom shelf were the diaries of Degas, one for every year of his military service. Dardalion opened them at random. The writing was perfectly rounded and showed a disciplined hand, while the words themselves gave evidence of the military mind.

One ten-year-old entry read:

Sathuli raiding party struck at Skarta outskirts on the eleventh. Two forces of Fifty sent to engage and destroy. Albar led the First, I the Second. My force trapped them on the slopes beyond Ekarlas. Frontal charge hazardous as they were well protected by boulders. I split the force into three sections and we climbed around and above them, dis-lodging them with arrows. They tried to break out at dusk, but by then I had deployed Albar's men in the arroyo below and all the raiders were slain. Regret to report we lost two men, Esdric and Garlan, both fine riders. Eighteen raiders were despatched.

Dardalion carefully replaced the diary, seeking the most recent.
The writing was more shaky now:

We enter the second month of siege and I see no hope of success. I am not able to sleep as I used. Dreams. Bad dreams fill my night hours.

And then:

Hundreds dying. I have started to experience the strangest visions. I feel that I am flying in the night sky, and I can see the lands of the Drenai below me. Nothing but corpses. Niallad dead. Egel dead. All the world is dead, and only we mock the world of ghosts.

Ten days earlier Degas had written:

My son Elnar died today, defending the gate tower. He was twenty-six and strong as a bull, but an arrow cut him down and he fell out over

130

the wall and on to the enemy. He was a good man and his mother, bless her soul, would have been proud of him. I am now convinced that we stand alone against Vagria and know we cannot hold for long. Kaem has promised to crucify every man, woman and child in Purdol unless we surrender. And the dreams have begun once more, whispering demons in my head. It is getting so hard to think clearly.

Dardalion flipped the pages.

Karnak arrived today with a thousand men. My heart soared when he told me Egel still fought, but then I realised how close I came to betraying everything I have given my life to protect. Kaem would have slain my men and the Drenai would have been doomed. Harsh words I heard from young Karnak, but richly deserved they were. I have failed.

And the last page:

The dreams have gone and I am at peace. It occurs to me now that through all my married life I never spoke to Rula of love. I never kissed her hand, as courtiers do, nor brought her flowers. So strange. Yet all men knew I loved her, for I bragged about her constantly. I once carved her a chair that had flowers upon it. It took me a month and she loved the chair. I have it still.

Dardalion closed the book and leaned back in the chair, gazing down on the lovingly carved and polished wood. It was a work of some artistry. Pushing himself to his feet, he walked to the bedroom where Degas lay on blood-soaked sheets, his knife still in his hand. His eyes were open and Dardalion gently closed the lids before covering the old man's face with a sheet.

'Lord of All Things,' said Dardalion, 'lead this man home.'

15

Cadoras watched as Waylander rode from the wagons, heading away to the north towards a range of low hills. The hunter lay flat on his belly, his chin in his hands; behind him, on the far side of the hill, his horse was tethered. He eased his way back from the hill-top, walked slowly to the steel-grey gelding and unbuckled the thick saddle roll, opening it out on the ground. Within the canvas wrapping was an assortment of weapons ranging from a dismantled crossbow to a set of ivory-handled throwing knives. Cadoras assembled the crossbow and selected ten bolts which he placed in a doeskin quiver at his belt. Then he carefully slid two throwing knives into each of his calf-length riding boots, and two more into sheaths at his side. His sword was strapped to his saddle, along with a Vagrian cavalry bow tipped with gold; the quiver for this hung on his saddle horn. Fully equipped, Cadoras returned the saddle roll to its place and buckled the straps. Then he took some dried meat from his saddlebags and sat back on the grass and stared at the sky, watching the gathering storm clouds drifting in from the east.

It was time for the kill.

There had been little joy in the hunting. He could have killed Waylander on a dozen occasions – but then it took two to play the game, and Waylander had refused to take part. At first this had irritated Cadoras, making him feel slightly as if his victim had held him in contempt. But as the days passed he had realised that Waylander simply did not care. And so Cadoras had not loosed the fatal shaft.

He wanted to know *why*. He was filled with an urge to ride in to the wagons and sit opposite Waylander, to ask him . . .

Cadoras had been a hunter for more than a decade and he knew the role better than any man alive. In the deadliest game of all he was a master – understanding every facet, every iron rule: the hunter stalked, the prey evaded or ran, or turned and fought back. But the prey *never* ignored.

Why?

Cadoras had expected Waylander to hunt him, had even set elaborate traps around his camp-site. Night after night he had hidden in trees, his bow slung, while his blankets lay by warm fires covering only rocks and branches.

Today would end the burning questions. He would kill Waylander and go home.

Home?

High walls and soul-less rooms, and cold-eyed messengers with offers of gold for death. Like a tomb with windows.

'Curse you, Waylander! Why did you make it so easy?'

'It was the only defence,' answered Waylander and Cadoras spun round as a sword of shining steel rested on his back. He froze and then relaxed, his right hand inching towards the hidden knives in his boot. 'Don't be foolish,' said Waylander. 'I can open your throat before you blink.'

'What now, Waylander?'

'I have not yet decided.'

'I should have killed you.'

'Yes, but then life is full of "should haves". Take off your boots . . . slowly.' Cadoras did as he was bid. 'Now your belt and jerkin.' Waylander moved the weapons and hurled them on to the grass.

'You planned this?' asked Cadoras, sitting back and resting on his elbows. Waylander nodded and sheathed his sword, sitting some ten feet from the hunter. 'You want some dried meat?' Cadoras enquired. Waylander shook his head and drew a throwing knife, balancing the blade in his right hand.

'Before you kill me, may I ask a question?'

'Of course.'

'How did you know I would wait this long?'

'I didn't, I merely hoped. You should know better than any man that the hunter has all the advantages. No man is safe from the assassin, be he king or peasant. But you had something to prove, Cadoras – and that made you an easy prey.'

'I had nothing to prove.'

'Truly? Not even to yourself?'

'Like what?'

'That you were the better man, the greatest hunter?'

Cadoras leaned back and stared at the sky. 'Pride,' he said. 'Vanity. It makes fools of us all.'

'We are all fools regardless – otherwise we would be farmers, watching our sons grow.'

Cadoras rolled to one elbow and grinned. 'Is that why you've decided to be a hero?'

'Perhaps,' admitted Waylander.

'Does it pay well?'

'I don't know. I haven't been one very long.'

'You know the Brotherhood will be back?'

'Yes.'

'You can't survive.'

'I know that too.'

'Then why do it? I've seen you with the woman – why don't you take her to Gulgothir and head east to Ventria?'

'You think it would be safe there?'

Cadoras shook his head. 'You have a point. But then at least you'd have a chance – on this quest you have none.'

'I am touched by your concern.'

'You may not believe it, but it is genuine. I respect you, Waylander, but I feel sorry for you. You are doomed . . . and by your own hand.'

'Why by mine?'

'Because the skills that are yours are now shackled. I do not know what has happened to you, but you are no longer Waylander the Slayer. If you were, I would now be dead. The Slayer would not have stopped to talk.'

'I cannot argue with that, but then the Cadoras of old would not have waited before loosing an arrow.'

'Maybe we are both getting old.'

'Collect your weapons and ride,' said Waylander, sheathing his knife and rising smoothly to his feet.

'I make no promises,' stated Cadoras. 'Why are you doing this?'

'Just ride.'

'Why not merely give me your knife and offer me your throat?' snapped Cadoras.

'Are you angry because I haven't killed you?'

'Think back to what you were, Waylander, then you'll know why I'm angry.' Cadoras strode to his weapons and retrieved them. Then he pulled on his boots, tightened his saddle cinch and mounted.

Waylander watched as the assassin rode south, then he wandered back over the hill-top to his own horse and stepped into the saddle. The wagons were lost in the heat haze to the north, but Waylander had no wish to catch up with them before nightfall.

He spent the day scouting the wooded hills, sleeping for two hours beside a rock pool shaded by spruce trees. Towards dusk he saw smoke curling into the sky in the north and a cold dread settled on him. Swiftly he saddled the gelding and raced for the trees, lashing the beast into a furious gallop. For almost a mile he pushed the pace, then sanity returned and he slowed the horse to a canter. His mind was numb and he knew what he would find before he crested the last hill. The smoke had been too great for a mere camp-fire, or even ten camp-fires. Sitting his horse atop the hill, he gazed down on the burnt-out wagons. They had been drawn into a rough semi-circle, as if the drivers had seen the danger with only seconds to spare and had tried to form a fighting circle. Bodies littered the ground and vultures had gathered in squabbling packs.

Waylander rode slowly down the hillside. Many of those now dead had been taken alive and cut to pieces – there had been, then, no prisoners. A child had been nailed to a tree and several women had been staked out with fires built on their chests. A little to the north Durmast's men lay in a rough circle, ringed by dead Nadir warriors. Already the vultures had begun their work and Waylander could not bear to search for Danyal's body. He turned his horse to the west.

The trail was not hard to follow, even under moonlight, and as he rode Waylander assembled his crossbow.

Images flickered in his mind and Danyal's face appeared . . .

Waylander blinked as tears stung his eyes. He swallowed back the sobs pushing at his throat, and something in him died. His back straightened as if a weight had been lifted from him and the recent past floated across his mind's eye like the dreams of another man. He saw the rescue of the priest, the saving of Danyal and the children, the battle at Masin and the promise made to Orien. He watched in astonishment as Cadoras was freed to strike again. Hearing himself talking to Cadoras about heroes, a dry chuckle escaped him. What a fool he must have sounded!

Hewla had been right – love was very nearly the downfall. But now the Nadir had killed Danyal and for that they would suffer. No matter that there were hundreds of them. No matter that he could not win.

Only one truth was of importance.

Waylander the Slayer was back.

Danyal knelt beside Durmast on the slopes of a hill overlooking a riverside town of rambling wooden buildings. The hill was thickly wooded and their horses were hidden in a hollow some sixty paces to the south.

She was tired. The previous day they had escaped from the Nadir raiders with seconds to spare and she had felt a deep sense of shame at their flight. Durmast had been scouting to the west and she had seen him galloping ahead of a Nadir war party, his axe in his hand. Arrows flashed by him as he thundered his bay gelding into line with the wagons, hauled on the reins alongside the baker's wagon and shouted for Danyal. Without thinking she had climbed alongside him and he had spurred his mount for the hills. She would be lying to herself if she claimed she had not known he was taking her to safety while those around her were doomed to savage and cruel deaths. And she hated herself for her weakness.

Four Nadir riders had pursued them into the hills. Once into the woods Durmast had dumped her from the saddle and swung his horse to meet their charge. The first had died as Durmast's axe smashed his rib-cage. The second had thrust out a lance which the giant brushed aside before slashing the man's head from his shoulders. The rest of the vicious action had been so swift and chaotic that Danyal could not take it in. Durmast had charged the remaining riders and the horses had gone down in a welter of flailing hooves. He had risen first, looming like a god of war with his silver axe flashing in the sunlight. With the four men dead, he had looted their saddlebags for food and water and without a word brought her a Nadir pony. Together they had headed north into the trees.

That night, with the temperature falling, they had slept under a single blanket and Durmast, still without a word, had removed his clothes and reached for her.

Turning into him she smiled sweetly, but his eyes widened as he felt the touch of cold steel at his loins.

'The knife is very sharp, Durmast. I would suggest you calm yourself – and sleep.'

'A simple "No" would have been sufficient, woman,' he said, his blue eyes cold with anger.

'Then I shall say "No". Do you give your word not to touch me?'

'Of course.'

'Since I know your word is as strong as a withered stick, let me tell you this: If you rape me, I shall do my best to kill you.'

'I am not a rapist, woman. Nor have I ever been.'

'The name is Danyal.' She withdrew the knife and turned her back to him.

135

He sat up and scratched his beard. 'You do not think highly of me, Danyal. Why?'

'Go to sleep, Durmast.'

'Answer me.'

'What a question! You led those people to slaughter and then fled without a backward glance. You are an animal – your own men stayed behind and died, but you just ran.'

'*We* just ran,' he pointed out.

'Yes – and don't think I don't hate myself for it.'

'What did you expect me to do, Danyal? Had I stayed I would have killed maybe six or seven Nadir, and then I would have died with the rest. There was no point.'

'You betrayed them all.'

'Yes, but then I was betrayed – I had an arrangement with the Nadir chieftain, Butaso.'

'You amaze me. The travellers paid you and had a right to expect loyalty – instead you sold them to the Nadir.'

'You have to pay a bounty to cross Nadir lands in safety.'

'Tell that to the dead.'

'The dead don't hear so well.'

She sat up and moved away from him, taking the blanket and wrapping it round her shoulders.

'They don't touch you, do they? The deaths?'

'Why should they? I lost no friends. All things die and their time had come.'

'They were people, families. They had put their lives in your hands.'

'What are you, my conscience?'

'You have one?'

'Your tongue is as sharp as your dagger. They paid me to guide them – am I responsible because some Nadir dog-eater breaks his word?'

'Why did you bother to rescue me?'

'Because I wanted to sleep with you. Is that a crime also?'

'No, it's just not a very attractive compliment.'

'Gods, woman, Waylander is welcome to you! No wonder he's changed – you're like acid on the soul. Now, can we share the blanket?'

The following day they had travelled in silence until they reached the last line of hills before the river. Halting the horses, Durmast had pointed to the distant blue mountains of the north-west.

'The tallest peak is Raboas, the Sacred Giant, and the river runs from that range and continues to the sea a hundred miles north of Purdol. It is called the Rostrias, the River of the Dead.'

'What are you planning?'

'There is a town yonder. There I shall book passage on a boat and head for Raboas.'

'What about Waylander?'

'If he is alive, we will see him there.'

'Why not wait in the town for him?'

'He won't come here – he'll strike north-west. We've moved north-east to avoid pursuit. Butaso is a Spear, a western tribe; this is Wolfshead land.'

'I thought you were travelling only as far as Gulgothir.'

'I've changed my mind.'

'Why?'

'Because I am a Drenai. Why should I not want to help Waylander regain the Armour of Bronze?'

'Because there's no profit in it for you.'

'Let's go,' he snapped, spurring his horse forward into the trees.

Hiding the horses in a hollow, Durmast crept to the crest of the hills overlooking the town. There were some twenty houses and seven warehouses built alongside a thick wooden jetty. Behind the warehouses was a long flat building with a shaded porch.

'That's the inn,' said Durmast, 'but it doubles as the main supply store. There don't seem to be any Nadir riders around.'

'Aren't those people Nadir?' asked Danyal, pointing to a group of men sitting beside the jetty.

'No. They are Notas – no tribe. Outcasts originally, now they farm and ply the river for trade and the Nadir come to them for iron tools and weapons, blankets and the like.'

'Are you known here?'

'I am known in most places, Danyal.'

Together they rode into the town, where they tied their horses to a hitching rail outside the inn. The inside was dimly lit and smelled of sweat, stale beer and food swimming in grease. Danyal moved to a table by a shuttered window; lifting the bar, she pushed the shutters open, rapping them firmly into the back of a man standing outside.

'You clumsy cow!' he shouted. Danyal turned away from him and sat down, but when he stormed into the inn, still shouting, she stood and drew her sword. The man stopped in his tracks as she advanced on him. He was stocky and dressed in a fur jacket with a thick black belt from which hung two long knives.

'Go away or I'll kill you,' snarled Danyal.

Durmast appeared behind the man and, grabbing his belt from the back, lifted him from his feet and carried him past Danyal.

'You heard the lady,' said Durmast. 'Go away!' Twisting, he hurled the man through the open window, watching in satisfaction as he crashed into the dust several feet beyond the wooden walkway. Then he turned to Danyal with a broad grin on his wide face.

'I see you are maintaining your reputation for sweetness.'

'I didn't need your help.'

'I am aware of that. I was doing him a favour. If he was lucky you would merely have stabbed him, but you might have lost your temper and used your acid tongue and he would never have recovered from that.'

'That's not very funny.'

'It depends on your standpoint. I have booked us passage on a sailing-boat which leaves tomorrow at mid-morning. I have also booked us a room . . . with *two* beds,' he added pointedly.

137

16

Butaso sat within his tent, gazing sullenly at the ancient shaman squatting before him. The old man spread out a section of tanned goatskin on the earth and casually tossed a dozen knuckle bones on to it. The bones had been shaped into rough cubes and strange symbols had been etched on each side. For a while the shaman stared at the bones – then he looked up, his dark slanted eyes burning with malicious humour.

'Your treachery has killed you, Butaso,' he said.

'Speak plainly.'

'Is that not plain enough? You are doomed. Even now a dark shadow hovers over your soul.'

'I am as strong as ever,' said Butaso, lurching to his feet. 'Nothing can harm me.'

'Why did you break your word to Ice-eyes?'

'I had a vision. I have many visions. The Chaos Spirit is with me – he guides me.'

'The Spirit of Dark Deeds is his Nadir name, Butaso. Why do you not use it? He is a deceiver.'

'So you say, old man. But he has brought me power and wealth, and many wives.'

'He has brought you death. What did he require of you?'

'To destroy the wagons of Ice-eyes.'

'Yet Ice-eyes lives. As does his friend, the Soul Stealer.'

'What is that to me?'

'Think you that I have no powers? Foolish mortal! Since the Soul Stealer filled your heart with fear that day, giving you your life, you have burned with the desire for vengeance. Now you have killed his friends and he hunts you. Do you not understand?'

'I understand that I have a hundred men scouring the Steppes for him. They will bring me his head by dawn.'

'This man is the prince of killers. He will evade your hunters.'

'That would please you, would it not, Kesa Khan? You have always hated me.'

'Your ego is bloated, Butaso. I do not hate you, I despise you – but that is neither here nor there. This man must be stopped.'

'You would help me?'

'He is a danger to future Nadir generations. He seeks the Armour of Bronze, the Nadir Bane; he must not live to fulfil his quest.'

'Use the Shapeshifters then – hunt him down.'

'They are a last resort,' snapped Kesa Khan, rising to his feet. 'I must think.' Replacing the knuckle bones in a goatskin sack, he moved outside the tent and stared up at the stars. Around him there was little movement, except among the sentries guarding Butaso; eight men ringed his tent with swords in hand, facing outwards silently, occasionally stamping their feet against the cold.

Kesa Khan walked to his own tent, where the slave girl Voltis had prepared a brazier of burning coals to warm the air. She had also poured a bowl of Lyrrd and placed three warmed rocks in his bed. He smiled at her and drank the Lyrrd in a single swallow, feeling the alcohol pouring fire into his veins.

'You are a fine girl, Voltis. I do not deserve you.'

'You have been kind,' she said, bowing.

'Would you like to return home?'

'No, Lord. I wish to serve you.' He was touched by her sincerity and leaning forward he lifted her chin . . . then froze.

Eight!

The guard on Butaso's tent was normally seven!

Butaso turned as the guard entered. 'What do you want?'

'The return of my gift,' said Waylander. Butaso spun on his heel, a scream beginning in his throat – a scream cut off by six inches of shimmering steel hammering into his neck. His fingers scrabbled for the blade, and his eyes widened in agony; then he fell to his knees, his gaze fixed on the tall figure standing impassively before him.

The last thing he heard as his eyes closed was the clash of steel as his guards rushed into the tent.

Waylander turned, his sword blocking a wild cut. Twisting his wrist, he sent his opponent's blade flying through the air. The guard wrenched a knife from its scabbard, but died as Waylander's sword lanced his ribs. More guards pushed forward, forcing the assassin back to the centre of the tent.

'Put down your sword,' hissed Kesa Khan from the entrance. Waylander gazed coolly at the ring of steel closing in on him.

'Come and take it,' he said.

As the Nadir surged forward, Waylander's sword flickered out and a man fell screaming. Then a blade crashed side on against his head and he fell. He struggled to rise, but pounding fists pushed him down and a sea of darkness washed over him . . .

Pain woke him – deep throbbing, insistent pain. His fingers were swollen and the sun beat mercilessly down on his naked body. He was hanging by his wrists from a pole at the centre of the Nadir camp; they had stripped him of his Nadir clothes and strung him in the sun, and already he could feel the burning of his marble-white skin. His face and arms were in no danger, burnt as they were to the colour of leather, but his body had never been exposed to harsh sunlight and already his chest and shoulders felt as if on fire. He tried to open his eyes, but only the left would function; the right was swollen shut. His mouth was dry, his tongue a stick.

His hands were throbbing and almost purple. Getting his feet under him he pushed himself upright, taking pressure from his swollen wrists. Immediately a fist lashed into his stomach and he winced and bit his swollen lip so hard that blood flowed to his chin.

139

'We have fine things in store for you, you round-eyed son of a slut,' said a voice. Waylander tilted his head to see before him a young man of middle height – his greasy black hair tied in a pony tail, his features obscured by the ash of mourning.

Waylander looked away and the man struck him again.

'Leave him!' ordered Kesa Khan.

'He is mine.'

'Obey me, Gorkai,' ordered the old man.

'He must die hard, and then serve my father in the Void.'

The young man walked away and Waylander looked at the old man.

'You did well, Soul Stealer, you took the life of a fool who would have led us to ruin.'

Waylander said nothing. His mouth was full of blood which moistened his dry tongue and eased his throat.

Kesa Khan smiled.

'Blood will not sustain you. Today we take you to the desert, where we will watch your soul drawn out by the burning sand.'

The long day wore on and the pain grew. Waylander closed his mind against the burning of his flesh and fought to stay calm, breathing slowly and deeply, conserving what energy he could against the moment when the Nadir released him. If they were to take him to the desert, then they must first cut him loose from the pole – at that moment he would attack and force them to kill him.

His mind drifted, flowing back over the years. He saw again the young, idealistic Dakeyras: the child who yearned to be a soldier, to serve in the army of Orien, the Warrior King of Bronze. He recalled the day when Orien had led his victorious force through the streets of Drenan, how the crowds had cheered and thrown flowers. The King had seemed like a giant to the ten-year-old Dakeyras as his armour blazed in the noon sun. Orien had carried his three-year-old son before him and the child, dismayed by the noise of the crowd, had burst into tears. Then the King had lifted him high and kissed him gently. Dakeyras had enjoyed that moment of warmth.

His mind tore his memory from the scene, and pictured once more the moment King Niallad fell with Waylander's bolt jutting from his back. The sight dragged him back to the present and the agony returned. How had the noble young child become the soul-less slayer? His wrists ached and he realised that his legs had given way once more; he forced himself upright and opened his good eye. A group of Nadir children squatted before him and one of them lashed at his leg with a stick.

A Nadir warrior stepped forward and sent the boy sprawling with a well-aimed kick.

Waylander drifted once more, his eyes closed. His heart sank as the vision returned of the child held high by the adoring father. With the kiss the boy had been comforted and had started to laugh, copying the King as he waved to the crowd. Tiny Niallad, the hope for tomorrow. One day, thought Dakeyras then, I will serve him as my father serves Orien.

140

'Waylander,' called a voice and he opened his eye. There was no one close, but the voice came again, deep in his mind. 'Close your eyes and relax.' Waylander did as he was bid, and his pain vanished as he sank into a deep sleep. He found himself standing on a bleak hillside under alien stars, bright and close and perfectly round. Two moons hung in the sky – one silver, one shot with blue and green like stained marble. On the hillside sat Orien, younger now and more like the king of Waylander's memory.

'Come, sit with me.'

'Have I died?'

'Not yet, though it is close.'

'I failed you.'

'You tried – a man can ask for no more.'

'They killed the woman I loved.'

'And you took your revenge. Was it sweet?'

'No, I felt nothing.'

'That is a truth you should have realised many years ago when you hunted down the men who slew your family. You are a weak man, Waylander, to be so manipulated by events. But you are not evil.'

'I killed your son. For money.'

'Yes. I had not forgotten.'

'It seems so futile to say that I am sorry, yet I am.'

'It is never futile. Evil is not like a rock, static and immobile – it is a cancer that builds on itself. Ask any soldier who has been to war. You never forget the first man you kill, but not all the gold in the world could get you to remember the tenth.'

'I can remember the tenth,' said Waylander. 'He was a raider named Kityan, a half-breed Nadir. I followed him to a small town east of Skeln . . .'

'And you killed him with your hands after putting out his eyes with your thumbs.'

'Yes. He was one of those who slew my wife and children.'

'Tell me, why did you not search for Danyal among the dead?'

Waylander turned away and swallowed hard. 'I have seen one woman I loved after the killers left her. I could not witness another such scene.'

'Had you found the strength to search, you would not now be tied to a Nadir pole. She lives, for Durmast rescued her.'

'No?'

'Would I lie, Waylander?'

'Can you help me escape?'

'No.'

'Then I will die.'

'Yes,' said Orien sadly. 'You are dying. But it is happening painlessly.'

Waylander nodded, then his head jerked round. 'You mean now?'

'Of course.'

'Return me, damn you!'

'You wish to return to agony and death?'

'It is my life, Orien. *Mine!* I have known pain and I can stand it, but until the moment of death I will not surrender. Not to you, not to the Nadir, not to anyone. Return me!'

'Close your eyes, Waylander, and prepare yourself for pain.'

Waylander groaned as the agony touched him, the sound tearing his dry, swollen throat. He heard a man laugh and opened his eyes to find a crowd had formed about him.

The young man, Gorkai, was grinning widely. 'I told you he was alive. Good! Give him a drink – I want him to feel every cut.' A squat warrior forced Waylander's head back, pouring water from a stone jug to his cracked lips. He could not swallow at first, but allowed the liquid to trickle into his dry throat.

'That's enough!' said Gorkai. 'Know this, assassin: we are going to cut your body very lightly and then smear you with honey. After that we bury you beside an ant's nest. You understand?' Waylander said nothing. His mouth was full of water and every few seconds he allowed a small amount to ease his throat.

Gorkai drew a curved knife and was moving forward when the sound of galloping hooves stopped him, causing him to turn. The crowd parted as a rider thundered into the camp and Waylander looked up, but the sun was directly behind the horseman.

The Nadir scattered as the rider approached and Gorkai, shading his eyes against the sun, screamed, 'Kill him!' The Nadir ran for their weapons; Gorkai gripped his knife tightly and turned on Waylander. The blade rose . . . But a crossbow shaft punched through his temple and he pitched to the earth. The horseman dragged on the reins beside the pole and a sword slashed through the ropes above Waylander's wrists. He slumped forward, recovered and staggered for the horse as two Nadir ran forward with blades in hand. Dropping his crossbow, the horseman hauled Waylander across his saddle; then he lashed out with his sword and the Nadir leapt back. Arrows flashed by the rider and he kicked his mount into a canter.

The pommel of the saddle cut into Waylander's side and he almost fell as the horse galloped towards the hills. He watched the tents flash by and twice saw Nadir archers bend their bows. The animal was breathing hard as they reached the trees. Behind them Waylander could hear the thunder of hooves and the furious screams of the pursuers. The rider dragged his mount to a stop in a hollow, then threw Waylander to the ground. He landed hard, then came to his knees; his hands were still tied.

Cadoras leaned over him as Waylander pushed out his arms; his sword sliced down and the ropes parted. Waylander glanced round, seeing that his own horse was tethered to a bush, his clothes and weapons tied to the saddle. By the trees was the naked corpse of the Nadir warrior he had slain the night before. He stumbled to his horse, pulled clear the reins and, with an effort, climbed into the saddle. Then they were off, hugging the tree-lined narrow trail.

Behind them the Nadir were closing and arrows flashed perilously close to the fugitives. Then the two men were out of the trees and found themselves riding across open ground.

'I hope your horse can jump,' yelled Cadoras.

Waylander strained to see ahead, fear rising in him as he saw the trail end in a sudden drop. Cadoras spurred on. 'Follow me!' he shouted.

His huge grey gelding sailed over the chasm and Waylander dug his heels into his mount's flanks and followed. The jump was less than ten feet. Far below them a river rushed over white rocks. Cadoras' horse landed well, slithering on the scree; Waylander almost fell as his own mount leapt, but hung on grimly. The horse stumbled on the far side, but found its feet and carried its rider out of bowshot. Waylander swung in the saddle to see the Nadir riders lining the chasm; the jump was too great for their ponies.

The two men headed deeper into the mountains, riding over rocks and through streams. Waylander swayed in the saddle, then lifted the canteen from the pommel and drank deeply. Turning, he pulled his cloak clear of the saddle rolls and swung it over his burning shoulders. Towards dusk, as they entered a thicker grove of trees, Cadoras suddenly pitched from his saddle. Waylander dismounted, tethered his horse and knelt by the fallen man. Only then did he see the three arrows that jutted from Cadoras' back. The man's cloak was drenched with blood. Gently Waylander eased him into a sitting position and Cadoras' head fell back against Waylander's chest. Glancing down, Waylander saw a fourth shaft deep in the man's left side.

Cadoras opened his eyes. 'Seems like a good place to camp,' he whispered.

'Why did you come back for me?'

'Who knows? Get me a drink.' With care Waylander eased the dying man against a tree before fetching a canteen. Cadoras drank deeply. 'I followed you. Found the Nadir you'd killed and saw that you had taken his clothes. I guessed then that you were engaged in some senseless act of folly.'

'You mean as senseless as attacking a Nadir camp singlehanded?'

Cadoras chuckled, then winced. 'Foolish, was it not? But then I've never been a hero. Thought I would try it just once – I don't think I'll ever do it again.'

'You want me to get those arrows out?'

'What would be the point? You'd rip me to pieces. Do you know . . . I have only been injured once in all these years, and that was merely a surface cut to the face which gave me this loathsome scar. Strange, is it not? I spend my life committing dark deeds, and the one time I try to do good I get killed. There's no justice!'

'Why did you do it? Truly, now?'

Cadoras leaned his head back and closed his eyes.

'I wish I knew. Do you think there's a heaven?'

'Yes,' lied Waylander.

'Do you think that one act can wipe out a lifetime of evil?'

'I don't know. I hope so.'

'Probably not. You know I never married? Never met anyone who liked me. Hardly surprising – I never liked myself much. Listen – don't trust

143

Durmast, he sold you out. He's taken a commission from Kaem to fetch the Armour.'

'I know.'

'You know? And yet you ride with him?'

'Life's a puzzle,' said Waylander. 'How do you feel?'

'That's a ridiculous question. I can't feel my legs and my back is burning like the devil. Have you ever had friends, Waylander?'

'Yes. Way back.'

'Was it a good feeling?'

'Yes.'

'I can imagine. I think you should go now. The Nadir will be here soon.'

'I'll stay awhile.'

'Don't be noble,' snapped Cadoras. 'Go and get that Armour! I would hate to think I was dying in vain. And take my horse with you – I don't want some dog-eating tribesman to have him. But watch out for him, he's a hateful beast; he'll take your hand off if he can.'

'I'll be careful.' Waylander lifted Cadoras' hand and squeezed it. 'Thank you, my friend.'

'Go away now. I want to die alone.'

17

The Drenai officer, Sarvaj, slept fitfully. He was huddled in the lee of the battlements with a thick blanket wrapped around him, his head resting on a ripped saddlebag he had found near the stables. He was cold and could feel each ring of his mailshirt, even through the leather backing and the woollen undershirt. Sleeping in armour was never comfortable, but add wind and rain and it becomes unbearable. Sarvaj turned over, catching his ear on a bronze buckle; he cursed and sat up, drawing his knife. After some minutes he sawed through the wet leather and hurled the offending metal out over the battlements.

Overhead thunder rolled impressively, and a fresh downpour lashed the grey stone walls. Sarvaj wished he had a rain cape of oiled leather, but even that would not have kept him dry in this storm. Beside him Vanek and Jonat slept on, blissfully unaware of the weather. In fact they had welcomed it, for it put a stop to the night attacks which wore down the spirit of the defenders.

Lightning speared the sky, illuminating the Keep which reared from the grey granite mountains like a broken tooth. Sarvaj stood and stretched. Turning, he gazed out over the harbour and the bay beyond. Vagrian triremes bobbed and swung on their anchors as the storm winds buffeted the bay. More than forty ships were now anchored at Purdol and Kaem's army had swelled to almost 60,000 fighting men – a sign, so Karnak assured the defenders, of growing desperation among the Vagrians.

Sarvaj was not so sure. Nearly a thousand men had died during the last fourteen bloody days, with almost the same number removed from the fighting by grievous wounds. When the wind changed you could hear the screams from the hospital.

Elban, a fine rider, had his leg amputated after gangrene set in, only to die during the ghastly operation. Sidrik, the jester of the regiment, took an arrow through the throat. The names spilled over in Sarvaj's mind, a rush of faces and jagged memories.

And Gellan seemed so tired. His hair shone with streaks of silver and his eyes were sunken and ringed with purple. Only Karnak seemed unchanged. Some of his fat had disappeared, yet he was still an awesome size. During a lull in the fighting the previous day he had wandered to Sarvaj's section.

'Another day closer to victory,' Karnak had said, a wide grin making him seem boyish in the dusk light.

'I hope so,' said Sarvaj, wiping his sword clean of blood and replacing it in its scabbard. 'You're losing weight, general.'

'I'll let you into a secret: a thin man couldn't keep up this pace! My father was twice my size and he lived to be over ninety.'

'That would be nice,' said Sarvaj, grinning. '*I'd* like to live to be twenty-five.'

'They won't beat us, they haven't the guts for it.'

It had seemed politic to agree and Karnak had walked off in search of Gellan.

Now Sarvaj listened to the thunder; it seemed to be moving towards the east. Stepping over the sleeping soldiers, he picked his way to the eastern gate tower and climbed the winding stair. Even here men slept, choosing to keep dry. He trod on someone's leg, but the man merely grunted and did not wake.

Walking out on to the high battlements, Sarvaj saw Gellan sitting on a stone seat staring out over the bay. The rain was now easing to a fine drizzle, as if some dark god had realised that dawn was but an hour away and the Vagrians needed good weather to scale the walls.

'Do you never sleep?' asked Sarvaj.

Gellan smiled. 'I do not seem to have the need of it. I doze now and then.'

'Karnak says we are winning.'

'Fine. I'll start to pack.'

Sarvaj slumped down beside him. 'It seems as if we've been here forever – as if all that's gone before is just a dream.'

'I know the feeling,' said Gellan.

'Two men ran at me yesterday, and I killed them both while thinking about a dance in Drenan last year. It was a weird experience, as if my body had taken over and my mind was free to wander.'

'Do not let it wander too far, my friend. We are none of us invulnerable.'

For a while they sat in silence and Gellan leaned his head back on the stone and dozed. Then Sarvaj spoke again.

'Wouldn't it be nice to wake up in Drenan?'

'Farewell to the bad dream?'

'Yes . . . Sidrik died today.'

'I hadn't heard.'

'Arrow through the throat.'

'Swift, then?'

'Yes, I hope I go as swiftly.'

'You die on me and I'll stop your pay,' said Gellan.

'I remember pay,' mused Sarvaj. 'Wasn't that something we used to get way back when the world was sane?'

'Just think how much you'll be worth when it's over!'

'Over?' muttered Sarvaj, his humour disappearing as swiftly as the storm. 'It will never be over. Even if we win, can you see us forgiving the Vagrians? We'll turn their land into a charnel-house and see how they stomach it.'

'Is that what you want?'

'Right now? Yes. Tomorrow . . . probably not. What would it achieve? I wonder how Egel is faring?'

'Dardalion says he is only a month from attempting a breakout. And the Lentrians have smashed the Vagrian army and advanced into the Drenai lands. You remember old Ironlatch?'

'The old man at the banquet?'

'Yes.'

'The one with no teeth who had to eat soup and soft bread?'

'The very same. Well, now he leads the Lentrian army.'

'I cannot believe it. We all laughed at him.'

'Laughter or not, he is pushing them back.'

'That must be hard for them to take. They're not used to losing.'

'That's their weakness,' said Gellan. 'A man or an army needs to lose once in a while. It's like putting steel through fire – if it doesn't break it comes out stronger.'

'Karnak has never lost.'

'I know.'

'So does your philosophy hold true with him?'

'You always manage to find the difficult questions. But yes, I think it does. When Karnak talks of the inevitability of victory he genuinely believes it.'

'And what about you?'

'You are my friend, Sarvaj, and I will not talk down to you. We have a chance – no more than that.'

'You are telling me no more than I know. What I want to know is: do you think we'll win?'

'Why should I be any more reliable in predictions than Karnak?'

'Because I trust you.'

'And I value that trust, but I can't answer you.'

'I think you already have.'

High in the Keep, Karnak was beginning to lose patience with the surgeon, Evris. Fighting to hold his temper, he cut across the man's argument by crashing his fist on the table.

'I will not have the wounded brought to the Keep! You understand? What do I need to say to you, Evris? Is my language not plain enough?'

'Oh, it is plain enough, general. I tell you that men are dying in their scores unnecessarily – and you do not care.'

'Care? Of course I care,' thundered Karnak. 'You impudent wretch! The audience is ended. Get out!'

'Audience, general? I thought one held those with kings. Not butchers!' In two strides Karnak rounded the table and grabbed the slightly-built surgeon by his blood-covered apron. Evris was hauled from his feet to dangle before the furious warrior.

Karnak held him high for several seconds and then hurled him against the far door. Evris hit hard and slid to the floor.

'Get out before I kill you,' hissed Karnak. Dundas, who had been watching the scene in silence, moved to his feet and assisted the surgeon, helping him out into the corridor.

'You went too far, surgeon,' said Dundas softly. 'Are you hurt?'

Evris wrenched himself clear of Dundas' supporting arms. 'No, I'm not

147

hurt, Dundas. I don't have gangrene spreading through my limbs. I don't have maggots breeding in my wounds.'

'Try to understand the wider view,' urged Dundas. 'We face many enemies, not least of which is the threat of plague. We cannot take the wounded into the Keep.'

'You think me so lacking in understanding of strategy that you must feed me the same simple line as your leader? I know what he is thinking and I would have respected him far more had he admitted it. We cannot hold the walls for much longer. Then the soldiers will retreat to the Keep. Karnak wants only fighting men there – he doesn't need a thousand or more wounded men clogging the space, needing to be fed . . . watered . . . cleansed and healed.'

Dundas said nothing and Evris smiled. 'Thank you for not disagreeing. When the retreat comes the Vagrians will kill every wounded man – butcher them in their beds.'

'Karnak has no choice.'

'I know that, damn you.'

'Then why did you rail against him?'

'Because he is there! It is his responsibility; it comes with power. And also because I detest him.'

'How can you say that when he is fighting to defend everything you have lived for?'

'Defending? You cannot defend what I have lived for with a sword. You cannot see it, can you, Dundas? There is no real difference between Karnak and Kaem. They are brothers of the Soul. But I cannot stand here talking to you when men are dying.' He stumbled away, then turned by the stairs.

'This morning I found three men dead in the stable cellar, where I had been forced to place them. Rats had eaten them alive.'

Then he was gone and Dundas sighed and returned to the general's rooms. He took a deep breath as he opened the door. Karnak was sitting at the table, his fury still present.

'Insipid worm!' he declared as Dundas entered. 'How dare he say that to me? When this is over, there will be a reckoning.'

'No, there won't, general,' said Dundas. 'You will honour him with medals and apologise.'

'Never! He accused me of forcing Degas to suicide – of not caring about my men.'

'He is a good surgeon and a caring man. And he knows why you will not allow the wounded into the Keep.'

'How? How does he know?'

'Because he is also a soldier.'

'If he knows, why in Hell's name did he attack me?'

'I don't know, general.'

Karnak grinned, and his anger passed. 'For a small man he certainly stood up to me.'

'He did that well enough.'

'I'll only give him a *small* medal – and no apology,' said Karnak. 'Now tell me, how is the water situation?'

'We've moved six hundred barrels into the Keep. That's the limit.'

'How long will that last?'

'It depends how many men we have left.'

'Say two thousand when the retreat comes?'

'Roughly six weeks, then.'

'It's not enough, not nearly enough. Why the Hell doesn't Egel break out?'

'It's not time; he's not ready.'

'He's too cautious.'

'He knows what he's doing, sir. He's a canny thinker.'

'He lacks flair.'

'You mean he isn't reckless?'

'Don't tell me what I mean,' snapped Karnak. 'Go away and get some rest.'

Dundas returned to his quarters and lay back on the narrow bed. There was no point in removing his armour; dawn was less than an hour away.

As he drifted towards sleep, images of Karnak and Egel floated in his mind. Both were men of awesome power. Karnak was like a storm, dramatic and inspiring, while Egel was more like an angry sea – deep, dark and deadly. They would never be friends. *Could* never be friends.

The images shifted and Dundas saw a tiger and a bear surrounded by snarling wolves. While the common enemy was close, the two animals would fight side by side.

But what would happen when the wolves departed?

Sarvaj buckled the chin-strap of his helmet and sharpened his sword with a black whetstone. Beside him Jonat was silent as the enemy raced forward carrying their ladders and coiled ropes. There were few archers now on the walls, the supply of arrows having been virtually drained three days before.

'What I'd give to be astride a horse with five thousand Legion riders,' muttered Vanek, staring down at the massed ranks of the infantry as they surged towards the fortress.

Sarvaj nodded. A cavalry charge would cut them apart like a lance slicing through pork fat. The first of the Vagrians reached the wall and the defenders took several paces back as the heavy grappling irons sailed over the ramparts, snagging tight.

'Another day begins,' said Vanek. 'You'd think they would be tired of it by now.'

Sarvaj found his mind wandering as he waited for the first enemy soldier to appear. Why would anyone want to be first? They always died. He wondered how he would feel as an attacker standing at the foot of the ladder. What did they think as they climbed towards death?

A hand reached over the ramparts, broad fingers clamping to the stone. Vanek's sword slashed down and the hand fell at Sarvaj's feet, fingers twitching. Scooping it up, he threw it over the ramparts. More warriors

149

appeared and Sarvaj stabbed out, his blade thrusting between a man's teeth and through the back of his neck. Dragging the blade clear, he back-handed it across the throat of another climber. Already his arm was weary and the battle proper had yet to begin.

For an hour the enemy were unable to get a foothold on the ramparts; then a huge warrior forced his way to the wall west of the gate tower, opening a gap behind him. Climbers surged over the ramparts and soon a fighting wedge had formed. Gellan saw the danger and took five men from the tower to launch a blistering attack to their flank. The massive Vagrian turned and aimed a slashing blow at the tall Drenai. Gellan ducked and lunged and his blade slid into the man's side. The Vagrian grunted, but was far from finished. His blade whistled down but Gellan blocked and moved.

'I'll kill you!' screamed the Vagrian. Gellan said nothing. The man lunged but Gellan sidestepped the blade and countered with a thrust to the throat. Choking on his blood, the warrior fell, but even as he died he lashed out, though his blade cut into the leg of the man beside Gellan. The Vagrians' wedge was collapsing in on itself and Gellan forced his way closer, drawing his dagger and stabbing an enemy soldier who had just climbed into view. The man fell back to be dashed on the rocks below. From the other side of the wedge Gellan could could hear Sarvaj shouting orders for the men to close in. Slowly the Vagrians were forced back and the wall cleared – only for a new wedge to open up thirty paces to the right.

This time Karnak led the counter-charge, swinging a double-headed battleaxe that smashed through armour, snapping ribs and disembowelling his assailants.

Sarvaj tripped over a body and fell heavily, rapping his head against the rampart steps. Rolling on to his back, he saw a sword-blade flash towards his face.

A second sword blocked the cut, deflecting the blade to strike the stone beside Sarvaj's head. Sarvaj rolled to his feet as Vanek killed the attacker, but there was no time for thanks as they hurled themselves once more into the fray.

A steady thudding boom rose above the noise of clashing steel and Sarvaj knew that the battering ram was once more in place, its bronze head crashing against the reinforced oak of the gates. The sun blazed down from a clear sky and he could feel the salt of his sweat stinging his eyes.

At noon the attack ceased and the Vagrians drew back, carrying their wounded with them, while the Drenai stretcher-bearers gathered the injured in the courtyard below. There was no longer room to carry them inside.

Other soldiers were toiling along the ramparts carrying buckets of water from which the defenders filled their canteens. Still others were washing the blood from the ramparts and spreading sawdust on the stone.

Sarvaj sent three men to fetch bread and cheese for the section, then sat down and removed his helmet. He remembered Vanek saving his life and looked round for the man, seeing him sitting by the wall of the gate tower. Pushing himself wearily to his feet he joined him.

'A tough morning,' he said.

Vanek smiled wearily. 'It will get tougher yet,' he responded.

'Thank you for saving me.'

'No problem. I wish someone had done the same for me.'

Sarvaj saw that Vanek's face was grey with pain and that he was sitting in a pool of blood with one hand clenched to his side.

'I'll get the stretcher-bearers,' said Sarvaj, half-rising.

'No . . . no point. Anyway, I don't want to be eaten by rats in the night. It doesn't matter – there's no pain, which I'm told is not a good sign.'

'I don't know what to say.'

'Don't worry about it. Did you hear that I left my wife?'

'Yes.'

'Stupid. I loved her too much to bear the sight of watching her grow old. You know? I took up with a young woman. Beautiful girl. She robbed me blind and had a young lover on the side. Why do we have to grow old?'

Sarvaj said nothing, but he drew closer for Vanek's voice was fading to a whisper.

'A year ago I would have seen that cut coming. Too slow . . . killed the bastard, though. Twisted my body to trap his blade, then cut his cursed throat. I think it was the twist that killed me. You know? Gods, I wish my wife was here! Isn't that stupid? Wanting to bring her here with all the bloodshed and death? Tell her for me, Sarvaj – tell her I was thinking about her. She was so beautiful once. People are like flowers . . . Gods! Look at that!'

Sarvaj swung round, but there was nothing to be seen.

'What is it?'

But Vanek was dead.

'They're coming back!' yelled Jonat.

151

18

Waylander had known much pain in his life and had always considered himself capable of withstanding any torment the world could inflict. Now he knew better. His blistered skin felt as if a thousand bees swarmed upon it, stabbing and stinging, while his head throbbed to the rhythms of the waves of nausea racking his body.

At first, as he rode away from the clearing and the dying Cadoras, the pain had been bearable but now, with the coming of night, it was insufferable. A fresh flood of agony struck him and he groaned, cursing himself for his weakness. He sat up, shivering, and moved deeper into the cave, where with trembling hands he shredded some bark for tinder and lit a small fire. His horses, tethered at the rear of the cave, whinnied and the sound ripped through him. He stood, staggered and then recovered his balance, moving to the beasts and patting their necks. Loosening the saddle cinch of his own mount, he spread a blanket over the beast's back before returning to the fire.

Adding thicker sticks to the blaze, he felt the warmth spread through him and slowly removed his shirt, wincing as the wool pulled clear of the blisters on his shoulders. Then he opened a leather pouch at his belt and drew out the long green leaves he had picked before dusk. There was danger in using Lorassium. In small quantities it eased pain and gave rise to colourful dreams; in large quantities it killed. And Waylander had no idea how much or how little to take – or how to prepare it. He crushed a leaf in his hand and smelled it, then placed it in his mouth and chewed slowly. It was bitter and he gagged. Anger rose in him, making his head pound, and he chewed faster. When after ten minutes there was no relief, he ate a second leaf.

Now flame dancers leapt above the tiny blaze, twisting and pirouetting, flinging their arms high with sparks streaming from their tiny fingers. The walls of the cave creaked and swelled and Waylander chuckled as his horse grew wings and horns. The chuckle faded as he saw his own hands had become scaled and taloned. Now the fire reshaped itself into a face, broad and handsome with flaming hair.

'Why do you seek to thwart me, man?' asked the fire.

'Who are you?'

'I am the Morning Star, the Lord of Dark Light.'

Waylander leaned back and threw a stick at the face. Fire leapt from its mouth and devoured the stick; the tongue of flame, Waylander noticed, was forked.

'I know you,' said the assassin.

'So you should, child, you have served me for many years. I am filled with sadness that you should betray me now.'

'I never served you. I have always been my own man.'

'Think you so? Then we will leave it at that.'

'No – tell me.'

'What is there to tell, Waylander? You have hunted and killed for many years. Do you think your actions aided the Source? They served the cause of Chaos. *My* cause! You are mine, Waylander – you have always been mine. And in my way I have protected you from harm, turned aside the daggers in the night. Even now I protect you from the Nadir huntsmen who have sworn to eat your heart.'

'Why would you do this for me?'

'I am a good friend to those who serve me. Did I not send Cadoras to you in your need?'

'I don't know. Yet I do know you are the Prince of Deceivers, so I doubt it.'

'Harsh words, mortal. Words of death, if I so choose.'

'What do you want from me?'

'I want to rid you of your taint. You are less of a man since Dardalion touched you with his weakness. I can remove it – I almost did when you went hunting Butaso – but now I see it reaffirming itself like a cancer in your heart.'

'How will you rid me of this taint?'

'Merely say that you desire it and it will be gone.'

'I do not desire it.'

'You think the Source will take you? You are defiled by the blood of the innocents you have slain. Why risk death for a God who despises you?'

'It is not for any God, it is for myself.'

'Death is not the end, Waylander – not for such as you. Your soul will enter the Void, be lost in the darkness, but I will find it and lash it with tongues of flame for eternity. Can you understand what you are risking?'

'I find your threats more acceptable than your promises. They are more in keeping with your reputation. Now leave me.'

'Very well, but know this: I am not an enemy you should desire, assassin. My reach is long and my talons deadly. Your death is already set; the scenario is written in the Book of Souls and I have read it with pleasure. But there is someone you should consider – Danyal. She travels with another whose soul is mine.'

'Durmast will not harm her,' said Waylander, though his words were empty and filled more with hope than conviction.

'We shall see.'

'Leave me, demon!'

'One last gift before I go. Watch and learn!' The face shimmered and shrank, the flames surged anew and within the blaze Waylander saw Durmast chasing Danyal through a dark wood. He caught her by the banks of a river and swung her round. She lashed at his face, but he parried the blow. Then he struck her and she fell; his hands ripped away her tunic . . .

Waylander watched the scene that followed, screaming only when Durmast drew his knife across her throat. Then he passed out.

And the pain ceased.

Dardalion and The Thirty knelt in the open courtyard by the stables, their minds joined, their concentration honed, their spirits seeping through the timbers and gullies below the stable.

The first rat was asleep, but its button eyes opened in alarm and it scurried away as it felt the presence of Man. Its nostrils quivered, but no scent of the enemy could be found in the dank air. It turned, filled with a terrible terror, squealed and ran for the open. More and more of its fellows joined it in the panic race for life. From gullies and drains and forgotten sewers the rats poured out into the courtyard, drawn to the circle of priests. The first rat ran to lie beside Astila, knowing only that here in the courtyard was an end to fear. Nothing could harm it while it lay thus, in the moon shadow of the Man. Others followed it and a great circle formed about the priests.

From the ramparts above Karnak watched in fascination, while around him officers and men made the sign of the Protective Horn.

Hundreds of rats clustered about the priests, clambering over their robes and on their shoulders. Sarvaj swallowed hard and looked away. Gellan shook his head and scratched his arm.

Dardalion slowly raised his arm and Gellan caught the movement.

'Open the gates. Gently now, only a foot or so!' Gellan glanced up at the soldier on the gate tower. 'What can you see?'

'No movement from the enemy, sir.'

As silently as they could, the soldiers by the gate removed the bronze reinforced bars from the gates and pulled them open.

The first rat blinked and shivered as the comforting blanket of safety slipped away from him. He scampered towards the gates and the horde followed.

The night air was cool as the black mass moved down the hill and into the silent streets of Purdol town, then on to the market squares and the pitched tents of the Vagrian army. On flowed the rats, over cobbled streets and into the tents.

One man awoke as a black rat scampered across his face; he sat up screaming and lashing out. Then a second one fell from his shoulder, landing in his lap with its teeth plunging into his thigh. Other screams filled the night as the rats moved on. Lunging men snapped tent poles and the white canvas billowed around them; others ran from the streets to hurl themselves into the sea. A burning brazier fell and flames licked at dry canvas, while the eastern breeze fanned the blaze and sent it leaping from tent to tent.

High on the Purdol walls Karnak's laughter echoed in the mountains, as the sounds of panic rose from the city below.

'It's not often that visiting relatives are greeted with such a display,' said Sarvaj. Jonat chuckled.

'Gods, what pandemonium,' said Gellan. 'Dardalion!' he called. 'Come up and view your handiwork.'

The priest in silver armour shook his head and led The Thirty back into the hospital building, where Evris was waiting.

'Mighty fine, young man,' he said, grasping Dardalion's hand. 'Mighty fine indeed. What can you do with cockroaches?'

Dardalion grinned. 'I think I'll leave that for another day, Evris, if you don't mind—'

Astila, alert as always, caught Dardalion as he fell.

'Carry him in here,' said Evris, pushing open the door to his own room. Astila laid Dardalion on the narrow bed and removed the silver armour, while Evris lifted Dardalion's wrist. 'The pulse is strong. I think he's just exhausted – how long since he slept?'

Astila shrugged. 'I don't know, surgeon. But I have only had three hours in the last eighty. There is so much to do – so many wounded and dying. And then at night . . .'

'I know. The Brotherhood stalks the darkness.'

'We will not hold them much longer. Soon we will die.'

'How many of them are there?'

'Who knows?' answered Astila wearily. 'They have been reinforced. Last night we almost lost Baynha and Epway. Tonight . . . ?'

'Get some rest. You are taking on too much.'

'It is the price of guilt, Evris.'

'You have nothing to feel guilty about, surely?'

Astila placed his hands on the surgeon's shoulders. 'It is all relative, my friend. We are taught that life is sacred. *All* life. I once got out of bed and trod on a beetle – I felt somehow defiled. How do you think I feel tonight, with scores of men dying in the town below? How do you think we all feel? There is no joy for us here, and the absence of joy is despair.'

Six men knelt before the shaman, six warriors with shining eyes and grim faces: Bodai, who had lost his right arm two years before; Askadi, whose spine was twisted following a fall from a cliff; Nenta, once a fine swordsman, now crippled with arthritis; Belikai the blind; Nontung the leper, fetched from the caves of Mithega; Lenlai the possessed, whose fits grew more frequent and who had bitten off his own tongue in a terrible spasm.

Kesa Khan, dressed now in a robe of human scalps, gave each man a draught of Lyrrd, spiced with the herbs of the mountains. He watched their eyes as they drank, noting the swelling of the pupils and the dawning of incomprehension.

'My children,' he said slowly, 'you are the Chosen. You whom life has robbed, you will be strong again. Sleek and strong. Power will flow in your veins. And then having tasted the strength you will die, and your souls will flow to the Void on a sea of joy. For you will have served the blood of your blood and fulfilled a Nadir destiny.' They sat still, their eyes fixed on his. Not a movement came from them – not a blink, seemingly not a breath. Satisfied, Kesa Khan clapped his hands lightly and six acolytes entered the cave, leading six grey timber wolves, muzzled and wary.

One by one, Kesa Khan approached the wolves, removing first the leash and then the muzzle. He laid his bony fingers across their eyes and each

155

sat obediently where he led them, until at last all six were squatting before the crippled warriors. The acolytes withdrew.

Kesa Khan closed his eyes, allowing his mind to flow around the cave and out into the darkness of the Nadir night, feeling the pulse of the land and tuning it to his own. He felt the vast elemental power of the mountains rushing into his mind, swelling within him, seeking to explode the frail man-shell that held it. The shaman opened his eyes, stilling the adrenal surge within his veins.

'In this cave the assassin rested. His scent is upon the rocks. Your last memory must be of this man: this tall, round-eyed Drenai who seeks to thwart the destiny of our race. Burn his image into your minds, even as the wolves feel the searing hatred of his scent in their nostrils. Waylander the Slayer. The Soul Stealer in the shadows. He is a strong man, this one – but not as strong as you will be. He is fast and deadly – but not as fast as you, my children.

'His flesh will be sweet, his blood like the wine of the mountains. No other flesh can sustain you. All other food will be poison to you. He alone is your life.'

Kesa Khan took a deep breath and stood, moving along the squatting wolves to touch each gently on the neck. As he touched them they tensed and growled, their eyes fixed on the silent men.

Suddenly the shaman screamed and the wolves leapt, their great fangs fastening on the throats before them. The men made no move as the fangs sliced through flesh and bone.

The wolves shuddered.

And swelled . . .

While the men shrank, their skin hanging in flapping folds, the wolves stretched, paws swelling into fur-covered fingers, nails darkening and curving into talons. Rib-cages expanded, bloated with new muscle; shoulders formed and the creatures loomed upright, dropping to the ground what appeared to be wizened sacks of old bones.

'Turn to me, my children,' said Kesa Khan. The six beasts obeyed him and he felt the power of their blood-red eyes upon him, felt the full savagery of their stares.

'Go forth and kill,' he whispered.

And six beasts padded into the night.

After a while the acolytes returned.

'Remove the bodies,' said the shaman.

'Can we call these things bodies?' asked a young man, his face ashen.

'Call them what you will, boy, but remove them.'

Kesa Khan watched them depart, then built a fire and wrapped himself in a goatskin robe. The ritual had drained him and he felt very old and very tired. There had been a day when only the strongest of warriors had been used, but that offended Kesa Khan. This way was better, for it gave a last glimpse of true life to men bowed by disaster.

They would hunt Waylander and devour him. Then they would die. If they drank water, it would choke them. If they ate meat, it would poison them. Within a month they would starve to death.

But they would have one last fine meal, as their great jaws closed upon the flesh of Waylander.

Kaem sat silently listening to the reports: sixty-eight men dead; forty-seven injured. Four hundred tents had been destroyed and two warehouses burnt to the ground, both containing meat and grain. One ship moored to the jetty had lost its sails in the blaze, but had otherwise survived intact. The rats, however, had infiltrated the remaining food stores and were overrunning the warehouses. Kaem dismissed the officers and turned to the black-coated figure beside him.

'Restore my good humour, Nemodes. Tell me once more how the Brotherhood is in sight of victory against the priests.'

Nemodes shrugged, his heavy-lidded eyes avoiding the general's gaze. The Brotherhood leader was a small, emaciated man with a thick fleshy nose which seemed out of place on his thin features. His mouth was lipless, his teeth like tombstones.

'Three of them died last night. The end is near,' he whispered.

'Three? I lost forty-eight.'

'The three are worth more than your scum,' snapped Nemodes. 'Soon they will lose the strength to keep us out and then we will work on Karnak as we destroyed Degas.'

'Your promises are as pig-wind,' said Kaem. 'Strong, but not lasting. Do you know how badly I need this fortress? Ironlatch has smashed our armies in the south and is advancing on Drenan. I cannot release men to stop him because Egel is still at large in Skultik and Karnak holds this last fortress. I cannot lose . . . and yet I cannot win.'

'We will kill the renegade priests,' Nemodes assured him.

'I don't want them dying of old age, Nemodes! You promised me the fortress would fall. It did not. You promised me the priests would be dead. They live. You promised me Waylander. What bad news have you on this front?'

'Cadoras betrayed us. He rescued the assassin from a Nadir village where his death would have been certain.'

'Why? Why would Cadoras do such a thing?'

Nemodes shrugged. 'It is beyond me. In all his life Cadoras never acted without self-interest. Perhaps he and Waylander struck a bargain. It matters not, for Cadoras is dead. However, nine of my brethren are currently approaching Raboas; they are the best warriors of my Order, and that means the best on the continent. And always we have Durmast.'

'I don't trust him.'

'That's why he *can* be trusted. Greed is the spur and that one will always sell to the highest bidder.'

'You depress me, Nemodes.'

'I do have some good news for you, general.'

'I can scarce believe that.'

'We have found the mountain entrance to the fortress – the route by which Karnak entered.'

Kaem took a deep breath and smiled. 'I want a thousand men ready to march in two hours.'

'I shall see that it is done,' promised Nemodes.

19

The wood was not large, but within it was a hollow where Waylander could build a fire. He was cold through, and though recovering fast from his ordeal still felt the effects of the fever caused by his tortured skin. For three days he had rested within the cave; then he had journeyed north, meeting a small group of Notas who sold him some foul-smelling salve which he smeared across his shoulders and upper back. While he was with them, a young woman had tended to the wound at his temple and the old Notas leader had given him a new name: Oxskull. Using a bronze mirror, Waylander had examined the wound. It was a swelling, purple and gross, the skin split across it in a jagged line. He remembered the sword-blade crashing against his head, and realised that it must have turned and struck him semi-flat. The swelling in his eye had reduced considerably, but he still found his vision troubled by harsh sunlight, which caused the eye to water heavily.

The Notas leader – a wizened, jovial ancient – examined his head, pressing and pushing.

'No crack, Oxskull. You live.'

'How far to Raboas?'

'Five days if you travel without care. Seven if your eyes are open.'

The girl moved forward with a pitcher of stone-cooled water and bathed Waylander's head. She was petite and pretty, her hands gentle.

'My youngest wife,' said the old man. 'Good, yes?'

'Good,' agreed Waylander.

'You carry many weapons, Oxskull. You are fighting a war?'

Waylander nodded. 'It would displease me to think I will leave here with less than I arrived.'

'Your black horse is ferocious,' countered the ancient leader. 'He bit my eldest son in the shoulder.'

'He is of uncertain temper. When your people gather my possessions back into one place, I will put them in my blanket roll. The horse will not bite me.'

The old man chortled and dismissed the girl, but his face lost its smile as the tent-flap settled back into place and he and the stranger were alone.

'You are a hunted man, Oxskull. Many, many riders seek you.'

'I know this.'

'Some Nadir. Some Southriders.'

'I know this also.'

'The Southriders wear black cloaks and their eyes are cold. They are like a cloud across the sun and our children fear them – the young are so perceptive.'

'They are evil men,' said Waylander. 'Their promises are dust, but their threats are sworn in blood.'

159

'This I know,' said the Notas leader. 'They promised gold for knowledge and death for silence.'

'When they return, tell them I was here.'

'This I would have done anyway. Why do they seek you? Are you a king in exile?'

'No.'

'What then?'

Waylander spread his hands. 'A man makes many enemies.'

The old man nodded grimly, his dark eyes fixed on the assassin.

'You know why I have lived this long?' he asked, leaning sideways and pouring a goblet of Lyrrd for his guest.

Waylander shrugged, accepted the goblet, and drank deeply.

'Because I am blessed. I see things within the mist of minds. I walk the spirit roads and view the births of mountains. Nothing is hidden from me. The Southriders worship the darkness and feed on the hearts of babes. They swallow the long green leaf and soar on the night winds. But you they cannot find. These men, who could hunt the smallest bat within a night-dark cavern, cannot find a rider on an arid plain. When I close my eyes I can see all things – the children playing beyond the tent, your horses cropping the grass, my youngest wife telling my oldest that she fears my touch for it reminds her of death. And yet I cannot see you, Oxskull. Why is that?'

'I don't know.'

'You speak the truth. *But I know*. Somewhere you have a friend – a friend of great power who has laid a charm over your spirit. Only with true eyes can you be seen.'

'I have such a friend.'

'Does he sit in a fortress under siege?'

'He may. I do not know.'

'He is in great danger.'

'I cannot help him.'

'You are the key, I think.'

'We shall see. How long ago did these riders come? Did they say they would return?'

'They did not say . . . but I know. They will ride into my camp at sunset.'

'From which direction?'

'From the east. Your journey to the north will avoid them – but only for now. Your paths will cross and nothing can change that. You need more friends, Oxskull – alone, you are lost.' The old Notas closed his eyes and shivered. When a sudden cool breeze sprang up within the tent, guttering the candles, he shook and trembled, his eyes flaring open.

'You must go from here and I must move camp,' he said, fear shining in his dark slanted eyes.

'What do you see?'

'Your enemies are powerful indeed. They have opened the ninth gate of Hell and the Shapeshifters are unleashed. You must ride far and fast, Oxskull.'

160

'What are the Shapeshifters?'

'I can tell you nothing more. Time is gone and every heartbeat brings us closer to destruction. Bear this in your soul: Do not try to fight them. Run! They are power and they are death. Run!'

The old man sprang to his feet and raced from the tent. Waylander could hear his shouted orders and the edge of panic in his voice. Finding that his possessions had been placed in a neat pile beside his horse, he packed them swiftly and rode from the camp, leaving Cadoras' mount in payment for the aid they had given him.

Now, camped some eight miles away, he pondered the old man's words: 'Do not fight. Run.'

But what were they, these Shapeshifters? Why could he not kill them? Did they lack a beating heart? What manner of thing could survive an encounter with Waylander the Slayer?

The old man was no coward. He had sensed the evil of the Brotherhood riders, but was not cowed by them. Yet this new threat had all but unmanned him. Why move his camp? Waylander added sticks to the blaze and warmed his hands. The night breeze rustled the branches of the trees, while in the distance a wolf howled.

The assassin looked to his weapons, honing the blades of his throwing knives. Then he checked his crossbow, a beautiful weapon designed to his specifications and fashioned by a Ventrian armourer. The stock was polished ebony and the two triggers were dulled bronze. The crafting of the weapon was beyond compare, and Waylander had paid the man a fortune in opals. That they were stolen gems took nothing from the gift and the armourer had blinked in astonishment when Waylander poured them into his outstretched hands.

'You are an artist, Arles, and this is a masterpiece.'

Suddenly Waylander's horse whinnied in terror and the assassin came smoothly to his feet, stringing the crossbow swiftly and slipping two bolts in place. The animal was tugging at the reins, seeking to pull them clear of the low-hanging branch to which they were tied. Its ears were flat to its skull and its eyes wide with fear.

'Do not fight. Run!' The old man's words hammered at him.

Scooping his blanket from beside the fire, Waylander rolled it and ran to his horse. It took some seconds to tighten the saddle cinch and settle the blanket in place, then he tugged the reins loose and vaulted into the saddle. He was almost thrown as the horse sprang to a gallop, then they were clear of the wood and racing north.

Waylander swivelled in the saddle – behind him several dark shapes had emerged from the wood. He blinked, but a cloud obscured the moon and they faded into darkness. He fought to control the mad gallop, hauling on the reins. It was madness to race across the Steppes in darkness. A pothole, a rabbit's burrow, a large rock – all could bring down his horse with a broken leg.

After about a mile the horse began to lose his wind and Waylander dragged him to a halt, then walked him gently. The beast's sides were lathered, his breathing ragged. Waylander stroked the long neck and whispered soothing words. He glanced back, but could see nothing. He had caught only a brief glimpse of his pursuers, but his memory was of huge men in wolfskin cloaks, running bent double. He shook his head – it must have been a trick of the light, for their speed was awesome. Now travelling at a more sedate pace, he stripped the bolts from the crossbow and loosed the strings.

Whatever men were behind him, they were on foot and would not catch him this night.

He dismounted and led his horse on towards the north, pausing only to wipe him clear of lather. 'I think you saved my life,' he whispered, stroking the velvet neck.

The clouds cleared and the moon shone silver above the distant mountains as Waylander walked the horse for about a mile before stepping into the saddle once more.

He rubbed his eyes and yawned, drawing his cloak tightly about him. The need to sleep rose in him like a warm blanket around his mind.

A night owl swooped overhead, then dropped like a stone with talons outstretched . . . a tiny rodent squealed as the owl struck.

A dark shadow moved to Waylander's right and he swung in the saddle, yet saw nothing but a screen of low bushes. Instantly alert, he glanced left to see two dark shapes emerging from the long grass at terrifying speed. His horse reared and came down running as Waylander's boots hammered into its side. Then it sprinted away with Waylander leaning low in the saddle.

A figure loomed ahead and the horse swerved. When the figure leapt, Waylander's blood chilled as he saw the demonic face, fangs bared, hurtling towards him. The assassin's fist lashed out to catch the creature on the side of the head; the horse's shoulder cannoned into the beast, sending it sprawling. This time Waylander made no effort to check its mad rush into the night. His own fear was as great, his mind filled with the image of those terrible red eyes and the dripping fangs. His heart was drumming against his chest as he rode. No wonder the old man was so desperate to move his camp – he was taking it away from Waylander's scent.

Three miles further on, Waylander regained control of himself. The horse had begun to tire badly and was now barely cantering. He slowed it and glanced back.

There was nothing to be seen, but he knew they were there; loping along his trail, smelling his fear. He searched the horizon for some hiding-place, but none was in sight. So he pushed on, knowing the beasts would run him down, for his horse was weary and, though faster on the short sprint, could not stay ahead on a long chase.

How many of the beasts were there? He had seen at least three. Three was not so terrible – surely he could handle three? He doubted it.

Anger flared in him. Dardalion had told him he was serving the Source, but what kind of a god left a man in such peril? Why did all the strength remain with the enemy?

'What do you want from me?' he shouted, staring up at the sky.

Ahead, a low line of hills rose gently from the plain; there were no

trees and little cover in sight. Slowly his horse plodded up the slope and
at the top Waylander pulled on the reins and studied his back trail. At
first he could see nothing, then in the distance he glimpsed them – six
dark shapes running together, hugging his trail. Only minutes separated
them now.

Waylander strung his crossbow, slipping the bolts into place. Two of
the beasts he could take swiftly, maybe a third with his sword.

He glanced over the brow of the hill and saw the river below, winding
towards the mountains like a silver ribbon. At the foot of the hills was a
shack and beyond it a small ferry. Hope rose within him and he urged
the horse onward.

Halfway down the hill he began to shout for the ferryman.

A lantern flared in the window of the shack and a tall man walked out
into the night.

'Take me across the river,' said Waylander.

'I'll take you in the morning,' replied the man. 'You can bed down in
the house.'

'In the morning we'll be dead. There are six beasts from Hell just behind
me. If you have family in the house, get them on the ferry.'

The man held up his lantern. He was tall, with wide shoulders and a
thick black beard; his eyes, though slanted, gave evidence of his mixed
blood. 'You'd better explain,' he said.

'Believe me, there is no time. I will give you twenty silver pieces for
the crossing, but if you don't move fast I'll make a try at swimming the
river.'

'You won't make it – the current is too strong. Wait here.'

The man walked back into the house and Waylander swore at his lack
of speed. Several minutes later he emerged leading three children; one
held a rag-doll clutched to her face. He led them to the ferry, lifting the
bar to allow Waylander's horse to scramble aboard. The assassin dismounted and locked the bar in place, then unhooked the ropes from the
jetty as the ferryman moved to the front, took a firm hold on the lead
rope and pulled. The ferry inched forward and the man leaned harder
into the rope as Waylander stood at the stern, watching the hillside.

The creatures came into sight and burst into a run.

The ferry was still only yards from the jetty.

'By all the Gods, what are they?' shouted the ferryman, letting go of
the rope.

'Pull if you want to live!' screamed Waylander and the man seized the
rope, throwing his full weight against it. The creatures plunged down the
slope and on to the jetty, in the lead a giant with glittering eyes. Talons
outstretched, it reached the end of the jetty and sprang. Waylander tugged
on the first trigger and the crossbow bolt flew into the beast's mouth,
punching through the bone above the throat and skewering the brain. The
creature crashed against the bar, snapping it in two. Waylander's horse
reared and whinnied in terror as a second beast leapt. A second bolt
bounced from its skull and it hit the ferry and staggered. Waylander ran

163

forward and leapt feet-first, his boots hammering into its chest so that it catapulted from the ferry into the swirling water of the river.

The other beasts howled in rage as Waylander came to his feet and snapped two bolts into place. He loosed one across the twenty-foot gap, watching it thud home in a fur-covered chest. The creature roared in anger, then plucked the bolt free and hurled it into the river.

A taloned hand fastened on Waylander's ankle. Dropping the crossbow, he dragged his sword from its scabbard and sliced downwards with all his strength. The blade bit deep into the creature's arm, but did not break the bone. Three times more Waylander hacked at the limb, until at last the talons loosened. Dragging his foot clear, he jumped back.

The creature rolled to its back, the crossbow bolt jutting from its mouth and blood pumping from its mutilated arm. It was lying on the edge of the ferry and Waylander ran forward and kicked it clear; the body sank like a stone.

'Where else can they cross?' asked Waylander

'About twenty miles upstream, fifteen down. What *were* they?'

'I don't know. I don't want to know.'

The children were huddled in the far corner of the ferry, too frightened for tears.

'You had better see to them,' said Waylander. 'I'll pull for a while.' The man left the rope and knelt by his children, talking to them in a low voice, taking them into his arms. Opening a chest fixed near the front of the ferry, he removed blankets and the children lay down on the deck, cuddled together.

It took just over an hour to cross the river, and Waylander was deeply grateful that he had not been forced to swim it. Out in the centre the current was too powerful for human endeavour.

The ferryman moved to the front, lifting a mooring rope as the jetty loomed. A second shack was built beyond the jetty and he and Waylander carried the now sleeping children inside, laying them on two beds pushed together by the far wall. The man prepared a fire and the two of them sat together as the blaze crackled to life.

'It's bad enough with the tribes,' said the ferryman suddenly, 'but now I think I'll move.'

'The beasts are hunting me. I do not think they will return to trouble you.'

'All the same, I have the children to think of – this is no place for them.'

'How long have you been here?'

'Three years. We moved when my wife died. I had a farm near Purdol, but raiders wiped me out – took all my seed-corn and the winter food store. So I set up here, helping an old Notas. He died last year, fell overboard.'

'The tribes don't bother you?'

'Not as long as I keep the ferry operating. But they don't like me. Mixed blood!'

'You are taller than most Nadir,' Waylander observed.

'My mother was a Vagrian woman. My father was Notas, so at least I'm in blood feud with no one. I hear there's a war in the south?'

'Yes.'

'And you are Waylander.'

'The riders have been, then. Which were they, Nadir or Vagrian?'

'Both,' said the man. 'But I won't betray you; I owe you four lives.'

'You owe me nothing – in fact the reverse. I led the creatures to you. When the riders come back, tell them what happened. Tell them I rode north.'

'Why should I do that?'

'Two reasons. First it is the truth, and second they know already where I am heading.'

The man nodded and stirred the blaze to fresh life before adding more fuel.

'If they know, why do you travel there? They will be waiting.'

'Because I have no choice.'

'That is nonsense. Life is all about choice. From here you can ride in any direction.'

'I gave my word.'

The ferryman smiled in understanding. 'That I cannot argue with. Nor would I try. But I am intrigued by it – what could make a man give such an oath?'

'Stupidity cannot be ruled out,' said Waylander.

'But you are not stupid.'

'All men are stupid. We plan as if we will live for ever. We think our efforts can match the mountains. But we fool ourselves – we count for nothing and the world never changes.'

'I detect bitterness, Waylander. But your deeds do not match your words. Whatever quest you are engaged upon must count. Else why risk your life?'

'Whether I succeed or fail, within a hundred years – maybe less – no one will remember the deed. No one will care. I can bring an hour's sunshine to a mountain-side; if I fail, it will bring an hour's rain. Does the mountain care?'

'Perhaps not,' said the ferryman, 'but *you* care. And that is enough. There is too little caring in the world – too much greed and violence. I like to see things grow. I like to hear laughter.'

'You are a romantic, ferryman.'

'My name is Gurion,' said the man, extending his hand.

Waylander took it and grinned. 'And I was once called Dakeyras.'

'You too are a romantic, Dakeyras, because only romantics stay true to their word despite the world. It ought to make us stronger, but it does not. Honour is a weighty chain that slows us down.'

'A philosopher *and* a romantic, Gurion? You should be a teacher, not a ferryman.'

'What is your quest, Dakeyras?'

'I seek the Armour of Bronze.'

'For what purpose?'

'There is a Drenai general named Egel and I am to deliver it to him. It will aid him in his war.'

'I have seen it.'

'You have been to Raboas?'

'Once, many years ago. It is a chamber deep in the caves. But it is guarded.'

'By the Nadir?'

'No, by creatures far worse – werebeasts that live in darkness at the centre of the mountain.'

'How then did you see it?'

'I was with my wife's people, the Wolfshead; there were fifty of us. It was a marriage ceremony: the Khan's youngest son. He wanted to see the legendary Armour.'

'I am surprised the Nadir did not remove it.'

'They could not,' said Gurion. 'Did you know? It does not exist.'

'Speak plainly, man.'

'The Armour is an image; you can pass your hands through it. The real Armour is said to be hidden somewhere in the mountain, but no man knows where. All that can be seen is a ghostly, shimmering vision and that is why it is worshipped.'

Waylander said nothing. He stared into the fire, lost in thought.

'I thought you knew where the real Armour was hidden,' said Gurion.

Waylander chuckled and shook his head, then he began to laugh. Gurion turned away as the sadness touched him.

'Curse all romantics,' said Waylander as the laughter left him. 'May they rot in seven hells!'

'You don't mean that,' said Gurion.

Waylander swept his fingers through his hair and stood.

'I cannot begin to tell you how tired I am. I feel I am drowning in a sea of quicksand, and my friends are helping me by tying rocks to my legs. You understand? I am a killer, who kills for money. Does that sound romantic? I am a hunter of men. Yet here I am being hunted . . . by men and beasts, and spirits of the dark. According to my friend Dardalion, my quest serves the Source. You have heard of the Source?' Gurion nodded. 'Well, let me tell you, my friend, that serving the Source is not easy. You cannot see him or hear him, and certainly he offers no help in his own cause.'

'He led you to my ferry,' offered Gurion.

Waylander chuckled. 'My enemies can soar into the night like invisible demons, conjure wolf-creatures from Hell and read minds. On our side is a God that can lead a man to a ferry!'

'And yet you still live.'

'For now, Gurion. Tomorrow is another day.'

20

Dardalion turned away from Astila and leaned on the broad-silled window. Like all the windows of the Keep it tapered from a broad base to a narrow slit, built for defence rather than for view or light. An archer could loose a shaft to the left, right or centre, covering a wide angle of attack; whereas the attackers could gain no access to the Keep through it nor, unless by a freak of chance, loose their arrows past the crack. Dardalion leaned on his elbows and stared at the ramparts below.

Once more blood and death stalked the walls, but the defenders were holding. Beyond the wall lay the charred remains of two Vagrian siege towers, blackened corpses scattered about them. A third siege tower was being hauled slowly towards the ramparts, and the defenders waited with oil and fire. Beyond the towers a second Vagrian army sat and waited the command to attack. Dardalion blinked and transferred his gaze to the grey stone of the window.

'Why will you not hear me, Dardalion?' asked Astila.

Dardalion turned. 'I hear you, my brother, but I cannot help you.'

'We need you here. We are dying. Seven now have gone to the Source and we need your strength.'

'Waylander also needs me. I cannot desert him.'

'We are losing heart, Dardalion.' Astila slumped to the narrow bed and sat with his head in his hands. For the first time Dardalion noticed the fatigue in the blond priest: the bowed shoulders, the purple smears under the once bright eyes. He left the window and sat beside Astila.

'I can only do so much, and there is so much to do. I truly believe that Waylander's quest is the answer for the Drenai. I cannot explain why. But through all my prayers the Armour returns to haunt me and night after night I see it shining in that dark cave. Yet despite its importance we have only one man seeking it for us. One man, Astila! And ranged against him are the Brotherhood, the Nadir, and now unholy creatures . . . He has no chance without me. Try to understand. Please try.'

Astila said nothing for a moment, then looked up and met Dardalion's gaze. His bright blue eyes were red-rimmed and hollow.

'You are the leader and I will follow you to death and beyond. But I tell you the end is very close. I say this without arrogance, but I am the strongest of the brothers and yet I am finished. If I travel the night, I shall not return. If that is your wish, so be it. But believe me, Dardalion, it is The Thirty or Waylander. I stand by your judgement.'

Dardalion laid his arm on Astila's shoulder. 'I also am at the limits of my power. It costs me greatly to hold the shield over Waylander. And I cannot break it, not even for you.'

'I understand,' said Astila dully. 'I will go and prepare for the night.'

'No. We must accept that we have lost the greater battle – merely put a shield on Karnak and those of his officers we can cover.'

'The Brotherhood will have the run of the fortress.'

'So be it. These are strong men, Astila. Good men. They will stand, even against the despair-clouds.'

'You believe that? Truly?'

'What else is there to believe when we are bereft of choice? Some will falter, some will die. Others will fight back. I cannot believe that evil will triumph. I cannot.'

'It has triumphed elsewhere and now the land is in ruins.'

'It has not triumphed here, Astila.'

'The war is not yet over, Dardalion.'

Jonat's sleep was plagued with bad dreams and he awoke with a start. He had seen his dead father dance as they cut him down from the gallows tree, his face purple, his tongue distended. Yet still he danced as the nobles laughed and threw copper coins – the nobles, dining on larks' tongues while his father begged for bread; paying more for a goblet of wine than his family saw in a month. Jeering, mocking.

He sat up, shivering. High on the walls Karnak walked with Gellan and Dundas. Jonat spat.

If only they had listened to him a year ago, the Vagrians would never have invaded. But the nobles thought differently. Cut down the Legion. Throw soldiers out of honest work. Let them starve, for the farms could not support them all. And who cared about the common soldier? No one. Least of all silk-robed noblemen with their gem-encrusted swords. What would they do if all the common soldiers went home? Both Vagrian and Drenai? Would the nobles fight among themselves? No. The game would be over, the fun spoiled.

He was jerked from his thoughts by Gellan's arrival. The officer sat down beside him.

'I saw you were awake. Mind if I join you?'

'Why not?'

'How are you faring?'

'Well enough.'

'I wish I was. I don't think I can handle too many days like today. You ever feel like that?'

'Sometimes. It'll pass, sir – when the first attack comes tomorrow.'

'I hope so. You did well today, Jonat; you held them together when all seemed lost. Not many men could have done that. It's a gift and I saw it in you from the first. I'm proud of you – I mean that. That's why I promoted you.'

'Not because I was a rabble-rouser?' snapped Jonat.

'No. You were what you were because you cared. You cared about the Legion, the real Legion, the men. And you had drive and energy and you commanded respect. An officer needs respect. The title is nothing unless the man is right. You were right. You *are* right.'

'But not right by birth,' said Jonat.

'I neither know nor care about your ancestry, but if it matters to you then let me tell you that my father was a fishmonger. No more than that. And I am proud of him, because he slaved to give me an education.'

'My father was a drunk – he was hung for riding a nobleman's horse.'

'You are not your father.'

'Damned right I am not! And I tell you this: I'll never serve another king.'

'Nor I. But that's a battle for another day. Now I am going to get some sleep.'

As Gellan stood, Jonat grinned. 'Was your father really a fishmonger?'

'No, he was an earl. I just said it to annoy you.'

'I would sooner believe that.'

'So would I. Good night, Jonat.'

'Good night, sir.'

'By the way, Dardalion says the priests can no longer hold back the power of the Brotherhood. He says to watch out for signs of despair among the men – the enemy will work on the weak. So keep an eye out.'

'I will.'

'I know. I have no worries about your section.'

Gellan moved away into the darkness and chuckled softly. His father had owned five fishing fleets and Gellan wondered how the earl would have relished the title of fishmonger.

Waylander slept for an hour, then saddled his horse and bade farewell to the ferryman. The night was clear and the distant mountains loomed like the wall at the end of the world.

'Take care,' offered Gurion, extending his hand.

'And you, my friend. Were I you, I'd head back across the river. Those beasts are hunting me – they'll not be back to trouble you.'

For three days he rode warily, covering his tracks as best he could, angling along swift-moving streams and over rocky slopes, disguising both his scent and his spoor. But he doubted his efforts would do more than delay his demonic pursuers. Added to this, he had to watch out for human foes.

Twice he stopped at Notas camps and once shared a meal with a small group of hunters. The four men had greeted him coolly and considered robbing him. But there was something about the tall southlander which kept them at bay – not his bow, his knives or his sword, more a calculating look in his eyes and a subtle confidence in his stance. So they had fed him and watched him depart with evident relief.

At nightfall a larger band of Nadir descended on the hunters, questioning them at length before killing them horribly.

The bodies were discovered the following day by nine Brotherhood warriors whose arrival disturbed the vultures. The riders did not stay long.

Towards dusk the first of the Shapeshifters came upon the scene, drawn by the scent of blood. Saliva dripped from its maw and its red eyes gleamed. The vultures scattered as it approached, their great wings flapping to lift their bloated bodies from the ground. Through superhuman efforts they made their way to the branches of surrounding trees, where they glowered down at the new invaders.

The other wolf-beasts emerged from the undergrowth and approached the remains. One pushed its snout into the bloody carcasses and, overcome by hunger, closed its jaws upon a piece of meat and bone. Then it coughed and spat the flesh from its mouth. Its howl rent the air.

And the four beasts loped towards the north.

Forty miles on, Waylander was close to the southern edge of the mountain range. Here the Steppes were jagged, deep canyons appearing and slashing across the land like gigantic knife-cuts. Trees and streams abounded within the canyons and, here and there, deserted huts and houses dotted the landscape. Wild sheep and goats grazed on the slopes, while to the north-east Waylander saw a herd of wild horses cropping grass beside a waterfall.

Urging his mount onward, he descended the slope into a shaded wood.

The land here was good, richer than the arid Steppes, the thick, black earth as fertile as any on the Sentran Plain. Yet there were no farms. No grain or wheat, nor fruit trees, nor golden corn.

For the Nadir were a nomadic race: hunters, warriors and killers who built nothing, caring little for the bleakness of their future. 'Conquer or die' was the most common phrase among the tribes. Though ultimately, Waylander realised, the phrase should have been conquer *and* die.

What future could there be for a people of no foundation?

Where were the books, the poems, the architecture, the philosophy? All the vast panoply of civilisation?

The Nadir were doomed – the future dust of history, bonded by blood and war and skimming across the surface of the planet like a vicious storm.

What purpose did they serve, he wondered? Scattered tribes full of hate, warring one upon the other, they could never be welded into one people.

That, at least, was a small blessing, for it meant that never would the tribesmen trouble the peoples of the south. But then they had troubles enough of their own.

Waylander made a brief camp in a cave at the far side of the canyon. Taking a stiff brush from his saddlebag, he worked to ease the burrs from his horse's back and then led him to water. He prepared a small fire and made some broth from his dried meat before snatching two hours' sleep. Back in the saddle, he started on the long climb out of the canyon. He studied his back trail often and now, for the first time since leaving the ferry, he saw his pursuers. As he crested the skyline to the north, they were entering the canyon from the south.

There appeared to be about twenty Nadir riders.

Waylander rode on. They were some four hours behind him, but he would increase that distance during the night.

He did not fear the pursuit, but ahead of him towered Raboas, the Sacred Giant, and here was the end of the journey where hunter and hunted were destined to meet.

His thoughts swung to Cadoras. Why had the assassin thrown his life away to rescue a man he hardly knew, a man he was pledged to kill? What had prompted an ice-cool killer to act in such a way?

Then he chuckled.

What had prompted Waylander to rescue Dardalion? Why had he fought so hard to protect Danyal and the children? Why was he now riding towards the certainty of the grave in such a foolhardy and impossible quest?

Danyal's face floated before his eyes, to be replaced in an instant by the bearded, heavy features of Durmast. He remembered once more the vision in the fire, but could not bring himself to believe it. Yet had not Durmast killed women? Children?

The horse plodded on and the sun sank beyond the western horizon. The night air was chill and Waylander pulled his cloak from his saddle roll and swept it over his shoulders. With the coming of night, his fear of the wolfbeasts grew. Where were they now?

His eyes flicked from left to right, and he swung in the saddle to study his back trail in the fast fading light. Hefting his crossbow, he resisted the temptation to load it. Lengthy stress on the metal arms would weaken the weapon, and for these beasts he needed it at full strength.

The moon blazed her white light as the clouds cleared, illuminating a thickly wooded hillside. Waylander had no wish to enter the trees during dark, but the tree-line stretched on far to the west and east. With a whispered curse, he flicked the reins and rode on.

Once inside the wood, he found his heart beating faster and his breathing increasing in speed as panic struggled to overcome him. Moonlight blazed ahead, silver shafts shining through the breaks in overhead branches. His horse's hooves thudded dully on the soft loam, and to the left a badger broke through the undergrowth and ambled across his trail, its fur bathed in light which turned it to silver armour. Waylander swore and gave in to the temptation to load his crossbow.

Suddenly a wolf's howl shattered the silence of the night. Waylander jerked and one of his bolts flew from the crossbow, slicing up through the branches overhead.

'You dolt!' he told himself. 'Get a grip, man!'

Slipping a second bolt home, he re-strung the bow. The howling came from some distance to the east, and from the sound Waylander guessed that a wolf-pack had cornered its quarry – possibly a stag – and the last battle was under way. The wolves would have chased the beast for many miles, tiring it and sapping the strength from its great muscles. Now it was at bay.

Waylander rode on, but the wolves fell silent and the assassin knew that the prey had eluded them once more. He dragged on the reins, not wishing to cross the line of the chase. His horse whinnied and tried to turn, but Waylander hauled him back.

A running figure emerged from the trees some thirty paces ahead. He was wounded, and dragged his left foot; in his hands was a huge wooden club. A wolf burst into view and leapt. The man turned, the club flashing in the moonlight to crunch against the wolf's ribs, stoving them in. It landed with a thud ten feet away from him.

He was big, bigger than any man Waylander had ever seen, and he appeared to be wearing a gruesome mask decorated with a white sphere at the forehead. The lower part of the mask had a lipless mouth, lined with fangs. Waylander could not see him clearly, but he did not look like a Nadir.

More wolves came into sight and the man bellowed his fury and frustration, then limped to a tree and turned to face the pack. They spread out in a cautious semi-circle and crept in upon him. Suddenly one darted from the right and he turned to meet it. Immediately another beast sprinted from the left and leapt. The man fell back as the jaws snapped shut just short of his throat. He lashed out with his club, but a third wolf ran forward.

A crossbow bolt flashed through its neck, and it slumped to the ground.

Waylander yelled at the top of his voice and spurred the horse into a gallop. The wolves scattered, but not before a second beast died with a bolt through its brain.

The man at the tree sagged and fell forward. Waylander sprang from the saddle and tied the reins to a stout bush. He reloaded the crossbow and scanned the undergrowth. The wolves were gone . . . for now.

He moved to the man, who was now kneeling, his hand clamped to a badly bleeding wound on his upper arm.

'You are lucky, my friend,' said Waylander.

The man looked up . . . and Waylander blanched.

He was wearing no mask. He had but a single eye at the centre of his forehead, wherein were two pupils each rimmed with gold iris. His nose was missing; two membrane-covered slits stretched beneath his eye. And his mouth was nightmare.

Shaped like an upturned V, it was lined with fangs sharp as arrow points. Once Waylander had seen a huge white fish with a mouth such as this, and he had never forgotten it. It had filled him with fear at the time, and made him vow never to enter the sea.

But *this*?

His crossbow was ready and he contemplated stepping back and loosing both bolts into the man-creature before it could attack him. But his great round eye closed and he slid to the ground.

It was almost too good an opportunity to miss and Waylander backed to his horse, ready to ride away. But he could not. Some contrariness in his nature made him stop and return to the wounded thing.

As he had with Dardalion so long before, Waylander stitched the wounds to the creature's arm and leg and then bandaged them as best he could. He was naked, but for a moth-eaten loincloth of old fur, and Waylander wrapped him in a blanket and prepared a fire.

After an hour the creature's eye opened and he sat up. Waylander offered him some dry meat and he took it without a word. The fangs closed on it and it disappeared.

'Can you talk?' asked Waylander.

The great eye merely looked at him. Waylander shrugged and passed more jerked beef which vanished instantly into the cavernous mouth.

'Can you understand me?'

The creature nodded.

'I cannot stay to help you. I am being hunted. Beasts and men. You understand?'

The creature lifted his hand and pointed south.

'That's right, they are coming from the south. I must go, but I will leave you food.'

Waylander walked to his horse, stood for a moment and then unpacked his blanket roll, removing two long hunting knives which were bone-handled and razor-sharp. He took them back to the fire. 'Here. You may need these.' The man-creature reached out. His fingers were incredibly long, the nails curved into dark talons which curled around the bone hilts as he raised the knives to his eye. His reflection came back at him and he blinked and looked away; then he nodded and pushed himself to his feet, towering over Waylander.

The assassin swallowed hard. It was difficult to read the expression on the monster's face, but Waylander was uncomfortably aware of the two knives in his hands.

'Goodbye, my friend,' he said, forcing a smile.

He went to his horse and stepped into the saddle, wrenching the reins clear of the bush. The creature moved forward, its jaws moving and a low grunting noise issuing forth which caused Waylander's mount to back away. The creature's head tilted to one side with the effort he was making.

'Udai rend,' he said. Not understanding, Waylander nodded and moved away.

'Urbye vrend.'

Understanding at last, Waylander turned in the saddle and waved.

'Goodbye, friend,' he called and rode into the darkness.

On the mountain pass east of Purdol, two young men ate a breakfast of cheese and bread while swapping tall stories concerning the legendary whores of Purdol Docks. The sun was shining and the taller of the two – a five-year soldier named Tarvic – stood up and walked to the edge of the cliff path, staring out over the desert to the north. He had been pleased to get this assignment; watching a cliff path was a lot less dangerous than defending a rampart.

He was still grinning when an arrow entered his throat and punched up through the roof of his mouth and into his brain.

The second soldier looked round as he staggered back, his hands twitching.

'What's wrong, Tarvic?' called Milis. As Tarvic fell back, his head bouncing from a jagged white rock, Milis saw the arrow and his mouth dropped open. The fear surged through him and he began to run. An arrow clipped him from the rock to his right and flashed by his face. Legs pumping hard, Milis sprinted towards the cave. Something hit him hard in the back, but it did not slow him.

The cave entrance loomed and twice more he was struck from behind, but there was no pain and he made his way into the security of the tunnel. Safe at last, he slowed his pace.

His face crashed into the rocky floor as the ground leapt up at him. He tried to rise, but his arms had no strength. He began to crawl, but hands pulled at him, turning him over.

'The Vagrians are coming,' he said.

'I know,' said the Vagrian, drawing his knife across Milis' throat.

He was alone, as he had always been alone. He sat by the murky waters of a lily-covered pond and stared at his reflection in the silver steel blade of the hunting knife. He knew he was a monster; the word had been hurled at him since the beginning – along with stones, spears and arrows. He had been hunted by horsemen carrying lances, by wolves with sharp fangs and cunning minds, and by the long-toothed snow tigers which came down from the mountains with the winter ice.

But he had never been caught. For his speed was legend and his strength terrifying.

He pushed his broad back against the bole of a willow and lifted his great head to stare at the twin moons high above the trees. He knew by now there was only one moon, but the pupils of his huge eye could never focus as true eyes. He had learned to live with that, as he had learned to live with the other savage gifts nature had bestowed on him.

For some reason his memory was sharper than most, although he did not realise it. He could remember vividly the moment of his birth, and the face of the old woman who guided him into the world from the black-red tunnel of the Void. She had screamed and let him fall and he had hurt himself, twisting his arm under his body and hitting the edge of a wooden bed.

A man entered then and picked him from the floor. He had taken a knife, but another woman's scream had stopped him dead.

For a little while he remembered feeding at the breast of a dark-haired, sad-eyed young girl. But then his teeth grew, pointed and sharp – red blood had mixed with the milk and the girl had cried as she fed him.

It was not long before he was carried out into the night and left under the stars, listening to the sound of hoofbeats fading into the distance. Fading, dying . . .

Still the sound of hooves on dry earth filled him with sadness.

He had no name and no future.

Yet something had come from the mountains and drawn him into the darkness . . .

There were many of them, skittering and screeching, touching and pinching, and he had grown among them through the Darkness years, rarely seeing the light of day.

And then, on a summer morning, he heard a lilting cry from Outside echoing down a crack in the rocks and reverberating in the tunnels of the mountain heart. He was lured by the sound and he climbed out into the light. High overhead, great white birds were wheeling and diving, and in their cries he felt his life encapsulated. From that moment he saw himself as Kai and he spent many hours each day lying on the high rocks watching for the white birds, waiting for them to call his name.

Then began the Long years as his strength grew. Nadir tribes would gather near the mountains and pass on to greener meadows and deeper streams. But while they camped he watched them, seeing the children at play, the women arm-in-arm and laughing as they strolled.

Sometimes he strayed too close and the laughter would become familiar screams and the hunters would ride. Kai would run, and then turn, and rend and tear until he was alone once more.

How many years, he wondered, had he lived thus?

The forest in which he now sat had been a small wood of slender trees. Was that a long time? He had no terms of reference. One tribe had camped for longer than most and he had watched one young girl as she grew to womanhood, her hair turning grey and her back becoming bent. They lived such short lives, these Nadir.

Kai stared at his hands. Special hands these, he knew. Slowly he unwrapped the bandage from his arm and plucked out the stitches Way-lander had placed there. Blood eased from the wound, then ran freely. Kai covered the gash with his hand and concentrated deeply. A strong sense of heat grew over the area, like a thousand tiny needles probing the flesh. After several minutes he removed his hand . . . And the gash was gone, the skin supple and unblemished by scab or scar. Removing the bandage and stitches from his leg, he repeated the process.

Strong again, he rose smoothly to his feet and breathed deeply. He could have killed the wolves eventually, but the man had helped him, and given him the knives.

Kai had no need of knives. He could run down an antelope and destroy it with his hands and tear its warm flesh with his fangs. What need of shiny metal?

But they were gifts, the first he had ever received, and the handles were pretty and handsomely carved. He had owned a knife once, but within a short time it had turned from shining grey to red-brown and had become brittle and useless.

He thought of the giver – the short, small man on the horse. Why had he not screamed and attacked? Why had he killed the wolves? Why had he bandaged the wounds? Why had he given him the knives?

All were mysteries.

Goodbye friend. What did it mean?

Over the years Kai had learned the language of men, piecing the jumble of sounds into linked sentences. He could not speak, for there was no one to listen, but he could understand. The man had said that he was hunted. Kai could understand that.

By beasts and men? Kai wondered why he had made the distinction.

He shrugged and sighed. Strangely he felt more alone today than yesterday.

He missed the small man.

Karnak was asleep on the floor of the great hall, a single blanket pulled across his massive frame. The log fire in the wide hearth had shrivelled to glowing cinders as the Drenai general lay on a goatskin rug, lost in dreams of childhood and the birth of ambition.

Despite their riches Karnak's family retained a puritan streak and early in their lives the children were taught of the necessity for self-sufficiency. Young Karnak had been apprenticed to a shepherd to the north of the family estates and one night, while camped high in the wooded hills, a great grey wolf had stalked the flock. Karnak, at the age of seven, took a stout staff of unshaped wood and walked towards the beast. For several seconds it stood its ground, yellow eyes fixed on the advancing child. then it had backed away and run into the darkness.

When Karnak returned home he told the tale to his father with great pride.

'I knew of it,' said his father coldly. 'But you have lessened the deed by bragging of it.'

For some reason he never forgot his father's dismissal and the scene returned time and time again to haunt his dreams. Sometimes he dreamt he fought off a dozen tigers, and crawled to his father dying of his wounds.

Always the old man responded with icy indifference.

'Why are you not dressed for dinner?' he would ask the blood-covered boy.

'I have been hurt by tigers, father.'

'Still bragging, Karnak?'

The sleeping man groaned and opened his eyes. The hall was silent, yet some sound had disturbed his slumber and now a faint drumming noise came to him. Karnak lay down, pressing his ear to the rug. Then he pulled the goatskin aside and pushed his ear to the stone.

Men were moving below ground . . . a lot of men.

Karnak swore and ran from the hall, snatching his axe from the great table of oak. In the corridor, several soldiers were rolling dice. And he called them to him and ran on towards the dungeon stairwell. A young warrior with a bandaged arm was just coming up the stairs and Karnak stopped him.

'Find Gellan and get him to bring a hundred men to the dungeons *now*. You understand? Now!'

With that the general hurled the man from him and raced down the stairs. Twice he almost slipped on the slime-covered stone and then he was into the narrow prison row. The door at the end of the row led to a wide chamber and from the back of this room Karnak could see the rough-hewed entrance to the mountain tunnel. Wiping his sweating palms on his green tunic, Karnak hefted his axe and ran through the torch-lit chamber and into the tunnel. The air was cold here and water glistened on the dark jagged walls. The tunnel was narrow; only three men could walk abreast. Karnak stopped to listen and a soldier walked into him from behind and cursed.

'Be silent!' hissed the general.

From some way ahead they could hear the whispering sound of stealthy footfalls on the rocky floor. Dancing torch shadows leapt from the far walls where the tunnel curved to the left.

Karnak lifted his axe and slowly, reverently, kissed both blades.

The Vagrians rounded the corner – to be met by an ear-piercing scream and a flashing axe of silver steel that smashed the ribs of the leading warrior. Torches were dropped as men scrambled for their swords, then more screams filled the tunnel as the axe swept and scythed the milling men. Booted feet trampled the torches to extinction and in the darkness terror grew. For Karnak the way was easy – he had fought his way in alone among the enemy, and anything he struck was likely to be hostile flesh. For the Vagrians it was a nightmare in which men stabbed comrades, or felt their swords clattering from stone walls. Confusion became chaos and the invaders fled.

Suddenly a short blade stabbed into Karnak's face, bouncing from his left cheekbone and lancing into his eye. He staggered back. The hurled knife fell to the floor and he clasped his hand to his face, where blood gushed from the eye-socket. With a curse he stumbled on after the Vagrians, screaming and yelling, the noise echoing ahead like the rage of an angry giant.

The pain of his ruined eye was intense and the darkness almost total, but still he ran, his axe held high. Ahead the tunnel widened and the darkness lifted slightly.

Three Vagrians, left as a rearguard, ran at him. The first died with his skull split in two. The second followed as the blade reversed and clove his ribs. The third dived at the general, who sidestepped and then whipped up his knee into the diving man's face; his head snapped back and he hit the floor unconscious. Karnak's axe hammered into his back.

He ran on, scanning the rocks for the support ropes and praying the Vagrians had not discovered them.

At the widest part of the tunnel he saw them, looped and partly hidden behind a jutting section of black rock. Moving to his left he lifted the rope and took in the slack. He began to play out the rope as he backed down the tunnel, but the Vagrians had seen at last that only one man faced them and now they came at him with a rush.

Karnak knew he was finished and a terrible anger welled in him. Dropping his axe, he took the rope in both hands and pulled with all his strength. A creaking sound from above gave evidence that the pulleys and winches were transmitting the power.

The Vagrians were now only twenty paces from the straining figure, their yells of rage deafening in the enclosed tunnel. Karnak pushed his right foot against the tunnel wall and tugged hard. A tortured groan came from the roof and a huge boulder toppled above the running soldiers. Then the entire roof gave way and a great crack sliced along the granite wall.

Karnak saw the Vagrians buried screaming under tons of rock and earth. Then he turned and began to run.

Rocks and boulders tumbled about him as he ran on into the dark, then he tripped and fell and something sharp and heavy hit his ribs. He rolled and coughed as swirling dust caught in his throat. It seemed alien and stupid to run into darkness and death, but still he forced himself on. The rock above him exploded and he was swept from his feet, his legs partially buried by rubble. Pulling himself clear, he staggered on until the ground tilted under him and he fell forward.

'Gellan!' he screamed, as the walls closed in and engulfed him. A rock struck his head . . . more covered his legs and waist. He threw his arms over his face and tried to move. Then something slammed into his forehead and his movements ceased.

For more than a full day and night Gellan had men toiling at the rocks, moving forward inch by dangerous inch, while outside on the walls the battle raged endlessly. Many of the officers were now dead and Gellan had promoted Sarvaj and Jonat to commands of 500 men apiece. The number of wounded had swelled to awesome proportions, and now fewer than 2,000 fighting men held the might of the Vagrian army at bay.

But Gellan himself remained in the treacherous tunnel, angrily shaking off the protest from brother officers.

'He's dead – what is the point?' argued one.

'We need him,' said Gellan.

'The roof has gone, man! Every foot we move forward only increases the risk of a further fall. It's madness!'

But he ignored them, refusing to allow their arguments to lodge in his mind where he knew he would be forced to accept their logic. It was a kind of madness, he knew. But he would not stop. Nor would the men.

They worked tirelessly, pushing their frail bodies into the blackness, ton upon ton of delicately balanced rock above and around them.

'How the hell will you find him? The men originally with him say he ran ahead. It would take years to dig your way through to the far side – and the ropes were a hundred paces from the first corner.'

'Get out and leave us alone.'

'You are insane, Gellan.'

'Leave or I'll kill you.'

By the second day even the most tireless of the workers had given up hope, but still they toiled on.

'We need you on the walls, Gellan. Despair is growing.'

This time the words got through, lodging where Gellan had no defence.

'One more hour,' he said, hope draining from him. 'I'll be there with you in one hour.'

The pain from his eye woke Karnak and he tried to move, panic welling in him as realisation struck home that he was trapped . . . buried alive. Madness surged in him and he struggled maniacally, stopping only when he felt the rocks move above him. He breathed slowly and deeply, fighting for calm.

'Why are you not dressed for dinner, Karnak?'

'A mountain fell on me, father.'

Manic laughter bubbled from his throat, but he fought it down and began to weep.

Stop it! You are Karnak, his strength told him.

I am a piece of flesh trapped in a tomb of rock, his weakness screamed.

All his plans were finished now and perhaps it was just as well, he thought. In his arrogance he had believed he could defeat the Vagrians, push them from the lands of the Drenai. His new-found heroic status would have guaranteed him leadership of the people. Egel could never have stood against him. Egel had no way with the mob – no charisma. And there were other ways to dispose of political enemies.

Waylander, and men like him, were easy to find.

But now there would be nothing. No purple robes. No public acclaim.

Why, he wondered, had he taken on the enemy single-handed?

Because he had not stopped to think. Dundas had seen through him: a hero who pretended to be otherwise.

Not exactly the death you would have chosen for yourself, Karnak, said his strength. Where was the drama? Where were the adoring crowds?

If a tree falls in the forest and no one hears, does it make a sound?

If a man dies unobserved, how will his death be chronicled?

'Damn you, father,' whispered Karnak. 'Damn you!'

Laughter shook him. Tears followed. 'Damn you!' he bellowed.

The rock beside him shifted and Karnak froze, waiting for the crushing death. Light fell on his face and a ragged cheer went up from the men. Karnak squinted against the torchlight, then forced a grin.

'You took your time, Gellan,' he whispered. 'I thought I'd have to dig myself out!'

179

22

Danyal lay back on the aft deck of the river barge, listening to the gentle lap of the waves against the hull. Some few paces to her left Durmast leaned on the rail, eyes scanning the river bank.

For some time she watched him, closing her eyes every time his shaggy head turned in her direction. For the last three days he had been either silent or surly, and whenever she glanced at him she found his glittering eyes focused on her. At first she had been irritated, but that had grown into fear, for Durmast was no ordinary man. Everything about him radiated power. In him was raw strength, and an innate savagery held in check by gossamer threads of reason and logic. All his life, she sensed, he had gained everything he desired by strength, or cunning, or calculated ruthlessness.

And he wanted her.

Danyal knew it – it was in his eyes, his movements, his lack of words.

There was little she could do to make herself less attractive. She had but the one tunic and that disguised her not at all.

Now he turned from the rail and approached her, looming in the darkness like a giant.

'What do you want?' she asked, sitting up.

He squatted beside her. 'I knew you weren't asleep.'

'You want to talk?'

'No . . . yes.'

'Then talk. I'm not going anywhere.'

'What does that mean?'

'It means I'm a captive listener.'

'You are not my captive. You can go or stay as you choose.'

He sat back and scratched his beard. 'Why do you twist everything into confrontation?'

'You bring out the worst in me, Durmast – put it down to that. How long before we disembark?'

'Tomorrow. We'll buy horses and be camped at Raboas by nightfall.'

'And then?'

'We'll wait for Waylander – if he is not already there.'

'I wish I could believe you,' she said bitterly.

'Why should you not?'

She laughed then and his hand shot out to grab her arm, dragging her to him. 'You bitch!' he hissed. In his eyes she saw insanity, the deadly madness of the berserker.

'Take your hand off me,' she said, fighting for calm.

'Why? I like to smell your fear.' He crushed her to him, holding her arms tight against her side. His face pushed against hers and she felt his breath against her cheek.

'I thought you said you were no rapist,' she whispered.

He groaned as he released her, pushing her from him.

'You make my head swim, woman. Your every movement, every look, urges me to take you – you want me, I know you do.'

'You misread me, Durmast. I want nothing to do with you.'

'Don't give me that! Women like you don't stay long without a man. I know what you need.'

'You know nothing; you are an animal.'

'You think Waylander is different? He and I are two sides of the same coin. We are killers. Why should you lust for one and not the other?'

'Lust?' she sneered. 'That's what you'll never understand. Lust has little to do with it. I love him as a man and I want to be with him. I want to talk to him, to touch him.'

'But not me?'

'Who could love you, Durmast?' she snapped. 'You are obsessed with yourself. You think you fooled me with your talk of helping Waylander? You want the Armour yourself and you'll sell it to the highest bidder.'

'So sure, are you?'

'Of course I am sure, I know you – you are physically strong, but morally you're less than a sewer rat.'

He moved towards her and she froze, realising she had gone too far, said too much. But he laid no hand upon her. Instead he smiled and his eyes cleared, humour replacing the malicious glint.

'Very well, Danyal, I'll admit to you: I do intend to sell the Armour to the highest bidder. And that will be Kaem and the Vagrians. I also intend to kill Waylander and collect the bounty. Now what will *you* do?'

Her hand flashed towards his face, the silver steel dagger clenched in her fist, but his arm snaked out to rap her wrist. The knife flew from her fingers.

'You can't kill me, Danyal,' he whispered. 'Waylander himself would find that difficult – and you are but an able student. You'll have to find another way.'

'To do what?' she asked, rubbing her numbed wrist.

'To outbid Kaem.'

Understanding struck her like a blow. 'You despicable swine. You wretch!'

He nodded. 'What is your offer?'

'You want me that badly?'

'Yes, I want you, woman. I always have, ever since watching you and Waylander make love in the hills above Delnoch.'

'And what will you give me, Durmast?'

'I'll let Waylander keep the Armour. And I won't try to kill him.'

'I agree,' she said softly.

'I thought you would,' he replied, reaching for her.

'Wait!' she commanded and this time he froze, for there was in her eyes a look of triumph. 'I agree to your terms, and I will pay you when Waylander rides away with the Armour. You and I will remain at Raboas.'

'You are asking for a lot of trust, Danyal.'

'Well, unlike you, Durmast, I can be trusted.'

He nodded. 'I think you can,' he asserted and moved away into the darkness.

Alone at last, the enormity of her promise swept over her.

Dundas, Gellan and Dardalion waited in the outer sitting-room while the surgeon, Evris, tended the now unconscious Karnak.

Gellan, still filthy from his days in the tunnel, sat slumped in a wide leather chair, seeming frail without his armour. Dundas paced the room from window to bedchamber door, occasionally stopping to listen as if to hear the surgeon's work. Dardalion sat silently, fighting off the urge to sleep; he could feel the tension in the two men and he relaxed his mind to flow with theirs.

He merged with Gellan, feeling first the man's inner strength – a power stretched to its limits and threatened by doubt. This was a good man, Dardalion knew, and the suffering among the men hurt him cruelly. He was thinking of Karnak and praying for his recovery, fearing some internal injury that would yet rob the Drenai of hope. He was thinking also of the wall and the dreadful toll it took daily.

Then Dardalion withdrew from Gellan and merged with the tall, blond Dundas. He too was praying for Karnak, but not only for friendship. The weight of responsibility towered over Dundas like a mountain. If Karnak should die he would lose not only his greatest friend, but would have to bear the full awesome responsibility for the defence. And here was a terrible quandary. The wall could not be held, but to retreat meant to doom a thousand wounded men. Dundas could picture the scene: the defenders watching from the transient safety of the Keep as the wounded were dragged out and slain before their eyes. Dundas was a soldier, and a good one, but he was also revered by the men for his natural kindness and understanding. As a man, these were qualities to be admired. As a warrior, they were weaknesses to be exploited.

Dardalion fell back on his own thoughts. He was no military man, no planner. What would he do, assuming the choice was laid at his door?

Fall back?

Hold?

He shook his head, as if to push the thoughts from him. He was tired and the effort of holding the shield over Waylander sapped him more by the hour. He closed his eyes and reached out, tasting the despair that permeated the fortress. The Brotherhood were everywhere: four men so far had committed suicide, while two others had been caught trying to open a blocked postern gate high on the north wall.

The bedchamber door opened and Evris came out, wiping his hands on a linen towel. Gellan surged to his feet, but the surgeon lifted his hands and said quietly, 'It's all right. He is resting.'

'What of his injuries?' asked Gellan.

'As far as I can tell, he has lost the sight of his left eye. But nothing more. Heavy bruising, maybe a cracked rib or two. He is passing no blood. His bulk saved him.'

Evris left the room to tend the other wounded and Dundas sank into a chair by an oval writing table.

'One bright ray of hope,' he said. 'Now if Egel were to arrive tomorrow with fifty thousand men, I would believe in miracles.'

'One miracle at a time suits me,' said Gellan. 'But we must make a decision – the wall cannot hold.'

'You think we should pull back?' asked Dundas.

'I think we must.'

'But the wounded . . .'

'I know.'

Dundas swore bitterly, then chuckled without humour. 'You know, I always wanted to be a general – a First Gan with a cavalry wing under my command. You know why? So that I could have a white horse and a red velvet cloak. Gods, I think I know how poor Degas felt!'

Gellan leaned back and closed his eyes. Dardalion watched the two men for a moment, then spoke. 'Wait for Karnak – let him make the decision,' he advised softly.

Gellan's eyes snapped open. 'Wouldn't that be easy? Hard decisions to make, so load them on the broadest shoulders. We are running short on arrows – if they're not flown already. There is no meat, the bread is maggoty, the cheese green with mould. The men are exhausted and some of them are fighting in a trance.'

'It is almost as hard for the Vagrians, Gellan,' said Dardalion. 'They may have the strength, but they are running short of food and disease is in their camp. They may have stopped Ironlatch in the south, but at great cost. They are stretched thin, and only two months from winter.'

'We do not have two months,' said Dundas. 'Once they take Purdol, they can sweep along the Delnoch range and down through Skoda to circle Ironlatch. Winter won't mean a damn then.'

'I have walked these walls,' said Dardalion, 'but not in the way you have. You see men at war. But I have walked the walls in spirit and I have felt the strength there. Do not be too sure of failure.'

'As you said, Dardalion,' snapped Gellan, 'you have not walked the walls as we have.'

'Forgive me, Gellan, I did not mean to be condescending.'

Gellan shook his head. 'Do not mind me, young priest. I know my men. They are stronger even than they believe and they have already performed miracles. No one could have expected them to last this long. I just wonder how much longer they can stand.'

'I agree with Gellan,' said Dundas. 'The decision is one we may rue for the rest of our lives, but it must be made. We must pull back.'

'You are the military men,' agreed Dardalion, 'and I am not trying to sway you. But the men are fighting like demons and there is no give in them. This morning, I am told, a man with his arm hacked off killed three Vagrians before pitching from the battlements. And when he fell, he dragged another enemy soldier with him. That does not sound like the attitude of defeat.'

'I saw that from the gate tower,' said Dundas. 'The man was a farmer, I spoke to him once – he'd lost his entire family to mercenaries.'

'One man doesn't alter the situation,' said Gellan. 'What we are asking of the men is inhuman and sooner or later they must crack.'

The door to the bedchamber swung open and the three men turned to see Karnak looming in the doorway, one huge hand steadying himself on the wooden frame.

'They won't crack, Gellan,' he said. Blood was seeping through the bandage over his eye and his face was ashen, but the power of the man dominated the scene.

'You should be resting, general,' said Dardalion.

'I had a rest in the tunnel. You've no idea what a rest it was, old lad! But I am back now. I've listened to all of you for some time, and there's something to be said for each argument. But my decision is the final one and it is this: We hold the wall. There will be no retreat to the Keep.

'Those men out there have been magnificent – they will continue to be so. But if we withdraw them to see their comrades butchered, they will lose that iron edge. Then the Keep would fall within days.'

He moved forward and slumped into a wide chair. 'Dundas, get some clothes for me – garish clothes. And find me a leather patch to wear over this bandage. And fetch me another axe. I'm going out on to the ramparts.'

'That is insane, sir,' said Gellan. 'You are in no condition to fight.'

'Fight? I am not going to fight, Gellan. I'm going to be *seen*. There's Karnak, they'll say. A mountain fell on him and he's back! Now get me the clothes!' He turned to Dardalion. 'One of your priests told me days ago that your powers to push back the Brotherhood have been cut so that you can hold some sort of magic shield over Waylander. Is that true?'

'It is, sir.'

'Where is Waylander now?'

'Close to the mountain.'

'Then lift the shield.'

'I cannot.'

'Listen to me, Dardalion, you believe in the power of the Source against all the forces of Chaos, and you have fought steadfastly in that belief.

'But now I think you are guilty of arrogance. I don't say that lightly, or even critically. I am an arrogant man myself. But you have decided that Waylander is more important to the Drenai than Purdol. Maybe you are right. But he is now close to the Armour and you have got him there. Let the Source bring him home.'

Dardalion looked up and met Karnak's stare. 'You must understand, sir, that the enemies Waylander faces are not all human. The Nadir and the Brotherhood trail him, yes, but there are others – beasts from the pit. If I lift the shield he will be alone.'

'Understand this: If he is alone it means only that there is no Source. You follow the reasoning?'

'I believe so, though I fear it is specious.'

'And that is your arrogance speaking. The Source existed before you

184

were born and will continue to exist after you are dead. You are not the only weapon he has.'

'But if you are wrong!'

'Then he dies, Dardalion. But trees will grow, streams will run to the seas and the sun will shine. Lift the damned shield!'

The priest pushed himself to his feet and moved towards the door.

'Will you do it?' said Karnak.

'It is done,' said Dardalion.

'Good! Now push the Brotherhood from Purdol!'

It was close to midnight and the last of the Vagrians limped back to their camp-fires. Jonat leapt to the ramparts and bellowed after them: 'Come back, you bastards, we're not finished with you yet.'

Along the wall stretcher-bearers carried away the wounded, while the dead were thrown from the battlements. Jonat sent a dozen men to fetch food and water before patrolling his section, checking casualties. For days now he had felt the burden of his new responsibilities weighing him down, and his own deep well of bitterness had brought him close to despair. The knowledge that the Brotherhood were at work had helped him a little, but tonight he felt free. The stars shone, the breeze from the sea was fresh and clean and the enemy were scurrying to their tents like whipped dogs. Jonat felt stronger than at any time in his life, and his grin was wide as he swapped jests with the soldiers around him. He even waved to Sarvaj at the gate tower, his intense dislike of the man submerged in his new-found good humour.

Suddenly a ragged cheer went up from the right and Jonat turned to see Karnak striding up the battlement steps. Behind him were four soldiers bearing flagons of wine.

'I see you, Jonat, you rascal,' roared Karnak. Jonat chuckled and caught the bottle Karnak lobbed in his direction. 'I take it you'll drink with me?'

'Why not, general?'

Karnak sat down and called the men to him. 'You've probably heard that I had to close the tunnel,' he said, grinning. 'It means the only way out is through the main gates. How do you feel about that?'

'Just let us know when you're ready to leave, general!' called a man at the back.

'Well, I would have said tonight, but the enemy seems downhearted enough,' said Karnak. 'After all, we don't want to rub their noses in it.'

'Is it true you caved in the mountain?' asked another man.

'I'm afraid so, old lad. My engineers left winches and pulleys in the tunnels and an elaborate set-up by one of the main beams. After all, you can't have an open road into a fortress.'

'We heard you were dead,' said Jonat.

'Good Gods, man, you think a mere mountain could kill me? What little faith you have! Anyway, how are you all faring?'

For some minutes Karnak sat and chatted with them, before moving further down the line. Two hours later he returned to his room, his eye a blistering agony, his strength all but gone. He lowered his body to the bed, rolled on to his back and groaned.

In the hall below Dardalion opened his eyes and looked about him. Eight priests met his gaze and nine more were stirring, but six lifeless bodies were slumped across the table.

'The Brotherhood are no longer a threat,' said Astila, 'but the price of victory is high.'

'The price is always high,' said Dardalion. 'Let us pray.'

'For what should we pray, Dardalion?' asked the young priest named Baynha. 'That we kill more enemies? More than sixty of the Brotherhood died tonight. I cannot take much more of this endless slaying.'

'You think we are wrong, Baynha?' questioned Dardalion gently.

'It is more a question of not knowing if we are right.'

'May I speak, Dardalion?' asked Astila and Dardalion nodded.

'I am not as intellectually gifted as some of our Order,' Astila began, 'but bear with me, brothers. I recall a phrase the Abbot used when I was a novitiate. He said: "When a fool sees himself as he is, then he is a fool no longer; and when a wise man learns of his own wisdom, then he becomes a fool." This caused me great trouble, for it seemed mere word play. But after many years I have come to this conclusion: that only in certainty is there moral danger. Doubt is the gift we must cherish, for it forces us to question our motives constantly. It guides us to truth. I do not know if we chose wisely the path we now walk. I do not know if we are right in what we do. But we walk it in faith.

'I despise the slaying, but I will continue to fight the Brotherhood with all the powers the Source has allowed me. But if you, Baynha, believe it is wrong, you should fight no longer.'

Baynha bowed his head briefly, then smiled.

'I am not wise, Astila. Does knowing this make me wise?'

'It makes you human, my brother, and I for one am glad of it. My biggest fear was that we would grow to love the battle.'

'I will fight on,' said Baynha, 'and on your advice will cherish my doubts. Yet I wonder what the future holds for us all. What happens if we win? Do we form a temple of warrior priests? Do we return to our former lives? We have begun something here which is new to the world. What is our purpose?'

Dardalion lifted his hand and they turned to him.

'My friends, these are great questions. But we should not attempt to answer them now. Those of us who survive must decide our future. Yet I must say now that I have had many dreams these past days, terror-filled dreams. But each has ended in the same way. I see a desert of broken souls and undead beasts. At the centre of this desert is an oasis – and beside it a tree. Beneath its branches men gather for shade, and rest, and peace. Not one of the undead beasts can gather near the tree, nor any creature of evil approach it.'

'And what does it mean, do you think?' asked Astila.

'The tree has Thirty branches,' said Dardalion.

23

Waylander slept and in his dreams he found himself once more upon the lonely hillside with the blind King Orien. He opened his eyes and gazed at the sky and the unfamiliar stars.

'Welcome!' said Orien.

Waylander sat up and the old man took his hand and patted it paternally.

'You have pleased me, Waylander. Restored my faith to full vigour. Your courage is great and you have proved to be a man of honour.'

'I am uncomfortable with compliments,' said Waylander, turning away and pulling free his hand.

Orien nodded. 'Then ask that which you fear.'

'Where is the Armour?'

'You will find it. Tomorrow, if the Source blesses you, you will ride upon the flanks of Raboas. There you will find a narrow path which winds to a cave. The cave is on a ledge, and there you will find a second path. These two roads are the only route to the mountain's heart. Enter the cave and you will see three tunnels. Take the right-hand entrance and journey on until you come to a wide, arching chamber. There is the Armour for all to see.'

'It is an image which cannot be taken,' said Waylander.

'It is real, but only the Chosen One can lift it.'

'And I am the Chosen One?'

'That you will know tomorrow.'

'Is Danyal safe?'

'I cannot say, for I do not know. I am not a God, Waylander.'

'Then what are you?'

'I am nothing but an image in your dreams.'

'You must be more than that.'

'Then think of me as the spirit of Orien, the last flickering evidence of the once-King. When you take the Armour I shall be gone, never to return.'

'Where will you go? Is paradise a reality? Does the Source exist?'

'I cannot answer your questions. Only you can decide. But you must go now, for your danger is great. Dardalion no longer shields you from the Brotherhood. Go now!'

Waylander opened his eyes a second time and jerked upright. He was back in his blankets at the foot of Raboas.

And his horse was gone.

He rolled to his feet and saw that the bush where his mount had been tethered had been uprooted. The beast must have been terrified. But by what?

Waylander strung his crossbow and scanned the undergrowth.

He could see nothing untoward, but closed his eyes and listened. From the right he heard a faint rustling.

He spun and loosed both bolts as the werewolf rose and charged. The bolts thudded home, but the corded muscles of the beast's great chest prevented them reaching the heart and lungs and its advance continued unchecked.

Waylander dived to his right, and a second beast reared above him. He rolled to his feet, his sword slicing out and bouncing from the creature's head.

He backed away as the four beasts advanced, their great jaws open, tongues lolling and red eyes fixed upon him. Gripping his sword two-handed, he raised it over his right shoulder, ready to take at least one of them with him.

A dark shadow reared up behind them and Waylander blinked as a massive hand grabbed a furry neck and squeezed. A terrible howl began and was cut short as the werewolf was lifted from the ground. A silver knife plunged between its ribs and the corpse was hurled ten feet into the bushes. The other beasts swung on the attacker, but with one bound he was among them and a second knife thudded home, disembowelling the creature which had been Lenlai the possessed. Fangs fastened on Kai's shoulder as a third beast leapt at him. He tore it loose, curling his huge hands around its throat and dangling it before him. Waylander winced as he heard the neck creak and snap, then Kai tossed the corpse aside.

The fourth werebeast had fled.

Waylander sheathed his sword and watched in grim fascination as the monster placed his hand over the gushing wound in his shoulder. Minutes later, when the hand was removed from the place, the wound had gone. Kai moved to the corpses, pulling clear the knives. His legs weak, Waylander sat down with his back to a tree. Kai approached him and squatted down, offering the knives hilt first. Waylander accepted them without comment.

Kai watched him for some seconds, then lifted his hand and tapped his enormous chest.

'Vrend,' he said.

'Friends,' agreed Waylander.

After a while Waylander moved to his pack, sharing out some jerked meat and dried fruit. The food disappeared swiftly, then Kai belched and tapped his chest once more.

'Kai,' he said, his head tilting with the effort of speech.

'Waylander.'

Kai nodded, then stretched himself out with head on arm and closed his great eye.

A noise in the undergrowth startled the assassin and he started to rise.

'Orsh,' said Kai, without moving.

Waylander's horse moved into the clearing. He patted its neck and fed it the last of the grain, before tethering it to a stout branch.

Taking his blanket, he lay down beside the man-monster and slept until dawn. When he awoke, he was alone. The bodies of the wolf-beasts had gone and so had Kai.

Waylander finished the last of his food, then saddled his horse. Moving from the clearing, he gazed up at the rearing bulk of Raboas.

The Sacred Giant.

A strange yet perfect sense of calm settled over Waylander as he guided his horse up the slopes of Raboas. The sun was shining through a lattice-work of cloud which gave incredible depth to the beauty of the sky, while overhead gulls swooped and dived like tiny living shreds of cloud. Waylander pulled on the reins and scanned the land about him. There was a beauty here he had never seen before: a savage elemental magnificence which spoke of the arrogance of eternity.

To his right a stream whispered across white rocks, gushing from a crack in the mountain. He dismounted and stripped his clothing; then he washed and shaved and combed his hair, tying it at the nape of the neck. The water was cold on his skin and he dressed again swiftly after shaking the dust of travel from his clothes. From his pack he took a shawl of black silk which he looped over his shoulders and head in the style of the Sathuli burnoose. Then he placed his mail-ringed shoulder-guard in place. From his pack he took two wrist-guards of silver which he buckled over his forearms, then a baldric carrying six sheathed throwing-knives. He sharpened his knives and his sword-blade and stood, facing the mountain.

Today he would die.

Today he would find peace.

In the distance he saw a dust-cloud heading towards Raboas. Many riders were galloping towards the mountain, but Waylander did not care.

This was his day. This glorious hour of beauty was his hour.

He stepped into the saddle and located the narrow path between the rocks, urging the horse onward.

All his life he had been heading for this path, he knew. Every experience of his existence had conspired to bring him here at this time.

From the moment he killed Niallad he had felt as if he had reached the peak of a mountain from which there was no return. All the paths had been closed to him, his only choice to step from the peak and fly!

Suddenly it did not matter whether he found the Armour, or indeed whether the Drenai won or died.

This was Waylander's hour.

For the first time in two decades he saw without anguish his beloved Tanya standing in the doorway of the farm and waving him home. He saw his son and his two daughters playing by the flower garden. He had loved them so much.

But to the raiders they had been no more than playthings. His wife they had raped and murdered; his children they had killed without thought or remorse. Their gain had been an hour of sated lust, several bags of grain and a handful of silver coin.

Their punishment had been death, hideous and vengeful – not one of them had died in less than an hour. For Dakeyras the farmer had died with his family. The raiders had created Waylander the Slayer.

But now the hatred was gone . . . vanished like smoke in the breeze. Waylander smiled as he remembered his first conversation with Dardalion.

'Once I was a lamb playing in a green field. Then the wolves came. Now I am an eagle and I fly in a different universe.'

'And now you kill the lambs?' Dardalion had accused.

'No, priest. No one pays for lambs.'

The path wound on and up, over jagged rocks between towering boulders.

Orien had said that werebeasts guarded the Armour, but Waylander did not care.

He would dismount and walk into the cave, fetch the Armour and wait for the enemy he could not slay.

His horse was breathing hard as they reached level ground. Ahead of him was a wide cave and before that a fire at which sat Durmast and Danyal.

'You took your time,' said the giant, grinning.

Waylander dismounted as Danyal ran to him; folding his arms around her he kissed her hair, closing his eyes to stem the tears. Durmast looked away.

'I love you,' said Waylander softly, his fingers touching the skin of her face. His words carried such overwhelming regret that Danyal pulled away from his arms.

'What is the matter?'

He shook his head. 'Nothing. You are well?'

'Yes. You?'

'Never better.' Taking her by the hand, he walked back to Durmast. The giant pushed himself to his feet, eyes flicking from one to the other.

'It is good to see you,' said Waylander. 'But I knew you would make it.'

'You too. Is everything all right with you?'

'Of course.'

'You seem strangely distant.'

'It has been a long journey and I am tired. You saw the dust-cloud?'

'Yes. We have less than an hour.'

Waylander nodded agreement.

Hobbling the horses, the trio prepared torches and entered the cave. It was dark and foul-smelling and, as Orien had promised, split into three tunnels. Waylander led the way and they moved deeper into the gloom.

Shadows leapt and swayed on the damp granite walls and Danyal, sword in hand, stayed close to the warriors. At one point they walked into a deep chamber where the flickering torchlight failed to pierce the darkness. Danyal pulled at Waylander's cloak and turned.

'What is it?'

At the furthest edges of the torchlight were scores of glittering, feral eyes.

'Ignore them,' said Waylander.

Durmast swallowed hard and drew his battleaxe from its sheath.

They walked on and the eyes closed in around them.

At last they reached the chamber Orien had described.

Inside, along the walls, were placed torch brackets containing sticks soaked with pitch. One by one Waylander lit them all until the chamber was bathed in light.

At the far end, on a wooden frame, stood the Armour of Bronze: winged helm, ornate breastplate bearing an eagle with wings spread, bronze gauntlets and two swords of rare beauty.

The three travellers stood silently before the Armour.

'It makes you believe in magic,' whispered Durmast.

'Who could lose, wearing such as that?' asked Danyal.

Waylander walked forward and reached out his hands.

They passed through the armour and he reached again.

But the image remained.

'Well, get it, man!' said Durmast.

'I cannot. I am not the Chosen One.'

'*What?*' hissed Durmast. 'What are you talking about?'

Waylander chuckled, then sat down before the Armour.

'There is a spell on it, Durmast. The old King, Orien, told me of it. Only the Chosen One can remove the Armour. It is a safeguard, I suppose – it is so vital to the Drenai that they could not risk it being taken by an enemy. But it does not matter.'

'Doesn't matter?' stormed Durmast. 'We've risked our lives to get this damned tin suit! Even now the Nadir are gathering – and I'm not too damned sure about those eyes out there. Of course it matters.'

'All that matters is that we tried,' said Waylander.

Durmast's response was short, vulgar and explosive. 'Horse dung! The world is full of sorry triers and I'll have no part of it. What do we do now? Wait for some golden-haired grinning Drenai hero who's been blessed in some magic fountain?'

Danyal approached the Armour and tried to touch it, but it remained ethereal.

'What do you think you're doing?' snapped Durmast.

'*You* try,' she said.

'What's the point? Do I look like a Drenai hero to you?'

'I *know* what you are, Durmast. Try anyway. What can you lose?'

The giant pushed himself upright and stalked to the Armour.

It looked so damned solid. He shrugged and his fingers snapped out . . .

And struck metal.

Danyal's jaw dropped. 'Gods! It *is* him!'

Durmast stood transfixed, then he swallowed hard and reached out once more. This time he lifted the helm and placed it reverently before Waylander. Then he stared at his hands – Waylander saw they were shaking uncontrollably. Piece by piece Durmast lifted the Armour from the stand. Then he sat beside Waylander, saying nothing.

The torches were guttering now and Danyal tapped Waylander's arm. 'We should go.'

Waylander and Durmast gathered up the Armour and followed Danyal to the doorway. Outside a sea of eyes gazed in at them. Danyal froze, then she lifted her torch and the eyes withdrew into the shadows.

'It's going to be a long walk,' muttered Durmast.

He stepped forward and the torchlight fell on the Armour of Bronze. A sibilant whispering rose up from all around them, then subsided into silence. But the eyes fell back and Danyal led the way out into the light.

Once in the open, Durmast and Waylander strapped the Armour to the back of Durmast's pack pony and covered the shining metal with a grey blanket.

The sound of hooves on stone brought a curse from Durmast and sweeping up his bow, he ran to the sloping path. Waylander joined him, crossbow in hand.

Two Nadir warriors rode into sight, lances in their hands. They catapulted from the saddle, one with a bolt through the eye, the other with a long shaft through the ribs.

'They are merely the vanguard; I think we are in trouble,' said Durmast, pulling a second arrow from his quiver. 'Unfortunately, I think we're trapped up here.'

'The second path may be clear,' said Waylander. 'Take Danyal and run. I'll hold them here and join you later.'

'*You* take her and run,' said Durmast. 'I have had enough of her company.'

'Listen to me, my friend. The Brotherhood are seeking me with all their powers. Wherever I run, they will follow. If I stay here I'll draw them to me like a beacon, which will give you a chance to get the Armour to Egel. Now go – before it's too late.'

Durmast swore, then backed away to Danyal.

'Saddle your horse,' he said. 'We're leaving.'

'No.'

'It's his idea – and it's a damn good one. Go and say goodbye; I'll saddle your damned horse.'

Danyal ran to Waylander.

'Is it true?' she asked, tears in her eyes.

'Yes, you must go. I am sorry, Danyal – sorry that we never had a chance at life together. But I am the better man for knowing you. Whether I run or stay, I am doomed . . . so I'll stay. But it will make it easier knowing I am helping you to succeed.'

'Durmast will betray you.'

'If he does, so be it. I have played my part and I can do no more. Please go.'

She reached for him, but at that moment a Nadir warrior ran forward. Waylander brushed her aside and loosed a bolt which took the man high in the shoulder; he fell and scrambled back under cover.

'I love you, Dakeyras,' whispered Danyal.

'I know. Go now.'

Waylander listened as the horses rode away, but he neither turned to watch them leave, nor saw Danyal straining for one last glimpse of him.

The Nadir came in a rush and two went down instantly. Two more fell as Waylander swept up Durmast's bow. Then they were on him and with a terrifying scream he leapt forward, his sword cleaving among them. The path was narrow and they could not circle him. The sword scythed among them and they backed away from his rage.

Six were now dead.

Waylander staggered back to his crossbow and loaded it, blood running freely now from a wound in his leg. He wiped the sweat from his eyes and listened.

The faintest sound of cloth on rock came to him and he glanced up as a Nadir warrior leapt from the boulder with knife raised. Waylander threw himself back, his finger jerking on the bronze triggers of the crossbow. Both bolts hammered into the diving warrior, but as he landed on top of the assassin his knife buried itself in Waylander's shoulder. Waylander pushed the corpse clear and rolled to his feet. The Nadir knife jutted from his flesh, but he left it where it was – to tear it loose would be to bleed to death. With difficulty he strung the crossbow.

The sun was dropping in the sky and the shadows lengthened.

The Nadir would wait for night . . .

And Waylander could not stop them.

The fingers of his left hand felt numb and he clenched them into a weak fist. Pain swept up and around the Nadir knife in his shoulder and Waylander swore. As best he could, he bound the wound in his thigh, but it continued to ooze blood.

He felt cold and began to shiver. As he lifted his hand to wipe the sweat from his eyes a Nadir bowman leapt into view and an arrow flashed from his bow. Waylander lurched left and fired and the archer vanished from sight. As Waylander sank back against the wall of the path he glanced down and saw that the black-feathered shaft had struck him above the left hip and punched its way through the flesh and muscle. Gingerly he reached behind him. The point of the arrow had exited high under his ribs and with a groan he snapped the shaft.

The Nadir charged . . .

Two bolts punched home and the enemy dropped behind the rocks.

But they were closer now and knew he was badly wounded. He struggled to re-string the crossbow, but his fingers were slippery with sweat and the effort tore at his wounded side.

How many more of them were there?

He found he could not remember how many he had slain.

Licking his lips with a dry tongue, he leaned against the wall. About twelve paces ahead of him was a round boulder and behind it, he knew, crouched a Nadir warrior. The wall beyond had a curving jut. Waylander aimed the crossbow and loosed the bolt, which struck the wall and ricocheted right. A piercing scream rent the air and a warrior loomed into sight with blood streaming from a wound at his temple. Waylander's second bolt plunged between his shoulder-blades and he fell without a sound.

Once more the assassin strung the bow. His left arm was now all but useless.

A sudden terrible cry froze Waylander's blood. He risked a glance down the path and saw the last of the werewolves surrounded by Nadir warriors. They hacked and cut at the beast, but its talons flashed among them and its great jaws tore at their flesh.

Six were down, with at least three dead for sure – and two men only remained to fight the beast. It leapt upon the first, who bravely tried to thrust his sword into its belly; the blade entered the fur-covered flesh just as the beast's fangs closed over the head of the warrior and his face disappeared in a crimson spray. The last Nadir fled down the slope.

And the werebeast advanced on Waylander.

The assassin pushed himself to his feet, staggered and regained balance.

The beast came on, slowly, painfully, blood pouring from countless wounds. It looked pitifully thin and its tongue was swollen and black. The Nadir sword jutted from its belly.

Waylander lifted his crossbow and waited.

The beast loomed above him, red eyes glittering.

Waylander squeezed the triggers and two black bolts flew into the beast's mouth, skewering its brain. It arched back and rolled over as Waylander fell to his knees.

The beast reared up once more, its taloned claw raking at the sky.

Then its eyes glazed and it pitched back down the path.

'And now you will rot in Hell,' said a voice.

Waylander turned.

The nine warriors of the Brotherhood emerged from the left-hand path with dark swords in their hands, their black armour seemingly ablaze in the fading light of the dying day as they moved forward. Waylander struggled to rise, but fell back against the cold stone, groaning as the arrow-head gouged back into his flesh. The Brotherhood warriors loomed closer, black helms covering their faces, black cloaks billowing behind them as the breeze picked up. Waylander tugged a throwing knife from its baldric sheath and hurled it, but the blade was contemptuously batted aside by a black-gauntleted hand.

Fear struck the assassin, overwhelming even his pain.

He did not want to die. The peace he had felt earlier evaporated, leaving him lost and as frightened as a child in the dark.

He prayed for strength. For deliverance. For bolts of lightning from the heavens . . .

And the Brotherhood laughed.

A booted foot cracked against Waylander's face and he was hurled to the ground.

'Pestilential vermin, you have caused us great trouble.'

A warrior knelt before him and grasped the broken shaft of the arrow in Waylander's side, twisting it viciously. Despite himself the assassin screamed. A bronze-studded leather gauntlet cracked against his face and he heard his nose break. His eyes filled with tears of pain and he felt himself hauled into a sitting position. Then as his vision cleared, he found himself gazing into the dark eyes of madness beyond the slit on the face of the black helm.

'Yours is the madness,' said the man, 'for believing you could stand against the power of the Spirit. What has it cost you, Waylander? Your life certainly. Durmast has the Armour – and your woman. And he will use both. Abuse both.'

The man took hold of the knife-hilt jutting from Waylander's shoulder.

'Do you like pain, assassin?' Waylander groaned as the man slowly exerted pressure on the knife. '*I* like pain.'

He lost consciousness, drifting back into a dark sea of tranquillity. But they found him even there and his soul fled across a jet-black sky, pursued by beasts with tongues of fire. He awoke to their laughter and saw that the moon had climbed high above Raboas.

'Now you understand what pain is,' said the leader. 'While you live you will suffer, and when you die you will suffer. What will you give me to end your pain?'

Waylander said nothing.

'Now you are wondering if you have the strength to draw a knife and kill me. Try it, Waylander! Please try. Here, I will help you. He pulled a throwing knife from the assassin's baldric sheath and pushed it into his hand. 'Try to kill me.'

Waylander could not move his hand, though he strained until blood bubbled from the wound in his shoulder. He sagged back, his face ashen.

'There is worse to come, Waylander,' promised the leader. 'Now stab yourself in the leg.'

Waylander watched his hand lift and turn . . . and he screamed as the blade plunged down into his thigh.

'You are mine, assassin. Body and soul.'

Another man knelt beside the leader and spoke. 'Shall we pursue Durmast and the girl?'

'No. Durmast is ours. He will take the Armour to Kaem.'

'Then if you permit, I would enjoy a conversation with the assassin.'

'Of course, Enson. How selfish of me. Pray continue.'

The man knelt over Waylander. 'Pull the knife from your leg,' he ordered. Waylander felt himself on the verge of begging, but gritted his teeth. His hand came down and wrenched the blade cruelly, but it would not come loose.

'Keep calm, Enson,' said the leader. 'Your excitement is lessening your power.'

'My apologies, Tchard. May I try again?'

'Of course.'

Once more Waylander's hand pulled at the blade, and this time the knife tore free of the wound.

'Very good,' said Tchard. 'Now try something a little more delicate. Get him to slowly put out one of his eyes.'

'Gods, no!' whispered Waylander. But the knife rose slowly, its blood-covered point inching inexorably towards the assassin's face.

'You stinking whoresons!' bellowed Durmast, and Tchard twisted to see the bearded giant standing by the path with a double-headed battleaxe in his hands. Enson turned also, and Waylander felt the spell that held him fall away. He stared at the knife blade only inches from his eye, and anger rose in him, blanketing the pain.

'Enson!' he said softly. As the man's helm turned back towards him, Waylander stabbed the knife through the eye-slit until the hilt slammed against the helm.

Tchard hammered a fist against Waylander's head and the assassin slumped to the ground beside the dead Enson.

Then the Brotherhood leader rose to his feet and faced Durmast.

'Why are you here?' he asked.

'I came for him.'

'There is no need, we have him. But if you are worried about the bounty, we will see that you get it.'

'I don't want the bounty. I want him . . . alive.'

'What is the matter with you, Durmast? This display is more than a little out of character.'

'Don't tell me about my character, you lump of chicken dung! Just move away from him.'

'Or else what?' snarled Tchard.

'Or else you die,' said Durmast.

'You think to kill eight members of the Brotherhood? Your wits are addled.'

'Try me,' urged Durmast, moving forward with axe raised.

Tchard moved to meet him, while the other seven warriors spread out in a semi-circle with swords drawn.

Suddenly Tchard pointed at Durmast. 'You cannot move!' he shouted and Durmast staggered and froze. Grim laughter came from Tchard as slowly he drew his sword and advanced.

'You great plodding fool! Of all the people unsuited to the part of hero, you take pride of place. You are like a great child among your elders and betters – and like all unruly children, you must be punished. I will listen to your song of pain for many, many hours.'

'You don't say,' said Durmast as his axe smashed down through Tchard's shoulder, exploding his ribs and exiting through his smashed hip.

'Any other speeches?' asked Durmast. 'Any more mind games? No? Then let's start killing one another!'

With a terrible cry he ran at the warriors, the axe swinging in a murderous arc of flashing silver. They leapt back, one falling to roll clear but another going down as the axe-blade tore into his skull. Waylander fought his way to his knees, but could not rise. Taking a throwing knife he waited, praying for the strength to aid the giant.

A sword slid into Durmast's back and he twisted, tearing the blade loose from the assailant's hand and backhanding the axe across his neck. Another sword lanced his chest, the wielder dying as Durmast hit him in the throat with his fist. The warriors closed in around the giant then, swords burying themselves deep in his huge body. But still the axe scythed into them. Only two of the Brotherhood were left now and these moved away from the wounded Durmast.

Waylander waited as they backed towards him. Wiping his fingers on his jerkin to free them of sweat and blood, he took the throwing knife in his fingers and hurled it. It thudded home under the helm of the warrior on the left, slicing down through the jugular. Blood pumped from the wound and the man lurched to the left, his hand clasped to his throat, seeking vainly to stem the red tide.

Durmast charged the only remaining warrior, who ducked under the sweeping axe to bury his blade in Durmast's belly. The giant dropped the axe and grabbed the warrior by the throat, snapping his neck with a surging twist of the wrists. Then he fell to his knees.

Waylander crawled agonisingly across the rocks to where the dying man knelt, his great hands closed around the sword-hilt protruding from his body.

'Durmast!'

The giant slid sideways to the ground beside Waylander. He smiled through bloody lips.

'Why?' whispered Durmast.

'What, my friend?'

'Why was *I* chosen?'

Waylander shook his head. Reaching out he took Durmast's hand, gripping it firmly. The giant's body was seeping blood from a score of wounds.

Durmast swore softly, then he smiled. 'It's a beautiful night.'

'Yes.'

'I bet the bastard was surprised when I cut him in half.'

'How did you do it?'

'Damned if I know!' Durmast winced and his head sagged back.

'Durmast?'

'I'm here . . . for a while. Gods, the pain is terrible! You think his power could not work against me because I am the Chosen One?'

'I don't know. Probably.'

'It would be nice.'

'Why did you come back?'

Durmast chuckled, but a coughing spasm struck him and blood bubbled from his mouth. He choked and spat. 'I came to kill you for the bounty,' he said at last.

'I don't believe you.'

'I don't believe myself sometimes!'

For a while they lay in silence.

'You think this counts as a decent deed?' asked Durmast, his voice little more than a whisper.

'I would think so,' said Waylander, smiling.

'Don't tell anybody,' said Durmast. His head rolled and a grating whisper of breath rattled in his throat.

A scraping sound caused Waylander to turn.

From the cave came a score of beasts, twisted and deformed. They ran to the bodies of the slain, cackling their delight. Waylander watched the corpses being dragged into the blackness of the inner mountain.

'I won't tell anybody,' he whispered to the dead Durmast.

And the creatures loomed above him.

24

Below the ramparts Gellan, Jonat and one hundred warriors waited, listening to the sounds of battle from above. All were dressed in the black armour of the Vagrian Hounds, blue capes over gilded breastplates. Gellan alone wore the officer's helm with its white horsehair plume.

It was almost midnight and the attack wore on. Gellan swallowed hard and tightened the helm's chinstrap.

'I still say this is madness,' whispered Jonat.

'I know – at this moment I'm inclined to agree with you.'

'But we'll go anyway,' muttered Jonat. 'One of these days someone is going to listen to my advice and I'll probably die of the shock!'

A Drenai soldier ran down the battlement steps, a bloody sword in his hand.

'They're retreating,' he said. 'Get ready!'

The man crouched on the steps, watching the ramparts.

'Now!' he shouted. Gellan waved his arm and the hundred soldiers followed him up the steps and over the wall. Ladders and ropes were still in place and Gellan took hold of a wooden slat and glanced down. Three men were still on the ladder and almost at the foot of the wall. Swinging his leg over the ramparts, he began to descend. Behind him some of the soldiers were waving their swords, pretending combat to fool any watchers in the Vagrian camp; Gellan found it unconvincing. Swiftly he climbed to the ground and waited for his men to join him. Then they began the long walk to the Vagrian camp.

Several enemy soldiers joined them, but there was no conversation. The men were bone-weary and demoralised following another grim, fruitless day.

Gellan flicked a glance at Jonat. The man was tense, yet his face was set and, as always, he had pushed his bitterness aside and was ready to give his all for the job in hand.

All around them men were sitting down by camp-fires, and to the right a unit of cooks were preparing a hot meal in three bubbling cauldrons.

The aroma swamped Gellan's sense and his dry mouth suddenly swam with saliva. No one at Purdol had eaten for three days.

The daring plan had been Karnak's. Masquerading as Vagrians, a party of Drenai warriors would raid the warehouse and carry back precious food to the starving defenders. It had sounded fine when sitting around the great table of the Purdol hall. But now, walking through the enemy camp, it seemed suicidal.

An officer stepped out of the darkness.

'Where are you going?' he asked Gellan.

'None of your damned business,' he replied, recognising the rank of the man by the bronze bars on his epaulettes.

'Just a moment,' said the officer in a more conciliatory manner, 'but I have been told no one is to enter the eastern quarter without authorisation.'

'Well, since we are due to be guarding the docks I would appreciate you telling me how we can accomplish that without being there.'

'Third wing are on dock duty,' said the man. 'I have it written down.'

'Fine,' said Gellan. 'In that case I shall ignore the First General's instructions and take my men back for some rest. But in case he asks me why I did so, what is your name?'

'Antasy, sixth wing,' replied the officer, snapping to attention. 'But I'm sure it won't be necessary to mention my name. Obviously there's been an error in the orders.'

'Obviously,' agreed Gellan, swinging away from him. 'Forward!'

As the men trooped wearily past the officer and on through the winding streets of the dockside, Jonat moved up alongside Gellan.

'Now comes the difficult part,' he said softly.

'Indeed it does.'

Ahead of them a party of six soldiers was stationed at the front of a wooden warehouse. Two were sitting on empty boxes while the other four were playing dice.

'On your feet!' bellowed Gellan. 'Who is in charge here?'

A red-faced young warrior ran forward, dropping the dice into a pouch at his side.

'I am, sir.'

'What is the meaning of this?'

'I'm sorry, sir. It was just . . . we were bored, sir.'

'Little chance of worrying about boredom with a hundred stripes on your back, boy!'

'No, sir.'

'You are not from my wing, and I do not intend getting involved with endless bickering and bureaucracy. Therefore I shall overlook your negligence. Tell me, are your friends at the back also engaged in dice?'

'I don't know, sir.'

'How many men are there?'

'Ten, sir.'

'When are you due for relief?'

The man glanced at the sky. 'Two hours, sir.'

'Very well. Open the warehouse.'

'I beg your pardon, sir?'

'Are you hard of hearing as well as negligent?'

'No, sir. It is just that we have no key.'

'You mean the key has not been sent?'

'What do you mean, sir?'

'The First General,' said Gellan, slowly and with infinite patience, 'has ordered us to transfer certain goods from this warehouse to his quarters. Your second officer . . . what is his name?'

'Erthold, sir.'

200

'Yes – Erthold – was due to meet me here, or to leave the key. Where is he?'

'Well . . .'

'Well what?'

'He is asleep, sir.'

'Asleep,' said Gellan. 'Why did I not consider such a possibility? A group of men lounging while on duty. Playing dice, no less, so that a hundred armed men could march up without being seen. Where else would the officer be but asleep? Jonat!'

'Yes, sir.'

'Be so good as to break open the door.'

'Yes, sir,' said Jonat joyously as with two other soldiers he ran forward. Within seconds they had splintered the side door, entered the building, lifted the bar of the main doors and pushed them wide.

Gellan waved his troops forward and the men surged into the warehouse.

'Erthold will be furious, sir,' said the soldier. 'Should I send someone to wake him?'

'As you please,' replied Gellan, smiling. 'But he might ask who gave permission for the man to leave his post. Is that your role?'

'You think it would be best not to disturb him?' asked the man.

'I leave that to you.'

'It would probably be best,' said the soldier, looking to Gellan for signs of approval. Gellan walked away from him, but turned as he heard the pounding of running feet. Ten men were sprinting from the rear of the warehouse with swords in hand.

They saw Gellan and halted. Three men saluted nervously and the others followed suit.

'Get back to your posts,' ordered Gellan.

The men glanced at their leader, who shrugged and waved them away.

'I'm sorry about all this, sir,' he said, 'but I am grateful to you for not taking us to task over the dice.'

'I have played on duty myself from time to time,' said Gellan.

The Drenai, heavily laden, began to leave the warehouse. Jonat supervised the food-gathering, making sure that only dried food was taken: flour, dried fruit, jerked meat, oats and salt.

He had also found a small medical store at the back and had packed three pouches of herbs he felt sure Evris would find useful.

Closing the great doors and replacing the bar, he was the last to leave. The men were standing in marching file, bulging packs upon their shoulders.

Jonat approached the sentry leader.

'I don't want anyone entering the warehouse, despite the broken door. If one drop of that spirit is consumed, there'll be trouble!' He winked broadly.

The man saluted and Gellan led the men back towards the Vagrian camp.

The column wound through deserted streets, on past the tents and the sentries, and out on to the broken ground before the fortress. There, glancing to his right, Gellan saw a sight that froze his blood.

In a dip beyond a row of houses hidden from the fort, three great machines were under construction. He had seen them in use while on a visit to Ventria. They were ballistae, great catapults capable of hurling huge rocks against a castle wall. The carnage would be intolerable once these were completed. The parts must have been sent from Vagria, round the Lentrian Horn, to be assembled here. He tapped Jonat on the shoulder and pointed to the work being undertaken by lantern light.

Jonat swore, then looked into Gellan's face. 'You are not thinking . . . ?'

'Take the men back to Purdol, Jonat. I'll see you later.'

'You can't . . .'

'No arguments. Get moving!'

Dardalion returned to the fortress and his sleeping body. His eyes flickered open and he swung his legs from the bed. Sadness engulfed him and he covered his face with his hands and wept.

He had watched Waylander's dying body being hauled into the mountain and had sensed the hunger of the mountain dwellers.

Astila entered the room silently and sat beside the weeping priest.

'Waylander is dead,' Dardalion told him.

'He was your friend,' said Astila. 'I am so sorry.'

'I do not know how friendship is judged under such circumstances. We were comrades, I suppose. He gave me new life, new purpose. From his gift of blood came The Thirty.'

'Did he fail in his quest?'

'Not yet. The Armour is safe at present, but a lone woman is carrying it across Nadir lands. I must reach her.'

'It is impossible, Dardalion.'

The warrior priest smiled suddenly. 'Everything we have attempted so far has seemed impossible at the outset.'

Astila closed his eyes. 'The men are coming back with food,' he said. 'Baynha reports there are no losses, but the officer has not yet returned.'

'Good. What of the Brotherhood?'

'There has been no attack tonight.'

'Are they marshalling their forces, or have we beaten them, I wonder?'

'I do not think they are beaten, Dardalion.'

'No,' said Dardalion sadly. 'That would be too much to hope for.'

Sensing that his leader wished to be alone, Astila left the room and Dardalion wandered to the high window to gaze out at the distant stars.

He felt a sense of calm as he looked into eternity, and Durmast's face loomed in his mind. He shook his head, remembering his own sense of shock as he had sped to Raboas anxious to observe Waylander. He had arrived to see the assassin being tortured and the giant Durmast confronting the Brotherhood.

With all his power, Dardalion had focused a shield over Durmast, blocking the mind spell of the man Tchard. But he could not prevent the terrible swords from plunging into the giant. He had listened as Waylander and Durmast spoke, and a great sorrow touched him as the giant talked.

'Do you think his power could not work against me because I am the Chosen One?'

Dardalion wished with all his heart that it could have been true, that it was not simply a case of happenstance: one man, one spirit in the right place at the right time.

Somehow, he felt, Durmast deserved more than that.

Dardalion found himself wondering whether the Source would accept Durmast. Did a lifetime of petty evil weigh more than a moment of heroism? Somehow it should, and yet . . .

The priest closed his eyes and prayed for the souls of the two men. Then he smiled. But what would such men make of the peaceful paradise promised by the ancients? An eternity of song and praise! Would they not prefer an end to existence?

One of the old religions promised a hall of heroes, where strong men were welcomed by warrior maidens who sang songs of the deeds of the brave.

Durmast would probably prefer that.

Dardalion stared at the moon . . . and trembled.

A single question lanced through his mind.

What is a miracle?

The simplicity of the answer dazzled him, as it leapt from the depths of his intellect to cover the unbidden question.

A miracle is something that happens unexpectedly at the moment it is needed. No more than that. No less.

His rescue of Durmast had been a miracle, for Durmast could never have expected such aid. And yet, why had Dardalion been on hand at just the right moment?

Because I chose to find Waylander, he told himself.

Why did you so choose?

The enormity of it all overcame the priest and he stepped back from the window and sat down on the bed.

Durmast had been chosen many years ago, even before his birth. But without Waylander, Durmast would have remained a killer and a thief. And without Dardalion, Waylander would have been nothing more than a hunted assassin.

It was all a pattern, created from an interweaving series of apparently random threads.

Dardalion fell to his knees, overcome with a terrible shame.

Gellan sat beyond the glare of the lanterns and watched the engineers constructing the ballistae. Some two hundred men were at work, hoisting the giant arms of the catapults into place and hammering home the wooden plugs against the resistance bar. At the top of each arm was a canvas pouch in which could be placed boulders weighing almost a quarter of a ton. Gellan had no real idea of the range of the Vagrian machines, but in Ventria he had seen rocks hurled hundreds of feet.

The ballistae were placed on wooden frames with two huge wheels at each corner. They would be hauled before the walls, probably in front of the gate tower.

The bronze-studded gates of oak had so far withstood all assaults. But they would not stand against these engines of destruction.

Gellan glanced at the fortress, silver-white now in the moonlight. The last of the men had been lifted to the ramparts; by now the food would be stored and bronze cauldrons would be sitting atop the cooking fires, bubbling with oats and meat.

Gellan wished he had said goodbye to Jonat. Somehow it seemed churlish to have sent him on his way without a word of farewell.

Pushing himself to his feet he walked boldly into the work area, stopping to study the constructions – peering into the massive joints and marvelling at the scale of the carpentry. He walked on, ignored by all, until he came to a storage hut. Stepping inside, he located the barrels of lantern oil and several buckets.

Removing his helm and breastplate, he filled the buckets with oil and carried them outside, placing them in front of the hut. When he had filled six buckets, he found an empty jar which he also filled with oil. Taking a lantern from a nearby post, he walked to the furthest of the siege engines and calmly poured oil into the wide joint that pinned the huge arm to the frame.

Then he moved to a second engine and emptied the jug over the wood. Pulling the glass from the lantern, Gellan held the flame to the saturated joint. Fire leapt from the frame.

'What are you doing?' screamed an engineer. Gellan ignored him and walked to the first engine, touching the flame to the oil.

The man grabbed him by the shoulder and spun him round, but Gellan's dagger slid between his ribs. Men were running now towards the engines.

'Quick!' shouted Gellan. 'Get water. Over there!'

Several men obeyed instantly, sweeping up the buckets Gellan had left by the hut.

A searing sheet of flame roared into the sky as the oil splashed on to the blaze. A second flare, though not quite as spectacular, streamed from the other machine.

With no time to destroy the third of the ballistae, Gellan backed away from the blazing engines, disbelieving his luck.

It had been so simple, but then he had moved about in an unhurried way and had thus escaped attention. Now he would make it to the fortress and enjoy a good meal.

He turned to run – and found himself facing a score of armed men, led by a dark-haired officer carrying a silver-steel sabre.

The officer walked forward, raising a hand to halt his soldiers. 'Gellan, isn't it?' he asked.

Slowly Gellan drew his own sword. 'It is.'

'We met two years ago when I was the guest of honour at the Silver Swords tourney in Drenan. You won, I believe.'

Gellan recognised the man as Dalnor, a Vagrian swordsman and aide to the general Kaem.

'It's pleasant to see you again,' said Gellan.

'I take it that you are not considering surrender?'

'The thought had not occurred to me. Do *you* wish to surrender?'

Dalnor smiled. 'I watched you fence, Gellan. You were very good – but suspect, I thought. There are certain gaps in your defences. May I demonstrate?'

'Please do.'

Dalnor stepped forward and presented his sword. Gellan touched blades and the two men sprang back and began to circle one another. Dalnor's slender sabre flicked forward, to be parried instantly; he in turn swiftly countered the riposte and the two men stepped apart.

Behind them the engines blazed and the duel was fought in the giant shadows cast by the flames.

The sabres clashed and sang time and again, with no wounds apparent on the warriors. First Dalnor feinted left and with a flick of the wrist scythed his blade to the right. This move Gellan blocked and countered with a stabbing thrust to the belly. Dalnor sidestepped, pushing the sword clear, then backhanded a cut to Gellan's head. Gellan ducked.

Again the sabres crossed and this time Dalnor feinted high and plunged his blade through Gellan's side above the right hip. The sabre landed through flesh and muscle and slid clear in a fraction of a second.

'You see, Gellan?' said Dalnor. 'The gap is in your low defence – you are too tall.'

'Thank you for pointing it out. I will work on it.'

Dalnor chuckled. 'I like you, Gellan. I wish you were a Vagrian.'

Gellan was weary and lack of food had sapped his strength. He did not answer, but presented his blade once more and Dalnor's eyebrows rose.

'Another lesson?' He stepped forward and the blades came together. For several seconds the duel was even, then Gellan made a clumsy block and Dalnor's sword slid between his ribs. Instantly Gellan slammed his fist round the blade to trap it in his body, then his own sabre licked out, slicing across Dalnor's jugular.

Dalnor fell back, gripping his throat.

Gellan fell forward, dropping his sabre.

'I enjoyed the lesson, Vagrian,' he said.

A Vagrian ran forward, cleaving his sword through Gellan's neck. Dalnor raised a hand as if to stop him, but his lifeblood frothed and bubbled from his throat and he fell beside the dead Drenai swordsman.

Beyond the scene the ballistae burned, a black plume of smoke rising above the grey fortress and curling like a huge fist above the defenders.

Kaem surveyed the wreckage after dawn. Two engines were destroyed.

But one remained.

It would be enough, Kaem decided.

25

Karnak watched the flames rearing high above the ridge and scanned the broken ground beyond for sign of Gellan. He did not expect to see him, yet the hope remained.

In terms of the future – if there was to be a future – it was probably just as well that Gellan had died. He would never have made a good follower; he was too independent of mind to slavishly align himself to any leader. And yet Karnak knew he would miss him; he was the thorn in the rose which reminds a man the flesh is weak.

'It looks like two fires,' said Dundas, moving alongside the general.

'Yet Jonat says there are three ballistae.'

'Still, two was a fine effort by a single man.'

'One man can do anything if he sets his heart on it,' said Karnak softly.

'We lost three hundred men today, general.'

Karnak nodded. 'Egel will be here soon.'

'You cannot believe that.'

'We will hold until he gets here, Dundas. We have no choice. Tell Jonat he must take Gellan's place.'

'Sarvaj is the senior man.'

'I know who the senior man is. Put Jonat in charge.'

'Yes, sir.' Dundas walked away, but Karnak stopped him.

'In peacetime I wouldn't put Jonat in charge of stable clearance. But this is a game of death.'

'Yes, sir.'

Karnak gazed from the gate tower ramparts, watching the men along the walls. Some were sitting and eating, others were spread out asleep; still more were sharpening sword-blades dulled by ceaseless combat.

Too few, he thought. He glanced back at the Keep.

Soon the hard decisions must be made.

On the wall below, Jonat sat with Sarvaj. For some while both men had watched for Gellan; now they knew he was either taken or slain.

'He was a good man,' said Sarvaj at last.

'He was a fool,' hissed Jonat. 'He didn't have to kill himself.'

'No,' agreed Sarvaj, 'but I shall miss him.'

'I won't! I couldn't care less how many officers die. I just wonder why I stay at this cursed fortress. I used to have a dream, an ambition if you like . . . Have you ever been up into the Skoda mountains?'

'No.'

'There are peaks there which have never been climbed; they are bathed in mist for nine months of the year. I wanted to build a home near one of those peaks – there is a glen, sheltered, where horses could be raised. I know about horses. I like horses.'

'I'm glad to hear there's something you like.'

'I like a lot of *things*, Sarvaj. But not many people.'

'Gellan liked you.'

'Stop it! I don't want to hear any more about Gellan. You understand?'

'I don't think that I do.'

'Because I care. Does that satisfy you? Is that what you wanted to hear? I am sorry that he's gone. There! And . . . I don't want to talk about it.'

Sarvaj removed his helmet and leaned back against the cold stone. 'I had a dream once too. There was a girl back in Drenan – bright, talented and available. Her father owned a fleet of traders which sailed from Mashrapur to the east. I was going to marry her and become a merchant.'

'What happened?'

'She married someone else.'

'Did she not love you?'

'She said she did.'

'You were better off without her.'

Sarvaj chuckled. 'Does this look like better off?'

'At least you are among friends,' said Jonat, extending his hand. Sarvaj took it.

'I always wanted to die among friends.'

'Well, that is one ambition you'll achieve.'

Danyal had been riding for four days across rough open country. In that time she had seen no one but now, as she rode through thick forest, she knew she was not alone. In the undergrowth to her right she had seen a dark shadow, moving from the thick cover and darting between the trees.

She had spurred her horse away, the pack pony following.

But still the shadower stayed in touch. She rarely caught more than a glimpse of him, but he moved with great speed and supernatural silence.

The light was fading and Danyal's fears grew. Her mouth was dry, but her hands were slick with sweat. She wished Waylander were here – or even Durmast.

Momentarily her fear eased as her last conversation with Durmast rose in her mind.

When they had travelled for some five miles, they had come across the party of warriors in black armour. Durmast had cursed and reached for his battleaxe, but they had ridden by with scarcely a glance at the two travellers.

Durmast's anger had been a sight to behold.

'They ignored me,' he had said.

'I'm glad,' she had told him. 'Did you want to fight them?'

'They were Brotherhood warriors seeking the Armour. They can read minds and they know we have it.'

'Then why did they not take it?'

He had dismounted and walked to a nearby rock where he sat and stared at the now distant mountain of Raboas.

Danyal joined him. 'We cannot stay here. Waylander is risking his life to give us time.'

'They knew,' said Durmast.

'Knew what?'

'They knew my thoughts.'

'I do not understand you.'

'You know what I am, Danyal . . . what I have been. There is no real strength in me except what I have in the muscles of this over-large body. I am a wretch, always have been. Take the Armour and go.'

'And what will you do?'

'I'll travel east – maybe go to Ventria. They say it is a rare experience to view the Opal Mountains in winter.'

'I cannot get through alone.'

'You don't understand, do you? I'll betray you, Danyal, and steal the Armour. It's worth a fortune.'

'You gave your word.'

'My word isn't worth pig-droppings.'

'You are going back to help Waylander.'

Durmast laughed. 'Do I look stupid? That would be the act of a madman. Go on. Ride! Go before I change my mind.'

As the days passed Danyal had hoped to see Waylander riding the back trail. She would not accept that he might be dead – could not accept it. He was strong. Invincible. No one could bring him down. She remembered the day when he had stood against the warriors in the forest. One man standing strong in the fading light, the red glow all around him. And he had won. He always won – he could not be dead.

She jerked back to the present as tears blurred her vision, blinking hard. The path was narrow and the darkness was gathering; she was loth to camp, but the horses were tired. Glancing to her right, she peered into the undergrowth, but there was no sign of the other traveller. Perhaps it had been a bear hunting for food. Perhaps her imagination had fuelled her fear.

Danyal rode on until she heard the sound of running water and then made camp by a shallow stream, determined to stay awake through the night, sword in hand.

She awoke with the dawn and stretched. Swiftly she washed in the icy stream, the water stinging the sleep from her. Then she tightened the saddle cinch of her mare and mounted. Durmast had told her to steer south-east until she reached the river. There was a ferry – cross that and head due south to Delnoch Pass.

The forest was silent as she rode and the day warm and close.

Four Nadir riders came into sight and Danyal jerked on the reins, her heart pounding as they came closer. One of them had a dead antelope roped across his saddle and the others carried bows. The lead rider halted before her.

'You are blocking the path,' he said.

Danyal steered the mare to the left and the men rode on.

That night she lit a small fire and fell asleep within seconds.

She awoke just after midnight to see a towering figure sitting by the fire, feeding branches to the flames. As silently as she could, she drew her dagger and pushed back the blanket. His back was to her, his naked

208

skin shining in the moonlight – he was big, and would dwarf even Durmast. She moved to her feet. He turned . . .

And she found herself staring into a single dreadful eye above a slitted nose and a fang-rimmed slash of a mouth.

'Vrend,' grunted Kai, tapping his chest. 'Vrend.'

Danyal's legs felt weak, but she took a deep breath and advanced with the knife outstretched. 'Go away,' she said.

Kai pushed out a taloned finger and began scratching at the earth. He was not looking at her. Tensing herself to spring and plunge the knife into him, she suddenly saw what he was doing: in the hard-baked clay, he had sketched a stick-figured man holding a small crossbow.

'Waylander,' said Danyal. 'You know Waylander?'

'Vrend,' said Kai, nodding. He pointed at her. 'Anyal.'

'Danyal. Yes, yes. I am Danyal. Is Waylander alive?'

'Vrend.' Kai curled his hand into a fist as if it held a dagger. Then he stabbed his shoulder and hip.

'He has been badly hurt? Is that what you are saying?'

The monster merely looked at her.

'The Brotherhood warriors. Did they find him? Tall men in black armour.'

'Dead,' said Kai, mimicking the actions of a sword or axe. Danyal sheathed her knife and sat beside Kai, reaching out and touching his arm. 'Listen to me. The man who killed them – is he alive?'

'Dead,' said Kai.

Danyal sat back and closed her eyes.

A few months ago she had been performing a dance in front of a king. Weeks later she had fallen in love with that king's assassin. Now she sat in a lonely forest with a monster who could not speak. She began to laugh at the lunacy of it all.

Kai listened to the laughter, heard it change and become weeping and watched the tears flow on her pretty cheeks. So pretty, he thought. Like the Nadir girl he had watched. So small, fragile and bird-boned.

Way back, Kai had wanted one of these soft beings as a friend. And he had seized a girl as she washed clothes by a stream, carrying her into the mountains where he had gathered fruit and pretty stones. But when they had arrived Kai had found her broken and lifeless, her ribs in shards where his arm had encircled her. Not all his healing power could help her.

He didn't touch them any more . . .

Six hundred men hauled the ballista into place some fifty paces from the gate. Then six carts came into view, pulled by teams of oxen; the Drenai watched as men milled around the carts, unyoking the beasts. Then a winch was set up behind the ballista.

Karnak called Dundas, Jonat and several other nearby officers to him.

'Get the majority of the men back into the Keep. Leave only a token force on the walls,' he instructed.

Within minutes the men had streamed back through the Keep gates, taking up positions on the battlements.

Karnak opened a leather pouch at his side and removed a hard cake of rolled oats and sugar. Tearing off a chunk, he chewed it thoughtfully as the preparations continued.

Several soldiers had manoeuvred a massive boulder to the rear of the cart and were tying ropes around it. At a signal, four soldiers winched it into place on the ballista. An officer raised an arm, a lever was swiftly pulled and the ballista arm shot forward.

Karnak watched the boulder soar through the air, seeming to grow as it approached. With a thundering crash it struck the wall beside the gate tower. Rocks exploded and an entire section of battlements crumbled under the impact.

The general finished his cake and walked to the rampart edge, stepping up on to the crenellated wall.

'Up here, you whoresons!' he bellowed. Then he stepped back and walked slowly down the stairwell to the main battlements.

'Get off the wall, you men,' he shouted. 'Back to the Keep!'

As a second section of wall exploded some thirty feet from the general, rocks and stones shrieked past his head. Two men were hurled from the battlements to smash against the cobbled courtyard.

Karnak cursed and ran down the steps to them. Both were dead.

A boulder struck the gate tower, sheering off to crash into the field hospital roof. Timbers cracked, but the boulder did not penetrate. Twice more the gate tower endured against the missiles, but on the third strike the entire structure shifted and sagged. With a creaking groan, the stone blocks gave way and the tower slid to the right to crash behind the gates.

In the hospital, Evris was completing the stitching of a stomach wound in a young soldier. The boy had been lucky; no vital organs had been sliced by the thrusting sword and now all he had to fear was gangrene.

The wall came apart and Evris' last sight was of an immense black cloud engulfing the room. The slight surgeon was crushed against the far wall beside the body of his patient. Four more boulders struck the hospital and a fallen lantern spread fire through a linen basket. The flames licked out through a door frame, and up between the walls of the hospital. Soon the blaze grew into an inferno. Many of the wards had no windows and smoke killed hundreds of wounded men. Orderlies struggled at first to control the fire, and then to carry their patients to safety; they succeeded only in trapping themselves.

The gates splintered as a huge rock punched through the oak beams. A second missile finished the work and the massive bronze hinges buckled; the left-hand gate sagged and fell.

Karnak spat and cursed loudly. Then he walked to the Keep gates.

'It's all over, general,' said a soldier as the general entered.

'It's not looking too hopeful,' agreed Karnak. 'Shut the gates.'

'Someone may get out of the hospital,' protested the man.

'No one will live through that inferno. Shut the gates.'

Karnak made his way to the great hall where Dardalion and the surviving twelve priests of the The Thirty were deep in prayer.

'Dardalion!'

The priest opened his eyes. 'Yes, general?'

'Tell me that Egel is on his way.'

'I cannot. The Brotherhood are everywhere and we cannot break out.'

'Without Egel, we are doomed. Finished. It will all have been for nothing.'

'We will have done our best, general. No one can ask for more.'

'I damn well can. Trying is for losers – all that counts is winning.'

'Waylander is dead,' said Dardalion suddenly, 'but the Armour is on its way to Egel.'

'The Armour is too late for us now, it was to have been a rallying point. If Egel has not yet raised an army, it will matter not at all.'

'Not to us, general. But Egel could link with Ironlatch.'

Karnak said nothing. The logic was irresistible and perhaps that had been Egel's plan all along. He must have known Karnak was a potential enemy in the long term – what better way to handle him than to allow the Vagrians to end his ambitions? And a link with Ironlatch would drive a wedge through the Vagrian forces, freeing the capital.

Purdol would wait.

Egel would have it all: the Armour, the army and the nation.

'He will come if he can, general,' said Dardalion.

'Why should he?'

'Egel is a man of honour.'

'What does that mean?' snapped Karnak.

'I hope that it means Egel will do exactly what you would if you were in his place.'

Karnak laughed, his good humour restored. 'I do hope not, Dardalion. I am rather counting on him getting here!'

As she slept, Danyal became aware of a voice piercing her dreams, blending with her sleeping thoughts. The awareness grew and she recognised Dardalion; he seemed thinner now and older, bowed down by enormous pressures.

'Danyal, can you hear me?'

'Yes,' she said and smiled wearily.

'Are you well?'

'I am unhurt, no more than that.'

'Do you have the Armour still?'

'Yes.'

'Where are you?'

'Less than a day from the river and the ferry. There is someone with me – a monster creature. He saw Waylander die.'

'Open your eyes and show me,' he said and Danyal sat up. Kai still sat by the fire, his great eye closed, his huge mouth hanging open.

'There is no evil in him,' said Dardalion. 'Now listen to me, Danyal –

I am going to try to reach Egel and urge him to send a troop to escort you home. Wait at the ferry until you hear from me.'

'Where are you?'

'I am at Dros Purdol, but the situation here is desperate and we are mere days from destruction. There are fewer than six hundred men to hold the fortress and we have barricaded ourselves within the Keep. The food is almost gone and the water is stale.'

'What can I do?'

'Wait at the ferry. May the Source bless you, Danyal.'

'And you, priest.'

'Priest no longer. The war has come to me and I have killed.'

'We are all sullied, Dardalion.'

'Yes. But the end is very near – then I shall know.'

'What will you know?'

'Whether I was right. I must go now. Wait at the ferry!'

Danyal and Kai found the crossing at dusk the following day. There was no sign of life and the ferry itself was moored on the far side of the river. Danyal unsaddled her horse and Kai carried the bulging pack containing the Armour into a small hut. She prepared a fire and some food, averting her eyes as Kai ate, spooning the oats into his mouth with his fingers.

She slept in a narrow bed while the monster sat, cross-legged before the fire.

Just after dawn she awoke to find herself alone. After a breakfast of dried fruit she wandered to the river and washed, removing her tunic and wading naked into the waist-deep water by the bank. The current was swift and she had difficulty in keeping her feet. After several minutes she returned to the shore and washed the tunic as best she could, beating it against a rock to dislodge the grit of travel.

Two men rose from the bushes to her left. Rolling to the right she scooped her sword into her hand, hurling aside the scabbard.

'She's feisty,' said the first man, a short, stout warrior wearing a brown leather jerkin and carrying a curved dagger. As he grinned at her, she saw he had lost his front two teeth; he was unshaven and dirty, as was his companion – a thickset man with a drooping moustache.

'Will you look at her!' said the first man. 'The body of an angel.'

'I'm looking,' said the second, grinning.

'You geldings never seen a woman before?' asked Danyal.

'Geldings? We'll show you who's a gelding,' snarled the gap-toothed warrior.

'You gutless dung-eater! You'll show me nothing but your entrails.'

Her sword came up and the men backed away.

'Take her, Cael!' ordered Gap-tooth. 'Take the sword away.'

'You take it.'

'You frightened?'

'No more than you.'

As they argued the immense figure of Kai rose behind them, his hands reaching out. His palms slammed their heads together with a sickening crack and both men slid to the ground. Kai leaned over to grab Gaptooth's belt and with a casual flick of his arm he hurled the unconscious man far out into the river. His companion followed and both sank from sight.

Kai ambled forward. 'Bad,' he said, shaking his head.

'Not any more,' said Danyal, 'but I could have handled it.'

That night as Danyal was carrying wood into the hut, her foot crashed through a rotted floorboard and the flesh of her leg was deeply gashed. Limping into the hut she began to bathe the wound, but Kai knelt by her and covered the place with his hand. Pain lanced her leg and she struggled to pull clear of his grasp. But the pain passed, and when he released her the wound had vanished.

'Gone!' he said, his head tilting to one side. Carefully she probed the leg; the skin was unbroken.

'How did you do that?'

He lifted his hand and pointed to the palm.

'Vrend,' he said. Then he tapped his shoulder and hip. 'Aynander.'

But she could not understand him.

A troop of Legion riders reached the opposite bank at noon the next day, and Danyal watched as they hauled the ferry across the river. She turned to Kai.

'You must go,' she said. 'They will not understand you.'

He reached out and lightly touched her arm. 'Urbye Anyal.'

'Goodbye, Kai. Thank you.'

He walked to the edge of the trees and turned as the ferry was docking, pointing north. 'Aynander,' he called and she waved and turned to the officer approaching her.

'You are Danyal?' he asked.

'Yes. The Armour is in the hut.'

'Who was the big man with the mask.'

'A friend, a good friend.'

'I wouldn't like anyone that big for an enemy.' He was a handsome young man with an easy smile and she followed him to the ferry. With the Armour aboard she sat back, relaxing for the first time in days. Then a sudden thought struck her and she ran to the rear of the ferry.

'Kai!' she shouted. 'Kai!'

But the forest was silent, the giant gone.

Aynander! Waylander.

The giant had cured him. That's what he had been trying to tell her.

Waylander was alive!

The Keep held the enemy at bay for five days before the bronze-headed battering ram finally cracked the timbers of the gates. Soldiers swarmed forward, tearing at the wood with axe and hook, ripping wide a gaping entrance to the Keep itself.

Beyond the gates, in the portcullis archway, Sarvaj waited with fifty swordsmen and a score of archers. The last of the arrows lay before the kneeling bowmen, and these they loosed as the gates opened and the

213

Vagrians filled the breach. The enemy front line fell as the shafts sliced home, but more warriors pushed forward with shields held high. The bowmen retired and Sarvaj led his swordsmen in a wild charge, blades flashing in the light streaming from the ruined gates.

The two groups crashed together, shield on shield, and for almost a minute the Vagrians gave way. Then their greater numbers began to push the Drenai back across the blood-covered cobblestones of the archway.

Sarvaj hacked and thrust his sword into the sea of bodies before him, his senses dulled by the screams and war-cries echoing alongside the clanging crash of sword and shield. A dagger rammed into his thigh and he chopped his sword across the neck of the wielder, watching him fall beneath the booted feet of his comrades. Sarvaj and a dozen others cut their way clear of the skirmish and tried to close the doors of the great Hall. More Drenai warriors ran from the battlements to aid them, but the Vagrians were too powerful and the Drenai were forced back into the Hall itself. There the enemy swarmed around the battling defenders, taunting them with their defeat. The Drenai formed a fighting circle and stood their ground, grim-eyed.

A Vagrian officer entered the hall and pointed at Sarvaj.

'Surrender now,' he said. 'It is over.'

Sarvaj glanced at the men around him. Fewer than twenty remained.

'Anyone feel like surrendering?' he asked.

'To that rabble?' replied one of the men.

The Vagrian waved his men forward.

Sarvaj stepped back as a warrior rushed at him, ducking under the sweeping blade to thrust his own sword into the man's groin, dragging it clear as a second warrior bore down on him. He parried a wild cut, then staggered as a lance clanged against his breastplate. A sword cut into his face and he fell, and rolled. Even then he stabbed upwards and a man screamed. But several warriors surrounded him, stabbing at his face again and again.

There was no pain, he realised, as his lifeblood rose up and choked him.

On the battlements above, Jonat – helmet gone, sword dulled – watched helplessly as the Vagrians swept over the ramparts. A warrior ran at him; he parried the blade and sent a dazzling riposte ripping through his throat. Dropping his sword, Jonat swept up the man's sabre and tested the edge. It was still keen and he grinned.

Drenai warriors backed away from the advancing enemy and fought a steady retreat down the winding stairwell to the next floor. From below Jonat could hear the sounds of battle and knew in that moment that the siege was over. Anger rose in him, and all the bitterness of his twenty-seven years washed over him. No one had ever listened. From the moment when, as a child, he had begged for his father's life, no one had ever really listened. Now was the final humiliation – to die in a lost war a mere five days after his greatest promotion. Had they won, Jonat would have been hailed as a hero and become one of the youngest First Dun officers in the Legion. In ten years he could have been a general.

Now there was nothing . . . he would not even make a footnote to history.

Dros Purdol, they would say – was not a battle once fought there?

Once out of the stairwell the Drenai formed a fighting wedge in the main corridor, but the Vagrians were now coming from above and below. Karnak and Dundas emerged from the left with a score of warriors and linked with Jonat's group.

'Sorry about this, old lad,' said Karnak. Jonat said nothing as the enemy charged from the left and Karnak met them with an insane counter-charge, his axe cleaving into their ranks. Dundas - beside him as always – fell with a spear through the heart, but Karnak's furious assault left him unmarked. Jonat cut and thrust at the advancing warriors, screaming his rage and despair. An axe hit his breastplate, careering up to crack sideways on against his head. Jonat went down, blood streaming from a shallow cut to his temple; he tried to rise but a Drenai warrior, his head cloven by an axe blow, fell across him. The sounds of battle receded and Jonat passed into darkness.

One by one the Drenai were cut down until only Karnak remained. He backed away, holding the great axe high as the Vagrians advanced with sword-points extended, shields raised. Karnak was breathing hard and blood ran from wounds in his arms and legs.

'Take him alive!' called an officer. 'The general wants him alive.'

The Vagrians rushed forward and the axe swept down. Fists rained upon the Drenai general and he slipped on the blood-covered floor. Booted feet thundered into his face and body and his head snapped back, striking the wall. His fist lashed out weakly, then finally he was still.

On the second floor the surviving priests of The Thirty had barricaded themselves within the Keep library. Dardalion listened to the hammering on the door, then called the priests to him. None of them was armed, save himself.

'It is over, my brothers,' he said.

Astila stepped forward. 'I will not fight them. But I want you to know, Dardalion, that I regret not an action, not a single deed.'

'Thank you, my friend.'

The young Baynha approached and took Dardalion's hand. 'I regret the use of the rats against common soldiers, but I feel no shame at our battles with the Brotherhood.'

'I think we should pray, my brothers, for time is short.'

Together in the centre of the library the small group knelt, and their minds swam together. They did not hear the final splintering of the door, nor the crash of the barricade, but they all felt the first sword-blade that pierced Astila's heart, that cut Baynah's head from his shoulders, and the other sharp swords which plunged into unresisting flesh. Dardalion was stabbed in the back and pain swept through him . . .

Beyond the dying fortress, Kaem stood on the balcony of his quarters watching with barely concealed glee as the battle moved into its final stages.

The bald Vagrian general was already planning the next move in his campaign. Leave a powerful force to hold Purdol and move his troops through Skultik forest to root out Egel, before turning south to deal with Ironlatch and the Lentrians.

Something bright and dazzling caught his eye and he glanced to the left where a low line of hills edged with trees heralded the entrance to Skultik. There, on a splendid black horse, sat a warrior with armour blazing in the noonday sun.

Bronze Armour! Kaem squinted against the glare, his mouth suddenly dry. The warrior raised his arm and suddenly the hill seemed to move as thousands of riders streamed towards the fortress. There was no time to organise a flank defence – Kaem watched in horror as rank after rank of fighting men swept over the hill.

Five thousand? Ten? Twenty?

On they came. The first Vagrian soldiers watched them approach and stood transfixed. Realisation hit them and they drew their swords, only to be swallowed up by the charging mass.

All was lost, Kaem knew. Numbers meant nothing now. The enemy would drive a wedge through his ranks and his army would be sundered and dispersed.

The Bronze Warrior sat atop the hill, his eyes fixed on the fortress. Kaem saw his head turn towards the harbour and knew with a sudden chill that the warrior was seeking him.

Kaem backed from the window, thinking rapidly. His ships were still docked nearby – he could escape the destruction at Purdol and join his southern forces. From there he could plot a holding action until winter, with a new offensive in the spring.

He turned . . .

Standing in the doorway was a hooded figure, tall and lean, a black cloak over his shoulders, in his hand a small, black crossbow.

Kaem could not see the face under the hood, but he knew. He knew.

'Don't kill me,' he begged. 'Don't!'

He backed away to the balcony, stepping out into the bright sunshine. The silent figure followed him.

Kaem turned and climbed the balcony wall, leaping for the cobbles thirty feet below. He landed on his feet, both legs snapping under the impact and his left thigh driving up through his hip into his stomach. He fell on his back and found himself staring up at the empty balcony. Agony seared him and he died screaming.

The hooded figure walked to the harbour and climbed down a rope ladder to a tiny sailboat. The wind was picking up and the craft skimmed over the waves and out of the harbour.

Inside the Keep, the Vagrians dragged Karnak along the blood-drenched corridors. His remaining eye was swollen and his lips were cut and bleeding. Down the steps they took him and through the carnage of the great Hall. Karnak struggled to walk, but his left leg was swollen and his ankle would take no weight.

Out in the sunshine the men stopped and blinked in surprise.

The courtyard was packed with Drenai soldiers and at the centre stood a man in the shining Bronze Armour carrying two swords.

'Release him,' ordered the warrior, his voice muffled and almost metallic.

The Vagrians stepped back.

Karnak staggered and almost fell, but the warrior in bronze moved forward to support him.

'The Vagrians are routed,' said Egel. 'The war has swung.'

'We did it?' whispered Karnak.

'By all the Gods, I swear it,' Egel told him.

'Kaem?'

'He killed himself.'

Karnak struggled to open his eyes, but tears swam in them.

'Take me away from here,' he said. 'Don't let anyone see me.'

Epilogue

With Kaem dead and the major Vagrian army surrendered, the war was over on the last day of autumn, when Egel and Karnak led the Drenai army to link with the Lentrian general Ironlatch on the outskirts of Drenan.

The following year, Karnak led the invasion of Vagria which saw the Emperor toppled.

The Drenai ruling houses refused all talk of monarchy and a republic was instituted, with Egel nominated to lead a government. The general refused, but took the title of the Earl of Bronze and returned to Delnoch, where he organised the construction of a mighty six-walled fortress across the Pass.

His adviser was a priest named Dardalion, who had been found seriously wounded in the library room at Purdol. Egel was much criticised for the expense of constructing Dros Delnoch, but maintained his faith in Dardalion's vision.

Five years after the success of Purdol, Egel was assassinated in his rooms at the fortress. In the civil war that followed, Karnak rose to rule the Drenai.

Jonat survived the siege of Purdol and became a general in the Legion. He died six years after the battle, leading a rebel force against Karnak in the civil war.

Danyal, with the gold Egel gave her for returning the Armour, bought a house in Skarta where she lived with Krylla and Miriel. But she was often seen riding in the Delnoch Pass and scanning the northern horizon.

Six months after the Vagrian defeat, she and the children vanished from home.

Two neighbours discussed the disappearance with the South Gate sentry.

'I watched her leave,' he said. 'She was riding with a companion. A man.'

'Did you recognise him?'

'No, he was a stranger. A waylander.'

DRUSS THE LEGEND

THE CHAOS WARRIOR

Decades after the passing of Egel and Karnak, a new hero rose among the Drenai. Slavers raided a mountain village, slaying the men and seizing the young women.

A newly married young farmer, felling timber in the woods when the raiders struck, was too late to prevent them taking his wife, Rowena. But armed with his father's axe he set off after them, on a quest that would take him across oceans, through barbarian lands and deserts, into savage jungles and over perilous mountains.

During the years that followed, his awesome skills and his rescue of Rowena made his name famous across the world.

In the west he was known as Druss, the Captain of the Axe. To the Ventrians he was the Chaos Warrior. The Nadir of the north called him Deathwalker.

But to the Drenai he was simply Druss the Legend.

Druss sat in the sunshine, watching the clouds glide slowly across the mountains, and thought of his life. Love and friendship had been with him always, the first with Rowena, the latter with Sieben, Eskodas and Bodasen. But the greater part of his forty-five years had been filled with blood and death, the screams of the wounded and dying.

He sighed. A man ought to leave more behind him than corpses, he decided. The clouds thickened, the land falling into shadow, the grass of the hillside no longer gleaming with life, the flowers ceasing to blaze with colour. He shivered. It was going to rain. The soft, dull, arthritic ache had begun in his shoulder. 'Getting old,' he said.

'Who are you talking to, my love?' He turned and grinned. Rowena seated herself beside him on the wooden bench, slipping her arm around his waist, resting her head on his shoulder. His huge hand stroked her hair, noting the grey at the temples.

'I was talking to myself. It's something that happens when you get old.'

She stared up into his grizzled face and smiled. 'You'll never get old. You're the strongest man in the world.'

'Once, princess. Once.'

'Nonsense. You hefted that barrel of sand at the village fair right over your head. No one else could do that.'

'That only makes me the strongest man in the village.'

Pulling away from him, Rowena shook her head, but her expression, as always, was gentle. 'You miss the wars and the battles?'

'No. I . . . I am happy here. With you. You give my soul peace.'

'Then what is troubling you?'

'The clouds. They move in front of the sun. They cast shadows. Then they are gone. Am I like that, Rowena? Will I leave nothing behind me?'

'What would you wish to leave?'

'I don't know,' he answered, looking away.

'You would have liked a son,' she said, softly. 'As would I. But it was not to be. Do you blame me for it?'

'No! No! Never.' His arms swept around her, drawing her to him. 'I love you. I always have. I always will. You are my wife!'

'I would have liked to have given you a son,' she whispered.

'It does not matter.'

They sat in silence until the clouds darkened and the first drops of rain began to fall.

Druss stood, lifting Rowena into his arms, and began the long walk to the stone house. 'Put me down,' she commanded. 'You'll hurt your back.'

'Nonsense. You are as light as a sparrow wing. And am I not the strongest man in the world?'

A fire was blazing in the hearth, and their Ventrian servant, Pudri, was preparing mulled wine for them. Druss lowered Rowena into a broad-backed leather armchair.

'Your face is red with the effort,' she chided him.

He smiled and did not argue. His shoulder was hurting, his lower back aching like the devil. The slender Pudri grinned at them both.

'Such children you are,' he said, and shuffled away to the kitchen.

'He's right,' said Druss. 'With you I am still the boy from the farm, standing below the Great Oak with the most beautiful woman in all the Drenai lands.'

'I was never beautiful,' Rowena told him, 'but it pleased me to hear you say it.'

'You were – and are,' he assured her.

The firelight sent dancing shadows on to the walls of the room as the light outside began to fail. Rowena fell asleep and Druss sat silently watching her. Four times in the last three years she had collapsed, the surgeons warning Druss of a weakness in her heart. The old warrior had listened to them without comment, his ice-blue eyes showing no expression. But within him a terrible fear had begun to grow. He had forsaken his battles and settled down to life in the mountains, believing that his presence nearby would hold Rowena to life.

But he watched her always, never allowing her to become too tired, fussing over her meals, waking in the night to feel her pulse, then being unable to sleep.

'Without her I am nothing,' he confided to his friend Sieben the Poet, whose house had been built less than a mile from the stone house. 'If she dies, part of me will die with her.'

'I know, old horse,' said Sieben. 'But I am sure the princess will be fine.'

Druss smiled. 'Why did you make her a princess? Are you poets incapable of the truth?'

Sieben spread his hands and chuckled. 'One must cater to one's audience. The saga of Druss the Legend had need of a princess. Who would want to listen to the tale of a man who fought his way across continents to rescue a farm girl?'

'Druss the Legend? Pah! There are no real heroes any more. The likes of Egel, Karnak and Waylander are long gone. Now they were heroes, mighty men with eyes of fire.'

Sieben laughed aloud. 'You say that only because you have heard the songs. In years to come men will talk of you in the same way. You and that cursed axe.'

The cursed axe.

Druss glanced up to where the weapon hung on the wall, its twin silver steel blades glinting in the firelight. Snaga the Sender, the blades of no return. He stood and moved silently across the room, lifting the axe from the brackets supporting it. The black haft was warm to the touch, and he felt, as always, the thrill of battle ripple through him as he hefted the weapon. Reluctantly he returned the axe to its resting place.

'They are calling you,' said Rowena. He swung and saw that she was awake and watching him.

'Who is calling me?'

'The hounds of war. I can hear them baying.' Druss shivered and forced a smile.

'No one is calling me,' he told her, but there was no conviction in his voice. Rowena had always been a mystic.

'Gorben is coming, Druss. His ships are already at sea.'

'It is not my war. My loyalties would be divided.'

For a moment she said nothing. Then: 'You liked him, didn't you?'

'He is a good king – or he was. Young, proud, and terribly brave.'

'You set too much store by bravery. There was a madness in him you could never see. I hope you never do.'

'I told you, it is not my war. I'm forty-five years old, my beard is going grey and my joints are stiff. The young men of the Drenai will have to tackle him without me.'

'But the Immortals will be with him,' she persisted. 'You said once there were no finer warriors in the world.'

'Do you remember all my words?'

'Yes,' she answered, simply.

The sound of hoofbeats came from the yard beyond, and Druss strode to the door, stepping out on to the porch.

The rider wore the armour of a Drenai officer, white plumed helm and silver breastplate, with a long scarlet cloak. He dismounted, tied the reins of his horse to a hitching rail and walked towards the house.

'Good evening. I am looking for Druss the Axeman,' said the man, removing his helm and running his fingers through his sweat-drenched fair hair.

'You found him.'

'I thought so. I am Dun Certak. I have a message from Lord Abalayn. He wonders if you would agree to ride east to our camp at Skeln.'

'Why?'

'Morale, sir. You are a legend. The Legend. It would boost the men during the interminable waiting.'

'No,' said Druss. 'I am retired.'

'Where are your manners, Druss?' called Rowena. 'Ask the young man to come in.'

Druss stepped aside and the officer entered, bowing deeply to Rowena.

'It is a pleasure to meet you, my lady. I have heard so much about you.'

'How disappointing for you,' she replied, her smile friendly. 'You hear of a princess and meet a plump matron.'

'He wants me to travel to Skeln,' said Druss.

'I heard. I think you should go.'

'I am no speechmaker,' growled Druss.

'Then take Sieben with you. It will do you good. You have no idea how irritating it is to have you fussing around me all day. Be honest, you will enjoy yourself enormously.'

'Are you married?' Druss asked Certak, his voice almost a growl.

'No, sir.'

'Very wise. Will you stay the night?'

'No, sir. Thank you. I have other despatches to deliver. But I will see you at Skeln . . . and look forward to it.' The officer bowed once more and backed away towards the door.

'You will stay for supper,' ordered Rowena. 'Your despatches can wait for at least one hour.'

'I'm sorry, my lady, but . . .'

'Give up, Certak,' advised Druss. 'You cannot win.'

The officer smiled and spread his hands. 'An hour then,' he agreed.

The following morning, on borrowed horses, Druss and Sieben waved farewell and headed east. Rowena waved and smiled until they were out of sight, then returned to the house, where Pudri was waiting.

'You should not have sent him away, lady,' said the Ventrian sadly. Rowena swallowed hard, and the tears began to flow. Pudri moved alongside her, his slender arms encircling her.

'I had to. He must not be here when the time comes.'

'He would want to be here.'

'In so many ways he is the strongest man I have ever known. But in this I am right. He must not see me die.'

'I will be with you, lady. I will hold your hand.'

'You will tell him that it was sudden, and there was no pain – even if it is a lie?'

'I will.'

Six days later, after a dozen changes of mount, Certak galloped into the camp. There were four hundred white tents set in unit squares in the shadow of the Skeln range, each housing twelve men. Four thousand horse were picketed in the surrounding fields, and sixty cookfires were blazing under iron pots. The odour of stew assailed him as he reined in outside the large red-striped tent used by the general and his staff.

The young officer handed over his despatches, saluted and left to rejoin his company at the northern edge of the camp. Leaving his lathered mount with a groom, he removed his helm and pushed aside the tent flap of his quarters. Inside his companions were dicing and drinking. The game broke up as he entered.

'Certak!' said Orases, grinning and rising to meet him. 'Well, what was he like?'

'Who?' asked Certak innocently.

'Druss, you moron.'

'Big,' said Certak, moving past the burly blond officer and throwing his helm to the narrow pallet bed. He unbuckled his breastplate, letting it drop to the floor. Freed of its weight, he took a deep breath and scratched his chest.

'Now don't be annoying, there's a good fellow,' said Orases, his smile fading. 'Tell us about him.'

'Do tell him,' urged the dark-eyed Diagoras. 'He's been talking about the axeman non-stop since you left.'

'That's not true,' muttered Orases, blushing. 'We've all been talking about him.' Certak slapped Orases on the shoulder, then ruffled his hair.

'You get me a drink, Orases, and then I'll tell you all.'

As Orases fetched a flagon of wine and four goblets, Diagoras moved smoothly to his feet and pulled up a chair, reversing it before sitting opposite Certak, who had stretched out on the bed. The fourth man, Archytas, joined them, accepting a goblet of light honey mead wine from Orases and draining it swiftly.

'As I said, he is big,' said Certak. 'Not as tall as the stories claim, but built like a small castle. The size of his arms? Well, his biceps are as large as your thighs, Diagoras. He is bearded and dark, though there is some grey in his hair. His eyes are blue, and they seem to look right through you.'

'And Rowena?' asked Orases eagerly. 'Is she as fabulously beautiful as the poem says?'

'No. She is nice enough, in a matronly sort of way. I suppose she would have been lovely once. It's hard to tell with some of these older women. Her eyes are gorgeous, though, and she has a pretty smile.'

'Did you see the axe?' asked Archytas, a wand-slender nobleman from the Lentrian border.

'No.'

'Did you ask Druss about his battles?' asked Diagoras.

'Of course not, you fool. He may be only a farmer now, but he's still Druss. You don't just march up and ask how many dragons he's downed.'

'There are no dragons,' said Archytas loftily.

Certak shook his head, staring at the man through narrowed eyes.

'It was a figure of speech,' he said. 'Anyway, they invited me to join them for supper and we chatted about horses and the running of the farm. He asked my opinion about the war, and I told him I thought Gorben would sail for Penrac Bay.'

'It's a safe bet,' said Diagoras.

'Not necessarily. If it's that safe, how come we're stuck here with five regiments?'

'Abalayn is over-cautious,' answered Diagoras, grinning.

'That's the trouble with you westerners,' said Certak. 'You live so long with your horses you start to think like them. Skeln Pass is a gateway to the Sentran Plain. If Gorben took that we would starve during the winter. So would half of Vagria, for that matter.'

'Gorben is no fool,' offered Archytas. 'He knows Skeln can be defended forever with two thousand men. The pass is too narrow for the numbers of his army to be of any real use. And there's no other way through. Penrac makes more sense. It's only three hundred miles from Drenan and the countryside around is as flat as a lake. There his army could spread and cause real problems.'

'I don't particularly care where he lands,' said Orases, 'as long as I'm close by to see it.'

Certak and Diagoras exchanged glances. Both had fought the Sathuli and had seen the true, bloody face of battle, and watched the crows peck out the eyes of dead friends. Orases was a newcomer who had urged his father to buy him a commission in Abalayn's lancers when news of the invasion fleet reached Drenan.

'What about the Cuckold King?' asked Archytas. 'Was he there?'

'Sieben? Yes, he arrived for supper. He looks ancient. I can't see the ladies swooning over him any longer. Bald as a rock and thin as a stick.'

'You think Druss will want to fight alongside us?' asked Diagoras. 'That would be something to tell the children.'

'No. He's past it. Tired. You can see it in him. But I liked him. He's no braggart, that's for sure. Down to earth. You'd never believe he was the subject of so many songs and ballads. They say Gorben has never forgotten him.'

'Maybe he sailed the fleet just for a reunion with his friend Druss,' said Archytas, with a sneer. 'Perhaps you should put that idea to the general. We could all go home.'

'It's an idea,' admitted Certak, biting back his anger. 'But if the regiments separate, we'd be deprived of your delightful company, Archytas. And nothing is worth that.'

'I could live with it,' said Diagoras.

'And I could do without being forced to share a tent with a pack of ill-bred hounds,' said Archytas. 'But needs must.'

'Well, woof, woof,' said Diagoras. 'Do you think we've been insulted, Certak?'

'Not by anyone worth worrying about,' he replied.

'Now that is an insult,' said Archytas, rising. A sudden commotion from outside the tent cut through the gathering drama. The flap was pulled aside. A young soldier pushed his head inside.

'The beacons are lit,' he said. 'The Ventrians have landed at Penrac.'

The four warriors leapt to their feet, rushing to gather their armour.

Archytas turned as he buckled his breastplate.

'This changes nothing,' he said. 'It is a question of honour.'

'No,' said Certak. 'It is a question of dying. And you'll do that nicely, you pompous pig.'

Archytas grinned mirthlessly back at him.

'We'll see,' he said.

Diagoras pulled down the earflaps of his bronze helmet and tied them under his chin. He leaned conspiratorially close to Archytas.

'A thought to remember, goat-face. If you kill him – which is extremely doubtful – I shall cut your throat while you're sleeping.' He smiled pleasantly and patted Archytas' shoulder. 'You see, I'm no gentleman.'

The camp was in uproar. Along the coast the warning beacons were blazing from the Skeln peaks. Gorben, as expected, had landed in the south. Abalayn was there with twenty thousand men. But he would be outnumbered at least two to one. It was a hard five days' ride to Penrac and the orders were being issued at speed, the horses saddled, and the tents packed away. Cooking fires were doused and wagons loaded as men scurried about the camp in seeming chaos.

By morning only six hundred warriors remained in the mouth of Skeln Pass, the bulk of the army thundering south to bolster Abalayn.

Earl Delnar, Warden of the North, gathered the men together just after dawn. Beside him stood Archytas.

'As you know, the Ventrians have landed,' said the Earl. 'We are to stay here in case they send a small force to harry the north. I know many of you would have preferred to head south, but, to state the obvious, someone has to stay behind to protect the Sentran Plain. And we've been chosen. The camp here is no longer suitable for our needs and we will be moving up into the pass itself. Are there any questions?'

There were none and Delnar dismissed the men, turning to Archytas.

'Why you have been left here I do not know,' he said. 'But I don't like you at all, lad. You are a troublemaker. I would have thought your skills would have been welcome at Penrac. However, be that as it may. You cause any trouble here and you will regret it.'

'I understand, Lord Delnar,' replied Archytas.

'Understand this also: As my aide I will require you to work, passing on my instructions exactly as I give them to you. I am told you are a man of surpassing arrogance.'

'That is hardly fair.'

'Perhaps. I cannot see that it should be true, since your grandfather was a tradesman and your nobility is scarce two generations old. You will find as you grow older that it is what a man does that counts, and not what his father did.'

'Thank you for your advice, my lord. I shall bear it in mind,' said Archytas stiffly.

'I doubt that you will. I do not know what drives you, but then I don't care overmuch. We should be here about three weeks and then I'll be rid of you.'

'As you say, my lord.'

Delnar waved him away, then glanced beyond him to the edge of the trees bordering the field to the west. Two men were walking steadily towards them. Delnar's jaw tightened as he recognised the poet. He called Archytas back.

'Sir?'

'The two men approaching yonder. Go out to meet them and have them brought to my tent.'

'Yes, sir. Who are they, do you know?'

'The large one is Druss the Legend. The other is the saga poet Sieben.'

'I understand you know him very well,' said Archytas, barely disguising his malice.

'It doesn't look much of an army,' said Druss, shading his eyes against the sun rising over the Skeln peaks. 'Can't be more than a few hundred of them.'

Sieben didn't answer. He was exhausted. Early the previous day Druss had finally tired of riding the tall gelding borrowed in Skoda. He had left it with a stock breeder in a small town thirty miles west, determined to walk to Skeln. In a moment – in which Sieben could only consider he had been struck by transient and massive stupidity – he had agreed to walk with him. He seemed to remember thinking it would be good for him. Now, even with Druss carrying both packs, the poet stumbled wearily alongside, his legs boneless and numb, his ankles and wrists swollen, his breathing ragged.

'You know what I think?' said Druss. Sieben shook his head, concentrating on the tents. 'I think we're too late. Gorben has landed at Penrac and the army's gone. Still, it's been a pleasant journey. Are you all right, poet?'

Sieben nodded, his face grey.

'You don't look it. If you weren't standing here beside me I'd think you were dead. I've seen corpses that looked in better health.' Sieben glared at him. It was the only response his fading strength would allow. Druss chuckled. 'Lost for words, eh? This was worth coming for.'

A tall young officer was making his way towards them, fastidiously avoiding small patches of mud and the more obvious reminders of the horses picketed in the field the night before.

Halting before them, he bowed elaborately.

'Welcome to Skeln,' he said. 'Is your friend ill?'

'No, he always looks like this,' said Druss, running his eyes over the warrior. He moved well, and handled himself confidently, but there was something about the narrow green eyes and the set of his features that nettled the axeman.

'Earl Delnar asked me to conduct you to his tent. I am Archytas. And you?'

'Druss. This is Sieben. Lead on.'

The officer set a fast pace which Druss made no effort to match on the last few hundred paces uphill. He walked slowly beside Sieben. The truth of it was that Druss himself was tired. They had walked most of the night, both trying to prove they still had a claim to youth.

Delnar dismissed Archytas and remained seated behind the small folding table on which were strewn papers and despatches. Sieben, oblivious of the tension, slumped to Delnar's narrow bed. Druss lifted a flagon of wine to his lips, taking three great swallows.

'He is not welcome here – and, therefore, neither are you,' said Delnar, as Druss replaced the flagon.

The axeman wiped his mouth with the back of his hand. 'Had I been sure you were here, I would not have brought him,' he said. 'I take it the army has moved on.'

'Yes. They travelled south. Gorben has landed. You may borrow two horses, but I want you gone by sundown.'

'I came to give the men something to think about besides waiting,' said Druss. 'They won't need me now. So I'll just rest up here for a couple of days then head back to Skoda.'

'I said you're not welcome here,' said Delnar.

The axeman's eyes grew cold as he stared at the Earl. 'Listen to me,' said Druss, as softly as he could. 'I know why you feel as you do. In your place I would feel the same. But I am not in your place. I am Druss. And I walk where I will. If I say I will stay here then I shall. Now I like you, laddie. But cross me and I'll kill you.'

Delnar nodded and rubbed his chin. The situation had gone as far as he could allow it. He had hoped Druss would leave, but he could not force him. What could be more ludicrous than the Earl of the North ordering Drenai warriors to attack Druss the Legend? Especially since the man had been invited to the camp by the Lord of Hosts. Delnar did not fear Druss, because he did not fear death. His life had been ended for him six years before. Since then his wife, Vashti, had shamed him with many more affairs. Three years ago she had delivered to him a daughter, a delightful child he adored, even if he doubted his part in her conception. Vashti had run away to the capital soon after, leaving the child at Delnoch. The Earl had heard his wife was now living with a Ventrian merchant in the rich western quarter. Taking a deep, calming breath, he met Druss' eyes.

'Stay then,' he said. 'But keep him from my sight.'

Druss nodded. He glanced down at Sieben. The poet was asleep.

'This should never have come between us,' said Delnar.

'These things happen,' said Druss. 'Sieben always had a weakness for beautiful women.'

'I shouldn't hate him. But he was the first I knew about. He was the man who destroyed my dreams. You understand?'

'We will leave tomorrow,' said Druss wearily. 'But for now let's walk in the pass. I need some sea air in my lungs.'

The Earl rose and donned his helm and red cape, and together the two warriors walked through the camp and on up the steep rocky slope to the mouth of the pass. It ran for almost a mile, narrowing at the centre to less than fifty paces, where the ground dropped away gently in a rolling slope down to a stream that flowed across the valley floor, angling towards the sea some three miles distant. From the mouth of the pass, through the jagged peaks, the sea glittered in the fragmented sunlight, glowing gold and blue. A fresh easterly wind cooled Druss' face.

'Good place for a defensive battle,' said the axeman, scanning the pass. 'At the centre any attacking force would be funnelled in and numbers would be useless.'

'And they would have to charge uphill,' said Delnar. 'I think Abalayn was hoping Gorben would land here. We could have sealed him in the bay. Left his army to starve, and brought the fleet round to harry his ships.'

'He's too canny for that,' said Druss. 'A more wily warrior king you will not find.'

'You liked him?'

'He was always fair with me,' said Druss, keeping his tone neutral.

Delnar nodded. 'They say he's become a tyrant.'

Druss shrugged. 'He once told me it was the curse of kings.'

'He was right,' said Delnar. 'You know your friend Bodasen is now one of his generals?'

'I wouldn't doubt it. He's a loyal man, with a good eye for strategy.'

'I should think you are relieved to miss this battle, my friend,' commented the Earl.

Druss nodded. 'The years I served with the Immortals were happy ones, I'll grant that. And I have other friends among them. But you are right, I would hate to come up against Bodasen. We were brothers in battle, and I love the man dearly.'

'Let's go back. I'll arrange some food for you.'

The Earl saluted the sentry at the mouth of the pass and the two men made their way up the slope to the camp. Delnar took him to a square white tent, lifting the flap for Druss to enter first. Within were four men. They leapt to their feet as the Earl followed Druss inside.

'Stand easy,' said Delnar. 'This is Druss, an old friend of mine. He'll be staying with us for a while. I'd like you to make him welcome.' He turned to Druss. 'I believe you know Certak and Archytas. Well, this black-bearded reprobate is Diagoras.' Druss liked the look of the man; his smile was quick and friendly, and the gleam in his dark eyes bespoke humour. But more than this he had what soldiers call 'the look of eagles' and Druss knew instantly he was a warrior born.

'Nice to meet you, sir. We've heard a lot about you.'

'And this is Orases,' said Certak. 'He's new with us. From Drenan.'

Druss shook hands with the young man, noting the fat around his middle and the softness of his grip. He seemed pleasant enough, but beside Diagoras and Certak he seemed boyish and clumsy.

'Would you like some food?' asked Diagoras, after the Earl had departed.

'I certainly would,' muttered Druss. 'My stomach thinks my throat's been sliced.'

'I'll get it,' said Orases swiftly.

'I think he's a little in awe of you, Druss,' said Diagoras as Orases raced from the tent.

'It happens,' said Druss. 'Why don't you ask me to sit down?'

Diagoras chuckled and pulled up a chair. Druss reversed it and sat. The others followed suit and the atmosphere eased. The world is getting younger, thought Druss, wishing he had never come.

'May I see your axe, sir?' asked Certak.

'Certainly,' said Druss, pulling Snaga smoothly from the oiled sheath. In the older man's hands the weapon seemed almost weightless, but as it passed to Certak the officer grunted.

'The blade that smote the Chaos Hound,' whispered Certak, turning it over in his hands, then returning it to Druss.

'Do you believe everything you hear?' said Archytas, sneering.

'Did it happen, Druss?' said Diagoras, before Certak could answer.

'Yes. A long time ago. But it scarce pierced its hide.'

'Was it true they were sacrificing a princess?' asked Certak.

'No. Two small children. But tell me about yourselves,' said Druss. 'Wherever I go people ask me the same questions and I get very bored.'

'If you're that bored,' said Archytas, 'why do you take the poet with you on all your adventures?'

'What does that mean?'

'Quite simply that it seems strange for a man as modest as you seem to be to take a saga master with him. Although it proved very convenient.'

'Convenient?'

'Well, he created you, didn't he? Druss the Legend. Fame and fortune. Surely any wandering warrior with such a companion could have been boosted into legend?'

'I suppose that's true,' said Druss. 'I've known a lot of men in my time whose deeds are forgotten, but who were worthy of remembrance in song or tale. I never really thought of it before.'

'How much of Sieben's great saga is exaggerated?' asked Archytas.

'Oh do shut up,' snapped Diagoras.

'No,' said Druss, lifting his hand. 'You've no idea how good this is. Always people ask me about the stories, and whenever I tell them they are – shall we say – rounded, they disbelieve me. But it's true. The stories are not about me. They are based in truth, but they have grown. I was the seed; they have become the tree. I never met a princess in my life. But to answer your first question, I never took Sieben on my quest. He just came. I think he was bored and wanted to see the world.'

'But did you slay the werebeast in the mountains of Pelucid?' said Certak.

'No. I just killed a lot of men in a lot of battles.'

'Then why do you allow the poems to be sung?' asked Archytas.

'If I could have stopped them I would,' Druss told him. 'The first few years of my return were a nightmare. But I've got used to it since. People believe what they want to believe. The truth rarely makes a difference. People need heroes, and if they don't have any, they invent them.'

Orases returned with a bowl of stew and a loaf of black bread. 'Have I missed anything?' he asked.

'Not really,' said Druss. 'We were just chatting.'

'Druss has been telling us that his legend is all lies,' said Archytas. 'It's been most revealing.'

Druss chuckled with genuine humour and shook his head. 'You see,' he told Diagoras and Certak, 'people believe what they want to believe, and hear only what they wish to hear.' He glanced across at the tight-lipped Archytas. 'Boy, there was a time when your blood would now be staining the walls of this tent. But I was younger then, and headstrong. Now I get no delight from killing puppies. But I am still Druss, so I tell you this, walk softly around me from now on.'

Archytas forced a laugh. 'You cause me no concern, old man,' he said. 'I don't think . . .'

Druss rose swiftly and backhanded him across the face. Archytas hurtled backwards over his chair to lie groaning on the tent floor, his nose smashed and leaking blood.

'No, you don't think,' said Druss. 'Now give me that stew, Orases. It must be getting cold.'

'Welcome to Skeln, Druss,' said Diagoras, grinning.

For three days Druss remained at the camp. Sieben had woken in Delnar's tent, complaining of chest pains. The regimental surgeon examined him and ordered him to rest, explaining to Druss and Delnar that the poet had suffered a serious spasm of the heart.

'How bad is it?' asked Druss.

The surgeon's eyes were bleak. 'If he rests for a week or two he could be fine. The danger is that the heart might cramp suddenly – and fail. He's not a young man, and the journey here was hard for him.'

'I see,' said Druss. 'Thank you.' He turned to Delnar. 'I am sorry, but we must stay.'

'Do not concern yourself, my friend,' responded the Earl, waving his hand. 'Despite what I said when you arrived, you are welcome. But, tell me, what happened between you and Archytas? It looks like a mountain fell on his face.'

'His nose tapped my hand,' grunted Druss.

Delnar smiled. 'He's a somewhat loathsome character. But you had better watch out for him. He's stupid enough to challenge you.'

'No, he won't,' said Druss. 'He may be foolish, but he's not in love with death. Even a puppy knows when to hide from a wolf.'

On the morning of the fourth day, as Druss sat with Sieben, one of the lookout sentries came running headlong into the camp. Within minutes chaos reigned as men raced for their armour. Hearing the commotion, Druss walked from the tent. A young soldier ran by. Druss' arm snaked out, catching the man's cloak and wrenching him to a stop.

'What's going on?' asked Druss.

'The Ventrians are here!' shouted the soldier, tearing himself loose and running towards the pass. Druss swore and strode after him. At the mouth of the pass he halted, staring out over the stream.

Standing in armoured line upon line, their lances gleaming, were the warriors of Gorben, filling the valley from mountainside to mountainside. At the centre of the mass was the tent of the king, and around it were massed the black and silver ranks of the Immortals.

Drenai warriors scurried past him as Druss made his slow way to Delnar's side.

'I told you he was cunning,' said Druss. 'He must have sent a token force to Penrac, knowing it would draw our army south.'

'Yes. But what now?'

'You're not left with many choices,' said Druss.

'True.'

The Drenai warriors spread out across the narrow centre of the pass in three ranks, their round shields glinting in the morning sun, their white horsehair-crested helms flowing in the breeze.

'How many here are veterans?' asked Druss.

'About half. I've placed them at the front.'

'How long will it take a rider to reach Penrac?'

'I've sent a man. The army should be back in about ten days.'

'You think we've got ten days?' asked Druss.

'No. But, as you say, there aren't too many choices. What do you think Gorben will do?'

'First he'll talk. He'll ask you to surrender. You'd better request a few hours to make up your mind. Then he'll send the Panthians in. They're an undisciplined bunch but they fight like devils. We should see them off. Their wicker shields and stabbing spears are no match for Drenai armour. After that he'll test all his troops on us . . .'

'The Immortals?'

'Not until the end, when we're weary and finished.'

'It's a gloomy picture,' said Delnar.

'It's a bitch,' agreed Druss.

'Will you stand with us, axeman?'

'Did you expect me to leave?'

Delnar chuckled suddenly. 'Why shouldn't you? I wish I could.'

In the first Drenai line Diagoras sheathed his sword, wiping his sweating palm on his red cloak.

'There are enough of them,' he said.

Beside him Certak nodded. 'Masterly understatement. They look like they could run right over us.'

'We'll have to surrender, won't we?' whispered Orases from behind them, blinking sweat from his eyes.

'Somehow I don't think that's likely,' said Certak. 'Though I admit it's a welcome thought.'

A rider on a black stallion forded the stream and galloped towards the Drenai line. Delnar walked through the ranks, Druss beside him, and waited.

The rider wore the black and silver armour of a general of the Immortals. Reining in before the two men, he leaned forward on the pommel of his saddle.

'Druss?' he said. 'Is that you?'

Druss studied the gaunt features, the silver-streaked dark hair hanging in two braids.

'Welcome to Skeln, Bodasen,' answered the axeman.

'I'm sorry to find you here. I was meaning to ride for Skoda as soon as we took Drenan. Is Rowena well?'

'Yes. And you?'

'As you see me. Fit and well. Yourself?'

'I'm not complaining.'

'And Sieben?'

'He's asleep in a tent.'

'He always knew when to avoid battles,' said Bodasen, forcing a smile. 'And that's what this is looking like unless commonsense prevails. Are you the leader?' he asked Delnar.

'I am. What message do you bring?'

'Merely this. Tomorrow morning my king will ride through this pass. He would consider it a courtesy if you could remove your men from his path.'

'We will think on it,' said Delnar.

'I would advise you to think well,' said Bodasen, turning his mount. 'I'll be seeing you, Druss. Take care!'

'You too.'

Bodasen spurred the stallion back towards the stream and on through the Panthian ranks.

Druss beckoned Delnar aside, away from the men. 'It's pointless standing here all day staring at them,' he said. 'Why don't you order them to stand down and we'll send half of them back to bring up some blankets and fuel?'

'You don't think they'll attack today?'

'No. Why should they? They know we'll not be reinforced tonight. Tomorrow will come soon enough.' Druss tramped back to the camp, stopping in to see the poet. Sieben was asleep. Druss pulled up a chair and stared down at the poet's lined face. Uncharacteristically he stroked the balding head. Sieben opened his eyes.

'Oh it's you,' he said. 'What's all the fuss about?'

'The Ventrians tricked us. They're on the other side of the mountain.'

Sieben swore softly. Druss chuckled. 'You just lie here, poet, and I'll tell you all about it once we've sent them running.'

'The Immortals are here too?' asked Sieben.

'Of course.'

'Wonderful. A nice little outing you promised me. A few speeches. And what do we get? Another war.'

'I saw Bodasen. He's looking well.'

'Marvellous. Maybe after he's killed us we can have a drink together and chat about old times.'

'You take things too seriously, poet. Rest now, and later I'll have some men carry you up to the pass. You'd hate to miss the action, now, wouldn't you?'

'Couldn't you get them to carry me all the way back to Skoda?'

'Later,' grinned Druss. 'Anyway, I must be getting back.'

The axeman walked swiftly up the mountain slopes and sat on a boulder at the mouth of the pass, gazing intently at the enemy camp.

'What are you thinking about?' asked Delnar, moving up to join him.

'I was remembering something I told an old friend a long time ago.'

'What was that?'

'If you want to win: Attack.'

Bodasen dismounted before the king and knelt, pressing his forehead to the earth. Then he rose. From a distance the Ventrian looked as he always had, powerful, black-bearded and keen of eye. But he could no longer stand close inspection. His hair and beard showed the unhealthy sheen of heavy, dark dye, his painted face glowed with unnatural colour and his eyes saw treachery in every shadow. His followers, even those like Bodasen who had served him for decades, knew never to stare into his face, addressing all their remarks to the gilded griffin on his breastplate. No one was allowed to approach him bearing a weapon, and he had not granted a private audience to anyone in years. Always he wore armour – even, it was said, when he slept. His food was tasted by slaves, and he had taken to wearing gloves of soft leather, in the belief that poison might be spread on the outside of his golden goblets.

Bodasen waited for permission to speak, glancing up swiftly to read the expression on the king's face. Gorben was staring moodily.

'Was that Druss?' he asked.

'Aye, my lord.'

'So even he has turned against me.'

'He is a Drenai, my lord.'

'Do you dispute with me, Bodasen?'

'No, sire. Of course not.'

'Good. I want Druss brought before me for judgement. Such treachery must be answered with swift justice. You understand?'

'Yes, sire.'

'Will the Drenai give us the way?'

'I think not, sire. But it will not take long to clear the path. Even with Druss there. Shall I order the men to stand down and prepare camp?'

'No. Let them stay in ranks for a while. Let the Drenai see their power and their strength.'

'Yes, sire.'

Bodasen backed away.

'Are you still loyal?' asked the king, suddenly.

Bodasen's mouth was dry. 'As I have always been, lord.'

'Yet Druss was your friend.'

'Even though that is true, sire, I will see him dragged before you in chains. Or his head presented to you, should he be slain in the defence.'

The king nodded, then turned his painted face to stare up at the pass.

'I want them dead. All dead,' he whispered.

In the cool of the pre-dawn haze the Drenai formed their lines, each warrior bearing a rounded shield and a short stabbing sword. Their sabres had been put aside, for in close formation a swinging longsword could be as deadly to a comrade standing close as to an enemy bearing down. The men were nervous, constantly rechecking breastplate straps, or discovering the bronze greaves protecting their lower legs were too tight, too loose, too anything. Cloaks were removed and left in tight red rolls by the mountain wall behind the ranks. Both Druss and Delnar knew this was the time a man's courage was under the greatest strain. Gorben could do many things. The dice were in his hands. All the Drenai could do was wait.

'Do you think he'll attack immediately the sun comes up?' asked Delnar.

Druss shook his head. 'I don't think so. He'll let the fear work for about an hour. But then again – you can never tell with him.'

The two hundred men in the front rank shared the same emotions now,

237

with varying intensity. Pride, for they had been singled out as the best; fear, for they would be first to die. Some had regrets. Many had not written home for weeks, others had left friends and relatives with bitter words. Many were the thoughts.

Druss made his way to the centre of the first line, calling for Diagoras and Certak to stand on either side of him.

'Move away from me a little,' he said. 'Give me swinging room.' The line shuffled apart. Druss loosened his shoulders, stretching the muscles of his arms and back. The sky lightened. Druss cursed. The disadvantage for the defenders – apart from the numbers of the enemy – was that the sun rose in their eyes.

Across the stream the black-skinned Panthians sharpened their spears. There was little fear among them. The ivory-skins facing them were few in number. They would be swept away like antelope before a veldt blaze. Gorben waited until the sun cleared the peaks, then gave the order to attack.

The Panthians surged to their feet, a swelling roar of hatred rising from their throats, a wall of sound that hurtled up into the pass, washing over the defenders.

'Listen to that!' bellowed Druss. 'That's not strength you hear. That's the sound of their terror!'

Five thousand warriors raced towards the pass, their feet drumming a savage beat on the rocky slopes, echoing high into the peaks.

Druss hawked and spat. Then he began to laugh, a rich, full sound that brought a few chuckles from the men around him.

'Gods, I've missed this,' he shouted. 'Come on, you cowsons!' he yelled at the Panthians. 'Move yourselves!'

Delnar, at the centre of the second line, smiled and drew his sword.

With the enemy a bare hundred paces distant, the men of the third line looked to Archytas. He raised his arm. The men dropped their shields and stooped, rising with barbed javelins. Each man had five of them at his feet.

The Panthians were almost upon them.

'Now!' yelled Archytas.

Arms flew forward and two hundred shafts of death hurtled into the black mass.

'Again!' bellowed Archytas.

The front ranks of the advancing horde disappeared screaming, to be trampled by the men behind them. The charge faltered as the tribesmen tripped and fell over fallen comrades. The mountain walls, narrowing like an hour-glass, slowed the attack still further.

Then the lines clashed.

A spear lunged for Druss. Blocking it with his axe blades, he dragged a back-hand cut that sheared through the wicker shield and the flesh beyond. The man grunted as Snaga clove through his ribcage. Druss tore the weapon clear, parried another thrust and hammered his axe into his opponent's face. Beside him Certak blocked a spear with his shield, expertly sliding his gladius into a gleaming black chest. A spear sliced his upper thigh, but there was no pain. He counter-thrust, and his attacker fell across the growing pile of corpses in front of the line.

The Panthians now found themselves leaping upon the bodies of their comrades in their desperation to breach the line. The floor of the pass became slippery with blood, but the Drenai held.

A tall warrior threw aside his wicker shield and hurdled the wall of dead, spear raised. He hurtled towards Druss. Snaga buried itself in his chest, but the weight of the man bore Druss back, tearing his axe from his hands. A second man leapt at him. Druss turned aside the thrusting spear with his mail-covered gauntlets, and smashed a cruel punch to the man's jaw. As the warrior crumpled Druss grabbed him by the throat and groin and hoisted the body above his head, hurling him back over the corpse wall into the faces of the advancing warriors. Twisting, he wrenched his axe clear of the first man's body.

'Come on, my lads,' he bellowed. 'Time to send them home!'

Leaping up on the corpses, he cut left and right, opening up a space in the Panthian ranks. Diagoras couldn't believe his eyes. He swore. Then leapt to join him.

The Drenai advanced, clambering over the Panthian dead, their swords red, their eyes grim.

At the centre the tribesmen struggled first to overcome the madman with the axe, then to get back from him, as other Drenai warriors joined him.

Fear flashed through their ranks like a plague.

Within minutes they were streaming back across the valley floor.

Druss led the warriors back into position. His jerkin was stained with blood, and his beard spotted with crimson. Opening his shirt, he removed a towel and wiped his sweating face. Doffing his helm of black and silver, he scratched his head.

'Well, lads,' he called out, his deep voice echoing in the crags, 'how does it feel to have earned your pay?'

'They're coming again!' someone shouted.

Druss' voice cut through the rising fear. 'Of course they are,' he bellowed. 'They don't know when they're beaten. Front rank fall back, second rank stand to. Let's spread the glory!'

Druss remained with the front line, Diagoras and Certak alongside him.

By dusk they had beaten off four charges for the loss of only forty men – thirty dead, ten wounded.

The Panthians had lost over eight hundred men.

It was a macabre scene that night as the Drenai sat around small camp-fires, the dancing flames throwing weird shadows across the wall of corpses in the pass making it seem as if the bodies writhed in the darkness. Delnar ordered the men to gather all the wicker shields they could find and recover as many javelins and spears as were still usable.

Towards midnight many of the veterans were asleep, but others found the excitement of the day too fresh, and they sat in small groups, talking in low tones.

Delnar walked from group to group, sitting with them, joking and lifting their spirits. Druss slept in the tent of Sieben, high in the mouth of the pass. The poet had watched part of the day's action from his bed, and fallen asleep during the long afternoon.

Diagoras, Orases and Certak sat with half a dozen other men as Delnar approached and joined them.

'How are you feeling?' asked the Earl.

The men smiled. What answer could they give?

'Can I ask a question, sir?' asked Orases.

'Certainly.'

'How is it that Druss has stayed alive so long? I mean, he has no defence to speak of.'

'It's a good point,' said the Earl, doffing his helm and running his fingers through his hair, enjoying the cool of the night. 'The reason is contained in your question. It is because he has no defence. That terrible axe rarely leaves a man with a non-mortal wound. To kill Druss you have to be prepared to die. No, not just prepared. You would have to attack Druss in the sure knowledge that he will kill you. Now, most men want to live. You understand?'

'Not really, sir,' admitted Orases.

'Do you know the one kind of warrior no one wants to face?' asked Delnar.

'No, sir.'

'The baresark, sometimes called the berserker, a man whose killing frenzy makes him oblivious to pain and uncaring about life. He throws his armour away and attacks the enemy, cutting and killing until he himself is cut to pieces. I saw a baresark once who had lost an arm. As the blood spewed from the stump he aimed it in the faces of his attackers and carried on fighting until he dropped.

'No one wants to fight such a man. Now, Druss is even more formidable than the berserker. He has all the virtues, but his killing frenzy is controlled. He can think clearly. And when you add the man's awesome strength he becomes a veritable machine of destruction.'

'But surely a chance thrust amid the melee,' said Diagoras. 'A sudden slip on a pool of blood. He could die as well as any other man.'

'Yes,' admitted Delnar. 'I do not say that he won't die in such a way; only that the odds are all with Druss. Most of you saw him today. Those who fought alongside him had no time to study his technique, but others of you caught a glimpse of the Legend. He's always balanced, always moving. His eyes are never still. His peripheral vision is incredible. He can sense danger even amid chaos. Today a very brave Panthian warrior hurled himself on the axe, dragging it from Druss' hand. A second warrior followed. Did anyone see it?'

'I did,' said Orases.

'But you didn't really learn from it. The first Panthian died to remove Druss' weapon. The second was to engage him while the others breached the line. Had they come through then, our force might have been split and pushed back into the walls of the mountain. Druss saw that instantly. That's why, although he could have just knocked his attacker senseless and retrieved his axe, he hurled the man back into the breach. Now think on this: in that instant Druss had seen the danger, formulated a plan of action, and carried it out. More even than this. He retrieved the axe and took the battle to the enemy. That's what broke them. Druss had judged exactly the right moment to attack. It's the instinct of the born warrior.'

'But how did he know we would follow him?' asked Diagoras. 'He could have been cut to pieces.'

'Even in this he was confident. That's why he asked you and Certak to stand alongside him. Now that's a compliment. He knew you would respond, and that others who might not follow him would follow you.'

'He has told you all this?' asked Certak.

The Earl chuckled. 'No. In a way Druss would be as surprised to hear it as you are. His actions are not reasoned. As I said, they are instinctive. If we live through this you will learn much.'

'Do you think we will?' asked Orases.

'If we are strong,' lied Delnar smoothly, surprised at himself.

The Panthians came again at dawn, creeping up through the pass as the Drenai waited, swords drawn. But they did not attack. Under the bewildered eyes of the defenders, they hauled away the bodies of their comrades.

It was a bizarre scene. Delnar ordered the Drenai back twenty paces to make room for the work, and the warriors waited. Delnar sheathed his sword and moved alongside Druss in the front line.

'What do you think?'

'I think they're preparing the ground for chariots,' said Druss.

'Horses will never attack a solid line. They'll pull up short,' the Earl pointed out.

'Take a look yonder,' muttered the axeman.

On the far side of the stream, the Ventrian army had parted, making way for the gleaming bronze chariots of the Tantrians. With their huge wheels bearing sickle blades, serrated and deadly, each chariot was drawn by two horses and manned by a driver and a spear carrier.

For an hour the clearing of bodies continued, while the chariots formed a line in the valley below. As the Panthians withdrew, Delnar ordered forward thirty men carrying the wicker shields retrieved from the battle the day before. The shields were spread in a line across the pass and doused with lantern oil.

Delnar placed his hand on Druss' shoulder. 'Take the line fifty paces forward, beyond the shields. When they attack, break formation left and right and make for the cover of the rocks. Once they are through we will fire the shields. Hopefully that will stop them. The second rank will engage the chariots while your line holds the following infantry.'

'Sounds good,' said Druss.

'If it doesn't work we won't try it again,' said Delnar.

Druss grinned.

Along the line of chariots the drivers were pulling silken hoods over the eyes of the horses. Druss led his two hundred men forward, hurdling the wall of wicker shields, Diagoras, Certak and Archytas beside him.

The thunder of hooves on the valley floor echoed through the crags as two hundred charioteers whipped their horses into the gallop.

With the chariots almost upon them Druss bellowed the order to break ranks. As men raced to the safety of the mountain walls on either side, the enemy thundered on towards the second line. Flaming torches were flung upon the wall of oil-soaked wicker shields. Black smoke billowed instantly, followed by dancing flames. The breeze carried the smoke towards the east, burning the flaring nostrils of the hooded horses. Whinnying their terror, they tried to turn, ignoring the biting whips of the charioteers.

Instantly all was confusion. The second line of chariots tore into the first, horses falling, vehicles overturning, hurling screaming men to the jagged rocks.

And into the milling chaos leapt the Drenai, hurdling the dying flames to fall upon the Ventrian spearmen, whose lances were useless at such close quarters.

Gorben, from his vantage point a half-mile away, ordered a legion of infantry into the fray.

Druss and the two hundred Drenai swordsmen re-formed across the pass, locking shields against the new attack, presenting a glittering wall of blades to the silver-armoured infantry.

Crushing the skull of one man and gutting a second, Druss stepped back, casting a lightning glance to left and right.

The line held.

More Drenai fell in this attack than on the previous day, but their numbers were few compared with the losses suffered by the Ventrians.

Only a handful of chariots burst back through the Drenai front line, there to crash and cut a path through their own infantry in their desire to be free of the pass.

Hour upon bloody hour the battle continued, savagely fought by both sides, with no thought of quarter.

The silver-clad Ventrian infantry continued to press their attack, but by dusk their efforts lacked conviction and weight.

Furious, Gorben ordered their general forward into the pass.

'Lead them hard, or you'll beg to be allowed to die,' he promised.

The general's body fell within the hour, and the infantry slunk back across the stream in the gathering gloom of twilight.

Ignoring the dancing troupe performing before him, Gorben lay back on the silk-covered couch, conversing in low tones with Bodasen. The king wore full battle-dress, and behind him stood the massively muscled Panthian bodyguard who for the last five years had been Gorben's executioner. He killed with his hands, sometimes by strangling his victims slowly, at other times gouging his thumbs through the eye sockets of the hapless prisoners. All executions were performed before the king, and scarcely a week passed without such a grisly scene.

The Panthian had once killed a man by crushing his skull between his hands, to the applause of Gorben and his courtiers.

Bodasen was sickened by it all, but he was caught within a web of his own making. Through the years, naked ambition had driven him to the heights of power. He now commanded the Immortals and was, under Gorben, the most powerful man in Ventria. But the position was perilous. Gorben's paranoia was such that few of his generals survived for long, and Bodasen had begun to feel the king's eyes upon him.

Tonight he had invited Gorben to his tent, promising him an evening of entertainment, but the king was in a surly, argumentative mood, and Bodasen trod warily.

'You thought the Panthians and the chariots would fail, did you not?' asked Gorben. The question was loaded with menace. If the answer was yes, the king would ask why Bodasen had not stated his view. Was he not the king's military advisor? What was the use of the advisor who gave no advice? If the answer was no, then his military judgement would prove to be lacking.

'We have fought many wars over the years, my lord,' he said. 'In most of them we have suffered reverses. You have always said "Unless we try we will never know how to succeed".'

'You think we should send in my Immortals?' asked Gorben. Always before the king had called them *your* Immortals. Bodasen licked his lips and smiled.

'There is no doubt they could clear the pass swiftly. The Drenai are fighting well. They are disciplined. But they know they cannot withstand the Immortals. But that decision is yours alone, my lord. Only you have the divine mastery of tactics. Men like myself are mere reflections of your greatness.'

'Then where are the men who can think for themselves?' snapped the king.

'I must be honest with you, sire,' said Bodasen quickly. 'You will not find such a man.'

'Why?'

'You seek men who can think as rapidly as you yourself, with your own penetrating insight. Such men do not exist. You are supremely gifted, sire. The gods would visit such wisdom on only one man in ten generations.'

'You speak truly,' said Gorben. 'But there is little joy in being a man apart, separated from his fellows by his god-given gifts. I am hated, you know,' he whispered, eyes darting to the sentries beyond the tent entrance.

'There will always be those that are jealous, sire,' said Bodasen.

'Are you jealous of me, Bodasen?'

'Yes, sire.'

Gorben rolled to his side, eyes gleaming. 'Speak on.'

'In all the years I have served and loved you, lord, I have always wished I could be more like you. For then I could have served you better. A man would be a fool not to be jealous of you. But he is insane if he hates you because you are what he never can be.'

'Well said. You are an honest man. One of the few I can trust. Not like Druss, who promised to serve me, and now thwarts my destiny. I want him dead, my general. I want his head brought to me.'

'It shall be done, sire,' said Bodasen.

Gorben leaned back, gazing around him at the tent and its contents. 'Your quarters are almost as lavish as my own,' he said.

'Only because they are filled with gifts from you, sire,' answered Bodasen swiftly.

Faces and armour blackened by dirt mixed with oil, Druss and fifty swordsmen silently waded the narrow stream under a moonless sky.

Praying the clouds would not part, Druss led the men single-file towards the eastern bank, axe in hand, blackened shield held before him. Once ashore Druss squatted at the centre of the small group, pointing towards two dozing sentries by a dying fire. Diagoras and two others ghosted from the group, approaching the sentries silently, daggers in hand. The men died without a sound. Removing torches hastily constructed from the wicker shields of Panthian warriors, Druss and the soldiers approached the sentries' fire.

Stepping over the bodies, Druss lit his torch and ran towards the nearest tent. His men followed suit, racing from tent to tent, until flames leapt thirty feet into the night sky.

Suddenly all was chaos, as screaming men burst from blazing canopies to fall before the swords of the Drenai. Druss raced ahead, cutting a crimson path through the confused Ventrians, his eyes fixed on the tent ahead, its glowing griffin outlined in the towering flames. Close behind came Certak and a score of warriors bearing torches. Wrenching open the flaps, Druss leapt inside.

'Damn,' he grunted, 'Gorben's not here! Curse it!'

Setting torch to silk, Druss shouted for his men to regroup, then led them back towards the stream. No concerted effort was made to stop them, as Ventrians milled in confusion, many of them half-clothed, others filling helms with water, forming human chains to battle the fierce inferno racing on the wings of the wind throughout the Ventrian camp.

A small group of Immortals, swords in hand, collided with Druss as he raced towards the stream. Snaga leapt forward, braining the first. The second died as Diagoras back-handed a slash across his throat. The battle was brief and bloody, but the element of surprise was with the Drenai. Bursting through the front line of swordsmen, Druss crashed his axe through one man's side before reversing a slashing swipe across another's shoulder.

Bodasen ran from his tent, sword in hand. Swiftly gathering a small group of Immortals, he raced past the flames towards the battle. A Drenai warrior loomed before him. The man aimed a thrust at Bodasen's unprotected body. The Ventrian parried and launched a devastating riposte that tore open the man's throat. Bodasen stepped over the body and led his men forward.

Druss killed two men, then bellowed for the Drenai to fall back.

244

The pounding of feet from behind caused him to swivel and face the new force. With the fire behind them Druss could not make out faces.

Nearby Archytas despatched a warrior, then saw Druss standing alone.

Without thinking, he raced towards the Immortals. In that instant Druss charged. His axe rose and fell, shearing through armour and bone. Diagoras and Certak joined him, with four other Drenai warriors. The battle was brief. Only one Ventrian broke clear, hurling himself to the right and rolling to his feet behind Archytas. The tall Drenai turned on his heel and engaged the man. Archytas grinned as their swords met. The man was old, though skilful, and no match for the young Drenai. Their swords glittered in the firelight: parry, riposte, counter, thrust and block. Suddenly the Ventrian seemed to trip. Archytas leapt forward. His opponent ducked and rolled to his feet in one flowing movement, his sword ramming into Archytas' groin.

'You live and learn, boy,' hissed Bodasen, dragging his blade clear. Bodasen turned as more Immortals ran forward. Gorben wanted Druss' head. Tonight he would give it to him.

Druss wrenched his axe from a man's body and sprinted for the stream and the relative sanctuary of the pass.

A warrior leapt into his path. Snaga sang through the air, smashing the man's sword to shards. A back-hand cut shattered his ribs. As Druss passed him, the man reached out, grabbing his shoulder. In the gleam of the flames, the axeman saw it was Bodasen. The dying Immortal general gripped Druss' jerkin, trying to slow him. Druss kicked him aside and ran on.

Bodasen fell heavily and rolled, watching the burly figure of the axeman and his companions fording the stream.

The Ventrian's vision swam. He closed his eyes. Weariness settled on him like a cloak. Memories danced in his mind. He heard a great noise like the crashing of the sea, and saw again the corsair ship bearing down upon them, gliding out of the past. Once more he raced with Druss to board her, carrying the fight to the aft deck.

Damn! He should have realised Druss would never change.

Attack. Always attack.

He opened his eyes, blinking to clear his vision. Druss was safely on the other side of the stream now, leading the warriors back to the Drenai line.

Bodasen tried to move, but agony lanced him. Carefully he probed the wound in his side, his sticky fingers feeling the broken ribs and the rush of arterial blood from the gaping gash.

It was over.

No more fear. No more insanity. No more bowing and scraping to the painted madman.

In a way he was relieved.

His whole life had been an anticlimax after that battle with Druss against the corsairs. In that one towering moment he had been alive, standing with Druss against . . .

They brought his body to the king in the pink light of dawn.

And Gorben wept.

Around them the camp was a shambles. Gorben's generals stood beside the throne, uneasy and silent. Gorben covered the body with his own cloak and dried his eyes on' a white linen towel. Then he turned his attention to the man kneeling before him, flanked by Immortal guards.

'Bodasen dead. My tent destroyed. My camp in flames. And you, you pathetic wretch, were the officer of the guard. A score of men invade my camp, killing my beloved general, and you still live. Explain yourself!'

'My lord, I sat with you in Bodasen's tent – by your order.'

'So now it is my fault the camp was attacked!'

'No, sire . . .'

'No, sire,' mimicked Gorben. 'I should think not. Your sentries were sleeping. Now they are dead. Do you not think it fitting for you to join them?'

'Sire?'

'Join them, I say. Take your blade and slice your veins.'

The officer drew his ornamental dagger, reversed it, then plunged the blade into his belly. For a moment there was no movement. Then the man began to scream and writhe. Gorben drew his sword, slashing the blade through the man's neck.

'He couldn't even do that right,' said Gorben.

Druss entered Sieben's tent and hurled his axe to the floor. The poet was awake, but lying silently watching the stars when Druss arrived. The axeman sat down on the floor, his great head slumped to his chest, staring at his hands, clenching and unclenching his fists. The poet sensed his despair. He struggled to sit up, the ache in his chest becoming a stabbing pain. He grunted. Druss' head came up, his back straightened.

'How are you feeling?' asked Druss.

'Fine. I take it the raid failed?'

'Gorben was not in his tent.'

'What is wrong, Druss?'

The axeman's head slumped forward and he didn't answer. Sieben climbed from the bed and made his way to Druss, sitting beside him.

'Come along, old horse, tell me.'

'I killed Bodasen. He came at me out of the shadows and I cut him down.'

Sieben put his arm on Druss' shoulder. 'What can I say?'

'You could tell me why – why it had to be me.'

'I can't tell you that. I wish I could. But you did not travel across the ocean, seeking to kill him, Druss. He came here. With an army.'

'I only ever had a few friends in my life,' said Druss. 'Eskodas died in my home. I've killed Bodasen. And I've brought you here to die for a pile of rock in a forgotten pass. I'm so tired, poet. I should never have come here.'

Druss rose and left the tent. Dipping his hands in the water-barrel outside, he washed his face. His back was painful, especially under the shoulder-blade where the spear had cut him so many years before. A swollen vein in his right leg nagged at him.

'I don't know if you can hear me, Bodasen,' he whispered, staring up at the stars, 'but I am sorry it had to be me. You were a good friend in happier days, and a man to walk the mountains with.'

Returning to the tent, he found Sieben had fallen asleep in the chair. Druss lifted him gently and carried him to his bed, covering him with a thick blanket. 'You're worn out, poet,' he said. He felt for Sieben's pulse. It was ragged but strong. 'Stay with me, Sieben,' he told him. 'I'll get you home.'

As the dawn's rays bathed the peaks Druss walked slowly down the rocky slope to stand again with the Drenai line.

For eight terrible days Skeln became a charnel house, littered with swelling corpses and the foul stench of putrefaction. Gorben threw legion after legion up into the pass, only to see them stumble back defeated and dejected. The dwindling band of defenders was held together by the indomitable courage of the black-garbed axeman, whose terrifying skill dismayed the Ventrians. Some said he was a demon, others a god of war. Old tales were recalled.

The Chaos Warrior walked again in the stories told around Ventrian camp-fires.

Only the Immortals stayed aloof from the fears. They knew it would fall to them to clear the pass, and they knew it would not be easy.

On the eighth night Gorben at last gave in to the insistent demands of his generals. Time was running out. The way had to be taken tomorrow lest the Drenai army trap them in this cursed bay.

The order was given and the Immortals honed their swords.

At dawn they rose silently, forming their black and silver line across the stream, staring stonily ahead at the three hundred men who stood between them and the Sentran Plain.

Tired were the Drenai, bone-weary and hollow-eyed.

Abadai, the new general of the Immortals, walked forward and lifted his sword in silent salute to the Drenai, as was the Immortal custom. The blade swept down and the line moved forward. To the rear three drummers began the doleful marching beat, and the Immortals' swords flashed into the air.

Grim were the faces as the cream of Ventria's army slowly marched towards the Drenai.

Druss, bearing a shield now, watched the advance, his cold blue eyes showing no expression, his jaw set, his mouth a tight line. He stretched the muscles of his shoulders, and took a deep breath.

This was the test. This was the day of days.

The spear-point of Gorben's destiny against the resolution of the Drenai.

He knew the Immortals were damned fine warriors, but they fought now for glory alone.

The Drenai, on the other hand, were proud men, and sons of proud men, descended from a race of warriors. They were fighting for their

247

homes, their wives, their sons, and sons yet unborn. For a free land and the right to make their own way, run their own lives, fulfil the destiny of a free race. Egel and Karnak had died for this dream, and countless more like them down through the centuries.

Behind the axeman, Earl Delnar watched the nearing enemy line. He was impressed by their discipline and, in a strangely detached way, found himself admiring them. He transferred his gaze to the axeman. Without him they could never have held this long. He was like the anchor of a ship in a storm, holding the prow into the wind, allowing it to ride clear and face the might of the elements without being broken upon the rocks or overturned by the power of the sea. Strong men drew courage from his presence. For he was a constant in a world of shifting change – a colossal force that could be trusted to endure.

As the Immortals loomed ever nearer, Delnar could feel the fear spreading among the men. The line shifted as shields were gripped more firmly. The Earl smiled. Time for you to speak, Druss, he thought.

With the instinct of a lifetime of war, Druss obliged. Raising his axe he bellowed at the advancing Immortals.

'Come in and die, you whoresons! I am Druss and this is death!'

Rowena was picking flowers in the small garden behind the house when the pain struck her, cutting beneath her ribs through to her back. Her legs collapsed beneath her and she toppled into the blooms. Pudri saw her from the meadow gate and ran to her side, shouting for help. Sieben's wife, Niobe, came running from the meadow and between them they lifted the unconscious woman and carried her into the house. Pudri forced a little foxglove powder into her mouth, then poured water into a clay goblet. Holding it to her lips, he pinched her nostrils, forcing her to swallow.

But this time the pain did not pass, and Rowena was carried upstairs to her bed while Niobe rode to the village for the physician.

Pudri sat by Rowena's bedside, his lined leathery face sunken and filled with concern, his large dark eyes moist with tears.

'Please do not die, lady,' he whispered. 'Please.'

Rowena floated from her body and opened her spirit eyes, gazing down with pity at the matronly form in her bed. She saw the wrinkled face and the greying hair, the dark rings below the eyes. Was this her? Was this tired, worn-out shell the Rowena that had been taken to Pelucid years before?

And poor Pudri, so shrunken and old. Poor devoted Pudri.

Rowena felt the pull of the Source. She closed her eyes and thought of Druss.

On the wings of the wind, the Rowena of yesterday's dreams soared above the farm, tasting the sweetness of the air, enjoying the freedom of those born to the sky. Lands swept below her, green and fertile, dappled with the gold of cornfields. Rivers became satin ribbons, seas rippling lakes, cities peopled with insects scurrying without purpose.

The world shrank until it became a plate studded with gems of blue and white, and then a stone, rounded as if by the sea, and finally a tiny jewel. She thought of Druss once more.

'Oh, not yet!' she begged. 'Let me see him once. Just once.'

Colours swam before her eyes, and she fell, twisting and spinning through the clouds. The land below her was gold and green, the cornfields and meadows of the Sentran Plain, rich and verdant. To the east it seemed as if a giant's cloak had been carelessly thrown on to the land, grey and lifeless, the mountains of Skeln merely folds in the cloth. Closer she flew until she hovered over the pass, gazing down on the embattled armies.

Druss was not hard to find.

He stood, as always, at the centre of the carnage, his murderous axe cutting and killing.

Sadness touched her then, a sorrow so deep it was like a pain in her soul.

'Goodbye, my love,' she said.

And turned her face to the heavens.

The Immortals hurled themselves on the Drenai line, and the clash of steel on steel sounded above the insistent drums. Druss hammered Snaga into a bearded face, then sidestepped a murderous thrust, disembowelling his assailant. A spear cut his face, a sword-blade ripped a shallow wound in his shoulder. Forced back a pace, Druss dug his heel into the ground, his bloody axe slashing into the black and silver ranks before him.

Slowly the weight of the Immortals forced back the Drenai line.

A mighty blow to Druss' shield split it down the middle. Hurling it from him, the axeman gripped Snaga with both hands, slashing a red swathe through the enemy. Anger turned to fury within him.

Druss' eyes blazed, power flooding his tired, aching muscles.

The Drenai had been pushed back nearly twenty paces. Ten more and the pass widened. They would not be able to hold.

Druss' mouth stretched in a death's-head grin. The line was bending like a bow on either side of him, but the axeman himself was immovable. The Immortals pushed towards him, but were cut down with consummate ease. Strength flowed through him.

He began to laugh.

It was a terrible sound, and it filled the veins of the enemy with ice. Druss lashed Snaga into the face of a bearded Immortal. The man was catapulted into his fellows. The axeman leapt forward, cleaving Snaga into the chest of the next warrior. Then he hammered left and right. Men fell back from his path, opening a space in the ranks. Bellowing his rage to the sky, Druss charged into the mass. Certak and Diagoras followed.

It was suicidal, yet the Drenai formed a wedge, Druss at the head, and sheared into the Ventrians.

The giant axeman was unstoppable. Warriors threw themselves at him from every side, but his axe flashed like quicksilver. A young soldier called Eericetes, only accepted into the Immortals a month before, saw Druss bearing down on him. Fear rose like bile in his throat. Dropping his sword he turned, pushing at the man behind him.

'Back,' he shouted. 'Get back!'

The men made way for him, and the cry was taken up by others, thinking it was an order from the officers.

'Back! Back to the stream!' The cry swept through the ranks and the Immortals turned, streaming towards the Ventrian camp.

From his throne Gorben watched in horror as his men waded the shallow stream, disorganised and bewildered.

His eyes flicked up to the pass, where the axeman stood waving Snaga in the air.

Druss' voice floated down to him, echoing from the crags.

'Where is your legend now, you eastern sons of bitches?'

Abadai, blood streaming from a shallow cut in his forehead, approached the king, dropping to his knees, head bowed.

'How did it happen?' demanded Gorben.

'I don't know, sire. One moment we were pushing them back, and then the axeman went mad, charging our line. We had them. We really had them. But somehow the cry went up to fall back, and then all was chaos.'

In the pass Druss swiftly honed the dulled blades of his axe.

'We beat the Immortals,' said Diagoras, slapping Druss on the shoulder. 'By all the gods in Missael, we beat the damned Immortals.'

'They'll be back, lad. And very soon. You'd better pray the army is moving at speed.'

With Snaga razor-edged once more, Druss looked to his wounds. The cut on his face stung like the devil, but the flow of blood had ceased. His shoulder was more of a problem, but he strapped it as best he could. If they survived the day, he would stitch it that night. There were several smaller cuts to his legs and arms but these had congealed and sealed themselves.

A shadow fell across him. He looked up. Sieben stood there, wearing breastplate and helm.

'How do I look?' asked the poet.

'Ridiculous. What do you think you are doing?'

'I'm getting into the thick of it, Druss old horse. And don't think you can stop me.'

'I wouldn't dream of it.'

'You're not going to tell me I'm being stupid?'

Druss stood and grabbed his friend's shoulders. 'These have been good years, poet. The best I could have wished for. There are few treasures in a man's life. One of them comes with the knowledge that a man has a friend to stand beside him when the hour grows dark. And let's be honest, Sieben. . . . It couldn't get much darker, could it?'

'Now you come to mention it, Druss my dear, it does seem a tiny bit hopeless.'

'Well, everybody has to die sometime,' said Druss. 'When death comes for you, spit in his eye, poet.'

'I'll do my best.'

'You always did.'

The drums sounded again and the Immortals massed. Fury was in their eyes now, and they glared balefully at the defenders. They would not be turned back. Not by Druss. Not by the pitiful two hundred facing them.

From the first clash the Drenai line was forced back. Even Druss, needing room to swing his axe, could find space only by retreating a pace. Then another. Then another. He battled on, a tireless machine, bloody and bloodied, Snaga rising in a crimson spray and falling with pitiless efficiency.

Time and again he rallied the Drenai. But ever on came the Immortals, striding across the bodies of their dead, their eyes grim, their mood resolute.

Suddenly the Drenai line broke, and the battle degenerated in moments to a series of skirmishes, small circles of warriors forming shield rings amid the black and silver sea filling the pass.

The Sentran Plain lay open to the conqueror.

The battle was lost.

But the Immortals were desperate to erase the memory of defeat. They blocked the pathway to the west, determined to kill the last of the defenders.

From his vantage point on the eastern hill Gorben threw down his sceptre in fury, turning on Abadai.

'They have won. Why are they not pushing on? Their bloodlust leaves them blocking the pass!'

Abadai could not believe his eyes. With time a desperate enemy waiting to betray them, the Immortals were unknowingly continuing the work of the defenders. The narrow pass was now gorged with warriors as the rest of Gorben's army jostled behind them, waiting to sweep through to the plain beyond.

Druss, Delnar, Diagoras and a score of others had formed a ring of steel by a cluster of jutting boulders. Fifty paces to the right Sieben, Certak and thirty men were surrounded and fighting furiously. The poet's face was grey and terrible pain grew in his chest. Dropping his sword he scrambled atop a grey boulder, pulling his throwing knife from its wrist sheath.

Certak parried one thrust, but a spear punched through his breastplate, ripping into his lungs. Blood welled in his throat and he fell. A tall Ventrian leapt to the boulder. Sieben hurled his blade. It took the man through the right eye.

A spear flashed through the air, lancing Sieben's chest. Strangely, far from causing him pain, it released the agony from his cramped heart. He toppled from the rock, to be swallowed by the black and silver horde.

Druss saw him fall – and went berserk.

Breaking from the shield ring, he launched his giant frame into the massed ranks of the warriors before him, cutting them aside like wheat before a scythe. Delnar closed the ring behind him, disembowelling a Ventrian lancer and locking shields with Diagoras.

Surrounded now by Immortals, Druss hammered his way forward. A spear took him high in the back. He swung round, braining the lancer. A sword bounced from his helm, gashing his cheek. A second spear pierced his side, and a clubbing blow from the flat of a sword thundered into his temple. Grabbing one assailant, he hauled him forward, butting him viciously. The man sagged in his grip. More enemies closed in around the axeman. Using the unconscious Ventrian as a shield, Druss dropped to the ground. Swords and spears slashed at him.

Then came the sound of bugles.

Druss struggled to rise, but a booted foot lashed into his temple and he fell into darkness.

He awoke and cried out. His face was swathed in bandages, his body racked with pain. He tried to sit, but a hand pushed gently on his shoulder.

'Rest, axeman. You've lost a lot of blood.'

'Delnar?'

'Yes. We won, Druss. The army arrived just in time. Now rest.'

The last moments of the battle surged back into Druss' mind. 'Sieben!'

'He is alive. Barely.'

'Take me to him.'

'Don't be a fool. By rights you should be dead. Your body was pierced a score of times. If you move, the stitches will open and you'll bleed to death.'

'Take me to him, damn you!'

Delnar cursed and helped the axeman to his feet. Calling an orderly who took the weight on the left side, he half-carried the wounded giant to the back of the tent and the still, sleeping form of Sieben the Sagamaster.

Lowering Druss into a seat by the bedside, Delnar and the orderly withdrew. Druss leaned forward, gazing at the bandages around Sieben's chest, and the slowly spreading red stain at the centre.

'Poet!' he called softly.

Sieben opened his eyes.

'Can nothing kill you, axeman?' he whispered.

'It doesn't look like it.'

'We won,' said Sieben. 'And I want you to note that I didn't hide.'

'I didn't expect you to.'

'I'm awfully tired, Druss old horse.'

'Don't die. Please don't die,' said the axeman, tears causing him to blink furiously.

'There are some things even you cannot have, old horse. My heart is almost useless. I don't know why I've lived this long. But you were right. They have been good years. I wouldn't change anything. Not even this. Look after Niobe and the children. And make sure some sagamaster does me justice. You'll do that?'

'Of course I will.'

'I wish I could be around to add to this saga. What a fitting climax.'

'Yes. Fitting. Listen, poet. I'm not good with words. But I want to tell you . . . I want you to know you've been like a brother to me. The best friend I ever had. The very best. Poet? Sieben?'

Sieben's eyes stared unseeing at the tent ceiling. His face was peaceful and looked almost young again. The lines seemed to vanish before Druss'

252

eyes. The axeman began to shake. Delnar approached and closed Sieben's eyes, covering his face with a sheet. Then he helped Druss back to his bed.

'Gorben is dead, Druss. His own men slew him as they ran. Our fleet has the Ventrians bottled up in the bay. At the moment one of their generals is meeting with Abalayn to discuss surrender. We did it. We held the pass. Diagoras wants to see you. He made it through the battle. Can you believe it, even fat Orases is still with us! Now, I'd have laid ten to one odds he wouldn't survive.'

'Give me a drink, will you,' whispered Druss.

Delnar came back to his side, bearing a goblet of cool water. Druss sipped it slowly. Diagoras entered the tent, carrying Snaga. The axe had been cleaned of blood and polished to shine like silver.

Druss gazed at it, but did not reach out. The dark-eyed young warrior smiled.

'You did it,' he said. 'I have never seen the like. I would not have believed it possible.'

'All things are possible,' said Druss. 'Never forget that, laddie.'

Tears welled in the axeman's eyes, and he turned his head away from them. After a moment he heard them back away. Only then did he allow the tears to fall.

LEGEND

This book is dedicated with love to three very special people. My father, Bill Woodford, without whom Druss the Legend would never have stood on the walls of Dros Delnoch. My mother, Olive, who instilled in me a love of stories in which heroes never lied, evil rarely triumphed and love was always true.

And my wife, Valerie, who showed me that life can be like stories.

Grateful thanks are also due to Russell Claughton, Tim Lenton, Tom Taylor, Nick Hopkins and Stella Graham for their help throughout the project.

Prologue

The Drenai herald waited nervously outside the great doors of the throne room, flanked by two Nadir guards who stared ahead, slanted eyes fixed on the bronze eagle emblazoned on the dark wood.

He licked dry lips with a dry tongue and adjusted his purple cape about his bony shoulders. He had been so confident in the council chamber at Drenan six hundred miles south when Abalayn asked him to undertake this delicate mission: a journey to distant Gulgothir to ratify the treaties made with Ulric, Lord of the Nadir tribes. Bartellus had helped to draft treaties in the past, and twice had been present at talks in western Vagria and south in Mashrapur. All men understood the value of trade and the necessity to avoid such costly undertakings as war. Ulric would be no exception. True he had sacked the nations of the northern plain, but then they had bled his people dry over the centuries with their taxes and raids; they had sown the seeds of their own destruction.

Not so the Drenai. They had always treated the Nadir with tact and courtesy. Abalayn himself had twice visited Ulric in his northern tent city – and been royally received.

But Bartellus had been shocked at the devastation in Gulgothir. That the vast gates had been sundered was no surprise, but many of the defenders had been subsequently mutilated. The square within the main keep boasted a small mound of human hands. Bartellus shivered and wrenched his mind from the memory.

For three days they had kept him waiting, but they had been courteous – even kindly.

He adjusted his cape again, aware that his lean, angular frame did little justice to the herald's garb. Taking a linen cloth from his belt, he wiped the sweat from his bald head. His wife constantly warned him that his head shone dazzlingly whenever he grew nervous. It was an observation he would have preferred left unspoken.

He slid a glance at the guard to his right, suppressing a shudder. The man was shorter than he, wearing a spiked helm fringed with goatskin. He wore a lacquered wooden breastplate and carried a serrated spear. The face was flat and cruel, the eyes dark and slanted. If Bartellus ever needed a man to cut off someone's hand . . .

He glanced to his left – and wished he hadn't, for the other guard was looking at him. He felt like a rabbit beneath a plunging hawk and hastily returned his gaze to the bronze eagle on the door.

Mercifully the wait ended and the doors swung open.

Taking a deep breath, Bartellus marched inside.

The room was long, twenty marble pillars supporting a frescoed ceiling. Each pillar carried a burning torch which cast gaunt dancing shadows to the walls beyond, and by each pillar stood a Nadir guard, bearing a spear.

Eyes fixed firmly ahead, Bartellus marched the fifty paces to the throne on the marble dais.

Upon it sat Ulric, Warlord of the North.

He was not tall, but he radiated power, and as Bartellus moved into the centre of the room he was struck by the sheer dynamism of the man. He had the high cheekbones and midnight hair of the Nadir, but his slanted eyes were violet and striking. The face was swarthy, a trident beard creating a demonic appearance which was belied by the warmth of the man's smile.

But what impressed Bartellus most was that the Nadir lord was wearing a white Drenai robe, embroidered with Abalayn's family crest: a golden horse rearing above a silver crown.

The herald bowed deeply.

'My Lord, I bring you the greetings of Lord Abalayn, elected leader of the free Drenai people.'

Ulric nodded in return, waving a hand for him to continue.

'My lord Abalayn congratulates you on your magnificent victory against the rebels of Gulgothir, and hopes that with the horrors of war now behind you, you will be able to consider the new treaties and trade agreements he discussed with you during his most enjoyable stay last spring. I have here a letter from Lord Abalayn, and also the treaties and agreements.' Bartellus stepped forward, presenting three scrolls. Ulric took them, placing them gently on the floor beside the throne.

'Thank you, Bartellus,' he said. 'Tell me, is there truly fear among the Drenai that my army will march on Dros Delnoch?'

'You jest, my lord?'

'Not at all,' said Ulric innocently, his voice deep and resonant. 'Traders tell me there is great discussion in Drenan.'

'Idle gossip merely,' said Bartellus. 'I helped to draft the agreements myself, and if I can be of any help with the more complex passages I would consider it a pleasure to assist you.'

'No, I am sure they are in order,' said Ulric. 'But you do realise my shaman Nosta Khan must examine the omens. A primitive custom, I know, but I am sure you understand?'

'Of course. Such things are a matter of tradition,' said Bartellus.

Ulric clapped his hands twice and from the shadows to the left came a wizened old man in a dirty goatskin tunic. Under his skinny right arm he carried a white chicken and in his left hand was a wide, shallow wooden bowl. Ulric stood as he approached, holding out his hands and taking the chicken by the neck and legs.

Slowly Ulric raised it above his head – then, as Bartellus' eyes widened in horror, he lowered the bird and bit through its neck, tearing the head from the body. The wings flapped madly and blood gushed and spattered, drenching the white robe. Ulric held the quivering carcass over the bowl, watching as the last of its life-blood stained the wood. Nosta Khan waited until the last drop oozed from the flesh and then lifted the bowl to his lips. He looked up at Ulric and shook his head.

The warlord tossed the bird aside and slowly removed the white robe.

Beneath it he wore a black breastplate and a belted sword. From beside the throne he lifted the war helm of black steel, fringed with silver fox fur, and placed it on his head. He wiped his bloody mouth on the Drenai robe and carelessly tossed it towards Bartellus.

The herald looked down at the blood-covered cloth at his feet.

'I am afraid the omens are not pleasant,' said Ulric.

1

Rek was drunk. Not enough to matter, but enough not to matter, he thought, staring at the ruby wine casting blood shadows in the lead crystal glass. A log fire in the hearth warmed his back, the smoke stinging his eyes, the acrid smell of it mixing with the odour of unwashed bodies, forgotten meals and musty, damp clothing. A lantern flame danced briefly in the icy wind as a shaft of cold air brushed the room. Then it was gone as a newcomer slammed shut the wooden door, muttering his apologies to the crowded inn.

Conversation which had died in the sudden blast of frosty air now resumed, a dozen voices from different groups merging into a babble of meaningless sounds. Rek sipped his wine. He shivered as someone laughed – the sound was as cold as the winter wind beating against the wooden walls. Like someone walking over your grave, he thought. He pulled his blue cloak more tightly about his shoulders. He did not need to be able to hear the words to know the topic of every conversation: it had been the same for days.

War.

Such a little word. Such a depth of agony. Blood, death, conquest, starvation, plague and horror.

More laughter burst upon the room. 'Barbarians!' roared a voice above the babble. 'Easy meat for Drenai lances.' More laughter.

Rek stared at the crystal goblet. So beautiful. So fragile. Crafted with care, even love; multi-faceted like a gossamer diamond. He lifted the crystal close to his face, seeing a dozen eyes reflected there.

And each accused. For a second he wanted to crush the glass into fragments, destroy the eyes and the accusation. But he did not. I am not a fool, he told himself. Not yet.

Horeb, the innkeeper, wiped his thick fingers on a towel and cast a tired yet wary eye over the crowd, alert for trouble, ready to step in with a word and a smile before a snarl and a fist became necessary. War. What was it about the prospect of such bloody enterprises that reduced men to the level of animals? Some of the drinkers – most, in fact – were well-known to Horeb. Many were family men: farmers, traders, artisans. All were friendly; most were compassionate, trustworthy, even kindly. And here they were talking of death and glory and ready to thrash or slay any suspected of Nadir sympathies. The Nadir – even the name spoke of contempt.

But they'll learn, he thought sadly. Oh, how they'll learn! Horeb's eyes scanned the large room, warming as they lighted upon his daughters who were clearing tables and delivering tankards. Tiny Dori blushing beneath her freckles at some ribald jest; Besa, the image of her mother, tall and fair; Nessa, fat and plain and loved by all, soon to marry the baker's

263

apprentice Norvas. Good girls. Gifts of joy. Then his gaze fell on the tall figure in the blue cloak seated by the window.

'Damn you, Rek, snap out of it,' he muttered, knowing the man would never hear him. Horeb turned away, cursed, then removed his leather apron and grasped a half-empty jug of ale and a tankard. As an afterthought he opened a small cupboard and removed a bottle of port he had been saving for Nessa's wedding.

'A problem shared is a problem doubled,' he said, squeezing into the seat opposite Rek.

'A friend in need is a friend to be avoided,' Rek countered, accepting the proffered bottle and refilling his glass. 'I knew a general once,' he said, staring at the wine, twirling the glass slowly with his long fingers. 'Never lost a battle. Never won one either.'

'How so?' asked Horeb.

'You know the answer. I've told you before.'

'I have a bad memory. Anyway, I like to listen to you tell stories. How could he never lose and never win?'

'He surrendered whenever threatened,' said Rek. 'Clever, eh?'

'How come men followed him if he never won?'

'Because he never lost. Neither did they.'

'Would you have followed him?' asked Horeb.

'I don't follow anyone any more. Least of all generals.' Rek turned his head, listening to the interweaving chatter. He closed his eyes, concentrating. 'Listen to them,' he said, softly. 'Listen to their talk of glory.'

'They don't know any better, Rek, my friend. They haven't seen it, tasted it. Crows like a black cloud over a battlefield feasting on dead men's eyes, foxes jerking at severed tendons, worms . . .'

'Stop it, damn you . . . I don't need reminding. Well, I'm damned if I'll go. When's Nessa getting married?'

'In three days,' answered Horeb. 'He's a good boy, he'll look after her. Keeps baking her cakes. She'll be like a tub before long.'

'One way or another,' said Rek, with a wink.

'Indeed yes,' answered Horeb, grinning broadly. The men sat in their own silence allowing the noise to wash over them, each drinking and thinking, secure within their circle of two. After a while Rek leaned forward.

'The first attack will be at Dros Delnoch,' he said. 'Do you know they've only 10,000 men there?'

'I heard it was less than that. Abalayn's been cutting back on the regulars and concentrating on militia. Still, there're six high walls and a strong keep. And Delnar's no fool – he was at the battle of Skeln.'

'Really?' said Rek. 'I heard that was one man against ten thousand, hurling mountains on the foe.'

'The saga of Druss the Legend,' said Horeb, deepening his voice. 'The tale of a giant whose eyes were death, and whose axe was terror. Gather round, children, and keep from the shadows lest evil lurks as I tell my tale.'

'You bastard!' said Rek. 'That used to terrify me. You knew him, didn't you – the Legend, I mean?'

'A long time ago. They say he's dead. If not, he must be over sixty. We were in three campaigns together, but I only spoke to him twice. I saw him in action once, though.'

'Was he good?' asked Rek.

'Awesome. It was just before Skeln and the defeat of the Immortals. Just a skirmish really. Yes, he was very good.'

'You're not terribly strong on detail, Horeb.'

'You want me to sound like the rest of these fools, jabbering about war and death and slaying?'

'No,' said Rek, draining his wine. 'No, I don't. You know me, don't you?'

'Enough to like you. Regardless.'

'Regardless of what?'

'Regardless of the fact that you don't like yourself.'

'On the contrary,' said Rek, pouring a fresh glass, 'I like myself well enough. It's just that I know myself better than most people.'

'You know, Rek, sometimes I think you ask too much of yourself.'

'No. No, I ask very little. I know my weaknesses.'

'It's a funny thing about weakness,' said Horeb. 'Most people will tell you they know their weaknesses. When asked, they tell you, "Well, for one thing I'm over-generous." Come on then, list yours if you must. That's what innkeepers are for.'

'Well, for one thing I'm over-generous – especially to innkeepers.'

Horeb shook his head, smiled and lapsed into silence.

Too intelligent to be a hero, too frightened to be a coward, he thought. He watched his friend empty his glass, lift it to his face and peer at his own fragmented image. For a moment Horeb thought he would smash it, such had been the anger on Rek's flushed face.

Then the younger man gently returned the goblet to the wooden table.

'I'm not a fool,' he said, softly. He stiffened as he realised he had spoken aloud. 'Damn!' he said. 'The drink finally got to me.'

'Let me give you a hand to your room,' offered Horeb.

'Is there a candle lit?' asked Rek, swaying in his seat.

'Of course.'

'You won't let it go out on me, will you? Not keen on the dark. Not frightened, you understand. Just don't like it.'

'I won't let it go out, Rek. Trust me.'

'I trust you. I rescued you, didn't I? Remember?'

'I remember. Give me your arm. I'll guide you to the stairs. This way. That's good. One foot in front of the other. Good!'

'I didn't hesitate. Straight in with my sword raised, didn't I?'

'Yes.'

'No, I didn't. I stood for two minutes shaking. And you got cut.'

'But you still came in, Rek. Don't you see? It didn't matter about the cut – you still rescued me.'

'It matters to me. Is there a candle in my room?'

265

Behind him was the fortress, grim and grey, outlined in flame and smoke. The sounds of battle filled his ears and he ran, heart pounding, his breathing ragged. He glanced behind him. The fortress was close, closer than it had been. Ahead were the green hills sheltering the Sentran Plain. They shimmered and retreated before him, taunting him with their tranquillity. He ran faster. A shadow fell across him. The gates of the fortress opened. He strained against the force pulling him back. He cried and begged. But the gates closed and he was back at the centre of the battle, a bloody sword in his shaking hand.

He awoke, eyes wide, nostrils flared, the beginning of a scream swelling his lungs. A soft hand stroked his face and gentle words soothed him. His eyes focused. Dawn was nearing, the pink light of a virgin day piercing the ice on the inside of the bedroom window. He rolled over.

'You were troubled in the night,' Besa told him, her hand stroking his brow. He smiled, pulled the goose-down quilt over his shoulder and drew her to him under the covers.

'I'm not troubled now,' said Rek. 'How could I be?' The warmth of her body aroused him and his fingers caressed her back.

'Not today,' she said, kissing him lightly on the forehead and pulling away. She threw back the quilt, shivered and ran across the room, gathering her clothes. 'It's cold,' she said. 'Colder than yesterday.'

'It's warm in here,' he offered, raising himself to watch her dress. She blew him a kiss.

'You're fine to romp with, Rek. But I'll have no children by you. Now, get out of that bed. We've a party of travellers coming in this morning and the room is let.'

'You're a beautiful woman, Besa. If I had any sense, I'd marry you.'

'Then it's a good job you have none, for I'd turn you down and your ego would never stand it. I'm looking for someone more solid.' Her smile took the sting from her words. Almost.

The door opened and Horeb bustled in bearing a copper tray containing bread, cheese and a tankard.

'How's the head?' he asked, placing the tray on the wooden table by the bed.

'Fine,' said Rek. 'Is that orange juice?'

'It is, and it'll cost you dear. Nessa waylaid the Vagrian trader as he left the ship. She waited an hour and risked frostbite just to get oranges for you. I don't think you're worth it.'

'True,' smiled Rek. 'Sad but true.'

'Are you really heading south today?' asked Besa, as Rek sipped his fruit juice. He nodded. 'You're a fool. I thought you'd had enough of Reinard.'

'I'll avoid him. Are my clothes cleaned?'

'Dori spent hours on them,' said Besa. 'And for what? So that you can get them filthy in Graven Forest.'

'That's not the point. One should always look one's best when leaving a city.' He glanced at the tray. 'I can't face the cheese.'

'Doesn't matter,' said Horeb. 'It's still on the bill!'

'In that case I'll force myself to eat it. Any other travellers today?'

'There's a spices caravan heading for Lentria – that will go through Graven. Twenty men, well-armed. They're taking the circular route south and west. There's a woman travelling alone – but she's already left,' said Horeb. 'Lastly there's a group of pilgrims. But they don't leave until tomorrow.'

'A woman?'

'Not quite,' said Besa. 'But almost.'

'Now, girl,' said Horeb, smiling broadly, 'it's not like you to be catty. A tall girl with a fine horse. And she's armed.'

'I could have travelled with her,' said Rek. 'It might have made the journey more pleasant.'

'And she could have protected you from Reinard,' said Besa. 'She looked the part. Now come on, Regnak, get dressed. I've not the time to sit here and watch you breakfast like a lord. You've caused enough chaos in this house.'

'I can't get up while you're here,' protested Rek. 'It wouldn't be decent.'

'You idiot,' she said, gathering up the tray. 'Get him up, father, else he'll lie there all day.'

'She's right, Rek,' said Horeb, as the door closed behind her. 'It's time for you to move, and knowing how long it takes you to prepare your public appearance I think I'll leave you to get on with it.'

'One must look one's best . . .'

'. . . when leaving a city. I know. That's what you always say, Rek. I'll see you downstairs.'

Once alone Rek's manner changed, the laughter lines about his eyes easing into marks of tension, sorrow almost. The Drenai were finished as a world power. Ulric and the Nadir tribes had already begun their march upon Drenan and they would ride into the cities of the plains on rivers of blood. Should every Drenai warrior kill thirty tribesmen, still there would be hundreds of thousands left.

The world was changing and Rek was running out of places to hide.

He thought of Horeb and his daughters. For six hundred years the Drenai race had stamped civilisation on a world ill suited to it. They had conquered savagely, taught wisely and, in the main, ruled well. But they had arrived at their sunset and a new empire was waiting, ready to rise from the blood and ashes of the old. He thought again of Horeb and laughed. Whatever happens, there is one old man who will survive, he thought. Even the Nadir need good inns. And the daughters? How would they fare when the hordes burst the city gates? Bloody images flooded his mind.

'Damn!' he shouted, rolling from the bed to push open the ice-sealed window.

The winter wind struck his bed-warmed body, snatching his mind back to the reality of today and the long ride south. He crossed to the bench on which his clothes had been laid out and swiftly dressed. The white woollen undershirt and the blue hose were gifts from gentle Dori; the tunic with gold embroidered collar a legacy of better days in Vagria; the reversed sheepskin jerkin and gold ties a present from Horeb and the thigh-length doeskin boots a surprise gift from a weary traveller at an outland inn. And he must have been surprised, thought Rek, remembering the thrill of fear and excitement as he had crept into the man's room to steal them only a month since. By the wardrobe stood a full-length bronze mirror, where Rek took a long look at his reflection. He saw a tall man, with shoulder-length brown hair and a well-trimmed moustache, cutting a fine figure in his stolen boots. He looped his baldric over his head and placed his longsword in the black and silver sheath.

'What a hero,' he told his reflection, a cynical smile on his lips. 'What a gem of a hero.' He drew the sword and parried and thrust at the air, one eye on his reflection. The wrist was still supple, the grasp sure. Whatever else you are not, he told himself, you are a swordsman. From the sill by the window he took the silver circlet talisman – his good luck charm since he stole it from a brothel in Lentria – and placed it over his forehead, sweeping his dark hair back over his ears.

'You may not actually be magnificent,' he told his reflection, 'but by all the gods in Missael you *look* it!'

The eyes smiled back at him. 'Don't you mock me, Regnak Wanderer,' he said. Throwing his cloak over his arm, he strolled downstairs to the long room, casting an eye over the early crowd. Horeb hailed him from the bar.

'Now that's more like it, Rek my lad,' he said, leaning back in mock admiration. 'You could have stepped straight from one of Serbar's poems. Drink?'

'No. I think I will leave it a while yet – like ten years. Last night's brew is still fermenting in my gullet. Have you packed me some of your vile food for the journey?'

'Maggoty biscuits, mildewed cheese and a two-year-old back of bacon that will come when you call it,' answered Horeb. 'And a flask of the worst . . .'

Conversation ceased as the seer entered the inn, his faded blue habit flapping against bony legs, his quarterstaff tapping on the wooden boards. Rek swallowed his disgust at the man's appearance and avoided glancing at the ruined sockets where once the man's eyes had been.

The old man pushed out a hand of which the third finger was missing. 'Silver for your future,' he said, his voice like a dry wind whispering through winter branches.

'Why do they do it?' whispered Horeb.

'Their eyes, you mean?' countered Rek.

'Yes. How can a man put out his own eyes?'

'Damned if I know. They say it aids their visions.'

'Sounds about as sensible as cutting off your staff in order to aid your sex life.'

'It takes all sorts, Horeb old friend.'

Drawn by the sound of their voices the old man hobbled nearer, hand outstretched. 'Silver for your future,' he intoned. Rek turned away.

'Go on, Rek,' urged Horeb. 'See if the journey bodes well. Where's the harm?'

'You pay. I will listen,' said Rek.

Horeb thrust a hand deep into the pocket of his leather apron and dropped a small silver coin into the old man's palm. 'For my friend here,' he said. 'I know my future.'

The old man squatted on the wooden floor and reached into a tattered pouch, producing a fistful of sand which he sprinkled about him. Then he produced six knuckle-bones bearing crafted runes.

'They're human bones, aren't they?' whispered Horeb.

'So they say,' answered Rek. The old man began to chant in the Elder tongue, his quavering voice echoing in the silence. He threw the bones to the sandy floor, then ran his hands over the runes.

'I have the truth,' he said at last.

'Never mind the truth, old man. Give me a tale full of golden lies and glorious maidens.'

'I have the truth,' said the seer, as if he had not heard.

'The hell with it!' said Rek. 'Tell me the truth, old man.'

'Do you desire to hear it, Man?'

'Never mind the damned ritual, just speak and begone!'

'Steady, Rek, steady! It's his way,' said Horeb.

'Maybe. But he's going a long way towards spoiling my day. They never give good news anyway. The old bastard's probably going to tell me I shall catch the plague.'

'He wishes the truth,' said Horeb, following the ritual, 'and will use it wisely and well.'

'Indeed he does not and will not,' said the seer. 'But destiny must be heard. You do not wish to hear words of your death, Regnak the Wanderer, son of Argas, and so I will withhold them. You are a man of uncertain character and only a sporadic courage. You are a thief and a dreamer and your destiny will both haunt and hunt you. You will run to avoid it, yet your steps will carry you towards it. But then this you know, Longshanks, for you dreamt it yester-eve.'

'Is that it, old man? That meaningless garbage? Is that fair trading for a silver coin?'

'The earl and the legend will be together at the wall. And men shall dream, and men shall die, but shall the fortress fall?'

The old man turned and was gone.

'What was your dream last night, Rek?' asked Horeb.

'You surely don't believe that idiocy, Horeb?'

'What was your dream?' the innkeeper persisted.

'I didn't dream at all. I slept like a log. Except for that bloody candle. You left it on all night and it stank. You must be more careful. It could have started a fire. Every time I stop here, I warn you about those candles. You never listen.'

2

Rek watched in silence as the groom saddled the chestnut gelding. He didn't like the horse – it had a mean eye and its ears lay flat against its skull. The groom, a young slim boy, was crooning gently to it as his shaking fingers tightened the girth.

'Why couldn't you get a grey?' asked Rek. Horeb laughed.

'Because it would have taken you one step too many towards farce. Understatement is the thing, Rek. You already look like a peacock and as it is, every Lentrian sailor will be chasing you. No, a chestnut's the thing.' More seriously he added, 'And in Graven you may wish to be inconspicuous. A tall white horse is not easily missed.'

'I don't think it likes me. See the way it looks at me?'

'Its sire was one of the fastest horses in Drenan; its dam was a war horse in Woundweaver's lancers. You couldn't get a better pedigree.'

'What is it called?' asked Rek, still unconvinced.

'Lancer,' answered Horeb.

'That has a nice ring to it. Lancer . . . Well, maybe . . . just maybe.'

'Daffodil's ready, sir,' said the groom, backing away from the chestnut. The horse swung its head, snapping at the retreating boy who stumbled and fell on the cobbles.

'Daffodil?' said Rek. 'You bought me a horse called *Daffodil*?'

'What's in a name, Rek?' answered Horeb innocently. 'Call it what you like – you must admit it's a fine beast.'

'If I didn't have a fine sense for the ridiculous, I would have it muzzled. Where are the girls?'

'Too busy to be waving goodbye to layabouts who rarely pay their bills. Now, be off with you.'

Rek advanced gingerly towards the gelding, speaking softly. It turned a baleful eye on him, but allowed him to swing into the high-backed saddle. He gathered the reins, adjusted his blue cloak to just the right angle over the horse's back and swung the beast towards the gate.

'Rek, I almost forgot . . .' called Horeb, pushing back towards the house. 'Wait a moment!' The burly innkeeper disappeared from sight, emerging seconds later carrying a short bow of horn and elm and a quiver of black-shafted arrows. 'Here. A customer left this behind in part payment some months ago. It looks a sturdy weapon.'

'Wonderful,' said Rek. 'I used to be a fine bowman.'

'Yes,' said Horeb. 'Just remember when you use it that the sharp end is pointed away from you. Now begone – and take care.'

'Thanks, Horeb. You too. And remember what I said about candles.'

'I will. On your way, boy. Be lucky now.'

Rek rode from the south gate as the watchmen trimmed the lantern wicks. The dawn shadows were shrinking on the streets of Drenan and young children played beneath the portcullis. He had chosen the southern route for the most obvious of reasons. The Nadir were marching from the North and the fastest way from a battle was a straight line in the opposite direction.

Flicking his heels, he urged the gelding forward towards the south. To his left the rising sun was breasting the blue peaks of the eastern mountains. The sky was blue, birds sang and the sounds of an awakening city came from behind him. But the sun was rising, Rek knew, on the Nadir. For the Drenai it was dusk on the last day.

Topping a rise he gazed down on Graven Forest, white and virginal under the winter snow. And yet it was a place of evil legends which normally he would have avoided. The fact that instead he chose to enter showed he knew two things: first, the legends were built around the activities of a living man; second, he knew that man.

Reinard.

He and his band of bloodthirsty cut-throats had their headquarters in Graven and were an open, festering sore in the body of trade. Caravans were sacked, pilgrims were murdered, women were raped. Yet an army could not seek them out, so vast was the forest.

Reinard. Sired by a prince of Hell, born to a noblewoman of Ulalia. Or so he told it. Rek had heard that his mother was a Lentrian whore and his father a nameless sailor. He had never repeated this intelligence – he did not, as the phrase went, have the guts for it. Even if he had, he mused, he would not keep them long once he tried it. One of Reinard's favourite pastimes with prisoners was to roast sections of them over hot coals and serve the meat to those poor unfortunates taken prisoner with them. If he met Reinard, the best thing would be to flatter the hell out of him. And if that didn't work, to give him the latest news, send him in the direction of the nearest caravan and ride swiftly from his domain.

Rek had made sure he knew the details of all the caravans passing through Graven and their probable routes. Silks, jewels, spices, slaves, cattle. In truth he had no wish to part with this information. Nothing would please him better than to ride through Graven quietly, knowing the caravanners' fate was in the lap of the gods.

The chestnut's hooves made little sound on the snow, and Rek kept the pace to a gentle walk in case hidden roots should cause the horse to stumble. The cold began to work its way through his warm clothing and his feet were soon feeling frozen within the doeskin boots. He reached into his pack and pulled out a pair of sheepskin mittens.

The horse plodded on. At noon, Rek stopped for a brief cold meal, hobbling the gelding by a frozen stream. With a thick Vagrian dagger he chipped away the ice, allowing the beast to drink, then gave him a handful of oats. He stroked the long neck and the chestnut's head came up sharply, teeth bared. Rek leapt backwards, falling into a deep snowdrift. He lay there for a moment, then smiled.

'I knew you didn't like me,' he said. The horse turned to look at him and snorted.

As he was about to mount, Rek glanced at the horse's hind-quarters. Deep switch scars showed by the tail.

Gently, his hand moved over them. 'So,' he said, 'someone took a whip to you, eh, Daffodil? Didn't break your spirit did they, boy?' He swung into the saddle. With luck, he reckoned, he should be free of the forest in five days.

Gnarled oaks with twisted roots cast ominous dusk shadows across the track and night breezes set the branches to whispering as Rek walked the gelding deeper into the forest. The moon was rising above the trees, casting a ghostly light on the trail. Teeth chattering, he began to cast about for a good camping site, finding one an hour later in a small hollow by an ice-covered pool. He built a stall in some bushes to keep the worst of the wind from the horse, fed it and then built a small fire by a fallen oak and a large boulder. Out of the wind, the heat reflected from the stone, Rek brewed tea to help down his dried beef; then he pulled his blanket over his shoulders, leaned against the oak and watched the flames dance.

A skinny fox poked its snout through a bush, peering at the fire. On impulse, Rek threw it a strip of beef. The animal flicked its eyes from the man to the morsel and back again, before darting out to snatch the meat from the frozen ground. Then it vanished into the night. Rek held out his hands to the fire and thought of Horeb.

The burly innkeeper had raised him after Rek's father had been killed in the northern wars against the Sathuli. Honest, loyal, strong and dependable – Horeb was all of these. And he was kind, a prince among men.

Rek had managed to repay him one well-remembered night when three Vagrian deserters had attacked him in an alley near the inn.

Luckily Rek had been drinking and when he first heard the sound of steel on steel he had rushed forward. Within the alley Horeb was fighting a losing battle, his kitchen knife no match for three swordsmen. Yet the old man had been a warrior and moved well. Rek had been frozen to the spot, his own sword forgotten. He tried to move forward, but his legs refused the order. Then a sword had cut through Horeb's guard, opening a huge wound in his leg.

Rek had screamed and the sound had released his terror.

The bloody skirmish was over in seconds. Rek took out the first assailant with a throat slash, parried a thrust from the second and shoulder-charged the third into a wall. From the ground Horeb grabbed the third man, pulling him down and stabbing out with his kitchen knife. The second man fled into the night.

'You were wonderful, Rek,' said Horeb. 'Believe me, you fight like a veteran.'

Veterans don't freeze with fear, thought Rek.

Now he fed some twigs to the flames. A cloud obscured the moon, an owl hooted. Rek's shaking hand curled round his dagger.

Damn the dark, he thought. And curse all heroes!

He had been a soldier for a while, stationed at Dros Corteswain, and had enjoyed it. But then the Sathuli skirmishes had become border war and the enjoyment palled. He had done well, been promoted; his senior officers had told him he had a fine feel for tactics. But they did not know about the sleepless nights. His men had respected him, he thought. But that was because he was careful – even cautious. He had left before his nerve could betray him.

'Are you mad, Rek?' Gan Javi had asked him when he resigned his commission. 'The war is expanding. We've got more troops coming and a fine officer like you can be sure of promotion. You'll lead more than a century in six months. You could be offered the Gan eagle.'

'I know all that, sir – and believe me, I'm really sorry I shall be missing the action. But it's a question of family business. Damn, I would cut off my right arm to stay, you know that.'

'I do, boy. And we'll miss you, by Missael. Your troop will be shattered. If you change your mind there will be a place for you here. Any time. You're a born soldier.'

'I'll remember that, sir. Thank you for all your help and encouragement.'

'One more thing, Rek,' said Gan Javi, leaning back in his carved chair. 'You know there are rumours that the Nadir are preparing a march on the south?'

'There are always rumours of that, sir,' answered Rek.

'I know, they've been circulating for years. But this Ulric is a canny one. He's conquered most of the tribes now and I think he's almost ready.'

'But Abalayn has just signed a treaty with him,' said Rek. 'Mutual peace in return for trade concessions and finance for his building programme.'

'That's what I mean, lad. I'll say nothing against Abalayn, he's ruled the Drenai for twenty years. But you don't stop a wolf by feeding it – believe me! Anyway, what I'm saying is that men like yourselves will be needed before long, so don't get rusty.'

The last thing the Drenai needed now was a man who was afraid of the dark. What they needed was another Karnak the One-eyed – a score of them. An Earl of Bronze. A hundred like Druss the Legend. And even if, by some miracle, this were to happen, would even these stem the tide of half a million tribesmen?

Who could even picture such a number?

They would wash over Dros Delnoch like an angry sea, Rek knew.

If I thought there was a chance, I still wouldn't go. Face it, he thought. Even if victory was certain, still he would avoid the battle.

Who will care in a hundred years whether the Drenai survived? It would be like Skeln Pass, shrouded in legend and glorified beyond truth.

War!

Flies settling like a black stain over a man's entrails as he weeps with the pain and holds his body together with crimson fingers, hoping for a miracle. Hunger, cold, fear, disease, gangrene, death!

War for soldiers.

The day he left Dros Corteswain he was approached by one of the Culs, who nervously offered him a tight-wrapped bundle.

'From the troop, sir,' he said.

He had opened it, embarrassed and empty of words, to see a blue cloak with an eagle clasp in crafted bronze.

'I don't know how to thank you all.'

'The men want me to say . . . well, we're sorry you're leaving. That's all, sir.'

'I'm sorry too, Korvac. Family business, you know?'

The man had nodded, probably wishing he had family business which would allow him to depart the Dros. But Culs had no commission to resign – only the Dun class could leave a fortress during a war.

'Well, good luck, sir. See you soon, I hope . . . we all hope.'

'Yes! Soon.'

That was two years ago. Gan Javi had died from a stroke and several of Rek's brother officers had been killed in the Sathuli battles. No message reached him of individual Culs.

The days passed – cold, gloomy, but mercifully without incident until the morning of the fifth day when, on a high trail skirting a grove of elm, he heard the one sound he disliked above all others – the clash of steel on steel. He should have ridden on, he *knew* he should. But for some reason his curiosity fractionally outweighed his fear. He hobbled the horse, swung the quiver to his back and strung the horn bow. Then carefully he worked his way through the trees and down into the snow-covered glen. Moving stealthily, with catlike care, he came to a clearing. Sounds of battle echoed in the glade.

A young woman, in armour of silver and bronze, stood with her back to a tree, desperately fending off a combined assault from three outlaws, burly men and bearded, armed with swords and daggers. The woman held a slender blade, a flickering, dancing rapier that cut and thrust with devastating speed.

The three, clumsy swordsmen at best, were hampering each other. But the girl was tiring fast.

These were Reinard's men, Rek knew, cursing his own curiosity. One of them cried out as the rapier lanced across his forearm.

'Take that, you dung beetle,' shouted the girl.

Rek smiled. No beauty, but she could fence.

He notched an arrow to his bow and waited for the right moment to let fly. The girl ducked under a vicious cut and flashed her blade through the eye of the swordsman. As he screamed and fell the other two fell back, more wary now; they moved apart, ready to attack from both flanks. The girl had been dreading this moment, for there was no defence but flight. Her gaze flickered from man to man. Take the tall one first, forget about the other and hope his first thrust is not mortal. *Maybe* she could take them both with her.

The tall one moved to the left while his comrade crossed to the right. At this moment Rek loosed a shaft at the tall outlaw's back, which lanced through his left calf. Swiftly he notched a second arrow, as the bewildered man spun round, saw Rek and hobbled towards him, screaming hatred.

Rek drew back the string until it touched his cheek, locked his left arm and loosed the shaft.

This time the aim was slightly better. He had been aiming for the chest – the largest target – but the arrow was high and now the outlaw lay on his back, the black shaft jutting from his forehead and blood bubbling to the snow.

'You took your time getting involved,' said the girl coolly, stepping across the body of the third outlaw and wiping her slender blade on his shirt.

Rek tore his eyes from the face of the man he had killed.

'I just saved your life,' he said, checking an angry retort.

She was tall and well-built – almost mannish, Rek thought; her hair long and mousy blonde, unkempt. Her eyes were blue and deep-set beneath thick dark brows which indicated an uncertain temper. Her figure was disguised by the silver steel mailshirt and bronze shoulder pads; her legs encased in shapeless green woollen troos laced to the thigh with leather straps.

'Well, what are you staring at?' she demanded. 'Never seen a woman before?'

'Well, that answers the first question,' he said.

'What does that mean?'

'You're a woman.'

'Oh, very dry!' She retrieved a sheepskin jerkin from beneath the tree, dusting off the snow and slipping it on. It did nothing to enhance her appearance, thought Rek.

'They attacked me,' she said. 'Killed my horse, the bastards! Where's your horse?'

'Your gratitude overwhelms me,' said Rek, an edge of anger in his voice. 'Those are Reinard's men.'

'Really? Friend of yours, is he?'

'Not exactly. But if he knew what I had done he would roast my eyes on a fire and serve them to me as an appetiser.'

'All right, I appreciate your point. I'm extremely grateful. Now, where's your horse?'

Rek ignored her, gritting his teeth against his anger. He walked to the dead outlaw and dragged his arrows clear, wiping them on the man's jerkin. Then he methodically searched the pockets of all three. Seven silver coins and several gold rings the richer, he then returned to the girl.

'My horse has one saddle. I ride it,' he said, icily. 'I've done about all I want to do for you. You're on your own now.'

'Damned chivalrous of you,' she said.

'Chivalry isn't my strong point,' he said, turning away.

'Neither is marksmanship,' she retorted.

'What?'

'You were aiming for his back from twenty paces and you hit his leg. It's because you closed one eye – ruined your perspective.'

'Thanks for the archery instruction. Good luck!'

'Wait!' she said. He turned. 'I need your horse.'

'So do I.'

'I will pay you.'

'He's not for sale.'

'All right. Then I will pay you to take me to where I can buy a horse.'

'How much?' he asked.

'One golden Raq.'

'Five,' he said.

'I could buy three horses for that,' she stormed.

'It's a seller's market,' he retorted.

'Two – and that's final.'

'Three.'

'All right, three. Now, where's your horse?'

'First the money, my lady.' He held out a hand. Her blue eyes were frosty as she removed the coins from a leather pouch and placed them in his palm. 'My name is Regnak – Rek to my friends,' he said.

'That's of no interest to me,' she assured him.

3

They rode in a silence as frosty as the weather, the tall girl behind Rek in the saddle. He resisted the urge to spur the horse on at speed, despite the fear gnawing at his belly. It would be unfair to say he was sorry he had rescued her – after all, it had done wonders for his self-esteem. His fear was of meeting Reinard now. This girl would never sit silent while he flattered and lied. And even if, by some stroke of good fortune, she did keep her mouth shut, she would certainly report him for giving information on caravan movements.

The horse stumbled on a hidden root and the girl pitched sideways. Rek's hand lanced out, catching her arm and hauling her back in the saddle.

'Put your arms around my waist, will you?' he said.

'How much will it cost me?'

'Just do it. It's too cold to argue.'

Her arms slid round him, her head resting against his back.

Thick, dark clouds bunched above them and the temperature began to drop.

'We ought to make an early camp,' he stated. 'The weather's closing in.'

'I agree,' she said.

Snow began to fall and the wind picked up. Rek dipped his head against the force of the storm, blinking against the cold flakes that blew into his eyes. He steered the gelding away from the trail and into the shelter of the trees, gripping the pommel of his saddle as the horse climbed a steep incline.

An open camp-site would be folly, he knew, in this freak storm. They needed a cave, or at least the lee of a rock face. For over an hour they moved on until at last they entered a clearing circled by oak and gorse. Within it was a crofter's hut of log walls and earthen roof. Rek glanced at the stone chimney: no smoke.

He heeled the tired gelding forward. At the side of the hut was a three-sided lean-to, with a wicker roof bent by the weight of the snow upon it. He steered the horse inside.

'Dismount,' he told the girl, but her hands did not move from his waist. He glanced down. The hands were blue and he rubbed at them furiously. 'Wake up!' he shouted. 'Wake up, damn you!' Pulling her hands free, he slid from the saddle and caught her as she fell. Her lips were blue, her hair thick with ice. Lifting her over one shoulder he removed the packs from the gelding, loosened the girth and carried the girl to the hut. The wooden door was open, snow drifting into the cold interior as he stepped inside.

The hut was one-roomed: he saw a cot in the corner beneath the only window, a hearth, some simple cupboards and a wood store – enough for two, maybe three nights – stacked against the far wall. There were three crudely made chairs and a bench table roughly cut from an elm trunk. Rek tipped the unconscious girl on to the cot, found a stick broom under the table and swept the snow from the room. He pushed the door shut, but a rotten leather hinge gave way and it tilted open again at the top. Cursing, he pulled the table to the doorway and heaved it against the frame.

Tearing open his pack, Rek pulled his tinder-box free and moved to the hearth. Whoever had owned or built the holding had left a fire ready laid, as was the custom in the wild. Rek opened his small tinder-pouch, making a mound of shredded dry leaves beneath the twigs in the grate. Over this he poured a little lantern oil from a leather flask and then struck his flint. His cold fingers were clumsy and the sparks would not take, so he stopped for a moment, forcing himself to take slow deep breaths. Then again he struck the flint and this time a small flame flickered in the tinder and caught. He leaned forward, gently blowing it, then as the twigs flared he turned to sort smaller branches from the store, placing them gently atop the tiny fire. Flames danced higher.

He carried two chairs to the hearth, placed his blankets over them before the blaze and returned to the girl. She lay on the crude cot, scarcely breathing.

'It's the bloody armour,' he said. He fumbled with the straps of her jerkin, turning her over to pull it loose. Swiftly he stripped off her clothing and set to work rubbing warmth into her. He glanced at the fire, placed three more logs to feed the blaze and then spread the blankets on the floor before it. Lifting the girl from the cot, he laid her before the hearth, turning her over to rub her back.

'Don't you die on me!' he stormed, pummelling the flesh of her legs. '-Don't you damn well dare!' He wiped her hair with a towel and wrapped her in the blankets. The floor was cold, frost seeped up from beneath the hut, so he pulled the cot to the hearth, then strained to lift her on to the bed. Her pulse was slow, but steady.

He gazed down at her face. It was beautiful. Not in any classic sense, he knew, for the brows were too thick and thunderous, the chin too square and the lips too full. Yet there was strength there, and courage and determination. But more than this: in sleep a gentle, childlike quality found expression.

He kissed her gently.

Buttoning his sheepskin jacket, he pulled the table aside and stepped out into the storm. The gelding snorted as he approached. There was straw in the lean-to; taking a handful he rubbed the horse's back.

'Going to be a cold night, boy. But you should be all right in here.' He spread the saddle blanket over the gelding's broad back, fed him some oats and returned to the hut.

The girl's colour was better now, and she slept peacefully.

Searching the cupboards, Rek found an old iron pan. Unclipping the canvas and steel canteen from his pack, he took out a pound of dried beef and set about making soup. He was warmer now, and removed his cloak and jacket. Outside the wind beat against the walls as the storm's fury grew, but inside the fire blazed warmth and a soft red light filled the cabin. Rek pulled off his boots and rubbed his toes. He felt good. Alive.

And damned hungry!

He took a leather-covered clay mug from his pack and tried the soup. The girl stirred and he toyed with the idea of waking her, but dismissed it. As she was, she was lovely. Awake, she was a harridan. She rolled over and moaned, a long leg pushing from the blanket. Rek grinned as he remembered her body. Not at all mannish! She was just big – but wonderfully proportioned. He stared at her leg, the smile fading. He pictured himself naked alongside her . . .

'No, no, Rek,' he said aloud. 'Forget it.'

He covered her with the blanket and returned to his soup. Be prepared, he told himself. When she wakes she will accuse you of taking advantage of her and cut your eyes out.

Taking his cloak, he wrapped it around himself and stretched out beside the fire. The floor was warmer now. Adding some logs to the blaze, he pillowed his head on his arm and watched the dancers in the flames circle and jump, twist and turn . . .

He slept.

He awoke to the smell of frying bacon. The hut was warm and his arm felt swollen and cramped. He stretched, groaned and sat up. The girl was nowhere in sight. Then the door opened and she stepped inside, brushing snow from her jerkin.

'I've seen to your horse,' she said. 'Are you fit to eat?'

'Yes. What time is it?'

'Sun's been up for about three hours. The snow's letting up.'

He pushed his aching body upright, stretching the tight muscles of his back. 'Too much time in Drenan in soft beds,' he commented.

'That probably accounts for the paunch,' she noted.

'Paunch? I've a curved spine. Anyway, it's relaxed muscle.' He looked down. 'All right, it's a paunch. A few more days of this and it will go.'

'I don't doubt it,' she said. 'Anyway, we were lucky to find this place.'

'Yes, we were.' The conversation died as she turned the bacon. Rek was uncomfortable in the silence and they began to speak at the same time.

'This is ridiculous,' she said finally.

'Yes,' he agreed. 'Bacon smells good.'

'Look . . . I want to thank you. There – it's said.'

'It was a pleasure. What about starting again, as if we had never met? My name is Rek.' He held out a hand.

'Virae,' she said, grasping his wrist in the warrior's grip.

'My pleasure,' he said. 'And what brings you to Graven Forest, Virae?'

'None of your damned business,' she snapped.

'I thought we were starting afresh?' he said.

279

'I'm sorry. Really! Look, it's not easy being friendly – I don't like you very much.'

'How can you say that? We've only said about ten words to each other. A bit early for character assessment, isn't it?'

'I know your kind,' she said. Taking two platters, she deftly flipped the bacon from the pan and handed him a plate. 'Arrogant. Think you're the gods' gift to the world. Footloose.'

'And what's wrong with that?' he asked. 'Nobody's perfect. I enjoy my life, it's the only one I've got.'

'It's people like you who have wrecked this country,' she told him. 'People who don't care; people who live for today. The greedy and the selfish. We used to be great.'

'Rubbish. We used to be warriors, conquering everybody, stamping Drenai rules on the world. A pox on it!'

'There was nothing wrong with that! The people we conquered prosper-ed, didn't they? We built schools, hospitals, roads. We encouraged trade and gave the world Drenai law.'

'Then you shouldn't be too upset,' he told her, 'that the world is changing. Now it will be Nadir law. The only reason the Drenai conquered was that the outlying nations had had their day. They were fat and lazy, full of selfish, greedy people who didn't care. All nations fall that way.'

'Oh, so you're a philosopher, are you?' she said. 'Well, I consider your opinions to be as worthless as you are.'

'Oh, now I'm worthless? What do you know of "worthless", prancing around dressed as a man? You're an imitation warrior. If you're so eager to uphold Drenai values, why don't you get off to Dros Delnoch with the other fools and wave your pretty little sword at the Nadir?'

'I've just come from there – and I'm going back as soon as I have accomplished what I set out to do,' she said, icily.

'Then you're an idiot,' he said, lamely.

'You were a soldier, weren't you?' she said.

'What's that to you?'

'Why did you leave the army?'

'None of your damned business.' He paused. Then, to break the awk-ward silence, went on, 'We should be at Glen Frenae by this afternoon; it's only a small village, but they do sell horses.'

They finished their meal without speaking, Rek feeling angry and uncomfortable yet lacking the skill to pierce the gap between them. She cleared the platters and cleaned out the pan, awkward in her mail-shirt.

Virae was furious with herself. She had not meant to quarrel with him. For hours as he slept she had crept about the cabin so as not to disturb him. At first when she woke she had been angry and embarrassed by what he had done, but she knew enough about frostbite and exposure to realise he had saved her life. And he had not taken advantage. If he had done so, she would have killed him without regret or hesitation. She had studied him as he slept. In a strange way he was handsome, she thought, then decided that although he was good-looking after a fashion, it was some indefinable quality which made him attractive – a gentleness, perhaps? A certain sensitivity? It was hard to pinpoint.

Why should he be so attractive? It angered her, she had no time now for romance. Then a bitter thought struck her: she had never had time for romance. Or was it that romance had never had time for her? She was clumsy as a woman, unsure of herself in the company of men – unless in combat or comradeship. His words came again in her mind: 'What do you know of "worthless", prancing around dressed as a man?'

Twice he had saved her life. Why had she said she disliked him? Because she was frightened?

She heard him walk from the hut, and then a strange voice.

'Regnak, my dear! Is it true you have a woman inside?'

She reached for her sword.

4

The Abbot placed his hands on the head of the young albino kneeling before him and closed his eyes. He spoke, mind to mind, in the manner of the Order.

'Are you prepared?'

'How can I tell?' answered the albino.

'Release your mind to me,' said the Abbot. The young man relaxed his control; in his mind the image of the Abbot's kindly face overlapped his thoughts. His thoughts swam, interweaving with the memories of the older man. The Abbot's powerful personality covered his own like a comforting blanket and he slept.

Release was painful and his fears returned as the Abbot woke him. Once again he was Serbitar and his thoughts were his own.

'Am I prepared?' he asked.

'You will be. The messenger comes.'

'Is he worthy?'

'Judge for yourself. Follow me to Graven.'

Their spirits soared, entwined, high above the monastery, free as the winter wind. Below them lay the snow-covered fields at the edge of the forest. The Abbot pulsed them onward, over the trees. In a clearing by a crofter's hut stood a group of men, facing a doorway in which stood a tall young man and behind him a woman, sword in hand.

'Which is the messenger?' asked the albino.

'Observe,' answered the Abbot.

Reinard had not had things going his way just recently. An attack on a caravan had been beaten off with heavy losses and then three more of his men had been found dead at dusk – among them his brother Erlik. A prisoner he had taken two days previously had died of fright long before the real entertainment could begin, and the weather had turned for the worse. Bad luck was haunting him and he was at a loss to understand why.

Damn the Speaker, he thought bitterly as he led his men towards the cabin. If he had not been in one of his three-day sleeps the attack on the caravan would have been avoided. Reinard had toyed with the idea of removing his feet as he slept, but good sense and greed had just held sway. Speaker was invaluable. He had come out of his trance as Reinard carried Erlik's body back to the camp.

'Do you see what has happened while you slept?' Reinard had stormed.

'You lost eight men in a bad raid and a woman slew Erlik and another after they killed her horse,' answered Speaker. Reinard stared hard at the old man, peering at the sightless sockets.

'A woman, you say?'

'Yes.'

'There was a third man killed. What of him?'

'Slain by an arrow through the forehead.'

'Who fired it?'

'The man called Regnak. The Wanderer who comes here on occasions.'

Reinard shook his head. A woman brought him a goblet of mulled wine and he sat on a large stone by a blazing fire. 'It can't be, he wouldn't dare! Are you sure it was him?'

'It was him,' said Speaker. 'And now I must rest.'

'Wait! Where are they now?'

'I shall find out,' said the old man, returning to his hut. Reinard called for food and summoned Grussin. The axeman squatted on the ground before him.

'Did you hear?' he asked.

'Yes. Do you believe it?' answered Grussin.

'It's ridiculous. But when has the old man been wrong? Am I getting old? When a craven like Rek can attack my men, I must be doing something wrong. I will have him roasted slowly over the fire for this.'

'We're getting short of food,' said Grussin.

'What?'

'Short of food. It's been a long winter and we needed that damn caravan.'

'There will be others. First, we will find Rek.'

'Is it worth it?' asked Grussin.

'Worth it? He helped some woman to kill my brother. I want that woman staked out and enjoyed by all the men. I want the flesh cut from her body in tiny strips from her feet to her neck. And then the dogs can have her.'

'Whatever you say.'

'You don't sound very enthusiastic,' said Reinard, hurling his now empty plate across the fire.

'No? Well, maybe *I'm* getting old. When we came here, there seemed to be a reason for it all. I'm beginning to forget what it was.'

'We came here because Abalayn and his mangy crew had my farm sacked and my family killed. And *I* haven't forgotten. You're not turning soft, are you?'

Grussin noted the gleam in Reinard's eyes.

'No, of course not. You're the leader and whatever you say is fine by me. We will find Rek – and the woman. Why don't you get some rest?'

'A curse on rest,' muttered Reinard. 'You sleep if you have to. We leave as soon as the old man gives us directions.'

Grussin walked to his hut and hurled himself on his fern-filled bed.

'You are troubled?' his woman, Mella, asked him as she kneeled by his side, offering him wine.

'How would you like to leave?' he asked, placing a huge hand on her shoulder. She leaned forward and kissed him. 'Wherever you go, I shall be with you,' she said.

'I'm tired of it,' he said. 'Tired of the killing. It gets more senseless with every day. He must be mad.'

'Hush!' she whispered, wary now. She leaned in to his bearded face and whispered in his ear: 'Don't voice your fears. We can leave quietly in the spring. Stay calm and do his bidding until then.'

He nodded, smiled and kissed her hair. 'You're right,' he said. 'Get some sleep.' She curled beside him and he gathered the blanket around her. 'I don't deserve you,' he said, as her eyes closed.

Where had it gone wrong? When they were young and full of fire Reinard's cruelty had been an occasional thing, a device to create a legend. Or so he had said. They would be a thorn in Abalayn's side until they achieved justice. Now it was ten years. Ten miserable bloody years.

And had the cause ever been just?

Grussin hoped so.

'Well, are you coming?' asked Reinard, from the doorway. 'They're at the old cabin.'

The march had been a long one and bitterly cold, but Reinard had scarcely felt it. Anger filled him with warmth and the prospect of revenge fed his muscles so that the miles sped by.

His mind filled with pictures of sweet violence and the music of screams. He would take the woman first and cut her with a heated knife. Arousal warmed his loins.

And as for Rek . . . He knew what Rek's expression would be as he saw them arrive.

Terror! Mind-numbing, bowel-loosening terror!

But he was wrong.

Rek had stalked from the hut, furious and trembling. The scorn on Virae's face was hard to bear. Only anger could blank it out. And even then, barely. He couldn't help what he was, could he? Some men are born to be heroes. Others to be cowards. What right had she to judge him?

'Regnak, my dear! Is it true you have a woman inside?'

Rek's eyes scanned the group. More than twenty men stood in a half-circle behind the tall, broad-shouldered outlaw leader. Beside him stood Grussin the Axeman, huge and powerful, his double-headed axe in his hand.

'Morning, Rein,' said Rek. 'What brings you here?'

'I heard you had a warm bedmate and I thought, "Good old Rek, he won't mind sharing". And I'd like to invite you to my camp. Where is she?'

'She's not for you, Rein. But I'll make a trade. There's a caravan headed . . .'

'Never mind the caravan!' shouted Reinard. 'Just bring out the woman.'

'Spices, jewels, furs. It's a big one,' said Rek.

'You can tell us about it as we march. Now I'm losing patience. Bring her out!'

Rek's anger blazed and his sword snaked from its scabbard.

'Come and get her then, you bastards!'

Virae stepped from the doorway to stand beside him, blade in hand, as the outlaws drew their weapons and advanced.

'Wait!' ordered Reinard, lifting his hand. He stepped forward, forcing a smile. 'Now listen to me, Rek. This is senseless. We've nothing against you. You've been a friend. Now, what's this woman to you? She killed my brother, so you see it's a matter of personal honour. Put up your sword and you can ride away. But I want her alive.' And you too, he thought.

'You want her – you take her!' said Rek. 'And me, too. Come on, Rein. You still remember what a sword's for, don't you? Or will you do what you normally do and scuttle back into the trees while other men do your dying for you? Run, you dung-worm!' Rek leapt forward and Reinard backed away at speed and stumbled into Grussin.

'Kill him – but not the woman,' he said. 'I want that woman.'

Grussin walked forward, his axe swinging at his side. Virae advanced to stand beside Rek. The axeman stopped ten paces short of the pair and his eyes met Rek's: there was no give there. He turned his gaze to the woman. Young, spirited – not beautiful – but a handsome lass.

'What are you waiting for, you ox!' screamed Reinard. 'Take her!'

Grussin turned and walked back to the group. A sense of unreality gripped him. He saw himself again as a young man, saving for his first holding; he had a plough which was his father's and the neighbours were ready to help him build his home near the elm grove. What had he done with the years?

'You traitor!' shouted Reinard, dragging his sword into the air.

Grussin parried the blow with ease. 'Forget it, Rein. Let's go home.'

'Kill him!' Reinard ordered. The men looked at one another, some starting forward while others hesitated. 'You bastard! You treacherous filth!' Reinard screamed, raising his sword once more. Grussin took a deep breath, gripped his axe in both hands and smashed the sword into shards, the axe blade glancing from the shattered hilt and hammering into the outlaw leader's side. He fell to his knees, doubled over. Then Grussin stepped forward; the axe raised and chopped and Reinard's head rolled to the snow. Grussin let the weapon fall, then walked back to Rek.

'He wasn't always as you knew him,' he said.

'Why?' asked Rek, lowering his blade. 'Why did you do it?'

'Who knows? It wasn't just for you – or her. Maybe something inside me had just had enough. Where was this caravan?'

'I was lying,' lied Rek.

'Good. We will not meet again. I'm leaving Graven. Is she your woman?'

'No.'

'You could do worse.'

'Yes.'

Grussin turned and walked to the body, retrieving his axe. 'We were friends for a long time,' he said. 'Too long.'

Without a backward glance he led the group back into the forest.

'I simply don't believe it,' said Rek. 'That was an absolute miracle.'

'Let's finish breakfast now,' said Virae. 'I'll brew some tea.'

Inside the hut Rek began to tremble. He sat down, his sword clattering to the floor.

'What's the matter?' asked Virae.

'It's just the cold,' he said, teeth chattering. She knelt beside him, massaging his hands, saying nothing.

'The tea will help,' she said. 'Did you bring any sugar?'

'It's in my pack, wrapped in red paper. Horeb knows I've a sweet tooth. Cold doesn't usually get to me like this – sorry!'

'It's all right. My father always says sweet tea is wonderful for . . . cold.'

'I wonder how they found us?' he said. 'Last night's snow must have covered our tracks. It's strange.'

'I don't know. Here, drink this.'

He sipped the tea, holding the leather-covered mug in both hands. Hot liquid splashed over his fingers. Virae busied herself clearing away and repacking his saddlebags. Then she raked the ashes in the hearth and laid a fire ready for the next traveller to use the hut.

'What are you doing at Dros Delnoch?' Rek asked, the warm sweet tea soothing him.

'I am Earl Delnar's daughter,' she said. 'I live there.'

'Did he send you away because of the coming war?'

'No. I brought a message to Abalayn, and now I've got a message for someone else. When I've delivered it, I'm going home. Are you feeling better?'

'Yes,' said Rek. 'Much better.' He hesitated, holding her gaze. 'It wasn't just the cold,' he said.

'I know: it doesn't matter. Everybody trembles after an action. It's what happens during it that counts. My father told me that after Skeln Pass he couldn't sleep without nightmares for a month.'

'You're not shaking,' he said.

'That's because I'm keeping busy. Would you like some more tea?'

'Yes. Thanks. I thought we were going to die. And just for a moment I didn't care – it was a wonderful feeling.' He wanted to tell her how good it was to have her standing beside him – but he couldn't. He wanted to walk across the room and hold her – and knew he would not. He merely looked at her while she refilled his mug, stirring in the sugar.

'Where did you serve?' she asked, conscious of his gaze and uncertain of its meaning.

'Dros Corteswain. Under Gan Javi.'

'He's dead now,' she said.

'Yes – a stroke. He was a fine leader. He predicted the coming war. I'm sure Abalayn wishes he had listened to him.'

'It wasn't only Javi who warned him,' said Virae. 'All the northern commanders sent reports. My father has had spies among the Nadir for years. It was obvious that they intended to attack us. Abalayn's a fool – even now he's sending messages to Ulric with new treaties. He won't accept that war's inevitable. Do you know we've only 10,000 men at Delnoch?'

'I had heard it was less,' said Rek.

'There are six walls and a town to defend. The complement in wartime should be four times as strong. And the discipline is not what it was.'

'Why?'

'Because they're all waiting to die,' she said, anger in her voice. 'Because my father's ill – dying. And because Gan Orrin has the heart of a ripe tomato.'

'Orrin? I've not heard of him.'

'Abalayn's nephew. He commands the troops, but he's useless. If I'd been a man . . .'

'I'm glad you're not,' he said.

'Why?'

'I don't know,' he said lamely. 'Just something to say . . . I'm glad you're not, that's all.'

'Anyway, if I had been a man I would have commanded the troops. I would have done a damned sight better than Orrin. Why are you staring at me?'

'I'm not staring. I'm listening, dammit! Why do you keep pressing me?'

'Do you want the fire lit?' she asked.

'What? Are we staying that long?'

'If you want to.'

'I'll leave it to you,' he said.

'Let's stay for today. That's all. It might give us time to . . . get to know each other better. We've made a pretty bad start, after all. And you have saved my life three times.'

'Once,' he said. 'I don't think you would have died of the cold, you're too tough. And Grussin saved us both. But, yes, I would like to stay just for today. Mind you, I don't fancy sleeping on the floor again.'

'You won't have to,' she said.

The Abbot smiled at the young albino's embarrassment. He released his hands from the mind hold and walked back to his desk. 'Join me, Serbitar,' he said, aloud. 'Do you regret your oath of celibacy?'

'Sometimes,' said the young man, rising from his knees. He brushed dust from his white cassock and seated himself opposite the Abbot.

'The girl is worthy,' Serbitar replied. 'The man is an enigma. Will their force be lessened by their lovemaking?'

'Strengthened,' said the Abbot. 'They need each other. Together they are complete, as in the Sacred Book. Tell me of her.'

'What can I tell?'

'You entered her mind. Tell me of her.'

'She is an earl's daughter. She lacks confidence in herself as a woman and she is a victim of mixed desires.'

'Why?'

'She doesn't know why,' he hedged.

'Of that I am aware. Do *you* know why?'

287

'No.'

'What of the man?'

'I did not enter his mind.'

'No. But what of the man?'

'He has great fears. He fears to die.'

'Is this a weakness?' asked the Abbot.

'It will be at Dros Delnoch. Death is almost certain there.'

'Yes. Can it be a strength?'

'I do not see how,' said Serbitar.

'What does the philosopher say of cowards and heroes?'

'The prophet says, "By nature of definition only the coward is capable of the highest heroism".'

'You must convene The Thirty, Serbitar.'

'I am to lead?'

'Yes. You shall be the Voice of The Thirty.'

'But who shall my brothers be?'

The Abbot leaned back in his chair. 'Arbedark will be the Heart. He is strong, fearless and true; there could be none other. Menahem shall be the Eyes, for he is gifted. I shall be the Soul.'

'No!' said the albino. 'It cannot be, master. I cannot lead you.'

'But you must. You will decide the other Numbers. I shall await your decision.'

'Why me? Why must I lead? I should be the Eyes. Arbedark should lead.'

'Trust me. All will be revealed.'

'I was raised at Dros Delnoch,' Virae told Rek as they lay before the blazing fire. His head rested on his rolled cloak, her head nestled on his chest. He stroked her hair, saying nothing. 'It's a majestic place. Have you ever been there?'

'No. Tell me about it.' He didn't really want to hear, but neither did he wish to speak.

'It has six outer walls, each of them twenty feet thick. The first three were built by Egel, the Earl of Bronze. But then the town expanded and gradually they built three more. The whole fortress spans the Delnoch Pass. With the exception of Dros Purdol to the west and Corteswain to the east, it is the only route for an army to pass through the mountains. My father converted the old keep and made it his home. The view is beautiful from the upper turrets. To the south in summer the whole of the Sentran Plain is golden with corn. And to the north you can see for ever. Are you listening to me?'

'Yes. Golden views. You can see for ever,' he said, softly.

'Are you sure you want to hear this?'

'Yes. Tell me about the walls again.'

'What about them?'

'How thick are they?'

'They are also up to sixty feet high, with jutting towers every fifty paces. Any army attacking the Dros would suffer fearful losses.'

'What about the gates?' he asked. 'A wall is only as strong as the gate it shields.'

'The Earl of Bronze thought of that. Each gate is set behind an iron portcullis and built of layered bronze, iron and oak. Beyond the gates are tunnels which narrow at the centre before opening out on to the level between walls. You could hold the tunnels against an enormous number of men. The whole of the Dros was beautifully designed; it's only the town which spoils it.'

'In what way?' he said.

'Originally Egel designed the gap between the walls to be a killing ground with no cover. It was uphill to the next wall, which would slow down the enemy. With enough bowmen you could have a massacre. It was good psychologically, too: by the time they came to take the next wall – if they ever did – they'd know there was more killing ground to come.'

'So how did the town spoil it?'

'It just grew. Now we have buildings all the way to wall six. The killing ground's gone. Quite the opposite in fact – now there's cover all the way.'

He rolled over and kissed her brow.

'What was that for?' she asked.

'Does it have to be for something?'

'There's a reason for everything,' she said.

He kissed her again. 'That was for the Earl of Bronze,' he said. 'Or the coming of spring. Or a vanished snowflake.'

'You don't make any sense,' she told him.

'Why did you let me make love to you?' he asked.

'What sort of a question is that?'

'Why?'

'None of your damned business!' she said.

He laughed and kissed her again. 'Yes, my lady. Quite right. None of my business.'

'You're mocking me,' she said, struggling to rise.

'Nonsense,' he said, holding her down. 'You're beautiful.'

'I'm not. I never have been. You *are* mocking me.'

'I will never mock you. And you *are* beautiful. And the more I look at you, the more beautiful you are.'

'You're a fool. Let me up.'

He kissed her again, easing his body close to hers. The kiss lingered and she returned it.

'Tell me about the Dros again,' he said, at last.

'I don't want to talk about it now. You're teasing me, Rek; I won't have it. I don't want to think about it tonight, not any more. Do you believe in fate?'

'I do now. Almost.'

'I'm serious. Yesterday, I didn't mind about going home and facing the Nadir. I believed in the Drenai cause and I was willing to die for it. I wasn't scared yesterday.'

'And today?' he asked.

'Today, if you asked me, I wouldn't go home.' She was lying, but she didn't know why. A surge of fear welled in her as Rek closed his eyes and leaned back.

'Yes, you would,' he said. 'You have to.'

'What about you?'

'It doesn't make sense,' he said.

'What doesn't?'

'I don't believe in what I'm feeling. I never have. I am almost thirty years old and I know the world.'

'What are you talking about?'

'I'm talking about fate. Destiny. An old man in tattered blue robes without any eyes. I'm talking about love.'

'Love?'

He opened his eyes, reached out and stroked her face.

'I can't tell you what it meant to me when you stood beside me this morning. It was the highest point in my life. Nothing else mattered. I could see the sky – it was more blue than ever I've seen it. Everything was in sharp focus. I was more aware of living than I have ever been. Does that make any sense?'

'No,' she said gently. 'Not really. Do you truly think I'm beautiful?'

'You are the most beautiful woman who ever wore armour,' he said, smiling.

'That's no answer. Why am I beautiful?'

'Because I love you,' he said, surprised at the ease with which he could say it.

'Does that mean you're coming with me to Dros Delnoch?'

'Tell me about those lovely high walls again,' he said.

5

The monastery grounds were split into training areas, some of stone, some of grass, others of sand or treacherous slime-covered slate. The abbey itself stood at the centre of the grounds, a converted keep of grey stone and crenellated battlements. Four walls and a moat surrounded the abbey, the walls a later and less war-like addition of soft, golden sandstone. By the western wall, sheltered by glass and blooming out of season were flowers of thirty different shades. All were roses.

The albino Serbitar knelt before his tree, his mind at one with the plant. He had struggled for thirteen years with the rose and understood it. There was empathy. There was harmony.

There was fragrance that pulsed for Serbitar alone. Greenfly upon the rose shrivelled and died as Serbitar gazed upon them, and the soft silky beauty of the blooms filled his senses like an opiate.

It was a white rose.

Serbitar sat back, eyes closed, mentally following the surge of new life within the tree. He wore full armour of silver mailshirt, sword and scabbard, leather leggings worked with silver rings; by his side was a new silver helm, bearing the figure One in Elder runes. His white hair was braided. His eyes were green – the colour of the rose leaves. His slender face, translucent skin over high cheekbones, had the mystic beauty of the consumptive.

He made his farewells, gently easing the gossamer panic of the plant. It had known him since its first leaf opened.

And now he was to die.

A smiling face grew in his mind and Serbitar sense-recognised Arbedark. We await you, pulsed the inner message.

I am coming, he answered.

Within the great hall a table had been set, a jug of water and a barley cake before each of thirty places. Thirty men in full armour sat silently as Serbitar entered, taking his place at the head of the table and bowing to the Abbot, Vintar, who now sat on his right.

In silence the company ate, each thinking his own thoughts, each analysing his emotions at this culmination of thirteen years' training.

Finally Serbitar spoke, fulfilling the ritual need of the Order.

'Brothers, the search is upon us. We who have sought must obtain that which we seek. A messenger comes from Dros Delnoch to ask us to die. What does the Heart of The Thirty feel on this matter?'

All eyes turned to black-bearded Arbedark. He relaxed his mind, allowing their emotions to wash over him, selecting thoughts, analysing them, forging them into one unifying concept agreed by all.

Then he spoke, his voice deep and resonant.

'The heart of the matter is that the children of the Drenai face extinction. Ulric has massed the Nadir tribes under his banner. The first attack on the Drenai empire will be at Dros Delnoch, which Earl Delnar has orders to hold until the autumn. Abalayn needs time to raise and train an army.

'We approach a frozen moment in the destiny of the continent. The Heart says we should seek our truths at Dros Delnoch.'

Serbitar turned to Menahem, a hawk-nosed young man, dark and swarthy, his hair braided in a single pony tail intertwined with silver thread. 'And how do the Eyes of The Thirty view this thing?'

'Should we go to the Dros the city will fall,' said Menahem. 'Should we refuse, the city will still fall. Our presence will merely delay the inevitable. Should the messenger be worthy to ask of us our lives, then we should go.'

Serbitar turned to the Abbot. 'Vintar, how says the Soul of The Thirty?'

The older man ran a slender hand through his thinning grey hair, then stood and bowed to Serbitar. He seemed out of place in his armour of silver and bronze.

'We will be asked to kill men of another race,' he said, his voice gentle, sad even. 'We will be asked to kill them, not because they are evil, merely because their leaders wish to do what the Drenai themselves did six centuries ago.

'We stand between the sea and the mountains. The sea will crush us against the mountain and thus we die. The mountain will hold us against the sea, allowing us to be crushed. Still we die.

'We are all weapon masters here. We seek the perfect death, to counterpoint the perfect life. True, the Nadir aggression does not pose a new concept in history. But their action will cause untold horror to the Drenai people. We can say that to defend those people we are upholding the values of our Order. That our defence will fail is no reason to avoid the battle. For it is the motive that is pure, and not the outcome.

'Sadly, the Soul says we must ride for Dros Delnoch.'

'So,' said Serbitar. 'We are agreed. I, too, feel strongly on this matter. We came to this Temple as outcasts from the world. Shunned and feared, we came together to create the ultimate contradiction. Our bodies would become living weapons, to polarise our minds to extremes of pacifism. Warrior-priests we are, as the Elders never were. There will be no joy in our hearts as we slay the enemy, for we love all life.

'As we die our souls will leap forward, transcending the world's chains. All petty jealousies, intrigues and hatreds will be left behind us as we journey to the Source.

'The Voice says we ride.'

A three-quarter moon hung in the cloudless night sky, casting pale shadows from the trees around Rek's camp-fire. A luckless rabbit, gutted and encased in clay, lay on the coals as Virae came back from the stream, wiping her naked upper body with one of Rek's spare shirts.

'If only you knew how much that cost me!' he said as she sat on a rock by the fire, her body glowing gold as the flames danced.

'It never served a better purpose,' she said. 'How much longer before that rabbit is ready?'

'Not long. You will catch your death of cold, sitting half-naked in this weather. My blood's chilling to ice just watching you.'

'Strange!' she said. 'Just this morning you were telling me how your blood ran hot just to look at me.'

'That was in a warm cabin with a bed handy. I've never been much for making love in the snow. Here, I've warmed a blanket.'

'When I was a child,' she said, taking the blanket and wrapping it round her shoulders, 'we used to have to run three miles across the downs in midwinter wearing only a tunic and sandals. That was bracing. And extremely cold.'

'If you're so tough, how was it that you turned blue before we found the cabin?' he asked, a broad smile robbing the question of malice.

'The armour,' she said. 'Too much steel, not enough wool beneath it. Mind you, if I had been riding in front I wouldn't have got so bored and fallen asleep. How long did you say that rabbit would be? I'm starving.'

'Soon. I think . . .'

'Have you ever cooked a rabbit this way before?' she asked.

'Not exactly. But it is the right way – I've seen it done. All the fur comes away as you crack the clay. It's easy.'

Virae was not convinced. 'I stalked that skinny beast for ages,' she said, recalling with pleasure the single arrow from forty paces which had downed it. 'Not a bad bow, if a little on the light side. It's an old cavalry bow, isn't it? We have several at Delnoch. The modern ones are all silver steel now – better range and a stronger poundage. I'm starving.'

'Patience aids the appetite,' he told her.

'You'd better not ruin that rabbit. I don't like killing the things at the best of times. But at least there's a purpose if one can eat it.'

'I'm not sure how the rabbit would respond to that line of reasoning,' said Rek.

'Can they reason?' asked Virae.

'I don't know, I didn't mean it literally.'

'Then why say it? You are a strange man.'

'It was just an abstract thought. Do you never have an abstract thought? Do you never wonder how a flower knows when it's time to grow? Or how the salmon finds its way back to the spawning grounds?'

'No,' she said. 'Is the rabbit cooked?'

'Well, what *do* you think about, when you're not planning how to kill people?'

'Eating,' she said. 'What about that rabbit?'

Rek tipped the ball of clay from the coals with a stick, watching it sizzle on the snow.

'Well, what do you do now?' she asked. He ignored her and picked up a fist-sized rock, then cracked it hard against the clay which split to disgorge a half-cooked, half-skinned rabbit.

'Looks good,' she said. 'What now?'

He poked the steaming meat with a stick.

'Can you face eating that?' he said.

'Of course. Can I borrow your knife? Which bit do you want?'

'I've got some oatcake left in my pack. I think I'll make do with that. Will you put some clothes on!'

They were camped in a shallow depression under a rock face – not deep enough to be a cave but large enough to reflect heat from the fire and cut out the worst of the wind. Rek chewed his oatcake and watched the girl devour the rabbit. It was not an edifying sight. She hurled the remnants of the carcass into the trees. 'Badgers should enjoy it,' she said. 'That's not a bad way to cook rabbit.'

'I'm glad you enjoyed it,' he said.

'You're not much of a woodsman, are you?' she told him.

'I manage.'

'You couldn't even gut the thing. You looked green when the entrails popped out.'

Rek hurled the rest of his oatcake in the direction of the hapless rabbit. 'The badgers will probably appreciate dessert,' he said. Virae giggled happily.

'You're wonderful, Rek. You're unlike any man I ever met.'

'I don't think I'm going to like what's coming next,' he said. 'Why don't we just go to sleep?'

'No. Listen to me. I'm serious. All my life I have dreamt of finding the right man: tall, kind, strong, understanding. Loving. I never thought he existed. Most of the men I've known have been soldiers – gruff, straight as spears and as romantic as a bull in heat. And I've met poets, soft of speech and gentle. When I was with soldiers I longed for poets, and when with poets I longed for soldiers. I had begun to believe the man I wanted could not exist. Do you understand me?'

'All your life you've been looking for a man who couldn't cook rabbits? Of course I understand you.'

'Do you really?' she asked, softly.

'Yes. But explain it to me anyway.'

'You're what I've always wanted,' she said, blushing. 'You're my Coward-Hero – my love.'

'I knew there would be something I wouldn't like,' he said.

As she placed some logs on the blaze he held out his hand. 'Sit beside me,' he said. 'You'll be warmer.'

'You can share my blanket,' she told him, moving round the fire and into his arms, resting her head on his shoulder. 'You don't mind if I call you my Coward-Hero?'

'You can call me what you like,' he said, 'so long as you're always there to call me.'

'*Always?*'

The wind tilted the flames and he shivered. 'Always isn't such a long time for us, is it? We only have as much time as Dros Delnoch holds. Anyway – you might get tired of me and send me away.'

'Never!' she said.

' "Never" and "always". I had not thought about those words much

294

until now. Why didn't I meet you ten years ago? The words might have meant something then.'

'I doubt it, I would only have been nine years old.'

'I didn't mean it literally. Poetically.'

'My father has written to Druss,' she said. 'That letter and this mission are all that keep him alive.'

'Druss? But even if he's alive he will be ancient by now; it will be obscene. Skeln was fifteen years ago and he was old then – they will have to carry him into the Dros.'

'Perhaps. But my father sets great store by the man. He was awed by him. He feels he's invincible. Immortal. He once described him to me as the greatest warrior of the age. He said Skeln Pass was Druss' victory and that he and the others just made up the numbers. He used to tell that story to me when I was young. We would sit by a fire like this and toast bread on the flames. Then he'd tell me about Skeln. Marvellous days.' She lapsed into silence, staring into the coals.

'Tell me the story,' he said, drawing her closer to him, his right hand pushing back the hair that had fallen across her face.

'You must know it. Everyone knows about Skeln.'

'True. But I've never heard the story from someone who was there. I've only seen the plays and listened to the saga-poets.'

'Tell me what you heard and I will fill in the detail.'

'All right. There were a few hundred Drenai warriors holding Skeln Pass while the main Drenai army massed elsewhere. It was the Ventrian king, Gorben, they were worried about. They knew he was on the march but not where he would strike. He struck at Skeln. They were outnumbered fifty to one, and they held on until reinforcements arrived. That's all.'

'Not quite,' said Virae. 'Gorben had an inner army of 10,000 men called the Immortals. They had never been beaten, but Druss beat them.'

'Oh, come,' said Rek. 'One man cannot beat an army. That's saga-poet stuff.'

'No, listen to me. My father said that on the last day, when the Immortals were finally sent in, the Drenai line had begun to fold. My father has been a warrior all his life. He understands battles and the shift and flow between courage and panic. The Drenai were ready to crack. But then, just as the line was beginning to give, Druss bellowed a battle cry and advanced, cutting and slashing with his axe. The Ventrians fell back before him. And then suddenly those nearest to him turned to run. The panic spread like brush-fire and the entire Ventrian line crumbled. Druss had turned the tide. My father says he was like a giant that day. Inhuman. Like a god of war.'

'That was *then*,' said Rek. 'I can't see a toothless old man being of much use. No man can resist age.'

'I agree. But can you see what a boost to morale it will be just to have Druss there? Men will flock to the banner. To fight a battle alongside Druss the Legend – there's an immortality in it.'

'Have you ever met the old man?' asked Rek.

'No. My father would never tell me, but there was something between them. Druss would never come to Dros Delnoch. It was something to do with my mother, I think.'

'She didn't like him?'

'No. Something to do with a friend of Druss'. Sieben, I think he was called.'

'What happened to him?'

'He was killed at Skeln. He was Druss' oldest friend. That's all I know about it.' Rek knew she was lying but let it rest. It was all ancient history anyway.

Like Druss the Legend . . .

The old man crumpled the letter and let it fall.

It was not age which depressed Druss. He enjoyed the wisdom of his sixty years, the knowledge accrued and the respect it earned. But the physical ravages of time were another thing altogether. His shoulders were still mighty above a barrel chest, but the muscles had taken on a stretched look – wiry lines which criss-crossed his upper back. His waist, too, had thickened perceptibly over the last winter. And almost overnight, he realised, his black beard streaked with grey had become a grey beard streaked with black. But the piercing eyes which gazed at their reflection in the silver mirror had not dimmed. Their stare had dismayed armies; caused heroic opponents to take a backward step, blushing and shamed; caught the imagination of a people who had needed heroes.

He was Druss the Legend. Invincible Druss, Captain of the Axe. The legends of his life were told to children everywhere – and most of them *were* legends, Druss reflected. Druss the Hero, immortal, god-like.

His past victories could have ensured him a palace of riches, concubines by the score. Fifteen years before Abalayn himself had showered him with jewels following his exploits at the Skeln Pass.

By the following morning, however, Druss had gone back to the Skoda mountains, high into the lonely country bordering the clouds. Among the pine and the snow leopards the grizzled old warrior had returned to his lair, to taste again of solitude. His wife of thirty years lay buried there. He had a mind to die there - though there would be no one to bury him, he knew.

During the past fifteen years Druss had not been inactive. He had wandered various lands, leading battle companies for minor princelings. Last winter he had retired to his high mountain retreat, there to think and die. He had long known he would die in his sixtieth year – even before the seer's prediction all those decades ago. He had been able to picture himself at sixty – but never beyond. Whenever he tried to consider the prospects of being sixty-one, he would experience only darkness.

His gnarled hands curled round a wooden goblet and raised it to his grey-bearded lips. The wine was strong, brewed himself five years before; it had aged well – better than he. But it was gone and he remained . . . for a little while.

The heat within his sparse furnished cabin was growing oppressive as the new spring sun warmed the wooden roof. Slowly he removed the sheepskin jacket he had worn all winter and the under-vest of horsehair. His massive body, criss-crossed with scars, belied his age. He studied the scars, remembering clearly the men whose blades had caused them: men who would never grow old as he had; men who had died in their prime beneath his singing axe. His blue eyes flicked to the wall by the small wooden door. There she hung, Snaga, which in the old tongue meant the Sender. Slim haft of black steel, interwoven with eldritch runes in silver thread, and a double-edged blade so shaped that it sang as it slew.

Even now he could hear its sweet song. One last time, Soul brother, it called to him. One last bloody day before the sun sets. His mind returned to Delnar's letter. It was written to the memory and not the man.

Druss raised himself from the wooden chair, cursing as his joints creaked. 'The sun has set,' whispered the old warrior, addressing the axe. 'Now only death waits and he's a patient bastard.' He walked from the cabin, gazing out over the distant mountains. His massive frame and grey-black hair mirrored in miniature the mountains he surveyed. Proud, strong, ageless and snow-topped, they defied the spring sun as it strove to deny them their winter peaks of virgin snow.

Druss soaked in their savage splendour, sucking in the cool breeze and tasting life, as if for the last time.

'Where are you, Death?' he called. 'Where do you hide on this fine day?' The echoes boomed around the valleys . . . DEATH, DEATH, Death, Death . . . DAY, DAY, Day, Day . . .

'I am Druss! And I defy you!'

A shadow fell across Druss' eyes, the sun died in the heavens and the mountains receded into mist. Pain clamped Druss' mighty chest, soul deep, and he almost fell.

'Proud mortal!' hissed a sibilant voice through the veils of agony. 'I never sought you. You have hunted me through these long, lonely years. Stay on this mountain and I guarantee you two score more years. Your muscles will atrophy, your brain will sink into dotage. You will bloat, old man, and I will only come when you beg it.

'Or will the huntsman have one more hunt?

'Seek me if you will, old warrior. I stand on the walls of Dros Delnoch.'

The pain lifted from the old man's heart. He staggered once, drew soothing mountain air into his burning lungs and gazed about him. Birds still sang in the pine, no clouds obscured the sun and the mountains stood, tall and proud, as they always had done.

Druss returned to the cabin and went to a chest of oak, padlocked at the onset of winter. The key lay deep in the valley below. He placed his giant hands about the lock and began to exert pressure. Muscles writhed on his arms; veins bulged on his neck and shoulders; and the metal groaned, changed shape and – split! Druss threw the padlock aside and opened the chest. Within lay a jerkin of black leather, the shoulders covered in a skin of shining steel, and a black leather skull-cap only relieved by a silver axe flanked by silver skulls. Long black leather gauntlets came into view, silver-skinned to the knuckles. Swiftly he dressed, coming finally to the long leather boots – a present from Abalayn himself so many years before.

Lastly he reached for Snaga, which seemed to leap from the wall to his waiting hand.

'One last time, Soul brother,' he told it. 'Before the sun sets.'

6

With Vintar standing beside him, Serbitar watched from a high balcony
as the two riders approached the monastery, cantering their horses towards
the northern gate. Grass showed in patches on the snow-covered fields as
a warm spring wind eased in from the west.

'Not a time for lovers,' said Serbitar, aloud.

'It is always a time for lovers, my son. In war most of all,' said Vintar.
'Have you probed the man's mind?'

'Yes. He is a strange one. A cynic by experience, a romantic by inclination and now a hero by necessity.'

'How will Menahem test the messenger?' asked Vintar.

'With fear,' answered the albino.

Rek was feeling good. The air he breathed was crisp and clean and a
warm westerly breeze promised an end to the harshest winter in years.
The woman he loved was beside him and the sky was blue and clear.

'What a great day to be alive!' he said.

'What's so special about today?' asked Virae.

'It's beautiful. Can't you taste it? The sky, the breeze, the melting
snow?'

'Someone is coming to meet us. He looks like a warrior,' she said.

The rider approached them and dismounted. His face was covered by
a black and silver helm crowned with a horsehair plume. Rek and Virae
dismounted and approached him.

'Good morning,' said Rek. The man ignored him; his dark eyes, seen
through the slits in the helm, focused on Virae.

'You are the messenger?' he asked her.

'I am. I wish to see Abbot Vintar.'

'First you must pass me,' he said, stepping back and drawing a longsword of silver steel.

'Wait a moment,' said Rek. 'What is this? One does not normally have
to fight one's way into a monastery.' Once again the man ignored him
and Virae drew her rapier. 'Stop it!' ordered Rek. 'This is insane.'

'Stay out of this, Rek,' said Virae. 'I will slice this silver beetle into tiny
pieces.'

'No, you won't,' he said, gripping her arm. 'That rapier is no good
against an armoured man. In any case, the whole thing is senseless. You
are not here to fight anybody. You simply have a message to deliver,
that's all. There must be a mistake here somewhere. Wait a moment.'

Rek walked towards the warrior, his mind racing, his eyes checking for
weak points in the armoured defences. The man wore a moulded breastplate over a mail-shirt of silver steel. Protecting his neck was a silver
torque. His legs were covered to the thigh in leather troos, cased with

silver rings, and upon his shins were leather greaves. Only the man's knees, hands and chin were open to attack.

'Will you tell me what is happening?' Rek asked him. 'I think you may have the wrong messenger. We are here to see the Abbot.'

'Are you ready, woman?' asked Menahem.

'Yes,' said Virae, her rapier cutting a figure-eight in the morning air as she loosened her wrist.

Rek's blade flashed into his hand. 'Defend yourself,' he cried.

'No, Rek, he's mine,' shouted Virae. 'I don't need you to fight for me. Step aside!'

'You can have him next,' said Rek. He turned his attention back to Menahem. 'Come on, then. Let's see if you fight as prettily as you look.'

Menahem turned his dark eyes on the tall figure before him. Instantly Rek's stomach turned over: this was death! Cold, final, worm in the eye-sockets, death. There was no hope in this contest. Panic welled in Rek's breast and his limbs began to tremble. He was a child again, locked in a darkened room, knowing the demons were hiding in the black shadows. Fear in the shape of bile rose in his throat as nausea shook him. He wanted to run . . . he needed to run.

Instead Rek screamed and launched an attack, his blade whistling towards the black and silver helm. Startled, Menahem hastily parried and a second blow almost got through. The warrior stepped backwards, desperately trying to regain the initiative, but Rek's furious assault had caught him off-balance. Menahem parried and moved, trying to circle.

Virae watched in stunned silence as Rek's blistering assault continued. The two men's swords glittered in the morning sunlight, a dazzling web of white light, a stunning display of skill. Virae felt a surge of pride. She wanted to cheer Rek on but resisted the urge, knowing the slightest distraction could sway the contest.

'Help me,' pulsed Menahem to Serbitar, 'or I may have to kill him.' He parried a blow, catching it only inches from his throat. 'If I can,' he added.

'How can we stop it?' Serbitar asked Vintar. 'The man is a baresark. I cannot get through to him. He will kill Menahem before much longer.'

'The girl!' said Vintar. 'Join with me.'

Virae shivered as she watched Rek growing in strength. Baresark! Her father had told her of such men, but never would she have placed Rek in their company. They were mad killers who lost all sense of reason and fear in combat, becoming the most deadly of opponents. All swordsmen gravitate between defence and attack, for despite a desire to win there is an equal desire not to lose. But the baresark loses all fear; his is all-out attack, and invariably he takes his opponent with him even if he falls. A thought struck her powerfully and suddenly she knew that the warrior was not trying to kill Rek – the contest was but a test.

'Put up your swords,' she screamed. 'Stop it!'

The two men battled on.

'Rek, listen to me!' she shouted. 'It's only a test. He's not trying to kill you.'

Her voice came to Rek as from a great distance, piercing the red mist before his eyes. Stepping back, he felt rather than saw the relief in the other man; then he took a deep breath and relaxed, his legs shaky, his hands trembling.

'You entered my mind,' he accused the warrior, fixing the man's dark eyes in a cold gaze. 'I don't know how. But if you ever do it again, I will kill you. Do you understand me?'

'I understand,' Menahem told him softly, his voice muffled within his helm. Rek sheathed his blade at the second attempt and turned to Virae who was looking at him strangely.

'It wasn't really me,' he said. 'Don't look at me like that, Virae.'

'Oh Rek, I'm sorry,' she said, tears in her eyes. 'I'm truly sorry.'

A new kind of fear hit him as she turned her face away. 'Don't leave me,' he said. 'It rarely happens and I would never turn on *you*. Never! Believe me.' She turned to face him, throwing her arms about his neck.

'Leave you? What are you talking about? It doesn't matter to me, you fool. I was just sorry for you. Oh, Rek – you're such an idiot. I'm not some tavern girl who squeals at the sight of a rat. I'm a woman who has grown up alongside men. Soldiers. Fighting men. Warriors. You think I would leave you because you are baresark?'

'I can control it,' he said, holding her tightly to him.

'Where we are going, Rek, you will not have to,' she said.

Serbitar left the monastery balcony and poured a goblet of spring water from a stone jug.

'How did he do it?'

Vintar sat back on a leather chair. 'There is a well of courage within him, fuelled by many things of which we can only guess. But when Menahem fed him fear, he responded with violence. Because what Menahem could not have understood is that the man fears fear itself. Did you glimpse that memory of his childhood during Menahem's probe?'

'The tunnels, you mean?'

'Yes. What do you make of a child who fears the dark and yet seeks out dark tunnels to travel through?'

'He tried to end his fears by facing them,' said Serbitar.

'He still does. And that's why Menahem almost died.'

'He will be useful at Dros Delnoch,' said Serbitar, smiling.

'More than you know,' said Vintar. 'More than you know.'

'Yes,' Serbitar told Rek as they sat within the oak-panelled study overlooking the courtyard. 'Yes, we can read minds. But I assure you we will not again attempt to read yours – or that of your companion.'

'Why did he do that to me?' asked Rek.

'Menahem is the Eyes of The Thirty. He had to see that you were worthy to ask of us . . . the service. You expect us to fight with your forces, to analyse enemy tactics and to use our skills in defence of a fortress about which we care nothing. The messenger has to be worthy.'

'But I am not the messenger, I am merely a companion.'

'We shall see . . . How long have you known of your . . . affliction?'

Rek turned his gaze to the window and the balcony beyond. A wren landed on the railing, sharpened his beak on the stone and then flew off. Light clouds were forming, fleece islands in the clear blue of the sky.

'It has happened only twice. Both times in the Sathuli wars. Once when we were surrounded after a dawn raid on a village, and the second time when I was part of a guard unit for a spices caravan.'

'It is common among warriors,' said Serbitar. 'It is a gift of fear.'

'It saved my life both times, but it scares me,' said Rek. 'It is as if someone else takes over my mind and body.'

'But that is not so, I assure you. It is you alone. Do not fear what you are, Rek – may I call you Rek?'

'Of course.'

'I did not wish to be overly familiar. It is a nickname, is it not?'

'A shortened form of Regnak. My foster-father, Horeb, shortened it when I was a child. It was a kind of joke. I disliked robust games and never wanted to explore or climb high trees. I wasn't reckless, he said; so he dropped the "less" and called me Rek. As I said, it's not much of a joke, but the name stuck.'

'Do you think,' asked Serbitar, 'that you will be comfortable at Dros Delnoch?'

Rek smiled. 'Are you asking me if I have the nerve?'

'Speaking bluntly? Yes, I suppose I am.'

'I don't know. Have you?'

The ghost of a smile hovered on the pale, fleshless face as the albino considered the question. His slender fingers tapped gently at the desk top.

'The question is a good one. Yes, I have the nerve. My fears are unconnected with death.'

'You have read my mind,' said Rek. 'You tell *me* if I have the nerve. I mean it. I don't know if I can stand a drawn-out siege; it is said that men fail under such pressure.'

'I cannot tell you,' Serbitar answered, 'if you will hold or fail. You are capable of both. I cannot analyse all the permutations of a siege. Ask yourself this: What if Virae fell? Would you stay on?'

'No,' said Rek instantly. 'I would saddle a fast horse and be gone. I don't care about Dros Delnoch. Or the Drenai empire.'

'The Drenai are finished,' said Serbitar. 'Their star has fallen.'

'Then you think the Dros will fall?'

'Ultimately it must. But I cannot see that far into the future as yet. The Way of the Mist is strange. Often it will show events still to come, but more often it will show events never to be. It is a perilous path which only the true mystic walks with certainty.'

'The Way of the Mist?' asked Rek.

'I'm sorry, why should you know? It is a road on another plane . . . a fourth dimension? A journey of the spirit like a dream. Only you direct the dream and see what you desire to see. It is a concept hard to verbalise to a non-Speaker.'

'Are you saying your soul can travel outside the body?' asked Rek.

'Oh yes, that is the easy part. We saw you in Graven Forest outside the cabin. We helped you then by influencing the axeman, Grussin.'

'You made him kill Reinard?'

'No. Our powers are not that great. We merely pushed him in a direction he was considering already.'

'I'm not sure I am entirely comfortable knowing you have that sort of power,' said Rek, avoiding the albino's green eyes.

Serbitar laughed, his eyes sparkling, his pale face mirroring his joy.

'Friend Rek, I am a man of my word. I promised never to use my gift to read your mind and I shall not. Nor will any of The Thirty. Do you think we would be priests, forsaking the world, if we wished harm to others? I am the son of an earl, but if I wished I could be a king, an emperor mightier than Ulric. Do not feel threatened. We must be at ease one with the other. More – we must be friends.'

'Why?' asked Rek.

'Because we are about to share a moment which comes only once in a lifetime,' said Serbitar. 'We are going to die.'

'Speak for yourself,' said Rek. 'I do not see that going to Dros Delnoch is just another way of committing suicide. It's a battle, that's all. No more, no less than that. A wall can be defended. A smaller force can hold a larger. History is full of examples: Skeln Pass, for example.'

'True,' said Serbitar. 'But they are remembered because they are exceptions. Let us deal in facts. The Dros is defended by a force less than a third of full complement. Morale is low, fear is rife. Ulric has a force in excess of half a million warriors all willing – lusting even – to die for him in battle. I am a weaponmaster and a student of war. Dros Delnoch will fall. Clear your mind of any other conclusion.'

'Then why come with us? What will you gain from it?'

'We die,' said Serbitar, 'and then live. But I shall say no more of that at this time. I do not wish to depress you, Rek. If it would serve a purpose, I would fill you with hope. But my whole battle strategy will be built around delaying the inevitable. Only then can I function – and serve your cause.'

'I hope you will keep that opinion to yourself,' said Rek. 'Virae believes we can hold. I know enough of warfare and morale to tell you plainly that if your theory were to spread among the men, there would be wholesale desertions; we would lose on the first day.'

'I am not a fool, Rek. I say this to *you* because it needs to be said. I shall be your advisor at Delnoch and you will need me to speak the truth. I shall have no real dealings with the soldiers, neither will The Thirty. Men will avoid us anyway, once they know what we are.'

'Perhaps. Why do you say you will be my advisor? Earl Delnar commands; I shall not even be an officer there.'

'Let us say,' said Serbitar, 'that I will be the advisor to your cause. Time will explain all far better than I. Have I depressed you?'

'Not at all. You have told me everything is hopeless, that we are all dead men and the Drenai are finished. Depressed? Not at all!'

Serbitar laughed and clapped his hands. 'I like you, Rek,' he said. 'I think you will hold firm.'

'I will hold firm all right,' said Rek, smiling. 'Because I will know that at the last wall I will have two horses waiting ready saddled. By the way, do you not have anything stronger than water to drink?'

'Sadly, no,' answered Serbitar. 'Alcohol inhibits our strength. If you need spirits, however, there is a village nearby and I can have someone ride out for you to purchase some.'

'You don't drink. There are no women. You eat no meat. What do you do for recreation?'

'We study,' said Serbitar. 'And we train, and we plant flowers and raise horses. Our time is well occupied, I can assure you.'

'No wonder you want to go away and die somewhere,' said Rek, with feeling.

Virae sat with Vintar in a small, sparsely furnished study awash with manuscripts and leather-bound tomes. There was a small desk littered with broken quills and scrawled parchment. She held back a smile as the older man fumbled with his breastplate strap. He could not have looked less a warrior.

'Can I help you?' she asked, standing up and leaning over the desk.

'Thank you, my dear,' he said. 'It weighs heavily.' He balanced the armour against the desk and poured himself some water, offering the jug to Virae who shook his head. 'I'm sorry the room is such a mess, but I have been hurrying to finish my diary. So much to say, so little time.'

'Bring it with you,' she said.

'I think not. Too many other problems to wrestle with once we are under way. You have changed since I saw you last, Virae.'

'Two years is a long time, Abbot,' she said, carefully.

'I think it is the young man with you,' he said, smiling. 'He has a great influence.'

'Nonsense. I am the same.'

'Your walk is more assured. You are less clumsy than I remember. He has given you something, I think.'

'Never mind that. What about the Dros?' she snapped, blushing.

'I am sorry, my dear. I did not wish to embarrass you.'

'You have not embarrassed me,' she lied. 'Now, about Dros Delnoch. How can you help us?'

'As I told your father two years ago, our help will be in organisation and planning. We will know the enemy's plans. We can aid you in thwarting them. Tactically we can organise the defences and militarily we can fight like a hundred. But our price is high.'

'My father has deposited 10,000 gold Raq in Ventria,' she said. 'With the merchant Asbidare.'

'Good. Then that is settled. We ride in the morning.'

'May I ask you something?' said Virae. He opened his hands and waited. 'Why do you need money?'

'For the next Temple of The Thirty. Each temple is financed by the death of the last.'

'Oh. What happens if you don't die? I mean, supposing we win?' His eyes searched her face for a matter of moments.

'Then we return the money,' he said.

'I see,' she said.

'You are unconvinced?'

'It doesn't matter. What do you think of Rek?'

'In what way?' asked Vintar.

'Let us not play games, Father Abbot. I know you can read minds. I want to know what you think of Rek?'

'The question is not precise enough – no, let me finish,' he said, watching her anger rise. 'Do you mean as a man, as a warrior or as a prospective husband for the daughter of an earl?'

'All three if you like. I don't know. Just tell me.'

'Very well. Do you believe in destiny?'

'Yes,' she said, remembering the same question she had asked of Rek. 'Yes, I do.'

'Then believe this. You were destined to meet. You are the perfect match. You boost his strengths and counter his weaknesses. What he does for you, you know already. As a man he is not unique, nor even very special. He has no great talents, is not a poet, a writer or a philosopher. As a warrior – well, he has a sporadic courage that hides great fears. But he is a man in love. And that will increase his strength, and his power to combat his fears. As a husband? In days of peace and plenty, I feel he would be wayward. But for now . . . he loves you, and is prepared to die for you. You can ask no more of a man than that.'

'Why did I meet him now, of all times?' she asked, tears stinging her eyes. 'I don't want him to die. I would kill myself, I think.'

'No, my dear. I don't think you would, though I agree that you would feel like doing so. Why now? Why not? Live or die, a man and a woman need love. There is a need in the race. We need to share. To belong. Perhaps you will die before the year is out. But remember this: to have may be taken from you, to have had never. Far better to have tasted love before dying, than to die alone.'

'I suppose so. But I would have liked children and a settled home. I would like to have taken Rek to Drenan and shown him off a little. I would like some of those bitches at court to see that a man could love me.' She bit her lip, straining to hold back the tears.

'They are inconsequential. Whether they see you or not will not alter the fact that they were wrong. And it is a little early for despair. It is spring, and it will be many weeks before we reach the Dros. All things can happen in that time. Ulric may have a heart attack, or fall from his horse and crush his skull. Abalayn may make another treaty. The attack may come at another fortress. Who knows?'

'I know. You are right. I don't know why I'm suddenly so full of self-pity. Meeting Rek was marvellous for me. You should have seen him standing up to Reinard's outlaws. You know of Reinard?'

305

'Yes.'

'Well, you won't have to worry about him any more. He's dead. Anyway, Rek stood up to twenty of them because they were going to take me. Twenty! He would have fought them all. Damn, I'm going to cry!'

'Why should you not cry? You are in love with a man who adores you, and the future looks bleak and empty of hope.' He walked to her, took her hand and pulled her to her feet. 'Virae, it is always harder for the young.'

She rested her head on his chest as the tears ran. He put his arms round her and patted her back. 'Can Dros Delnoch hold?' she asked him.

'All things can happen. Did you know Druss is on his way there?'

'He agreed? That is good news.' She sniffed and wiped her eyes on the sleeve of her shirt. Then Rek's words came back to her. 'He's not senile, is he?'

Vintar laughed aloud. 'Druss! Senile? Certainly not. What a wonderful thought! That is one old man who will never be senile. It would mean giving in to something. I used to believe that if Druss wanted night to last longer, he would just reach up and drag the sun back down over the horizon.'

'You knew him?'

'Yes. And his wife, Rowena. A beautiful child. A Speaker of rare talent. Gifted, even beyond Serbitar.'

'I always thought Rowena was just part of the legend,' said Virae. 'Did he really cross the world to find her?'

'Yes,' said Vintar, releasing Virae and returning to his desk. 'She was taken prisoner soon after they wed, when the village was attacked by slavers. He hunted her for years. They were a blissfully happy couple. Like you and Rek, I shouldn't wonder.'

'What happened to her?'

'She died. Soon after Skeln Pass. A weak heart.'

'Poor Druss,' she said. 'But he is still strong, you say?'

'When he stares, valleys tremble,' quoted Vintar, 'where he walks, beasts are silent, when he speaks, mountains tumble, when he fights, armies crumble.'

'But can he still fight?' she pressed.

'I think he will manage a skirmish or two,' said Vintar, roaring with laughter.

7

Two days and twenty-seven leagues from Skoda, and Druss, with a mile-eating soldier's stride, was nearing the lush valleys at the edge of Skultik Forest. He was three days' march from Dros Delnoch, and evidence of the coming war met his eyes everywhere. Deserted homes, untended fields and the people he did meet were wary and mistrustful of strangers. They wore defeat like a cloak, Druss thought. Topping a small rise he found himself looking down on a village of maybe thirty homes, some crudely built, others showing signs of more careful construction. At the centre of the hamlet was a square, an inn and a stable.

Druss rubbed his thigh, trying to ease the rheumatic pain in his swollen right knee. His right shoulder ached, but this was a dull throbbing he could live with, a reminder of past battles when a Ventrian spear had cut under his shoulder blade. But the knee! This would not bear him many more leagues without rest and an ice pack.

He hawked and spat, wiping a huge hand across his bearded lips. You're an old man, he told himself. There is no point in pretending otherwise. He limped down the hill towards the inn, wondering once more whether he should purchase a mount. His head told him yes, his heart said no. He was Druss the Legend and he never rode. Tireless, he could walk all night and fight all day. It would be good for morale when Druss walked into Dros Delnoch. Men would say: 'Great Gods, the old boy's walked from Skoda.' And others would answer: 'Of course he has. That's Druss. He never rides.'

But his head told him to buy a horse and leave it at the forest's edge, a mere ten miles from the Dros. And who would be the wiser?

The inn was crowded, but the innkeeper had rooms to spare. Most of the customers were passing through, heading south, or west into neutral Vagria. Druss paid his money, took a canvas sack of ice to his room and sat on the hard bed pressing it to his swollen knee. He had not been in the main room for long, but long enough to hear some of the conversations and to recognise many of the men there as soldiers. Deserters.

Always in war, he knew, there were men who would sooner ride than die. But many of the young men downstairs had seemed more demoralised than cowardly.

Were things so bad at Delnoch?

He removed the ice and massaged the fluid away from the joint, his thick fingers pressing and probing, his teeth gritted hard against the pain. Satisfied at last, he opened his small-pack and removed a length of sturdy cotton bandage which he wound tightly about the knee, tucking the end into the fold. Then he rolled down his woollen leggings and pulled his black boot on to his foot, grunting as the injured knee tensed. He stood and walked to the window, pushing it open. His knee felt better – not much, but enough. The sky was cloudless and blue, and a soothing breeze ruffled his beard. High overhead an eagle circled.

Druss returned to his pack, removing the crumpled letter from Delnar. He walked to the window for better light and smoothed the parchment open.

The script was writ large and Druss chuckled again. He was no reader, and Delnar knew it.

My Dearest Comrade,
Even as I write I receive messages about the Nadir army being gathered at Gulgothir. It is plain that Ulric is ready to expand south. I have written to Abalayn, pleading for more men. There are none to be had. I have sent Virae to Vintar – you remember the Abbot of Swords? – to request The Thirty. I clutch at straws, my friend.

I do not know in what health this letter will find you, but it is written in desperation. I need a miracle, or the Dros will fall. I know you swore never again to enter the gates, but old wounds heal and my wife is dead. As is your friend Sieben. You and I are the only men living to know the truth of the matter. And I have never spoken of it.

Your name alone will stop the desertions and restore morale. I am plagued on all sides by poor officers, politically appointed, but my heaviest load is Gan Orrin, the commander. He is Abalayn's nephew and a martinet. He is despised and yet I cannot replace him. In truth, I no longer command.

I have a cancer. It consumes me daily.

It is unfair of me to tell you of it, for I know I am using my own impending death to ask of you a favour.

Come and fight with us. We need you, Druss. Without you, we are lost. Just as at Skeln. Come as soon as you can.

Your comrade in arms.

Earl Delnar

Druss folded the letter, pushing it into a deep pocket inside his leather jerkin.

'An old man with a swollen knee and arthritic back. If you've pinned your hopes on a miracle, my friend, you will need to seek elsewhere.'

A silvered mirror stood next to a wash-basin on an oak chest and Druss stared hard at his reflection. The eyes were piercing blue, the beard square-cut, the jaw beneath it firm. He pulled his leather helm from his head and scratched the thick mat of grey hair. His thoughts were sombre as he replaced the helm and strode downstairs.

At the long bar he ordered ale and listened to the talk around him.

'They say Ulric has a million men,' said one tall youngster. 'And you heard what he did at Gulgothir. When the city refused to surrender, and he had taken it, he had every second defender hanged and quartered. Six thousand men. They say the air was black with crows. Imagine! Six thousand!'

'Do you know why he did it?' Druss asked, breaking into the conversation. The men looked at one another, then back at Druss.

'Of course I know. He's a bloodthirsty savage, that's why.'

'Not at all,' said Druss. 'Join me in a drink?' He called the innkeeper and ordered more ale. 'He did it so that men like you could spread the word to other cities. Wait! Mistake me not,' said Druss, as the man's anger flushed his face. 'I do not criticise you for telling the story. It is natural for these tales to be passed on. But Ulric is a canny soldier. Assume he took the city and treated the defenders heroically? Other cities would defend just as hard. But this way he sends fear ahead of him. And fear is a great ally.'

'You talk like an admirer,' said another man, shorter, with a curling blond moustache.

'But I am,' said Druss, smiling. 'Ulric is one of the greatest generals of the age. Who else in a thousand years has united the Nadir? And with such simplicity. It is the Nadir way to fight anyone not of their tribe. With a thousand tribes thinking this way, they could never become a nation. Ulric took his own tribe, the Wolfshead, and changed the style of Nadir war. To each tribe he conquered, he offered a choice: join him or die. Many chose to die, but many more chose to live. And his army grew. Each tribe keeps its own customs, and they are honoured. You cannot take such a man lightly.'

'The man is a treacherous cur,' offered a man from another group of speakers. 'He signed a treaty with us. Now he is to break it.'

'I am not defending his morals,' said Druss equably. 'Merely pointing out that he's a good general. His troops worship him.'

'Well, I don't like the way you speak, old man,' said the tallest of the listeners.

'No?' said Druss. 'Are you a soldier, then?'

The man hesitated, glanced at his companions, then shrugged. 'It doesn't matter,' he said. 'Forget it.'

'Are you a deserter, then?'

'I said to forget it, old man,' stormed the youngster.

'Are you all deserters?' asked Druss, leaning back against the bar and scanning the thirty or so men gathered there.

'No, not all,' said one young man, emerging from the throng. He was tall and slim, dark hair braided beneath a helm of bronze. 'But you cannot blame those who are.'

'Don't bother with it, Pinar,' said one. 'We have talked it over.'

'I know. Interminably,' said Pinar. 'But it doesn't change the situation. The Gan is a pig. Worse, he is incompetent. But in leaving, you are just making sure your comrades have no chance at all.'

'They haven't any chance anyway,' said the short one with the blond moustache. 'If they had any sense, they would leave with us.'

'Dorian, you are being selfish,' said Pinar gently. 'When the fighting starts, Gan Orrin will have to forget his idiot rules. We will all be too busy to worry about them.'

'Well, I've had enough of it already,' said Dorian. 'Shining armour.

Dawn parades. Forced marches. Midnight inspections. Penalties for sloppy salutes, uncombed crests, talking after lights out. The man's mad.'

'If you're caught, you will be hung,' said Pinar.

'He doesn't dare to send anyone after us. They would desert too. I came to Dros Delnoch to fight the Nadir. I left a farm, a wife and two daughters. I didn't come here for all that shining armour garbage.'

'Then go, my friend,' said Pinar. 'I hope you do not live to regret it.'

'I do regret it already. But my mind is set,' said Dorian. 'I am heading south to join Woundweaver. Now there's a soldier!'

'Is Earl Delnar still alive?' asked Druss. The young warrior nodded absently. 'How many men still hold their positions?'

'What?' said Pinar, realising Druss was speaking to him.

'How many men have you at Delnoch?'

'What concern is it of yours?'

'It's where I am heading.'

'Why?'

'Because I have been asked, young laddie,' said Druss. 'And in more years than I care to remember, I have never turned down a request from a friend.'

'This friend asked you to join us at Dros Delnoch? Is he mad? We need soldiers, archers, pikemen, warriors. I haven't time to be respectful, old man. But you should go home – we have no need of greybeards.'

Druss smiled grimly. 'You are a blunt speaker, boy. But your brains are in your breeches. I have handled an axe for twice your lifetime. My enemies are all dead, or wished they were.' His eyes blazed and he stepped closer towards the younger man. 'When your life has been spent in one war after another for forty-five years, you have to be pretty handy to survive. Now you, laddie – your lips scarce dry from your mother's milk – are just a beardless boy to me. Your sword looks pretty there at your side. But if I chose, I could kill you without breaking sweat.'

A silence had fallen on the room and the watchers noted the bright sheen on Pinar's brow.

'Who invited you to Dros Delnoch?' he said at last.

'Earl Delnar.'

'I see. Well, the earl has been ill, sir. Now you may or may not be a mighty warrior still. And I most certainly am a beardless boy to you. But let me tell you this: Gan Orrin commands at Dros Delnoch, and he will not allow you to stay, Earl Delnar or no. I am sure your heart is in the right place, and I am sorry if I sounded disrespectful. But you are too old for a war.'

'The judgement of youth!' said Druss. 'It is seldom of value. All right, much as it goes against the grain, I can see I still have to prove myself. Set me a task, boy!'

'I don't understand you,' said Pinar.

'Set me a task. Something no man here can do. And we will see how "the old man" fares.'

'I have no time for these games. I must return to the Dros.' He turned to go, but Druss' words hit him like a blow, chilling his blood.

310

'You don't understand, boy. If you do not set me that task, I will have to kill you. For I will not be shamed.'

The young man turned again. 'As you say. Very well, shall we adjourn to the market-place?'

The inn emptied, the crowd forming a circle about the two men in the deserted village square. The sun beat down and Druss sucked in a deep breath, glorying in the warmth of spring.

'It will be pointless giving you a test of strength,' said Pinar, 'for you are built like a bull. But war, as you know, is a test of stamina. Do you wrestle?'

'I have been known to,' said Druss, doffing his jerkin.

'Good! Then you may test your skill, one at a time, against three men of my choice. Do you agree?'

'All too simple against these soft, fat runners,' said Druss. An angry murmur arose from the crowd but Pinar silenced them with a raised hand.

'Dorian. Hagir. Somin. Will you give old father here a trial?'

The men were the first three Dross had met at the bar. Dorian removed his cloak and tied his shoulder-length hair behind his neck with a leather thong. Druss, unnoticed, tested his knee: it was not strong.

'Are you ready?' asked Pinar.

Both men nodded and immediately Dorian rushed the older man. Druss lashed out, grabbing the other's throat, then stooped to push his right hand between the man's legs and lifted. With a grunt and a heave, he hurled him ten feet through the air to land like a sack on the hard-packed earth. Dorian half rose, than sat back shaking his head. The crowd hooted with laughter.

'Who's next?' asked Druss.

Pinar nodded to another youngster; then, observing the fear on the lad's face, he stepped forward. 'You have made your point, greybeard. You are strong and I am at fault. But Gan Orrin will not allow you to fight.'

'Laddie, he will not stop me. If he tries, I will tie him to a fast horse and send him back to his uncle.' All eyes turned as a hoarse cry split the air.

'You old bastard!' Dorian had gathered up his longsword and was advancing towards Druss, who stood with arms folded, waiting.

'No,' said Pinar. 'Put up your blade, Dorian.'

'Back off or draw your sword,' Dorian told him. 'I have had enough of these games. You think you are a warrior, old man? Then let us see you use that axe. Because if you don't, I will put some air in your belly.'

'Boy,' said Druss, his eyes cold, 'think well about this venture. For make no mistake, you cannot stand before me and live. No man ever has.' The words were spoken softly, yet no one disbelieved the old man.

Except Dorian.

'Well, we shall see. Draw your blade!'

Druss slipped Snaga from its sheath, his broad hand curling round its black haft. Dorian attacked!

And died.

He lay on the ground, head half-severed from his neck. Druss hammered Snaga deep into the earth, cleansing the blade of blood, while Pinar stood in stunned silence. Dorian had not been a great swordsman, but he was certainly skilled. Yet the old man had batted aside the slashing sword and in one flowing motion had returned the attack – all without moving his feet. Pinar looked down at the body of his former companion. You should have stayed at the Dros, he thought.

'I did not want that to happen,' said Druss, 'but I gave him fair warning. The choice was his.'

'Yes,' said Pinar. 'My apologies for speaking the way I did. You will be a great help to us, I think. Excuse me, I must help them to remove the body. Will you join me for a drink?'

'I will see you in the long bar,' said Druss.

The tall dark-haired youngster whom Druss had been scheduled to wrestle approached him as he walked through the crowd.

'Excuse me, sir,' he said. 'I am sorry about Dorian. He's hot-tempered. Always has been.'

'Not any more,' said Druss.

'There will be no blood feud,' said the man.

'Good. A man with wife and daughters has no place losing his temper. The man was a fool. Are you a friend of the family?'

'Yes. My name is Hagir. Our farms are close. We are . . . were . . . neighbours.'

'Then, Hagir, when you get home I hope you will see that his wife is cared for.'

'I am not going home. I'm going back to the Dros.'

'What changed your mind?'

'With respect, you did, sir. I think I know who you are.'

'Make your own decisions, don't place them on my shoulders. I want good soldiers at Dros Delnoch, but also I want men who will stand.'

'I didn't leave because I was frightened. I was just fed up with the crazy rules. But if men like you are prepared to be there, I will stick it out.'

'Good. Join me for a drink later. Now I am going to have a hot bath.'

Druss pushed his way past the men in the doorway and went inside.

'Are you really going back, Hagir?' asked one of the men.

'Yes. Yes, I am.'

'But why?' urged another. 'Nothing has changed. Except that we shall all be on report and probably flogged.'

'It's him – *he's* going there. The Captain of the Axe.'

'Druss! That was Druss?'

'Yes, I am sure of it.'

'How sickening!' said the other.

'What do you mean, Somin?' asked Hagir.

'Dorian – Druss was Dorian's hero. Don't you remember him talking about him? Druss this and Druss that. It is one reason he joined up – to be like Druss, and maybe even to meet him.'

'Well, he met him,' said Hagir sombrely.

Druss, dark-haired Pinar, tall Hagir and blunt-featured Somin sat at a corner table in the long room of the inn. Around them a crowd gathered, drawn by the legend of the grizzled old man.

'Just over nine thousand, you say. How many archers?'

Dun Pinar waved a hand. 'No more than six hundred, Druss. The rest are remnants of cavalry lancers, infantrymen, pikers and engineers. The bulk of the complement is made up of volunteer farmers from the Sentran Plain. They're plucky enough.'

'If I remember aright,' said Druss, 'the first wall is four hundred paces long and twenty wide. You will need a thousand archers on it. And I don't just mean a thousand bows. We need men who can pick a target from a hundred paces.'

'We just haven't got them,' said Pinar. 'On the credit side, we do have almost a thousand Legion Riders.'

'Some good news at least. Who leads them?'

'Gan Hogun.'

'The same Hogun who routed the Sathuli at Corteswain?'

'Yes,' said Pinar, pride in his voice. 'A skilled soldier, strong on discipline and yet worshipped by his men. He's not very popular with Gan Orrin.'

'He wouldn't be,' said Druss. 'But that's a matter we shall settle at Delnoch. What of supplies?'

'There we have a few problems. There is enough food for a year, and we discovered three more wells, one as far back as the keep. We have close to six hundred thousand arrows, a multitude of javelins and several hundred spare mail-shirts.

'But the biggest problem is the town itself. It has spread from Wall Three down to Wall Six, hundreds of buildings from wall to wall. There is no killing ground, Druss. Once over Wall Six, the enemy has cover all the way to the keep.'

'We will tackle that, too, when I arrive. Are there still outlaws in Skultik?'

'Of course. When have there not been?' answered Pinar.

'How many?'

'Impossible to say. Five or six hundred, perhaps.'

'Do they have a known leader?'

'Again, hard to say,' said Pinar. 'According to rumour, there is a young nobleman who heads the largest band. But you know how these rumours grow. Every outlaw leader is an ex-nobleman or a prince. What are you thinking?'

'I'm thinking they are archers,' said Druss.

'But you cannot enter Skultik now, Druss. Anything could happen. They could kill you.'

'True. All things could happen. My heart could give out, my liver fail. Disease could strike me. A man cannot spend his life worrying about the unexpected. I need archers. In Skultik there are archers. It's that simple, boy.'

'But it's not that simple. Send someone else. You are too valuable to lose like this,' Pinar told him, gripping the old man's arm.

'I'm too long in the tooth to change my ways now. Direct action pays off, Pinar. Believe me. And there's more to it, which I will tell you about some other time.

'Now,' he said, leaning back and addressing the crowd, 'you know who I am, and where I am heading. I will speak plainly to you; many of you are Runners, some are frightened, others are demoralised. Understand this: when Ulric takes Dros Delnoch the Drenai lands will become Nadir lands. The farms you are running to will be Nadir farms. Your wives will become Nadir women. There are some things no man can run from. I know.

'At Dross Delnoch you risk death. But all men die.

'Even Druss. Even Karnak the One-Eyed. Even the Earl of Bronze.

'A man needs many things in his life to make it bearable. A good woman. Sons and daughters. Comradeship. Warmth. Food and shelter. But above all these things, he needs to be able to know that he is a man.

'And what is a man? He is someone who rises when life has knocked him down. He is someone who raises his fist to heaven when a storm has ruined his crop – and then plants again. And again. A man remains unbroken by the savage twists of fate.

'That man may never win. But when he sees himself reflected, he can be proud of what he sees. For low he may be in the scheme of things: peasant, serf, or dispossessed. But he is unconquerable.

'And what is death? An end to trouble. An end to strife and fear.

'I have fought in many battles. I have seen many men die. And women too. In the main, they died proud.

'Bear this in mind, as you decide your future.'

The old man's fierce blue eyes scanned the faces in the crowd, gauging reaction. He knew he had them. It was time to leave.

He bade his farewells to Pinar and the rest, settled his bill despite the protestations of the innkeeper and set off for Skultik.

He was angry as he walked, feeling the stares on his back as the inn emptied to watch him go. He was angry because he knew his speech had been a falsehood, and he was a man who liked the truth. Life, he knew, breaks many men. Some as strong as oak wither as their wives die, or leave them, as their children suffer or starve. Other strong men break if they lose a limb; or worse, the use of their legs or their eyesight. Each man has a breaking point, no matter how strong his spirit. Somewhere, deep inside him, there is a flaw that only the fickle cruelty of fate can find. A man's strength is ultimately born of his knowledge of his own weakness, Druss knew.

His own fear was of dotage and senility. The thought of it set him to trembling. Did he really hear a voice at Skoda, or was it merely his own terror booming inside him?

Druss the Legend. Mightiest man of his era. A killing machine, a warrior. And why?

Because I never had the courage to be a farmer, Druss told himself.

Then he laughed, dismissing all sombre thoughts and self doubt. It was a talent he had.

Today had a good feel about it. He felt lucky. If he kept to known trails he would certainly meet outlaws. One old man alone was a package not to be missed. They would be a sorely inefficient lot if he were to pass through the forest unnoticed – and unattended.

The woods were becoming thicker now, as he reached the outskirts of Skultik. Huge, gnarled oaks, graceful willows and slender elm interlinked their branches for as far as the eye could see – and greatly beyond, Druss knew.

The noon sun made shafts of shimmering light through the branches and the breeze carried the sounds of miniature waterfalls from hidden streams. It was a place of enchantment and beauty.

To his left a squirrel ceased its hunt for food and gazed warily at the old man as he marched past. A fox crouched in the undergrowth and a snake slithered beneath a fallen trunk as he approached. Overhead birds sang, a chorus full of the sounds of life.

Throughout the long afternoon Druss marched on, occasionally bursting into song, full-bodied and lusty versions of battle hymns from a score of nations.

Towards dusk he became aware that he was being watched.

How he was aware he could never explain. A tightening of the skin on his neck, a growing awareness that his back made a broad target. Whatever it was, he had learned to trust his senses in the matter. He loosened Snaga in her sheath.

Some moments later he entered a small clearing in a grove of beech trees, slender and wand-like against a background of oak.

At the centre of the clearing, on a fallen trunk, sat a young man, dressed in homespun garments of green tunic and brown leather leggings. Upon his legs lay a longsword, and by his side was a longbow and a quiver of goose-feathered arrows.

'Good day, old man,' he said, as Druss appeared. Lithe and strong, thought Druss, noting with a warrior's eye the cat-like grace of the man as he stood, sword in hand.

'Good day, laddie,' said Druss, spotting a movement to his left in the undergrowth. Another whisper of branch on cloth came from his right.

'And what brings you to our charming forest?' asked the young man. Druss casually walked to a nearby beech and sat, leaning his back against the bark.

'A desire for solitude,' he said.

'Ah yes. Solitude! And now you have company. Perhaps this is not a lucky time for you.'

'One time is as lucky as another,' said Druss, returning the other's smile. 'Why don't you ask your friends to join us? It must be damp skulking in the bushes.'

'How rude of me, to be sure. Eldred, Ring, come forward and meet our guest.' Sheepishly two other young men pushed their way through the greenery to stand beside the first. Both were dressed in identical clothing of green tunic and leather leggings. 'Now we are all here,' said the first.

'All except the bearded one with the longbow,' said Druss.

The young man laughed. 'Come out, Jorak. Old father here misses nothing, it seems.' The fourth man came into the open. He was large – a head taller than Druss and built like an ox, his massive hands dwarfing the longbow.

'Now, dear sir, we are all here. Be so kind as to divest yourself of all your valuables, for we are in a hurry. There is a stag roasting at camp, and sweet new potatoes, garnished with mint. I don't want to be late.' He smiled, almost apologetically.

Druss bunched his powerful legs beneath him, rising to his feet, his blue eyes glinting with battle joy.

'If you want my purse, you will have to earn it,' he said.

'Oh damn!' said the young man, smiling and reseating himself. 'I told you, Jorak, that this old fellow had a warrior look about him.'

'And I told you that we should have merely shot him down and then taken his purse,' said Jorak.

'Unsporting,' said the first. He turned to Druss. 'Listen, old man, it would be churlish of us to shoot you down from a distance and that sets us a pretty problem. We must have your purse, don't you see? No point in being a robber else?' He paused, deep in thought, then spoke once more. 'You're obviously not a rich man, so whatever we get will not be worth a great deal of effort. How about spinning a coin? You win, you keep your money, we win, we take it. And I'll throw in a free meal. Roast stag! How does that sound?'

'How about if I win I get your purses, *and* a meal?' asked Druss.

'Now, now, old horse! No point in taking liberties when we're trying to be friendly. All right! How about this? Honour needs to be satisfied. How about a little skirmish with Jorak here? You look quite strong, and he's a dab hand at bare-knuckle squabbles.'

'Done!' said Druss. 'What are the rules?'

'Rules? Whoever is left standing wins. Win or lose, we'll stand you a supper. I rather like you – you remind me of my grandfather.'

Druss grinned broadly, reached into his pack and pulled on his black gauntlets. 'You don't mind do you, Jorak?' he asked. 'It's the old skin on my knuckles – it tends to split.'

'Let's get it over with,' said Jorak, advancing.

Druss stepped in to meet him, taking in the awesome breadth of the man's shoulders. Jorak lunged, hurling a right cross. Druss ducked and crashed his own right fist into the other's belly. A whoosh of air exploded from the giant's mouth. Stepping back, Druss thundered a right hook to the jaw and Jorak hit the ground face first. He twitched once, then lay still.

'The youth of today,' said Druss sadly, 'have no stamina!'

The young leader chuckled. 'You win, Father Time. But look, for the sake of my fast diminishing prestige, give me the opportunity of besting you at something. We will have a wager: I wager my purse against yours that I am a better archer.'

'Hardly a fair bet, laddie. I will concede that point. But I will make a wager with you: strike the trunk of the tree behind me with one arrow, and I'll pay up.'

'Come now, dear sir, where is the art in that? Less than fifteen paces, and the bole is three hands wide.'

'Try it and see,' offered Druss.

The young outlaw shrugged, hefted his bow and drew a long arrow from his doeskin quiver. With a fluid motion his strong fingers drew back the string and released the shaft. As the outlaw's bow bent, Druss drew Snaga and the axe sang through the air in a glittering arc of white light as he sliced the blade to his right. The outlaw's shaft splintered as the axe struck. The young man blinked and swallowed. 'I would have paid to have seen that,' he said.

'You did!' said Druss. 'Where is your purse?'

'Sadly,' said the young man, pulling his pouch from his belt, 'it is empty. But the purse is yours as we agreed. Where did you learn that trick?'

'In Ventria, years ago.'

'I've seen some axe work in the past. But that bordered on the incredible. My name is Bowman.'

'I am Druss.'

'I know that, old horse. Actions speak louder than words.'

8

Hogun swallowed back despair, his mind working furiously. He and 200 of his Legion Riders faced more than a thousand Nadir dog-soldiers, the cavalry wing of Ulric's forces.

Sent out to gauge the strength and disposition of the Nadir horde, Hogun was over 150 miles from Delnoch. He had all but pleaded with Orrin to forsake this plan, but the First Gan was not to be dissuaded.

'A refusal to obey a direct order is punishable by instant dismissal for any of Gan rank. Is that what you wish, Hogun?'

'You know that's not what I'm saying. What I am telling you is that this mission is futile. We know from our spies and countless refugees the strength of Ulric's forces. Sending 200 men into that wasteland is insane.'

Orrin's brown eyes had blazed with anger, his fat chin trembling in a bid to suppress his fury. 'Insane, is it? I wonder. Is it just that you don't like the plan, or is the famed Corteswain warrior afraid to meet the Nadir?'

'The Black Riders are the only seasoned troops of proven worth you have here, Orrin,' he said, as persuasively as he could. 'You could lose all 200 men with such a scheme, and learn from it no more than we already know. Ulric has 500,000 men, and more than twice that in camp followers, cooks, engineers and whores. He will be here within six weeks.'

'Hearsay,' muttered Orrin. 'You leave at first light.'

Hogun had come close to killing him then, close enough for Orrin to sense danger.

'I am your senior officer,' he said, his voice close to a whine. 'You will obey me.'

And Hogun had. With 200 of his finest men, mounted on black horses – bred for generations as the finest war mounts on the continent – he had thundered his troop northwards as the dawn sun breasted the Delnoch mountains.

Out of sight of the Dros he had slowed the column and signalled the men to ride at ease, free to talk to their riding companions. Dun Elicas cantered alongside him, reining his horse to a walk.

'A bad business, sir.'

Hogun smiled, but did not answer. He liked young Elicas. The man was a warrior born, and a fine lieutenant. He sat a horse as if he had been born on one, a true centaur. And a hellion in battle, with his custom-made silver steel sabre, two inches shorter than the standard version.

'What are we supposed to be finding out?' he asked.

'The size and disposition of the Nadir army,' answered Hogun.

'We know that already,' said Elicas. 'What is the fat fool playing at?'

'Enough of that, Elicas,' he said sternly. 'He wants to be sure the spies were not . . . exaggerating.'

'He's jealous of you, Hogun; he wants you dead. Face it, man. No one can hear us. You know what he is – a courtier. And he has no guts. The Dros won't last a day, he'll open the gates for sure.'

'He's a man under terrible pressure. The whole of the Drenai cause rests on his shoulders,' said Hogun. 'Give him time.'

'We don't have time. Look Hogun, send me to Woundweaver. Let me explain our situation. He could be replaced.'

'No. Believe me, Elicas, it would achieve nothing. He's Abalayn's nephew.'

'That old man has a lot to answer for,' snarled Elicas. 'If we do somehow get out of this business alive, he will fall for sure.'

'He has ruled for thirty years. It's too long. But, as you say, if we do get out alive it will be because of Woundweaver. And it's certain he will take control.'

'Then let me ride to him now,' urged Elicas.

'The time isn't right. Woundweaver cannot act. Now, leave it alone. We will do our job, and, with luck, get away without being spotted.'

But luck had not been with them. Five days out from Delnoch they had come across three Nadir outriders. They had killed only two, the third ducking down over the neck of his Steppes pony and riding like the wind into a nearby wood. Hogun had ordered an immediate withdrawal, and might have pulled it off had he enjoyed an ounce of luck. Elicas has been the first to spot the mirror messages flashing from peak to peak.

'What do you think, sir?' he asked, as Hogun reined in.

'I think we will need good fortune. It depends how many dog soldiers they have in the vicinity.'

The answer was not long in coming. Towards late afternoon they saw the dust-cloud south of them. Hogun glanced over his back trail.

'Lebus!' he called and a young warrior cantered alongside.

'You have eyes like a hawk. Look back there, what do you see?'

The young soldier shielded his eyes from the sun, then squinted at their back trail.

'Dust, sir. From maybe two thousand horses.'

'And ahead?'

'Perhaps a thousand.'

'Thank you. Rejoin the troop. Elicas!'

'Sir?'

'Cloaks furled. We will take them with lances and sabres.'

'Yes, sir.' He cantered back down the column. The black cloaks were unpinned and folded to be strapped to saddles. The black and silver armour glinted in the sunlight as man after man began to prepare for the charge. From saddlebags each rider removed a black and silver forearm guard and slipped it in place. Then small round bucklers were lifted from saddle horns to be fitted to the left arm. Straps were adjusted, armour tightened. The approaching Nadir could now be seen as individuals, but the sound of their battle cries was muffled by the pounding of horses' hooves.

'Helms down!' yelled Hogun. 'Wedge formation!'

Hogun and Elicas formed the point of the wedge, the other riders slipping expertly into position a hundred on either side.

'Advance!' yelled Elicas. The troop broke into a canter; then, at full gallop, the lances tilted. As the distance narrowed, Hogun felt his blood racing and could hear his pounding heart in time with the rolling thunder of the black horses' iron-shod hooves.

Now he could pick out individual Nadir faces, and hear their screams.

The wedge smashed into the Nadir ranks, the larger black war horses cleaving a path through the mass of smaller hill ponies. Hogun's lance speared a Nadir chest, and snapped as the man catapulted from his pony. Then his sabre slashed into the air; he cut one man from his mount, parried a thrust from the left and back-handed his blade across the throat of the horseman. Elicas screamed a Drenai war cry from his right, his horse rearing, the front hooves caving the chest of a piebald pony who ditched his rider beneath the milling mass of Black Riders.

And then they were through, racing for the distant, fragile safety of Dros Delnoch.

Glancing back, Hogun saw the Nadir reform and canter to the north. There was no pursuit.

'How many men did we lose?' he asked Elicas as the troop slowed to a walk.

'Eleven.'

'It could have been worse. Who were they?'

Elicas recounted the names. All good men, survivors of many battles.

'That bastard Orrin will pay for this,' said Elicas bitterly.

'Forget it! He was right. More by luck than any judgement, but he was right.'

'What do you mean "right"? We've learned nothing and we've lost eleven men,' said Elicas.

'We have learned that the Nadir are closer than we believed. Those dog soldiers were Wolfshead tribe. That's Ulric's own, they're his personal guard. He'd never send them that far ahead of his main force. I'd say we now have a month – if we're lucky.'

'Damn! I was going to gut the pig and take the consequences.'

'Tell the men no fires tonight,' said Hogun.

Well, fat man, he thought, this is your first good decision.

May it not be the last.

9

The forest had an ageless beauty that touched Druss' warrior soul.
Enchantment hung in the air. Gnarled oaks became silent sentinels in the
silver moonlight, majestic, immortal, unyielding. What cared they for
man's wars? A gentle breeze whispered through the interwoven branches
above the old man's head. A shaft of moonlight bathed a fallen log,
granting it momentarily an ethereal splendour. A lone badger, caught in
the light, shuffled into the undergrowth.

A raucous song began among the men crowded around the blazing
camp fire and Druss cursed softly. Once again the forest was merely forest,
the oaks outsize plants. Bowman wandered across to him carrying two
leather goblets and a winesack.

'Finest Ventrian,' he said. 'It'll turn your hair black.'

'I'm all for that,' said Druss. The young man filled Druss' goblet, then
his own.

'You look melancholy, Druss. I thought the prospect of another glorious
battle would lighten your heart.'

'Your men are the worst singers I have heard in twenty years. They're
butchering that song,' Druss replied, leaning his back against the oak,
feeling the wine ease his tension.

'Why are you going to Delnoch?' asked Bowman.

'The worst were a bunch of captured Sathuli. They just kept chanting
the same bloody verse over and over again. We let them go in the end –
we thought that if they sang like that when they got home, they'd break
the fighting spirit of their tribe in a week.'

'Now look here, old horse,' said Bowman, 'I am a man not easily
thrown. Give me an answer – any answer! Lie if you like. But tell me
why you travel to Delnoch.'

'Why do you want to know?'

'It fascinates me. A man with half an eye could see that Delnoch will
fall, and you're a man with enough experience to know the truth when
you see it. So why go?'

'Have you any idea, laddie, how many such lost causes I have been
involved in during the past forty or so years?'

'Precious few,' said Bowman. 'Or you would not be here to tell of
them.'

'Not so. How do you decide a battle is lost? Numbers, strategic advantage, positioning? It's all worth a sparrow's fart. It comes down to men
who are willing. The largest army will founder if its men are less willing
to die than to win.'

'Rhetoric,' snorted Bowman. 'Use it at the Dros. The fools there will
lap it up.'

'One man against five, and the one disabled,' said Druss, holding his temper. 'Where would your money go?'

'I'm ahead of you, old man. What if the one was Karnak the One-Eyed. Yes? Well, then my money would be on him. But how many Karnaks are there at Dros Delnoch?'

'Who knows? Even Karnak was unknown once. He made his name on a bloody battlefield. There will be many heroes come the last at Dros Delnoch.'

'Then you admit it? The Dros is doomed,' said Bowman, grinning in triumph. 'At the last, you said.'

'Damn you, boy! Don't put words in my mouth,' snarled Druss, cursing himself. Where are you now, Sieben, he thought? Now that I need you with your glib words and ready wit.

'Then don't try to treat me like a fool. Admit that the Dros is doomed.'

'As you say,' admitted Druss, 'anyone with half an eye could see it. But I don't give a damn, laddie. Until the actual moment when they cut me down, I shall still be looking to win. And the gods of war are fickle at best. Where do you stand on the matter?'

Bowman smiled and refilled both goblets. For a while he was silent, enjoying the wine and the old man's discomfort.

'Well?' said Druss.

'Now we come to it,' answered Bowman.

'Come to what?' said Druss, ill at ease under the young archer's cynical gaze.

'The reason for this visit to my woods,' said Bowman, spreading his hands, his smile now open and friendly. 'Come now, Druss, I've too much respect for you to fence any longer. You want my men for your insane battle. And the answer is no. But enjoy the wine anyway.'

'Am I so transparent?' asked the old warrior.

'When Druss the Legend takes a stroll through Skultik on the eve of the End, he's looking for more than acorns.'

'Is this all you want from life?' asked Druss. 'You sleep in a wattle hut and eat when you can find game. When you cannot, you starve. In winter you're cold. In summer the ants crawl into your clothes and the lice prosper. You were not made for a life like this.'

'We are not made for life at all, old horse. It is made for us. We live it. We leave it. I'll not throw my life away in your bloody madness. I leave such heroics to men like you. All your years have been spent in one squalid war after another. And what has changed? Have you thought that if you had not defeated the Ventrians fifteen years ago at Skeln, we would now be part of a mighty empire and *they* would have had to worry about the Nadir?'

'Freedom's worth fighting for,' said Druss.

'Why? No one can take away the freedom of a man's soul.'

'Liberty, then?' offered Druss.

'Liberty is only valued when it is threatened, therefore it is the threat that highlights the value. We should be grateful to the Nadir, since they heighten the value of our liberty.'

322

'You've lost me, damn you, with your pretty words. You're like those politicians in Drenan, as full of wind as a sick cow. Don't tell me my life has been wasted, I won't have that! I loved a good woman and I've always been true to my principles. I never did a shameful thing, nor yet a cruel one.'

'Ah, but Druss, not all men are you. I will not criticise your principles if you do not try to graft them on to me. I have no time for them. A pretty hypocrite I would be as a robber outlaw with principles.'

'Then why did you not let Jorak shoot me down?'

'As I said, it was unsporting. It lacked a sense of style. But on another day, when I was colder, or more bad-tempered . . .'

'You are a nobleman, aren't you?' said Druss. 'A rich boy playing at robbers. Why do I sit here and argue with you?'

'Because you need my archers.'

'No. I have given up on that thought,' said Druss, offering his goblet to the green-garbed outlaw. Bowman filled it, a cynical smile once more upon his mouth.

'Given up? Nonsense. I will tell you what you're thinking. You will argue some more, offer me wages and a pardon for my crimes. If I refuse, you will kill me and take your chances with the same offer to my men.'

Druss was shaken, but his face showed nothing.

'Do you also read palms?' he asked, sipping his wine.

'You're too honest, Druss. And I like you. That's why I would like to point out that Jorak is behind the bushes there with an arrow notched.'

'Then I have lost,' said Druss. 'You keep your archers.'

'Tut, tut, dear man, I didn't expect such defeatism from Druss the Legend. Put your offer.'

'I've no time for your games. I had a friend like you, Sieben the Saga Master. He could talk all day and convince you the sea was sand. I never won an argument with him. He talked about having no principles – and like you, he lied.'

'He was the poet who wrote the Legend. He made you immortal,' said Bowman, softly.

'Yes,' said Druss, his mind drifting back over the long years.

'Did you really hunt your woman across the world?'

'That part at least was true. We were wed when we were very young. Then my village was attacked by a slaver called Harib Ka, who sold her to an eastern merchant. I missed the attack, as I was working in the woods. But I followed them. In the end it took me seven years and when I found her, she was with another man.'

'What happened to him?' asked Bowman, softly.

'He died.'

'And she came back with you to Skoda.'

'Aye. She loved me. She really did.'

'An interesting addendum to your saga,' said Bowman.

Druss chuckled. 'I must be getting melancholy in my old age. I don't usually prattle on about the past.'

'What happened to Sieben?' asked the outlaw.

'He died at Skeln.'

'You were close?'

'We were like brothers.'

'I can't think why I remind you of him,' said Bowman.

'Maybe it is because you both hide a dark secret,' said Druss.

'Perhaps,' admitted the outlaw. 'However, make your offer.'

'A pardon for every man, and five gold Raq a head.'

'Not enough.'

'It's my best offer, I'll go no further.'

'Your offer must be this: A pardon, five gold Raq a head for all 620 men, and an agreement that when Wall Three falls we leave with our money and our pardons stamped with the Earl's seal.'

'Why Wall Three?'

'Because that will be the beginning of the end.'

'Something of a strategist, are you, boy?'

'You could say that. By the way, how do you feel about women warriors?'

'I have known a few. Why do you ask?'

'I shall be bringing one.'

'So? What difference does it make as long as she can aim a bow?'

'I didn't say it made a difference. I just thought I ought to mention it.'

'Is there something about this woman that I should know?' asked Druss.

'Only that she's a killer,' said Bowman.

'Then she's perfect and I will welcome her with open arms.'

'I wouldn't recommend it,' said Bowman, softly.

'Be at Delnoch in fourteen days, and I'll welcome you all with open arms.'

Rek awoke to see the new sun breasting the distant mountains. His body adjusted swiftly from dreamless sleep and he stretched and slid from the covers, then walked to the tower window of the bedroom. In the courtyard below The Thirty were assembling their mounts, great beasts with short-cropped manes and braided tails. Apart from the sound of steel hooves on cobbles an eerie silence hung over the scene. None of the men spoke. Rek shivered.

Virae moaned in her sleep, her arm stretching across the wide bed.

Rek watched the men below check their armour and tighten saddle girths. Strange, he thought. Where are the jokes, the laughter, all the sounds soldiers usually make as they prepare for war? Jests to ease the fear, curses to ease the tension?

Serbitar appeared, a white cloak over his silver armour, his braided white hair covered by a silver helm. The Thirty saluted him. Rek shook his head. It was uncanny. Identical timing: like the same salute in thirty mirrors.

Virae opened her eyes and yawned. She rolled over and saw Rek's back silhouetted against the morning sun. She smiled.

'Your belly is receding into memory,' she said.

'Mock not,' he said, smiling. 'Unless you are going to appear in front of thirty warriors in your skin, you need to hurry. They are already in the courtyard.'

'It's one way to find out if they're human,' she said, sitting up. Rek tore his eyes from her body.

'You have the strangest effect on me,' he said, gazing into her eyes. 'You always make me think of love-making at the wrong times. Now get dressed.'

In the courtyard Serbitar led the men in prayer, a silent joining of minds. Vintar watched the young albino fondly, pleased with his swift adjustment to the responsibility of leadership.

Serbitar ended the prayer and returned to the tower. He was uneasy – out of harmony. He mounted the circular stone steps to the tower bedroom, smiling as he remembered his promise to the tall Drenai and his woman. It would have been so much easier to Speak than to mount these stairs to check if they were ready.

He knocked on the iron-studded door. Rek opened it, beckoning him in.

'I see you are ready,' he said. 'We won't be long.'

Serbitar nodded. 'The Drenai have met the Nadir,' he said.

'They are already at Delnoch?' asked Rek, alarmed.

'No, no,' answered Serbitar. 'The Legion met them in the outlands. They did well. Their leader is called Hogun. He, at least, is quality.'

'When was this?'

'Yesterday.'

'Your powers again?'

'Yes. Does it distress you?'

'It makes me uncomfortable. But only because I do not share the talent.'

'A wise observation, Rek. It will come to be more acceptable, believe me.' Serbitar bowed as Virae entered from the rear wash-room.

'I am sorry to have kept you waiting,' she said. Dressed in her armour, silver mail-shirt, with bronze shoulder pads, she now also sported a silver helm, raven-winged, and a white cloak – gifts from Vintar. Her fair hair was braided on either side of her face.

'You look like a goddess,' Rek told her.

They joined The Thirty in the courtyard, checked their mounts and rode alongside Serbitar and Menahem, heading for the Drinn estuary.

'Once there,' Menahem told them, 'we will book passage on a Lentrian ship to Dros Purdol. It will save two weeks of travel. From Purdol we travel by river and road and should reach Delnoch in four weeks at the outside. I fear battle will be joined before we arrive.'

As the hours passed the ride became a personal nightmare for Rek. His back was bruised and his buttocks numb before Serbitar called for a noon break. It was a short one, and the pain had become intense by dusk.

They camped in a small grove of trees near a stream. Virae almost fell from the saddle, fatigue – deep and numbing – showing in her every movement. But she was enough of a horsewoman to tend her mount before slumping to the ground, her back against a tree. Rek took more time wiping the lather from Lancer's back and shoulders. *He* didn't need to sit! He covered the horse with a blanket, then walked to the stream. Lancer was bearing up as well as the priests' mounts, Rek thought with pride.

But he was still wary around the gelding. It had a tendency to snap at him even now. Rek smiled, thinking back.

'A fine mount,' Serbitar had said that morning, stepping forward to stroke the mane. Lancer snapped and Serbitar leapt backwards. 'May I Speak with him?' Serbitar had asked.

'With a horse?'

'It is more an empathic bond. I shall tell him I mean no harm.'

'Go ahead.'

After a little while Serbitar smiled. 'He is being very friendly, but he is waiting to snap at me again. That, my friend, is a cantankerous animal.'

Rek walked back to the camp-site to find four fires glowing merrily and the riders eating their oatcakes. Virae was asleep beneath a tree, wrapped in a red blanket, her head resting on her white cloak. He joined Serbitar, Vintar and Menahem at their fire. Arbedark was talking softly to a nearby group.

'We're pushing hard,' said Rek. 'The horses won't last.'

'We can rest aboard ship,' said Serbitar. 'And we will be aboard the Lentrian vessel *Wastrel* early tomorrow. It sails with the morning tide, hence the urgency.'

'Even my bones are tired,' said Rek. 'Is there any more news from Delnoch?'

'We will see later,' said Menahem, smiling. 'I am sorry, friend Rek, for my testing of you. It was a mistake.'

'Please forget it – and what I said. The words were spoken in anger.'

'That is gracious. Before you joined us we were talking of the Dros. It is our belief that under existing leadership it cannot last a week. Morale is low and their leader Orrin is overwhelmed by his position and responsibility. We need a fair wind and no delays.'

'You mean it could be over before we arrive?' said Rek, his heart leaping.

'I think not,' said Vintar. 'But the end may be near. Tell me, Regnak, why do you travel to Delnoch?'

'The possibility of stupidity can never be ruled out,' Rek told him, without humour. 'Anyway, we might not lose. Surely there is at least a faint chance?'

'Druss will be there soon,' said Vintar. 'Much will depend on his reception. If it is good, and we can arrive while the first wall holds, we should be able to harness the strengths of the defenders and guarantee resistance for about a month. I cannot see a mere 10,000 men holding for longer.'

'Woundweaver may send reinforcements,' said Menahem.

'Perhaps,' said Serbitar. 'But unlikely. Already his marshals are scouring the empire. Virtually the entire army is gathered at Delnoch, with 3,000 men holding Dros Purdol and another thousand at Corteswain.

'Abalayn has been foolish these last years, running down the army and cultivating trade agreements with Ulric. It was folly. Had it not been the Nadir attacking now, it would have been Vagria before long.

'My father would love to humble the Drenai. He has dreamed about it long enough.'

'Your father?' queried Rek.

'Earl Drada of Dros Segril. Did you not know?' said Serbitar.

'No, I didn't. But Segril is only eighty miles west of Delnoch. Surely he will send men when he knows you are there?'

'No. My father and I are not friends; my talent unnerves him. However, if I am killed he will be in blood feud with Ulric. That means he will swing his forces to Woundweaver. It may help the Drenai – but not Dros Delnoch.'

Menahem tossed twigs to the fire, holding his dark-skinned hands towards the blaze. 'Abalayn has at least got one thing right. This Lentrian Woundweaver is quality. A warrior of the old school, tough, determined, and practical.'

'There are times, Menahem,' Vintar said, smiling gently, age sitting heavily on him following the hard ride, 'when I doubt you will achieve your aim. Warriors of the old school, indeed!'

Menahem grinned broadly. 'I can admire a man for his talents, while debating his principles,' he said.

'Indeed you can, my boy. But did I not note the merest hint of empathy?' asked Vintar.

'You did, master Abbot. But only a hint, I assure you.'

'I hope so, Menahem. I would not want to lose you before the Journey. Your soul must be sure.'

Rek shivered. He had no idea what they were talking about. On reflection he had no wish to know.

Dros Delnoch's first line of defence was the wall Elbidar, spreading snake-like for almost a quarter of a mile across the Delnoch Pass. Forty-eight feet high when viewed from the north, a mere five feet from the south, like a giant step carved from the heart of a mountain in seamed granite.

Cul Gilad sat on the battlements, gazing sombrely past the few trees towards the northern plains. His eyes scanned the shimmering distant horizon, searching for the tell-tale dust clouds that would herald the invasion. There was nothing to see. His dark eyes narrowed as he caught sight of an eagle high in the morning sky. Gilad smiled.

'Fly, you great golden bird. Live!' he shouted. Gilad pushed himself to his feet and stretched his back. His legs were long and slim, his movements fluid, graceful. The new army shoes were half a size too large and packed with paper. His helm, a wondrous thing of bronze and silver, slipped over one eye. Cursing, he hurled it to the floor. One day he would write a battle hymn about army efficiency, he thought. His belly rumbled and he cast his eyes about for his friend Bregan, gone to fetch their mid-morning food: black bread and cheese – bound to be. Endless wagons of supplies arriving daily at Delnoch, yet the mid-morning meal was always black bread and cheese. Shielding his eyes, he could just make out Bregan's tubby form ambling from the mess hall bearing two platters and a jug. Gilad smiled. Good-natured Bregan. A farmer, a husband, a father. All these things he did well in his own soft, kindly, easygoing way. But a soldier?

'Black bread and creamed cheese,' said Bregan, smiling. 'We've only had it three times and I'm already tired of it.'

'Are the carts still coming in?' asked Gilad.

'By the score. Still, I expect they know best what a warrior needs,' said Bregan. 'I wonder how Lotis and the boys are bearing up.'

'News should be in later. Sybad always gets letters.'

'Yes. I've only been here two weeks and yet I miss the family terribly,' said Bregan. 'I only joined up on the spur of the moment, Gil. That officer's speech just got to me, I suppose.'

Gilad had heard it before – almost every day for the two weeks since first they had been issued with armour. Bregan shouldn't be at Delnoch, he knew; he was tough enough, but in a way he lacked the heart. He was a farmer, a man who loved growing things. To destroy was alien to him.

'By the way,' said Bregan suddenly, his face echoing his excitement, 'you'll never guess who's just arrived!'

'Who?'

'Druss the Legend. Can you believe it?'

'Are you sure, Bregan? I thought he was dead.'

'No. He arrived an hour ago. The whole mess hall is buzzing with the news. They say he's bringing five thousand archers and a legion of axemen.'

'Don't count on it, my friend,' said Gilad. 'I've not been here long, but I would like a copper coin for every story I've heard about reinforcements, peace plans, treaties and leave.'

'Well, even if he brings no one it's still good news, isn't it? I mean, he is a hero, isn't he?'

'He certainly is. Gods, he must be about seventy, though. That's a bit old, isn't it?'

'But he's a *hero*.' Bregan stressed the word, his eyes gleaming. 'I've heard stories about him all my life. He was a farmer's son. And he's never lost, Gil. Not ever. And he will be with us. Us! The next song about Druss the Legend will have us in it. Oh, I know we won't be named – but we'll know, won't we? I'll be able to tell little Legan that I fought beside Druss the Legend. It makes a difference, doesn't it?'

'Of course it does,' said Gilad, dipping his black bread into the cheese and scanning the horizon. Still no movement. 'Does your helmet fit?' he asked.

'No, it's too small. Why?'

'Try mine.'

'We've been through that, Gil. Bar Kistrid says it's against the rules to swap.'

'A pox on Bar Kistrid and his stupid rules. Try it on.'

'They all have numbers stamped inside.'

'Who cares? Try it on, for Missael's sake.'

Bregan carefully looked around, reached across and tried on Gilad's helm.

'Well?' asked Gilad.

'It's better. Still a little tight, but much better.'

'Give me yours.' Gilad placed Bregan's helm over his own head; it was close to perfect. 'Wonderful!' he said. 'This will do.'

'But the rules . . .'

'There is no rule that says a helm must not fit,' said Gilad. 'How's the swordplay coming along?'

'Not bad,' said Bregan. 'It's when it's in the scabbard that I feel stupid. It keeps flapping between my legs and tripping me.' Gilad burst into laughter, a fine lilting sound that echoed high into the mountains.

'Ah, Breg, what are we doing here?'

'Fighting for our country. It's nothing to laugh at, Gil.'

'I'm not laughing at you,' he lied. 'I'm laughing at the whole stupid business. We face the biggest threat in our history and they give me a helmet too big, and you a helmet too small, and tell us we can't exchange them. It's too much. Really. Two farmers on a high wall tripping over their swords.' He giggled, then laughed aloud again.

'They probably won't notice we've swapped,' said Bregan.

'No. All I need now is to find a man with a large chest wearing my breastplate.' Gilad leaned forward, the laughter hurting his side.

'It is good news about Druss, isn't it?' said Bregan, mystified by Gilad's sudden good humour.

'What? Oh yes.' Gilad took a deep breath, then smiled at his friend. Yes, it was good news, if it could so lift a man like Bregan, he thought. A hero indeed. Not a hero, Bregan, you fool. Just a warrior. You are the hero. You have left the family and the farm you love to come here and die in order to protect them. And who will sing your song – or mine? If they remember Dros Delnoch at all in years to come, it will be because a white-maned old man died here. He could hear the psalmists and saga-poets chanting their rhymes. And the teachers telling young children – Nadir children and Drenai – the tale of Druss: 'And at the end of a long, glorious life, Druss the Legend came at last to Dros Delnoch, where he fought mightily, and fell.'

'They say in the mess hall,' said Bregan, 'that after a month this bread is riddled with worms.'

'Do you believe everything they tell you?' snapped Gilad, suddenly angry. 'If I was sure I'd be alive in a month, I would be glad to eat wormy bread.'

'Not me,' said Bregan. 'It can poison you, so they say.'

Gilad bit back his anger.

'You know,' said Bregan thoughtfully, 'I don't know why so many people seem to think we're doomed. Look at the height of this wall. And there are six of them. And at the end of it there's still the Dros itself. Don't you think?'

'Yes.'

'What's wrong, Gil? You're acting so strangely. Laughing one minute, angry the next. It's not like you, you've always been so . . . cool, I suppose.'

'Don't mind me, Breg. I'm just frightened.'

'So am I. I wonder if Sybad got a letter. It's not the same, I know – as seeing them, I mean. But it lifts me to hear they're well. I'll bet Legan isn't sleeping too well, without me there.'

'Don't think about that,' said Gilad, sensing the emotional shift in his friend and knowing his tears were not far away. Such a soft man. Not weak. Never weak. But soft, gentle and caring. Not like himself. He hadn't come to Delnoch to defend the Drenai and his family – he came because he was bored. Bored with his life as a farmer, cold to his wife and uncaring about the land. Up at first light to tend the animals and prepare the fields, tilling and planting until late afternoon. Repairing fences, or leather hinge-straps or leaking buckets until long after dusk. Then slipping into a rush-mattressed bed beside a fat, carping woman, whose complaints would drone on long after sleep had carried him on the all too short journey to a new sunrise.

He had believed nothing could be worse, but he could not have been more wrong.

He thought of Bregan's words about Dros Delnoch's strength. His mind's eye pictured hundreds of thousands of barbarian warriors swarming like ants over a thin line of defenders. It's funny, he thought, how different people view the same event. Bregan can't see how they can take Delnoch.

I can't see how they can fail.

All in all, he thought, smiling, I think I would rather be Bregan.

'I'll bet it's cooler at Dros Purdol,' said Bregan. 'The sea air blowing in and all that. This pass seems to make even the spring sun burn.'

'It blocks the east wind,' said Gilad, 'and the grey marble reflects the heat down on to us. I expect it's pleasant in winter, though.'

'Well, I shall not be here to see that,' said Bregan. 'I only signed on for the summer and I'm hoping to be back in time for the harvest supper. That's what I told Lotis.'

Gilad laughed, his tension flowing from him. 'Never mind Druss,' he said. 'I'm glad you're with me, Breg, I really am.'

Bregan's brown eyes searched Gilad's face for any sign of sarcasm. Satisfied, he smiled. 'Thanks for saying that. We never had much to do with one another at the village and I always felt you thought I was dull.'

'I was wrong. Here, take my hand on it. We will stick together, you and I, see off the Nadir and journey back to the Supper with tall tales.'

Bregan gripped his hand, grinning, then: 'Not like that,' he said suddenly. 'It has to be the warrior's grip, wrist to wrist.'

Both men chuckled.

'Never mind about saga-poets,' said Gilad. 'We will compose our own song. Bregan of the Broadsword and Gilad, the demon of Dros Delnoch. How's that?'

'I think you ought to find another name for yourself. My Legan has always been afraid of demons.'

The sound of Gilad's laughter reached the eagle high above the pass. It banked sharply and flew to the south.

10

Druss paced impatiently in the great hall of the keep, gazing absently at the marble statues of past heroes flanking the high walls. No one had questioned him as he entered the Dros, and everywhere soldiers were sitting in the spring sunshine, some dicing their meagre wages, others asleep in the shade. The city folk moved about their business as usual and a dull, apathetic air hung over the fortress. The old man's eyes had blazed with a cold fury. Officers chatted among the enlisted men – it was almost more than the old warrior could bear. Angry beyond endurance, he had marched to the Keep and hailed a young officer in a red cloak who stood in the shade of the portcullis gate.

'You! Where will I find the Earl?'

'How should I know?' answered the man, walking past the black-garbed axeman. A mighty hand curled round the folds of the red cloak and tugged, contemptuously. The officer checked in his stride, lost his footing and crashed back into the old man, who grabbed him by the belt and hoisted him from the floor. His breastplate clanged as his back hit the gateway.

'Maybe you didn't hear me, you son of a slut!' hissed Druss. The young man swallowed hard.

'I think he's in the great hall,' he said. 'Sir!' he added hurriedly. The officer had never seen battle nor any degree of violence, yet he knew instinctively the threat contained in the ice-cold eyes. He's insane, he thought as the old man slowly lowered him to the ground.

'Lead me to him and announce me. The name is Druss. Do you think you can remember it?'

The young man nodded so vigorously that his horse-hair crested helm slipped over his eyes.

Minutes later Druss paced in the great hall, his anger barely held in check. Was this how empires fell?

'Druss, old friend, how you delight my eyes!' If Druss had been surprised by the state of the fortress, he was doubly shocked by the appearance of Earl Delnar, Lord Warden of the North. Supported by the young officer, the man would not pass for the shadow he had cast at Skeln Pass a scant fifteen years before. His skin stretched like parchment over a skull-like countenance, yellow and dry, his eyes burning brightly – feverishly – in dark sockets. The young officer brought him close to the old warrior and the Earl extended a hand like a claw. Gods of Missael, thought Druss. He is five years younger than I!

'I do not find you in good health, my lord,' said Druss.

'Still the blunt speaker, I see! No, you do not. I am dying, Druss.' He patted the young soldier's arm. 'Ease me into that chair by the sunlight, Mendar.' The young man pulled the chair into place. Once settled, the

Earl smiled his thanks and dismissed him to fetch wine. 'You frightened the boy, Druss. He was shaking more than I – and I have good reason.' He stopped speaking and began to take deep, shuddering breaths. His arms trembled. Druss leaned forward, resting a huge hand on the frail shoulder, wishing he could pour strength into the man. 'I will not last another week. But Vintar came to me in a dream yesterday. He rides with The Thirty and my Virae. They will be here within the month.'

'So will the Nadir,' said Druss, pulling up a high-backed chair to sit opposite the dying Earl.

'True. In the interim I would like you to take over the Dros. Prepare the men. Desertions are high. Morale is low. You must . . . take over.' Once more the Earl paused to breathe.

'I cannot do that – even for you. I am no general, Delnar. A man must know his limitations. I am a warrior – sometimes a champion, but never a Gan. I understand little of the clerk's work involved in running this city. No, I cannot do that. But I will stay and fight – that will have to be enough.'

The Earl's fever-sick eyes focused on the ice-blue orbs of the axeman. 'I know your limitations, Druss, and I understand your fears. But there is no one else. When The Thirty arrive they will plan and organise. Until then, it is as a warrior that you will be needed. Not to fight, although the gods know how well you do that, but to train: to pass on your years of experience. Think of the men here as a rusty weapon which needs a warrior's firm hand. It needs to be sharpened, honed, prepared. It's useless else.'

'I may have to kill Gan Orrin,' said Druss.

'No! You must understand that he is not evil, nor even wilful. He is a man out of his depth, and struggling hard. I don't think he lacks courage. See him and then judge for yourself.'

A racking cough burst from the old man's lips, his body shuddering violently. Blood frothed at his mouth as Druss leapt to his side. The Earl's hand fluttered towards his sleeve and the cloth held there. Druss pulled it clear and dabbed the Earl's mouth, easing him forward and gently tapping his back. At last the fit subsided.

'There is no justice when such as you must die like this,' said Druss, hating the feeling of helplessness that overwhelmed him.

'None of us . . . can choose . . . the manner of our passing. No, that is not true . . . For you are here, old warhorse. I see that you at least have chosen wisely.'

Druss laughed, loud and heartily. The young officer, Mendar, returned with a flagon of wine and two crystal goblets. He poured for the Earl, who produced a small bottle from a pocket in his purple tunic; he uncorked it and poured several drops of dark liquid into his wine. As he drank, a semblance of colour returned to his face.

'Darkseed,' he said. 'It helps me.'

'It is habit forming,' said Druss, but the Earl chuckled.

'Tell me, Druss,' he said, 'why did you laugh when I said you had chosen your death?'

'Because I am not ready to give in to the old bastard yet. He wants me, but I will make it damned hard for him.'

'You have always seen death as your own personal enemy. Does he exist, do you think?'

'Who knows? I like to think so. I like to think this is all a game. All life is a test between him and me.'

'But *is* it?'

'No. But it gives me an edge. I have six hundred archers joining us within fourteen days.'

'That is wonderful news. How in heavens did you manage it? Woundweaver sent word he could spare not a man.'

'They are outlaws and I have promised them a pardon – and five gold Raq a head.'

'I don't like it, Druss. They are mercenaries and not to be trusted.'

'You have asked me to take over,' said Druss. 'So trust me; I won't let you down. Order the pardons to be drawn up and prepare notes against the treasury in Drenan.' He turned to the young officer standing patiently by the window. 'You, young Mendar!'

'Sir?'

'Go, and tell . . . ask . . . Gan Orrin if he will see me in an hour. My friend and I have much to talk over, but tell him that I would be grateful for a meeting. Understand?'

'Yes, sir.'

'Then get on with it.' The officer saluted and left. 'Now, before you tire, my friend, let us get down to business. How many fighting men have you?'

'Just over nine thousand. But six thousand of those are recruits, and only a thousand – The Legion – are battle-hardened warriors.'

'Surgeons?'

'Ten, led by Calvar Syn. You remember him?'

'Aye. A point on the credit side.'

For the rest of the hour Druss questioned the Earl, and by the end of the time he was visibly weaker. He began to cough blood once more, eyes squeezed shut against the pain that racked him. Druss lifted him from his chair. 'Where is your room?' he asked. But the Earl was unconscious.

Druss strode from the hall, bearing the limp form of the Warden of the North. He hailed a passing soldier, gained directions and ordered Calvar Syn to be summoned.

Druss sat at the foot of the Earl's bed as the elderly surgeon ministered to the dying man. Calvar Syn had changed little; his shaven head still gleamed like polished marble, and his black eye-patch looked even more tattered than Druss remembered.

'How is he?' asked Druss.

'How do you think he is, you old fool?' answered the surgeon. 'He is dying. He cannot last another two days.'

'I see you have retained your good humour, doctor,' said Druss, grinning.

'What is there to be good-humoured about?' queried the surgeon. 'An old friend is dying, and thousands of young men will follow him within the next few weeks.'

'Perhaps. It is good to see you, anyway,' said Druss, rising.

'Well it's not good to see you,' said Calvar Syn, a gleam in his eye and a faint smile on his lips. 'Where you go, the crows gather. Anyway, how is it that you seem so ridiculously healthy?'

'You're the doctor – you tell me.'

'Because you are not human! You were carved out of stone on a winter's night and given life by a demon. Now get out! I have work to do.'

'Where will I find Gan Orrin?'

'Main Barracks. Now *go*!' Druss grinned and left the room.

Dun Mendar took a deep breath. 'You don't like him, sir?'

'Like him? Of course I like him!' snapped the surgeon. 'He kills men clean, boy. Saves me work. Now you get out, too.'

As Druss walked across the parade ground before the main barracks building, he became aware of the stares of the soldiers and the muted whispers as he passed. He smiled inwardly. It had begun! From now on he would be unable to relax for a moment. Never could he show these men a glimpse of Druss the Man. He was The Legend. The invincible Captain of the Axe. Indestructible Druss.

He ignored the salutes until he reached the main entrance, where two guards snapped to attention.

'Where will I find Gan Orrin?' he asked the first.

'Third doorway of the fifth corridor on the right,' answered the soldier, back straight, eyes staring ahead.

Druss marched inside, located the room and knocked on the door.

'Come!' said a voice from within and Druss entered. The desk was immaculately tidy, the office spartanly furnished but smart. The man behind the desk was tubby, with soft, doelike dark eyes. He looked out of place in the gold epaulettes of a Drenai Gan.

'You are Gan Orrin?' asked Druss.

'I am. You must be Druss. Come in, my dear fellow, and have a seat. You have seen the Earl? Yes, of course you have. Of course you have. I expect he has told you about our problems here. Not easy. Not easy at all. Have you eaten?' The man was sweating and ill at ease and Druss felt sorry for him. He had served under countless commanders in his lifetime. Many were fine, but as many were incompetent, foolish, vain or cowardly. He did not know as yet into which category Orrin fell, but he sympathised with his problems.

On a shelf by the window stood a wooden platter bearing black bread and cheese. 'I will have some of that, if I may?' said Druss.

'But of course.' Orrin passed it to him. 'How is the Earl? A bad business. Such a fine man. A friend of his, weren't you? At Skeln together. Wonderful story. Inspiring.'

Druss ate slowly, enjoying the gritty bread. The cheese was good too, mellow and full-flavoured. He rethought his original plan to tackle Orrin by pointing out the shambles into which the Dros had fallen, the apathy and the ram-shackle organisation. A man must know his limitations, he thought. If he exceeds them, nature has a way of playing cruel tricks. Orrin should never have accepted Gan rank, but in peacetime he would be easily absorbed. Now he stood out like a wooden horse in a charge.

'You must be exhausted,' Druss said at last.

'What?'

'Exhausted. The workload here is enough to break a lesser man. Organisation of supplies, training, patrols, strategy, planning. You must be completely worn out.'

'Yes, it is tiring,' said Orrin, wiping the sweat from his brow, his relief evident. 'Not many people realise the problems of command. It's a nightmare. Can I offer you a drink?'

'No, thank you. Would it help if I took some of the weight from your shoulders?'

'In what way? You are not asking me to stand down, are you?'

'Great Missael, no,' said Druss, with feeling. 'I would be lost. No, I meant nothing of that kind.

'But time is short and no one can expect you to bear this burden alone. I would suggest you turn over to me the training and all the responsibility for preparing the defence. We need to block those tunnels behind the gates, and set work parties to razing the buildings from Wall Four to Wall Six.'

'Block the tunnels? Raze the buildings? I don't understand you, Druss,' said Orrin. 'They are all privately owned. There would be an uproar.'

'Exactly!' said the old warrior, gently. 'And that is why you must appoint an outsider to take the responsibility. Those tunnels behind the gates were built so that a small rearguard could hold an enemy force long enough to allow the defenders to move back to the next wall. I propose to destroy the buildings between Walls Four and Six and use the rubble to block the tunnels. Ulric will expend a lot of men in order to breach the gates. And it will avail him nothing.'

'But why destroy the buildings?' asked Orrin. 'We can bring rubble in from the south of the pass.'

'There is no killing ground,' said the old warrior. 'We must get back to the original plan of the Dros. When Ulric's men breach the first wall, I want every archer in the Dros peppering them. Every yard of open ground will be littered with Nadir dead. We're outnumbered five hundred to one and we have to level the odds somehow.'

Orrin bit his lip and rubbed his chin, his mind working furiously. He glanced at the white-bearded warrior seated calmly before him. As soon as he had heard Druss had arrived, he had prepared for the certainty that he would be replaced – sent back to Drenan in disgrace. Now he was being offered a lifeline. He should have thought of razing the buildings and blocking the tunnels; he knew it, just as he knew he was miscast as a Gan. It was a hard fact to accept.

Throughout the last five years, since his elevation, he had avoided self-examination. However, only days before he had sent Hogun and 200 of his Legion Lancers into the outlands. At first he had held to the belief that it was a sensible military decision. But as the days passed and no word came he had agonised over his orders. It had little to do with strategy, but everything to do with jealousy. Hogun, he had realised with sick horror, was the best soldier in the Dros. When he had returned and told Orrin that his decision had proved a wise one, far from bolstering Orrin it had finally opened his eyes to his own inadequacy. He had considered resigning, but could not face the disgrace. He had even contemplated suicide, but could not bear the thought of the dishonour it would bring to his uncle, Abalayn. All he could do was to die on the first wall. And this he was prepared for. He had feared Druss would rob him even of that.

'I have been a fool, Druss,' he said, at last.

'Enough of that talk!' snapped the old man. 'Listen to me. You are the Gan. From this day on no man will speak ill of you. What you fear, keep to yourself, and believe in me. Everyone makes mistakes. Everyone fails at something. The Dros will hold, for I will be damned if I will let it fall. If I had felt you were a coward, Orrin, I would have tied you to a horse and sent you packing. You have never been in a siege, nor led a troop into battle. Well, now you will do both, and do it well, for I will be beside you.

'Get rid of your doubts. Yesterday is dead. Past mistakes are like smoke in the breeze. What counts is tomorrow, and every tomorrow until Woundweaver gets here with reinforcements. Make no mistake, Orrin. When we survive and the songs are sung, you will be worth your place in them and no one will sneer. Not a soul. Believe it!

'Now I have talked enough. Give me your seal on parchment and I will start today with my duties.'

'Will you want me with you today?'

'Best not,' said Druss. 'I have a few heads to crack.'

Minutes later, Druss marched towards the officers' mess flanked by two Legion guards, tall men and well-disciplined. The old man's eyes blazed with anger and the guards exchanged a glance as they marched. They could hear the sounds of singing coming from the mess, and were set to enjoy the sight of Druss the Legend in action.

He opened the door and stepped into the lavishly furnished interior. A trestle bar had been set up against the far wall, stretching out into the centre of the room. Druss pushed his way past the revellers, ignoring the complaints, then placed one hand beneath the trestle and hurled it into the air, scattering bottles, goblets, and food to shower on the officers. Stunned silence was followed by an angry surge of oaths and curses. One young officer pushed his way to the front of the crowd; dark-haired, sullen-eyed and haughty, he confronted the white-bearded warrior.

'Who the hell do you think you are, old man?' he said.

Druss ignored him, his eyes scanning the thirty or so men in the room. A hand grabbed his jerkin.

'I said who . . .' Druss backhanded the man across the room to crash into the wall and slither to the floor, half-stunned.

'I am Druss. Sometimes called Captain of the Axe. In Ventria they call me Druss the Sender. In Vagria I am merely the Axeman. To the Nadir I am Deathwalker. In Lentria I am the Silver Slayer.

'But who are you? You dung-eating lumps of offal! Who the hell are *you*?' The old man drew Snaga from her sheath at his side. 'I have a mind to set an example today. I have a mind to cut the fat from this ill-fated fortress. Where is Dun Pinar?'

The young man pushed himself from the back of the crowd, a half-smile on his face, a cool look in his dark eyes. 'I am here, Druss.'

'Gan Orrin has appointed me to take charge of the training and preparation of the defences. I want a meeting with all officers on the training ground in an hour. Pinar, you organise it. The rest of you, clear up this mess and get yourselves ready. The holiday is over. Any man who fails me will curse the day he was born.' Beckoning Pinar to follow him, he walked outside. 'Find Hogun,' he said, 'and bring him to me at once in the main hall of the Keep.'

'Yes, sir! And sir . . .'

'Out with it, lad.'

'Welcome to Dros Delnoch.'

The news flashed through the town of Delnoch like a summer storm, from tavern to shop to market stall. Druss was here! Women passed the message to their men, children chanted his name in the alleys. Tales of his exploits were retold, growing by the minute. A large crowd gathered before the barracks, watching the officers milling at the parade ground. Children were lifted high, perched on men's shoulders to catch a glimpse of the greatest Drenai hero of all time.

When he appeared, a huge roar went up from the crowd and the old man paused and waved.

They couldn't hear what he told the officers, but the men moved with a purpose as he dismissed them. Then, with a final wave he returned to the Keep.

Within the main hall once more, Druss removed his jerkin and relaxed in a high-backed chair. His knee was throbbing and his back ached like the devil. And still Hogun had not appeared.

He ordered a servant to prepare him a meal and enquired after the Earl. The servant told him the Earl was sleeping peacefully. He returned with a huge steak, lightly done, which Druss wolfed down, following it with a bottle of finest Lentrian Red. He wiped the grease from his beard and rubbed his knee. After seeing Hogun, he would have a hot bath, ready for tomorrow. He knew his first day would tax him to his limits – and he mustn't fail.

'Gan Hogun, sir,' announced the servant. 'And Dun Elicas.'

The two men who entered lifted Druss' heart. The first – it had to be Hogun – was broad-shouldered and tall, clear-eyed, with a square jaw.

And Elicas, though slimmer and shorter, had the look of eagles about him. Both men wore the black and silver of The Legion, without badges of rank. It was a long-standing custom, going back to the days when the Earl of Bronze had formed them for the Vagrian Wars.

'Be seated, gentlemen,' said Druss.

Hogun pulled up a chair, reversing it in order to lean on the back. Elicas perched himself on the edge of the table, arms folded across his chest.

Elicas watched the two men carefully. He had not known what to expect from Druss, but he had begged Hogun to allow him to be present at the meeting. He worshipped Hogun, but the grim old man seated before him had always been his idol.

'Welcome to Delnoch, Druss,' said Hogun. 'You have lifted morale already. The men speak of nothing else. I am sorry to have missed you earlier, but I was at the first wall supervising an archery tourney.'

'I understand you have already met the Nadir?' said Druss.

'Yes. They will be here in less than a month.'

'We shall be ready. But it will need hard work. The men are badly trained – if trained at all. That must change. We have only ten surgeons, no medical orderlies, no stretcher-bearers and only one hospital – and that is at Wall One, which is no good to us. Comments?'

'An accurate appraisal. All I can add is that – apart from my men – there are only a dozen officers of worth.'

'I have not yet decided the worth of any man here. But let us stay positive for the moment. I need a man of mathematical persuasion to take charge of the food stores and to prepare ration rotas. He will need to shift his equations to match our losses. He must also be responsible for liaison and administration with Gan Orrin.' Druss watched as the two men exchanged glances, but said nothing of it.

'Dun Pinar is your man,' said Hogun. 'He virtually runs the Dros now.'

Druss' eyes were cold as he leaned towards the young general. 'There will be no more comments like that, Hogun. It does not become a professional soldier. We start today with a clean slate. Yesterday is gone. I shall make my own judgements and I do not expect my officers to make sly comments about each other.'

'I would have thought you would want the truth,' interposed Elicas, before Hogun could answer.

'The truth is a strange animal, laddie. It seems to vary from man to man. Now keep silent. Understand me, Hogun, I value you. Your record is a good one. But from now on, no one speaks ill of the First Gan. It is not good for morale, and what is not good for our morale is good for the Nadir. We have enough problems.' Druss stretched out a length of parchment and pushed it to Elicas with a quill and ink. 'Make yourself useful, boy, and take notes. Put Pinar at the top, he is our quartermaster. Now, we will need fifty medical orderlies and two hundred stretcher-bearers. The first Calvar Syn can choose from volunteers, but the bearers will need someone to train them. I want them to be able to run all day. Missael knows they will need to when the action gets warm. These men will need stout hearts. It is no easy thing to run about on a battlefield lightly armed. For they will not be able to carry swords and stretchers.

'So who do you suggest to pick and train them?'

Hogun turned to Elicas, who shrugged.

'You must be able to suggest someone,' said Druss.

'I don't know the men of Dros Delnoch that well, sir,' said Hogun, 'and no one from the Legion would be appropriate.'

'Why not?'

'They are warriors. We shall need them on the wall.'

'Who is your best ranker?'

'Bar Britan. But he's a formidable warrior, sir.'

'That is why he is the man. Listen well: the stretcher-bearers will be armed with daggers only, and they will risk their lives as much as the men battling on the walls. But it is not a glorious task, so the importance of it must be highlighted. When you name your best ranker as the man to train the bearers and work with them during the battle, this will come home to them. Bar Britan must also be given fifty men of his choice as a moving troop to protect the bearers as best he can.'

'I bow to your logic, Druss,' said Hogun.

'Bow to nothing, son. I make mistakes as well as any man. If you think me wrong, be so good as to damn well say so.'

'Put your mind at rest on that score, Axeman!' snapped Hogun.

'Good! Now, as to training. I want the men trained in groups of fifty. Each group is to have a name – choose them from legends, names of heroes, battlefields, whatever, as long as the names stir the blood.

'There will be one officer to each group and five rankers, each commanding ten men. These under-leaders will be chosen after the first three days' training. By then we should have taken their mark. Understood?'

'Why names?' asked Hogun. 'Would it not be simpler if each group had a number? Gods, man, that's 180 names to find!'

'There is more to warfare, Hogun, than tactics and training. I want proud men on those walls. Men who know their comrades and can identify with them. "Group Karnak" will be representing Karnak the One-Eyed, where "Group Six" would be merely identified.

'Throughout the next few weeks we will set one group against another, in work, play and mock combat. We will weld them into units – proud units. We will mock and cajole them, sneer at them even. Then, slowly, when they hate us more than they do the Nadir, we will praise them. In as short a time as possible, we must make them think of themselves as an elite force. That's half the battle. These are desperate, bloody days; days of death. I want men on those walls; strong men, fit men – but most of all, proud men.

'Tomorrow you will choose the officers and allocate the groups. I want the groups running until they drop, and then running again. I want sword practice and wall scaling. I want demolition work done by day and night. After ten days we will move on to unit work. I want the stretcher-bearers running with loads of rock until their arms burn and their muscles tear.

'I want every building from Wall Four to Wall Six razed to the ground and the tunnels blocked.

'I want one thousand men at a time working on the demolition in three-hour shifts. That should straighten backs and strengthen sword arms.

'Any questions?'

Hogun spoke: 'No. Everything you wish for will be done. But I want to know this: do you believe the Dros can hold until the autumn?'

'Of course I do, laddie,' lied Druss easily. 'Why else would I bother? The point is, do *you* believe it?'

'Oh yes,' lied Hogun, smoothly. 'Without a doubt.'

The two men grinned.

'Join me in a glass of Lentrian Red,' said Druss. 'Thirsty work, this planning business!'

11

In a wooden loft, its window in the shadow of the great Keep, a man waited, drumming his fingers on the broad table. Behind him, pigeons ruffled their feathers within a wickerwork coop. The man was nervous. On edge.

Footsteps on the stairs made him reach for a slender dagger. He cursed and wiped his sweating palm on his woollen trousers.

A second man entered, pushed the door shut and sat opposite the first. The newcomer spoke: 'Well? What orders are there?'

'We wait. But that may change when word reaches them that Druss is here.'

'One man can make no difference,' said the newcomer.

'Perhaps not. We shall see. The tribes will be here in five weeks.'

'Five? I thought . . .'

'I know,' said the first man. 'But Ulric's firstborn is dead. A horse fell on him. The funeral rites will take five days; and it's a bad omen for Ulric.'

'Bad omens can't stop a Nadir horde from taking this decrepit fortress.'

'What is Druss planning?'

'He means to seal the tunnels. That's all I know so far.'

'Come back in three days,' said the first man. He took a small piece of paper and began to write in tiny letters upon it. He shook sand on the ink, blew it, then re-read what he had written:

Deathwalker here. Tunnels sealed. Morale higher.

'Perhaps we should kill Druss,' said the newcomer, rising.

'If we are told to,' said the first man. 'Not before.'

'I will see you in three days then.'

At the door he adjusted his helm, sweeping his cloak back over his shoulder badge.

He was a Drenai Dun.

Cul Gilad lay slumped on the short grass by the wall of the cookhouse at Eldibar, breath heaving from his lungs in convulsive gasps. His dark hair hung in lank rats' tails which dripped sweat to his shoulders. He turned on his side, groaning with the effort. Every muscle in his body seemed to be screaming at him. Three times he and Bregan, with forty-eight others of Group Karnak, had raced against five other groups from Wall One to Wall Two, scaled the knotted ropes, moved to Wall Three, scaled the knotted ropes, moved to Wall Four . . . An endless, mindless agony of effort.

Only his fury kept him going, especially after the first wall. The white-bearded old bastard had watched him beat 600 men to Wall Two, his burning legs and tired arms pumping and pulling in full armour. First man! And what did he say? 'A staggering old man followed by staggering old women. Well, don't just lie there, boy. On to Wall Three!'

Then he had laughed. It was the laugh that did it.

Gilad could have killed him then – slowly. For five miserable endless days, the soldiers of Dros Delnoch had run, climbed, fought, torn down buildings in the teeth of hysterical curses from the dispossessed owners, and trundled cart upon cart of rubble into the tunnels at Walls One and Two. Working by day and night, they were bone weary. And still that fat old man urged them on.

Archery tourneys, javelin contests, sword-play, dagger work and wrestling in between the heavy work made sure that few of the Culs bothered to frequent the taverns near the Keep.

Damned Legion did, though. They glided through the training with grim smiles, and hurled scornful jests at the farmers who sought to keep up with them. Let them try working eighteen hours in the fields, thought Gilad. Bastards!

Grunting with pain he sat up, pushing his back against the wall, and watched others training. He had ten minutes yet before the next shift was required to fill the rubble carts. Stretcher-bearers toiled across the open ground, bearing rocks twice the weight of an injured man. Many had bandaged hands. Alongside them the black-bearded Bar Britan shouted them on.

Bregan tottered towards him and slumped to the grass. His face was cherry red. Silently he handed Gilad an orange half – it was sweet and fresh.

'Thanks, Breg.' Gilad's eyes moved over the other eight men in his group. Most were lying silently, though Midras had begun to retch. The idiot had a girl in the town and had visited her the night before, creeping back into barracks for an hour's sleep before daybreak.

He was paying for it now. Bregan was bearing up well: a little faster, a little fitter. And he never complained, which was a wonder.

'Almost time, Gil,' he said. Gilad glanced towards the tunnel where the work was slowing down. Other members of Group Karnak were moving towards the partly demolished homes.

'Come on, lads,' said Gilad. 'Let's be sitting up. Let's start taking some deep breaths.' Groans followed the order and there was scarce a movement from the men. 'Come on, now. Group Kestrian are already moving. Bastards!' Gilad pushed himself to his feet, pulling Bregan up with him. Then he moved to each of the men. Slowly they rose and began to move towards the tunnel.

'I think I'm dying,' said Midras.

'You will if you let us down today,' muttered Gilad. 'If that old swine laughs at us one more time . . .'

'A pox on him,' said Midras. 'You don't see him working up a sweat, do you?'

At dusk the weary men trooped away from the tunnels towards the peace and relative sanctity of the barracks. They hurled themselves on to narrow cots and began to unbuckle breastplates and greaves.

343

'I don't mind the work,' said Baile, a stocky farmer from a village neighbouring Gilad's, 'but I don't see why we have to do it in full armour.'

No one answered him.

Gilad was almost asleep when a voice bellowed: 'Group Karnak to the parade ground!'

Druss stood in the parade-ground square, hands on hips, his blue eyes scanning the exhausted men who stumbled from the barracks, their eyes squinting against the torch-light. Flanked by Hogun and Orrin, he smiled grimly as the men shambled into ranks.

The fifty men of Group Karnak were joined by Group Kestrian and Group Sword.

Silently they waited for whatever foul idea Druss had now dreamed up.

'You three groups,' said Druss, 'are to run the length of the wall and back. The last man's group will run again. Go!'

As the men set off for the gruelling half-mile, someone yelled from the crowd: 'What about you, fat man? Coming?'

'Not this time,' Druss yelled back. 'Don't be last.'

'They're exhausted,' said Orrin. 'Is this wise, Druss?'

'Trust me. When the attacks come, men will be dragged from sleep fast enough. I want them to know their limits.'

Three more days passed. Tunnel one was almost filled, and work had begun on tunnel two. No one cheered now as Druss walked by, not even among the townsfolk. Many had lost their homes, others were losing business. A deputation had visited Orrin, begging for demolition to cease. Others found that sight of the clear ground between walls only emphasised that Druss expected the Nadir to take the Dros. Resentment grew, but the old warrior swallowed his anger and pushed on with his plan.

On the ninth day something happened which gave the men a fresh topic of conversation.

As Group Karnak assembled for their run Gan Orrin approached Dun Mendar, the officer commanding.

'I shall be running with your group today,' he said.

'You are taking over, sir?' said Mendar.

'No, no. Just running. A Gan must be fit too, Mendar.'

A sullen silence greeted Orrin as he joined the ranks, his bronze and gold armour setting him apart from the waiting soldiers.

Throughout the morning he toiled with the men, scaling ropes, sprinting between walls. Always he was last. As he ran some of the men laughed, others jeered. Mendar was furious. The man's making an even greater fool of himself, he thought. And he's making us the laughing stock, too. Gilad ignored the Gan, except at one point to pull him over the battlements when it looked as if he might fall.

'Let him drop,' yelled a man further along the wall.

Orrin gritted his teeth and carried on, staying with the troop throughout the day and even working on the demolition. By afternoon he was working at half the speed of the other soldiers. No one had yet spoken to him. He ate apart from the other men, but not by choice – where he sat, they did not.

At dusk he made his way to his quarters, body trembling, muscles on fire and slept in his armour.

At daybreak he bathed, put on his armour and rejoined Group Karnak. Only at sword practice did he excel, but even then he half thought the men were letting him win. And who could blame them?

An hour before dusk Druss arrived with Hogun, ordering four groups to assemble by the gate of Wall Two: Karnak, Sword, Egel and Fire.

From atop the battlements Druss called down to the two hundred men: 'A little race to stretch your muscles, lads. It's a mile from this gate round the perimeter and back. You will run it twice. Last man's group runs again. Go!'

As they hurtled off, bunching and pushing, Hogun leaned forward.

'Damn!' he said.

'What's wrong?' asked Druss.

'Orrin. He's running with them. I thought he would have had enough yesterday. What's the matter with the man? Is he mad?'

'You run with the men,' said Druss. 'Why not him?'

'Come on, Druss, what sort of a question is that? I'm a soldier and I train every day of my life. But him! Look at him – he's last already. You will have to pick the last man apart from Orrin.'

'I can't do that, lad. It would shame him. He made his choice and I expect he has his reasons.'

At the first mile Orrin was thirty yards behind the last man and struggling hard. He fastened his gaze to the back of the man's breastplate, and ran on, ignoring the pain in his side. Sweat stung his eyes and his white horse-hair crested helm fell from his head. It was a relief.

At a mile and a half he was forty yards adrift.

Gilad glanced back from the centre of the leading pack, eased out and turned, jogging back to the breathless Gan. Once alongside he joined him stride for stride.

'Listen,' he said, breathing easily. 'Unclench your fists, it will help with the breathing. Think of nothing else except sticking to me. No, don't try to answer me. Count your breaths. Take a deep breath and blow out as fast as possible. That's it. A deep breath every two strides. And keep counting. Think of nothing except the number of breaths. Now stay with me.'

He moved in front of the general, keeping to the same slow pace, then increased it gently.

Druss sat back on the battlements as the race drew near its end. Orrin was being drawn along by the slim under-leader. Most of the men had finished the race and were spread out watching the last few runners. Orrin was still last, but only ten yards adrift of the tiring Cul from Group Fire. Men started yelling for the Cul to sprint. Every group except Karnak was willing him on.

Thirty yards to go. Gilad dropped back alongside Orrin. 'Give it everything,' he said. 'Run, you fat son of a bitch!'

Gilad increased his pace and sped by the Cul. Orrin gritted his teeth and took after him. Anger gave him strength. Fresh adrenalin flowed to tired muscles.

Ten yards to go and now he was at the man's shoulder. He could hear the encouragement screamed from the crowd. The man beside him pulled ahead with a last effort, his face twisted in agony.

Orrin drew level in the shadow of the gate and lurched ahead. He hurled himself forward, crashing to the earth and rolling into the crowd. He couldn't get up, but hands grabbed him, hauling him to his feet and pounding his back. He fought for breath . . . A voice said: 'Keep walking. It will help. Come on, move your legs.' Supported on both sides, he began to walk. Druss' voice came down from the battlements.

'That man's group, one more circuit.'

Group Fire set off, this time at a slow jog.

Gilad and Bregan helped Orrin to a jutting foundation block and sat him upon it. His legs were shaking, but his breathing was less ragged.

'I am sorry I insulted you,' said Gilad. 'I wanted to make you angry. My father always said anger helps the strength.'

'You don't have to make excuses,' said Orrin. 'I shall take no action.'

'It's not an excuse. I could do that run ten times over; so could most of my men. I just thought it would help.'

'It did. Thank you for dropping back.'

'I think you did wonderfully well,' said Bregan. 'I know how you felt. But we've been doing this for nearly two weeks. Today is only your second day.'

'Will you join us again tomorrow?' asked Gilad.

'No. I should like to, but I do have other work to do.' He smiled suddenly. 'On the other hand,' he said, 'Pinar is very good at paperwork, and I am damned tired of having complaining deputations knocking at my door every five minutes. Yes, I'll be here.'

'May I make a suggestion?' said Gilad.

'Of course.'

'Get yourself some ordinary armour. You will stand out less.'

'I'm supposed to stand out,' said Orrin, smiling. 'I am the Gan.'

High above them, Druss and Hogun shared a bottle of Lentrian Red.

'It took nerve for him to come out today after the jeering yesterday,' said Druss.

'Yes, I suppose so,' said Hogun. 'No, dammit, I'll agree with you and praise the man. But it goes against the grain. You gave him the backbone.'

'You can't give a man something that isn't there,' said Druss. 'He just never looked for it.' Druss grinned and took a long swig from the bottle, passing it to Hogun half-drained.

'I like the little man,' said Druss. 'He's game!'

Orrin lay back on his narrow bunk, his back cushioned by soft pillows, his hand curled around a clay cup. He tried to tell himself there was no glory in coming second from last. Happily he failed. He had never been athletic, even as a child. But he came from a family of warriors and Drenai leaders and his father had insisted he take part in all soldierly pursuits.

He had always handled a sword well, which, in his father's eyes, made up for the other, mightier, shortcomings. Like not being able to stand physical pain. Or not being able to understand, even after patient explanation, the great mistake made by Nazredas at the battle of Plettii. He wondered if his father would have been pleased at his hurling himself to the floor in order to beat a Cul in a foot race. He smiled: he would think him mad.

The sound of knuckles rapping at his door brought him back to the present.

'Come!'

It was Druss, minus his black and silver jerkin. Strange how he looked like an old man, thought Orrin, without his legendary garb. The warrior's beard was combed and he wore a flowing white shirt-tunic with billowing sleeves gathered in at the wrists. About his middle was a thick black belt with silver buckle. He was carrying a large bottle of Lentrian Red.

'I thought, if you were awake, I might join you for a drink,' said Druss, pulling up a chair and reversing it, as Orrin had seen Hogun do on many occasions.

'Why do you do that?' asked Orrin.

'What?' said Druss.

'Turn the chair round.'

'Old habits die hard – even among friends. It's a warrior's habit. With your legs astride the chair, it is easier to rise. Also it puts a thick layer of wood between your belly and the man you are talking to or sitting with.'

'I see,' said Orrin. 'I had always meant to ask Hogun, but I never got round to it. What makes men adopt habits like that?'

'The sight of a friend with a knife in his belly!' said Druss.

'I can see that it would. Will you teach me your tricks, Druss, before the Nadir arrive?'

'No. You will have to learn them the hard way. Little things I will help you with at the right time – they may make a difference.'

'Little things? You intrigue me, Druss. Tell me something now.' Orrin accepted a cup of Lentrian and settled back. Druss drank from the bottle.

'All right,' said the axeman, half the bottle drained, 'answer me this: why are the men issued with oranges every morning?'

'It keeps them fit and helps prevent dysentery. It's refreshing and cheap. Is that it?' asked Orrin puzzled.

'Some of it,' said Druss. 'The Earl of Bronze introduced oranges to the army, partly for the reasons you mention, but mainly because if you rub the juice into the palm of your hand your sword will not slip as the hand sweats. Also, if you rub it on your brow, sweat will not drop into your eyes.'

'I never knew that. I expect I should have done, but I didn't. How simple! Give me another.'

'No,' said Druss, 'another time. Tell me, why have you joined in the training with the Culs?'

Orrin sat up, his dark eyes fixed on Druss' face. 'You don't think it's a good idea?'

'It depends on what you are trying to achieve. Are you seeking respect?'

'Great Gods, no!' said Orrin. 'I have left it too late for that, Druss. No, it was something you said the other night when the men were turfed out of bed for that night run. I asked you if it was wise and you said, "They need to know their limitations." Well, so do I. I've never been in a battle. I want to know what it's like to be woken from sleep after a full day's training and to be expected to fight again.

'I've let down a lot of people here. I may let them down again when the Nadir are scaling the wall, though I hope not. But I need to be fitter and faster. And I shall be.

'Is that such a bad idea?'

Druss tilted the bottle, licked his lips and smiled.

'No. It's a good idea. But when you are a little fitter, spread yourself around the groups more. It will pay off.'

'Pay off?'

'You'll see.'

'Have you seen the Earl?' asked Orrin suddenly. 'Syn says he's bad. Very bad indeed.'

'I don't think I have seen worse. He's constantly delirious now – how he hangs on I don't know.'

The two men talked on for over an hour, Orrin questioning the old man about his life and the many battles he had taken part in, returning always to the immortal story of Skeln and the fall of King Gorben.

When the Keep alarm bell sounded, both men reacted instantly. Druss cursed, threw the bottle aside and raced for the door. Orrin heaved himself from his bunk and followed. Across the parade ground square and up the short hill to the Keep Druss ran, pounding under the portcullis gate and up the long winding stone stairs to the Earl's bedchamber. Calvar Syn was at his bedside, with Dun Mendar, Pinar and Hogun. An old servant stood weeping by the window.

'Is he dead?' asked Druss.

'No. Soon,' answered Calvar Syn.

Druss moved to the bedside, sitting beside the frail figure. The Earl's eyes opened and blinked twice.

'Druss?' he called, his voice weak. 'Are you there?'

'I am here.'

'He's coming. I see him. He is hooded and black.'

'Spit in his eye for me,' said Druss, his huge hand stroking the Earl's fevered brow.

'I thought . . . after Skeln . . . I would live for ever.'

'Be at peace, my friend. One thing I have learned about Death is that his bark's worse than his bite.'

'I can see them, Druss. The Immortals. They're sending in the Immortals!' The dying man grabbed Druss' arm, and tried to haul himself upright. 'Here they come! Gods, will you look at them, Druss!'

'They're just men. We will see them off.'

'Sit by the fire, child, and I'll tell you of it. But don't tell your mother I told you – you know how she hates the bloodthirsty tales. Ah, Virae, my little love! You will never understand what it has meant to me just being your father . . .' Druss bowed his head as the old Earl rambled on, his voice thin and wavering. Hogun gritted his teeth and closed his eyes, Calvar Syn sat slumped in an armchair and Orrin stood by the door, remembering his own father's death so many years before.

'We were at the pass for many days, holding out against everything they could throw at us. Tribesmen, chariots, infantry, cavalry. But always the threat of the Immortals hung over us. Never beaten! Old Druss stood at the centre of our first line, and as the Immortals marched towards us we froze. You could feel panic in the air. I wanted to run and I could see the same feeling reflected on the faces around me. Then old Druss lifted his axe in the air and bellowed at the advancing line. It was wonderful. Magical almost. The spell broke. The fear passed. He raised his axe for them to see, then he shouted. I can hear him now: "Come on, you fat-bellied whoresons! I am Druss, and this is Death!"'

'Virae? Virae? I waited for you . . . just one more time. See you. So much . . . So much wanted . . .' The frail body trembled, then lay still. Druss closed the dead man's eyes and wiped a hand across his own.

'He should never have sent her away,' said Calvar Syn. 'He loved that girl, she was all he lived for.'

'Maybe that's why he sent her,' said Hogun.

Druss pulled the silk sheet up and over the Earl's face, and walked to the window. Now he was alone – the last survivor of Skeln. He leaned on the window sill and sucked in the night air.

Outside the moon bathed the Dros in eldritch light, grey and ghostly, and the old man gazed towards the north. Overhead a fluttering pigeon flew in and circled a loft beneath the Keep. It had come out of the north.

He turned from the window.

'Bury him quietly tomorrow,' he said. 'We will not interrupt training for a full funeral.'

'But Druss, this is Earl Delnar!' said Hogun, eyes blazing.

'That,' said Druss, pointing at the bed, 'is a cancer-ridden corpse. It isn't anyone. Just do as I say.'

'You cold-hearted bastard,' said Dun Mendar.

Druss turned his icy gaze on the officer.

'And just you remember that, laddie, the day you – or any of you – go against me.'

12

Rek leaned on the starboard rail with one arm about Virae's shoulders and stared at the sea. Strange, he thought, how night changed the mood of the ocean. A vast, semi-solid mirror reflecting the stars, while the moon's twin floated, fragmented and ethereal, a mile or so away. Always a mile or so away. A gentle breeze billowed the triangular sail as the *Wastrel* cut a white path through the waves, gently dipping and rising with the swell. Aft stood the mate at the spoked wheel, his silver eye-patch glinting in the moonlight. Forward a young seaman cast his lead into the waves, calling out the changes in depth as they passed over the hidden reef.

All was tranquillity, peace, and harmony. The steady lapping of the waves added to the feeling of isolation that enveloped Rek as he stared out to sea. With stars above and below them they could be floating on the tides of the galaxy, far from the all too human struggle that awaited them.

This is contentment, thought Rek.

'What are you thinking?' asked Virae, slipping an arm round his waist.

'I love you,' he said. A dolphin surfaced below them, calling out a musical welcome before again seeking the depths. Rek watched his lithe form swimming among the stars.

'I know you love me,' said Virae, 'but I was asking you what you were thinking?'

'That's what I was thinking. I am content. At peace.'

'Of course you are. We're on a ship and it's a lovely night.'

'Woman, you have no soul,' he said, kissing her brow.

She looked up at him and smiled. 'If you think that – you are a fool! I'm just not as practised as you at telling pretty lies.'

'Hard words, my lady. Would I lie to you? You would cut my throat.'

'I would too. How many women have heard you say you love them?'

'Hundreds,' said Rek, watching her eyes and seeing the smile fade from them.

'So why should I believe you?'

'Because you do.'

'That's no answer.'

'Of course it is. You're not some dimwitted milk-maid fooled by an easy smile. You know the truth when you hear it. Why do you suddenly doubt it?'

'I don't doubt you, you oaf! I just wanted to know how many women you've loved.'

'Slept with, you mean?'

'If you want to be coarse.'

'I don't know,' he lied. 'It's not my habit to keep count. And if your

350

next question is, "How do I compare?", you will find yourself alone, because I shall go below.'

It was. But he did not.

The mate by the tiller watched them, listened to their easy laughter and smiled with them, although he could not hear the cause of their good humour. At home he had a wife and seven children, and it made him feel good to watch the young man and his woman. He waved as they went below deck, but they did not see him.

'Nice to be young and in love,' said the captain, moving silently from the shadows by his cabin door to stand beside the mate.

'Nice to be old and in love,' answered the mate, grinning.

'A calm night, but the breeze is picking up. I don't like the look of the clouds to the west.'

'They will pass us by,' said the mate. 'But we'll have bad weather, for sure. It will be behind us, pushing us on. We may pick up a couple of days. Did you know they are headed for Delnoch?'

'Yes,' said the captain, scratching his red beard and checking their course by the stars.

'Sad,' said the mate, with real feeling. 'They say Ulric has promised to raze it to the ground. You heard what he did at Gulgothir? Killed every second defender and a third of the women and children. Just lined them up and had his warriors cut them down.'

'I heard. It's not my business. We've traded with the Nadir for years; they're all right as people – much the same as anyone else.'

'I agree. I had a Nadir woman once. A real hellion – ran off with a tinker. Later I heard she cut his throat and stole his wagon.'

'Most likely she only wanted the horse,' said the captain. 'She could buy herself a real Nadir man for a good horse.' Both men chuckled, then stood in silence for a while enjoying the night air.

'Why are they going to Delnoch?' asked the mate.

'She's the Earl's daughter. I don't know about him. If she was my daughter I would have made sure she didn't come back. I'd have sent her to the farthest southern point of the empire.'

'The Nadir will reach there – and beyond – before long. It's only a matter of time.'

'Well, a lot can happen in that time. The Drenai are sure to surrender long before then. Look! That damned albino and his friend. They make my flesh creep.'

The mate glanced along the deck to where Serbitar and Vintar stood at the port rail.

'I know what you mean – they never say anything. I'll be glad to see the back of them,' said the mate, making the sign of the Claw above his heart.

'That won't ward off their kind of demons,' said the captain.

Serbitar smiled as Vintar pulsed: 'We are less than popular, my boy.'

'Yes. Always it is thus. It is hard to hold back contempt.'

'But you must.'

'I said hard, not impossible.'

'Word play. Even to notice that it is hard is an admission of defeat,' said Vintar.

'Always the scholar, Father Abbot.'

'As long as the world has pupils, master priest.'

Serbitar grinned, a rare sight. A gull wheeled and circled above the ship; the albino casually mind-touched it as it arced above the mast.

Within its mind was nothing of joy or sorrow or hope. Only hunger and need. And frustration, that the ship offered no sustenance.

A feeling of fierce exultation suddenly swept over the young priest in a mind pulse of incredible power, a sense of ecstasy and fulfilment flooding his body. He gripped the rail hard and reached back along the path, shutting off his probe as it neared the door of Rek's cabin.

'Their emotions are very strong,' pulsed Vintar.

'It is unseemly to dwell on it,' replied Serbitar primly, a blush apparent even in the moonlight.

'Not so, Serbitar, my friend. This world has few redeeming features, and one is the capacity for the people upon it to love one another with great and enduring passion. I rejoice in their love-making. It is a beautiful thing for them.'

'You are a voyeur, Father Abbot,' said Serbitar, smiling now. Vintar laughed aloud.

'It is true. They have such energy, the young.'

Suddenly Arbedark's slim, serious face appeared in both men's minds, his features set hard.

'I am sorry,' he pulsed. 'There is grave news from Dros Delnoch.'

'Speak,' said Serbitar.

'The Earl is dead. And there are traitors within the Dros. Ulric has ordered Druss killed.'

'Form a circle round me,' shouted Druss, as the exhausted men staggered from the wall. 'Now sit down before you fall down.'

His blue eyes scanned the circle, then he snorted with contempt. 'You dregs! Call yourselves soldiers? Finished after a few runs. How the hell do you think you're going to feel after three days' fighting, day and night, against a Nadir force that outnumbers you fifty to one? Eh?'

No one answered him. The question was all too obviously rhetorical. Indeed most of the men were delighted to be berated thus – it meant a further respite from the interminable training.

Druss pointed at Gilad. 'You! Which four groups are represented here?'

Gilad swung round checking the faces. 'Karnak, Bild, and Gorbadac . . . er . . . I don't know the other one.'

'Well!' bellowed the old man. 'Will not one of you beggars own up? Which is the other damned group?'

'Falcon,' piped a voice from the back.

'Good! Group officers step forward,' said Druss. 'The rest of you, take a breather.' He walked a little distance from the men, beckoning the officers to follow.

'Right, before I tell you what I want, will the officer from Group Falcon make himself known?'

'I am the officer, sir. Dun Hedes,' said a young man who was short but well-built.

'Then why did *you* not announce your group when I asked. Why was it some spotty farm boy?'

'I am partially deaf, sir, and when I am tired and the blood is pounding I can hardly hear.'

'Then, Dun Hedes, consider yourself relieved of Group Falcon.'

'You can't do that to me! I have always served well. You cannot disgrace me!' said the young man, his voice rising.

'Listen to me, you young fool. There is no disgrace in being deaf. And you can feel free to walk with me on the battlements if you will, when the Nadir arrive. But how well can you serve me as a leader if you can't hear my damned instructions?'

'I will manage,' said Dun Hedes.

'And how well will your men manage when they try to ask for advice? What happens if we sound the retreat and you don't hear it? No! The decision's made. Stand down.'

'I request the right to see Gan Orrin!'

'As you will. But at the end of today I will have a new Dun for Falcon. Now to business. I want each of you – you included, Hedes – to pick your two strongest men. The best you have at hand-to-hand wrestling, bare-knuckle, whatever. They will have their chance to knock me from my feet. That should lighten the mood. Get to it!'

Dun Mendar called Gilad to him as he returned to his group, then squatted down among the men to outline Druss' idea. Chuckles came from various soldiers as men volunteered swiftly. The noise grew as men clamoured for the right to down the old warrior, and Druss laughed aloud as he sat apart from the men, peeling an orange. At last the pairs were selected and he heaved himself to his feet.

'There is an object to this little exercise, but I shall explain that later on. For now, look upon it as light entertainment,' said Druss, hands on hips. 'However, I find the audience is always more alert if there is some-thing to be won, so I will offer a free afternoon to any group whose champions down me.' A cheer greeted this and he went on, 'Mind you, those that don't down me will run an additional two miles,' and grinned again as the groans erupted.

'Don't be such faint-hearts. What do you have before you? Here is one old, fat man. We will start with the Bild pair.'

The men could have been twins; both were huge, black-bearded, with massively muscled arms and shoulders. Stripped of their armour, they appeared as formidable a pair of warriors as could be seen among the groups.

'Right, my lads,' said Druss, 'you can wrestle, or punch, or kick or gouge. Begin when you're ready.' The old man doffed his jerkin as he spoke and the Bild pair circled slowly, relaxed and smiling. Once on either side of the old man they lunged. Druss dropped to one knee, ducking under a round-house right, then slammed his hand up into the man's groin, grabbing his shirt-front with the other hand and hurling him into his comrade. Both men collapsed to the ground, arms entwined.

Curses exploded from the Bild men seated around the circle, to be drowned by jeers from the other groups.

'Next, Gorbadac!' announced Druss. The two advanced more warily than their predecessors, then the tallest one dived towards Druss' middle with arms outstretched. The axeman's knee came up to meet him and he sagged to the grass. The second attacked almost immediately, only to be backhanded contemptuously across the cheek. He tripped over his fallen comrade and fell heavily. The first man was unconscious and had to be carried to the back of the circle.

'Now, Falcon!' said Druss. This time he watched them advance, then bellowed at the top of his voice and charged. The first man's mouth fell open in surprise, the second took a backward step and tripped. Druss hit the first man with a straight left; he went down and lay still.

'Karnak?' said Druss. Gilad and Bregan entered the circle. Druss had seen the dark one before and liked the look of him. A born warrior, the old man had thought. He enjoyed seeing the look of hatred the boy threw at him every time he laughed at him, and liked the way he had dropped back to help Orrin. Druss flicked his gaze to the second man. Surely here was an error? The chubby one was no fighter, nor would ever be – good-natured and tough, but never a warrior.

Gilad launched himself forward and checked as Druss raised his fists. Druss twisted to keep him in vision; then hearing a sound from behind, he whirled to see the fat one attack, trip, and fall sprawling at his feet. Chuckling he swung back to Gilad – turning into a flying kick that hammered into his chest. He took a backward step to brace himself, but the fat one had rolled behind him and Druss hit the ground with a grunt.

A massive roar rose from two hundred throats. Druss smiled and rolled to his feet smoothly, holding up a hand for silence.

'I want you to think about what you've seen today, my lads,' said Druss, 'for it wasn't only fun. You have seen what one man can do, and you have also seen what a simple bit of teamwork can achieve.

'Now, when the Nadir are swarming over the walls you will all be hard pressed to defend yourselves – but you've got to do more than that. You've got to protect your comrades where you can, for no warrior has a defence against a sword in the back. I want each of you to find a sword brother. You don't have to be friends – that will come. But you need understanding and you need to work at it. You will protect each other's backs when the assault comes, so make your choices well. Those of you who lose a sword brother when the fighting starts, find another. Failing that, do what you can for the men around you.

'I have been a warrior for more than forty years – twice as long as most of you have lived. Bear that in mind. What I say is of value – for I have survived.

'There is only one way to survive in war, and that is by being willing to die. You will find soon that fine swordsmen can be downed by untutored

354

savages who would slice their fingers if asked to carve meat. And how? Because the savage is willing. Worse, he may be baresark.

'The man who takes a backward step against a Nadir warrior is stepping into eternity. Meet them head to head, savage to savage.

'You have heard it said that this is a lost cause and you will hear it again. I have heard it a thousand times in a hundred lands.

'Mostly you hear it from faint-hearts, and can ignore it. Often, however, you will hear it from seasoned veterans. Ultimately such prophecies are worthless.

'There are half a million Nadir warriors. An awesome figure! One to numb the mind. But the walls are only so long and so wide. They cannot all come over at once. We will kill them as they do, and we will kill hundreds more as they climb. And day by day we will wear them down.

'You are going to lose friends, comrades, brothers. You are going to lose sleep. You are going to lose blood. Nothing about the next few months will be easy.

'I am not going to talk about patriotism, duty, liberty and the defence of freedom – because that's all dung to a soldier.

'I want you to think about survival. And the best way you can do that is to look down on the Nadir when they arrive and think to yourselves: "There are fifty men down there just for me. And one by one, by all the Gods, I'll cut them down."

'As for me . . . well, I'm a seasoned campaigner. I'll take a hundred.' Druss took a deep breath, allowing time for his words to sink in.

'Now,' he said, at last, 'you can get back to your duties – with the exception of Group Karnak.' Turning, he saw Hogun and as the men hauled themselves to their feet, he walked back towards the mess hall of Wall One with the young general.

'A nice speech,' said Hogun. 'It sounded very similar to the one you gave this morning at Wall Three.'

'You haven't been very attentive, laddie,' said Druss. 'I have given that speech six times since yesterday. And I've been knocked down three times. I'm as dry as a sand lizard's belly.'

'I will stand you a bottle of Vagrian in the mess hall,' said Hogun. 'They don't serve Lentrian at this end of the Dros – it's too pricey.'

'It will do. I see you have regained your good humour.'

'Aye. You were right about the Earl's burial. Just too damned quick about being right, that's all,' said Hogun.

'What does that mean?'

'Just what it says. You have a way, Druss, of turning your emotions on and off. Most men lack that. It makes you seem what Mendar called you – cold-hearted.'

'I don't like the phrase – but it fits,' said Druss, pushing open the door to the mess hall. 'I mourned Delnar as he lay dying. But once dead, he's gone. And I'm still here. And there's a damned long way to go yet.'

The two men sat at a window table and ordered drinks from a steward. He returned with a large bottle and two goblets; both men sat silently for a while watching the training.

Druss was deep in thought. He had lost many friends in his life, but none more dear than Sieben and Rowena – the one his sword brother, the other his wife. Thoughts of them both were as tender as open wounds. When I die, he thought, everyone will mourn for Druss the Legend.

But who will mourn for *me*?

13

'Tell us what you saw,' said Rek, as he joined the four leaders of The Thirty in Serbitar's cabin. He had been woken from a deep sleep by Menahem, who had swiftly explained the problems facing the Dros. Now alert, he listened as the blond warrior priest outlined the threat.

'The Captain of the Axe is training the men. He has demolished all buildings from Wall Three and created killing ground. He has also blocked the gate tunnels back to Wall Four – he has done well.'

'You mentioned traitors,' said Rek.

Serbitar lifted a hand. 'Patience!' he said. 'Go on, Arbedark.'

'There is an innkeeper called Musar, originally from the Nadir Wolfs-head tribe. He has been at Drós Delnoch for eleven years. He and a Drenai officer are planning to kill Druss. I think there may be others. Ulric has been told of the tunnel blocking.'

'How?' asked Rek. 'Surely there is no travel to the north?'

'He keeps pigeons,' said Arbedark.

'What can you do?' Rek asked Serbitar, who shrugged and looked to Vintar for support. The Abbot spread his hands. 'We tried to make contact with Druss, but he is not receptive and the distance is still very great. I do not see how we can help.'

'What news of my father?' asked Virae. The men looked at one another; ill at ease, Serbitar spoke at last.

'He is dead. I am deeply sorry.'

Virae said nothing, her face showing no emotion. Rek put an arm on her shoulder, but she pushed it away and stood. 'I'm going on deck,' she said softly. 'I'll see you later, Rek.'

'Shall I come with you?'

'No. It's not for sharing.'

As the door closed behind her Vintar spoke, his voice gentle and sorrowful. 'He was a fine man after his fashion. I contacted him before the end; he was at peace and in the past.'

'In the past?' said Rek. 'What does that mean?'

'His mind had vanished into happier memories. He died well. I think the Source will have him – I shall pray to that effect. But what of Druss?'

'I tried to reach the general, Hogun,' said Arbedark, 'but the danger was great. I almost lost my bearings. The distance . . .'

'Yes,' said Serbitar. 'Did you manage to ascertain how the assassination is to be attempted?'

'No. I could not enter the man's mind, but before him was a bottle of Lentrian Red that he was re-sealing. It could be poison, or an opiate of some kind.'

'There must be something you can do,' said Rek, 'with all your power.'

'All power – but one – has limits,' said Vintar. 'We can only pray.

Druss has been a warrior for many years – a survivor. It means he is not only skilful but lucky. Menahem, you must journey to the Dros and watch for us. Perhaps the attempt will be delayed until we are closer.'

'You mentioned a Drenai officer,' said Rek to Arbedark. 'Who? Why?'

'I know not. As I completed the journey, he was leaving the house of Musar. He acted furtively and this aroused my suspicions. Musar was in the loft and upon the table beside him lay a note written in the Nadir tongue. It said, "Kill Deathwalker." That is the name by which Druss is known to the tribes.'

'You were lucky to see the officer,' said Rek. 'In a fortress city of that size, the chances of seeing a single act of treachery must be amazing.'

'Yes,' said Arbedark. Rek saw the look that passed between the blond priest and the albino.

'Is there more to it than luck?' he asked.

'Perhaps,' said Serbitar. 'We will talk of it soon. For now we are helpless. Menahem will watch the situation and keep us informed. If they delay the attempt for two more days we may be in a position to help.'

Rek looked at Menahem, sitting upright at the table, eyes closed and breathing shallow.

'Has he gone?' he asked.

Serbitar nodded.

Druss managed to look interested as the speeches wore on. Three times since the banquet ended the old warrior had heard how grateful were the townsfolk, burghers, merchants and lawyers that he had come among them. How it showed up the faint-hearts ever ready to write off the might of the Drenai empire. How, when the battle was won – speedily – Dros Delnoch would attract sightseers from all over the continent. How new verses would be added to Serbar's saga of The Legend. The words droned on, the praise growing more fulsome as the wine flowed.

Some two hundred of Delnoch's richest and most influential families were present at the Great Hall, seated around the massive round table normally reserved for state occasions. The banquet was the brainchild of Bricklyn, the Master Burgher, a short self-obsessed businessman who had bent Druss' ear throughout the meal and was now taking the liberty of bending it again in the longest speech so far.

Druss kept his smile firmly fixed, nodding here and there where he felt it appropriate. He had attended many such functions in his life, though they normally followed rather than preceded a battle.

As had been expected, Druss had opened the speeches with a short talk on his life, concluding it with a stirring promise that the Dros would hold if only the soldiers would show the same courage as those families sitting round the table. As had also been expected, he received a tumultuous ovation.

As was his wont on these occasions Druss drank sparingly, merely sipping the fine Lentrian Red placed before him by the stout innkeeper Musar, the banquet's master of ceremonies.

With a start Druss realised that Bricklyn had finished his speech, and he applauded vigorously. The short grey-haired man sat down at his left, beaming and bowing as the applause continued.

'A fine speech,' said Druss. 'Very fine.'

'Thank you. Yours, I think, was better,' said Bricklyn, pouring himself a glass of Vagrian White from a stone jug.

'Nonsense. You are a born speaker.'

'It's strange you should say that. I remember when I gave a speech in Drenan for the wedding of Count Maritin . . . you know the count, of course? . . . Anyway, he said . . .' And so it went on, with Druss smiling and nodding, Bricklyn finding more and more stories to outline his qualities.

Towards midnight as prearranged, Delnar's elderly servant, Arshin, approached Druss and announced – loudly enough for Bricklyn to overhear – that Druss was needed on Wall Three to supervise a new detachment of archers and their placement. It was not before time. Throughout the evening Druss had drunk no more than a single goblet, yet his head swam and his legs shook as he pushed himself upright. He made his apologies to the stout burgher, bowed to the assembly and marched from the room. In the corridor outside he stopped and leaned against a pillar.

'Are you all right, sir?' asked Arshin.

'The wine was bad,' muttered Druss. 'It's hit my stomach worse than a Ventrian breakfast.'

'You'd better get to bed, sir. I will take a message to Dun Mendar to attend you in your room.'

'Mendar? Why the hell should he attend me?'

'I'm sorry, sir. I couldn't mention it in the Hall as you had told me what to say when I approached you, but Dun Mendar asked if you could spare him a moment. He has a serious problem, he said.'

Druss rubbed his eyes and took several deep breaths. His belly felt weak, disconnected and fragile. He toyed with the idea of sending Arshin to explain to the young Karnak officer, but then realised word would get round that Druss was sick. Or worse, that he couldn't hold his wine.

'Maybe the air will do me good. Where is he?'

'He said he would meet you at the inn by Unicorn Alley. Turn right outside the Keep until you reach the first market square, then turn left by the miller's. Walk on through Baker's Row until you reach the armoury repair shop, then turn right. That's Unicorn Alley and the inn is at the far end.'

Druss asked the man to repeat the directions, then pushed himself from the wall and staggered out into the night. The stars were bright, the sky cloudless. He sucked in the crisp air and felt his stomach turn.

'Damn this,' he said angrily, and found a secluded spot by the Keep, away from the sentries, where he made himself vomit. Cold sweat covered his brow and his head ached as he pushed himself upright, but at least his stomach seemed more settled. He headed towards the first square, located the miller's store and turned left. Already the smell of baking bread was coming from the ovens in Baker's Row.

The smell made him retch again. Angry now at his condition, he hammered on the first door he came to. A short, fat baker in a white cotton apron opened the door and peered nervously at him.

'Yes?' he said.

'I am Druss. Do you have a loaf ready?'

'It's only just past midnight. I have some bread from yesterday, but if you wait for a while I will have fresh. What's the matter? You look green.'

'Just get me a loaf – and hurry!' Druss clamped a hand to the door frame, pulling himself upright. What the hell was wrong with that wine? Or maybe it was the food. He hated rich food. Too many years on dried beef and raw vegetables. His body couldn't take it, but it had never reacted like this before.

The man trotted back down the short hallway bearing a hefty chunk of black bread and a small phial.

'Drink this,' he said. 'I have an ulcer and Calvar Syn says it settles the stomach faster than anything else.' Gratefully Druss downed the contents of the phial. It tasted like charcoal. Then he tore a great bite from the bread, sliding gratefully to the floor with his back against the door. His stomach rebelled, but he gritted his teeth and finished the loaf; within a few minutes he was feeling better. His head ached like the devil and his vision was a little blurred, but his legs felt fine and he had strength enough to bluff his way through a short chat with Mendar.

'My thanks, baker. What do I owe you?'

The baker was about to ask for two copper coins, but realised in time that the old man had no pockets visible, and no money sack. He sighed and said what was expected.

'No money necessary from you, Druss. Naturally.'

'Decent of you,' said Druss.

'You should get back to your quarters,' said the baker. 'And get a good night's sleep.' He was about to add that Druss was no youngster any more, but thought better of it.

'Not yet. Got to see one of my officers.'

'Ah, Mendar,' said the baker, smiling.

'How did you know?'

'I saw him not twenty minutes since with three or four others heading down towards The Unicorn. We don't see many officers here at this time of night. The Unicorn's a soldiers' drinking house.'

'Yes. Well, thanks again. I'll be on my way.'

Druss stood in the doorway for a few moments after the baker had returned to his oven. If Mendar was with three or four others, they might expect him to join them for a drink, and he racked his brains to think of a reason for refusing. Unable to come up with a convincing excuse, he cursed and started down Baker's Row.

All was darkness now and silence. The silence jarred him, but his head ached too hard to consider it.

Ahead he could see the anvil sign of the armoury repairer gleaming in the moonlight. He stopped again, blinking as the sign shimmered and distorted and shook his head.

Silence . . . What was it about the damned silence?

He walked on, ill at ease, loosening Snaga in her sheath more as a reflex habit than as a conscious awareness of danger. He turned right . . .

Something swished through the air. Light exploded in his eyes as the club hit him – he went down hard and rolled in the dirt as a dark figure sprang forward. Snaga sang through the air slicing through the man's thigh, crunching on bone which splintered and broke, tearing a scream from the assassin. Druss lurched to his feet as more shapes came from the shadows. His vision blurred, he could still make out the gleam of steel in the moonlight. Bellowing a war cry, he lunged forward. A sword arced towards him, but he batted it aside and clove his axe through the skull of the swordsman, simultaneously kicking out at a second man. A sword blade cut through his shirt, nicking his chest. He hurled Snaga and turned to meet the third man.

It was Mendar!

Druss moved sideways with arms outstretched like a wrestler. The young officer, sword in hand, advanced confidently. Druss glanced at the second man; he was lying groaning on the ground, his weakening fingers desperately trying to pull the axe from his belly. Druss was angry with himself. He should never have hurled the axe – he blamed it on the headache and sickness. Now Mendar leapt and swung his sword, and Druss jumped backwards as the silver steel swished by him, an inch from his neck.

'You can't back away much longer, old man!' said Mendar, grinning.

'Why are you doing this?' asked Druss.

'Playing for time? Sorry? You wouldn't understand.'

Once more he leapt and slashed and once more Druss jumped clear. But now his back was against a building and there was nowhere to run.

Mendar laughed. 'I didn't realise it would be so easy to kill you, Druss,' he said, and lunged. Druss twisted, slammed his hand against the flat of the sword, then leapt forward as the weapon sliced the skin over his ribs, and hammered a fist into Mendar's face. The tall officer staggered back with blood pouring from his mouth. A second blow crashed under his heart, snapping a rib. He went down, losing his grip on his sword, but huge fingers gripped his throat and hauled him upright. He blinked – the grip relaxed just enough for him to squeeze air through his windpipe.

'Easy, boy? Nothing in life is easy.'

A whisper of sound came from behind him.

Druss grabbed Mendar and swung him round. A double-headed axe clove through the officer's shoulder, lodging against the breastbone. Druss hurdled the body and shoulder-charged the assassin as he struggled to free his weapon. The man was hurled backwards. As Druss clambered to his feet the killer turned and sprinted out into Baker's Row.

Druss cursed and returned to the dying officer. Blood poured from the ghastly wound, soaking into the hard-packed earth.

'Help me,' said Mendar. 'Please!'

'Think yourself lucky, you whoreson. I would have killed you much more slowly. Who was he?'

But Mendar was dead. Druss retrieved Snaga from the other dead assassin, then searched for the man whose leg he had wounded. Following a trail of blood into a narrow alley, he found the man lying back against a wall – a dagger rammed to the hilt in his heart, his fingers still curled about the handle.

Druss rubbed his eyes and his hand came away sticky. He ran his fingers over his temple. A lump the size of an egg, tender and broken, made him curse once more.

Was nothing simple in the world any more?

In his day a battle was a battle, army against army.

Pull yourself together, he told himself. There have always been traitors and assassins.

It was just that he had never been a target before.

Suddenly he laughed as he remembered the silence. The inn was empty. As he turned into Unicorn Alley he should have realised the danger. Why would five men be waiting for him after midnight in a deserted alley?

You old fool, he told himself. You must be getting senile.

Musar sat alone in his loft, listening to the pigeons as they ruffled their feathers to greet the new dawn. He was calm now, tranquil almost and his large hands no longer trembled. He walked to the window, leaning far out over the sill to gaze north. His one all-consuming ambition had been to see Ulric ride in to Dros Delnoch and on to the rich southlands – to see the rise, at long last, of the Nadir empire.

Now his Drenai wife and his eight-year-old son lay below, their sleep deepening towards death as he savoured his last dawn.

It had been hard watching them sip their poisoned drinks, listening to his wife's amiable chatter about her plans for tomorrow. When his son had asked him if he could go riding with Brentar's boy, he had said that he could.

He should have followed his first instincts and poisoned the old warrior, but Dun Mendar had convinced him otherwise. Suspicion would then have fallen instantly on the master of ceremonies. This way was surer, Mendar had promised: drug him and kill him in a dark alleyway. So simple!

How could one so old move so swiftly?

Musar had felt he could bluff it out. He knew Druss would never recognise him as the fifth assassin, for his face had been half-covered by a dark scarf. But the risks were too great, maintained his Nadir lord, Surip. The last message had congratulated him on his work over these last twelve years, and concluded: Peace on you, brother, and your family.

Musar filled a deep bucket with warm water from a large copper kettle.

Then he took a dagger from a shelf at the rear of the loft and sharpened it on a small whetstone. The risks were too great? Indeed they were. Musar knew the Nadir had another man at Delnoch, more highly placed than he. On no account would he be compromised.

He plunged his left arm into the bucket, then holding the dagger firmly with his right he severed the arteries of the wrist. The water changed colour.

He had been a fool to marry, he thought, tears shining in his eyes.

But she had been so lovely . . .

Hogun and Elicas watched as men from the Legion cleared away the bodies of the assassins. Spectators looked on from nearby windows, calling down questions, but the Legion ignored them.

Elicas tugged at his small gold earring as Lebus the Tracker outlined the skirmish. Elicas had never lost his fascination for the Tracker's skill. On a trail Lebus could tell you the sex of the horses, the age of the riders and damned near the conversations around the camp-fires. It was a science beyond his understanding.

'The old man entered the alley over there. The first man was hidden in the shadows. He struck him, and Druss fell. He rose fast. See the blood there? An axe cut across the thigh. Then he charged the other three, but he must have thrown his axe because he backed away to the wall there.'

'How did he manage to kill Mendar?' asked Hogun, who already knew from Druss. But he too appreciated Lebus' skill.

'That had me puzzled, sir,' said the tracker. 'But I think I have it. There was a fifth attacker who stayed back during the struggle. There is some indication that Druss and Mendar had ceased to fight and were standing close. The fifth man must have moved in then. See the heel-mark there, that belongs to Druss. See the deep round imprint? I would say he swung Mendar round to block the fifth man.'

'Good work, Lebus,' said Hogun. 'The men say you could track a bird in flight and I believe them.'

Lebus bowed and moved away.

'I begin to believe Druss is everything they say he is,' said Elicas. 'Astonishing!'

'True,' said Hogun, 'but worrying. To have an army the size of Ulric's opposing us is one thing; traitors at the Dros is quite another. And as for Mendar . . . it is almost beyond belief.'

'From a good family, I understand. I have put it around that Mendar aided Druss against Nadir infiltrators. It may work. Not everyone has Lebus' talent, and anyway the ground will be well trodden over by full daylight.'

'The Mendar story is a good one,' said Hogun. 'But word will get out.'

'How is the old man?' asked Elicas.

'Ten stitches in his side and four in his head. He was asleep when I left. Calvar Syn says it's a miracle the skull didn't crack.'

'Will he still judge the Open Swords?' asked the younger man. Hogun merely raised an eyebrow. 'Yes, I thought he would. That's a shame.'

'Why?' asked Hogun.

'Well, if he hadn't judged it you would have done so. And then I would have missed the pleasure of beating you.'

'You conceited pup!' said Hogun laughing. 'The day has not yet come when you could breach my guard – even with a wooden sword.'

'There's a first time for everything. And you're not getting any younger, Hogun. Why, you must be over thirty. One foot in the grave!'

'We shall see. A side bet, perhaps?'

'A flagon of Red?' said Elicas.

363

'Done, my lad! Nothing tastes sweeter than wine another man has paid for.'

'As I shall no doubt find out this evening,' retorted Elicas.

14

The marriage was a simple one – performed by the Abbot of Swords, Vintar, and witnessed by the captain and mate of the *Wastrel*. The sea was calm, the night sky cloudless. Overhead gulls wheeled and dived, a sure sign of approaching land.

Antaheim, one of The Thirty, tall and slender, his dark features showing his Vagrian descent, supplied the ring: an unadorned band of gold.

Now as the dawn neared and the others slept, Rek stood alone at the prow, starlight glinting on his silver head-band, wind streaming his hair like a dark banner.

The die was cast now. He was chained by his own hand to the Delnoch cause. Sea spray stung his eyes and he stepped back, sitting down with his back to the rail and hugging his cloak tight about him. All his life he had sought direction and an escape from fear, an end to trembling hands and an unsteady heart. Now his fears had vanished like candle wax before a flame.

Earl Regnak of Dros Delnoch, Warden of the North.

At first Virae had refused his offer, but ultimately he knew she would be forced to accept. If she had not married him, Abalayn would have sent a husband post-haste. It was inconceivable that Delnoch should lack a leader, and equally inconceivable for a woman to take on the duties.

The captain had sprinkled their heads with sea water in the ritual blessing, but Vintar, a lover of truth, had omitted the blessing of fertility and replaced it with the more simple: 'Be happy, my children, now and until the end of your lives.'

Druss had escaped the attempt on his life, Gan Orrin had found his strength, and The Thirty were only two days from Dros Purdol and the last stage of their journey. The winds had been kind and *Wastrel* was two, maybe three days ahead of schedule.

Rek studied the stars and remembered the sightless seer and his prophetic verse.

'The earl and the legend will be together at the wall, and men shall dream, and men shall die, but shall the fortress fall?'

In his mind's eye Rek pictured Virae as she had been when he left her almost an hour ago, her light hair tangled upon the pillow, her eyes closed and her face peaceful in rest. He had wanted to touch her, to pull her close and feel her arms about him. Instead he had covered her gently with a blanket, dressed and quietly climbed to the deck. Away to starboard he could hear the dolphins' ghostly music.

Now he pulled himself upright and returned to his cabin. Once more Virae had kicked away the blanket. Rek undressed slowly and eased himself down beside her.

And this time he touched her.

Amidships, the leaders of The Thirty finished their prayers and broke bread together, which Vintar blessed. They ate in silence, breaking the bond of unity to enjoy their own thoughts. At last Serbitar leaned back and signalled the opening. Their minds blended together.

'The old man is a fearsome warrior,' said Menahem.

'But he is no strategist,' said Serbitar. 'His method of holding the Dros will be to man the walls and do battle until a conclusion is reached.'

'There is little choice,' said Menahem. 'We will offer no other option.'

'That is true. What I am saying is that Druss will merely pack the walls with men, which is not a serviceable idea. He has ten thousand men and to defend efficiently he will only be able to use seven thousand at any given time. The other walls must be manned, essential services run, messengers assigned. There must also be a floating force ready to offer instant aid to any weak spot.

'Our strength must be to achieve maximum efficiency with total economy of effort. Withdrawals must be meticulously timed. Every officer must be not only aware but totally sure of his role.'

'And we must,' said Arbedark, 'develop an aggressive attitude to defence. We have seen ourselves that Ulric is stripping whole forests in order to build his ballistae and siege towers. We must have inflammables, also containers for them.'

For over an hour, as the dawn breasted the eastern horizon, the leaders set about their plans: eliminating some ideas, refining and expanding others.

Finally Serbitar called on them to join hands. Arbedark, Menahem and Vintar relaxed their control, drifting down into the darkness, as Serbitar drew their power to him.

'Druss! Druss!' he pulsed, his mind soaring across the ocean, past Dros Purdol, the port fortress, on along the Delnoch range past the Sathuli settlements, over the vast Sentran Plain – faster and faster he flew.

Druss awoke with a start, blue eyes scanning the room, nostrils flared to scent danger in the air. He shook his head. Someone was saying his name, but there was no sound. Swiftly he made the sign of the Claw over his heart. Still someone called him.

Cold sweat appeared on his brow.

He reached across the bed, snatching Snaga from the chair by the wall.

'Listen to me, Druss,' pleaded the voice.

'Get out of my head, you whoreson!' bellowed the old man, rolling from the bed.

'I am of The Thirty. We are travelling to Dros Delnoch to aid you. Listen to me!'

'Get *out* of my head!'

Serbitar had no choice, for the pain was incredible. He released the old warrior and returned to the ship.

Druss staggered to his feet, fell and rose again. The door opened and Calvar Syn moved swiftly to him.

'I told you not to get up before noon,' he snapped.

'Voices,' said Druss. 'Voices . . . Inside my head!'

'Lie down. Now listen. You are the Captain and you expect men to obey you. That's what discipline is about. I am the Surgeon and I expect to be obeyed by my patients. Now tell me about the voices.'

Druss laid his head on the pillow and closed his eyes. His head ached abominably and his stomach was still queasy. 'There was only one voice. It said my name. Then it said it was from The Thirty and that they were coming to aid us.'

'Is that all?'

'Yes. What is happening to me, Calvar? I've never had this before from a blow on the head.'

'It could be the blow; concussion can cause some very strange effects – including seeing visions and hearing voices. But they rarely last. Take my advice, Druss. The worst thing you can do at the moment is get over-excited. You could black out . . . Or worse. Blows to the head can be fatal, even after a period of several days. I want you to rest and relax, and if the voice comes again listen to it – even reply to it. But do not become alarmed. Understand?'

'Of course I understand,' said Druss. 'I don't normally panic, doctor, but some things I do *not* like.'

'I know that, Druss. Do you need something to help you sleep now?'

'No. Wake me at noon. I have to judge a contest of swordsmanship. And don't fret,' he said, seeing the gleam of annoyance in the surgeon's one good eye, 'I shall not get excited, and I will come straight back to bed afterwards.'

Outside the room, Hogun and Orrin waited. Calvar Syn joined them, signalled for silence and beckoned them to a nearby office.

'I'm not happy,' he told them. 'He's hearing voices, and believe me, that is not a good sign. But he's strong as a bull.'

'Is he in any danger?' asked Hogun.

'It's hard to say. This morning I didn't think so. But he has been under a lot of strain recently and that may not help his condition. And, although it is easy to forget, he is no longer a young man.'

'What about the voices?' said Orrin. 'Could he go mad?'

'I think I would bet against that,' replied Calvar. 'He said it was a message from The Thirty. Earl Delnar told me he had sent Virae to them with a message and it could be that they have a Speaker among them. Or it could be someone of Ulric's; he also has Speakers among his shaman. I have told Druss to relax and listen to any future voices, and report them to me.'

'That one old man is vital to us,' said Orrin, softly. 'Do everything you can, Calvar. It would be a hammer blow to morale if anything happened to him.'

'Do you think I don't know that?' snapped the surgeon.

The banquet to celebrate the Open Swords was a raucous affair. All who had reached the Last Hundred were invited; officers and enlisted men were seated side by side, swapping jests, tales and tall, tall, stories.

Gilad was seated between Bar Britan, who had beaten him soundly, and Dun Pinar, who had in turn vanquished Britan. The black-bearded Bar was cursing Pinar good-humouredly, and complaining that the latter's wooden sword lacked the balance of his own cavalry sabre.

'I'm surprised you didn't ask to be allowed to fight on horseback,' said Pinar.

'But I did,' protested Britan, 'and they offered me the target pony.' The three men burst into laughter which others joined as the joke spread around the table. The target pony was a saddle, tied to a moving rail and pulled by ropes. It was used for archery practice and jousting.

As the wine flowed Gilad relaxed. He had seriously considered missing the banquet, fearing that his background would leave him ill at ease with the officer class. He had only agreed to come when the men of his group had lobbied him, pointing out that he was the only member of Karnak who had reached the Last Hundred. Now he was glad he had been persuaded. Bar Britan was a dry, witty companion, while Pinar, despite his breeding – or perhaps because of it – made Gilad feel among friends.

At the far end of the table sat Druss, flanked by Hogun and Orrin, while beside them sat the archer leader from Skultik. Gilad knew nothing about the man, save that he had brought 600 bowmen to the Dros.

Hogun, in full Legion dress armour of silver breastplate edged with ebony, and black and silver mail-shirt, stared at the silver sword lying on the table before Druss.

The final had been watched by more than five thousand soldiers as Hogun and Orrin took their places. The first strike had been Hogun's, a neat parry and riposte after a four-minute duel. The second had been Orrin's, following a feint to the head. Hogun had blocked swiftly, but a subtle twist of the wrist sent his opponent's wooden blade down to touch Hogun's side. After some twenty minutes Hogun led by two strikes to one – one strike from victory.

During the first break Druss strolled to where Hogun and his seconds sat drinking watered wine in the shade of Wall One.

'Nice work,' said Druss. 'He's good, though.'

'Yes,' said Hogun, wiping the sweat from his brow with a white towel. 'But he is not as strong on the right.'

'True. But you are slow against the leg cut.'

'A Lancer's main fault. It comes from too much work in the saddle,' said Hogun. 'He is shorter than I, which gives him an advantage in that respect.'

'True. It has done Orrin good to reach the final. His cheers outnumber yours, I think?'

'Yes, but that will not disturb me,' said Hogun.

'I hope it does not,' said Druss. 'Still, nothing could be better for morale than seeing the Fortress Gan perform so well.' Hogun glanced up, holding Druss' gaze, then the old warrior smiled and moved back to his judge's seat.

'What was that about?' asked Elicas, walking behind Hogun and kneading the muscles of his neck and shoulder. 'Encouraging words?'

'Yes,' said Hogun. 'Do some work on the forearm, will you? The muscles are knotted there.'

The young general grunted as Elicas probed the flesh with his powerful thumbs. Was Druss asking him to lose? Surely not. And yet . . .

It would do no harm for Orrin to win the Silver Sword and would certainly increase his growing standing with the troops.

'What are you thinking?' asked Elicas.

'I'm thinking that he's weak on the right.'

'You will take him, Hogun,' said the young officer. 'Try that vicious parry-riposte you used on me.'

At two strikes even, Hogun's wooden blade snapped. Orrin stepped back, allowing a replacement, and offered his opponent a swift practice with the new weapon. Hogun was unhappy with the balance and changed the sword again. He needed time to think. *Had* Druss suggested he lose?

'You're not concentrating,' said Elicas sternly. 'What's the matter with you? The Legion has a lot of wages tied up in this tourney.'

'I know.'

His mind cleared. No matter what the reason, he could not fight to lose.

He threw everything he could into the last attack, blocked a back-hand sweep and lunged. Just before his blade thudded against Orrin's belly, however, the Gan's sword tapped his neck. Orrin had read the move and lured him in. In real combat both men would have died, but this was not real combat and Orrin had won. The two men shook hands as the cheering soldiers swarmed forward.

'That's my money gone,' said Elicas. 'Still, there is a bright side.'

'What's that?' said Hogun, rubbing at his burning forearm.

'I cannot afford to settle our own bet. You will have to stand for the wine. It's the least you can do, Hogun, after letting down the Legion!'

The banquet lifted Hogun's spirits and the speeches from Bar Britan on behalf of the soldiers and Dun Pinar for the officers were witty and short; the food was good, the wine and ale plentiful, and the camaraderie reassuring. It is hardly the same Dros, thought Hogun.

Outside at the portcullis gates, Bregan stood sentry duty with a tall young Cul from Group Fire. Bregan didn't know his name and couldn't ask, since sentries were forbidden to talk on duty. A strange rule, thought Bregan, but there to be obeyed.

The night was chill but he barely noticed it. His thoughts were back in the village with Lotis and the children. Sybad had received a letter that day, and all was well. Legan, Bregan's five-year-old son, was mentioned. It seemed that when he climbed a tall elm and couldn't get down, he had cried and called for his father. Bregan had asked Sybad to write a few words for him in his next letter home. He had wanted him to say how much he loved and missed them all, but he couldn't bring himself to ask Sybad to pen such endearments. Instead, he asked him to tell Legan to be a good boy and obey his mother. Sybad took notes from all the villagers and spent the early evening composing the letter, which was sealed in wax and delivered to the mail room. A rider would carry it south with other letters and army despatches for Drenan.

Lotis would have banked the fire by now and doused the lamps, Bregan thought. She would be lying in their rush-filled bed, probably asleep. Legan would be asleep beside her, he knew, for Lotis always found it difficult to sleep alone when Bregan was away.

'You will stop the savages, daddy, won't you?'

'Yes,' Bregan had told him. 'But they probably won't come. The politicians will sort it out, just like they have always done before.'

'Will you be home soon?'

'I'll be back for Harvest Supper.'

'Promise?'

'I promise.'

The banquet over, Druss invited Orrin, Hogun, Elicas and Bowman to the Earl's study above the great hall. The servant Arshin brought them wine and Druss introduced the outlaw to the fortress leaders. Orrin shook hands coolly, his eyes showing his distaste. For two years he had sent patrols into Skultik with orders to catch and hang the outlaw leader. Hogun was less concerned with Bowman's pedigree and more interested in the skills the outlaws could bring. Elicas had no preconceived opinion, but instinctively liked the blond archer.

Once seated, Bowman cleared his throat and told them the size of the Nadir horde gathered at Gulgothir.

'How do you come by this intelligence?' asked Orrin.

'Three days ago we . . . met . . . some travellers in Skultik. They were journeying from Dros Purdol to Segril and had come across the northern desert. They were waylaid near Gulgothir and taken into the city, where they stayed for four days. Because they were Vagrian merchants they were treated civilly, but questioned by a Nadir officer called Surip. One of them is a former Vagrian officer, and he made the estimate of their strength.'

'But half a million?' said Orrin. 'I thought the figure was exaggerated.'

'Underplayed, if anything,' said Bowman. 'Outlying tribes were still coming in when he left. I'd say you will have quite a battle on your hands.'

'I don't wish to be pedantic,' said Hogun, 'but do you not mean *we* have a battle on our hands?'

Bowman glanced at Druss. 'Have you not told them, old horse? No? Ah, what a deliciously embarrassing moment, to be sure.'

'Told us what?' asked Orrin.

'That they are mercenaries,' said Druss, uneasily. 'They stay only until the fall of Wall Three. It has been agreed.'

'And for this . . . this pitiful aid they expect pardons!' shouted Orrin, rising to his feet. 'I will see them swing first.'

'After Wall Three we will have less need of archers,' said Hogun calmly. 'There is no killing ground.'

'We need archers, Orrin,' said Druss. 'We need them badly. And this man has 600 of the finest. We know walls will fall, and we will need every

370

shaft. The postern gates will be sealed by then. I don't like this situation either, but needs must . . . Better to have cover for the first three walls than to have none at all. Do you agree?'

'And if I don't?' said the Gan, still angry.

'Then I shall send them away,' said Druss. Hogun began an angry outburst, but was silenced by a wave of Druss' hand. 'You are the Gan, Orrin. It is your decision.'

Orrin sat down, breathing deeply. He had made many mistakes before Druss arrived – he knew that now. This situation angered him deeply, but he had no choice but to back the axeman and Druss knew it too. The two men exchanged glances and smiled.

'They shall stay,' said Orrin.

'A wise decision,' said Bowman. 'How soon will the Nadir arrive, do you think?'

'Too damned soon,' muttered Druss. 'Some time within the next three weeks, according to our scouts. Ulric lost a son, which has given us a few more days. But it's still not enough.'

For some time the men discussed the many problems facing the defenders. Finally Bowman spoke, this time hesitantly.

'Look here, Druss, there is something I feel I should mention, but I don't want to be thought . . . strange. I've been toying with the idea of not mentioning it, but . . .'

'Speak on, laddie. You're among friends . . . mostly.'

'I had a strange dream last night and you appeared in it. I would have dismissed it – but seeing you today made me think again. I dreamed I was woken from a deep sleep by a warrior in silver armour. I could see right through him, as if he was a ghost. He told me that he had been trying to contact you, but without success. When he spoke it was like a voice in my mind. He said that his name was Serbitar and that he was travelling with his friends and a woman called Virae.

'He said it was important for me to tell you to collect inflammables and containers, since Ulric has built great siege towers. He also suggested fire gullies across the spaces between walls. In my mind he showed me a vision of you being attacked. He told me a name: Musar.

'Does any of it make any sense?'

For a moment no one spoke, although Druss seemed hugely relieved.

'Indeed it does, laddie. Indeed it does!'

Hogun poured a fresh glass of Lentrian and passed it to Bowman.

'What did this warrior look like?' he asked.

'Tall, slender. I think his hair was white, though he was young.'

'It is Serbitar,' said Hogun. 'The vision is a true one.'

'You know him?' asked Druss.

'Of him only. He is the son of Earl Drada of Dros Segril. It is said that the boy was fey and had a demon; he could read men's thoughts. He is an albino, and as you know the Vagrians consider this an ill omen. He was sent to the Temple of The Thirty, south of Drenan, when he was about thirteen. It is also said that his father tried to smother him when he was a babe, but that the child sensed him coming and hid outside his bedroom window. These, of course, are but stories.'

'Well, his talents have grown, it seems,' said Druss. 'But I don't give a damn. He'll be useful here – especially if he can read Ulric's mind.'

15

For ten days work progressed. Fire gullies ten yards wide were dug four feet deep across the open ground between Walls One and Two, and again between Walls Three and Four. These were filled with brushwood and small timber, while vats were placed along each gully ready to pour oils to the dry wood.

Bowman's archers hammered white stakes in the open ground at various points between walls, and also out on the plain before the fortress. Each line of stakes represented sixty paces, and his men practised for several hours each day, black clouds of shafts slicing the air above each row as the commands were shouted.

Target dummies were set up on the plain, only to be splintered by scores of arrows, even at 120 paces. The skills of the Skultik archers were formidable.

Hogun rehearsed withdrawals, timing the men by drumbeats as they dashed from the battlements, across the plank bridges of the fire gullies to scale the ropes to the next wall. Each day they became more swift.

Minor points began to occupy more time as the overall fitness and readiness of the troops increased.

'When do we add the oil?' Hogun asked Druss, as the men took an afternoon break.

'Between Walls One and Two, it will have to be filled on the day of the first attack. Until the first day we will have no real idea of how well the men will stand up to the assault.'

'There remains the problem,' added Orrin, 'of who lights the gullies and when. For example, if the wall is breached we could have Nadir tribesmen racing side by side with our own men. No easy decision to throw in a lighted torch.'

'And if we give men the duty,' said Hogun, 'what happens if they are killed on the wall?'

'We will have to have a torch duty,' said Druss. 'And the decision will be relayed by a bugler from Wall Two. An officer of cool nerve will be needed to judge the issue. When the bugle sounds the gully goes up – no matter who is left behind.'

Matters such as these occupied Druss more and more, until his head swam with plans, ideas, stratagems and ploys. Several times during such discussions the old man's temper flared and his huge fists hammered the table, or else he strode around the room like a caged bear.

'I'm a soldier – not a damned planner,' he would announce, and the meeting would be adjourned for an hour.

Combustibles were carted in from outlying villages, a seemingly endless number of despatches arrived from Drenan and Abalayn's panicked government, and a multitude of small problems – concerning delayed

mail, new recruits, personal worries and squabbles between groups –
threatened to overwhelm the three men.

One officer complained that the latrine area of Wall One was in danger
of causing a health hazard, since it was not of regulation depth and lacked
an adequate cess pit.

Druss set a working party to enlarge the area.

Abalayn himself demanded a complete strategic appraisal of all Dros
Delnoch's defences, which Druss refused since the information could be
leaked to Nadir sympathisers. This in turn brought a swift rebuke from
Drenan and a firm request for an apology. Orrin penned this, claiming it
would keep the politicians off their backs.

Then Woundweaver sent a requisition for the Legion's mounts, claiming
that since the order was to hold to the last man, the horses would be of
little use at Delnoch. He allowed that twenty should be retained for
dispatch purposes. This so enraged Hogun that he was unapproachable
for days.

Added to this, the burghers had begun to complain about the rowdy
behaviour of the troops in civilian areas. All in all Druss was beginning
to feel at the end of his tether, and had begun to voice openly his desire
that the Nadir would arrive and the devil with the consequences!

Three days later his wish was partly answered.

A Nadir troop, under a flag of truce, galloped in from the north. Word
spread like wildfire, and by the time it reached Druss in the main hall of
the Keep an air of panic was abroad in the town.

The Nadir dismounted in the shadow of the great gates and waited.
They did not speak. From their pack-saddles they took dried meat and
water sacks and sat together, eating and waiting.

By the time Druss arrived with Orrin and Hogun they had completed
their meal. Druss bellowed down from the battlements.

'What is your message?'

'Open the gates!' called back the Nadir officer, a short barrel-chested
man, bow-legged and powerful.

'Are you the Deathwalker?' called the man.

'Yes.'

'You are old and fat. It pleases me.'

'Good! Remember that when next we meet, for I have marked you,
Loudmouth, and my axe knows the name of your spirit. Now, what is
your message?'

'The Lord Ulric, Prince of the North, bids me to tell you that he will
be riding to Drenan to discuss an alliance with Abalayn, Lord of the
Drenai. He wishes it known that he expects the gates of Dros Delnoch to
be open to him; that being so, he guarantees there will be no harm to
any man, woman, or child, soldier or otherwise within the city. It is the
Lord Ulric's wish that the Drenai and the Nadir become as one nation.
He offers the gift of friendship.'

'Tell the Lord Ulric,' said Druss, 'that he is welcome to ride to Drenan
at any time. We will even allow an escort of 100 warriors, as befits a
prince of the north.'

'The Lord Ulric allows no conditions,' said the officer.

'These are *my* conditions – they shall not change,' said Druss.

'Then I have a second message. Should the walls be contested and the gates closed, the Lord Ulric wishes it known that every second defender taken alive will be slain, that all the women will be sold into slavery and that one in three of all citizens will lose his right hand.'

'Before that can happen, laddie, the Lord Ulric has to take the Dros. Now you give him this message from Druss the Deathwalker: In the north the mountains may tremble as he breaks wind, but this is Drenai land, and as far as I am concerned he is a pot-bellied savage who couldn't pick his own nose without a Drenai map.

'Do you think you can remember that, laddie. Or shall I carve it on your arse in large letters?'

'Inspiring as your words were, Druss,' said Orrin, 'I must tell you that my stomach turned over as you spoke them. Ulric will be furious.'

'Would that he were,' said Druss bitterly, as the Nadir troop galloped back to the north. 'If that were the case, he would truly be just a pot-bellied savage. No! He will laugh . . . loud and long.'

'Why should he?' asked Hogun.

'Because he has no choice. He has been insulted and should lose face. When he laughs, the men will laugh with him.'

'It was a pretty offer he made,' said Orrin, as the three men made the long walk back to the Keep. 'Word will spread. Talks with Abalayn . . . One empire of Drenai and Nadir . . . Clever!'

'Clever and true,' said Hogun. 'We know from his record that he means it. If we surrender, he will march through and harm no one. Threats of death can be taken and resisted – offers of life are horses of a different colour. I wonder how long it will be before the burghers demand another audience.'

'Before dusk,' predicted Druss.

Back on the walls, Gilad and Bregan watched the dust from the Nadir horsemen dwindle into the distance.

'What did he mean, Gil, about riding to Drenan for discussions with Abalayn?'

'He meant he wants us to let his army through.'

'Oh. They didn't look terribly fierce, did they? I mean they seem quite ordinary really, save that they wear furs.'

'Yes, they are ordinary,' said Gilad, removing his helm and combing his hair with his fingers, allowing the cool breeze to get to his head. 'Very ordinary. Except that they live for war. Fighting comes as naturally to them as farming does to you. Or me,' he added as an afterthought, knowing this to be untrue.

'I wonder why?' said Bregan. 'It has never made much sense to me. I mean, I understand why some men become soldiers: to protect the nation and all that. But a whole race of people living to be soldiers seems . . . unhealthy? Does that sound right?'

Gilad laughed. 'Indeed it sounds right. But the northern steppes make poor farmland. Mainly they breed goats and ponies. Any luxuries they desire, they must steal. Now to the Nadir, so Dun Pinar told me at the banquet, the word for stranger is the same as the word for enemy. Anyone not of the tribe is simply there to be killed and stripped of goods. It is a way of life. Smaller tribes are wiped out by larger tribes. Ulric changed the pattern; by amalgamating beaten tribes into his own, he grew more and more powerful. He controls all the northern kingdoms now, and many to the east. Two years ago he took Manea, the sea kingdom.'

'I heard about that,' said Bregan. 'But I thought he had withdrawn after making a treaty with the king.'

'Dun Pinar says the king agreed to be Ulric's vassal and Ulric holds the king's son hostage. The nation is his.'

'He must be a pretty clever man,' said Bregan. 'But what would he do if he ever conquered the whole world? I mean, what good is it? I would like a bigger farm and a house with several floors. That I can understand. But what would I do with ten farms? Or a hundred?'

'You would be rich and powerful. Then you could tell your tenant farmers what to do and they would all bow as you rode past in your fine carriage.'

'That doesn't appeal to me, not at all,' said Bregan.

'Well, it does to me,' said Gilad. 'I've always hated it when I had to tug the forelock for some passing nobleman on a tall horse. The way they look at you, despising you because you work a smallholding; paying more money for their hand-made boots than I can earn in a year of slaving. No, I wouldn't mind being rich – so pig-awful rich that no man could ever look down on me again.'

Gilad turned his face away to stare out over the plains – his anger fierce, almost tangible.

'Would you look down on people then, Gil? Would you despise me because I wanted to remain a farmer?'

'Of course not. A man should be free to do what he wants to do, as long as it doesn't hurt others.'

'Maybe that's why Ulric wants to control everything. Maybe he is sick of everyone looking down on the Nadir.'

Gilad turned back to Bregan and his anger died within him.

'Do you know, Breg, that's just what Pinar said, when I asked him if he hated Ulric for wanting to smash the Drenai. He said, "Ulric isn't trying to smash the Drenai, but to raise the Nadir." I think Pinar admires him.'

'The man I admire is Orrin,' said Bregan. 'It must have taken great courage to come out and train with the men as he has done. Especially being as unpopular as he was. I was so pleased when he won back the Swords.'

'Only because you won five silver pieces on him,' Gilad pointed out.

'That's not fair, Gil! I backed him because he was Karnak; I backed you too.'

'You backed me for a quarter-copper and him for a half-silver, according to Drebus who took your bet.'

376

Bregan tapped his nose, smiling. 'Ah, but then you don't pay the same price for a goat as for a horse. But the thought was there. After all, I knew you couldn't win.'

'I damn near had that Bar Britan. It was a judge's decision at the last.'

'True,' said Bregan. 'But you would never have beaten Pinar, or that fellow with the earring from the Legion. But what's even more to the point, you never could have beaten Orrin. I've seen you both fence.'

'Such judgement!' said Gilad. 'It's small wonder to me that you didn't enter yourself, so great is your knowledge.'

'I don't have to fly in order to know that the sky is blue,' said Bregan 'Anyway, who did you back?'

'Gan Hogun.'

'Who else? Drebus said you had placed two bets,' said Bregan innocently.

'You know very well. Drebus would have told you.'

'I didn't think to ask.'

'Liar! Well, I don't care. I backed myself to reach the last fifty.'

'And you were so close,' said Bregan. 'Only one strike in it.'

'One lucky blow and I could have won a month's wages.'

'Such is life,' said Bregan. 'Maybe next year you can come back and have another try?'

'And maybe corn will grow on the backs of camels!' said Gilad.

Back at the Keep, Druss was struggling to keep his temper as the City Elders argued back and forth about the Nadir offer. Word had spread to them with bewildering speed, and Druss had barely managed to eat a chunk of bread and cheese before a messenger from Orrin informed him that the Elders had called a meeting.

It was a Drenai rule, long established, that except in time of battle the Elders had a democratic right to see the city lord and debate matters of importance. Neither Orrin nor Druss could refuse. No one could argue that Ulric's ultimatum was unimportant.

Six men constituted the City Elders, an elected body which effectively ruled all trade within the city. The Master Burgher and chief elder was Bricklyn, who had entertained Druss so royally on the night of the assassination attempt. Malphar, Backda, Shinell and Alphus were all merchants, while Beric was a nobleman, a distant cousin of Earl Delnar and highly-placed in city life. Only lack of real fortune kept him at Delnoch and away from Drenan, which he loved.

Shinell, a fat, oily silk merchant, was the main cause of Druss' anger. 'But surely we have a right to discuss Ulric's terms and must be allowed a say in whether they are accepted or rejected,' he said again. 'It is of vital interest to the city, after all, and by right of law our vote must carry.'

'You know full well, my dear Shinell,' said Orrin smoothly, 'that the City Elders have full rights to discuss all civil matters. This situation hardly falls within that category. Nevertheless, your point of view is noted.'

Malphar, a red-faced wine dealer of Lentrian stock, interrupted Shinell as he began his protest. 'We are getting nowhere with this talk of rules and precedent. The fact remains that we are virtually at war. Is it a war we can win?' His green eyes scanned the faces around him and Druss tapped his fingers on the table-top, the only outward sign of his tensions. 'Is it a war we can carry long enough to force an honourable peace? I don't think it is,' continued Malphar. 'It is all a nonsense. Abalayn has run the army down until it is only a tenth of the size it was a few years ago. The navy has been halved. This Dros was last under siege two centuries ago, when it almost fell. Yet our records tell us that we had forty thousand warriors in the field.'

'Get on with it, man! Make your point,' said Druss.

'I shall, but spare me your harsh looks, Druss. I am no coward. What I am saying is this: If we cannot hold and cannot win, what is the point of this defence?'

Orrin glanced at Druss and the old warrior leaned forward. 'The point is,' he said. 'that you don't know whether you've lost – until you've lost. Anything can happen: Ulric could suffer a stroke; plague could hit the Nadir forces. We have to try to hold.'

'What about the women and children?' asked Backda, a skull-faced lawyer and property owner.

'What about them?' said Druss. 'They can leave at any time.'

'To go where, pray? And with what monies?'

'Ye gods!' thundered Druss, surging to his feet. 'What will you be wanting me to do next? Where they go, if they do, how they go – is their concern and yours. I am a soldier and my job is to fight and kill. And believe me, I do that very well. We have been ordered to fight to the last and that we will do.

'Now, I may not know very much about law and all the little niceties of city politics, but I do know this: Any man who speaks of surrender during the coming siege is a traitor.

'And I will see him hang.'

'Well said, Druss,' offered Beric, a tall middle-aged man with shoulder-length grey hair. 'I couldn't have put it better myself. Very stirring.' He smiled as Druss sank back to his seat. 'There is one point, though. You say you have been asked to fight to the end. That order can always be changed; politics being what it is, the question of expediency comes into it. At the moment, it is expedient for Abalayn to ask us to prepare for war. He may feel it gives him greater bargaining power with Ulric. Ultimately, though, he must consider surrender. Facts are facts: the tribes have conquered every nation they have attacked and Ulric is a general above comparison.

'I suggest we write to Abalayn and urge him to reconsider this war.'

Orrin shot Druss a warning glance.

'Very well put, Beric,' he said. 'Obviously Druss and I, as loyal military men, must vote against; however, feel free to write and I will see the petition is forwarded with the first available rider.'

'Thank you, Orrin. That is very civilised of you,' said Beric. 'Now can we move on to the subject of the demolished homes?'

Ulric sat before the brazier, a sheepskin cloak draped over his naked torso. Before him squatted the skeletal figure of his shaman, Nosta Khan.

'What do you mean?' Ulric asked him.

'As I said, I can no longer travel over the fortress. There is a barrier to my power. Last night as I floated above Deathwalker I felt a force, like a storm wind. It pushed me back beyond the outer wall.'

'And you saw nothing?'

'No. But I sensed . . . felt . . .'

'Speak!'

'It is difficult. In my mind I could feel the sea and a slender ship. It was a fragment only. Also there was a mystic with white hair. I have puzzled long over this. I believe Deathwalker has called upon a white temple.'

'And their power is greater than yours?' said Ulric.

'Merely different,' hedged the shaman.

'If they are coming by sea, then they will make for Dros Purdol,' said Ulric, staring into the glimmering coals. 'Seek them out.'

The shaman closed his eyes, freed the chains of his spirit and soared free of his body. Formless he raced high above the plain, over hills and rivers, mountains and streams, skirting the Delnoch range until at last the sea lay below him, shimmering beneath the stars. Far he roved before sighting *Wastrel*, picking out the tiny glint of her aft lantern.

Swiftly he dropped from the sky to hover by the mast. By the port rail stood a man and a woman. Gently he probed their minds, then drifted down through the wooden deck, beyond the hold and on to the cabins. These he could not enter, however. As lightly as the whisper of a sea breeze, he touched the edge of the invisible barrier. It hardened before him, and he recoiled. He floated to the deck, closing on the mariner at the stern, smiled, then raced back towards the waiting Nadir warlord.

Nosta Khan's body trembled and his eyes opened.

'Well?' asked Ulric.

'I found them.'

'Can you destroy them?'

'I believe so. I must gather my acolytes.'

On *Wastrel* Vintar rose from his bed, his eyes troubled, his mind uneasy. He stretched.

'You felt it too,' pulsed Serbitar, swinging his long legs clear of the second bed.

'Yes. We must be wary.'

'He did not try to breach the shield,' said Serbitar. 'Was that a sign of weakness or confidence?'

'I don't know,' answered the Abbot.

Above them at the stern the second mate rubbed his tired eyes, slipped a looped rope over the wheel and transferred his gaze to the stars. He had always been fascinated by these flickering, far-off candles. Tonight they were brighter than usual, like gems strewn on a velvet cloak. A priest had once told him they were holes in the universe, through which the bright eyes of the gods gazed down on the peoples of the earth. It was a pretty nonsense, but he had enjoyed listening.

Suddenly he shivered. Turning, he lifted his cloak from the aft rail and slung it about his shoulders. He rubbed his hands.

Floating behind him, the spirit of Nosta Khan lifted its hands, focusing power upon the long fingers. Talons grew, glinting like steel, serrated and sharp. Satisfied, he closed in on the mariner, plunging his hands into the man's head.

Searing agony blanketed the brain within as the man staggered and fell, blood pouring from his mouth and ears and seeping from his eyes. Without a sound he died. Nosta Khan loosened his grip. Drawing on the power of his acolytes, he willed the body to rise, whispering words of obscenity in a language long erased from the minds of ordinary men. Darkness swelled around the corpse, shifting like black smoke to be drawn in through the bloody mouth. The body shuddered.

And rose.

Unable to sleep Virae dressed silently, climbed to the deck and wandered to the port rail. The night was cool, the soft breeze soothing. She gazed out over the waves to the distant line of land silhouetted against the bright, moonlit sky.

The view always calmed her, the blending of land and sea. As a child at school in Dros Purdol she had delighted in sailing, especially at night when the land mass appeared to float like a sleeping monster of the deep, dark and mysterious and wonderfully compelling.

Suddenly she narrowed her eyes. Was the land moving? To her left the mountains seemed to be receding, while on the right the shoreline seemed closer. No, not *seemed*. *Was*. She glanced at the stars. The ship had veered north-west; yet they were days from Purdol.

Puzzled, she walked aft towards the second mate as he stood with hands on the wheel.

'Where are we heading?' she asked him, mounting the four steps to the stern and leaning on the rail.

His head turned towards her. Blank, blood-red eyes locked on hers as his hands left the wheel and reached for her.

Fear entered her soul like a lance, only to be quelled by rising anger. She was not some Drenai milk-maid to be terrified thus – she was Virae, and she carried the blood of warriors in her veins.

Dropping her shoulder, she threw a right-hand punch to his jaw. His head snapped back but still he came on. Stepping inside the groping arms, she grabbed his hair and smashed a head butt into his face. He took it without a sound, his hands curling round her throat. Twisting desperately before the grip tightened, she threw him with a rolling hip lock and he hit the deck hard on his back. Virae staggered. He rose slowly and came for her again.

Running forward, she leapt into the air and twisted, hammering both feet into his face. He fell once more.

And rose.

Panicked now, Virae searched for a weapon but there was nothing. Smoothly she vaulted the wheel rail to land on the deck. He followed her.

'Move away from him!' screamed Serbitar, racing forward with sword drawn. Virae ran to him.

'Give me that!' she said, tearing the sword from his hand. Confidence surged in her as her hand gripped the ebony hilt. 'Now, you son of a slut!' she shouted, striding towards the mariner.

He made no effort to avoid her, and the sword flashed in the moonlight, slicing into his exposed neck. Twice more she struck, and the grinning head toppled from the body. But the corpse did not fall.

Oily smoke oozed from the severed neck to create a second head, formless and vague. Coal-red eyes glittered within the smoke.

'Get back!' shouted Serbitar. 'Get away from him!'

This time she obeyed, backing towards the albino.

'Give me the sword.'

Vintar and Rek had joined them.

'What on earth is it?' whispered Rek.

'Nothing on earth,' replied Vintar.

The thing stood its ground, arms folded across its chest.

'The ship is heading for the rocks,' said Virae and Serbitar nodded.

'It is keeping us from the wheel. What do you think, Father Abbot?'

'The spell was planted in the head, which must be thrown overboard. The beast will follow it,' replied Vintar. 'Attack it.'

Serbitar moved forward, supported by Rek. The corpse bent its body, right hand closing on the hair of the severed head. Holding the head to its chest, it waited for the attack.

Rek leapt forward, slashing a cut at the arm. The corpse staggered. Serbitar ran in, slicing the tendons behind the knee. As it fell, Rek hammered the blade two-handed across its arm. The arm fell clear, the fingers releasing the head which rolled across the deck. Dropping his sword Rek dived at it. Swallowing his revulsion, he lifted it by the hair and hurled it over the side. As it hit the waves the corpse on the deck shuddered. As if torn by a great wind the smoke flowed from the neck to vanish beneath the rail and into the darkness of the deep.

The captain came forward from the shadows by the mast.

'What was it?' he asked.

Vintar joined him, placing a hand gently on the man's shoulder.

'We have many enemies,' he said. 'They have great powers. But fear not, we are not powerless and no harm will befall the ship again. I promise you.'

'And what of his soul?' asked the captain, wandering to the rail. 'Have they taken it?'

'It is free,' said Vintar. 'Believe me.'

'We will all be free,' said Rek, 'if someone doesn't turn the ship away from those rocks.'

In the darkened tent of Nosta Khan the acolytes silently backed out, leaving him sitting in the centre of the circle chalked on the dirt floor. Lost in thought, Nosta Khan ignored them – he was drained and angry.

For they had bested him and he was a man unused to defeat. It tasted bitter in his mouth.

He smiled.

There would be another time . . .

16

Blessed by a following wind, *Wastrel* sped north until at last the silver grey towers of Dros Purdol broke the line of the horizon. The ship entered the harbour a little before noon, piloting past the Drenai war triremes and the merchant vessels anchored in the bay.

On the milling docks street traders sold charms, ornaments, weapons and blankets to mariners, while burly dockers carried provisions up swaying gangplanks, stacking cargo and checking loads. All was noise and apparent confusion.

The harbour-side was rich in colour and the hectic pace of city life and Rek felt a pang of regret to be leaving the ship. As Serbitar led The Thirty ashore, Rek and Virae said their goodbyes to the captain.

'With one exception, it has been a more than pleasant voyage,' Virae told him. 'I thank you for your courtesy.'

'I was glad to be of service, my lady. I will forward the marriage papers to Drenan on my return. It was a "first" for me. I have never taken part in the wedding of an earl's daughter – much less conducted one. I wish you well.' Bending forward he kissed her hand.

He wanted to add, 'Long life and happiness,' but he knew their destination.

Virae strode down the gangplank as Rek gripped the captain's hand. He was surprised when the man embraced him.

'May your sword arm be strong, your spirit lucky and your horse swift when the time comes,' he said.

Rek grinned. 'The first two I will need. As to the horse, do you believe *that* lady will consider flight?'

'No, she's a wonderful lass. Be lucky.'

'I will try hard,' said Rek.

At the quayside a young red-caped officer eased his way through the crowd to confront Serbitar.

'Your business in Dros Purdol?' he asked.

'We are travelling to Delnoch as soon as we can obtain horses,' answered the albino.

'The fortress will soon be under siege, sir. Are you aware of the coming war?'

'We are. We travel with the Lady Virae, daughter of Earl Delnar, and her husband Regnak.'

Seeing Virae, the officer bowed: 'A pleasure, my lady. We met at your eighteenth birthday celebration last year. You probably won't remember me.'

'On the contrary, Dun Degas! We danced and I trod on your foot. You were most kind and took the blame.'

Degas smiled and bowed again. How she had changed, he thought!

Where was the clumsy girl who had contrived to trip on the hem of her skirt? Who had blushed as red as the wine when, during a heated conversation, she had crushed a crystal goblet, drenching the woman to her right. What had changed? She was the same woman-girl he remembered – her hair mousey blonde, her mouth too wide, her brows thunder-dark over deep-set eyes. He saw her smile as Rek stepped forward and his question was answered. She had become desirable.

'What are you thinking, Degas?' she asked. 'You look far away.'

'My apologies, my lady. I was thinking Earl Pindak will be delighted to receive you.'

'You will have to convey my regrets,' said Virae, 'for we must leave as soon as possible. Where can we purchase mounts?'

'I am sure we can find you good horses,' said Degas. 'It is a shame you did not arrive sooner, since four days ago we sent three hundred men to Delnoch to aid the defence. You could have travelled with them – it would have been safer. The Sathuli have grown bold since the Nadir threat.'

'We shall get there,' said the tall man with Virae. Degas' eyes measured him: a soldier, he thought, or has been at some time. Carries himself well. Degas directed the party to a large inn, promising to supply the horses within two hours.

True to his word, he returned with a troop of Drenai cavalrymen riding thirty-two horses. They were not of the pedigree of the mounts left behind in Lentria, being mustangs bred for mountain work, but they were sturdy animals. When the horses had been allocated and the provisions packed, Degas approached Rek.

'There is no charge for these mounts, but I would be obliged if you could deliver these despatches to the Earl. They came by sea from Drenan yesterday and missed our force. The one with the red seal is from Aba-layn.'

'The Earl will receive them,' said Rek. 'Thank you for your help.'

'It is nothing. Good luck!' The officer moved on to make his farewells to Virae. Pushing the letters into the saddle-bag of his roan mare, Rek mounted and led the party west from Purdol along the line of the Delnoch mountains. Serbitar cantered alongside him as they entered the first of the deep woods beyond the town.

'You look troubled,' said Rek.

'Yes. There will be outlaws, renegades, perhaps deserters, and certainly Sathuli tribesmen along our route.'

'But that is not what troubles you?'

'You are perceptive,' said Serbitar.

'How true. But then I saw the corpse walk.'

'Indeed you did,' said Serbitar.

'You have hedged about that night for long enough,' said Rek. 'Now give me the truth of it. Do you know what it was?'

'Vintar believes it to be a demon summoned by Nosta Khan. He is the head shaman to Ulric's Wolfshead tribe – and therefore Lord of all Nadir shaman. He is old and it is said he first served Ulric's great-grandfather. He is a man steeped in evil.'

'And his powers are greater than yours?'

'Individually, yes. Collectively? I don't think so. We are presently stopping him from entering Delnoch, but he in turn has cast a veil over the fortress and we cannot enter.'

'Will he attack us again?' asked Rek.

'Assuredly. The question is what method he will choose.'

'I think I will leave you to worry about that,' said Rek. 'I can only take in so much gloom in one day.'

Serbitar did not answer him. Rek reined his mount and waited for Virae.

That night they camped by a mountain stream, but lit no fires. In the early evening Vintar recited poetry, his voice soft and melodious, his words evocative.

'They are his own work,' Serbitar whispered to Virae, 'though he will not own to them. I know not why. He is a fine poet.'

'But they are so sad,' she said.

'All beauty is sad,' replied the albino. 'For it fades.'

He left her and retreated to a nearby willow, sitting with his back to the tree, a silver ghost in the moonlight.

Arbedark joined Rek and Virae, handing them honey cakes he had purchased at the port. Rek glanced over at the lonely figure of the albino.

'He travels,' said Arbedark. 'Alone.'

As the dawn bird-song began, Rek groaned and eased his aching body away from the probing tree roots which were denting his side. His eyes opened. Most of The Thirty were still asleep, though tall Antaheim stood sentry by the stream. At the willow Serbitar remained where he had been during the recital.

Rek sat up and stretched, his mouth dry. Pushing back his blanket he walked to the horses, removed his pack, rinsed his mouth with water from his canteen and went to the stream. Taking out a bar of soap, he stripped the shirt from his chest and knelt by the swift rushing water.

'Please don't do that,' said Antaheim.

'What?'

The tall warrior walked across to him, squatting by his side. 'The soap bubbles will carry on downstream. It is not wise thus to announce our movements.'

Rek cursed himself for a fool and apologised swiftly.

'That is not necessary. I am sorry to have intruded. Do you see that plant there, by the lichen rock?' Rek twisted, then nodded. 'It is a lemon mint. Wash in the water, then crush some of the leaves and clean your body. It will refresh you and create . . . a more pleasant aroma.'

'Thank you. Is Serbitar still travelling?'

'He should not be. I will seek him.' Antaheim closed his eyes for several seconds. When they opened again, Rek recognised panic and the warrior ran from the stream. In that moment all members of The Thirty surged from their blankets and raced to Serbitar by the willow.

Rek dropped his shirt and soap on the bank and moved to join them.

Vintar was bending over the albino's still form; he closed his eyes and placed his hands on the young leader's slender face. For long moments he remained thus. Sweat broke out upon his forehead and he began to sway. When he lifted a hand, Menahem joined him instantly, raising Serbitar's head. The swarthy warrior lifted the albino's right eyelid: the iris was red as blood.

Virae dropped to her knees beside Rek. 'His eyes are green normally,' she said. 'What is happening?'

'I don't know,' said Rek.

Antaheim rose from the group and sprinted for the undergrowth, returning minutes later with what appeared to be an armful of vine leaves which he tipped to the ground. Gathering dried twigs, he fashioned a small fire; then, setting up a tripod of branches, he hung a pot above the flames, filled it with water and crushed the leaves between his palms, dropping them into the pot. Soon the water began to bubble and a sweet aroma filled the air. Antaheim lifted the pan from the flames, adding cold water from his canteen, then transferred the green liquid to a leather-covered pottery mug which he passed to Menahem. Slowly they opened Serbitar's mouth and, while Vintar held the albino's nostrils, they poured in the liquid. Serbitar gagged and swallowed and Vintar released his nose. Menahem laid his head back on the grass and Antaheim swiftly killed the fire. There had been no smoke.

'What's going on?' asked Rek as Vintar approached him.

'We will talk later,' said Vintar.'Now I must rest.' He stumbled to his blankets and lay down, slipping instantly into a deep, dreamless sleep.

'I feel like a one-legged man in a foot race,' said Rek.

Menahem joined them, his dark face grey with exhaustion as he sipped water from a leather canteen. He stretched his long legs out on the grass and lay on his side, supporting himself on his elbow. He turned towards Rek.

'I didn't mean to eavesdrop,' he said, 'but I did overhear you. You must forgive Vintar. He is older than the rest of us and the strain of the hunt proved too much for him.'

'The hunt? What hunt?' asked Virae.

'We sought Serbitar. He had journeyed far and the path was sundered. He could not return and we had to find him. Vintar guessed rightly that he had retreated into the mists and taken his chances. He had to seek him.'

'I'm sorry, Menahem. You look worn out,' said Rek, 'but try to remember that we do not know what you are talking about. Into the mists? What the devil does that mean?'

Menahem sighed. 'How can one explain colours to a blind man?'

'One says,' snapped Rek, 'that red is like silk, blue is like cool water, and yellow is like sunshine on the face.'

'Forgive me, Rek. I am tired, I did not mean to be rude,' said Menahem. 'I cannot explain the mists to you as I understand them. But I will try to give you some idea.

'There are many futures but only one past. When we travel beyond ourselves we walk a straight path, journeying much as we are doing now. We direct ourselves over vast distances. But the path back remains solid, for it is locked in our memories. Do you understand?'

'So far,' said Rek. 'Virae?'

'I'm not an idiot, Rek.'

'Sorry. Go on, Menahem.'

'Now try to imagine there are other paths. Not just from, say, Drenan to Delnoch, but from today into tomorrow. Tomorrow has not yet happened and the possibilities for it are endless. Each one of us makes a decision that will affect tomorrow. But let us say we do travel into tomorrow. Then we are faced with a multitude of paths, gossamer-thin and shifting. In one tomorrow Dros Delnoch has already fallen, in another it has been saved, or is about to fall or about to be saved. Already we have four paths. Which is true? And when we tread the path, how do we return to today, which from where we are standing is a multitude of yesterdays? To which do we return? Serbitar journeyed far beyond tomorrow. And Vintar found him as we held the path in sight.'

'You used the wrong analogy,' said Rek. 'It is nothing like explaining colours to a blind man. Rather is it more like teaching archery to a rock. I haven't the remotest idea what you are talking about. Will Serbitar be all right?'

'We don't know yet. If he lives, he will have information of great value.'

'What happened to his eyes? How did they change colour?' asked Virae.

'Serbitar is an albino – a true albino. He needs certain herbs in order to maintain his strength. Last night he journeyed too far and lost his way. It was foolhardy. But his heartbeat is strong and he is now resting.'

'Then he won't die?' said Rek.

'That we cannot say. He travelled a path which stretched his mind. It could be he will suffer the Pull; this happens sometimes to Travellers. They move so far from themselves that they just drift, like smoke. If his spirit is broken, it will pass from him and return to the mist.'

'Can't you do anything?'

'We have done all we can. We cannot hold him forever.'

'When will we know?' asked Rek.

'When he awakes. If he awakes.'

The long morning wore on and Serbitar still lay unmoving. The Thirty volunteered no conversation and Virae had walked upstream to bathe. Bored and tired, Rek took the despatches from his pouch. The bulky scroll sealed in red wax was addressed to Earl Delnar. Rek broke the seal and spread the letter wide. In flowing script the message read:

My dear friend,

Even as you read this, our intelligence is that Nadir will be upon you. We have tried repeatedly to secure peace, having offered all that we have save the right to govern ourselves as a free people. Ulric will have none of this – he wishes to secure for himself a kingdom stretching between the northern and southern seas.

I know the Dros cannot hold and I therefore rescind my order that you fight to the last. It will be a battle without profit and without hope.

Woundweaver is – needless to say – against this policy, and has made it clear that he will take his army into the hills as a raiding force should the Nadir be allowed to pass to the Sentran Plain.

You are an old soldier and the decision must be yours.

Pin the blame for surrender upon me. It is mine by right, since I have brought the Drenai people to this parlous state.

Do not think of me unkindly. I have always tried to do that which was best for my people.

But perhaps the years have told more heavily upon me than I realised, for my wisdom has been lacking in my dealings with Ulric.

It was signed simply 'Abalayn', and below the signature was the red seal of the Drenai dragon.

Rek re-folded the scroll and returned it to his saddle bag.

Surrender . . . A helping hand at the brink of the abyss.

Virae returned from the stream, her hair dripping and her features flushed.

'Ye gods, that was good!' she said, sitting beside him. 'Why the long face? Serbitar not awake yet?'

'No. Tell me, what would your father have done if Abalayn had told him to surrender the Dros?'

'He would never have given that order to my father.'

'But if he had?' insisted Rek.

'The point does not arise. Why do you always ask questions that have no relevance?'

He put a hand on her shoulder. 'Listen to me. What would he have done?'

'He would have refused. Abalayn would know that my father is the lord of Dros Delnoch, the High Warden of the North. He can be relieved of command – but not ordered to give up the fortress.'

'Suppose Abalayn had then left the choice to Delnar. What then?'

'He would have fought to the last; it was his way. Now will you tell me what all this is about?'

'The despatch Degas gave me for your father. It is a letter from Abalayn withdrawing his "fight to the last" order.'

'How dare you open that?' stormed Virae. 'It was addressed to my father and should have been given to me. How *dare* you!' Her face red with fury, she suddenly struck out at him. When he parried the blow, she launched another and without thinking he struck her, flat-handed, sprawling her to the grass.

She lay there, eyes blazing.

'I'll tell you how I dare,' he said, suppressing his anger with great effort. 'Because *I* am the Earl. And if Delnar is dead, then it was addressed to me. Which means that the decision to fight is mine. As is the decision to open the gates to the Nadir.'

'That's what you want, isn't it? A way out?' She rose to her feet, snatching up her leather jerkin.

'Think what you like,' he said. 'It doesn't matter to me. Anyway, I should have known better than to talk to you about the letter. I'd forgotten how much this war means to you. You can't wait to see the crows feast, can you? Can't wait for the bodies to start swelling and rotting! You hear me?' he shouted at her back as she walked away.

'Trouble, my friend?' asked Vintar as he sat down opposite the angry Rek.

'Nothing whatsoever to do with you,' snapped the new Earl.

'Of that I don't doubt,' said Vintar calmly. 'But I might be able to help. After all, I've known Virae for many years.'

'I'm sorry, Vintar. That was unforgivable of me.'

'I have found in my life, Rek, that there are a few actions which are unforgivable. And certainly there are no words said that carry such a penalty. It is a man's lot, I fear, to strike out when he has suffered hurt. Now, can I help?'

Rek told him about the despatch and Virae's reaction.

'A thorny problem, my boy. What will you do?'

'I have not yet made up my mind.'

'That is as well. No one should make a hasty decision over such a weighty matter. Do not be too hard on Virae, she is now sitting by the stream and feeling very miserable. She is desperately sorry for what she said and is merely waiting for you to apologise so that she can tell you it was all her own fault.'

'I'll be damned if I will apologise,' said Rek.

'It will be a frosty ride if you do not,' said the Abbot.

A soft moan came from the sleeping Serbitar. Instantly Vintar, Menahem, Arbedark and Rek moved over to him. The albino's eyes fluttered and opened . . . Once more they were the green of rose leaves. He smiled at Vintar.

'Thank you, Lord Abbot,' he whispered. Vintar patted his face gently.

'Are you all right?' asked Rek.

Serbitar smiled. 'I am well. Weak but well.'

'What happened?' asked Rek.

'Nosta Khan. I tried to force entry at the fortress and was flung into the outer mists. I was lost . . . broken. I saw futures that were terrible and chaos beyond all imagining. I fled.' He lowered his eyes. 'I fled in panic, I know not where or when.'

'Speak no more, Serbitar,' said Vintar. 'Rest now.'

'I cannot rest,' said the albino, struggling to rise. 'Help me, Rek.'

'Maybe you should rest, as Vintar says,' Rek told him.

'No. Listen to me. I did enter Delnoch and I saw death there. Terrible death!'

'The Nadir are there already?' asked Rek.

'No. Be silent. I could not see the man clearly, but I saw the Musif well being poisoned behind Wall Two. Anyone who drinks from that well will die.'

'But we should arrive before the fall of Wall One,' said Rek. 'And surely they will not need the Musif well until then?'

'That is not the point. Eldibar, or Wall One as you call it, is indefensible. It is too wide; any capable commander will give it up. Don't you understand? That's why the traitor poisoned the other well. Druss is bound to fight his first battle there and the men will be fed that day at dawn. By midday the deaths will begin, and by dusk you will have an army of ghosts.'

'We must ride,' said Rek. 'Now! Get him on a horse.'

Rek ran to find Virae as The Thirty saddled their mounts. Vintar and Arbedark helped Serbitar to his feet.

'There was more, was there not?' said Vintar.

'Aye, but some tragedies are best left unspoken.'

For three days they rode in the shadow of the Delnoch range into deep glens, and over wooded hills. They rode swiftly but with caution, Menahem scouting ahead and pulsing messages to Serbitar. Virae had said little since the argument and avoided Rek studiously. He in turn gave no ground and made no attempt to breach the silence, though it hurt him deeply.

On the morning of the fourth day, as they breasted a small hill above thick woods, Serbitar held up a hand to halt the column.

'What's wrong?' asked Rek, drawing alongside.

'I have lost contact with Menahem.'

'Trouble?'

'I don't know. He could have been thrown from his horse.'

'Let us go and find out,' said Rek, spurring the mare.

'No!' called Serbitar, but the horse was already on the move downhill and gathering speed. Rek tugged at the reins to bring the animal's head up, then leaned back in the saddle as the beast slithered to the foot of the hill. Once more on firm ground Rek glanced about him. Amongst the trees he could see Menahem's grey standing with head down, and beyond, the warrior himself lying face down on the grass. Rek cantered the mare towards him, but as he passed under the first tree a whisper of movement alerted him and he flung himself from his saddle as a man leapt from the branches. Rek landed on his side, rolled and regained his feet, dragging his sword free of its scabbard. His attacker was joined by two others; all wore the flowing white robes of the Sathuli.

Rek backed towards the fallen Menahem and glanced down. The warrior's head was bleeding at the temple. Slingshot, Rek realised, but had no chance to check if the priest was still alive. Other Sathuli now crept from the undergrowth, their broad tulwars and long knives in hand.

Slowly they advanced, grins splitting their dark, bearded features. Rek grinned back.

'This is a good day to die,' he said. 'Why don't you join me?'

He slid his right hand further up the hilt of his sword, making room for his left. This was no time for fancy sword-play; it would be hack and stand, two-handed. Once again he felt a strange sense of departure that heralded the baresark rage. This time he welcomed it.

With an ear-piercing scream he attacked them all, slashing through the throat of the first man as his mouth opened in astonishment. Then he was among them, his blade a whistling arc of bright light and crimson death. Momentarily stunned by his assault they fell back, then leapt forward again screaming their own war cries. More tribesmen burst from the undergrowth behind him as the thunder of hooves was heard.

Rek was not aware of the arrival of The Thirty. He parried a blow and back-handed his blade across the face of his assailant, stepping over the corpse to engage yet another tribesman.

Serbitar fought in vain to establish a defensive ring that could include Rek. His slender blade swept out, kissing and killing with surgical precision. Even Vintar, the oldest and least capable swordsman, found little difficulty in slaying the Sathuli warriors. Savage as they were, they were untutored in fencing skills, relying on ferocity, fearlessness and weight of numbers to wear down a foe. And this tactic would work again, Vintar knew, for they were outnumbered perhaps four to one with no avenue of retreat open to them.

The clash of steel on steel and the cries of the wounded echoed in the small clearing. Virae, cut across the upper arm, disembowelled one man and ducked beneath a slashing tulwar as a new attacker stormed in. Tall Antaheim stepped forward to block a second slash. Arbedark moved through the battle like a dancer; a short sword in each hand, he choreographed death and destruction like a silver ghost of elder legends.

Rek's anger grew. Was it all for this? Meeting Virae, coming to terms with his fears, taking the mantle of Earl? All so that he could die on a tribesman's tulwar in an unnamed wood? He hammered his blade through the clumsy guard of the Sathuli before him, then kicked the falling corpse into the path of a new attacker.

'Enough!' he yelled suddenly, his voice ringing through the trees. 'Put up your swords, all of you!' The Thirty obeyed instantly, stepping back and forming a ring of steel about the fallen Menahem, leaving Rek standing alone. The Sathuli slowly lowered their swords, glancing nervously one to another.

All battles, as they knew, followed the same pattern: fight and win, fight and die or fight and run. There was no other way. But the tall one's words were spoken with power and his voice held them momentarily.

'Let your leader step forth,' ordered Rek, plunging his sword blade into the ground at his feet and folding his arms, though the Sathuli blades still ringed him.

The men before him stepped aside as a tall broad-shouldered man in robes of blue and white moved forward. He was as tall as Rek, though hawk-nosed and swarthy. A trident beard gave him a sardonic look and the sabre scar from brow to chin completed the impression.

'I am Regnak, Earl of Dros Delnoch,' said Rek.

'I am Sathuli – Joachim Sathuli – and I shall kill you,' replied the man grimly.

'Matters like this should be settled by men such as you and I,' said Rek. 'Look about you – everywhere are Sathuli corpses. How many of my men are among them?'

'They will join them soon,' said Joachim.

'Why do we not settle this like princes?' said Rek. 'You and I alone.'

The man's scarred eyebrow lifted. 'That would only equal the odds against you. You have no bargaining power, wherefore should I grant you this?'

'Because it will save Sathuli lives. Oh, I know they give their lives gladly, but for what? We carry no provisions, no gold. We have only horses and the Delnoch ranges are full of them. This is now a matter of pride, not of booty. Such matters are for you and I to decide.'

'Like all Drenai, you talk a good fight,' said the Sathuli, turning away.

'Has fear turned your bowels to water?' asked Rek, softly.

The man turned back, smiling. 'Ah, now you seek to anger me. Very well! We will fight. When you die, your men will lay down their swords?'

'Yes.'

'And if I die, we allow you to pass?'

'Yes.'

'So be it. I swear this on the soul of Mehmet, Blessed be His Name.'

Joachim drew a slender scimitar and the Sathulis around Rek moved back to form a circle about the two men. Rek drew his blade from the earth and the battle began.

The Sathuli was an accomplished swordsman and Rek was forced back as soon as the fight started. Serbitar, Virae and the others watched calmly as blade met blade time and again. Parry, riposte, thrust and parry, slash and check. Rek defended frantically at first, then slowly began to counter. The battle wore on, with both men sweating freely. It was obvious to all that they were evenly matched in skill, and virtually identical in strength and reach. Rek's blade sliced the skin above Joachim's shoulder. The scimitar licked out to open a wound on the back of Rek's hand. Both men circled warily, breathing deeply.

Joachim attacked; Rek parried, launching a riposte. Joachim jumped back and they circled again. Arbedark, the finest swordsman of The Thirty, was lost in wonder at their technique.

Not that he could not match it, for he could; rather that his skill was honed by mental powers which the two combatants would never comprehend on a conscious level. Yet both were using the same skills subconsciously. It was as much a battle of minds as of blades, yet even here the men were well-matched.

Serbitar pulsed a question to Arbedark. 'It is too close for me to judge. Who will win?'

'I know not,' replied Arbedark. 'It is fascinating.'

Both men were tiring fast. Rek had established a two-handed grip on his longsword, his right arm no longer able to bear the full weight of the blade. He launched an attack which Joachim parried desperately; then his sword caught the scimitar an inch above the hilt – and the curved blade snapped. Rek stepped forward, touching the point of his sword to Joachim's jugular. The swarthy Sathuli did not move but merely gazed back defiantly, his brown eyes meeting Rek's gaze.

'And what is your life worth, Joachim Sathuli?'

'A broken sword,' answered Joachim. Rek held out his hand and received the useless hilt.

'What is the meaning of this?' asked the surprised Sathuli leader.

'It is simple,' answered Rek. 'All of us here are as dead men. We ride for Dros Delnoch to face an army the like of which has not been seen before in this world. We shall not survive the summer. You are a warrior, Joachim, and a worthy one. Your life is worth more than a broken blade. We proved nothing by this contest, save that we are men. Before me I have nothing but enemies and war.

'Since we will meet no more in this life, I would like to believe that I have left at least a few friends behind me. Will you take my hand?' Rek sheathed his sword and held out his hand.

The tall Sathuli smiled. 'There is a strangeness in this meeting,' he said, 'for as my blade broke I wondered, in that moment when death faced me, what would I have done had your sword snapped. Tell me, why do you ride to your death?'

'Because I must,' said Rek simply.

'So be it, then. You ask me for friendship and I give it, though I have sworn mighty oaths that no Drenai would feel safe on Sathuli land. I give you this friendship because you are a warrior, and because you are to die.'

'Tell me, Joachim, as one friend to another, what would you have done if *my* blade had broken?'

'I would have killed you,' said the Sathuli.

17

The first of the spring storms burst over the Delnoch mountains as Gilad relieved the watch sentry on Wall One. Thunder rumbled angrily overhead while crooked spears of jagged lightning tore the night sky, momentarily lighting the fortress. Fierce winds whistled along the walls, shrieking sibilantly.

Gilad hunched himself under the overhang of the gate tower, tugging the small brazier of hot coals into the lee of the wall. His cape was wet through, and water dripped steadily from his drenched hair on to his shoulders to trickle inside his breastplate, soaking the leather of his mailshirt. But the wall reflected the heat from the brazier and Gilad had spent worse nights on the Sentran Plain, digging out buried sheep in the winter blizzards. He regularly raised himself to peer over the wall to the north, waiting for a flash of lightning to illuminate the plain. Nothing moved there.

Further down the wall an iron brazier exploded as lightning struck it and showers of hot coals fell close to him. What a place to be wearing armour, he thought. He shuddered and hunched closer to the wall. Slowly the storm moved on, swept over the Sentran Plain by the fierce wind from the north. For a while the rain remained, sheeting against the grey stone battlements and running down the tower walls, hissing and spitting as random drops vaporised on the coals.

Gilad opened his small-pack and removed a strip of dried meat. He tore off a chunk and began to chew. Three more hours – then a warm bunk for three more.

From the darkness behind the battlements came the sound of movement. Gilad spun round, scrabbling for his sword, phantom childhood fears flooding his mind. A large figure loomed into the light from the brazier.

'Stay calm, laddie! It's only me,' said Druss, seating himself on the other side of the brazier. He held out his huge hands to the flames. 'Fire now, is it?'

His white beard was wet through, his black leather jerkin gleaming as if polished by the storm. The rain had petered to a fine drizzle, and the wind had ceased its eerie howling. Druss hummed an old battle hymn for a few moments as the heat warmed him. Gilad, tense and expectant, waited for the sarcastic comments to follow. 'Cold, are we? Need a little fire to keep away the phantoms, do we?' Why pick my watch, you old bastard? he thought. After a while the silence seemed oppressive and Gilad could bear it no longer.

'A cold night to be out walking, sir,' he said, cursing himself for the respectful tone.

'I have seen worse. And I like the cold. It's like pain – it tells you you're alive.'

The firelight cast deep shadows on the old warrior's weatherbeaten face and for the first time Gilad saw the fatigue etched there. The man is bone-tired, he thought. Beyond the legendary armour and the eyes of icy fire, he was just another old man. Tough and strong as a bull, maybe, but old. Worn out by time, the enemy that never tired.

'You may not believe it,' said Druss, 'but this is the worst time for a soldier – the waiting before the battle. I've seen it all before. You ever been in a battle, lad?'

'No, never.'

'It's never as bad as you fear it will be – once you realise that dying is nothing special.'

'Why do you say that? It's special to me. I have a wife and a farm which I'd like to see again. I've a lot of living to do yet,' said Gilad.

'Of course you have. But you could survive this battle and come down with the plague, or be killed by a lion, or develop a cancer. You could be robbed and killed or fall from a horse. Ultimately you will die anyway. Everyone dies. I'm not saying you should give up and just open your arms to welcome it. You must fight it all the way. An old soldier – a good friend of mine – told me early in my life that he who fears to lose will never win. And it's true. You know what a baresark is, boy?'

'A strong warrior,' said Gilad.

'Yes he is. But he's more than that: he's a killing machine who cannot be stopped. Do you know why?'

'Because he's insane?'

'Yes, there is that to him. But more. He doesn't defend, because when he's fighting he doesn't care. He just attacks, and lesser men – who do care – die.'

'What do you mean by lesser men? A man doesn't have to be a killer to be great.'

'That's not what I meant . . . But I suppose it could have been. If I tried to farm – as your neighbour – men would say that I was not as good as you. They would look down on me as a bad farmer. On these battlements men will be judged by how long they stay alive. Lesser men, or lesser soldiers if you will, either change or fall.'

'Why did you come here, Druss?' asked Gilad, meaning to ask why the axeman had chosen to interrupt his watch. But the warrior misunderstood.

'I came to die,' he said softly, warming his hands and staring into the coals. 'To find some spot on the battlements to make a stand, and then to die. I didn't expect to have to take over the damned defence. A pox on it! I'm a soldier, not a general.'

As Druss talked on, Gilad realised the axeman was not talking to him – not to Cul Gilad, the former farmer. He was chatting to just another soldier at just another fire at just another fortress. In microcosm this scene was Druss' life, the wait before the war.

'I always promised her that I would stop and tend the farm, but always someone, somewhere, had a battle to fight. I thought for years that I was representing something – liberty, freedom, I don't know. The truth was always much more simple. I love to fight. She knew, but had the good grace never to point it out. Can you imagine what it's like to be a Legend – THE damned Legend? Can you, boy?'

'No, but it must make you feel proud,' said Gilad, uncertain.

'It makes you tired. It saps your strength when it should raise it. Because you can't afford to be tired. You're Druss the Legend and you're invulnerable, invincible. You laugh at pain. You can march for ever. With one blow you can topple mountains. Do I look as if I can topple mountains?'

'Yes,' said Gilad.

'Well, I damned well can't. I'm an old man with a weak knee and an arthritic back. My eyes are not so good as they were either.

'When I was young and strong, the bruises always healed quickly. I was tireless then. I could fight all damned day. As I grew older I learned to fake it and snatch rest where I could. To use my experience in battle where before I had just powered my way through. In my fifties I was careful, and anyway by that time the Legend made men tremble. Three times since, I have fought men who could have beaten me, but they beat themselves because they knew who I was and were afraid.

'Do you think I'm a good leader?'

'I don't know. I'm a farmer, not a soldier,' said Gilad.

'Don't hedge with me, boy. I asked for an opinion.'

'No, you're probably not. But you *are* a great warrior. I suppose in years gone by you would have been a war chief. I can't tell. You've done wonders with the training; there's a new spirit at the Dros.'

'There were always leaders in my day,' said Druss. 'Strong men with quick minds. I have tried to remember all their lessons. But it's hard, boy. Do you see? It's hard. I've never been afraid of enemies I can face with an axe or my hands, if needs be. But the enemies at this fortress are not the same. Morale, preparation, fire gullies, supplies, liaison, organisation. It saps the soul.'

'We'll not fail you, Druss,' said Gilad, his heart reaching out to the older man. 'We will stand firm beside you. You have given us that, though I hated you for most of the training.'

'Hate breeds strength, laddie. Of course you will hold. You're men. Did you hear about Dun Mendar?'

'Yes, it was tragic. A good job that he was there to aid you,' said Gilad.

'He was there to kill me, boy. And he almost did.'

'What?' said Gilad, shocked.

'You heard me. And I don't expect you to repeat it. He was in the pay of the Nadir and he led the assassins.'

'But . . . that means you stood alone against them all,' said Gilad. 'Five of them and you survived?'

'Aye, but they were a motley crew, and ill-trained. Do you know why I told you that . . . about Mendar?'

'Because you wanted to talk?'

'No. I've never been much of a talker, and I have little need for sharing my fears. No, I wanted you to know that I trust you. I want you to take over Mendar's role. I'm promoting you to Dun.'

'I don't want it,' said Gilad fiercely.

'Do you think I want this responsibility? Why do you think I've spent this time here? I am trying to make you understand that often – more often than not – we are forced into doing what we fear. You will take over as of tomorrow.'

'Why? Why me?'

'Because I have watched you and I think you have a talent for leadership. You've impressed me in leading your ten. And you helped Orrin in that race. That was pride. Also I need you, and others like you.'

'I've no experience,' said Gilad, knowing it sounded lame.

'That will come. Think on this: your friend Bregan is no soldier and some of your men will die at the first attack. Having a good officer will save some of them.'

'All right. But I can't afford to dine in the officers' mess or run up an armourer's bill. You will have to supply me with the uniform.'

'Mendar's gear should fit you, and you will put it to more noble use.'

'Thank you. You said earlier on that you came here to die. Does that mean you think we cannot win?'

'No, it doesn't. Forget what I said.'

'Damn you, Druss, don't patronise me! You just talked about trust. Well, I'm an officer now and I asked you a straight question. I won't repeat the answer. So trust me.'

Druss smiled and his eyes met the fierce gaze of the young sentry.

'Very well. We have no chance in the long term. Every day brings us closer to a Nadir victory. But we will make them pay dearly. And you can believe that, laddie, for that's Druss the Legend talking.'

'Never mind the Legend,' said Gilad, returning the other's smile. 'That's the man who took on five assassins in a darkened alley.'

'Don't build me up too high because of that, Gilad. All men have talents. Some build, some paint, some write, some fight. For me it is different. I have always had a way with death.'

The girl moved along the battlements, ignoring the comments of the soldiers; her auburn hair glinting in the morning sun, her long legs, slender and bronzed, the objects of many of the friendly though intimate comments from the troops. She smiled once, when one of the men she passed murmured to a companion, 'I think I'm in love.' She blew him a kiss and winked.

Bowman smiled, gently shaking his head. He knew Caessa was making a meal of her entrance, but with a body like hers who would blame her? As tall as most men, willowy and graceful, her every movement combined to promise pleasure to any man watching. Physically, Bowman thought, she is the perfect woman. The ultimate female.

He watched her string her longbow. Jorak looked at him questioningly but he shook his head. The rest of the archers stood back. This was

Caessa's moment, and after an entrance like that she deserved a little applause.

Straw dummies had been set up one hundred paces from the wall. The heads were painted yellow, the torsos red. It was a standard distance for a fine archer, but shooting down from a battlement added several degrees to the difficulty.

Caessa reached over her shoulder to the doeskin quiver and drew a black feathered shaft. She checked it for line, then notched it to the string.

'Head,' she said.

With one flowing movement she drew back the string and as it touched her cheek, she loosed the shaft. It flashed through the morning air and hammered into the neck of the nearest dummy. The watching men burst into rapturous applause and Caessa glanced at Bowman. He raised an eyebrow.

Five more arrows lanced into the straw target before Bowman raised a hand to signal the other archers forward. Then he called Caessa to him and walked from the battlements.

'You took your time getting here, lady,' he said, smiling.

She linked her arm in his and blew him a kiss. As always he felt arousal stirring. As always he suppressed it.

'Did you miss me?' Her voice was deep and throaty, a sound as full of sexual promise as her body was a vision.

'I always miss you,' he said. 'You raise my spirits.'

'Only your spirits?'

'Only my spirits.'

'You lie. I can see it in your eyes,' she said.

'You see nothing that I do not want you to see – or anyone else. You are safe with me, Caessa. Have I not told you? But allow me to say that for a woman who does not seek the company of men, you make a very spectacular entrance. Where are your trousers?'

'It was hot. The tunic is decorous enough,' she said, absently tugging at the hem.

'I wonder if you really know what you want,' he said.

'I want to be left alone.'

'Then why do you seek my friendship?'

'You know what I mean.'

'Yes, *I* do,' he told her, 'but I'm not sure that you do.'

'You are very serious today, O Lord of the Forest. I can't think why. We are all being paid. We have our pardons and the quarters are a sight better than Skultik.'

'Where have they placed you?' he asked.

'The young officer . . . Pinar? . . . insisted that I have a room in the main barracks. He wouldn't hear of me sharing with the rest of the men. It was quite touching really. He even kissed my hand!'

'He's all right,' said Bowman. 'Let's have a drink.' He led her into the Eldibar mess hall and on through the officers' section at the rear, ordering a bottle of white wine. Seated by the window, he drank in silence for a while, watching the men train.

'Why did you agree to this?' she asked him, suddenly. 'And don't give me any of that rubbish about pardons. You don't give a damn about that, or about the money.'

'Still trying to read me? It can't be done,' he said, sipping his wine. Then he turned and called out for bread and cheese. She waited until the serving soldier had left.

'Come on, tell me!'

'Sometimes, my dear, as you will no doubt find when you are a little older, there are no simple reasons for a man's actions. Impulse. An act spurred by the moment. Who knows why I agreed to come here? I certainly do not!'

'You're lying again. You just won't say. Is it that old man, Druss?'

'Why are you so interested? In fact, why are you here?'

'Why not? It should be exciting and not terribly dangerous. We are leaving, aren't we, when the third wall goes?'

'Of course. That was the agreement,' he said.

'You don't trust me, do you?' she said, smiling.

'I don't trust anybody. You know, sometimes you do act just like every other woman I have known.'

'Is that a compliment, O Master of the Green Wood?'

'I think not.'

'Then what does it mean? After all, I am a woman. How do you expect me to act?'

'There you go again. Let's get back to trust. What made you ask?'

'You won't say why you came, and then you lie about leaving. Do you think I'm a complete fool? You have no intention of quitting this doomed pile of rock. You will stay to the end.'

'And where do you come by this remarkable intelligence?' he asked.

'It's written all over your face. But don't worry, I won't let on to Jorak or any of the others. But don't count on me to stay. I have no intention of dying here.'

'Caessa, my little dove, you only prove how little you know me. Anyway, for what it's worth . . .' Bowman ceased his explanation as the tall figure of Hogun entered the doorway and the Gan threaded his way through the tables towards them. It was Caessa's first sight of the Legion general and she was impressed. He moved with grace, one hand resting on his sword hilt. His eyes were clear, his jaw strong and his features fair – handsome almost. She disliked him instantly. Her view was strengthened when he pulled up a chair, reversed it and sat facing Bowman, ignoring her totally.

'Bowman, we must talk,' he said.

'Go ahead. First, let me introduce Caessa. Caessa, my dear, this is Gan Hogun of the Legion.' He turned and nodded once in her direction.

'Do you mind if we talk alone?' he asked Bowman. Caessa's green eyes blazed with anger but she kept silent and stood, desperate for a parting remark that would sting the man.

399

'I will see you later,' said Bowman, as she opened her mouth. 'Get yourself some food now.' As she turned on her heel and left the room, Bowman watched her, delighting in the feline grace of her walk.

'You've upset her,' he said.

'Me? I didn't even speak to her,' said Hogun, removing his black and silver helm and placing it on the table. 'Anyway, that's immaterial. I want you to speak to your men.'

'What about?'

'They spend a lot of their time loafing around and jeering at the soldiers as they train. It's not good for morale.'

'Why shouldn't they? They are civilian volunteers. It will all stop when the fighting starts.'

'The point is, Bowman, that the fighting may start before the Nadir arrive. I have just stopped one of my men from gutting that black-bearded giant, Jorak. Much more of this and we will have murder on our hands.'

'I'll talk to them,' said Bowman. 'Calm yourself and have a drink. What did you think of my lady archer?'

'I really didn't look too closely. She seemed pretty.'

'I think it must be true what they say about the cavalry,' said Bowman. 'You are all in love with your horses! Great gods, man, she's more than merely pretty!'

'Talk to your men now. I will feel a lot better then. Tensions are rising pretty badly and the Nadir are only two days away.'

'I said I would. Now, have a drink and relax. You're getting as edgy as your men and that can't be good for morale.'

Hogun grinned suddenly. 'You're right. It's always like this before a fight. Druss is like a bear with a sore head.'

'I hear you lost the Open Swords to the fat one,' said Bowman, grinning. 'Tut, tut, old horse! This is no time to be currying favour with the hierarchy.'

'I didn't let him win, he's a fine swordsman. Don't judge him too harshly, my friend; he may yet surprise you. He certainly surprised me. What did you mean when you said I upset the girl?'

Bowman smiled, then laughed loudly. He shook his head and poured another glass of wine.

'My dear Hogun, when a woman is beautiful she comes to expect a certain . . . how shall I say? . . . a certain reverence from men. You should have had the good grace to be thunderstruck by her beauty. Stunned into silence, or better still into a babbling fool. Then she would have merely ignored you and answered your devotion with arrogant disdain. Now you have slighted her and she will hate you. Worse than this, she will do all in her power to win your heart.'

'I don't think that makes a great deal of sense. Why should she try to win my heart if she hates me?'

'So that she can be in a position to treat you with disdain. Do you know nothing about women?'

'I know enough,' said Hogun. 'I also know that I don't have time for this foolishness. Should I apologise to her, do you think?'

'And let her know you know how slighted she was? My dear boy, your education has been sadly lacking!'

18

Druss welcomed the arrival of the Dros Purdol riders – not so much for their numbers, more for the fact that their arrival proved that the Dros had not been forgotten by the outside world.

Yet still, Druss knew, the defenders would be badly stretched. The first battle on Eldibar, Wall One, would either raise the men - or destroy them. The Delnoch fighting edge was sharp enough, but spirit was a different thing. You could fashion the finest steel into a sword blade of passing excellence, but occasionally the move from fire to water would cause it to crack where blades of lesser metal survived. An army was like that, Druss knew. He had seen highly trained men panic and run, and farmers stand their ground, armed with picks and hoes.

Bowman and his archers practised daily now on Kania, Wall Three, which had the longest stretch of ground between the mountains. They were superb. The 600 archers could send 3,000 arrows arcing through the air every ten heartbeats. The first charge would bring the Nadir into range for nearly two minutes before the siege ladders could reach the walls. The attacking warriors would suffer terrible losses over the open ground. It would be bloody carnage. But would it be enough?

They were about to see the greatest army ever assembled, a horde that within twenty years had built an empire stretching across a dozen lands and five-score cities. Ulric was on the verge of creating the largest empire in known history, a mighty achievement for a man not yet out of his forties.

Druss walked the Eldibar battlements, chatting to individual soldiers, joking with them, laughing with them. Their hatred of him had vanished like dawn mist during these last days. They saw him now for what he was: an iron old man, a warrior from the past, a living echo of ancient glories.

They remembered then that he had chosen to stand with them. And they knew why. This was the only place in all the world for the last of the old heroes: Druss the Legend, standing with the last hopes of the Drenai on the battlements of the greatest fortress ever built, waiting for the largest army in the world. Where else would he be?

Slowly the crowds gathered about him, as more men made their way to Eldibar. Before long Druss was threading his way through massed ranks on the battlements, while even more soldiers gathered on the open ground behind them. He climbed to the crenellated battlement wall and turned to face them. His voice boomed out, silencing the chatter.

'Look about you!' he called, the sun glinting from the silver shoulder guards on his black leather jerkin, his white beard glistening. 'Look about you now. The men you see are your comrades – your brothers. They will live with you and die for you. They will protect you and bleed for you. Never in your lives will you know such comradeship again. And if you live to be as old as I am, you will always remember this day and the days to follow. You will remember them with a clearness you would never have believed. Each day will be like crystal, shining in your minds.

'Yes, there will be blood and havoc, torture and pain, and you will remember that too. But above all will be the sweet taste of life. And there is nothing like it, my lads.

'You can believe this old man when he says it. You may think life is sweet now, but when death is a heartbeat away then life becomes unbearably desirable. And when you survive, everything you do will be enhanced and filled with greater joy: the sunlight, the breeze, a good wine, a woman's lips, a child's laughter.

'Life is nothing unless death has been faced down.

'In times to come, men will say "I wish I had been there with them." By then the cause won't matter.

'You are standing at a frozen moment in history. The world will be changed when this battle is over – either the Drenai will rise again, or a new empire will dawn.

'You are now men of history.' Druss was sweating now, and strangely tired, but he knew he had to go on. He was desperate to remember Sieben's saga of the elder days and the stirring words of an elder general. But he could not. He breathed in deeply, tasting the sweet mountain air.

'Some of you are probably thinking that you may panic and run. You won't! Others are worried about dying. Some of you will. But all men die. No one ever gets out of this life alive.

'I fought at Skeln Pass when everyone said we were finished. They said the odds were too great but I said be damned to them! For I am Druss and I have never been beaten, not by Nadir, Sathuli, Ventrian, Vagrian or Drenai.

'By all the gods and demons of this world, I will tell you now – I do not intend to be beaten here either!' Druss was bellowing at the top of his voice as he dragged Snaga into the air. The axe blade caught the sun and the chant began.

'DRUSS THE LEGEND! DRUSS THE LEGEND!' The men on other battlements could not hear Druss' words, but they heard the chant and took it up. Dros Delnoch echoed to the sound, a vast cacophony of noise that crashed and reverberated through the peaks, scattering flocks of birds which took to the skies in fluttering panic. At last Druss raised his arms for silence and gradually the chant subsided, though more men were running from Wall Two to hear his words. By now almost five thousand men were gathered about him.

'We are the Knights of Dros Delnoch, the siege city. We will build a new legend here to dwarf Skeln Pass. And we will bring death to the Nadir in their thousands. Aye, in their hundreds of thousands. WHO ARE WE?'

'KNIGHTS OF DROS DELNOCH!' thundered the men.

'And what do we bring?'

'DEATH TO THE NADIR!'

Druss was about to continue when he saw men's heads turn to face

403

down into the valley. Columns of dust in the distance created clouds which rose to challenge the sky, like a gathering storm. Like the father of all storms. And then, through the dust could be seen the glinting spears of the Nadir, filling the valley from all sides, sweeping forward, a vast dark blanket of fighting men, with more following. Wave after wave of them came into sight. Vast siege towers pulled by hundreds of horses; giant catapults, leather-covered battering rams; thousands of carts and hundreds of thousands of horses; vast herds of cattle and more men than the mind could total.

Not one heart among the watchers failed to miss a beat at the sight. Despair was tangible and Druss cursed softly. He had nothing more to say. And he felt he had lost them. He turned to face the Nadir horsemen bearing the horse-hair banners of their tribes. By now their faces could be seen, grim and terrible. Druss raised Snaga into the air and stood, legs spread, a picture of defiance. Angry now, he stared at the Nadir outriders.

As they saw him they pulled up their horses and stared back. Suddenly the riders parted to allow a herald through. Galloping his steppe pony forward he rode towards the gates, swerving as he came beneath the wall where Druss stood. He dragged on the reins and the horse skidded to a stop, rearing and snorting.

'I bring this command from the Lord Ulric,' he shouted. 'Let the gates be opened and he will spare all within, save the white-bearded one who insulted him.'

'Oh, it's you again, lard-belly,' said Druss. 'Did you give him my message as I said it?'

'I gave it, Deathwalker. As you said it.'

'And he laughed, did he not?'

'He laughed. And swore to have your head. And my Lord Ulric is a man who always fulfils his desires.'

'Then we are two of a kind. And it is my desire that he should dance a jig on the end of a chain, like a performing bear. And I will have it so, even if I have to walk into your camp and chain him myself.'

'Your words are like ice on the fire, old man – noisy and without worth,' said the herald. 'We know your strength. You have maybe 11,000 men. Mostly farmers. We know all there is to know. Look at the Nadir army! How can you hold? What is the point? Surrender yourself. Throw yourself on the mercy of my Lord.'

'Laddie, I have seen the size of your army and it does not impress me. I have a mind to send half my men back to their farms. What are you? A bunch of pot-bellied, bow-legged northerners. I hear what you say. But don't tell me what you can do. Show me! And that's enough of talk. From now on *this* will talk for me.' He shook Snaga before him, sunlight flashing from the blade.

Along the line of defenders Gilad nudged Bregan. 'Druss the Legend!' he chanted and Bregan joined him with a dozen others. Once more the sound began to swell as the herald wheeled his mount and raced away. The noise thundered after him:

'DRUSS THE LEGEND! DRUSS THE LEGEND!'

Druss watched silently as the massive siege engines inched towards the wall, vast wooden towers sixty feet high and twenty feet wide; ballistae by the hundred, ungainly catapults on huge wooden wheels. Countless numbers of men heaved and strained at thousands of ropes, dragging into place the machines that had conquered Gulgothir.

The old warrior studied the scene below, seeking out the legendary warmaster Khitan. It did not take long to find him. He was the still centre of the whirlpool of activity below, the calm amid the storm. Where he moved, work ceased as his instructions were given, then began again with renewed intensity.

Khitan glanced up at the towering battlements. He could not see Death-walker, but felt his presence and grinned.

'You cannot stop my work with one axe,' he whispered.

Idly he scratched the scarred stump at the end of his arm. Strange how, after all these years, he could still feel his fingers. The gods had been kind that day when the Gulgothir tax-gatherers sacked his village. He had been barely twelve years old and they had slain his family. In an effort to protect his mother, he had run forward with his father's dagger. A slashing sword sent his hand flying through the air to land beside the body of his brother. The same sword had lanced into his chest.

To this day he could not explain why he had not died along with the other villagers, nor indeed why Ulric had spent so long trying to save him. Ulric's raiders had surprised the killers and routed them, taking two prisoners. Then a warrior checking the bodies had found Khitan, barely alive. They had taken him into the steppes, laying him in Ulric's tent. There they had sealed the weeping stump with boiling tar and dressed the wound in his side with tree moss. For almost a month he remained semi-conscious, delirious with fever. He had one memory of that terrible time: a memory he would carry to the day he died.

His eyes had opened to see above him a face, strong and compelling. The eyes were violet and he felt their power.

'You will not die, little one. Hear me?' The voice was gentle, but as he sank once more into the nightmares and delirium he knew that the words were not a promise. They were a command.

And Ulric's commands were to be obeyed.

Since that day Khitan had spent every conscious moment serving the Nadir lord. Useless in combat, he had learned to use his mind, creating the means by which his lord could build an empire.

Twenty years of warfare and plunder. Twenty years of savage joy.

With his small entourage of assistants, Khitan threaded his way through the milling warriors and entered the first of the twenty siege towers. They were his special pride. In concept they had been startlingly simple. Create a wooden box, three-sided and twelve feet high. Place wooden steps inside against the walls leading to the roof. Now take a second box and place it atop the first. Secure it with iron pins. Add a third and you have a tower. It was relatively easy to assemble and dismantle and the component parts could be stacked on wagons and carried wherever the general needed them.

But if the concept was simple, the practicalities had been plagued by complexities. Ceilings collapsed under the weight of armed men, walls gave way, wheels splintered and worst of all, once over thirty feet high the structure was unstable and prone to tip.

Khitan recalled how for more than a year he had worked harder than his slaves, sleeping less than three hours a night. He had strengthened the ceilings, but this had merely made the entire structure more heavy and less stable. In despair he had reported to Ulric. The Nadir warlord had sent him to Ventria, to study at the University of Tertullus. He felt that he had been disgraced, humiliated. Nevertheless he obeyed; he would suffer anything to please Ulric.

But he had been wrong and the year he had spent studying under Rebow, the Ventrian lecturer, proved to be the most glorious time of his life.

He learned of mass centres, parallel vectors and the need for equilibrium between external and internal forces. His appetite for knowledge was voracious and Rebow found himself warming to the ugly Nadir tribesman. Before long the slender Ventrian invited Khitan to share his home, where studies could be carried on long into the night. The Nadir was tireless. Often Rebow would fall asleep in his chair, only to wake several hours later and find the small, one-armed Khitan still studying the exercises he had set him. Rebow was delighted. Rarely had a student showed such aptitude, and never had he found a man with such a capacity for work.

Every force, learnt Khitan, has an equal and opposite reaction, so that, for example, a jib exerting a push at its top end must also exert an equal and opposite push at the foot of its supporting post. This was his introduction to the world of creating stability through understanding the nature of stress.

For him the University of Tertullus was a kind of paradise.

On the day he had left for home the little tribesman wept as he embraced the stricken Ventrian. Rebow had begged him to reconsider; to take a post at the university, but Khitan had not the heart to tell him he was not in the least tempted. He owed his life to one man, and dreamed of nothing but serving him.

At home once more, he set to work. Under construction the towers would be tiered, creating an artificial base five times the size of the structure. While being moved into position, only the first two levels would be manned, creating a mass weight low to the ground. Once positioned by a wall, ropes would be hurled from the centre of the tower and iron pins hammered into the ground, creating stability. The wheels would be iron-spoked and rimmed, and there would be eight to a tower, to distribute the weight.

Using his new knowledge, he designed catapults and ballistae. Ulric was well pleased and Khitan ecstatic.

Now, bringing his mind back to the present, Khitan climbed to the top of the tower, ordering the men to lower the hinged platform at the front. He gazed at the walls three hundred paces distant and saw the black-garbed Deathwalker leaning on the battlements.

The walls were higher than at Gulgothir and Khitan had added a section to each tower. Ordering the platform to be raised once more, he tested the tension in the support ropes and climbed down through the five levels, stopping here and there to check struts or ties.

Tonight his four hundred slaves would go to work beneath the walls, chipping away at the rocky floor of the Pass and placing the giant pulleys every forty paces. The pulleys, six feet high and cast around greased bearings, had taken months to design and years to construct to his satisfaction, finally being completed at the ironworks of Lentria's capital a thousand miles to the south. They had cost a fortune and even Ulric had blanched when the final figure was estimated. But they had proved their worth over the years.

Thousands of men would pull a tower to within sixty feet of a wall. Thereafter the line would shrink as the gap closed; the three-inch diameter ropes could be curled round the pulleys, passed under the towers and hauled from behind.

The slaves who dug and toiled to create the pulley beds were protected from archers by movable screens of stretched oxhide. But many were slain by rocks hurled from the walls above. This was of no concern to Khitan. What did concern him was possible damage to the pulleys, and these were not protected by iron casing.

With one last lingering look at the walls, he made his way back to his quarters in order to brief the engineers. Druss watched him until he entered the city of tents which now filled the valley for over two miles.

So many tents. So many warriors. Druss ordered the defenders to stand down and relax while they could, seeing in their faces the pinched edge of fear, the wide eyes of barely controlled panic. The sheer scale of the enemy had cut into morale. He cursed softly, stripped off his black leather jerkin, stepped back from the battlements and lowered his huge frame to the welcoming grass beyond. Within moments he was asleep. Men nudged one another and pointed; those closest to him chuckled as the snoring began. They were not to know that it was his first sleep for two days, nor that he lay there for fear that his legs would not carry him back to his quarters. They knew only he was Druss: the Captain of the Axe.

And that he held the Nadir in contempt.

Bowman, Hogun, Orrin and Caessa also left the walls for the shade of the mess hall, the green-clad archer pointing at the sleeping giant.

'Was there ever such a one?' he said.

'He just looks old and tired to me,' said Caessa. 'I can't see why you regard him with such reverence.'

'Oh yes, you can,' said Bowman. 'You are just being provocative as usual, my dear. But then that's the nature of your gender.'

'Not so,' said Caessa, smiling. 'What is he after all? He is a warrior. Nothing more, nothing less. What has he ever done to make him such a hero? Waved his axe? Killed men? I have killed men. It is no great thing. No one has written a saga about me.'

'They will, my lovely, they will,' said Bowman. 'Just give them time.'

'Druss is more than just a warrior,' said Hogun, softly. 'I think he always has been. He is a standard, an example if you like . . .'

'Of how to kill people?' offered Caessa.

'No, that's not what I meant. Druss is every man who has refused to quit; to surrender when life offered no hope; to stand aside when the alternative was to die. He is a man who has shown other men there is no such thing as guaranteed defeat. He lifts the spirit merely by being Druss, and being seen to be Druss.'

'Just words!' said Caessa. 'You men are all the same. Always lofty words. Would you sing the praises of a farmer who fought for years against failed crops and floods?'

'No,' admitted Hogun. 'But then it is the life of a man like Druss which inspires the farmers to battle on.'

'Garbage!' sneered Caessa. 'Arrogant garbage! The farmer cares nothing for warriors or war.'

'You will never win, Hogun,' said Bowman, holding open the mess hall door. 'Give up now, while you can.'

'There is a fundamental error in your thinking, Caessa,' said Orrin suddenly, as the group seated themselves around a trestle table. 'You are ignoring the simple fact that the vast majority of our troops here *are* farmers. They have signed on for the duration of this war.' He smiled gently and waved his hand for the mess servant.

'Then the more fool them,' said Caessa.

'We are all fools,' agreed Orrin. 'War is a ridiculous folly, and you are right: men love to prove themselves in combat. I don't know why, for I have never desired it myself. But I have seen it too often in others. But even for me Druss is, as Hogun describes him, an example.'

'Why?' she asked.

'I cannot put it into words, I'm afraid.'

'Of course you can.'

Orrin smiled and shook his head. He filled their goblets with white wine, then broke the bread and passed it round. For a while they ate in silence, then Orrin spoke again.

'There is a green leaf called Neptis. When chewed it will relieve toothache, or head pain. No one knows why, it just does. I suppose Druss is like that. When he is around, fear seems to fade. That's the best I can do to explain.'

'He doesn't have that effect on me,' said Caessa.

On the tower battlements, Bregan and Gilad watched the Nadir preparations. Along the wall Dun Pinar supervised the setting of notched poles to repel siege ladders, while Bar Britan oversaw the plugging of scores of pottery jugs containing oil. Once filled and plugged, the jugs were placed in wicker baskets at various points along the walls. The mood was grim. Few words were exchanged as men checked their weapons, sharpened already sharp swords, oiled armour or checked each shaft in their quivers.

Hogun and Bowman left the mess hall together, leaving Orrin and Caessa deep in conversation. They sat on the grass some twenty paces from the axeman, Bowman lying on his side and resting on his elbow.

'I once read some fragments from the Book of Elders,' said the archer. 'One line in particular strikes me now. "Come the moment, come the man." Never did a moment call for a man more desperately than this. And Druss has arrived. Providence, do you think?'

'Great gods, Bowman! You're not turning superstitious, are you?' asked Hogun, grinning.

'I should say not. I merely wonder whether there is such a thing as fate that such a man should be supplied at such a time.'

Hogun plucked a stem of couch grass and placed it between his teeth. 'All right, let us examine the argument. Can we hold for three months until Woundweaver gathers and trains his army?'

'No. Not with these few.'

'Then it matters not whether Druss' arrival was coincidence or otherwise. We may hold for a few more days because of his training, but that is not enough.'

'Morale is high, old horse, so best not repeat those sentiments.'

'Do you think me a fool? I will stand and die with Druss when the time comes, as will the other men. I share my thoughts with you because you will understand them. You are a realist – and moreover, you remain only until the third wall falls. With you I can be frank, surely?'

'Druss held Skeln Pass when all others said it would fall,' said Bowman.

'For eleven days – not three months. And he was fifteen years younger then. I don't belittle what he did; he is worthy of his legends. Knights of Dros Delnoch! Have you ever seen such knights? Farmers, peasants and raw recruits. Only the Legion have seen real action, and they are trained for hit-and-run charges from horseback. We could fold on the first attack.'

'But we won't, will we!' said Bowman, laughing. 'We are Druss' knights and the ingredients of a new legend.' His laughter sang out, rich and full of good humour. 'Knights of Dros Delnoch! You and me, Hogun. They will sing about us in days to come. Good old Bowman, he came to the aid of an ailing fortress for love of liberty, freedom and chivalry . . .'

'. . . and gold. Don't forget the gold,' said Hogun.

'A minor point, old horse. Let us not ruin the spirit of the thing.'

'Of course not, I do apologise. However, surely you have to die heroically before you can be immortalised in song and saga?'

'A moot point,' admitted Bowman. 'But I'm sure I will find a way round it.'

Above them on Musif, Wall Two, several young Culs were ordered to help fetch buckets for the tower well. Grumbling, they left the battlements to join the line of soldiers waiting by the stores.

Each armed with four wooden buckets, the men filed from the building towards the shallow cave beyond where the Musif well nestled in the cold shadows. Attaching the buckets to a complicated system of pulleys, they lowered them slowly towards the dark water below.

'How long is it since this has been used?' asked one soldier as the first bucket reappeared, covered in cobwebs.

'Probably about ten years,' answered the officer, Dun Garta. 'The people who had homes here used the centre well. A child died in here once and the well was polluted for over three months. That and the rats kept most people away.'

'Did they ever get the body out?' asked the Cul.

'Not as I heard. But don't worry, lad. It's only bones by now and won't affect the taste. Go on, try some.'

'Funnily enough I don't feel very thirsty.'

Garta laughed and dipped his hands into the bucket, lifting the water to his mouth.

'Spiced with rat droppings and garnished with dead spiders!' he said. 'Are you sure you won't have some?'

The men grinned, but none stepped forward.

'All right, the fun's over,' said Garta. 'The pulleys are working, the buckets are ready and I should say the job's done. So let's lock the gate and get back to work.'

Garta awoke in the night, pain ripping at him like an angry rat trapped in his belly. As he rolled from the bed and struggled to rise, his groaning woke the other three men sharing the room. One of them rushed to his side.

'What is it, Garta?' he said, turning the writhing man on to his back. Garta drew up his knees, his face purple. His hand snaked out, grabbing the other's shirt.

'The . . . water! Water!' He started to choke.

'He wants water!' yelled the man supporting him.

Garta shook his head. Suddenly his back arched as pain seared him.

'Great gods! He's dead,' said his companion as Garta slumped in his arms.

19

Rek, Serbitar, Virae and Vintar sat around a small camp-fire an hour before dawn. The camp had been made late the night before in a secluded hollow on the south side of a wooded hill.

'Time is short,' said Vintar. 'The horses are exhausted and it is at least a five-hour ride to the fortress. We might get there before the water is issued and we might not. Indeed, it may already be too late. But we do have one other choice.'

'Well, what is it?' said Rek.

'It must be your decision, Rek. None other can make it.'

'Just tell me, Abbot. I am too tired to think.'

Vintar exchanged glances with the albino.

'We can – The Thirty can – join forces and seek to pierce the barrier around the fortress.'

'Then try it,' said Rek. 'Where is the problem?'

'It will take all our powers and may not succeed. If it does not, we will not have the strength to ride on. Indeed, even if we do succeed we will need to rest for most of the day.'

'Do you think you can pierce the barrier?' said Virae.

'I do not know. We can only try.'

'Think what happened when Serbitar tried,' said Rek.

'You could all be hurled into the . . . whatever. What then?'

'We die,' answered Serbitar, softly.

'And you say it is *my* choice?'

'Yes,' answered Vintar, 'for the rule of The Thirty is a simple one. We have pledged our service to the master of Delnoch; you are that master.'

Rek was silent for several minutes, his weary brain numbed by the weight of the decision. He found himself thinking of so many other worries in his life which at the time had seemed momentous. There had never been a choice like this. His mind clouded with fatigue and he could not concentrate.

'Do it!' he said. 'Break the barrier.' Pushing himself to his feet he walked away from the fire, ashamed that such an order should be forced from him at a time when he could not think clearly.

Virae joined him, her arm circling his waist.

'I'm sorry,' she said.

'For what?'

'For what I said when you told me about the letter.'

'It doesn't matter. Why should you think well of me?'

'Because you are a man and you act like one,' she said. 'Now it's your turn.'

'My turn?'

'To apologise, you dolt! You struck me.'

He pulled her to him, lifting her from her feet, and kissed her.

'That wasn't an apology,' she said. 'And you scratched my face with your stubble.'

'If I apologise, will you let me do it again?'

'Strike me, you mean?'

'No, kiss you!'

Back at the hollow The Thirty formed a circle around the fire, removing their swords and plunging them into the ground at their feet.

The communion began, their minds flowing, streaming into Vintar. He welcomed each by name in the halls of his subconscious.

And merged. The combined power rocked him and he struggled to retain the memory of himself. He soared like a ghostly giant, a new being of incredible power. The tiny thing that was Vintar clung on inside the new colossus, forcing down the combined essence of twenty-nine personalities.

Now there was only one.

It called itself Temple and was born under the Delnoch stars.

Temple reared high under the clouds, stretching ethereal arms across the Delnoch crags.

He soared exultant, new eyes drinking in the sights of the universe. Laughter welled within him. Vintar reeled at the centre, driving himself deeper into the core.

At last Temple became aware of the Abbot, more as a tiny thought niggling at the edge of his new reality.

'Dros Delnoch. West.'

Temple flew west, high over the crags. Beneath him the fortress lay silent, grey and ghostly in the moonlight. He sank towards it and sensed the barrier.

Barrier?

To him?

He struck at it – and was hurled into the night, angry and hurt. His eyes blazed and he knew fury: the barrier had touched him with pain.

Again and again Temple launched himself towards the Dros, striking blows of fearful power. The barrier trembled and changed.

Temple drew back, confused, watching.

The barrier drew in on itself like swirling mist, reforming. Then it darkened into a thick plume, blacker than the night. Arms emerged, legs formed and a horned head grew with seven slanted red eyes.

Temple had learned much during his few minutes of life.

Joy, freedom, and knowledge of life had come first. Then pain and fury.

Now he knew fear and gained the knowledge of evil.

His enemy flew at him, curving black talons slashing the sky. Temple met him head on, curling his arms around its back. Sharp teeth tore at his face, talons ripping his shoulders. His own huge fists locked together at the creature's spine, drawing it in upon itself.

Below on Musif, Wall Two, three thousand men took up their positions. Despite all arguments, Druss had refused to surrender Wall One without a fight and waited there with six thousand men. Orrin had raged at him that such action was stupidity; the width of the wall made for an impossible task. Druss was obstinate, even when Hogun backed Orrin.

'Trust me,' Druss urged them. But he lacked the words to convince them. He tried to explain that the men needed a small victory on the first day in order to hone that final edge to their morale.

'But the risk, Druss!' said Orrin. 'We could *lose* on the first day. Can't you see that?'

'You are the Gan,' snarled Druss then. 'You can overrule me if you wish.'

'But I will not, Druss. I will stand beside you on Eldibar.'

'And I,' said Hogun.

'You will see that I am right,' said Druss. 'I promise you.'

Both men nodded, smiling to mask their despair.

Now the duty Culs were queuing by the wells, gathering the water buckets and making their way along the battlements, stepping over the legs and bodies of men still sleeping.

On Wall One Druss dipped a copper dish into a bucket and drank deeply. He wasn't sure that the Nadir would attack today. His instincts told him Ulric would allow another full day of murderous tension, the sight of his army preparing for battle draining the defenders of courage and sapping them of hope. Even so Druss had little choice. The move was Ulric's: the Drenai would have to wait.

Above them Temple suffered the fury of the beast, his shoulders and back shredded, his strength fading. The horned creature was also weakening. Death faced them both.

Temple did not want to die – not after such a short bitter-sweet taste of life. He wanted to see at close hand all those things he had glimpsed from afar, the coloured lights of expanding stars, the silence at the centre of distant suns.

His grip tightened. There would be no joy in the lights, no thrill amid the silence if this thing was left alive behind him. Suddenly the creature screamed – a high terrible sound, eerie and chilling. Its back snapped and it faded like mist.

Semi-conscious within Temple's soul, Vintar cried out.

Temple looked down, watching the men, tiny frail creatures, preparing to break their fast with dark bread and water. Vintar cried out again and Temple's brow furrowed.

He pointed his finger at the wall.

Men began to scream, hurling water cups and buckets from the Musif battlements. In each vessel black worms wriggled and swam. Now more men surged to their feet, milling and shouting.

'What the devil's happening up there?' said Druss, as the noise flowed down to him. He glanced down at the Nadir and saw that men were streaming back from the siege engines towards the tent city. 'I don't know what's going on,' said Druss. 'But even the Nadir are leaving. I'm going back to Musif.'

In the city of tents Ulric was no less angry as he shouldered his way

413

through to the wide tent of Nosta Khan. His mind was icy calm as he confronted the sentry outside.

The news was spreading through the army like a steppe gorse-fire: as dawn broke, the tents of Nosta Khan's sixty acolytes had been filled with soul-searing screams. Guards had rushed in to find men writhing broken-backed on the dirt-floors, their bodies bent like overstrung bows.

Ulric knew that Nosta Khan had marshalled his followers, drawing on their combined power to thwart the white templars, but he had never truly understood the appalling dangers.

'Well?' he asked the sentry.

'Nosta Khan is alive,' the man told him.

Ulric lifted the flap and stepped into the stench of Nosta Khan's home. The old man lay on a narrow pallet bed, his face grey with exhaustion, his skin bathed in sweat. Ulric pulled up a stool and sat beside him.

'My acolytes?' whispered Nosta Khan.

'All dead.'

'They were too strong, Ulric,' said the old man. 'I have failed you.'

'Men have failed me before,' said Ulric. 'It matters not.'

'It matters to me!' shouted the shaman, wincing as the effort stretched his back.

'Pride,' said Ulric. 'You have lost nothing, you have merely been beaten by a stronger enemy. It will avail them little, for my army will still take the Dros. They cannot hold. Rest yourself – and take no risks, shaman. I order it!'

'I will obey.'

'I know that. I do not wish you to die. Will they come for you?'

'No. The white templars are filled with notions of honour. If I rest, they will leave me be.'

'Then rest. And when you are strong, we will make them pay for your hurt.'

Nosta Khan grinned. 'Aye.'

Far to the south Temple soared towards the stars. Vintar could not stop him and fought to stay calm as Temple's panic washed over him, seeking to dislodge him. With the death of the enemy, Vintar had tried to summon The Thirty from within the new mind of the colossus. In that moment Temple looked inside himself and discovered Vintar.

Vintar had tried to explain his presence and the need for Temple to relinquish his individuality. Temple absorbed the truth and fled from it like a comet, seeking the heavens.

The Abbot again tried to summon Serbitar, seeking the niche in which he had placed him in the halls of his subconscious. The spark of life that was the albino blossomed under the Abbot's probing and Temple shuddered, feeling as if part of himself had been cut free. He slowed in his flight.

'Why are you doing this to me?' he asked Vintar.

'Because I must.'

'I will die!'

'No. You will live in all of us.'

414

'Why must you kill me?'

'I am truly sorry,' said Vintar gently. With Serbitar's aid he sought Arbedark and Menahem. Temple shrank and Vintar closed his heart with grief to the overwhelming despair. The four warriors summoned the other members of The Thirty, and with heavy hearts returned to the hollows.

Rek hurried across to Vintar as the Abbot opened his eyes and moved.

'Were you in time?' he asked.

'Yes,' muttered Vintar, wearily. 'Let me rest now.'

It was an hour short of dusk when Rek, Virae and The Thirty rode under the great portcullis gate set beneath the Delnoch Keep. Their horses were weary, lather-covered and wet-flanked. Men rushed to greet Virae, soldiers doffing helms and citizens asking for news from Drenan. Rek stayed in the background until they were inside the Keep. A young officer escorted The Thirty to the barracks while Rek and Virae made their way to the topmost rooms. Rek was exhausted.

Stripping off his clothes, he bathed himself with cold water and then shaved, removing the four-day stubble and cursing as the keen razor – a gift from Horeb – nicked his skin. He shook most of the dust from his garments and dressed once more. Virae had gone to her own rooms and he had no idea where these were. Strapping on his sword belt, he made his way back to the main hall, stopping twice to ask servants the way. Once there he sat alone, gazing at the marble statues of ancient heroes. He felt lost: insignificant and overpowered.

As soon as they had arrived, they heard the news that the Nadir horde was before the walls. There was a tangible air of panic among the townsfolk and they had seen refugees leaving by the score with carts piled high – a long, sorrowful convoy heading south.

Rek was unsure whether tiredness or hunger was predominant in him at that moment. He heaved himself to his feet, swayed slightly, then cursed loudly. Near the door was a full-length oval mirror. As he stood before it, the man who stared back at him appeared tall, broad-shouldered and powerful. His grey-blue eyes were purposeful, his chin strong, his body lean. The blue cape, though travel-worn, still hung well and the thigh-length doeskin boots gave him the look of a cavalry officer.

As Rek gazed at the Earl of Dros Delnoch, he saw himself as others would see him. They were not to know of his inner doubts and would see only the image he had created.

So be it.

He left the hall and stopped the first soldier he met to ask him where Druss was to be found. Wall One, the soldier said, and he described the location of the postern gates. The tall young Earl set out for Eldibar as the sun sank; going through the town, he stopped to buy a small loaf of honey cake which he ate as he walked. It was growing darker as he reached the postern gate of Wall Two, but a sentry showed him the way through and at last he entered the killing ground behind Wall One. Clouds obscured the moon and he almost fell into the fire-pit that stretched across the pass. A young soldier hailed him and showed him the first wooden bridge across it.

'One of Bowman's archers, are you?' asked the soldier, not recognising the tall stranger.

'No. Where is Druss?'

'I have no idea. He could be on the battlements, or you might try the mess hall. Messenger, are you?'

'No. Which is the mess hall?'

'See the lights over there? That's the hospital. Past there is the store room; keep walking until you hit the smell of the latrines, then turn right. You can't miss it.'

'Thank you.'

'It's no trouble. Recruit, are you?'

'Yes,' said Rek. 'Something like that.'

'Well, I'd better come with you.'

'There is no need.'

'Yes, there is,' said the man and Rek felt something sharp in the small of his back. 'This is a Ventrian dagger, and I suggest you just walk along with me for a short way.'

'What's the point of all this?'

'First, someone tried to kill Druss the other day – and second, I don't know you,' said the man. 'So walk on and we will find him together.'

The two men moved on towards the mess hall. Now that they were closer, they could hear the sounds from the buildings ahead. A sentry hailed them from the battlements; the soldier answered, then asked for Druss.

'He's on the wall near the gate tower,' came the answer.

'This way,' said the soldier, and Rek climbed the short steps to the battlement walls. Then he stopped dead. On the plain thousands of torches and small fires illuminated the Nadir army. Siege towers straddled the pass like wooden giants from mountain wall to mountain wall. The whole valley was lit as far as the eye could see – it was like a view of the second level of hell itself.

'Not a pretty sight, is it?' said the soldier.

'I don't think it will look any better by daylight,' said Rek.

'You are not wrong,' agreed the other. 'Let's move.'

Ahead of them Druss was seated on the battlements talking to a small group of soldiers. He was telling a wonderfully embroidered tall story which Rek had heard before. The punch line evoked the desired effect and the night silence was broken by the sound of laughter.

Druss laughed heartily with the men, then noticed the newcomers. He turned and studied the tall man in the blue cape.

'Well?' he asked the soldier.

'He was looking for you, captain, so I brought him along.'

'To be more precise,' said Rek, 'he thought I might be an assassin. Hence the dagger behind me.'

Druss raised an eyebrow. 'Well, are you an assassin?'

'Not recently. Can we talk?'

416

'We appear to be doing just that.'

'Privately.'

'You start talking and I will decide how private it is to be,' said Druss.

'My name is Regnak. I have just arrived with warriors from the Temple of The Thirty and Virae, the daughter of Delnar.'

'We will talk privately,' decided Druss. The men wandered away out of earshot.

'So speak,' said Druss, his cold grey eyes fixed on Rek's face.

Rek seated himself on the battlement wall and stared out over the glowing valley.

'A little on the large side, isn't it?'

'Scare you, does it?'

'To the soles of my boots. However, you're obviously in no mood to make this an easy meeting, so I will simply spell out my position. For better or worse, I am the Earl. I'm not a fool, nor yet a general – though often the two are synonymous. As yet I will make no changes. But bear this in mind . . . I will take a back seat to no man when decisions are needed.'

'You think that bedding an Earl's daughter gives you that right?' asked Druss.

'You know it does! But that's not the point. I have fought before and my understanding of strategy is as sound as any here. Added to that I have The Thirty, and their knowledge is second to none. But even more important: if I have to die at this forsaken place it will not be as a bystander. I shall control my own fate.'

'You seek to take a lot on yourself, laddie.'

'No more than I can handle.'

'Do you really believe that?'

'No,' said Rek frankly.

'I didn't think you did,' said Druss with a grin. 'What the hell made you come here?'

'I think fate has a sense of humour.'

'She always had in my day. But you look like a sensible young fellow. You should have taken the girl to Lentria and set up home there.'

'Druss, nobody takes Virae anywhere she does not want to go. She has been reared on war and talk of war; she can cite all your legends and the facts behind every campaign you ever fought. She's an Amazon – and this is where she wants to be.'

'How did you meet?'

Rek told him about the ride from Drenan, through Skultik, the death of Reinard, the Temple of The Thirty, the shipboard wedding and the battle with the Sathuli. The old man listened to the straightforward story without comment.

'. . . and here we are,' concluded Rek.

'So you're baresark,' said Druss.

'I didn't say that!' retorted Rek.

'But you did, laddie – by not saying it. It doesn't matter. I have fought

417

beside many such. I am only surprised the Sathuli let you go; they're not known for being an honourable race.'

'I think their leader – Joachim – is an exception. Listen, Druss, I would be obliged if you could keep quiet about the baresark side.'

Druss laughed. 'Don't be a fool boy! How long do you think it will stay a secret once the Nadir are on the walls? You stick by me and I will see that you don't swat anyone from our side.'

'That's good of you – but I think you could be a little more hospitable. I'm as dry as a vulture's armpit.'

'There is no doubt,' said Druss, 'that talking works up more of a thirst than fighting. Come on, we will find Hogun and Orrin. This is the last night before the battle, so it calls for a party.'

20

As the dawn sky lightened on the morning of the third day, the first realities of apocalypse hammered home on the walls of Dros Delnoch. Hundreds of ballistae arms were pulled back by thousands of sweating warriors. Muscles bunching and knotting, the Nadir drew back the giant arms until the wicker baskets at their heads were almost horizontal. Each basket was loaded with a block of jagged granite.

The defenders watched in frozen horror as a Nadir captain raised his arm. The arm swept down and the air became filled with a deadly rain that crashed and thundered amidst and around the defenders. The battlements shook as the boulders fell. By the gate tower, three men were smashed to oblivion as a section of crenellated battlement exploded under the impact of one huge rock. Along the wall men cowered, hurling themselves flat, hands over their heads. The noise was frightening, the silence that followed was terrifying. For as the first thunderous assault ceased and soldiers raised their heads to gaze below, it was only to see the same process being casually repeated. Back, and further back went the massive wooden arms. Up went the captain's hand. Down it went.

And the rain of death bore down.

Rek, Druss and Serbitar stood above the gate tower, enduring the first horror of war along with the men. Rek had refused to allow the old warrior to stand alone, though Orrin had warned that for both leaders to stand together was lunacy. Druss had laughed. 'You and the lady Virae shall watch from the second wall, my friend. And you will see that no Nadir pebble can lay me low.'

Virae, furious, had insisted that she be allowed to wait on the first wall with the others, but Rek had summarily refused. An argument was swiftly ended by Druss: 'Obey your husband, woman!' he thundered. Rek had winced at that, closing his eyes against the expected outburst. Strangely Virae had merely nodded and retired to Musif, Wall Two, to stand beside Hogun and Orrin.

Now Rek crouched by Druss and gazed left and right along the wall. Swords and spears in hand, the men of Dros Delnoch waited grimly for the deadly storm to cease.

During the second reloading Druss ordered half the men back to stand beneath the second wall, out of range of the catapults. There they joined Bowman's archers.

For three hours the assault continued, pulverising sections of the wall, butchering men and obliterating one overhanging tower, which collapsed under the titanic impact and crumbled slowly into the valley below. Most of the men leapt to safety and only four were carried screaming over the edge to be broken on the rocks below.

Stretcher-bearers braved the barrage to carry wounded men back to the

Eldibar field hospital. Several rocks had hit the building, but it was solidly built and so far none had broken through. Bar Britan, black-bearded and powerful, raced alongside the bearers with sword in hand, urging them on.

'Gods, that's bravery!' said Rek, nudging Druss and pointing. Druss nodded, noting Rek's obvious pride at the man's courage. Rek's heart went out to Britan as the man ignored the lethal storm.

At least fifty men had been stretchered away. Fewer than Druss had feared. He raised himself to stare over the battlements.

'Soon,' he said. 'They are massing behind the siege towers.'

A boulder crashed through the wall ten paces away from him, scattering men like sand in the wind. Miraculously only one failed to rise, the rest rejoining their comrades. Druss raised his arm to signal Orrin. A trumpet sounded and Bowman and the rest of the men surged forward. Each archer carried five quivers of twenty arrows as they raced across the open ground, over the fire-gully bridges and on towards the battlements.

With a roar of hate, almost tangible to the defenders, the Nadir swept towards the wall in a vast black mass, a dark tide set to sweep the Dros before it. Thousands of the barbarians began to haul the huge siege towers forward, while others ran with ladders and ropes. The plain before the walls seemed alive as the Nadir poured forward, screaming their battle cries.

Breathless and panting, Bowman arrived to stand beside Druss, Rek and Serbitar. The outlaws spread out along the wall.

'Shoot when you're ready,' said Druss. The green-clad outlaw swept a slender hand through his blond hair and grinned.

'We can hardly miss,' he said. 'But it will be like spitting into a storm.'

'Every little helps,' said the axeman.

Bowman strung his yew bow and notched an arrow. To the left and right of him, the move was repeated a thousand times. Bowman sighted on a leading warrior and released the string, the shaft slashing the air to slice and hammer through the man's leather jerkin. As he stumbled and fell, a ragged cheer went up along the wall. A thousand arrows followed, then another thousand and another. Many Nadir warriors carried shields, but many did not. Hundreds fell as the arrows struck, tripping the men behind. But still the black mass kept coming, trampling the wounded and dead beneath them.

Armed with his Vagrian bow, Rek loosed shaft after shaft into the horde, his lack of skill an irrelevant factor since, as Bowman had said, one could hardly miss. The arrows were a barbed mockery of the clumsy ballistae attack so recently used against them. But it was taking a heavier toll.

The Nadir were close enough now for individual faces to be clearly seen. Rough looking men, thought Rek, but tough and hardy – raised to war and blood. Many of them lacked armour, others wore mail-shirts, but most were clad in black breastplates of lacquered leather and wood. Their screaming battle cries were almost bestial; no words could be heard, only

420

their hate could be felt. Like the angry scream of some vast, inchoate monster, thought Rek as the familiar sensation of fear gripped his belly.

Serbitar raised his helm visor and leaned over the battlements, ignoring the few arrows that flashed up and by him.

'The ladder men have reached the walls,' he said, softly.

Druss turned to Rek. 'The last time I stood beside an Earl of Dros Delnoch in battle, we carved a legend,' he said.

'The odd thing about sagas,' offered Rek, 'is that they very rarely mention dry mouths and full bladders.'

A grappling hook whistled over the wall.

'Any last words of advice?' asked Rek, dragging his sword free from its scabbard.

Druss grinned, drawing Snaga. 'Live!' he said.

More grappling irons rattled over the walls, jerking taut instantly and biting into the stone as hundreds of hands applied pressure below. Frantically the defenders lashed razor-edged blades at the vine ropes until Druss bellowed at the men to stop.

'Wait until they're climbing!' he shouted. 'Don't kill ropes – kill *men*!'

Serbitar, a student of war since he was thirteen, watched the progress of the siege towers with detached fascination. The obvious idea was to get as many men on the walls as possible by using ropes and ladders, then to pull in the towers. The carnage below among the men pulling the tower ropes was horrific as Bowman and his archers peppered them with shafts. But more always rushed in to fill the places of the dead and dying.

On the walls, despite the frenzied slashing of ropes, the sheer numbers of hooks and throwers had enabled the first Nadir warriors to gain the battlements.

Hogun, with five thousand men on Musif, Wall Two, was sorely tempted to forget his orders and race to the aid of Wall One. But he was a professional soldier, reared on obedience, and he stood his ground.

Tsubodai waited at the bottom of the rope as the tribesmen slowly climbed above him. A body hurtled by him to splinter on the jagged rocks and blood splashed his lacquered leather breastplate. He grinned, recognising the twisted features of Nestzan, the race runner.

'He had it coming to him,' he said to the man beside him. 'Now, if he'd been able to run as fast as he fell, I wouldn't have lost so much money!'

Above them the climbing men had stopped now, as the Drenai defenders forced the attackers back towards the ramparts. Tsubodai looked up at the man ahead of him.

'How long are you going to hang there, Nakrash?' he called. The man twisted his body and looked down.

'It's these Green Steppe dung-eaters,' he shouted. 'They couldn't gain a foothold on a cow pat.'

Tsubodai laughed happily, stepping away from the rope to see how the other climbers were moving. All along the wall it was the same: the climbing had stopped, the sounds of battle echoing down from above. As bodies crashed to the rocks around him, he dived back into the lee of the wall.

'We'll be down here all day,' he said. 'The Khan should have sent the Wolfshead in first. These Greens were useless at Gulgothir, and they're even worse here.'

His companion grinned and shrugged. 'Line's moving again,' he said.

Tsubodai grasped the knotted rope and pulled himself up beneath Nakrash. He had a good feeling about today – maybe he could win the horses Ulric had promised to the warrior who would cut down the old greybeard everyone was talking about.

'Deathwalker.' A pot-bellied old man without a shield.

'Tsubodai,' called Nakrash. 'You don't die today, hey? Not while you still owe me on that foot race.'

'Did you see Nestzan fall?' Tsubodai shouted back. 'Like an arrow. You should have seen him swinging his arms. As if he wanted to push the ground away from him.'

'I'll be watching you. Don't die, do you hear me?'

'You watch yourself. I'll pay you with Deathwalker's horses.'

As the men climbed higher more tribesmen filled the rope beneath him. Tsubodai glanced down.

'Hey you!' he called. 'Not a lice-ridden Green are you?'

'From the smell you must be Wolfshead,' replied the climber, grinning.

Nakrash scaled the battlements, dragging his sword clear and then turning to pull Tsubodai alongside him. The attackers had forced a wedge through the Drenai line, and still neither Tsubodai nor Nakrash could join the action.

'Move away! Make room!' called the man behind them.

'You wait there, goat-breath,' said Tsubodai. 'I'll just ask the round-eyes to help you over. Hey, Nakrash, stretch those long legs of yours and tell me where Deathwalker is.'

Nakrash pointed to the right. 'I think you will soon get a chance at those horses. He looks closer than before.' Tsubodai leapt lightly to the ramparts, straining to see the old man in action.

'Those Greens are just stepping up and asking for his axe, the fools.' But no one heard him above the clamour.

The thick wedge of men ahead of them was thinning fast, and Nakrash leapt into a gap and slashed open the throat of a Drenai soldier who was trying desperately to free his sword from a Nadir belly. Tsubodai was soon beside him hacking and cutting at the tall round-eyed southerners.

Battle lust swept over him, as it had during ten years of warfare under Ulric's banner. He had been a youngster when the first battle began, tending his father's goats on the granite steppes far to the north. Ulric had been a war leader for only a few years at that time. He had subdued the Long Monkey tribe and offered their men the chance to ride with his forces under their own banner. They had refused and died to a man. Tsubodai remembered that day: Ulric had personally tied their chieftain to two horses and ordered him torn apart. Eight hundred men had been beheaded and their armour handed over to youngsters like Tsubodai.

On the next raid he had taken part in the first charge. Ulric's brother Gat-sun had praised him highly and given him a shield of stretched cow-hide, edged with brass. He had lost it in a knuckle-bone game the same night, but he still remembered the gift with affection. Poor Gat-sun! Ulric had him executed the following year for trying to lead a rebellion. Tsubodai had ridden against him and been among the loudest to cheer as his head fell. Now, with seven wives and forty horses Tsubodai was, by any reckoning, a rich man. And still to see thirty.

Surely the gods loved him?

A spear grazed his shoulder. His sword snaked out, half-severing the arm. Oh, how the gods loved him! He blocked a slashing cut with his shield.

Nakrash came to his rescue, disembowelling the attacker who fell screaming to the ground to vanish beneath the feet of the warriors pushing from behind.

To his right the Nadir line gave way and he was pushed back as Nakrash took a spear in the side. Tsubodai's blade slashed the air, taking the lancer high in the neck; blood spurted and the man fell back. Tsubodai glanced at Nakrash, lying at his feet writhing, his hands grasping the slippery lance shaft.

Leaning down, he pulled his friend clear of the action. There was nothing more he could do, for Nakrash was dying. It was a shame, and put a pall on the day for the little tribesman. Nakrash had been a good companion for the last two years. Looking up, he saw a black-garbed figure with a white beard cleaving his way forward, a terrible axe of silver steel in his blood-splashed hands.

Tsubodai forgot about Nakrash in an instant. All he could see were Ulric's horses. He pushed forward to meet the axeman, watching his movements, his technique. He moved well for one so old, thought Tsubodai, as the old man blocked a murderous cut and back-handed his axe across the face of a tribesman who was hurled screaming over the battlements.

Tsubodai leapt forward, aiming a straight thrust for the old man's belly. From then on, it seemed to him that the scene was taking place under water. The white-bearded warrior turned his blue eyes on Tsubodai and a chill of terror seeped into his blood. The axe seemed to float against his sword blade, sweeping the thrust aside, then the blade reversed and with an agonising lack of speed clove through Tsubodai's chest.

His body slammed back into the ramparts and slid down to rest beside Nakrash. Looking down he saw bright blood, replaced by dark arterial gore. He pushed his hand into the gash, wincing as a broken rib twisted under his fist.

'Tsubodai?' said Nakrash softly. Somehow the sound carried to him.

He hunched his body over his friend, resting his head on his chest.

'I hear you, Nakrash.'

'You almost had the horses. Very close.'

'Damn good, that old man, hey?' said Tsubodai.

423

The noise of the battle receded. Tsubodai realised it had been replaced by a roaring in his ears, like the sea gathering shingle.

He remembered the gift Gat-sun had given him, and the way he had spat in Ulric's eye on the day of his execution.

Tsubodai grinned. He had liked Gat-sun.

He wished he hadn't cheered so loudly.

He wished . . .

Druss hacked at a rope and turned to face a Nadir warrior who was scrambling over the wall. Batting aside a sword thrust, he split the man's skull, then stepped over the body and tackled a second warrior, gutting him with a back-hand slash. Age vanished from him now. He was where he was always meant to be – at the heart of a savage battle. Behind him Rek and Serbitar fought as a pair, the slim albino's slender rapier and Rek's heavy longsword cutting and slashing.

Druss was joined now by several Drenai warriors, and they cleared their section of the wall. Along the wall on both sides similar moves were being repeated as the five thousand warriors held. The Nadir could feel it too, as slowly the Drenai inched them back. The tribesmen fought with renewed determination, cutting and killing with savage skill. They had only to hold on until the siege tower ledges touched the walls, then thousands more of their comrades could swarm in to reinforce them. And they were but a few yards away.

Druss glanced behind. Bowman and his archers were fifty paces back, sheltering behind small fires which had been hastily lit. Druss raised his arm and waved at Hogun, who ordered a trumpet sounded.

Along the wall, several hundred men pulled back from the fighting to gather up wax-sealed clay pots and hurl them at the advancing towers. Pottery smashed against wooden frames, splashing dark liquid to stain the wood.

Gilad, with sword in one hand and clay pot in the other, parried a thrust from a swarthy axeman, crashed his sword into the other's face and threw his globe. He just had time to see it shatter in the open doorway at the top of the tower, where Nadir warriors massed, before two more invaders pressed forward to tackle him. The first he gutted with a stabbing thrust, only to find his sword trapped in the depths of the dying man's belly. The second attacker screamed and slashed at Gilad, who released his grip on his sword hilt and leapt backwards. Instantly another Drenai warrior intercepted the Nadir, blocked his attack and all but beheaded him with a reverse stroke. Gilad tore his sword free of the Nadir corpse and smiled his thanks to Bregan.

'Not bad for a farmer!' yelled Gilad, forcing his way back into the battle and slicing through the guard of a bearded warrior carrying an iron-pitted club.

'Now, Bowman!' shouted Druss.

The outlaws notched arrows whose tips were partially covered by oil-soaked cloth and held them over the flames of the fires. Once burning, they fired them over the battlements to thud into the siege tower walls. Flames sprang up instantly and black smoke, dense and suffocating, was whipped upwards by the morning breeze. One flaming arrow flashed through the open doorway of the tower where Gilad's globe of oil had struck, to pierce the leg of a Nadir warrior whose clothes were oil-drenched. Within seconds the man was a writhing, screaming human torch, blundering into his comrades and setting them ablaze.

More clay pots sailed through the air to feed the flames on the twenty towers, and the terrible stench of burning flesh was swept over the walls by the breeze.

With the smoke burning his eyes, Serbitar moved among the Nadir, his sword weaving an eldritch spell. Effortlessly he slew, a killing machine of deadly, awesome power. A tribesman reared up behind him, knife raised, but Serbitar twisted and opened the man's throat in one smooth motion.

'Thank you, brother,' he pulsed to Arbedark on Wall Two.

Rek, while lacking Serbitar's grace and lethal speed, used his sword to no less effect, gripping it two-handed to bludgeon his way to victory beside Druss. A hurled knife glanced from his breastplate, slicing the skin over his bicep. He cursed and ignored the pain, as he ignored other minor injuries received that day: the gashed thigh and the ribs bruised by a Nadir javelin which had been turned aside by his breastplate and mail-shirt.

Five Nadir burst through the defences and raced on towards the defence-less stretcher-bearers. Bowman skewered the first from forty paces, and Caessa the second, then Bar Britan raced to intercept them with two of his men. The battle was brief and fierce, the blood from Nadir corpses staining the earth.

Slowly, almost imperceptibly, a change was coming over the battle. Fewer tribesmen were gaining the walls, for their comrades had been forced back to the battlements, and there was little room to gain purchase. The Nadir now fought not to conquer, but to survive. The tide of war – fickle at best – had turned and they had become the defenders.

But the Nadir were grim men, and brave. For they neither cried out nor sought to surrender, but stood their ground and died fighting.

One by one they fell, until the last of the warriors was swept from the battlements to lie broken on the rocks below.

Silently now the Nadir army retired from the field, stopping out of bowshot to slump to the ground and stare back at the Dros with dull, unremitting hatred. Black plumes of smoke rose from the smouldering towers and the stink of death filled their nostrils.

Rek leaned on the battlements and rubbed his face with a bloodied hand. Druss walked forward, wiping Snaga clean with a piece of torn cloth. Blood flecked the iron grey of the old man's beard and he smiled at the new Earl.

'You took my advice then, laddie?'

'Only just,' said Rek. 'Still, we didn't do too badly today?'

'This was just a sortie. The real test will come tomorrow.'

Druss was wrong. Three time more the Nadir attacked that day before dusk sent them back to their camp fires, dejected and temporarily defeated. On the battlements weary men slumped to the bloody ground, tossing aside helmets and shields. Stretcher-bearers carried wounded men from the scene, while the corpses were left to lie for the time being; their needs no longer being urgent. Three teams were detailed to check the bodies of Nadir warriors; the dead were hurled from the battlements, the living despatched with speed and their bodies pitched to the plain below.

Druss rubbed his tired eyes. His shoulder burned with fatigue, his knee was swollen and his limbs felt leaden. But he had come through the day better than he had hoped. He glanced around. Some men lay sprawled asleep on the stone. Others merely sat with their backs to the walls, eyes glazed and minds wandering. There was little conversation. Further along the wall the young Earl was talking to the albino. They had both fought well and the albino seemed fresh; only the blood which spattered his white cloak and breastplate gave evidence of his day's work. Regnak, though, seemed tired enough for both. His face, grey with exhaustion, looked older, the lines more deeply carved. Dust, blood and sweat merged together on his features, and a rough bandage on his forearm was beginning to drip blood to the stones.

'You'll do, laddie,' said Druss softly.

'Druss, old horse, how are you feeling?' Bowman asked.

'I have had better days,' snarled the old man, lurching upright and gritting his teeth against the pain from his knee. The young archer almost made the mistake of offering Druss an arm to lean on, but checked himself in time. 'Come and see Caessa,' he said.

'About the last thing I need now is a woman. I'll get some sleep,' answered Druss. 'Just here will be fine.' With his back to the wall he slid gently to the ground, keeping his injured knee straight. Bowman turned and walked back to the mess hall where he found Caessa and explained the problem. After a short argument, she gathered some linen while Bowman sought a jug of water, and in the gathering twilight they walked back to the battlements. Druss was asleep, but he awoke as they approached him.

The girl was a beauty, no doubt about that. Her hair was auburn, but gold-tinted in the moonlight, matching the tawny flecks in her eyes. She stirred his blood as few women had the power to do now. But there was something else about her: something unattainable. She crouched down by him, her slender fingers probing gently at the swollen knee. Druss grunted as she dug more deeply. Then she removed his boot and rolled up the trouser leg. The knee was discoloured and puffy, the veins in the calf below swollen and tender.

'Lie back,' she told him. Moving alongside him, left hand curled around his thigh, she lifted the leg and held his ankle in her right hand. Slowly she flexed the joint.

'There is water on the knee,' she said, as she set down his leg and began to massage the joint. Druss closed his eyes. The sharpness of the pain receded to a dull ache. The minutes passed and he dozed. She woke him with a light slap on the calf and he found his knee was tightly bandaged.

'What other problems do you have?' she asked, coolly.

'None,' he said.

'Don't lie to me, old man. Your life depends on it.'

'My shoulder burns,' he admitted.

'You can walk now. Come with me to the hospital and I will ease the pain.' She gestured to Bowman, who leaned forward and helped the axeman to his feet. The knee felt good, better than it had in weeks.

'You have real skill, woman,' he said. 'Real skill.'

'I know. Walk slowly – it will feel a little sore by the time we get there.'

In a side room at the hospital, she told him to remove his clothes. Bowman smiled, and leaned back against the door with arms folded across his chest.

'All of them?' asked Druss.

'Yes. Are you shy?'

'Not if you're not,' said Druss, slipping from his jerkin and shirt, then sitting on the bed to remove his trousers and boots.

'Now what?' he asked.

Caessa stood before him, examining him critically, running her hands over his broad shoulders and probing his muscles.

'Stand up,' she told him, 'and turn round.' He did so and she scrutinised his back. 'Move your right arm above your head – slowly.' As the examination continued Bowman watched the old warrior, marvelling at the number of scars he carried. Everywhere: front and back; some long and straight, others jagged; some stitched, others blotchy and overlapped. His legs, too, showed evidence of many light wounds. But by far the greatest number were in the front. Bowman smiled. You have always faced your enemies, Druss, he thought.

Caessa told the warrior to lie on the bed, face down, and began to manipulate the muscles of his back, easing out knots, and pummelling crystals under the shoulder-blades.

'Get me some oil,' she asked Bowman, without looking round. He fetched liniment from the stores, then left the girl to her work. For over an hour she massaged the old man, until at last her own arms burned with fatigue. Druss had fallen asleep long since, and she covered him with a blanket and silently left the room. In the corridor outside she stood for a moment, listening to the cries of the wounded in the makeshift wards and watching the orderlies assisting the surgeons. The smell of death was strong here and she made her way out into the night.

The stars were bright, like frozen snowflakes on a velvet blanket, the moon a bright silver coin at the centre. She shivered. Ahead of her a tall man in black and silver armour strode towards the mess hall. It was Hogun. He saw her and waved, changed direction and came towards her. She cursed under her breath; she was tired and in no mood for male company.

'How is he?' asked Hogun.

'Tough!' she said.

'I know that, Caessa. The whole world knows it. But how is he?'

'He's old, and he's tired – exhausted. And that's after only one day. Don't pin too many hopes on him. He has a knee which could collapse under him at any time, a bad back which will grow worse and too many crystals in too many joints.'

'You paint a pessimistic picture,' said the general.

'I tell it as it is. It is a miracle that he's alive tonight. I cannot see how a man of his age, with the physical injuries he's carrying, could fight all day and survive.'

'And he went where the fighting was thickest,' said Hogun. 'As he will do tomorrow.'

'If you want him to survive, make sure he rests the day after.'

'He will never stand for it,' said Hogun.

'Yes, he will. He *may* get through tomorrow – and that I doubt. But by tomorrow night he will hardly be able to move his arm. I will help him, but he will need to rest one day in three. And an hour before dawn tomorrow, I want a hot tub set up in his room here. I will massage him again before the battle begins.'

'You're spending a lot of time over a man you described as "old and tired", and whose deeds you mocked only a short time since.'

'Don't be a fool, Hogun. I am spending this time with him because he *is* old and tired, and though I do not hold him in the same reverence as you, I can see that the men need him. Hundreds of little boys playing at soldiers to impress an old man who thrives on war.'

'I will see that he rests after tomorrow,' said Hogun.

'If he survives,' Caessa added grimly.

21

By midnight the final toll for the first day's battle was known. Four hundred and seven men were dead. One hundred and sixty-eight were wounded and half of those would not fight again.

The surgeons were still working and the head count was being double-checked. Many Drenai warriors had fallen from the battlements during the fighting, and only a complete roll call would supply their numbers.

Rek was horrified, though he tried not to show it during the meeting with Hogun and Orrin in the study above the great hall. There were seven present at this meeting: Hogun and Orrin representing the warriors; Bricklyn for the townsfolk; Serbitar, Vintar and Virae. Rek had managed to snatch four hours' sleep and felt fresher for it; the albino had slept not at all and seemed no different.

'These are grievous losses for one day's fighting,' said Bricklyn. 'At that rate, we could not hold out for more than two weeks.' His greying hair was styled after the fashion of the Drenai court, swept back over his ears and tight-curled at the nape of the neck. His face, though fleshy, was handsome and he had a highly-practised charm. The man was a politician, and therefore not to be relied upon, thought Rek.

Serbitar answered Bricklyn. 'Statistics mean nothing on the first day,' he said. 'The wheat is being separated from the chaff.'

'What does that mean, Prince of Dros Segril?' asked the burgher, the question more sharp in the absence of his usual smile.

'No disrespect was intended to the dead,' replied Serbitar. 'It is merely a reality in war that the men with the least skill are those first to fall. Losses are always greater at the outset. The men fought well, but many of the dead lacked skill – that is why they are dead. The losses will diminish, but they will still be high.'

'Should we not concern ourselves with what is tolerable?' asked the burgher, turning to Rek. 'After all, if we should believe that the Nadir will breach the walls eventually, what is the point of continued resistance? Are lives worth nothing?'

'Are you suggesting surrender?' asked Virae.

'No, my lady,' replied Bricklyn smoothly. 'That is for the warriors to decide and I will back any decision they make. But I believe we must examine alternatives. Four hundred men died today and they should be honoured for their sacrifice. But what of tomorrow? And the day after. We must be careful that we do not put pride before reality.'

'What is he talking about?' Virae asked Rek. 'I cannot understand any of it.'

'What are these alternatives you speak of?' said Rek. 'As I see it, there are only two. We fight and win, or we fight and lose.'

'These are the plans uppermost at this time,' said Bricklyn. 'But we must think of the future. Do we believe we can hold out here? If so, we must fight on by all means. But if not, then we must pursue an honourable peace, as other nations have done.'

'What is an honourable peace?' asked Hogun, softly.

'It is where enemies become friends and quarrels are forgotten. It is where we receive the Lord Ulric into the city as an ally to Drenan, having first obtained from him the promise that no harm will come to the inhabitants. Ultimately all wars are so concluded – as evidenced by the presence here of Serbitar, a Vagrian prince. Thirty years ago, we were at war with Vagria. Now we are friends. In thirty years' time, we may have meetings like this with Nadir princes. We must establish perspectives here.'

'I take your point,' said Rek, 'and it is a good one. . .'

'You may think so. Others may not!' snapped Virae.

'It is a good one,' continued Rek smoothly. 'These meetings are no place for sabre-rattling speeches. We must, as you say, examine realities. The first reality is this: we are well-trained, well-supplied and we hold the mightiest fortress ever built. The second reality is that Magnus Wound-weaver needs time to train and build an army to resist the Nadir even if Delnoch falls. There is no point in discussing surrender at this time, but we will bear it in mind for future meetings.

'Now is there any other town business to discuss, for the hour is late and we have kept you over-long, my dear Bricklyn?'

'No, my lord, I think we have concluded our business,' answered the burgher.

'Then may I thank you for your help – and your sage counsel – and bid you goodnight.'

The burgher stood, bowed to Rek and Virae and left the room. For several seconds they listened to his departing footsteps. Virae, flushed and angry, was about to speak when Serbitar broke the silence.

'That was well said, my lord Earl. He will be a thorn in our side.'

'He is a political animal,' said Rek. 'He cares nothing for morality, honour or pride. But he has his place and his uses. What of tomorrow, Serbitar?'

'The Nadir will begin with at least three hours of ballistae bombardment. Since they cannot advance their army while such an assault is in progress, I would suggest we retire all but fifty men to Musif an hour before dawn. When the barrage ceases we will move forward.'

'And what,' said Orrin, 'if they launch their second assault at dawn? They will be over the walls before our force can reach the battlements.'

'They do not plan such a move,' said the albino simply.

Orrin was unconvinced, but felt uncomfortable in the presence of Serbitar. Rek noted his concern.

'Believe me, my friend, The Thirty have powers beyond the ken of normal men. If he says it, then it is so.'

'We shall see, my lord,' said Orrin doubtfully.

'How is Druss?' asked Virae. 'He looked quite exhausted when I saw him at dusk.'

'The woman Caessa tended to him,' said Hogun, 'and she says he will be well. He is resting at the hospital.'

Rek wandered to the window, opened it and breathed in the crisp night air. From here he could see far down into the valley, where the Nadir camp-fires blazed. His eyes rested on the Eldibar hospital, where lamps still burned.

'Who would be a surgeon?' he said.

At Eldibar Calvar Syn, waist wrapped in a bloody leather apron, moved like a sleepwalker. Fatigue bit deep into his bones as he moved from bed to bed, administering potions.

The day had been a nightmare – more than a nightmare – for the bald, one-eyed surgeon. In thirty years he had seen death many times. He had watched men die who should have lived and seen men survive wounds which should have slain them outright. And often his own very special skills had thwarted death where others could not even staunch the wound. But today had been the worst day of his life. Four hundred strong young men, this morning fit and in their prime, were now rotting meat. Scores of others had lost limbs or fingers. Those with major wounds had been transferred to Musif. The dead had been carted back behind Wall Six for burial beyond the gates.

Around the weary surgeon orderlies flung buckets of salted water to the bloody floor, brushing away the debris of pain.

Calvar Syn walked silently into Druss' room and gazed down on the sleeping figure. By the bedside hung Snaga, the silver slayer. 'How many more, you butcher?' said Calvar. The old man stirred, but did not wake.

The surgeon stumbled into the corridor and made his way to his own room. There he hurled the apron across a chair and slumped to his bed, lacking even the energy to pull a blanket across his body. Sleep would not come. Nightmare images of agony and horror flitted across his mind and he began to sob. A face entered his mind, elderly and gentle. The face grew, absorbing his anguish and radiating harmony. Larger and larger it became, until like a warm blanket it covered his pain. And he slept, deep and dreamless.

'He rests now,' said Vintar, as Rek turned away from the window in the Keep.

'Good,' said Rek. 'He won't rest much tomorrow. Serbitar, have you had any more thoughts about our traitor?'

The albino shook his head. 'I don't know what we can do. We are watching the food and the wells. There is no other way he can affect us. You are guarded, as are Druss and Virae.'

'We must find him,' said Rek. 'Can you not enter the mind of every man in the fortress?'

'Of course! We would surely have an answer for you within three months.'

'I take the point,' Rek said, smiling ruefully.

Khitan stood silently watching the smoke billow up from his towers. His

431

face was expressionless, his eyes dark and shrouded. Ulric approached him, placing a hand on his shoulder.

'They were just wood, my friend.'

'Yes, my lord. I was thinking that in future we need a false-fronted screen of soaking hides. It should not be too difficult, though the increased weight could prove a problem in terms of stability.'

Ulric laughed. 'I thought to find you broken with grief. And yet already you plan.'

'I feel stupid, yes,' answered Khitan. 'I should have foreseen the use of the oil. I knew the timbers would never burn merely from fire arrows, and gave no thought to other combustibles. No one will beat us like that again.'

'Most assuredly, my learned architect,' said Ulric, bowing.

Khitan chuckled. 'The years are making me pompous, my lord. Death-walker did well today. He is a worthy opponent.'

'Indeed he is – but I don't think today's plan was his. They have white templars among them who destroyed Nosta Khan's acolytes.'

'I thought there was some devilry in that,' muttered Khitan. 'What will you do with the defenders when we take the fortress?'

'I have said that I will slay them.'

'I know. I wondered if you had changed your mind. They are valiant.'

'And I respect them. But the Drenai must learn what happens to those who oppose me.'

'So, my lord, what will you do?'

'I shall burn them all on one great funeral pyre – all save one who shall live to carry the tale.'

An hour before dawn, Caessa slipped silently into Druss' room and approached the bedside. The warrior was sleeping deeply, lying on his belly with his massive forearms cradling his head. As she watched him Druss stirred. He opened his eyes, focusing on her slender legs clad in thigh-length doeskin boots. Then his gaze travelled upwards. She wore a body-hugging green tunic with a thick, silver-studded leather belt that accentuated her small waist. By her side hung a short sword with an ebony handle. He rolled over and met her gaze – there was anger in her tawny eyes.

'Finished your inspection?' she snapped.

'What ails you, girl?'

All emotion left her face, withdrawing like a cat into shadows.

'Nothing. Turn over, I want to check your back.'

Skilfully she began to knead at the muscles of his shoulder-blade, her fingers like steel pins, causing him to grunt occasionally through gritted teeth.

'Turn over again.'

With Druss once more on his back she lifted his right arm, locked her own arms around it and gave a sharp pull and twist. A violent cracking sound followed and for a fraction of a second Druss thought she had broken his shoulder. Releasing his arm, she rested it on his left shoulder, then crossed his left arm to sit on the right shoulder. Leaning forward to pull him on his side, she placed her clenched fist under his spine between the shoulder-blades, then rolled him back. Suddenly she threw her weight across his chest, forcing his spine into her fist. Twice more he grunted as alarming sounds filled the air which he identified as a kind of crunching snap. Sweat beaded his forehead.

'You're stronger than you look, girl.'

'Be quiet and sit up, facing the wall.'

This time she seemed almost to break his neck, placing her hands under his chin and over his ear, wrenching first to the left and then to the right. The sound was like a dry branch snapping.

'Tomorrow you rest,' she said as she turned to leave.

He stretched and moved his injured shoulder. He felt good – better than he had in weeks.

'What were those cracking sounds?' he asked, halting her at the door.

'You have arthritis. The first three dorsals were locked solid, therefore blood could not flow properly. Also, the muscle under the shoulder blade had knotted, causing spasms which reduced the strength to your right arm. But heed me, old man, tomorrow you must rest. That or die.'

'We all die,' he said.

'True. But you are needed.'

'Do you dislike me – or all men?' he asked as her hand touched the door handle.

She turned to look at him, smiled, pushed the door shut and came back into the room, stopping within inches of his burly naked frame.

'Would you like to sleep with me, Druss?' she asked sweetly, laying her left arm across his shoulder.

'No,' he said, softly, gazing into her eyes. The pupils were small, unnaturally so.

'Most men do,' she whispered, moving closer.

'I am not most men.'

'Are you dried-up then?' she asked.

'Perhaps.'

'Or is it boys you lust after? We have some like that in our band.'

'No, I can't say I have ever lusted after a man. But I had a real woman once, and since then I have never needed another.'

She stepped away from him. 'I have ordered a hot bath for you, and I want you to stay in it until the water cools. It will help the blood to flow through those tired muscles.' With that she turned and was gone. For a few moments Druss stared at the door, then he sat down on the bed and scratched his beard.

The girl disturbed him. There was something in her eyes. Druss had never been good with women, not intuitive as some men are. Women were another race to him, alien and forbidding. But this child was something else again – in her eyes was madness, madness and fear. He shrugged and did what he always had done when a problem eluded him: forgot about it.

After the bath he dressed swiftly, combed his hair and beard, then snatched a hasty breakfast in the Eldibar mess hall and joined the fifty

433

volunteers on the battlements as the dawn sunlight pierced the early morning mist. It was a crisp morning, fresh with the promise of rain. Below him the Nadir were gathering, carts piled with boulders making their slow way to the catapults. Around him there was little conversation – on days such as this a man's thoughts turned inward. Will I die today? What is my wife doing now? Why am I here?

Further along the battlements Orrin and Hogun walked among the men. Orrin said little, leaving the Legion general to make jokes and ask questions. He resented Hogun's easy style with the enlisted men, but not too deeply; it was probably more regret than resentment.

A young Cul – Bregan, was it? – made him feel better as they passed the small group of men near the gate tower.

'Will you be fighting with Karnak today, sir?' he asked.

'Yes.'

'Thank you, sir. It is a great honour – for all of us.'

'It is nice of you to say so,' said Orrin.

'No, I mean it,' said Bregan. 'We were talking about it last night.'

Embarrassed and pleased, Orrin smiled and walked on.

'Now that,' offered Hogun, 'is a greater responsibility than checking supply lines.'

'In what way?'

'They respect you. And that man hero-worships you. It is not an easy thing to live up to. They will stand beside you when all have fled. Or they will flee with you when all else stand.'

'I won't run away, Hogun,' said Orrin.

'I know you won't, that's not what I meant. As a man, there are times when you want to lie down, or give in, or walk away. It's usually left to the individual, but in this case you are no longer one man. You are fifty. You are Karnak. It is a great responsibility.'

'And what of you?' asked Orrin.

'I am the Legion,' he answered simply.

'Yes, I suppose you are. Are you frightened today?'

'Of course.'

'I'm glad of that,' said Orrin, smiling. 'I wouldn't like to be the only one.'

As Druss had promised the day brought fresh horror: stone missiles obliterating sections of battlements, then the terrible battle cries and the surging attack with ladders to the wall, and a snarling horde breasting the granite defence to meet the silver steel of the Drenai. Today it was the turn of three thousand men from Musif, Wall Two, to relieve warriors who had fought long and hard the day before. Swords rang, men screamed and fell and chaos descended for long hours. Druss strode the walls like a fell giant, blood-spattered and grim, his axe cleaving the Nadir ranks, his oaths and coarse insults causing the Nadir to centre upon him. Rek fought with Serbitar beside him, as on the previous day, but with them now were Menahem and Antaheim, Virae and Arbedark.

By afternoon the twenty-foot-wide battlements were slippery with blood

434

and cluttered by bodies; yet still the battle raged. Orrin, by the gate towers, fought like a man possessed, side by side with the warriors from Group Karnak. Bregan, his sword broken, had gathered a Nadir axe, two-headed and long-handled, which he wielded with astonishing skill.

'A real farmer's weapon!' yelled Gilad during a brief lull.

'Tell that to Druss!' shouted Orrin, slapping Bregan on the back.

At dusk the Nadir fell back once more, sent on their way by jeers and catcalls. But the toll had been heavy. Druss, bathed in crimson, stepped across the bodies and limped to where Rek and Serbitar stood cleaning their weapons.

'The wall's too damned wide to hold for long,' he muttered, leaning forward to clean Snaga on the jerkin of a dead Nadir.

'Too true,' said Rek, wiping the sweat from his face with the edge of his cloak. 'But you are right, we cannot just give it to them yet.'

'At present,' said Serbitar, 'we are killing them at a rate of three to one. It is not enough. They will wear us down.'

'We need more men,' said Druss, sitting back on the battlements and scratching his beard.

'I sent a messenger last night to my father at Dros Segril,' said Serbitar. 'We should have reinforcements in about ten days.'

'Drada hates the Drenai,' said Druss. 'Why should he send men?'

'He must send my personal bodyguard. It is the law of Vagria, and though my father and I have not spoken for twelve years, I am still his first-born son. It is my right. Three hundred swords will join me here – no more than that, but it will help.'

'What was the quarrel?' asked Rek.

'Quarrel?' queried the albino.

'Between you and your father.'

'There was no quarrel. He saw my talents as "Gifts of Darkness" and tried to kill me. I would not allow it. Vintar rescued me.' Serbitar removed his helm, untied the knot that bound his white hair and shook his head. The evening breeze ruffled his hair. Rek exchanged glances with Druss and changed the subject.

'Ulric must realise by now that he has a battle on his hands.'

'He knew that anyway,' answered Druss. 'It won't worry him yet.'

'I don't see why not, it worries me,' said Rek, rising as Virae joined them with Menahem and Antaheim. The three members of The Thirty left without a word and Virae sat beside Rek, hugging his waist and resting her head on his shoulder.

'Not an easy day,' said Rek, gently stroking her hair.

'They looked after me,' she whispered. 'Just like you told them to, I suppose.'

'Are you angry?'

'No.'

'Good. We have only just met and I don't want to lose you yet.'

'You two ought to eat,' said Druss. 'I know you don't feel like it, but take the advice of an old warrior.' The old man stood, glanced back once at the Nadir camp and walked slowly towards the mess hall. He was tired. Almighty tired.

Ignoring his own advice, he skirted the mess hall and made for his room at the hospital. Inside the long building he paused to listen to the moans from the wards. The stench of death was everywhere. Stretcher-bearers pushed past him bearing bloodied corpses, orderlies hurled buckets of water to the floor, others with mops or buckets of sand prepared the ground for tomorrow. He spoke to none of them.

Pushing open the door of his room, he stopped. Caessa sat within. 'I have food for you,' she said, avoiding his eyes. Silently he took the platter of beef, red beans and thick black bread and began to eat.

'There is a bath for you in the next room,' she said as he finished. He nodded and stripped off his clothing.

He sat in the hip bath and cleaned the blood from his hair and beard. When cold air touched his wet back, he knew she had entered. She knelt by the bath and poured an aromatic liquid into her hands, then began washing his hair. He closed his eyes, enjoying the sensation of her fingers on his scalp. Rinsing his hair with warm fresh water, she rubbed it dry with a clean towel.

Back in his room, Druss found that she had laid out a clean undervest and black woollen trousers and had sponged his leather jerkin and boots. She poured him a goblet of Lentrian wine before leaving. Druss finished the wine and lay back on the bed, resting his head on his hand. Not since Rowena had a woman tended to him in this fashion, and his thoughts were mellow.

Rowena, his child bride, taken by slavers soon after the wedding at the great oak. Druss had followed them, not even stopping to bury his parents. For months he had travelled the land until, at last, in the company of Sieben the Poet, he had discovered the slavers' camp. Having found out from them that Rowena had been sold to a merchant who was heading east, he slew the leader in his tent and set out once more. For five years he wandered across the continent, a mercenary, building a reputation as the most fearsome warrior of his time, becoming at last the champion of Ventria's God-king, Gorben.

Finally he had found his wife in an eastern palace and had wept. For without her he had always been only half a man. She alone made him human, stilling for a while the dark side of his nature, making him whole, showing him the beauty in a field of flowers, where he looked for perfection in a blade of steel.

She used to wash his hair, and stroke the tension from his neck and the anger from his heart.

Now she was gone and the world was empty, a shifting blur of shimmering grey where once had been colours of dazzling brightness.

Outside a gentle rain began to fall. For a while Druss listened to it pattering on the roof. Then he slept.

Caessa sat in the open air, hugging her knees. Had anyone approached her, they could not have seen where the rain ended and the tears began.

436

22

For the first time all members of The Thirty manned Eldibar as the Nadir massed for the charge. Serbitar had warned Rek and Druss that today would be different: no ballistae bombardment, merely an endless series of charges to wear down the defenders. Druss had refused all advice to rest for the day and stood at the centre of the wall. Around him were The Thirty in their silver steel armour and white cloaks. With them was Hogun, while Rek and Virae stood with the men of Group Fire forty paces to the left. Orrin remained with Karnak on the right. Five thousand men waited, swords in hands, shields buckled, helms lowered.

The sky was dark and angry, huge clouds bunching to the north. Above the walls a patch of blue waited for the storm. Rek smiled suddenly as the poetry of the moment struck him.

The Nadir began to move forward in a seething furious mass, their pounding feet sounding like thunder.

Druss leapt to stand on the crenellated battlements above them.

'Come on, you whoresons!' he bellowed. 'Deathwalker waits!' His voice boomed out over the valley, echoed by the towering granite walls. At that moment lightning split the sky, a jagged spear above the Dros. Thunder followed.

And the blood-letting began.

As Serbitar had predicted, the centre of the line suffered the most ferocious of attacks, wave upon wave of tribesmen breasting the walls to die under the steel defence of The Thirty. Their skill was consummate. A wooden club knocked Druss from his feet and a burly Nadir warrior aimed an axe blow at his skull. Serbitar leapt forward to block the blow, while Menahem despatched the man with a throat slash. Druss, exhausted, stumbled over a fallen body and pitched to the feet of three attackers. Arbedark and Hogun came to the rescue as he scrabbled for his axe.

The Nadir burst through the line on the right, forcing Orrin and Group Karnak away from the battlements and back on to the grass of the killing ground. As Nadir reinforcements swept over the wall unopposed, Druss saw the danger first and bellowed a warning. He cut two men from his path and raced alone to fill the breach. Hogun desperately tried to follow him, but his way was blocked.

Three young Culs from Karnak joined the old man as he hammered and cut his way to the walls, but they were soon surrounded. Orrin – his helm lost, his shield splintered – stood his ground with the remnants of his group. He blocked a wide, slashing cut from a bearded tribesman and lanced a return thrust through the man's belly. Then he saw Druss. And knew that save for a miracle he was doomed.

'With me, Karnak!' he yelled, hurling himself into the advancing mass. Behind him Bregan, Gilad and twenty others surged forward, joined by

Bar Britan and a squad of stretcher guards. Serbitar, with fifteen of The Thirty, clove a path along the walls.

The last of Druss' young companions fell with a broken skull and the old warrior stood alone as the Nadir circle closed about him. He ducked beneath a swinging sword, grabbed the man's jerkin and smashed a head butt to his nose. A sword blade cut his upper arm and another sliced his leather jerkin above the hip. Using the stunned Nadir as a shield, Druss backed to the battlements, but an axe blade thudded into the trapped tribesman and tore him from Druss' grasp. With nowhere to go, Druss braced his foot against the battlements and dived forward into the mass; his great weight carried them back and several tumbled to the earth with him. He lost hold of Snaga, grabbed at the neck of the warrior above him and crushed his windpipe, then hugging the body to him waited for the inevitable killing thrust. As the body was kicked away, Druss lashed out at the leg beside him, sweeping the man from his feet.

'Whoa, Druss! It's me – Hogun.'

The old man rolled over and saw Snaga lying several yards away. He stood and snatched up the axe.

'That was close,' said the Legion Gan.

'Yes,' said Druss. 'Thank you! That was good work!'

'I would like to take the credit, but it was Orrin and the men from Karnak. They fought their way to you, though I don't know how.'

It had begun to rain and Druss welcomed it, turning his face to the sky with mouth open, eyes closed.

'They're coming again!' someone yelled. Druss and Hogun walked to the battlements and watched the Nadir charge. It was hard to see them through the rain.

To the left Serbitar was leading The Thirty from the wall, marching silently back towards Musif.

'Where in hell's name are *they* going?' muttered Hogun.

'There's no time to worry about that,' snarled Druss, cursing silently as his shoulder flamed with fresh agonies.

The Nadir horde swept forward. Then thunder rumbled and a huge explosion erupted at the centre of the Nadir ranks. Everything was confusion as the charge faltered.

'What happened?' asked Druss.

'Lightning struck them,' said Hogun, removing his helm and unbuckling his breastplate. 'It could happen here next – it's all this damned metal.'

A distant trumpet sounded and the Nadir marched back to their tents. At the centre of the plain was a vast crater surrounded by blackened bodies. Smoke rose from the hole.

Druss turned and watched The Thirty enter the postern gate at Musif.

'They *knew*,' he said softly. 'What manner of men are they?'

'I don't know,' answered Hogun. 'But they fight like devils, and at the moment that's all I care about.'

'They knew,' Druss said again, shaking his head.

'So?'

'How much more do they know?'

'Do you tell fortunes?' the man asked Antaheim as they crouched together beneath the makeshift canvas roof with five others from Group Fire. Rain pattered on the canvas and dripped steadily to the stones below. The roof, hastily constructed, was pinned to the battlements behind them and supported by spears at the two front corners. Within, the men huddled together. They had seen Antaheim walking alone in the rain, and one of the men, Cul Rabil, had called him over, despite the warnings of his comrades. Now an uncomfortable atmosphere existed within the canvas shelter.

'Well, do you?' asked Rabil.

'No,' said Antaheim, removing his helm and untying the battle knot in his long hair. He smiled. 'I am not a magician. Merely a man as you – all of you – are. My training is different, that is all.'

'But you can speak without talking,' said another man. 'That's not natural.'

'It is to me.'

'Can you see into the future?' asked a thin warrior, making the sign of the Protective Horn beneath his cloak.

'There are many futures. I can see some of them, but I do not know which will come to pass.'

'How can there be many futures?' asked Rabil.

'It is not an easy concept to explain, but I will try. Tomorrow an archer will shoot an arrow. If the wind drops, it will hit one man – if the wind rises, it will hit another. Each man's future therefore depends on the wind. I cannot predict which way the wind will blow, for that too depends on many things. I can look into tomorrow and see both men die, whereas only one may actually fall.'

'Then what is the point of it all? Your talent, I mean?' asked Rabil.

'Now that is an excellent question, and one which I have pondered for many years.'

'Will we die tomorrow?' asked another.

'How can I tell?' answered Antaheim. 'But all men must die eventually. The gift of life is not permanent.'

'You say "gift",' said Rabil. 'This implies a giver?'

'Indeed it does.'

'Which then of the gods do you follow?'

'We follow the Source of all things. How do you feel after today's battle?'

'In what way?' asked Rabil, pulling his cloak closer about him.

'What emotions did you feel as the Nadir fell back?'

'It's hard to describe. Strong.' He shrugged. 'Filled with power. Glad to be alive.' The other men nodded at this.

'Exultant?' offered Antaheim.

'I suppose so. Why do you ask?'

Antaheim smiled. 'This is Eldibar, Wall One. Do you know the meaning of the word "Eldibar"?'

'Is it not just a word?'

'No, it is far more. Egel, who built this fortress, had names carved on

439

every wall. "Eldibar" means "Exultation". It is there that the enemy is first met. It is there he is seen to be a Man. Power flows in the veins of the defenders. The enemy falls back against the weight of our swords and the strength of our arms. We feel, as heroes should, the thrill of battle and the call of our heritage. We are exultant! Egel knew the hearts of men. I wonder did he know the future?'

'What do the other names mean?'

Antaheim shrugged. 'That is for another day. It is not good luck to talk of Musif while we shelter under the protection of Eldibar.' Antaheim leaned back into the wall and closed his eyes, listening to the rain and the howling wind.

Musif. The Wall of Despair! Where strength has not been great enough to hold Eldibar, how can Musif be held? If we could not hold Eldibar, we cannot hold Musif. Fear will gnaw at our vitals. Many of our friends will have died at Eldibar and once more we will see, in our minds, the laughing faces. We will not want to join them. Musif is the test.

And we will not hold. We will fall back to Kania, the Wall of Renewed Hope. We did not die on Musif and Kania is a narrower fighting place. And anyway, are there not three more walls? The Nadir can no longer use their ballistae here, so that is something, is it not? In any case, did we not always know we would lose a few walls?

Sumitos, the Wall of Desperation, will follow. We are tired, mortally weary. We fight now by instinct, mechanically and well. Only the very best will be left to stem the savage tide.

Valteri, Wall Five, is the Wall of Serenity. Now we have come to terms with mortality. We accept the inevitability of our deaths, and find in ourselves depths of courage we would not have believed possible. The humour will begin again and each will be a brother to each other man. We will have stood together against the common enemy, shield to shield, and we will have made him suffer. Time will pass on this wall more slowly. We will savour our senses, as if we have discovered them anew. The stars will become jewels of beauty we never saw before, and friendship will have a sweetness never previously tasted.

And finally Geddon, the Wall of Death . . .

I shall not see Geddon, thought Antaheim.

And he slept.

'Tests! All we keep hearing about is that the real test will come tomorrow. How many damn tests are there?' stormed Elicas. Rek raised a hand, as the young warrior interrupted Serbitar.

'Calm down!' he said. 'Let him finish. We have only a few moments before the City Elders arrive.'

Elicas glared at Rek, but was silent after looking at Hogun for support and seeing his almost imperceptible shake of the head. Druss rubbed his eyes and accepted a goblet of wine from Orrin.

'I am sorry,' said Serbitar, gently. 'I know how irksome such talk is. For eight days now we have held the Nadir back, and it is true I continue to speak of fresh tests. But you see, Ulric is a master strategist. Look at his army – it is twenty thousand tribesmen. This first week has seen them blooded on our walls. They are not his finest troops. Even as we have trained our recruits, so does he. He is in no hurry; he has spent these days culling the weak from his ranks, for he knows there are more battles to come when, and if, he takes the Dros. We have done well – exceedingly well. But we have paid dearly. Fourteen hundred men have died and four hundred more will not fight again.

'I tell you this. Tomorrow his veterans will come.'

'And where do you gain this intelligence?' snapped Elicas.

'Enough, boy!' roared Druss. 'It is sufficient that he has been right till now. When he is wrong, you may have your say.'

'What do you suggest, Serbitar?' asked Rek.

'Give them the wall,' answered the albino.

'What?' said Virae. 'After all the fighting and dying? That is madness.'

'Not so, my lady,' said Bowman, speaking for the first time. All eyes turned to the young archer, who had forsaken his usual uniform of green tunic and hose. Now he wore a splendid buckskin top-coat, heavy with fringed thongs, sporting an eagle crafted from small beads across the back. His long blond hair was held in place by a buckskin headband, and by his side hung a silver dagger with an ebony haft shaped like a falcon, whose spread wings made up the knuckle guard.

He stood. 'It is sound good sense. We knew that walls would fall. Eldibar is the longest and therefore the most difficult to hold. We are stretched there. On Musif we would need fewer men, and therefore would lose fewer. And we have the killing ground between the walls. My archers could create an unholy massacre among Ulric's veterans before even a blow is struck.'

'There is another point,' said Rek, 'and one equally important. Sooner or later we will be pushed back from the wall, and despite the fire gullies our losses will be enormous. If we retire during the night, we will save lives.'

'And let us not forget morale,' Hogun pointed out. 'The loss of the wall will hit the Dros badly. If we give it up as a strategic withdrawal, however, we will turn the situation to our advantage.'

'What of you, Orrin? How do you feel about this?' asked Rek.

'We have about five hours. Let's get it started,' answered the Gan.

Rek turned lastly to Druss. 'And you?'

The old man shrugged. 'Sounds good,' he said.

'It's settled then,' said Rek. 'I leave you to begin the withdrawal. Now I must meet the Council.'

Throughout the long night the silent retreat continued. Wounded men were carried on stretchers, medical supplies loaded on to hand-carts and personal belongings packed hastily into kitbags. The more seriously injured had long since been removed to the Musif field hospital, and Eldibar barracks had been little used since the siege began.

By dawn's first ghostly light the last of the men entered the postern gates at Musif and climbed the long winding stairways to the battlements. Then began the work of rolling boulders and rubble on to the stairs to block the entrances. Men heaved and toiled as the light grew stronger. Finally, sacks of mortar powder were poured on to the rubble and then packed solid into the gaps. Other men with buckets of water doused the mixtures.

'Given a day,' said Maric the Builder, 'that mass will be almost immovable.'

'Nothing is immovable,' said his companion. 'But it will take them weeks to make it passable, and even then the stairways were designed to be defensible.'

'One way or the other, I shall not see it,' said Maric. 'I leave today.'

'You are early, surely?' said his friend. 'Marrissa and I also plan to leave. But not until the fourth wall falls.'

'First wall, fourth wall, what is the difference? All the more time to put distance between myself and this war. Ventria has need of builders. And their army is strong enough to hold the Nadir for years.'

'Perhaps. But I will wait.'

'Don't wait too long, my friend,' said Maric.

Back at the Keep, Rek lay staring at the ornate ceiling. The bed was comfortable and Virae's naked form nestled into him, her head resting on his shoulder. The meeting had finished two hours since and he could not sleep. His mind was alive with plans, counter-plans and all the myriad problems of a city under siege. The debate had been acrimonious, and pinning down any of those politicians was like threading a needle under water. The consensus opinion was that Delnoch should surrender.

Only the red-faced Lentrian, Malphar, had backed Rek. That oily serpent, Shinell, had offered to lead a delegation to Ulric personally. And what of Beric, who felt himself tricked by fate in that his bloodline had been rulers of Delnoch for centuries, yet he had lost out by being a second son? Bitterness was deep within him. The lawyer, Backda, had said little, but his words were acid when they came.

'You seek to stop the sea with a leaking bucket.'

Rek had struggled to hold his temper. He had not seen any of them standing on the battlements with sword in hand. Nor would they. Horeb had a saying that matched these men:

'In any broth, the scum always rises to the top.'

He had thanked them for their counsel and agreed to meet in five days' time to answer their proposals.

Virae stirred beside him. Her arm moved the coverlet, exposing a rounded breast. Rek smiled, and for the first time in days thought about something other than war.

Bowman and a thousand archers stood on the ramparts of Eldibar watching the Nadir mass for the charge. Arrows were loosely notched to the string, hats tilted at a jaunty angle to keep the right eye in shadow against the rising sun.

The horde screamed their hatred and surged forward.

Bowman waited. He licked his dry lips.

'Now!' he yelled, smoothly drawing back the string to touch his right cheek. The arrow leapt free with a thousand others, to be lost within the surging mass below. Again and again they fired until their quivers were empty. Finally Caessa leapt to the battlements and fired her last arrow straight down at a man pushing a ladder against the wall. The shaft entered at the top of the shoulder and sheared through his leather jerkin, lancing through his lung and lodging in his belly. He dropped without a sound.

Grappling-irons clattered to the ramparts.

'Back!' yelled Bowman, and began to run across the open ground, across the fire-gully bridges and the trench of oil-soaked brush. Ropes were lowered and the archers swiftly scaled them. Back at Eldibar the first of the Nadir had gained the wall. For long moments they milled in confusion before they spotted the archers clambering to safety. Within minutes the tribesmen had gathered several thousand strong. They hauled their ladders over Eldibar and advanced on Musif. Then arrows of fire arced over the open ground to vanish within the oil-soaked brush. Instantly thick smoke welled from the gully, closely followed by roaring flames twice the height of a man.

The Nadir fell back. The Drenai cheered.

The brush blazed for over an hour, and the four thousand warriors manning Musif were stood down. Some lay in groups on the grass; others wandered to the three mess halls for a second breakfast. Many sat in the shade of the rampart towers.

Druss strolled among the men, swapping jests here and there; accepting a chunk of black bread from one man, an orange from another. He saw Rek and Virae sitting alone near the eastern cliff and wandered across to join them.

'So far, so good!' he said, easing his huge frame to the grass. 'They're not sure what to do now. Their orders were to take the wall, and they've accomplished that.'

'What next, do you think?' asked Rek.

'The old boy himself,' answered Druss. 'He will come. And he'll want to talk.'

'Should I go down?' asked Rek.

'Better if I do. The Nadir know me. "Deathwalker". I'm part of their legends. They think I'm an ancient god of death stalking the world.'

'Are they wrong, I wonder?' said Rek, smiling.

'Maybe not. I never wanted it, you know. All I wanted was to get my wife back. Had slavers not taken her I would have been a farmer. Of that I am sure – though Rowena doubted it. There are times when I do not much like what I am.'

'I'm sorry, Druss. It was a jest,' said Rek. 'I do not see you as a death-god. You are a man and a warrior. But most of all, a man.'

'It's not you, boy; your words only echo what I already feel. I shall die soon . . . Here at this Dros. And what will I have achieved in my life? I have no sons nor daughters. No living kin . . . Few friends. They will say, "Here lies Druss. He killed many and birthed none." '

'They will say more than that,' said Virae suddenly. 'They'll say, "Here lies Druss the Legend, who was never mean, petty, nor needlessly cruel.

Here was a man who never gave in, never compromised his ideals, never betrayed a friend, never despoiled a woman and never used his strength against the weak." They'll say "He had no sons, but many a woman asleep with her babes slept more soundly for knowing Druss stood with the Drenai." They'll say many things, whitebeard. Through many generations they will say them, and men with no strength will find strength when they hear them.'

'That would be pleasant,' said the old man, smiling.

The morning drifted by and the Dros shone in the warm sunlight. One of the soldiers produced a flute and began to play a lilting springtime melody that echoed down the valley, a song of joy in a time of death.

At midday Rek and Druss were summoned to the ramparts. The Nadir had fallen back to Eldibar, but at the centre of the killing ground was a man seated on a huge purple rug. He was eating a meal of dates and cheese, and sipping wine from a golden goblet. Thrust into the ground behind him was a standard sporting a wolf's head.

'He's certainly got style,' said Rek, admiring the man instantly.

'I ought to go down before he finishes the food,' said Druss. 'We lose face as we wait.'

'Be careful!' urged Rek.

'There are only a couple of thousand of them,' answered Druss with a broad wink.

Hand over hand, he lowered himself to the Eldibar ground below and strolled towards the diner.

'I am a stranger in your camp,' he said.

The man looked up. His face was broad and clean-cut, the jaw firm. The eyes were violet and slanted beneath dark brows; they were eyes of power.

'Welcome, stranger, and eat,' said the man. Druss sat cross-legged opposite him. Slowly the man unbuckled his lacquered black breastplate and removed it, laying it carefully at his side. Then he removed his black greaves and forearm straps. Druss noted the powerful muscles of the man's arms and the smooth, catlike movements. A warrior born, thought the old man.

'I am Ulric of the Wolfshead.'

'I am Druss of the Axe.'

'Well met! Eat.'

Druss took a handful of dates from the silver platter before him and ate slowly. He followed this with goat's-milk cheese and washed it down with a mouthful of red wine. His eyebrows rose.

'Lentrian Red,' said Ulric. 'Without poison.'

Druss grinned. 'I'm a hard man to kill. It's a talent.'

'You did well. I am glad for you.'

'I was grieved to hear of your son. I have no sons, but I know how hard it is for a man to lose a loved one.'

'It was a cruel blow,' said Ulric. 'He was a good boy. But then all life is cruel, is it not? A man must rise above grief.'

Druss was silent, helping himself to more dates.

444

'You are a great man, Druss. I am sorry you are to die here.'

'Yes. It would be nice to live for ever. On the other hand, I am beginning to slow down. Some of your men have been getting damn close to marking me – it's an embarrassment.'

'There is a prize for the man who kills you. One hundred horses, picked from my own stable.'

'How does the man prove to you that he slew me?'

'He brings me your head and two witnesses to the blow.'

'Don't allow that information to reach my men. They will do it for fifty horses.'

'I think not! You have done well. How is the new Earl settling in?'

'He would have preferred a less noisy welcome, but I think he is enjoying himself. He fights well.'

'As do you all. It will not be enough, however.'

'We shall see,' said Druss. 'These dates are very good.'

'Do you believe you can stop me? Tell me truly, Deathwalker.'

'I would like to have served under you,' said Druss. 'I have admired you for years. I have served many kings. Some were weak, others wilful. Many were fine men, but you . . . you have the mark of greatness. I think you will get what you want eventually. But not while I live.'

'You will not live long, Druss,' said Ulric gently. 'We have a shaman who knows these things. He told me that he saw you standing at the gates of Wall Four – Sumitos, I believe it is called – and the grinning skull of Death floated above your shoulders.'

Druss laughed aloud. 'Death always floats where I stand, Ulric! I am he who walks with death. Does your shaman not know your own legends? I may choose to die at Sumitos. I may choose to die at Musif. But wherever I choose to die, know this: as I walk into the Valley of Shadows I will take with me more than a few Nadir for company on the road.'

'They will be proud to walk with you. Go in peace.'

23

Bloody day followed bloody day, an endless succession of hacking, slaying and dying; skirmishes carrying groups of Nadir warriors out on to the killing ground before Musif, and threatening to trap the Drenai army on the walls. But always they were beaten back and the line held. Slowly, as Serbitar had predicted, the strong were separated from the weak. It was easy to tell the difference. By the sixth week only the strong survived. Three thousand Drenai warriors were either dead or had been removed from the battle with horrifying injuries.

Druss strode like a giant along the ramparts day after day, defying all advice to rest, daring his weary body to betray him, drawing on hidden reserves of strength from his warrior's soul. Rek also was building a name, though he cared not. Twice his baresark attacks had dismayed the Nadir and shattered their line. Orrin still fought with the remnants of Karnak, now only eighteen strong. Gilad fought beside him on the right and on his left was Bregan, still using the captured axe. Hogun had gathered fifty of the Legion about him and stood back from the rampart line, ready to fill in any gap that developed.

The days were full of agony and the screams of the dying. And the list in the Hall of the Dead grew longer at every sunrise. Dun Pinar fell, his throat torn apart by a jagged dagger. Bar Britan was found under a mound of Nadir bodies, a broken lance jutting from his chest. Tall Antaheim of The Thirty was struck by a javelin in the back. Elicas of the Legion was trapped by the rampart towers as he hurled himself at the Nadir screaming defiance and fell beneath a score of blades. Jorak, the huge outlaw, had his brains dashed out by a club – and, dying, grabbed two Nadir warriors and threw himself from the battlements, dragging them screaming to their deaths on the rocks below.

Amid the chaos of slashing swords many deeds of individual heroism passed unseen. One young soldier battling back to back with Druss saw an enemy lancer bearing down on the old man. Unthinking he threw himself in the way of the flashing steel point, to die writhing among the other broken bodies on the ramparts. Another soldier, an officer named Portitac, leapt into the breach near the gate tower and stepped on to the ramparts, where he seized the top of a ladder and flung himself forward, pulling the ladder out from the wall. Twenty Nadir near the top died with him on the rocks and five others broke limbs. Many were such tales of bravery.

And still the battles raged. Rek now sported a slanting scar from eyebrow to chin, gleaming red as he battled on. Orrin had lost three fingers from his left hand, but after only two days behind the lines had joined his men once more on the wall.

From the capital at Drenan the messages came endlessly:

Hold on.
Give Woundweaver time.
Just one more month.
And the defenders knew they could not hold.
But still they fought on.

Twice the Nadir tried night attacks, but on both occasions Serbitar warned the defenders and the assailants paid dearly for their efforts. At night hand-holds were difficult to find and the long climb to the battlements was fraught with peril. Hundreds of tribesmen died without need for the touch of Drenai steel or a black-shafted arrow.

Now the nights were silent and in some ways as bad as the days. For the peace and tranquillity of the moon darkness acted as a weird counterpoint to the crimson agonies of the sunlight. Men had time to think: to dream of wives, children, farms, and even more potently of a future that might have been.

Hogun and Bowman had taken to walking together on the battlements at night, the grim Legion general and the bright witty outlaw. Hogun found that in Bowman's company he could forget the loss of Elicas; he could even laugh again. For his part, Bowman felt a kinship with the Gan, for he too had a serious side although he kept it well hidden.

But on this particular night Bowman was in a more melancholy mood and his eyes were distant.

'What ails you, man?' asked Hogun.

'Memories,' answered the archer, leaning over the ramparts to stare at the Nadir camp-fires below.

'They must be either very bad or very good to touch you so.'

'These are very bad, my friend. Do you believe in gods?'

'Sometimes. Usually when my back is against a wall and the enemy surrounds me,' said Hogun.

'I believe in the Twin Powers of Growth and Malevolence. I believe that on rare occasions each of these powers chooses a man, and in different ways destroys him.'

'And these powers have touched you, Bowman?' asked Hogun gently.

'Perhaps. Think back on recent history – you will find examples.'

'I do not need to. I know where this tale is leading,' said Hogun.

'What do you know?' asked the archer, turning to face the dark-cloaked officer. Hogun smiled gently, though he noted that Bowman's fingers were curled around the hilt of his dagger.

'I know that you are a man whose life has been marred by some secret tragedy: a wife dead, a father slain . . . something. There may even be some dark deed which you perpetrated and cannot forget. But even if that were the case, the very fact you remember it with such pain means that you acted out of character. Put it behind you, man! Who among us can change the past?'

'I wish I could tell you,' said Bowman. 'But I cannot. I am sorry, I am not fit company this evening. You go on. I will stay here a while.'

Hogun wanted to clap his hand on the other's shoulder and say some-

447

thing witty to break the mood, as Bowman had so often done for him. But he could not. There were times when a grim-faced warrior was needed, even loved, but this was not one of them and he cursed himself and left silently.

For over an hour Bowman stood on the ramparts, staring out over the valley, listening to the faint songs of the Nadir women drifting out from the far camp below.

'You are troubled?' said a voice.

Bowman swung round to face Rek. The young Earl was dressed in the clothes in which he had arrived – thigh-length doeskin boots, a high-collared tunic with gold embroidered collar and a reversed sheepskin jerkin. By his side was his longsword.

'I am merely tired,' said Bowman.

'I too. Is my scar fading?'

Bowman peered closely at the jagged red line from brow to chin. 'You were lucky not to lose an eye,' he commented.

'Useless Nadir steel,' said Rek. 'I made a perfect block and his blasted sword snapped and lashed across my face. Good gods, man, have you any idea how long I've protected my face?'

'It's too late to worry about that now,' said Bowman, grinning.

'Some people are born ugly,' said Rek. 'It's not their fault, and I for one have never held it against a man that he is ugly. But others – and I count myself among them – are born with handsome features. That is a gift which should not be lightly taken away.'

'I take it you made the perpetrator pay for his deed?'

'Naturally! And you know, I think he was smiling even as I slew him. But then he was an ugly man. I mean really ugly. It's not right.'

'Life can be so unfair,' agreed Bowman. 'But you must look on the bright side, my lord Earl. You see, unlike me, you were never stupendously handsome. Merely well-featured. The brows were too thick, the mouth a shade too wide. And your hair is now growing a little thinner. Now, had you been blessed with the near miraculous good looks possessed by such as I, you would have truly had something to grieve over.'

'There is something in what you say,' said Rek. 'You have indeed been greatly blessed. It was probably nature's way of making up to you for being short.'

'Short? I am almost as tall as you.'

'Ah, but what a large word *almost* is. Can a man be almost alive? Almost right? In the question of height, my friend, we do not deal in subtle shades of grey. I am taller, you are shorter. But I would concur there is not a more handsome short man at the fortress.'

'Women have always found me the perfect height,' said Bowman. 'At least when I dance with them I can whisper love words in their ears. With your long shanks their heads would nestle near your armpit.'

'Get a lot of time for dancing in the forest, do you?' asked Rek amiably.

'I didn't always live in the forest. My family . . .' Bowman stuttered to silence.

448

'I know your family background,' said Rek. 'But it's about time you talked about it – you've carried it too long.'

'How could you know?'

'Serbitar told me. As you know, he has been inside your mind . . . When you carried his messages to Druss.'

'I suppose the entire damned fortress knows?' said Bowman. 'I will leave at dawn.'

'Only Serbitar and I know the story – and the truth of it. But leave if you will.'

'The truth of it is that I killed my father and brother.' Bowman was white-faced and tense.

'Twin accidents – you know it well!' said Rek. 'Why must you torture yourself?'

'Why? Because I wonder at accidents in life. I wonder how many are caused by our own secret desires. There was a foot-racer once – the finest I ever saw. He was preparing for the Great Games, to run for the first time against the fastest men from many nations. On the day before the race he fell and twisted his ankle. Was it really an accident – or was he frightened to face the great test?'

'Only he will ever know,' said Rek. 'But therein lies the secret. He knows and so should you. Serbitar tells me that you were hunting with your father and brother. Your father was to the left, your brother to the right, when you followed a deer into the thicket. A bush before you rustled, and you aimed and let the arrow fly. But it was your father, who had come unannounced. How could you know he would do such a thing?'

'The point is that he taught us never to shoot until we saw the target.'

'So you made a mistake. What else is new on the face of the world?'

'And my brother?'

'He saw what you had done, misunderstood and ran at you in a rage. You pushed him away and he fell, striking his head on a rock. No one could wish such a burden on themselves. But you have nursed it, and it is now time for you to release it.'

'I never loved my father or my brother,' said Bowman. 'My father killed my mother. He left her alone for months and had many mistresses. When my mother took one lover he had him blinded and her slain . . . horribly.'

'I know. Don't dwell on it.'

'And my brother was made in his image.'

'This also I know.'

'And do you know what I felt when they were both lying dead at my feet?'

'Yes. You were exultant.'

'And is that not terrible?'

'I don't know if you have considered this, Bowman, but think on it. You blame the gods for bringing a curse upon you – but the curse really fell on the two men who deserved it.

'I don't know yet whether I fully believe in fate, but certain things do happen in a man's life which he cannot explain. My being here, for instance. Druss' conviction that he will die here, for he has made a pact with death. And you . . . But I do believe that you were merely the instrument of . . . who knows? . . . a law of natural justice perhaps.

'Whatever you believe about yourself, know this: Serbitar searched your heart and he found no malice there. And he *knows*.'

'Perhaps,' said Bowman. Then he grinned suddenly. 'Have you noticed that when Serbitar removes that horsehair helm he is shorter than I am?'

The room was spartanly furnished: a rug, a pillow and a chair, all bunched beneath the small window by which the albino stood, naked and alone. Moonlight bathed his pale skin and the night breeze ruffled his hair. His shoulders were bowed, his eyes closed. Weariness was upon him like no other weariness he had felt in all his young life. For it was born of the spirit and the truth.

The philosophers often talked of lies sitting under the tongue like salted honey. This, Serbitar knew, was true enough. But more often the hidden truth was worse. Far worse. For it settled in the belly and grew to engulf the spirit.

Below him were the Vagrian quarters which housed Suboden and the three hundred men who had come from Dros Segril. For several days he had fought alongside his personal bodyguard and become again the Prince of Dros Segril, son of Earl Drada. But the experience had been painful, for his own men had made the sign of the Protective Horn as he approached. They rarely spoke to him, and then only to answer a direct question speedily. Suboden, blunt-speaking as always, had asked the albino to return to his comrades.

'We are here, Prince Serbitar, because it is our duty. This we will accomplish best without you beside us.'

More painful than this, however, was the long discussion he had had with the Abbot of Swords – the man he revered, loved as a father, mentor and friend.

Serbitar closed his eyes and opened his mind, soaring free of the body prison and sweeping aside the curtains of time.

Back he travelled, back and further back. Thirteen long, wearisome, joy-filled years flowed past him and he saw again the caravan which had brought him to the Abbot of Swords. Riding at the head of ten warriors is the giant, red-bearded Drada, the young Earl of Segril – battle-hardened, volatile, a pitiless enemy but a true friend. Behind him ten of his most trusted warriors, men who would die for him without a moment's hesitation, for they love him above life. At the rear is a cart upon which, on a straw pallet covered with silken sheets, lies the young prince, a canvas screen shielding his ghost-white face from the sun.

Drada wheels the black horse round and gallops back to the cart. He leans on his saddle horn and glances down at the boy. The boy looks up; framed against the bright sky, he can see only the flaring wings of his father's battle helmet.

The cart is moving again, into the shade of the ornate black gates. They swing open and a man appears.

'I bid you welcome, Drada,' he says, the voice at variance with the silver armour he wears, for it is a gentle sound, the voice of a poet.

'I bring you my son,' answers the Earl – his voice gruff, soldierly.

Vintar moves to the cart and looks down on the boy. He places a hand on the pale forehead, smiles and pats the boy's head.

'Come walk with me, boy,' he says.

'He cannot walk,' says Drada.

'But he can,' says Vintar.

The boy turns his red eyes towards Vintar, questioningly, and for the first time in his lonely life feels a touching of minds. There are no words. Vintar's gentle poet's face enters with a promise of strength and friendship. The fragile muscles on Serbitar's skeletal body begin to shake, as an infusion of power regenerates wasted cells.

'What is the matter with the boy?' Drada's voice fills with alarm.

'Nothing. Say farewell to your son.'

The red-bearded warrior turns his horse's head to the north, and gazes down at the white-haired child. 'Do as you are told. Be good.' He hesitates . . . pretends his horse is skittish. He is trying to find words for a final farewell, but he cannot. Always he has found difficulty with this red-eyed child. 'Be good,' he says again; then raises an arm and leads his men northward on the long journey home.

As the wagon pulls away, bright sunlight streams on to the pallet and the boy reacts as if lanced. His face mirrors pain, his eyes squeeze shut. Vintar gently seeks his mind and pulses: 'Stand now and follow the pictures I will place on your eyelids.'

At once the pain eases and the boy can see, more clearly than ever before. And his muscles lift him at last – a sensation he thought he had forgotten since a year ago when he collapsed in the snow of the Delnoch mountains. From that moment to this he has lain paralysed, unspeaking.

Now he stands, and with eyes tight shut, he sees more clearly. Without guilt he realises he has forgotten his father and is happy for it.

The spirit of the older Serbitar tastes again the total joy which flooded the youth that day as, arm-in-arm with Vintar the Soul, he walked across the courtyard until at last, in a bright-lit corner, they came to a tiny rose cutting nestling by a high stone wall.

'This is your rose, Serbitar. Love it. Cherish it and grow with it. One day a flower will form on that tiny plant. And its fragrance will be for you alone.'

'Is it a white rose?'

'It is whatever you will it to be.'

And through the years that followed Serbitar found peace and joy in comradeship, but never more than the experience of true contentment with Vintar the Soul on that first day.

Vintar had taught him to recognise the herb Lorassium, and eat of its leaves. At first they had made him drowsy and filled his mind with colours. But as the days passed his powerful young mind mastered the visions and the green juices had strengthened his weak blood. Even his eyes changed colour to reflect the power of the plant.

And he learned to run again, savouring the joy of the wind in his face, to climb and wrestle, to laugh and live.

And he had learned to speak without speaking, move without moving and see without seeing.

Through all these blissful years Serbitar's rose had blossomed and grown.

A white rose . . .

And now it had all come to this! One glimpse into the future had destroyed thirteen years of training and belief. One speeding shaft, viewed through the mists of time, had changed his destiny.

Serbitar had stared horror-struck at the scene below him, on the battle-scarred walls of the Dros. His mind had recoiled from the violence he saw there and he had fled, comet-swift, to a far corner of a distant universe, losing himself and his sanity among exploding stars and new suns' birthing.

And still Vintar had found him.

'You must return.'

'I cannot. I have seen.'

'As have I.'

'Then you know that I would rather die than see it again.'

'But you must, for it is your destiny.'

'Then I refuse my destiny.'

'And your friends? Do you refuse them also?'

'I cannot watch you die again, Vintar.'

'Why not? I myself have seen the scene a hundred times. I have even written a poem about it.'

'As we are now – shall we be again, after death? Free souls?'

'I do not know, but I would have it so. Now return to your duty. I have pulsed The Thirty. They will keep your body alive for as long as they can.'

'They always have. Why should I be the last to die?'

'Because we would have it so. We love you, Serbitar. And always have. A shy child you were, who had never tasted friendship. Suspicious you were, of the slightest touch or embrace – a soul crying alone in a cosmic wilderness. Even now you are alone.'

'But I love you all.'

'Because you need our love.'

'Not so, Vintar!'

'Do you love Rek and Virae?'

'They are not of The Thirty.'

'Neither were you, until we made it so.'

And Serbitar had returned to the fortress and felt ashamed. But the shame he had felt earlier was as nothing compared with the feeling he now experienced.

Was it but an hour since that he had walked the ramparts with Vintar, and complained of many things, and confessed to many sins?

'You are wrong, Serbitar. So wrong. I also feel blood-lust in battle. Who does not? Ask Arbedark or Menahem. While we are still men, we will feel as other men do.'

'Then is it for nothing that we are priests?' cried Serbitar. 'We have spent years of our lives studying the insanity of war, man's lust for power, his need for bloodshed. We raise ourselves above the common man with powers that are almost god-like. Yet in the final analysis we come to this; lusting after battle and death. It *is* for nothing!'

'Your conceit is colossal, Serbitar,' said Vintar, an edge to his voice and the suggestion of anger showing in his eyes. 'You speak of "god-like". You speak of the "common man". Where in your words is the humility we strive for?

'When you first came to the Temple you were weak and lonely, and several years the youngest. But you learned the more swiftly. And you were chosen as the Voice. Did you only acquire the disciplines and forego the philosophy?'

'It would appear so,' answered Serbitar.

'You are wrong again. For in wisdom there is suffering. You are pained not because you disbelieve, but because you believe. Let us return to basics. Why do we travel to a distant war?'

'To die.'

'Why do we choose this method? Why not simply allow ourselves to starve?'

'Because in war a man's will to live is strongest. He will fight hard to stay alive. He will learn again to love life.'

'And what will that force US to face?'

'Our doubts,' whispered Serbitar.

'But you never thought that such doubt would come to you, so sure were you of your god-like powers?'

'Yes, I was sure. Now I am not. Is this such a great sin?'

'You know it is not. Why am I alive, my boy? Why did I not die with Magnar's Thirty two decades ago?'

'You were the One chosen to found the new temple.'

'Why was I chosen?'

'You were the most perfect. It has to be so.'

'Then why was I not the leader?'

'I do not understand you.'

'How is the leader chosen?'

'I know not. You have never said.'

'Then guess, Serbitar.'

'Because he is the best choice. The most . . .'

'Perfect?'

'I would have said so, but I see where you are leading. If you were the most perfect, why did Magnar lead? Well, why did he?'

'You have seen the future, you should have seen and heard this conversation. You tell me.'

453

'You know that I did not,' said Serbitar. 'There was no time for study of the minutiae.'

'Oh, Serbitar, still you will not understand! What you saw and chose to examine *was* the minutiae, the meaningless and the trivial. What does it mean to the history of this planet that this Dros falls? How many other castles have fallen throughout the ages? Of what cosmic importance was their failure? How vital are our deaths?'

'Tell me then, my lord Abbot, how is the leader chosen?'

'Have you not guessed at it, my son?'

'I believe so.'

'Then speak.'

'He is the least perfect of the acolytes,' said Serbitar, softly, his green eyes searching Vintar's face and begging denial.

'He is the least perfect,' echoed Vintar sadly.

'But why?' asked Serbitar.

'So that his task will be the more difficult, the more demanding. To give him the chance to rise and match the position he holds.'

'And I have failed?'

'Not yet, Serbitar. Not yet.'

24

Day by day more people left the siege city, piling their possessions on to carts, wagons or the backs of mules and forming convoys that snaked their way inland towards the relative security of the Skoda mountains and the capital beyond.

With each departure now, fresh problems faced the defenders. Fighting men had to be seconded to other duties such as latrine clearance, stores supply and food preparation. Now the drain on resources came on two fronts.

Druss was furious and insisted the gates be closed, the evacuation stopped. Rek pointed out that even more soldiers would then be needed to police the south road.

Then the first disaster of the campaign struck the defenders.

On the High Day of Summer – ten weeks after the battle began – Musif fell and chaos reigned. The Nadir breached the wall at the centre, driving a wedge into the killing ground beyond. The men, threatened with encirclement, fell back and raced for the fire gullies. Running skirmishes began as discipline fled, and two gully bridges collapsed as warriors milled upon them.

On Kania, Wall Three, Rek waited as long as he dared before ordering the gullies lit with flame arrows. Druss, Orrin and Hogun scrambled to safety just as the blaze took. But beyond the gully more than eight hundred Drenai warriors battled on hopelessly in tight shield rings which grew smaller moment by moment. Many on Kania turned away, unable to bear the sight of their friends' futile battles. Rek stood with fists clenched and watched in despair. The fighting did not last long. Hopelessly outnumbered, the Drenai were engulfed and the battle song of victory was sung by thousands of tribesmen.

They gathered before the flames chanting, waving blood-stained swords and axes in the air. Few on the walls understood the words, but understanding was unnecessary. The message was primal, the meaning clear. It struck the heart and soul with blistering clarity.

'What do they sing?' Rek asked Druss, as the old man recovered his breath following the long rope climb to the ramparts.

'It's their Glory chant:

> Nadir we,
> Youth-born,
> Blood-letters
> Axe-wielders,
> Victors still.

Beyond the fire tribesmen burst into the field hospital, slaying men in

455

their beds and dragging others out into the sunlight where they could be seen by their comrades on the wall. Then they were peppered with arrows, or slowly dismembered. One was even nailed to the window shutters of the barracks, to hang screaming for two hours before being disembowelled and beheaded.

The Drenai dead, stripped of their weapons and armour, were hurled into the fire gullies, and the stench of burning flesh filled the air and stung the eyes.

The evacuation at the south gates became a flood as the city emptied. Soldiers joined in, discarding their weapons and mingling with the crowds. No effort was made to stop them, on Rek's direct order.

In a little house, near the street of Millers, Maerie tried to comfort the small child sobbing in her arms. The noise in the street outside frightened her, as families loaded their possessions on to carts and wagons tethered with oxen or milk cows. It was pandemonium.

Maerie cuddled the child, crooning a lullaby tune and kissing the tight curls on his head.

'I must go back to the wall,' said her husband, a tall young man with dark hair and wide, gentle blue eyes. How tired he looked, hollow-eyed and gaunt.

'Don't go, Carin,' she said, as he strapped his sword-belt about his waist.

'Don't go? I must.'

'Let us leave Delnoch. We have friends in Purdol and you could find work there.'

He was not an intuitive man and he missed the note of desperation in her voice, failed to sense the rising panic behind her eyes.

'Don't let these fools frighten you, Maerie. Druss is still with us and we will hold Kania. I promise you.'

The sobbing child clutched his mother's dress, soothed by the gentle strength of his father's voice. Too young to understand the words yet he was comforted by the pitch and tone. The noise outside receded from him and he slept on his mother's shoulder. But Maerie was older and wiser than the child and to her the words were just words.

'Listen to me, Carin. I want to leave. Today!'

'I can't talk now. I must go back. I will see you later. It will be all right.' Leaning forward he kissed her, then stepped into the chaos of the street.

She looked around her, remembering: the chest by the door a gift from Carin's parents. The chairs made by her uncle, Damus; fashioned with care like all his work. They had brought the chairs and chest with them two years before.

Good years?

Carin was kind, thoughtful, loving. There was so much goodness to him. Easing the child into his cot, she wandered to the small bedroom, shutting the window against the noise. Soon the Nadir would come. The door would be smashed in and filthy tribesmen would come for her, tearing at her clothing . . .

She shut her eyes.

Druss was still here, he had said.

Stupid Carin! Kind, loving, thoughtful, stupid Carin! Carin the miller.

She had never been truly happy with him, though without this war she might never have realised it. She had been so close to contentment. Then he had joined the defenders, coming home so proudly in that ludicrous breastplate and oversized helm.

Stupid Carin. Kind Carin.

The door opened and she turned to see her friend Delis, her blonde hair covered in a travel shawl and a heavy cloak over her shoulders.

'Are you coming?' she asked.

'Yes.'

'Is Carin coming with you?'

'No.'

Swiftly she gathered her belongings, pushing them into a canvas bag issued to Carin. Delis carried the bag to the wagon outside while Maerie lifted her son from his cot, wrapping him in a second blanket. Stooping, she pulled open the small chest, pushing aside the linen and pulling clear the small bag of silver which Carin had hidden there.

She didn't bother to close the door.

In the Keep Druss raged at Rek, swearing to kill any deserter he recognised.

'It's too late for that,' said Rek.

'Damn you, boy!' muttered Druss. 'We have fewer than three thousand men. How long do you think we will hold if we allow desertions?'

'How long if we don't?' snapped Rek. 'We are finished, anyway! Serbitar says Kania can be held for maybe two days, Sumitos perhaps three, Valteri the same and Geddon less. Ten days in all. Ten miserable days!' The young Earl leaned on the balcony rail above the gates and watched the convoys start south. 'Look at them, Druss! Farmers, bakers, tradesmen. What right have we to ask them to die? What will it matter to them if we fail? The Nadir will not kill every baker in Drenan – it will just mean a change of masters.'

'You give up too easily,' snarled Druss.

'I'm a realist. And don't give me any Skeln Pass lectures. I'm not going anywhere.'

'You might as well,' said Druss, slumping into a leather chair. 'You have already lost hope.'

Rek turned from the window, eyes blazing. 'What is it with you warriors? It is understandable that you talk in clichés, but unforgivable if you think in them. Lost hope, indeed! I never *had* any hope. This enterprise was doomed from the start, but we do what we can and what we must. So a young farmer with wife and children decides to go home. Good! He shows a sense which men like you and I will never understand. They will sing songs about us, but he will ensure that there are people to sing them. He plants. We destroy.

'Anyway, he has played his part and fought like a man. It is criminal that he should feel the need to flee in shame.'

'Why not give them all the chance to go home?' asked Druss. 'Then you and I could stand on the walls and invite the Nadir to come at us one at a time like sportsmen.'

Suddenly Rek smiled, tension and anger flowing from him. 'I won't argue with you, Druss,' he said softly. 'You are a man I admire above all others. But in this I think you are wrong. Help yourself to wine – I shall be back soon.'

Less than an hour later the Earl's message was being read to all sections.

Bregan brought the news to Gilad as he ate in the shade offered by the field hospital under the towering cliff face of West Kania.

'We can go home,' said Bregan, his face flushed. 'We can be there by Harvest Supper!'

'I don't understand,' said Gilad. 'Have we surrendered?'

'No. The Earl says that any who wish to leave can now do so. He says that we can leave with pride, that we have fought like men – and as men, we must be given the right to go home.'

'Are we going to surrender?' asked Gilad, puzzled.

'I don't think so,' said Bregan.

'Then I shall not go.'

'But the Earl says it's all right!'

'I don't care what he says.'

'I don't understand this, Gil. Lots of the others are going. And it is true that we've played our part. Haven't we? I mean, we've done our best.'

'I suppose so.' Gilad rubbed his tired eyes and turned to watch the smoke from the fire gully drift lazily skyward. 'They did their best too,' he whispered.

'Who did?'

'Those who died. Those who are still going to die.'

'But the Earl says it's all right. He says that we can leave with our heads held high. Proud.'

'Is that what he says?'

'Yes.'

'Well, my head wouldn't be high.'

'I don't understand you, I really don't. You have said all along that we can't hold this fortress. Now we have a chance to leave. Why can't you just accept it and come with us?'

'Because I'm a fool. Give my love to everyone back there.'

'You know I won't go unless you come too.'

'Don't you start being a fool, Breg! You've got everything to live for. Just picture little Legan toddling towards you and all the stories you will be able to tell. Go on. *Go!*'

'No. I don't know why you're staying, but I shall stay too.'

'That you must not do,' said Gilad gently. 'I want you to go back, I

458

really do. After all, if you don't there will be no one to tell them what a hero I am. Seriously, Breg, I would feel so much better if I knew that you were away from all this. The Earl's right. Men like you have played their part. Magnificently.

'And as for me . . . well, I just want to stay here. I've learned so much about myself, and about other men. I'm not needed anywhere but here. I'm not necessary. I will never be a farmer, and I have neither the money to be a businessman nor the breeding to be a prince. I'm a misfit. This is where I belong . . . with all the other misfits. Please, Bregan. Please go!'

There were tears in Bregan's eyes and the two men embraced. Then the curly-haired young farmer rose. 'I hope everything works out for you, Gil. I'll tell them all – I promise I will. Good luck!'

'And to you, farmer. Take your axe. They can hang it in the village hall.'

Gilad watched him walk back towards the postern gates and the Keep beyond. Bregan turned once, and waved. Then he was gone.

Altogether, six hundred and fifty men chose to leave.

Two thousand and forty remained. Added to these were Bowman, Caessa and fifty archers. The other outlaws, having fulfilled their promise, returned to Skultik.

'Too damned few now,' muttered Druss, as the meeting ended.

'I never liked crowds anyway,' said Bowman lightly.

Hogun, Orrin, Rek and Serbitar remained in their seats as Druss and Bowman wandered out into the night.

'Don't despair, old horse,' said Bowman, slapping Druss on the back. 'Things could be worse, you know.'

'Really? How?'

'Well, we could be out of wine.'

'We *are* out of wine.'

'We are? That's terrible. I would never have stayed had I known. Luckily, however, I do just happen to have a couple of flagons of Lentrian Red stored in my new quarters. So at least we can enjoy tonight. We might even be able to save some for tomorrow.'

'That's a good idea,' said Druss. 'Maybe we could bottle it, and lay it down for a couple of months to age a little. Lentrian Red, my foot! That stuff of yours is brewed in Skultik from soap, potatoes and rats' entrails. You would get more taste from a Nadir slop-bucket.'

'You have the advantage of me there, old horse, having never tasted a Nadir slop-bucket. But my brew does hit the spot rather.'

'I think I'd rather suck a Nadir's armpit,' muttered Druss.

'Fine! I'll drink it all myself,' snapped Bowman.

'No need to get touchy, boy. I'm with you. I have always believed that friends should suffer together.'

The artery writhed under Virae's fingers like a snake, spewing blood into the cavity of the stomach.

'Tighter!' ordered Calvar Syn, his own hands deep in the wound, pushing aside blue, slimy entrails as he sought frantically to stem the bleeding within. It was useless, he knew it was useless, but he owed it to the man beneath him to use every ounce of his skill. Despite all his efforts he could feel the life oozing between his fingers. Another stitch, another small pyrrhic victory.

The man died as the eleventh stitch sealed the stomach wall.

'He's dead?' asked Virae. Calvar nodded, straightening his back. 'But the blood is still flowing,' she said.

'It will do so for a few moments.'

'I really thought he would live,' she whispered. Calvar wiped his bloody hands on a linen cloth and walked round beside her. He put his hands on her shoulders, turning her towards him.

'His chances were one in a thousand, even if I had stopped the bleeding. The lance cut his spleen and gangrene was almost certain.'

Her eyes were red, her face grey. She blinked and her body shook, but there were no tears as she looked down at the dead face.

'I thought he had a beard,' she said, confused.

'That was the one before.'

'Oh, yes. He died too.'

'You should rest.' Putting his arms round her, he led her from the room and out into the ward, past the stacked rows of triple-tiered bunk beds. Orderlies moved quietly among the rows. Everywhere the smell of death and the sweet, nauseous odour of putrefaction was mixed with the antiseptic bitterness of Lorassium juice and hot water scented with lemon mint.

Perhaps it was the unwelcome perfume, but she was surprised to find that the well was not dry and tears could still flow.

He led her to a back room, filled a basin with warm water and washed the blood from her hands and face, dabbing her gently as if she were a child.

'He told me that I love war,' she said. 'But it's not true. Maybe it was then. I don't know any more.'

'Only a fool loves war,' said Calvar, 'or a man who has never seen it. The trouble is that the survivors forget about the horrors and remember only the battle lust. They pass on that memory, and other men hunger for it. Put on your cloak and get some air. Then you will feel better.'

'I don't think I can come back tomorrow, Calvar. I will stay with Rek at the wall.'

'I understand.'

'I feel so helpless watching men die in here.' She smiled. 'I don't like feeling helpless, I'm not used to it.'

He watched her from the doorway, her tall figure draped in a white cloak, the night breeze billowing her hair.

'I feel helpless too,' he said softly.

The last death had touched him more deeply than it should, but then he had known the man, whereas others were but nameless strangers.

Carin, the former miller. Calvar remembered that the man had a wife and son living at Delnoch.

'Well, at least someone will mourn for you, Carin,' he whispered to the stars.

Rek sat and watched the stars shining high above the Keep tower and the passage of an occasional cloud, black against the moonlit sky. The clouds were like cliffs in the sky, jagged and threatening, inexorable and sentient. Rek pulled his gaze from the window and rubbed his eyes. He had known fatigue before, but never this soul-numbing weariness, this depression of the spirit. The room was dark now. He had forgotten to light the candles, so intent had he been on the darkening sky. He glanced about him. So open and welcoming during the hours of daylight, the room was now shadow haunted and empty of life. He was an interloper. He drew his cloak about him.

He missed Virae, but she was working at the field hospital with the exhausted Calvar Syn. Nevertheless the need in him was great and he rose to go to her. Instead he just stood there. Cursing, he lit the candles. Logs lay ready in the fireplace, so he lit the fire – though it was not cold – and sat in the firm leather chair watching the small flames grow through the kindling and eat into the thicker logs above. The breeze fanned the flame, causing the shadows to dance, and Rek began to relax.

'You fool,' he said to himself as the flames roared and he began to sweat. He removed his cloak and boots and pulled the chair back from the blaze.

A soft tap at the door roused Rek from his thoughts. He called out and Serbitar entered the room. For a moment Rek did not recognise him; he was without his armour, dressed in a tunic of green, his long white hair tied at the nape of the neck.

'Am I disturbing you, Rek?' he said.

'Not at all. Sit down and join me.'

'Thank you. Are you cold?'

'No. I just like to watch fires burn.'

'I do too. It helps me to think. A primal memory perhaps, of a warm cave and safety from predatory animals?' said Serbitar.

'I wasn't alive then – despite my haggard appearance.'

'But you were. The atoms that make up your body are as old as the universe.'

'I have not the faintest idea what you're talking about, though I don't doubt that it is all true,' said Rek.

An uneasy silence developed, then both men spoke at once and Rek laughed. Serbitar smiled and shrugged.

'I am unused to casual conversation. Unskilled.'

'Most people are when it comes down to it. It's an art,' said Rek. 'The thing to do is relax and enjoy the silences. That's what friends are all about – they are people with whom you can be silent.'

'Truly?'

461

'My word of honour as an Earl.'

'I am glad to see you retain your humour. I would have thought it impossible to do so under the circumstances.'

'Adaptability, my dear Serbitar. You can only spend so long thinking about death – then it becomes boring. I have discovered that my great fear is not of dying but of being a bore.'

'You are seldom boring, my friend.'

'Seldom? "Never" is the word I was looking for.'

'I beg your pardon. Never is the word which I was, of course, seeking.'

'How will tomorrow be?'

'I cannot say,' answered Serbitar swiftly. 'Where is the lady Virae?'

'With Calvar Syn. Half of the civilian nurses have fled south.'

'You cannot blame them,' said Serbitar. He stood and walked to the window. 'The stars are bright tonight,' he said. 'Though I suppose it would be more accurate to say that the angle of the earth makes visibility stronger.'

'I think I prefer "the stars are bright tonight",' said Rek who had joined Serbitar at the window.

Below them Virae was walking slowly, a white cloak wrapped about her shoulders and her long hair flowing in the night breeze.

'I think I will join her, if you'll excuse me,' said Rek.

Serbitar smiled. 'Of course. I will sit by the fire and think, if I may!'

'Make yourself at home,' said Rek, pulling on his boots.

Moments after Rek had left Vintar entered. He too had forsaken armour for a simple tunic of white wool, hooded and thick.

'That was painful for you, Serbitar. You should have allowed me to come,' he said, patting the younger man's shoulder.

'I could not tell him the truth.'

'But you did not lie,' whispered Vintar.

'When does evasion of the truth become a lie?'

'I do not know. But you brought them together, and that was your purpose. They have this night.'

'Should I have told him?'

'No. He would have sought to alter that which cannot be altered.'

'Cannot or must not?' asked Serbitar.

'Cannot. He could order her not to fight tomorrow and she would refuse. He cannot lock her away – she is an Earl's daughter.'

'If we told her?'

'She would refuse to accept it, or else defy fate.'

'Then she is doomed.'

'No. She is merely going to die.'

'I will do everything in my power to protect her, Vintar. You know that.'

'As will I. But we will fail. Tomorrow night you must show the Earl Egel's secret.'

'He will be in no mood to see it.'

Rek put his arm about her shoulders, leaned forward and kissed her cheek.

'I love you,' he whispered.

She smiled and leaned into him, saying nothing.

'I simply can't say it,' said Virae, her large eyes turned full upon him.

'That's all right. Do you feel it?'

'You know that I do. I just find it hard to say. Romantic words sound . . . strange . . . clumsy when I use them. It's as if my throat wasn't made to form the sounds. I feel foolish. Do you understand what I'm saying?' He nodded and kissed her again. 'And anyway, I haven't had your practice.'

'True,' he said.

'What does that mean?' she snapped.

'I was just agreeing with you.'

'Well, don't. I'm in no mood for humour. It's easy for you – you're a talker, a storyteller. Your conceit carries you on. I want to say all the things I feel, but I cannot. And then, when you say them first my throat just seizes up and I know I should say something, but I still can't.'

'Listen, lovely lady, it doesn't matter! They are just words as you say. I'm good with words, you're good with actions. I know that you love me; I don't expect you to echo me every time I tell you how I feel. I was just thinking earlier about something Horeb told me years ago. He said that for every man there is the one woman, and that I would know mine when I saw her. And I do.'

'When I saw you,' she said, turning in to him and hugging his waist, 'I thought you were a popinjay.' She laughed.

'You should have seen your face as that outlaw charged towards you!'

'I was concentrating. I've told you before that marksmanship was never my strong point.'

'You were petrified.'

'True.'

'But you still rescued me?'

'True. I'm a natural hero.'

'No, you're not – and that's why I love you. You're just a man who does his best and tries to be honourable. That is rare.'

'Despite my conceit – and you may find this hard to believe – I get very uncomfortable when faced with compliments.'

'But I want to say what I feel, it's important to me. You are the first man I ever really felt comfortable with as a woman. You brought me to life. I may die during this siege, but I want you to know that it has been worth it.'

'Don't talk about dying. Look at the stars. Feel the night. It's beautiful, isn't it?'

'Yes, it is. Why don't you take me back to the Keep and than I can show you how actions speak louder than words?'

'Why don't I just do that!'

They made love without passion, but gently, lovingly and fell asleep watching the stars through the bedroom window.

The Nadir captain, Ogasi, urged his men on, baying the war chant of Ulric's Wolfshead tribe and smashing his axe into the face of a tall defender. The man's hands scrabbled at the wound as he fell back. The hideous battle song carried them forward, cleaving the ranks and gaining a foothold on the grass beyond.

But, as always, Deathwalker and the white templars rallied the defenders.

Ogasi's hatred gave him power as he cut left and right trying to force his way towards the old man. A sword cut his brow and he staggered momentarily, recovering to disembowel the swordsman. On the left the line was being pushed back, but on the right it was sweeping out like the horn of a bull.

The powerful Nadir wanted to scream his triumph to the skies.

At last they had them!

But again the Drenai rallied. Pushing himself back into the throng in order to wipe away the blood from his eyes, Ogasi watched the tall Drenai and his sword-maiden block the horn as it swung. Leading maybe twenty warriors, the tall man in the silver breastplate and blue cape seemed to have gone mad. His laughter sang out over the Nadir chant and men fell back before him.

His baresark rage carried him deep among the tribesmen, and he used no defence. His red-drenched sword-blade sliced, hammered and cut into their ranks. Beside him the woman ducked and parried, protecting his left, her own slender blade every bit as deadly.

Slowly the horn collapsed in upon itself and Ogasi found himself being drawn back to the battlements. He tripped over the body of a Drenai archer who was still clutching his bow. Kneeling, Ogasi dragged it from the dead hand and pulled a black-shafted arrow from the quiver. Leaping lightly to the battlements, he strained for sight of Deathwalker, but the old man was at the centre and obscured by Nadir bodies. Not so the tall baresarker – men were scattering before him. Ogasi notched the arrow to the string, drew, aimed and with a whispered curse let fly.

The shaft skinned Rek's forearm – and flew on.

Virae turned, seeking Rek, and the shaft punched through her mail-shirt to bury itself below her right breast. She grunted at the impact, staggered and half-fell. A Nadir warrior broke through the line, racing towards her.

Gritting her teeth she drew herself upright, blocked his wild attack and opened his jugular with a back-hand cut.

'Rek!' she called, panic welling within her as her lungs began to bubble, absorbing the arterial blood. But he could not hear her. Pain erupted and she fell, twisting her body away from the arrow so as not to drive it deeper.

Serbitar ran to her side, lifting her head.

'Damn!' she said. 'I'm dying!'

He touched her hand and immediately the pain vanished.

'Thank you, friend! Where's Rek?'

'He is baresark, Virae. I could not reach him now.'

'Oh, gods! Listen to me – don't let him be alone for a while after . . . you know. He is a great romantic fool, and I think he might do something silly. You understand?'

'I understand. I will stay with him.'

'No, not you. Send Druss – he is older and Rek worships him.' She turned her eyes to the sky. A solitary storm cloud floated there, lost and angry. 'He warned me to wear a breastplate – but it's so damned heavy.' The cloud seemed larger now – she tried to mention it to Serbitar, but the cloud loomed and the darkness engulfed her.

Rek stood at the balcony window, gripping the rail, tears streaming from his eyes and uncontrollable sobs bursting through gritted teeth. Behind him lay Virae, still, cold and at peace. Her face was white, her breast red from the arrow wound which had pierced a lung. The blood had stopped flowing now.

Shuddering breaths filled Rek's lungs as he fought to control his grief. Blood dripped from a forgotten wound in his forearm. He rubbed his eyes and turned back to the bed; sitting beside her he lifted her arm and felt for a pulse, but there was nothing.

'Virae!' he said softly. 'Come back. Come back. Listen. I love you! You're the one.' He leaned over her, watching her face. A tear appeared there, then another . . . But they were his own. He lifted her head and cradled it in his arms. 'Wait for me,' he whispered. 'I'm coming.' He fumbled at his belt, pulling the Lentrian dagger from its sheath, and held it to his wrist.

'Put it down, boy,' said Druss from the doorway. 'It would be meaningless.'

'Get out!' shouted Rek. 'Leave me.'

'She's gone, lad. Cover her.'

'Cover her? Cover my Virae! No! No, I can't. Oh gods in Missael, I can't just cover her face.'

'I had to once,' said the old man as Rek slumped forward, tears stinging his eyes and silent sobs racking his frame. 'My woman died. You are not the only one to face death.'

For a long while Druss stood silently in the doorway, his heart aching. Then he pushed the door shut and walked into the room.

'Leave her for a while and talk to me, boy,' he said, taking Rek by the arm. 'Here by the window. Tell me again how you met.'

And Rek told him of the attack in the forest, the killing of Reinard, the ride to the Temple and the journey to Delnoch.

'Druss!'

'Yes.'

'I don't think I can live with this.'

'I have known men who couldn't. But there is no need to cut your wrists. There's a horde of tribesmen out here who will do it for you gladly.'

'I don't care about them any more – they can have the damned place. I wish I had never come here.'

'I know,' said Druss, gently. 'I spoke to Virae yesterday in the hospital. She told me she loved you. She said . . .'

'I don't want to hear it.'

'Yes you do, because it's a memory you can hold. And it keeps her alive in your mind. She said that if she died, it would be worth it just to have met you. She worshipped you, Rek. She told me of the day you stood by her against Reinard and all his men – she was so proud of you. I was too when I heard about it. You had something, boy, that few men ever possess.'

'And now I've lost it.'

'But you *had* it! That can never be taken away from you. Her only regret was she was never really able to tell you how she felt.'

'Oh, she told me – it didn't need words. What happened to you when your wife died? How did it feel?'

'I don't think I need to tell you. You know how I felt. And don't think it's any easier after thirty years. If anything, it becomes harder. Now, Serbitar is waiting to see you in the Hall. He says it's important.'

'Nothing is important any more. Druss, will you cover her face? I couldn't bear to do it.'

'Yes. Then you must see the albino. He has something for you.'

Serbitar was waiting at the bottom of the stairs as Rek slowly descended to the main Hall. The albino wore full armour and helm topped with white horse-hair. The visor was down, shielding his eyes. He looked, Rek thought, like a silver statue. Only his hands were bare and these were white as polished ivory.

'You wanted me?' said Rek.

'Follow me,' said Serbitar. Turning on his heel, he strode from the Hall towards the spiral stone stairwell leading to the dungeons below the Keep. Rek had been ready to refuse any request, but now he was forced to follow and his anger grew. The albino stopped at the top of the stairs and removed a flaming torch from a copper wall bracket.

'Where are we going?' asked Rek.

'Follow me,' repeated Serbitar.

Slowly and carefully the two men descended the cracked, worn steps until at last they reached the first level of dungeons. Long disused, the hallway glittered with water-sodden cobwebs and wet moss-covered arches. Serbitar moved on until they reached an oak door, a rusty bolt holding it fast. He struggled with the bolt for some moments, finally working it free, then both men had to haul on the door before it creaked and groaned and opened. Another stairwell beyond yawned dark before them.

Once again Serbitar started down. The steps ended in a long corridor, ankle-deep in water. They waded through to a final door, shaped like an oak-leaf and bearing a gold plaque with inscribed lettering in the Elder tongue.

'What does it say?' asked Rek.

'It says: "To the worthy – welcome. Herein lies Egel's secret, and the soul of the Earl of Bronze".'

'What does it mean?'

Serbitar tried the door handle but the door was locked, seemingly from within since no bolt, chain, or keyhole could be seen.

'Do we break it down?' said Rek.

'No. You open it.'

'It is locked. Is this a game?'

'Try it.'

Rek turned the handle gently and the door swung open without a sound. Soft lights sprang up within the room, glowing globes of glass set in the recesses of the walls. The room was dry, though now the water from the corridor outside flowed in and spread across the richly carpeted floor.

At the centre of the room, on a wooden stand, was a suit of armour unlike anything Rek had ever seen. It was wonderfully crafted in bronze, the overlapping scales of metal glittering in the light. The breastplate carried a bronze eagle, with wings flaring out over the chest and up to the shoulders. Atop this was a helmet, winged and crested with an eagle's head. Gauntlets there were, scaled and hinged, and greaves. Upon the table before the armour lay a bronze-ringed mail-shirt lined with softest leather, and mail leggings with bronze hinged kneecaps. But above all, Rek was drawn to the sword encased in a block of solid crystal. The blade was golden and over two feet in length; the hilt double-handed, the guard a pair of flaring wings.

'It is the armour of Egel, the first Earl of Bronze,' said Serbitar.

'Why was it allowed to lie here?'

'No one could open the door,' answered the albino.

'It was not locked,' said Rek.

'Not to you.'

'What does that mean?'

'The meaning is clear: you and no other were meant to open the door.'

'I can't believe that.'

'Shall I fetch you the sword?' asked Serbitar.

'If you wish.'

Serbitar walked to the crystal cube, drew his own sword and hammered at the block. Nothing happened. His blade clanged back into the air, leaving no mark upon the crystal.

'You try,' said Serbitar.

'May I borrow your sword?'

'Just reach for the hilt.'

Rek moved forward and lowered his hand to the crystal, waiting for the cold touch of glass which never came. His hand sank into the block, his fingers curling round the hilt. Effortlessly he drew the blade forth.

'Is it a trick?' he asked.

'Probably. But it is none of mine. Look!' The albino put his hands on the now empty crystal and heaved himself up upon it. 'Pass your hands below me,' he said.

467

Rek obeyed – for him the crystal did not exist.

'What does it mean?'

'I do not know, my friend. Truly I do not.'

'Then how did you know it was here?'

'That is even more difficult to explain. Do you remember that day in the grove when I could not be awakened?'

'Yes.'

'Well, I travelled far across the planet, and even beyond, but in my travels I breasted the currents of time and I visited Delnoch. It was night and I saw myself leading you through the hall and down to this room. I saw you take the sword and I heard you ask the question you have just asked. And then I heard my answer.'

'So, at this moment you are hovering above us listening?'

'Yes.'

'I know you well enough to believe you, but answer me this: that may explain how you are here now with me, but how did the first Serbitar know the armour was here?'

'I genuinely cannot explain it, Rek. It is like looking into the reflection of a mirror, and watching it go on and on into infinity. But I have found in my studies that often there is more to this life than we reckon with.'

'Meaning?'

'There is the power of the Source.'

'I am in no mood for religion.'

'Then let us instead say that all those centuries ago, Egel looked into the future and saw this invasion, so he left his armour here, guarded by magic which only you – as the Earl – could break.'

'Is your spirit image still observing us?'

'Yes.'

'Does it know of my loss?'

'Yes.'

'Then you knew she would die?'

'Yes.'

'Why did you not tell me?'

'It would have been a waste of joy.'

'What does that mean?' said Rek, anger building inside him and pushing away the grief.

'It means that were you a farmer anticipating long life, I might have warned you – to prepare you. But you are not; you are fighting a savage horde and your life is at risk every day. As was Virae's. You knew that she might die. Had I told you this was certain, not only would it have gained you nothing, but also robbed you of the joy you had.'

'I could have saved her.'

'No, you could not.'

'I don't believe that.'

'Why would I lie? Why would I wish her dead?'

Rek did not answer. The word 'dead' entered his heart and crushed his soul. Tears welled in him again and he fought them back, concentrating on the armour.

'I will wear that tomorrow,' he said through gritted teeth. 'I will wear it and die.'

'Perhaps,' answered the albino.

26

The dawn was clear, the air fresh and sweet as two thousand Drenai warriors prepared for the assault on Kania. Below them the Nadir shaman were moving through the ranks of tribesmen, sprinkling the blood of chickens and sheep on the bared blades which the warriors held before them.

Then the Nadir massed and a great swelling chant came from thousands of throats as the horde moved forward, bearing ladders, knotted ropes and grappling-irons. Rek watched from the centre of the line. He lifted the bronze helm and placed it over his head, buckling the chin-strap. To his left was Serbitar, to his right Menahem. Others of The Thirty were spread along the wall.

And the carnage began.

Three assaults were turned back before the Nadir gained a foothold on the battlements. And this was short-lived. Some two-score tribesmen breached the defence, only to find themselves faced with a madman in bronze and two silver ghosts who strode among them dealing death. There was no defence against these men, and the bronze devil's sword could cut through any shield or armour; men died under that terrible blade screaming as if their souls were ablaze. That night the Nadir captains carried their reports to the tent of Ulric and the talk was all of the new force upon the battlements. Even the legendary Druss seemed more human – laughing as he did in the face of Nadir swords – than this golden machine of destruction.

'We felt like dogs being beaten from his path with a stick,' muttered one man. 'Or weaponless children being thrust aside by an elder.'

Ulric was troubled and, though he lifted their spirits at last by pointing out again and again that it was merely a man in bronze armour, after the captains had left he summoned the ancient shaman, Nosta Khan, to his tent. Squatting before a blazing brazier of coals the old man listened to his warlord, nodding the while. At last he bowed and closed his eyes.

Rek was asleep, exhausted by battle and sorrow. The nightmare came slowly, enveloping him like black smoke. His dream eyes opened and before him was a cave mouth, black and terrible. Fear emanated from it like a tangible force. Behind him was a pit, stretching down into the fiery bowels of the earth, from which came strange sounds, whimpers and screams. In his hand was no sword, upon his body no armour. A slithering sound came from the pit and Rek turned to see oozing up from it a gigantic worm, slime-covered and putrescent. The stench made him reel back. The mouth of the worm was huge and could swallow a man with ease; around it were triple rows of pointed fangs and lodged between one set was the arm of a man, bloody and broken. Rek backed towards the cave mouth, but a hissing made him spin round. From the blackness of the cave came a spider, its giant maw dripping poison. Within its mouth was a face, green and shimmering and from the mouth of the face flowed words of power. As each word sounded Rek grew weaker, until he could hardly stand.

'Are you just going to stand there all day?' said a voice.

Rek turned to see Virae. By his side, dressed in a flowing gown of white. She smiled at him.

'You're back!' he said, reaching out for her.

'No time for that, you fool! Here! Take your sword.' Her arms reached towards him and the bronze sword of Egel appeared in her hands. A shadow fell across them as Rek snatched the sword, spinning round to face the worm which was towering above them. The blade swept through three feet of the creature's neck as the mouth descended and green gore spouted from the wound. Rek struck again and again until the creature, almost cut in two, flopped backwards into the pit.

'The spider!' yelled Virae and he spun once more. The beast was upon him, its huge mouth mere paces away. Rek hurled his sword into the gaping maw and it flew like an arrow to split the green face within like a melon. The spider reared into the air and toppled backwards. A breeze blew up, and the beast became black smoke which drifted into the air and then was gone.

'I suppose you would have gone on standing there if I hadn't come along?' said Virae.

'I think so,' answered Rek.

'You fool,' she said, smiling and he moved forward tentatively, holding out his arms.

'Can I touch you?' he asked.

'An odd request for a husband to make.'

'You won't disappear?'

Her smile faded. 'Not yet, my love.'

His arms crushed her to him, tears spilling from his eyes. 'I thought you were gone for ever. I thought I would never see you again.'

For a while they said nothing, but merely stood together embracing.

Finally she gently pushed him away. 'You must go back,' she said.

'Back?'

'To Delnoch. You are needed there.'

'I need you more than I need Delnoch. Can we not stay here? Together?'

'No. There is no "here". It doesn't exist. Only you and I are real. Now you must return.'

'I will see you again, won't I?'

'I love you, Rek. I will always love you.'

He awoke with a start, eyes focusing on the stars outside his window. Her face could still be seen, fading against the midnight sky.

'Virae!' he shouted. 'Virae!' The door opened and Serbitar ran to the bedside.

'Rek, you're dreaming. Wake up!'

471

'I am awake. I saw her. She came to me in a dream and rescued me.'

'All right, but she's gone now. Look at me.'

Rek gazed into Serbitar's green eyes. He saw concern there, but this soon faded and the albino smiled.

'You are all right,' said Serbitar. 'Tell me of the dream.'

Afterwards Serbitar questioned him about the face. He wanted every detail that could be remembered. Finally he smiled.

'I think you were the victim of Nosta Khan,' he said. 'But you held him off – a rare feat, Rek.'

'Virae came to me. It was not a dream?'

'I think not. The Source released her for a time.'

'I would like to believe that, I truly would.'

'I think you should. Have you looked for your sword?'

Rek swung out of the bed and padded over to the table where his armour lay. The sword was gone.

'How?' whispered Rek. Serbitar shrugged.

'It will return. Never fear!'

Serbitar lit the candles and stoked the fire to life in the hearth. As he finished a gentle tapping came at the door.

'Come in,' called Rek.

A young officer entered, bearing the sword of Egel.

'I am sorry to disturb you, sir, but I saw the light. One of the sentries found your sword upon the Kania battlements, so I brought it here. I wiped the blood from it first, sir.'

'Blood?'

'Yes, sir. It was covered in blood. Strange how wet it still was.'

'Thank you again.' Rek turned to Serbitar. 'I don't understand.'

In the tent of Ulric the candles flickered. The warlord sat transfixed, staring at the headless body on the floor before him. The sight was one which would haunt him for the rest of his days. One moment the shaman had been sitting in trance before the coals, the next a red line had been drawn across his neck and his head toppled into the fire.

Finally Ulric called his guards to remove the corpse, having first wiped his own sword blade across the bloody neck.

'He angered me,' he told the guards.

The Nadir chieftain left his tent and walked out under the stars. First the legendary axeman, then the warriors in silver. Now a bronze devil whose magic was greater than Nosta Khan. Why did he feel this chill in his soul? Dros was just another fortress. Had he not conquered a hundred such? Once past the gates of Delnoch, the Drenai empire was his. How could they hold against him? The answer was simple – they could not! One man – or devil – in bronze could not stem the Nadir tribes.

But what new surprises does this Dros hold? he asked himself.

He glanced up at the towering walls of Kania.

'You will fall!' he shouted. His voice echoed through the valley. 'I shall bring you down!'

472

In the ghostly light of the pre-dawn, Gilad made his way from the mess canteen with a bowl of hot broth and a chunk of crusty black bread. Slowly he threaded his way through the ranks of men lining the walls until he came to his own position above the blocked postern tunnel. Togi was already there, sitting hunched and round-shouldered with his back to the wall. He nodded as Gilad squatted beside him, then spat on the whetstone in his calloused hand and continued to sharpen his long cavalry sabre.

'Feels like rain,' said Gilad.

'Aye. It'll slow their climbing.'

Togi never initiated a conversation, yet always found a point others would miss. Theirs was a strange friendship: Togi, a taciturn Black Rider of fifteen years' standing and Gilad, a volunteer farmer from the Sentran Plain. Gilad could not remember quite how they had come into contact, for Togi's face was scarcely memorable. He had just grown aware of the man. Men of the Legion had now been spread along the wall, joining other groups. No one had said why, but it was obvious to Gilad: these were the warrior elite, and they added steel to the defence wherever they were placed. Togi was a vicious warrior, who fought silently. No screams or war cries, merely a ruthless economy of movement and rare skill that left Nadir warriors dead or dismembered.

Togi did not know his own age, only that as a youth he had joined the Riders as a stable boy, and later had won his black cloak in the Sathuli wars. He had had a wife years back, but she had left him, taking their son with her. He had no idea where they had gone, and professed not to care overmuch. He had no friends that he spoke of and cared little for authority. Gilad had asked him once what he thought of the Legion officers.

'They fight as well as the rest of us,' he said. 'But it is the only thing we will ever do together.'

'What do you mean?' asked Gilad.

'Nobility. You can fight or die for them, but you will never be one of them. To them we don't exist as people.'

'Druss is accepted,' Gilad pointed out.

'Aye. By me also,' answered Togi, a fierce gleam in his dark eyes. 'That's a man, that one. But it alters nothing. Look at the silver men who fight under the albino – not one of them is from a lowly village. An Earl's son leads them; nobles all of them.'

'Then why do you fight for them, if you hate them so much?'

'Hate them? I don't hate them. It's just the way life is. I don't hate anybody and they don't hate me. We understand each other, that's all. To me the officers are no different from the Nadir; they're both different races. And I fight because that's what I do – I'm a soldier.'

'Did you always want to be a soldier?'

'What else was there?'

Gilad spread his hands. 'Anything you chose.'

'I'd like to have been a king.'

'What kind of king?'

'A bloody tyrant!' answered Togi. He winked but did not smile. He rarely smiled, and when he did it was the merest flicker of movement around the eyes.

The day before, as the Earl of Bronze made his dramatic entrance on to the walls, Gilad had nudged Togi and pointed.

'New armour – it suits him,' said the Rider.

'It looks old,' said Gilad.

Togi merely shrugged. 'So long as it does the job . . .'

That day Togi's sabre had snapped six inches above the hilt. He had hurled himself on the leading Nadir and rammed the broken blade into his neck, snatching the man's short sword and laying about him ferociously. His speed of thought and quicksilver movements amazed Gilad. Later, during a lull between assaults, he had retrieved a second sabre from a dead soldier.

'You fight well,' Gilad had said.

'I'm alive,' answered Togi.

'Is that the same thing?'

'It is on these walls, though good men have fallen. But that is a matter of luck. The bad or the clumsy do not need bad luck to kill them, and even good luck wouldn't save them for long.'

Now Togi stowed the whetstone in his pouch and wiped the curving blade with an oiled cloth. The steel shone blue-white in the gathering light.

Further along the line Druss was chatting to the warriors, lifting their spirits with jests. He made his way towards them and Gilad pushed himself to his feet, but Togi remained where he was. Druss, white beard ruffled by the breeze, stopped and spoke quietly to Gilad.

'I'm glad you stayed,' he said.

'I had nowhere to go,' answered Gilad.

'No. Not many men appreciate that,' said the old warrior. He glanced down at the crouching Rider. 'I see you there, Togi, you young pup. Still alive, then?'

'So far,' he said, looking up.

'Stay that way,' said Druss and he walked on along the line.

'That is a great man,' said Togi. 'A man to die for.'

'You knew him before this?'

'Yes.' Togi would say no more and Gilad was about to press him when the blood-chilling sound of the Nadir war chant signalled the dawn of one more red day.

Below the walls, among the Nadir, was a giant called Nogusha. Ulric's champion for ten years, he had been sent forward with the first wave and with him as personal bodyguards were twenty Wolfshead tribesmen. Their duty was to protect him until he could meet and kill Deathwalker. Strapped to his back was a three-foot sword, the blade six inches wide; by his side were two daggers in twin sheaths. An inch over six feet, Nogusha was the tallest warrior in the Nadir ranks and the most deadly: a veteran of three hundred hand-to-hand contests.

The horde reached the walls. Ropes swirled over the battlements, ladders rattled on the grey stone. Nogusha barked commands to the men around him and three tribesmen climbed above him, the others swarming alongside. The bodies of the first two above him plummeted down to the rocks below, but the third created a space for Nogusha before being hacked to death. Gripping the battlements with one huge hand, Nogusha's sword flashed into the air while on either side of him the bodyguards closed in. The massive sword cleaved a passage as the group formed a wedge driving towards Druss some twenty paces distant. Although the Drenai closed in behind Nogusha's band, blocking the wall, none could approach the giant tribesman. Men died beneath his flashing broadsword. On either side of him his bodyguards were faring less well: one by one they fell until at last only Nogusha still stood. By now he was only paces away from Druss, who turned and saw him, battling alone and soon to fall. Their eyes met and understanding was there instantly. This was a man Druss would be hard put not to recognise: Nogusha the Swordsman, Ulric's executioner, a man whose deeds were the fabric of fresh Nadir legends – a living younger counterpart to Druss himself.

The old man leapt lightly from the ramparts to the grass beyond, where he waited. He made no move to halt the attack on the Nadir warrior. Nogusha saw Druss waiting, slashed a path and jumped clear. Several Drenai warriors made to follow him, but Druss waved them back.

'Well met, Nogusha,' said the old man.

'Well met, Deathwalker.'

'You will not live to collect Ulric's reward,' said Druss. 'There is no way back.'

'All men must die. And this moment for me is as close to paradise as I could wish for. All my life you have been there before me, making my deeds seem shadows.'

Druss nodded solemnly. 'I too have thought of you.'

Nogusha attacked with stunning speed. Druss hammered the sword aside, stepped in and struck a blow of awesome power with his left fist. Nogusha staggered, but recovered swiftly, blocking the downward sweep of Druss's axe. The battle that followed was brief and viciously fought. No matter how high the skill, a contest between an axeman and a swordsman could never last long. Nogusha feinted to the left, then swept his sword up under Druss's guard. With no time for thought, Druss hurled himself under the arcing blade, slamming his shoulder into Nogusha's midriff. As the tribesman was hurled backwards the sword's blade sliced the back of Druss's jerkin, gashing the skin and flesh of his upper back. The old man ignored the sudden pain and threw himself across the body of the fallen swordsman. His left hand clamped over the right wrist of his opponent and Nogusha did likewise.

The struggle was now titanic as each man strained to break the other's grip. Their strength was near identical, and while Druss had the advantage of being above the fallen warrior, and thus in a position to use his weight to bear down, Nogusha was younger and Druss had been cut deep. Blood welled down his back, pooling above the thick leather belt around his jerkin.

'You . . . cannot hold . . . against me,' hissed Nogusha through clenched teeth.

Druss, face purple with effort, did not answer. The man was right – he could feel his strength ebbing. Nogusha's right arm began to lift, the sword blade glinting in the morning sun. Druss' left arm was beginning to shake with the effort and would give out at any moment. Suddenly the old man lifted his head and rammed his forehead down on to Nogusha's helpless face. The man's nose splintered as the edge of his adversary's silver-rimmed helm crashed upon it. Thrice more Druss butted the tribesman and Nogusha began to panic. Already his nose and one cheekbone were smashed. He twisted, released Druss' arm and exploded a mighty punch to his chin, but Druss rode it and hammered Snaga into the man's neck. Blood burst from the wound, and Nogusha ceased to struggle. His eyes met the old man's, but no word was said: Druss had no breath, Nogusha had no vocal chords. The tribesman transferred his gaze to the sky, and died. Druss slowly pulled himself upright; then taking Nogusha by the feet, he dragged him up the short steps to the battlements. Meanwhile the Nadir had fallen back ready for another charge. Druss called two men and ordered them to pass up Nogusha's body, then he climbed on to the ramparts.

'Hold on to my legs, but do not let yourselves be seen,' Druss whispered to the soldiers behind him. In full view of the Nadir massed below, he pulled the body of Nogusha upright in a tight bear-hug, took hold of his neck and groin and, with a mighty effort, raised the huge body above his head. With a heave and a scream he hurled the body out over the walls. But for the men holding him, he would have fallen. They helped him down, their faces anxious.

'Get me to the hospital before I bleed to death,' he whispered.

27

Caessa sat beside the bed, silent but watchful, her eyes never leaving the sleeping Druss. Thirty stitches laced the wound on the axeman's broad back, the line curving alongside the shoulder-blade and over the shoulder itself where the cut was deepest. The old man was asleep, drugged with poppy wine. The blood loss from the wound had been prodigious and he had collapsed on the way to the hospital. Caessa stood by Calvar Syn as the stitches were inserted. She said nothing. Now she merely sat.

She could not understand her fascination for the warrior. Certainly she did not desire him – men had never raised desire in her. Love? Was it love? She had no way of knowing, no terms of reference to gauge her feelings by. Her parents had died horribly when she was seven. Her father, a peaceful placid farmer, had tried to stop raiders from robbing his barn and they had cut him down without a moment's thought. Caessa's mother seized her by the hand and raced for the woods above the cliff. But they were seen and the chase was short. The woman could not carry the child, for she was pregnant. And she would not abandon her. She had fought like a wild-cat, but had been over-powered, abused and slain. All the while the child sat beneath an oak tree, frozen with terror, unable even to scream. A bearded man with foul breath had finally come to her, lifted her brutally by the hair, carried her to the cliff edge and hurled her out over the sea.

She had missed the rocks, though her head was gashed in the fall and her right leg broken. A fisherman saw her plunge and pulled her clear. From that day on she changed.

The laughing child laughed no more, nor danced, nor sang. Sullen she was and vicious she became. Other children would not play with her, and as she grew older she found herself more and more alone. At the age of fifteen she killed her first man, a traveller who had chattered to her by a river's edge, asking directions. She crept into his camp and cut his throat while he slept, sitting beside him to watch him die.

He was the first of many.

The death of men made her cry. In her tears she became alive. For Caessa, to live was the most important single objective of her life. And so men died.

In later years, since her twentieth birthday, Caessa had devised a new method of selecting victims: those who were attracted to her. They would be allowed to sleep with her but later, as they dreamed – perhaps of the pleasures they had enjoyed – she would draw a sharpened blade gently across their throats. She had killed no one since joining Bowman some six months before, for Skultik had become her last refuge.

Yet now she sat beside the bed of an injured man and wished for him to live. Why?

She drew her dagger and pictured its blade drawing across the old man's throat. Usually this death-fantasy made her warm with desire, but now it created a sense of panic. In her mind's eye she saw Druss sitting beside her in a darkened room, a log fire burning in the hearth. His arm was over her shoulder and she was nestling into his chest. She had pictured the scene many times, but now she saw it afresh, for Druss was so large – a giant in her fantasy. And she knew why.

She was seeing him through the eyes of a seven-year-old.

Orrin slipped quietly into the room. He was thinner now, drawn and haggard, yet stronger. An indefinable quality marked his features. Lines of fatigue had aged him, but the change was more subtle – it emanated from the eyes. He had been a soldier, longing to be a warrior; now he was a warrior longing to be anything else. He had seen war and cruelty, death and dismemberment. He had watched the sharp beaks of crows at work on dead men's eyes, and the growth of worms in pus-filled sockets. And he had found himself, and wondered no longer.

'How is he?' he asked Caessa.

'He will recover. But he will not fight for weeks.'

'Then he will not fight again, for we have only days. Prepare him to be moved.'

'He cannot be moved,' she said, turning to look at him for the first time.

'He must be. We are giving up the wall and we draw back tonight. We lost over four hundred men today. Wall Four is only a hundred yards long – we can hold that for days. Get him ready.'

She nodded and rose. 'You are tired too, general,' she said. 'You should rest.'

'I will soon,' he answered, and smiled. The smile sent a shiver down her back. 'We will all rest soon, I think.'

Bearers transferred Druss to a stretcher, lifting him gently and covering him with white blankets against the night cold. With other wounded men they made a convoy to Wall Four where ropes were lowered and the stretchers silently raised. No torches were lit, only the light of the stars bathed the scene. Orrin climbed the last rope and hauled himself over the battlements. A helping hand reached out and pulled him upright – it was Gilad.

'You always seem on hand to help me, Gilad. Not that I'm complaining.'

Gilad smiled. 'With the weight you've lost, general, you would win that race now.'

'Ah, the race! It seems like a different age. What happened to your friend. The one with the axe?'

'He went home.'

'A wise man. Why did you stay?'

Gilad shrugged. He had grown tired of the question.

'It's a nice night, the best yet,' said Orrin. 'Strange, I used to lie in bed at night and watch the stars. They always made me sleepy. Now I have no need of sleep. I feel I'm throwing away life. Do you feel that?'

'No, sir. I sleep like a baby.'

'Good. Well, I'll say goodnight then.'

'Goodnight, sir.'

Orrin walked away slowly, then turned. 'We didn't do too badly, did we?' he said.

'No, sir,' replied Gilad. 'I think the Nadir will remember us without affection.'

'Yes. Goodnight.' He had begun the walk down the short rampart steps when Gilad stepped forward.

'Sir!'

'Yes?'

'I . . . I wanted to say . . . Well, just that I have been proud to serve under you. That's all, sir.'

'Thank you, Gilad. But I am the one who should be proud. Goodnight.'

Togi said nothing as Gilad returned to the wall, but the young officer could feel the Rider's eyes upon him.

'Well, say it,' said Gilad. 'Get it over with.'

'Say what?'

Gilad looked at his friend's blank face and searched his eyes for signs of humour or contempt. Nothing showed. 'I thought you would think . . . I don't know,' he said, lamely.

'The man has shown quality and courage and you told him so. There is no harm in that, although it wasn't your place. In peacetime I'd think you were crawling, currying favour with a comment like that. Not here. There is nothing to gain and he knew that. So it was well said.'

'Thank you,' said Gilad.

'For what?'

'For understanding. You know, I believe he is a great man – greater than Druss perhaps. For he has neither Druss' courage nor Hogun's skill, yet he is still here. Still trying.'

'He'll not last long.'

'None of us will,' said Gilad.

'No, but he won't see the last day. He's too tired – up here he's too tired.' Togi tapped his temple.

'I think you're wrong.'

'No, you don't. That's why you spoke to him as you did. You sensed it too.'

Druss floated on an ocean of pain, burning, searing his body. His jaw clamped shut, teeth grinding against the insistent agony creeping like slow acid through his back. Words were almost impossible, hissed through gritted teeth, and the faces of those around his bed shivered and swam, blurring beyond recognition.

He became unconscious, but the pain followed him down into the depths of dreams where gaunt, shadow-haunted landscapes surrounded him and jagged mountains reared black against a grey, brooding sky. Druss lay on the mountain, unable to move against the pain, his eyes focused on a small grove of lightning-blasted trees some twenty paces from where he lay. Standing before them was a man dressed in black. He was lean, and his eyes were dark. He moved forward and sat on a boulder, gazing down at the axeman.

'So, it comes to this,' he said. The voice had a hollow ring, like wind whistling through a cavern.

'I shall recover,' hissed Druss, blinking away the sweat dripping into his eyes.

'Not from this,' said the man. 'You should be dead now.'

'I have been cut before.'

'Ah, but the blade was poisoned – green sap from the northern marches. Now you are riddled with gangrene.'

'No! I will die with my axe in my hand.'

'Think you so? I have waited for you, Druss, through these many years. I have watched the legions of travellers cross the dark river at your hands. And I have watched you. Your pride is colossal, your conceit immense. You have tasted glory and prized your strength above all else. Now you will die. No axe. No glory. Never to cross the dark river to the Forever Halls. There is satisfaction for me in this, can you understand that? Can you comprehend it?'

'No. Why do you hate me?'

'Why? Because you conquer fear. And because your life mocks me. It is not enough that you die. All men die, peasants and kings – all are mine, come the end. But you, Druss, you are special. Were you to die as you desire, you would mock me still. So for you, I have devised this exquisite torture.

'You should by now be dead from your wound. But I have not yet claimed you. And now the pain will grow more intense. You will writhe . . . You will scream . . . Finally your mind will snap and you will beg. *Beg* for me. And I shall come and take you by the hand and you will be mine. Men's last memories of you will be of a mewling, weeping wreck.They will despise you and your legend will be tainted at the last.'

Druss forced his massive arms beneath him and struggled to rise. But the pain drove him down once more, forcing a groan through clenched teeth.

'That's it, axeman. Struggle on. Try harder. You should have stayed on your mountain and enjoyed your dotage. Vain man! You could not resist the call of blood. Suffer – and bring me joy.'

In the makeshift hospital Calvar Syn lifted the hot towels from Druss' bare back, replacing them swiftly as the stench filled the room. Serbitar stepped forward and also examined the wound.

'It is hopeless,' said Calvar Syn, rubbing his hand over the polished dome of his skull. 'Why is he still alive?'

'I don't know,' said the albino softly. 'Caessa, has he spoken?'

The girl glanced up from her bedside chair, her eyes dulled with fatigue. She shook her head. The door opened and Rek moved inside silently. He lifted his eyebrows in a question to the surgeon, but Calvar Syn shook his head.

'Why?' asked Rek. 'The wound was no worse than he has had before.'

'Gangrene. The wound will not close and the poison has spread through his body. He cannot be saved. All the experience I have gained in forty years says he should now be dead. His body is putrefying at an amazing rate.'

'He is a tough old man. How long can he last?'

'He will not live to see tomorrow,' answered the surgeon.

'How goes it on the wall?' asked Serbitar. Rek shrugged. His armour was bloody, his eyes tired.

'We are holding for the moment, but they are in the tunnel beneath us and the gate will not stand. It's a damned shame we had no time to fill the gate tunnel. I think they will be through before dusk. They have already burst a postern gate, but Hogun and a few others are holding the stairwell.

'That's why I came, doctor. I'm afraid you will have to prepare once more for evacuation. From now on the hospital will be at the Keep. How soon can you move?'

'How can I say? Men are being brought in all the time.'

'Begin your preparations, anyway. Those who are too badly hurt to be moved must be despatched.'

'What?' shouted the surgeon. 'Murdered, you mean?'

'Exactly so. Move those who can move. The others . . . how do you think the Nadir will treat them?'

'I will move everyone, regardless. If they die during the evacuation, it will still be better than knifing them in their beds.'

'Then begin now. We are wasting time,' said Rek.

On the wall Gilad and Togi joined Hogun at the postern stair-well. The stairs were littered with corpses, but more Nadir warriors rounded the bend in the spiral and scrambled over the bodies. Hogun stepped forward, blocking a thrust, and disembowelled the leading man. He fell, tripping the warrior behind him. Togi slashed a two-handed stroke through the second man's neck as he fell in turn. Two more warriors advanced, holding round ox-hide shields before them. Behind, others pushed forward.

'It's like holding back the sea with a bucket,' yelled Togi.

Above them the Nadir gained a foothold on the ramparts, driving a wedge into the Drenai formation. Orrin saw the danger and raced forward with fifty men of the new Group Karnak. Below them to the right the battering ram thundered against the giant gates of oak and bronze. So far the gates held, but ominous cracks had appeared beneath the crossed centre beams, and the wood groaned under the impact.

Orrin battled his way to the Nadir wedge, using his sword two-handed, cutting and slashing with no attempt at defence. Beside him a Drenai warrior fell, his throat gashed. Orrin back-handed a cut to the attacker's face, then blocked a blow from his left.

It was three hours to dusk.

Bowman knelt on the grass behind the battlements, three quivers of arrows before him on the ground. Coolly he notched shaft to his bow, drew and let fly. A man to the left of Orrin fell, the arrow piercing his temple. Then a second Nadir fell to Orrin's sword, before another arrow downed a third. The wedge was falling apart as the Drenai hacked their way forward.

At the stairwell Togi was bandaging a long gash in his forearm while a fresh squad of Legion warriors held the entrance. Gilad leaned against a boulder, wiping sweat from his brow.

'A long day,' he said.

'It will be longer yet,' muttered Togi. 'They can sense how close they are to taking the wall.'

'Yes. How is the arm?'

'All right,' answered Togi. 'Where now?'

'Hogun said to fill in where we're needed.'

'That could be anywhere. I'm for the gate – coming?'

'Why not?' answered Gilad, smiling.

Rek and Serbitar cleared a section of battlements, then raced to join Orrin and his group. All along the wall the defensive line was bending. But it held.

'If we can hold out until they re-form for another charge, we may yet have time to get everyone back behind Valteri,' yelled Orrin as Rek fought his way alongside.

For another hour the battle raged, then the huge bronze head of the battering ram breached the timbers of the gate. The great beam at the centre sagged as a crack appeared, then with a tearing groan it slid from its sockets. The ram was withdrawn slowly, to clear the way for the fighting men beyond.

Gilad sent a runner to the battlements to inform Rek, or either of the Gans, then he drew his sword and waited with fifty others to hold the entrance.

As he rocked his head from side to side to ease the aching muscles of his shoulders, he glanced at Togi. The man was smiling.

'What is so funny?'

'My own stupidity,' answered Togi. 'I suggested the gates to get a bit of rest. Now I'm going to encounter death.'

Gilad said nothing. Death! His friend was right – there would be no escape to Wall Five for the men at the gate. He felt the urge to turn and run and suppressed it. What did it matter anyway? He'd seen enough of death in the last few weeks. And if he survived, what would he do, where would he go? Back to the farm and a dull wife? Grow old somewhere, toothless and senile, telling endlessly boring stories of his youth and courage.

'Great gods!' said Togi suddenly. 'Just look at that!'

Gilad turned. Coming slowly towards them across the grass was Druss, leaning on the girl outlaw, Caessa. He staggered and almost fell, but she held him. As they came closer Gilad swallowed back the horror he felt. The old man's face had a sunken look; it was pallid and tinged with blue, like a two-day-old corpse. The men stepped aside as Caessa steered Druss to the centre of the line, then she drew a short sword and stood with him.

The gates opened and the Nadir poured through. Druss, with great effort, drew Snaga. He could hardly see through the mists of pain and each step had been a new agony as the girl brought him forward. She had dressed him carefully, crying all the while, then helped him to his feet. He himself had begun to weep, for the pain was unbearable.

'I can't make it,' he had whimpered.

'You can,' she told him. '*You must.*'

'The pain . . .'

'You have had pain before. Fight through it.'

'I cannot. I'm finished.'

'Listen to me, damn you! You are Druss the Legend, and men are dying out there. One last time, Druss. *Please*. You mustn't give up like an ordinary man. *You are Druss*. You can do it. Stop them. You must stop them. My mother's out there!'

His vision cleared momentarily and he saw her madness. He could not understand it, for he knew nothing of her life, but he sensed her need. With an effort that tore an agonising scream from him, he bunched his legs beneath him and stood, clamping a huge hand to a shelf on the wall to hold himself upright. The pain grew, but he was angry now and used the pain to spur himself on.

Druss took a deep breath. 'Come on, little Caessa, let's find your mother,' he said. 'But you will have to help me; I'm a little unsteady.'

The Nadir swept through the gates and on to the waiting blades of the Drenai. Above them, Rek received word of the calamity. For the moment the attack on the wall had ceased as men massed below in the gate tunnel.

'Back!' he shouted. 'Get to Wall Five.' Men began to run across the grass, through the deserted streets of outer Delnoch, streets which Druss had cleared of people so many days before. There would be no killing ground now between walls, for the buildings still stood, haunted and empty.

Warriors raced for the transient security of Wall Five, giving no thought to the rearguard at the broken gate. Gilad did not blame them and, strangely, had no wish to be with them.

Only Orrin, as he ran, noticed the rearguard. He turned to join them, but Serbitar was beside him, grasping his arm. 'No,' he said. 'It would be useless.'

They ran on. Behind them the Nadir breasted the wall and raced in pursuit.

In the gateway the carnage continued. Druss, fighting from memory, hacked and slashed at the advancing warriors. Togi died as a short lance hammered into his chest; Gilad did not see him fall. For Caessa the scene was different: there were ten raiders and Druss was battling against them all. Each time he killed a man she smiled. Eight . . . Nine . . .

The last of the raiders, a man she could never forget for he had killed her mother, came forward. He had a gold earring and a scar running from eyebrow to chin. Lifting her sword she hurled herself forward, ramming the blade into his belly. The squat Nadir toppled backwards, pulling the girl with him. A knife sliced between her shoulder blades. But she did not feel it. The raiders were all dead, and for the first time since childhood she was safe. Her mother would come out of the trees now and take her

483

home, and Druss would be given a huge meal and they would laugh. And she would sing for him. She would . . .

Only seven men still stood around Druss and the Nadir surrounded them. A lance thrust out suddenly, crushing Druss' ribs and piercing a lung. Snaga lashed back a murderous reply, cutting the lancer's arm from his shoulder. As he fell Gilad sliced his throat. Then Gilad himself fell, pierced through the back, and Druss stood alone. The Nadir fell back as one of their captains moved forward.

'Remember me, Deathwalker?' he said.

Druss tore the lance from his side, hurling it away from him.

'I remember you, lard-belly. The herald!'

'You said you would have my soul, yet I stand here and you die. What think you of that?'

Suddenly Druss lifted his arm to fling Snaga forward and the blade split the herald's head like a pumpkin.

'I think you talk too much,' said Druss. He toppled to his knees and looked down to see the lifeblood flowing from him. Beside him Gilad was dying, but his eyes were open. 'It was good to be alive, wasn't it, boy?'

Around them the Nadir stood, but no move was made against them. Druss looked up and pointed at a warrior.

'You, boy,' he said in guttural dialect, 'fetch my axe.' For a moment the warrior did not move, then he shrugged and pulled Snaga from the head of the herald. 'Bring it here,' ordered Druss. As the young soldier advanced, Druss could see that he intended to kill him with his own weapon, but a voice barked out a command and the warrior stiffened. He handed Druss the axe and moved back.

Druss' eyes were misting now and he could not make out the figure looming before him.

'You did well, Deathwalker,' said Ulric. 'Now you can rest.'

'If I had just one more ounce of strength I would cut you down,' muttered Druss, struggling with his axe. But the weight was too great.

'I know that. I did not know Nogusha carried poison on his blade. Will you believe that?'

Druss' head bowed, and he toppled forward.

Druss the Legend was dead.

28

Six hundred Drenai warriors watched silently as the Nadir gathered about the body of Druss and lifted it gently, bearing it back through the gates he had striven to hold. Ulric was the last man to pass the portals. In the shadow of the broken timbers he turned, his violet eyes scanning the men at the wall, stopping at last to rest on a figure of bronze. Ulric lifted his hand as if in greeting, then slowly pointed at Rek. The message was clear enough.

First the Legend, now the Earl.

Rek made no reply, but merely watched as the Nadir warlord strode into the shadows of the gate and out of sight.

'He died hard,' said Hogun as Rek turned and sat back on the ramparts, lifting his helm visor.

'What did you expect?' asked Rek, rubbing tired eyes with weary fingers. 'He lived hard.'

'We will follow him soon,' said Hogun. 'There's not a day's fighting left in the men we have. The city is deserted now: even the camp baker has left.'

'What of the Council?' asked Rek.

'Gone, all of them. Bricklyn should be back in the next day or two with words from Abalayn. I think he will be bringing his message direct to Ulric – he'll be based in the Keep by then.'

Rek did not answer – there was no need. It was true: the battle was over. Only the massacre remained.

Serbitar, Vintar and Menahem approached silently, their white cloaks tattered and bloody. But there was no mark of wounds upon them. Serbitar bowed.

'The end is come,' he said. 'What are your orders?'

Rek shrugged. 'What would you have me say?'

'We could fall back to the Keep,' offered Serbitar, 'but we have not enough men to hold even that.'

'Then we will die here,' said Rek. 'One place is as good as another.'

'Truly,' said Vintar, gently. 'But I think we have a few hours' grace.'

'Why?' asked Hogun, loosening the bronze brooch at his shoulder and removing his cloak.

'I think the Nadir will not attack again today. Today they have slain a mighty man, a legend even among their ranks. They will feast and celebrate. Tomorrow, when we die, they will feast again.'

Rek removed his helm, welcoming the cool breeze on his sweat-drenched head. Overhead the sky was clear and blue, the sun golden. He drew in a deep breath of clear mountain air, feeling its power soaking into tired limbs. His mind flew back to days of joy with Horeb in the inn at Drenan – long-gone days, never to be revisited. He swore aloud, then laughed.

'If they don't attack, we should have a party of our own,' he said. 'Gods, a man can die but once in a lifetime! Surely it's worth celebrating?' Hogun grinned and shook his head but Bowman, who had approached unnoticed, clapped Rek on the shoulder.

'Now that is my kind of language,' he said. 'But why not do it properly, go the whole way?'

'The whole way?' asked Rek.

'We could join the Nadir party,' said Bowman. 'Then they would have to buy the drinks.'

'There's some truth in that, Earl of Bronze,' said Serbitar. 'Shall we join them?'

'Have you gone mad?' said Rek, looking from one to the other.

'As you said, Rek, we only die once,' suggested Bowman. 'We have nothing to lose. Anyway, we should be protected by the Nadir laws of hospitality.'

'This is insanity!' said Rek. 'You're not serious?'

'Yes, I am,' said Bowman. 'I think I would like to pay my last respects to Druss. And it will make a grand exit for Nadir poets to sing about in later years. Drenai poets are almost bound to pick it up too. I like the idea – it has a certain poetic beauty to it. Dining in the dragon's lair.'

'Damn it, I'm with you then,' said Rek. 'Though I think my mind must be unhinged. When should we leave?'

Ulric's ebony throne had been set outside his tent, and the Nadir warlord sat upon it dressed in eastern robes of gold thread upon silk. Upon his head was the goatskin-fringed crown of the Wolfshead tribe, and his black hair was braided after the fashion of the Ventrian kings. Around him, in a vast circle many thousands strong, sat his captains; beyond them were many other circles of men. At the centre of each circle Nadir women danced in a frenzy of motion, in tune to the rippling rhythms of a hundred drums. In the circle of captains, the women danced around a funeral pyre ten feet high on which lay Druss the Legend, arms crossed and axe upon his chest.

Outside the circles countless fires blazed and the smell of burning meat filled the air. Everywhere camp women carried yokes bearing buckets of Lyrrd, an alcohol brewed from goat's milk. Ulric himself drank Lentrian Red in honour of Druss. He didn't like the drink; it was too thin and watery for a man reared on the more potent of liquors brewed on the northern steppes. But he drank it anyway. It would be bad manners to do less, for the spirit of Druss had been invited among them: a spare goblet was filled to the brim beside Ulric's own, and a second throne had been set to the right of the Nadir warlord.

Ulric stared moodily over the rim of his goblet, focusing his gaze on the body atop the pyre.

'It was a good time to die, old man,' he said softly. 'You will be remembered in our songs, and men will talk of you around our camp-fires for generations to come.'

The moon shone brightly in a cloudless sky, and the stars gleamed like distant candles. Ulric sat back and gazed into eternity. Why this black mood? What was the weight his soul carried? Rarely before had he felt this way, and certainly never on the eve of such a victory.

Why?

His gaze returned to the body of the axeman.

'You have done this to me, Deathwalker,' he said. 'For your heroics have made me the dark shadow.'

In all legends, Ulric knew, there were bright heroes and dark, dark evil. It was the very fabric of each tale.

'I am not evil,' he said. 'I am a warrior born, with a people to protect and a nation to build.' He swallowed another mouthful of Lentrian and refilled his goblet.

'My Lord, is something wrong?' asked his carle-captain, Ogasi, the thickset steppe rider who had slain Virae.

'He accuses me,' said Ulric, pointing to the body.

'Shall we light the pyre?'

Ulric shook his head. 'Not until midnight. The Gates must be open when he arrives.'

'You do him great honour, Lord. Why then does he accuse you?'

'With his death. Nogusha carried a poisoned blade – I had the story from his tent servant.'

'That was not at your command, Lord. I was there.'

'Does it matter? Am I no longer responsible for those who serve me? I have tainted my legend in order to end his. A dark, dark deed, Ulric Wolfshead.'

'He would have died tomorrow anyway,' said Ogasi. 'He lost only a day.'

'Ask yourself, Ogasi, what that day meant. Men like Deathwalker come perhaps once in twenty lifetimes. They are rare. So what is that day worth to ordinary men? A year? Ten years? A lifetime? Did you see him die?'

'I did, Lord.'

'And will you forget it?'

'No, Lord.'

'Why not? You have seen brave men die before.'

'He was special,' said Ogasi. 'Even when he fell at the last, I thought he would rise. Even now some of the men cast fearful glances at his pyre, expecting to see him stand again.'

'How could he have stood against us?' asked Ulric. 'His face was blue with gangrene. His heart should have stopped long since. And the pain . . .'

Ogasi shrugged. 'While men compete in war, there will be warriors. While there are warriors, there will be princes among warriors. Among the princes will be kings, and among the kings an emperor. You said it yourself, my Lord. Such as he come once in twenty lifetimes. You would expect him to die in his bed?'

'No. I had thought to let his name die. Soon I will control the mightiest empire known to men. History will *be* as I write it.

'I could erase him from the memory of men, or worse still sully his name until his legend reeks. But I shall not. I will have a book written about his life and men shall know how he thwarted me.'

'I would expect nothing less from Ulric,' said Ogasi, his dark eyes gleaming in the firelight.

'Ah, but then you know me, my friend. There are others among the Drenai who will be expecting me to dine on Druss' mighty heart. Eater of Babies, the Plague That Walks, the Barbarian of Gulgothir.'

'Names you yourself invented, my Lord, I think.'

'True. But then a leader must know all the weapons of war. And there are many which owe nothing to the lance and sword, the bow and the sling. The Word steals men's souls, while the sword kills only their bodies. Men see me and know fear – it is a potent device.'

'Some weapons turn on their users, my Lord. I have . . .' The man suddenly stuttered to silence.

'Speak, Ogasi! What ails you?'

'The Drenai, my Lord! They are in the camp!' said Ogasi, his eyes wide in disbelief. Ulric spun in his chair. Everywhere the circles were breaking as men stood to watch the Earl of Bronze striding towards the Lord of the Nadir.

Behind him in ranks came sixteen men in silver armour, and behind them a Legion Gan walking beside a blonde warrior bearing a longbow.

The drums petered to silence and all eyes swung from the Drenai group to the seated warlord. Ulric's eyes narrowed as he saw that the men were armed. Panic welled in his breast but he forced it down, his mind racing. Would they just walk up and slay him? He heard the hiss of Ogasi's blade leaving its scabbard and raised a hand.

'No, my friend. Let them approach.'

'It is madness, Lord,' whispered Ogasi, as the Drenai drew nearer.

'Pour wine for our guests. The time to kill them will come after the feast. Be prepared.'

Ulric gazed down from his raised throne into the grey-blue eyes of the Earl of Bronze. The man had forsaken his helm but otherwise was fully armoured, the great sword of Egel hanging at his side. His companions stood back, awaiting events. There was little sign of tension, though the Legion general Ulric knew as Hogun had his hand resting lightly on his sword hilt and was watching Ogasi keenly.

'Why are you here?' asked Ulric. 'You are not welcome in my camp.'

The Earl looked slowly about him and then returned the gaze of the Nadir warlord.

'It is strange,' he said, 'how a battle can change a man's perspectives. Firstly, I am not in your camp, I am standing on Delnoch ground and that is mine by right – it is you who are on *my* lands. Be that as it may, for tonight you are welcome. As to why I am here? My friends and I have come to bid farewell to Druss the Legend – Deathwalker. Is Nadir hospitality so poor that no refreshment is offered us?'

Ogasi's hand strayed towards his sword once more. The Earl of Bronze did not move.

'If that sword is drawn,' he said softly, 'I will remove his head.'

Ulric waved Ogasi back.

'Do you think to leave here alive?' he asked Rek.

'If I so choose – yes,' replied the Earl.

'And I have no say in this matter?'

'None.'

'Truly? Now you intrigue me. All around you are Nadir bowmen. At my signal, your bright armour will be hidden by black-shafted arrows. And you say I cannot?'

'If you can, then order it,' demanded the Earl. Ulric moved his gaze to the archers. Arrows were ready and many bows were already bent, their iron points glittering in the firelight.

'Why can I not order it?' he asked.

'Why have you not?' countered the Earl.

'Curiosity. What is the real purpose of your visit? Have you come to slay me?'

'No. If I wished, I could have slain you as I killed your shaman: silently, invisibly. Your head would now be a worm-filled shell. There is no duplicity here – I came to honour my friend. Will you offer me hospitality or shall I return to my fortress?'

'Ogasi!' called Ulric.

'My Lord?'

'Fetch refreshments for the Earl and his followers. Order the archers back to their fires and let the entertainment continue.'

'Yes, Lord,' said Ogasi dubiously.

Ulric gestured the Earl to the throne at his side. Rek nodded and turned to Hogun: 'Go and enjoy yourselves. Return for me in an hour.'

Hogun saluted and Rek watched his small group wander off around the camp. He smiled as Bowman leaned over a seated Nadir and lifted a goblet of Lyrrd. The man stared when he saw his drink disappear, then laughed as Bowman drained it without a splutter.

'Damn good, hey?' said the warrior. 'Better than that red vinegar from the south.'

Bowman nodded and pulled a flask from his hip pouch, offering it to the man. Suspicion was evident in the hesitant way the Nadir accepted the flask, but his friends were watching.

Slowly he removed the top, then took a tentative sip, followed by a full-blown swallow.

'This is damn good too,' said the man. 'What is it?'

'They call it Lentrian Fire. Once tasted, never forgotten!'

The man nodded, then moved aside to make a place for Bowman.

'Join us, Longbow. Tonight no war. We talk, yes?'

'Decent of you, old horse. I think I will.'

Seated on the throne, Rek lifted Druss' goblet of Lentrian Red and raised it towards the pyre. Ulric also raised his goblet and both men silently toasted the fallen axeman.

'He was a great man,' said Ulric. 'My father told me tales of him and his lady. Rowena, wasn't it?'

'Yes, he loved her greatly.'

'It is fitting,' said Ulric, 'that such a man should know great love. I am sorry he is gone. It would be a fine thing if war could be conducted as a game where no lives were lost. At the end of a battle combatants could meet – even as we are doing – and drink and talk.'

'Druss would not have had it so,' said the Earl. 'Were this a game where the odds mattered, Dros Delnoch would already be yours. But Druss was a man who could change the odds and make nonsense of logic.'

'Up to a point – for he is dead. But what of you? What manner of man are you, Earl Regnak?'

'Just a man, Lord Ulric – even as you.'

Ulric leaned closer, his chin resting on his hand. 'But then I am not an ordinary man. I have never lost a battle.'

'Nor yet have I.'

'You intrigue me. You appear from nowhere, with no past, married to the dying Earl's daughter. No one has ever heard of you and no man can tell me of your deeds. Yet men die for you, as they would for a beloved king. Who are you?'

'I am the Earl of Bronze.'

'No. That I will not accept.'

'Then what would you have me say?'

'Very well, you are the Earl of Bronze. It matters not. Tomorrow you may return to your grave – you and all those who follow you. You began this battle with ten thousand men; you now boast perhaps seven hundred. You pin your faith on Magnus Woundweaver, but he cannot reach you in time – and even if he did, it would matter not. Look about you. This army is bred on victory. And it grows. I have four armies like this – can I be stopped?'

'Stopping you is not important,' said the Earl. 'It never was.'

'Then what are you doing?'

'We are *trying* to stop you.'

'Is this a riddle which I should understand?'

'Your understanding is not important. It may be that destiny intends you to succeed. It may be that a Nadir empire will prove vastly beneficial to the world. But ask yourself this: were there no army here when you arrived, save Druss alone, would he have opened the gate to you?'

'No. He would have fought and died,' said Ulric.

'But he would not have expected to win. So why would he do it?'

'Now I understand your riddle, Earl. But it saddens me that so many men must die when it is futile to resist. Nevertheless I respect you. I will see that your pyre is as high as that of Druss.'

'Thank you, no. If you do kill me, lay my body in a garden beyond the Keep. There is already a grave there, surrounded by flowers, within which lies my wife. Put my body beside it.'

Ulric fell silent for several minutes, taking time to refill the goblets.

'It shall be as you wish, Earl of Bronze,' he said at last. 'Join me in my tent now. We shall eat a little meat, drink a little wine and be friends. I shall tell you of my life and my dreams, and you may talk of the past and your joys.'

'Why only the past, Lord Ulric?'

'It is all you have left, my friend.'

29

At midnight, as the flames from the funeral pyre blazed against the night sky, the Nadir horde drew their weapons, holding them aloft in silent tribute to the warrior whose soul, they believed, stood at the gates of Paradise.

Rek and the company of Drenai followed suit, then he turned and bowed to Ulric. Ulric returned the bow and the company set off to return to the postern gate of Wall Five. The return journey was made in silence, each man's thoughts his own.

Bowman thought of Caessa, and of her death at Druss' side. He had loved her in his way, though never spoke of it. To love her was to die.

Hogun's mind reeled with the awesome picture of the Nadir army seen from close range; numberless and mighty. Unstoppable!

Serbitar thought of the journey he would make with the remnants of The Thirty at dusk on the morrow. Only Arbedark would be missing, for they had convened the night before and declared him an Abbot. Now he would journey from Delnoch alone to found a new temple in Ventria.

Rek fought against despair. Ulric's last words echoed again and again in his mind:

'Tomorrow you will see the Nadir as never before. We have paid homage to your courage by attacking only in daylight, allowing you to rest at night. Now I need to take your Keep and there will be no rest until it falls. Day and night we will come at you until none are left alive to oppose us.'

Silently the group mounted the postern steps, making their way to the mess hall. Rek knew sleep would not come to him this night. It was his last night upon the earth, and his tired body summoned fresh reserves so that he could taste life and know the sweetness of drawing breath.

The group sat around a trestle table and Rek poured wine. Of The Thirty, only Serbitar and Vintar remained. For many minutes the five men said little, until at last Hogun broke the uncomfortable silence.

'We knew it would come to this, did we not? There was no way to hold indefinitely.'

'Very true, old horse,' said Bowman. 'Still, it is a trifle disappointing, don't you think? I must own that I always kept alive a small hope that we would succeed. Now that it is gone, I feel a tiny twinge of panic.' He smiled gently, and finished his drink at a single swallow.

'You are not pledged to stay,' said Hogun.

'True. Perhaps I will leave in the morning.'

'I don't think you will – though I don't know why,' said Hogun.

'Well, if truth be told, I promised that Nadir warrior, Kaska, that I would have another drink with him once they took the Keep. Nice chap

– if a trifle maudlin in his cups. He has six wives and twenty-three children. It is a wonder he has the time to come to war.'

'Or the strength!' added Hogun, grinning. 'And what of you, Rek. Why do you stay?'

'Hereditary stupidity,' answered Rek.

'That is not enough,' said Bowman. 'Come on, Rek – the truth, if you please.'

Rek scanned the group swiftly, noting the fatigue on all their faces and realising for the first time that he loved them all.

His eyes met Vintar's and understanding flowed between them. The older man smiled.

'I think,' said Rek, 'that only the Abbot of Swords can answer that question – for all of us.'

Vintar nodded and closed his eyes for several moments. Each man knew he was searching their hearts and minds, yet there was no fear, no embarrassment, no desire any longer to be alone.

'All things that live must die,' said Vintar. 'Man alone, it seems, lives all his life in the knowledge of death. And yet there is more to life than merely waiting for death. For life to have meaning, there must be a purpose. A man must pass something on – otherwise he is useless.

'For most men, that purpose revolves around marriage and children who will carry on his seed. For others it is an ideal – a dream, if you like. Each of us here believes in the concept of honour: that it is man's duty to do that which is right and just; that might alone is not enough. We have all transgressed at some time. We have stolen, lied, cheated – even killed – for our own ends. But ultimately we return to our beliefs. We do not allow the Nadir to pass unchallenged because we cannot. We judge ourselves more harshly than others can judge us. We know that death is preferable to betrayal of that which we hold dear.

'Hogun, you are a soldier and you have faith in the Drenai cause. You have been told to stand, and will do so without question. It would not occur to you that there were any alternatives but to obey. And yet you understand when others think differently. You are a rare man.

'Bowman, you are a romantic – and yet a cynic. You mock the nobility of man, for you have seen that too often nobility gives way to more base desires. Yet you have secretly set yourself standards which other men will never understand. You, more than any of the others, desire to live. The urge is strong in you to run away. But you will not – not as long as a single man stands to defend these walls. Your courage is great.

'Rek, you are the most difficult to answer for. Like Bowman you are a romantic, but there is a depth to you which I have not tried to plumb. You are intuitive and intelligent, but it is your intuition that guides you. You know it is right that you stay – and also senseless that you stay. Your intellect tells you that this cause is folly, but your intuition forces you to reject your intellect. You are that rare animal, a born leader of men. And you cannot leave.

'All of you are bound together in chains a thousand times stronger than steel.

'And finally there is one – who comes now – for which all I have said remains true. He is a lesser man than any here and yet a greater, for his fears are greater than yours, and yet he also will stand firm and die beside you.'

The door opened and Orrin entered, his armour bright and freshly oiled. Silently he sat among them, accepting a goblet of wine.

'I trust Ulric was in good health,' he said.

'He has never looked better, old horse,' answered Bowman.

'Then we will give him a bloody nose tomorrow,' said the general, his dark eyes gleaming.

The dawn sky was bright and clear as the Drenai warriors ate a cold breakfast of bread and cheese, washed down with honeyed water. Every man who could stand manned the walls, blades to the ready. As the Nadir prepared to advance, Rek leapt to the battlements and turned to face the defenders.

'No long speeches today,' he shouted. 'We all know our plight. But I want to say that I am proud – more proud than I could ever have imagined. I wish I could find words . . .' He stammered to silence, then lifted his sword from its scabbard and held it high.

'By all the gods that ever walked, I swear that you are the finest men I ever knew. And if I could have chosen the end of this tale, and peopled it with heroes of the past, I would not change a single thing. For no one could have given more than you have.

'And I thank you.

'But if any man here wishes to leave now, he may do so. Many of you have wives, children, others depending on you. If that be the case, leave now with my blessing. For what we do here today will not affect the outcome of the war.'

He leapt lightly to the ramparts to rejoin Orrin and Hogun.

Further along the line a young Cul shouted: 'What of you, Earl of Bronze. Will you stay?'

Rek stepped to the wall once more. 'I must stay, but I give you leave to go.'

No man moved, though many considered it.

The Nadir war cry rose and the battle began.

Throughout that long day, no foothold could be gained by the Nadir and the carnage was terrible.

The great sword of Egel lunged and slew, cleaving armour, flesh and bone, and the Drenai fought like demons, cutting and slaying ferociously. For these, as Serbitar had predicted so many weeks ago, were the finest of the fighting men, and death and fear of death had no place in their minds. Time and again the Nadir reeled back, bloodied and bemused.

But as dusk approached the assault on the gates strengthened, and the great barrier of bronze and oak began to buckle. Serbitar led the last of The Thirty to stand, as Druss had done, in the shadow of the gate porch. Rek raced to join them, but a withering mind pulse from Serbitar ordered him back to the wall. He was about to resist when Nadir warriors scram-

494

bled over the ramparts behind him. Egel's sword flashed, beheading the first, and Rek was once more in the thick of battle.

In the gateway Serbitar was joined by Suboden, the captain of his Vagrian bodyguard. Only some sixty men were still alive out of the force which had originally arrived.

'Go back to the walls,' said Serbitar.

The fair-haired Vagrian shook his head. 'I cannot. We are here as your carle-guard and we will die with you.'

'You bear me no love, Suboden. You have made that plain.'

'Love has little to do with my duty, Lord Serbitar. Even so, I hope you will forgive me. I thought your powers were demon-sent, but no man possessed would stand as you do now.'

'There is nothing to forgive, but you have my blessing,' Serbitar told the blond carle-captain.

The gates splintered suddenly and with a roar of triumph the Nadir burst through, hurling themselves upon the defenders spearheaded by the white-haired templar.

Drawing a slender Ventrian dagger, Serbitar fought two-handed – blocking, stabbing, parrying and cutting. Men fell before him, but always more leapt to fill the breach he created. Beside him the slim Vagrian carle-captain hacked and hammered at the oncoming barbarians. An axe splintered his shield, but hurling aside the fragments, he took a double-handed grip on his sword, bellowed his defiance and launched himself forward. An axe crushed his ribs and a lance tore into his thigh. He fell into the seething mass, stabbing left and right. A kick sent him sprawling to his back and three spears buried themselves in his chest. Feebly he sought to lift his sword for one last time, but an iron-studded boot stamped on his hand, while a blow from a wooden club ended his life.

Vintar fought coolly, pushing himself alongside the albino, waiting for the arrow he knew would be loosed at any second. Ducking beneath a slashing sword, he disembowelled his opponent and turned.

In the shadows of the sundered gates an archer drew back on his string, his fingers nestling against his cheek. The shaft leapt from the bow to take Vintar in the right eye and he fell against the Nadir spears.

The remaining defenders fought in an ever tightening circle as dusk deepened into night. The Nadir cries were silenced now, the battle tense and silent but for the sounds of steel on steel on flesh.

Menahem was lifted from his feet by the force of a stabbing spear that tore into his lungs. His sword whistled down towards the neck of the kneeling lancer – and stopped.

Lightly he touched the blade to the man's shoulder. Unable to believe his luck, the warrior dragged his spear free and buried it once more in the priest's chest.

Now Serbitar was alone.

Momentarily the Nadir fell back, staring at the blood-covered albino. Much of the blood was his own. His cloak was in tatters, his armour gashed and dented, his helm long since knocked from his head.

He took three deep shuddering breaths, looked inside himself and saw

495

that he was dying. Reaching out with his mind, he sought Vintar and the others.

Silence.

A terrible silence.

It was all for nothing then, he thought, as the Nadir tensed for the kill. He chuckled wryly.

There was no Source.

No centre to the universe.

In the last seconds left to him, he wondered if his life had been a waste.

He knew it had not. For even if there was no Source, there ought to have been. For the Source was beautiful.

A Nadir warrior sprang forward. Serbitar flicked aside his thrust, burying his dagger in the man's breast, but the pack surged in, a score of sharp blades meeting inside his frail form. Blood burst from his mouth and he fell.

From a great distance came a voice:

'Take my hand, my brother. We Travel.'

It was Vintar!

The Nadir surged and spread towards the deserted Delnoch buildings and the score of streets that led to Geddon and the Keep beyond. In the front line Ogasi raised his sword, bellowing the Nadir victory chant. He began to run, then skidded to a halt.

Ahead of him on the open ground before the buildings stood a tall man with a trident beard, dressed in the white robes of the Sathuli. He carried two tulwars, curved and deadly. Ogasi advanced slowly, confused.

A Sathuli within the Drenai fortress?

'What do you do here?' yelled Ogasi.

'Merely helping a friend,' replied the man. 'Go back! I shall not let you pass.'

Ogasi grinned. So the man was a lunatic. Lifting his sword, he ordered the tribesmen forward. The white-robed figure advanced on them.

'Sathuli!' he yelled.

From the buildings came a mighty answering roar as three thousand Sathuli warriors, their white robes ghostly in the gathering darkness, streamed to the attack.

The Nadir were stunned and Ogasi could not believe his eyes. The Sathuli and the Drenai were lifelong enemies. He knew it was happening, but his brain would not drink it in. Like a white tide on a dark beach, the Sathuli front line crashed into Nadir.

Joachim sought Ogasi, but the stocky tribesman was lost amid the chaos.

The savage twist to events, from certain victory to certain death, dismayed the tribesmen. Panic set in and a slow withdrawal became a rout. Trampling their comrades, the Nadir turned and ran with the white army at their backs, harrying them on with screams as bestial as any heard on the Nadir steppes.

On the walls above, Rek was bleeding from wounds in his upper arms and Hogun had suffered a sword cut to his scalp, blood running from the gash and skin flapping as he lashed out at his attackers.

Now Sathuli warriors appeared on the battlements and once more the Nadir fled their terrible tulwars, backing to the walls and seeking escape down the ropes.

Within minutes it was over. Elsewhere on the open ground small pockets of Nadir warriors were surrounded and despatched.

Joachim Sathuli, his white robes stained with crimson, slowly mounted the rampart steps, followed by his seven lieutenants. He approached Rek and bowed. Turning, he handed his bloody tulwars to a dark-bearded warrior. Another man passed him a scented towel. Slowly, elaborately he wiped his face and then his hands. Finally he spoke:

'A warm welcome,' he said, his face unsmiling but his eyes full of humour.

'Indeed,' said Rek. 'It is lucky the other guests had to leave, otherwise there would not have been any room.'

'Are you so surprised to see me?'

'No, not surprised. Astonished sounds more accurate.'

Joachim laughed. 'Is your memory so short, Delnoch? You said we should part as friends and I agreed. Where else should I be in a friend's hour of need?'

'You must have had the devil's own task convincing your warriors to follow you.'

'Not at all,' answered Joachim, an impish gleam in his eyes. 'Most of their lives they have longed to fight inside these walls.'

The tall Sathuli warrior stood on the high walls of Geddon, gazing down at the Nadir camp beyond the deserted battlements of Valteri. Rek was asleep now and the bearded prince strode the walls alone. Around him were sentries and soldiers of both races, but Joachim remained solitary.

For weeks Sathuli scouts atop the Delnoch range had watched the battle raging below. Often Joachim himself had scaled the peaks to view the fighting. Then a Nadir raiding party had struck at a Sathuli village and Joachim had persuaded his men to follow him to Delnoch. Added to this, he knew of the traitor who dealt with the Nadir, for he had witnessed a meeting in a high, narrow pass between the traitor and the Nadir captain, Ogasi.

Two days later the Nadir had tried to send a force over the mountains and the Sathuli had repulsed them.

Joachim heard the news of Rek's loss with sadness. Fatalistic himself, he could still share the feelings of a man whose woman had died. His own had died in childbirth two years before and the wound was still fresh.

Joachim shook his head. War was a savage mistress, but a woman of power nonetheless. She could wreak more havoc in a man's soul than time.

The Sathuli arrival had been timely and not without cost. Four hundred of his men were dead – a loss scarcely bearable to a mountain people who numbered a mere thirty thousand, many of these being children and ancients.

But a debt was a debt.

The man Hogun hated him, Joachim knew. But this was understandable, for Hogun was of the Legion and the Sathuli had spilt Legion blood for years. They reserved their finest tortures for captured Riders. This was an honour, but Joachim knew the Drenai could never understand. When a man died he was tested – the harder the death, the greater the rewards in Paradise. Torture advanced a man's soul and the Sathuli could offer no greater reward to a captured enemy.

He sat upon the battlements and stared back at the Keep. For how many years had he longed to take this fortress? How many of his dreams had been filled with pictures of the Keep in flames?

And now he was defending it with the lives of his followers.

He shrugged. A man with his eyes on the sky does not see the scorpion below his feet. A man with his eyes on the ground does not see the dragon in the air.

He paced the ramparts, coming at last to the gate tower and the stone inscription carved there: GEDDON.

The Wall of Death.

The air was thick with the smell of death and the morning would see the crows fly in to the feast. He should have killed Rek in the woods. A promise to an unbeliever was worth nothing, so why had he kept it? He laughed suddenly, accepting the answer: because the man had not cared.

And Joachim liked him.

He passed a Drenai sentry who saluted him and smiled. Joachim nodded, noting the uncertainty of the smile.

He had told the Earl of Bronze that he and his men would stay for one more day and then return to the mountains. He had expected a plea to remain – offers, promises, treaties. But Rek had merely smiled.

'It is more than I would have asked for,' he said.

Joachim was stunned, but he could say nothing. He told Rek of the traitor and of the Nadir attempt to cross the mountains.

'Will you still bar the way?'

'Of course. That is Sathuli land.'

'Good! Will you eat with me?'

'No, but I thank you for the offer.'

No Sathuli could break bread with an unbeliever.

Rek nodded. 'I think I will rest now,' he said. 'I will see you at dawn.'

In his high room in the Keep Rek slept, dreaming of Virae, always of Virae. He awoke hours before dawn and reached out for her. But the sheets beside him were cold and, as always, he felt the loss anew. On this night he wept, long and soundlessly. Finally he rose, dressed, and descended the stairs to the small hall. The manservant, Arshin, brought him a breakfast of cold ham and cheese, with a flagon of cold water, laced with honey mead. He ate mechanically until a young officer approached with the news that Bricklyn had returned with despatches from Drenan.

The burgher entered the hall, bowed briefly and approached the table, laying before Rek several packages and a large sealed scroll. He seated himself opposite Rek and asked if he could pour himself a drink. Rek nodded as he opened the scroll. He read it once, smiled, then laid it aside and looked across at the burgher. He was thinner and perhaps even greyer than the first time Rek had seen him. He was still dressed in riding clothes, and his green cloak was dust-covered. Bricklyn drained the water in two swallows and refilled his cup; then he noticed Rek's eyes upon him.

'You have seen the message from Abalayn?' he asked.

'Yes. Thank you for bringing it. Will you stay?'

'But of course. Surrender arrangements must be made and Ulric welcomed to the Keep.'

'He has promised to spare no one,' said Rek softly.

Bricklyn waved his hand. 'Nonsense! That was war talk. Now he will be magnanimous.'

'And what of Woundweaver?'

'He has been recalled to Drenan and the army disbanded.'

'Are you pleased?'

'That the war is over? Of course. Though I am naturally saddened that so many had to die. I hear that Druss fell at Sumitos. A great shame. He was a fine man and a magnificent warrior. But it was as he would wish to go, I am sure. When would you like me to see Lord Ulric?'

'As soon as you wish.'

'Will you accompany me?'

'No.'

'Then who will?' asked Bricklyn, noting with pleasure the resignation mirrored in Rek's face.

'No one.'

'No one? But that would not be politic, my lord. There should be a deputation.'

'You will travel alone.'

'Very well. What terms shall I negotiate?'

'You will negotiate nothing. You will merely go to Ulric and say that I have sent you.'

'I do not understand, my lord. What would you have me say?'

'You will say that you have failed.'

'Failed? In what? You speak in riddles. Are you mad?'

'No. Just tired. You betrayed us, Bricklyn, but then I expect nothing less from your breed. Therefore I am not angry. Or vengeful. You have taken Ulric's pay and now you may go to him. The letter from Abalayn is a forgery and Woundweaver will be here in five days with over fifty thousand men. Outside there are three thousand Sathuli and we can hold the wall. Now be gone! Hogun knows that you are a traitor and has told me that he will kill you if he sees you. Go now.'

For several minutes Bricklyn sat stunned, then he shook his head. 'This is madness! You cannot hold! It is Ulric's day, can you not see it? The Drenai are finished and Ulric's star shines. What do you hope to achieve?'

Rek slowly drew a long, slender dagger and placed it on the table before him.

'Go now,' he repeated quietly.

Bricklyn rose and stormed to the door. He turned in the doorway.

'You fool!' he spat. 'Use the dagger on yourself, for what the Nadir will do when they take you will make merry viewing.' Then he was gone.

Hogun stepped from behind a tapestry-covered alcove and moved to the table. His head was bandaged and his face pale. In his hand he held his sword.

'How could you let him go, Rek? How?'

Rek smiled. 'Because I couldn't be bothered to kill him.'

30

The last candle guttered and died as a light autumn wind billowed the curtains. Rek slept on, head resting on his arms at the table where only an hour before he had sent Bricklyn to the Nadir. His sleep was light, but dreamless. He shivered as the room became cooler, then awoke with a start in the darkness. Fear touched him and he reached for his dagger. He shivered again: it was cold . . . so cold. He glanced at the fire. It was blazing, but no heat reached him. He stood and walked towards it, squatting in front of it and opening his hands to the heat. Nothing. Confused, he stood once more and turned back to the table, and then the shock hit him.

Head resting on his arms, the figure of Earl Regnak still slept there. He fought down panic, watching his sleeping form, noting the weariness in the gaunt face, the dark-hollowed eyes and the lines of strain about the mouth.

Then he noticed the silence. Even at this late hour of deepest darkness, some sounds should be heard from sentries, or servants or the few cooks preparing the morning's breakfast. But there was nothing. He moved to the doorway and beyond into the darkened corridor, then beyond that into the shadow of the portcullis gate. He was alone – beyond the gate were the walls, but no sentries paced them. He walked on in the darkness, and the clouds cleared and the moon shone brightly.

The fortress was deserted.

From the high walls of Geddon he looked to the north. The plain was empty. No Nadir tents were pitched there.

So he was truly alone. Panic left him and a deep sense of peace covered his soul like a warm blanket. He sat on the ramparts, gazing back at the Keep.

Was this a taste of death, he wondered? Or merely a dream? He cared not. Whether a foretaste of tomorrow's reality or the result of a needed fantasy was immaterial. He was enjoying the moment.

And then, with a deep sense of warmth, he knew that he was not alone. His heart swelled and tears came to his eyes. He turned and she was there: dressed as he had first seen her, with a bulky sheepskin jerkin and woollen troos, she opened her arms and walked into his embrace. He held her tightly to him, pressing his face into her hair. For a long time they stood thus, while deep sobs racked his body. Finally the crying subsided and he gently released her. She looked up at him and smiled.

'You have done well, Rek,' she said. 'I am so proud of you.'

'Without you it is meaningless,' he said.

'I wouldn't change anything, Rek. If they told me that I could have my life again, but not meet you, I would refuse. What does it matter that we had only months? What months they were!'

'I never loved anyone as I loved you,' he said.

'I know.'

They talked for hours, but the moon shone from the same place and the stars were static, the night eternal. Finally she kissed him to stem his words.

'There are others you must see.'

He tried to argue, but she held her fingers to his mouth. 'We will meet again, my love. For now, speak to the others.'

Around the walls was now a mist, swirling and thick. Overhead the moon shone in a cloudless sky. She walked into the mist and was gone. He waited and soon a figure in silver armour came towards him. As always he looked fresh and alert, his armour reflected the moonlight and his white cloak was spotless. He smiled.

'Well met, Rek,' said Serbitar. They clasped hands in the warrior's grip.

'The Sathuli came,' said Rek. 'You held the gate just long enough.'

'I know. Tomorrow will be hard, and I will not lie to you. All futures have I seen, and in only one do you survive the day. But there are forces here which I cannot explain to you and even now their magic is at work. Fight well!'

'Will Woundweaver arrive?' asked Rek.

Serbitar shrugged. 'Not tomorrow.'

'Then we will fall?'

'It is likely. But if you do not, I want you to do something for me.'

'Name it,' said Rek.

'Go once more to Egel's room where there is a last gift for you. The servant Arshin will explain.'

'What is it? Is it a weapon. I could use it tomorrow.'

'It is not a weapon. Go there tomorrow night.'

'Serbitar?'

'Yes, my friend.'

'Was all as you dreamed it would be? The Source, I mean?'

'Yes! And so much more. But I cannot speak of it now. Wait for a while longer. There is another who must speak with you.'

The mist deepened and Serbitar's white form drew back until he merged and was gone.

And Druss was there. Mighty and strong, his black jerkin glistening, his axe at his side.

'He gave me a fine send-off,' said Druss. 'How are you, boy? You look tired.'

'I am tired, but all the better for seeing you.'

Druss clapped him on the shoulder and laughed.

'That Nogusha used a poisoned blade on me. I tell you, laddie, it hurt like hell. Caessa dressed me. I don't know how she got me to my feet. Still . . . she did.'

'I saw it,' said Rek.

'Aye, a grand exit, was it not? That young lad Gilad fought well. I have not seen him yet, but I expect I shall. You're a good boy, Rek. Worthy! It was good to know you.'

'And you, Druss. I never met a better man.'

'Of course you did, boy. Hundreds! But it's nice of you to say it. However, I didn't come here to exchange compliments. I know what you are facing and I know tomorrow will be hard – damned hard. But don't give ground. Do not retreat to the Keep – whatever happens, hold the wall. Much rests on it. Keep Joachim beside you; if he dies, you are finished. I must go. But remember. *Hold the wall. Do not retreat to the Keep.*'

'I will remember. Goodbye, Druss.'

'Not goodbye. Not yet,' said Druss. 'Soon.'

The mist moved forward, enveloping the axeman and sweeping over Rek. Then the moonlight faded and dark descended on the Earl of Bronze.

Back in the Keep, Rek awoke. The fire still burned and he was hungry again.

In the kitchens Arshin was preparing breakfast. The old man was tired, but he brightened when Rek walked in.

He liked the new Earl and remembered when Virae's father, Delnar, had been a young man, proud and strong. There seemed a similarity, but perhaps – Arshin thought – the long years had distorted his memory.

He handed the Earl some toasted bread and honey which he wolfed down, following it with watered wine.

Back in his quarters, Rek buckled his armour into place and made his way to the battlements. Hogun and Orrin were already there, supervising the barricade within the gate tunnel.

'This is the weak spot,' said Orrin. 'We should retire to the Keep. At least the gates will hold for some hours.'

Rek shook his head. 'We will stand on Geddon. There must be no retreat.'

'Then we shall die here,' said Hogun. 'For that barricade will hold them not at all.'

'Perhaps,' said Rek. 'We shall see. Good morning, Joachim Sathuli.'

The bearded warrior nodded and smiled. 'You slept well, Earl of Bronze?'

'Well indeed. I thank you for giving us this day of your time.'

'It is nothing. The payment of a small debt.'

'You owe me nothing. But I tell you this, if we survive this day there shall be no more war between us. The rights to the high Delnoch passes are mine, though you dispute the rights of the Drenai to them. Therefore, before these witnesses, I give them to you.

'There is also a scroll bearing my seal at the Keep. When you leave tonight, you shall have it. A copy will go to Abalayn in Drenan.

'I know that the gesture will have little meaning if the Nadir win through today – but it is all I can do.'

Joachim bowed. 'The gesture is enough in itself.'

The talk ceased as the Nadir drums sounded and the warriors of Dros Delnoch spread out along the wall to receive the attackers. Rek lowered his helm visor and drew the sword of Egel. Below, in the barricaded gate tunnel, stood Orrin and one hundred warriors. The tunnel was only twenty feet wide at the centre and Orrin reckoned to hold it for the greater part of the morning. After that, with the barricades torn down, the sheer weight of the Nadir horde would push them back into the open ground behind the ramparts.

And so the last bloody day began at Dros Delnoch.

31

Wave after wave of screaming tribesmen scaled ropes and ladders throughout the morning, finding that only cold, terrible death awaited them under the slashing swords and tulwars of the defenders. Men fell screaming to the rocks below the walls, or died trampled beneath the feet of battling men on the ramparts. Side by side, Sathuli and Drenai brought death to the Nadir.

Rek cut and slashed two-handed, the sword of Egel cleaving the ranks of the Nadir like a scythe through wheat. Beside him Joachim fought with two short swords, whirling and killing.

Below, Orrin's men were being pushed slowly back into the wider section of the tunnel, though the Nadir paid dearly for every inch of ground.

Blocking a thrusting lance, Orrin backhanded a slashing cut to a warrior's face. The man disappeared in the milling mass and another attacker took his place.

'We can't hold!' yelled a young officer to Orrin's right.

Orrin had no time to answer.

Suddenly the leading Nadir warrior screamed in horror, pushing back into his comrades. Others followed his gaze, looking back beyond the Drenai at the tunnel mouth.

A gap opened between the Drenai and the Nadir, and widened as the tribesmen turned and fled down into the open grounds between Valteri and Geddon.

'Great gods of Missael!' said the officer. 'What's going on?' Orrin turned and saw what had filled the Nadir with terror.

Behind them in the darkened tunnel stood Druss the Legend, Serbitar and The Thirty. With them were many departed warriors. Druss' axe was in his hand and the joy of battle in his eyes. Orrin swallowed, then licked his lips. He replaced his sword in its scabbard at the third attempt.

'I think we will leave them to hold the tunnel,' he said. The remaining men bunched behind him as he walked towards Druss.

The ghostly defenders appeared not to notice them, their eyes fixed on the tunnel beyond. Orrin tried to speak to Druss, but the old man just stared ahead. When Orrin reached out a shaking hand and tried to touch the axeman, his hand met nothing – only cold, cold air.

'Let us get back to the wall,' he said. He closed his eyes and walked blindly through the ranks of the spirits. By the time he reached the tunnel mouth he was shivering. The other men with him said nothing.

No one looked back.

He joined Rek on the wall and the battle continued. Moments later, during a brief lull, Rek shouted: 'What's happening in the tunnel?'

'Druss is there,' replied Orrin. Rek merely nodded and turned again as fresh Nadir warriors breasted the ramparts.

Bowman, bearing short sword and buckler, fought beside Hogun. Though not as skilled with the blade as with the bow, he was no mean warrior.

Hogun blocked an axe blow – and his sword snapped. The axe head crushed his shoulder, burying itself in his chest. He hammered the broken sword into the belly of the axeman and fell with him to the ground.

A lance licked out, spearing the Legion general's back as he struggled to rise. Bowman's short sword disembowelled the lancer, but more Nadir pressed forward and Hogun's body was lost in the mêlée.

By the gate tower Joachim Sathuli fell, his side pierced by a thrown spear. Rek half-carried him beyond the ramparts, but had to leave him, for the Nadir had almost broken through. Joachim gripped the spear with both hands, sweat breaking out on his forehead, and examined the wound. The point had passed through just above the right hip, and broken the skin of his back. The head, he knew, was barbed and there would be no drawing it out. He gripped the spear more firmly, rolled to his side then pushed it further into the wound until the whole of the spear-head cleared his back. He passed out for several minutes, but the gentle touch of a hand roused him. A Sathuli warrior named Andisim was beside him.

'Remove the head of the spear,' Joachim hissed. 'Quickly!'

Wordlessly the man took his dagger and as gently as possible levered the spear-head from the shaft. At last it was done. 'Now,' whispered Joachim, 'pull the shaft clear.' Standing above him, the man slowly withdrew the spear as Joachim grunted against the agony. Blood gushed out, but Joachim ripped his robe and plugged the wound, allowing Andisim to do the same for the hole in his back.

'Get me to my feet,' he ordered, 'and fetch me a tulwar.'

Beyond the walls of Eldibar, within his tent, Ulric watched the sands fall in the huge glass. Beside him was the scroll he had received that morning from the north.

His nephew Jahingir had declared himself Kan – overlord of the north. He had slain Ulric's brother, Tsubodi, and taken Ulric's mistress Hasita as hostage.

Ulric could not blame him and felt no anger. His family were born to lead and blood ran true among them.

But he could not dally here and so had set the glass. If the wall had not fallen by the time the sand ran out, he would lead his army north again, win back his kingdom and return to take Dros Delnoch on another day.

He had received the message about Druss holding the tunnel and had shrugged. Alone once more, he had smiled.

So, not even Paradise can keep you from the battle, old man!

Outside his tent stood three men bearing rams' horns, waiting for his signal. And the sands flowed on.

On the wall of Geddon the Nadir broke through to the right. Rek screamed for Orrin to follow him and cut a path along the ramparts. To the left more Nadir gained the ramparts and the Drenai fell back, leaping to the grass and re-forming. The Nadir swarmed forward.

The day was lost.

Sathuli and Drenai waited, swords ready, as the Nadir massed before them. Bowman and Orrin stood beside Rek, and Joachim Sathuli limped towards them.

'I'm glad we are only offering you one day,' grunted Joachim, clutching the bloody bandage wedged into his side.

The Nadir spread out before them and charged.

Rek leaned on his sword blade, breathing deeply and saving what was left of his strength. There was no longer the energy inside him to promote a baresark rage, nor the will.

All his life he had feared this moment, and now that it was upon him it was as meaningless as dust upon the ocean. Wearily he focused his gaze on the charging warriors.

'I say, old horse,' muttered Bowman, 'do you think it's too late to surrender?'

Rek grinned. 'Just a little,' he said. His hands curled around the sword hilt, he twisted his wrist and the blade hissed into the air.

The front ranks of the Nadir were less than twenty paces from them when the sound of distant rams' horns echoed up from the valley.

The charge slowed . . .

And stopped. Less than ten paces apart, both sides stood listening to the insistent wailing.

Ogasi cursed and spat, sheathing his sword. He stared sullenly into the astonished eyes of the Earl of Bronze. Rek removed his helm and plunged his sword into the ground before him as Ogasi stepped forward.

'It is over!' he said. He lifted his arm, waving the Nadir back to the walls. Then he turned. 'Know this, you round-eyed bastard, it was I, Ogasi, who slew your wife.'

It took a few seconds for the words to register, then Rek took a deep breath and removed his gauntlets.

'Do you think it matters, amid all this,' said Rek, 'to know who fired one arrow? You want me to remember you? I shall. You want me to hate you? I cannot. Maybe tomorrow. Or next year. Maybe never.'

For a moment Ogasi stood silent, then he shrugged.

'The arrow was meant for you,' he said, weariness settling on him like a dark cloak. Turning on his heel, he followed the departing warriors. Silently they climbed down the ladders and ropes – none took the path through the gate tunnel.

Rek unbuckled his breastplate and walked slowly to the tunnel mouth. Coming towards him were Druss and The Thirty. Rek lifted a hand in greeting, but a wind blew and the warriors vanished into mist and were gone.

'Goodbye, Druss,' he said softly.

Later that evening Rek bade farewell to the Sathuli and slept for several hours, hoping for another meeting with Virae. He awoke refreshed – but disappointed.

Arshin brought him food and he ate with Bowman and Orrin. They said little. Calvar Syn and his orderlies had found Hogun's body, and the surgeon was labouring to save the hundreds of wounded men now being carried to the Geddon hospital.

Rek made his way to his room around midnight and removed his armour; then he remembered Serbitar's gift. He was too tired to care, but sleep would not come, so he rose and dressed, took a torch from a wall bracket and made his way slowly down into the bowels of the Keep. The door to Egel's room was closed once more, but it opened to him as before.

The lights blazed within as Rek placed his torch against the wall and stepped inside. His breath caught in his throat as he gazed on the crystal block. Within it lay Virae! Upon her body was no mark, no arrow wound; she lay naked and peaceful, seemingly asleep, floating within the transparent crystal. He walked to the block, reached inside and touched her. She did not stir and her body was cold. Stooping, he lifted her clear and placed her on a nearby table. Then he removed his cloak, wrapped it around her and lifted her again. Gathering up the torch he made his slow way back to his room above the Keep hall.

He summoned Arshin and the old retainer blanched as he saw the still form of the Earl's wife. He looked at Rek, then gazed at the floor.

'I am sorry, my lord. I do not know why the white-haired one placed her body in the magic crystal.'

'What happened?' asked Rek.

'The prince Serbitar and his friend the Abbot came to see me on the day she died. The Abbot had had a dream, he said. He would not explain it to me, but he said it was vital that my lady's body be placed within the crystal. He said something about the Source . . . I didn't understand it. I still don't, my lord. Is she alive or dead? And how did you find her? We laid her upon this crystal block and she gently sank into it. Yet when I touched it, it was solid. I understand nothing any more.' Tears welled in the old man's eyes and Rek moved to him, placing a hand on his bony shoulder.

'It is all hard to explain. Fetch Calvar Syn. I will wait here with Virae.'

A dream of Vintar's – what could it mean? The albino had said there were many tomorrows and that no one could ever tell which would come to pass. But he had obviously seen one in which Virae lived and had ordered her body to be preserved. And somehow the wound had been healed inside the crystal. But did that mean she would live?

Virae alive!

His mind reeled. He could neither think nor feel and his body seemed numb. Her death had all but destroyed him, yet now, with her here once more, he was afraid to hope. If life had taught him anything, it had shown him that every man has a breaking point. He knew he was now facing his. He sat by the bed and lifted her cold hand, his own hand shaking with tension, and felt for a pulse. Nothing. Crossing the room, he fetched another blanket and covered her, then went to work building a fire in the hearth.

It was nearly an hour before he heard Calvar Syn on the stairs outside. The man was cursing Arshin loudly. Wearing a stained blue tunic and a blood-covered leather apron, the surgeon stepped into the room.

'What fool nonsense is this, Earl?' he thundered. 'I have men who are dying for want of my skills? What . . .' He stammered to silence as he saw the girl in the bed. 'So, the old man was not lying. Why, Rek? Why have you brought her body back?'

'I don't know. Truly. Serbitar came to me in a dream and told me he had left a gift for me. This is what I found. I don't know what's happening – is she dead?'

'Of course, she's dead. The arrow pierced her lung.'

'Look at her, will you? There's no wound.'

The surgeon pulled back the sheet and lifted her wrist. For several moments he stood in silence. 'There is a pulse,' he whispered, 'but it is faint – and very, very slow. I cannot wait with you – there are men dying. But I will return in the morning. Keep her warm, that's all you can do.'

Rek sat beside the bed, holding her hand. Sometime, though he knew not when, he fell asleep beside her. The dawn broke bright and clear and the rising sun's light entered the eastern window, bathing the bed in golden light. At its touch Virae's cheeks gained colour and her breathing deepened. A soft moan came from her lips and Rek was instantly awake.

'Virae? Virae, can you hear me?'

Her eyes opened, then closed again, her lashes fluttering.

'Virae!' Once more her eyes opened, and she smiled.

'Serbitar brought me back,' she said. 'So tired . . . Must sleep.' She turned over, hugged the pillow and fell asleep, just as the door opened and Bowman stepped inside.

'Gods, it's true then,' he said.

Rek ushered him from the room into the corridor.

'Yes. Somehow Serbitar saved her, I cannot explain it. I don't even care how it happened. What is going on outside?'

'They've gone! All of them – every damned one of them, old horse. The camp is deserted; Orrin and I have been there. All that's left is a Wolfshead standard and the body of that Burgher Bricklyn. Can you make any sense out of it?'

'No,' said Rek. 'That standard means that Ulric will return. The body? I can't say. I sent him to them – he was a traitor and obviously they had no more use for him.'

A young officer came running up the spiral stairs.

'My lord! There is a Nadir rider waiting at Eldibar.'

Rek and Bowman walked together to Wall One. Below them on a grey steppe pony sat Ulric, Lord of the Nadir, dressed in fur-rimmed helmet, woollen jerkin and goatskin boots. He looked up as Rek leaned over the ramparts.

'You fought well, Earl of Bronze,' he shouted. 'I came to bid you farewell. There is civil war in my own kingdom and I must leave you for a while. I wanted you to know that I shall return.'

509

'I will be here,' said Rek. 'And next time your reception will be even warmer. Tell me, why did your men retire when we were beaten?'

'Do you believe in fate?' asked Ulric.

'I do.'

'Then let us call it a trick of fate. Or perhaps it was a cosmic jest, a joke played by the gods. I care not. You are a brave man. Your men are brave men. And you have won. I can live with that, Earl of Bronze – a poor man would I be if I could not. But for now, farewell! I shall see you again in the Spring.'

Ulric waved, turned his pony's head and galloped off into the north.

'Do you know,' said Bowman, 'although it may sound grotesque, I think I like the man.'

'Today I could like anybody,' said Rek, smiling. 'The sky is clear, the wind is fresh and life tastes very fine. What will you do now?'

'I think I will become a monk and devote my entire life to prayer and good works.'

'No,' said Rek. 'I mean, what will you do today?'

'Ah! Today I'll get drunk and go whoring,' said Bowman.

Throughout the long day Rek periodically visited the sleeping Virae. Her colour was good, her breathing deep and even. Late in the evening, as he sat alone in the small hall before a dying fire, she came to him, dressed in a light green woollen tunic. He stood and took her into his arms, kissed her, then sat down in the leather chair and pulled her to his lap.

'The Nadir have really gone?' she asked.

'They have indeed.'

'Rek, did I truly die? It seems like a dream now. Hazy. I seem to remember Serbitar bringing me back, and my body lay in a glass block beneath the Keep.'

'It was not a dream,' said Rek. 'Do you remember coming to me as I fought a giant worm and a huge spider?'

'Vaguely. But it's fading even as I remember it.'

'Don't worry about it. I will tell you everything during the next fifty years or so.'

'Only fifty years?' she said. 'So you will desert me when I'm old and grey?'

The sound of laughter echoed through the Keep.

Epilogue

Ulric never returned to Dros Delnoch. He defeated Jahingir in a pitched battle at Gulgothir Plain and then took his army to invade Ventria. During the campaign he collapsed and died. The tribes fled back to the north, and without his influence Nadir unity was broken. Civil war came once more to the north, and the people of the rich southlands breathed again.

Rek was welcomed as a hero in Drenan, but soon tired of the city life and returned with Virae to Delnoch. Their family grew over the years, with three sons and two daughters. The sons were Hogun, Orrin and Horeb. The daughters were Susay and Besa. Grandfather Horeb brought his family from Drenan to Delnoch, taking over the inn of the traitor Musar.

Orrin returned to Drenan and resigned from the army. His uncle Abalayn retired from public life and Magnus Woundweaver was elected to lead the Council. He chose Orrin as his deputy.

Bowman remained at Delnoch for a year, then travelled to Ventria to fight the Nadir once more. He did not return.

THE KING BEYOND THE GATE

This book is dedicated with love to my children Kathryn and Luke, as a small return for the gift of their company.

Acknowledgements:
Without the help of friends there would be no joy in writing. Many thanks to Tom Taylor for his help with the story, Stella Graham for the proof-reading, and Jean Maund for the copy-editing. Thanks also to Gary, Russ, Barbara, Philip, George, John D., Jimmy, Angela, Jo, Lee and Iona and all the staff of the *Hastings Observer* who created the good years.

And to Ross Lempriere for storming the stairs.

Prologue

The trees were laced with snow and the forest lay waiting below him like a reluctant bride. For some time he stood among the rocks and boulders, scanning the slopes. Snow gathered on his fur-lined cloak and on the crown of his wide-brimmed hat, but he ignored it, as he ignored the cold seeping through his flesh and numbing his bones. He could have been the last man alive on a dying planet.

He half wished that he were.

At last, satisfied that there were no patrols, he moved down from the mountainside, placing his feet carefully on the treacherous slopes. His movements were slow and he knew the cold to be a growing danger. He needed a camp-site and a fire.

Behind him the Delnoch range reared under thickening clouds. Before him lay Skultik forest, an area of dark legend, failed dreams and childhood memories.

The forest was silent, save for the occasional crack of dry wood as thickening ice probed the branches, or the silky rushing of snow falling from overburdened boughs.

Tenaka turned to look at his footprints. Already the sharp edges of his tracks were blurring and within minutes they would be gone. He pushed on, his thoughts sorrowful, his memories jagged.

He made camp in a shallow cave away from the wind and lit a small fire. The flames gathered and grew, red shadow-dancers swaying on the cave walls. Removing his woollen gloves he rubbed his hands above the blaze; then he rubbed his face, pinching the flesh to force the blood to flow. He wanted to sleep, but the cave was not yet warm enough.

The Dragon was dead. He shook his head, and closed his eyes. Ananais, Decado, Elias, Beltzer. All dead. Betrayed because they believed in honour and duty above all else. Dead because they believed that the Dragon was invincible and that good must ultimately triumph.

Tenaka shook himself awake, adding thicker branches to the fire.

'The Dragon is dead,' he said aloud, his voice echoing in the cave. How strange, he thought – the words were true, yet he did not believe them.

He gazed at the fire shadows, seeing again the marbled halls of his palace in Ventria. There was no fire there, only the gentle cool of the inner rooms, the cold stone keeping at bay the strength-sapping heat of the desert sun. Soft chairs and woven rugs; servants bearing jugs of iced wine, carrying buckets of precious water to feed his rose garden and ensure the beauty of his flowering trees.

The messenger had been Beltzer. Loyal Beltzer – the finest Bar-ranking warrior in the Wing.

'We are summoned home, sir,' he had said, standing ill-at-ease in the wide library, his clothes sand-covered and travel-stained. 'The rebels have defeated one of Ceska's regiments in the north and Baris has issued the call personally.'

'How do you know it was Baris?'

'His seal, sir. His personal seal. And the message: "The Dragon calls".'

'Baris has not been seen for fifteen years.'

'I know that, sir. But his seal . . .'

'A lump of wax means nothing.'

'It does to me, sir.'

'So you will go back to Drenai?'

'Yes, sir. And you?'

'Back to what, Beltzer? The land is in ruins. The Joinings are undefeatable. And who knows what foul, sorcerous powers will be ranged against the rebels? Face it, man! The Dragon was disbanded fifteen years ago and we are all older men. I was one of the younger officers and I am now forty. You must be nearer fifty – if the Dragon still survived you would be in your pension year.'

'I know that,' said Beltzer, drawing himself stiffly to attention. 'But honour calls. I have spent my life serving the Drenai and now I cannot refuse the call.'

'I can,' said Tenaka. 'The cause is lost. Give Ceska time and he will destroy himself. He is mad. The whole system is falling apart.'

'I am not good with words, sir. I have ridden two hundred miles to deliver the message. I came seeking the man I served, but he is not here. I am sorry to have troubled you.'

'Listen, Beltzer!' said Tenaka, as the warrior turned for the door. 'If there was the smallest chance of success, I would go with you gladly. But the thing reeks of defeat.'

'Do you not think I know that? That we all know it?' said Beltzer. And then he was gone.

The wind changed and veered into the cave, gusting snow to the fire. Tenaka cursed softly. Drawing his sword he went outside, cutting down two thick bushes and dragging them back to screen the entrance.

As the months passed he had forgotten the Dragon. He had estates to minister, matters of importance in the real world.

Then Illae had fallen sick. He had been in the north, arranging cover patrols to guard the spice route, when word had reached him and he hurried home. The physicians said she had a fever that would pass and that there was no cause for concern. But her condition worsened. Lung blight, they told him. Her flesh melted away until at last she lay in the wide bed, her breathing ragged, her once beautiful eyes shining now with the image of death. Day after day he sat beside her, talking, praying, begging her not to die.

And then she had rallied and his heart leapt. She was talking to him about her plans for a party, and had stopped to consider whom to invite.

'Go on,' he had said. But she was gone. Just like that. Ten years of shared memories, hopes and joys vanished like water on the desert sand.

He had lifted her from the bed, stopping to wrap her in a white woollen shawl. Then he carried her into the rose garden, holding her to him.

'I love you,' he kept saying, kissing her hair and cradling her like a child. The servants gathered, saying nothing, until after an hour two of them had come forward and separated them, leading the weeping Tenaka to his room. There he found the sealed scroll that listed the current state of his business investments, and beside it a letter from Estas, his accountant. These letters contained advice about areas of investment, with sharp political insights into places to ignore, exploit or consider.

Unthinking he had opened the letter, scanning the list of Vagrian settlements, Lentrian openings and Drenai stupidities until he came to the last sentences:

Ceska routed the rebels south of the Sentran Plain. It appears he has been bragging about his cunning again. He sent a message summoning old soldiers home; it seems he has feared the Dragon since he disbanded it fifteen years ago. Now his fears are behind him – they were destroyed to a man. The Joinings are terrifying. What sort of world are we living in?

'Living?' Tenaka said. 'No one is living – they are all dead.'

He stood up and walked to the western wall, stopping before an oval mirror and gazing at the ruin of his life.

His reflection stared back at him, the slanted violet eyes accusing, the tight-lipped mouth bitter and angry.

'Go home,' said his reflection, 'and kill Ceska.'

1

The barracks buildings stood shrouded in snow, the broken windows hanging open like old, unhealed wounds. The square once trodden flat by ten thousand men was now uneven, as the grass pushed against the snow above it.

The Dragon herself had been brutally treated: her stone wings smashed from her back, her fangs hammered to shards and her face daubed with red dye. It seemed to Tenaka as he stood before her in silent homage that she was crying tears of blood.

As Tenaka gazed at the square, memory flashed bright pictures to his mind: Ananais shouting commands to his men, contradictory orders that had them crashing into one another and tumbling to the ground.

'You dung-rats!' bellowed the blond giant. 'Call yourselves soldiers?'

The pictures faded against the ghostly white emptiness of reality and Tenaka shivered. He moved to the well where an old bucket lay, its handle still tied to a rotting rope. He dropped the bucket into the well and heard the ice break, then hauled it up and carried it to the dragon.

The dye was hard to shift, but he worked at it for almost an hour, scraping the last traces of red from the stone with his dagger.

Then he jumped to the ground and looked at his handiwork.

Even without the dye she looked pitiful, her pride broken. Tenaka thought once more of Ananais.

'Maybe it is better you died, rather than living to see this,' he said.

It began to rain, icy needles that stung his face. Tenaka scooped his pack to his shoulder and ran for the deserted barracks. The door hung open and he stepped inside the old officers' quarters. A rat scurried into the dark as he passed but Tenaka ignored it, pushing on to the wider rooms at the rear. He dumped his pack in his old room and then chuckled as he saw the fireplace: it was stacked with wood, the fire laid.

On the last day, knowing that they were leaving, someone had come into his room and laid the fire.

Decado, his aide?

No. There was no romantic element in his make-up. He was a vicious killer, held in check only by the iron discipline of the Dragon and his own rigid sense of loyalty to the regiment.

Who else?

After a while he stopped scanning the faces his memory threw at him. He would never know.

After fifteen years the wood should be dry enough to burn without smoke, he told himself, and placed fresh tinder below the logs. Soon the tongues of flame spread and the blaze took hold.

On a sudden impulse he moved to the panelled wall, seeking the hidden niche. Where once it had sprung open at the touch of a button, now it

521

creaked on a rusted spring. Gently he prised open the panelling. Behind was a small recess, created by the removal of a stone slab many years before the disbanding. On the back wall, in Nadir script, was written:

Nadir we,
Youth born,
Blood letters,
Axe wielders,
Victors still.

Tenaka smiled for the first time in months and some of the burden he carried lifted from his soul. The years swept away and he saw himself once more as a young man, fresh from the Steppes, arriving to take up his commission with the Dragon; felt again the stares of his new brother officers and their scarcely veiled hostility.

A Nadir prince in the Dragon? It was inconceivable – some even thought obscene. But his *was* a special case.

The Dragon had been formed by Magnus Woundweaver after the First Nadir Wars a century before, when the invincible warlord Ulric had led his hordes against the walls of Dros Delnoch, the most powerful fortress in the world, only to be turned back by the Earl of Bronze and his warriors.

The Dragon was to be the Drenai weapon against future Nadir invasions.

And then, like a nightmare come true – and while memories were still fresh of the Second Nadir War – a tribesman had been admitted to the regiment. Worse, he was a direct descendant of Ulric himself. And yet they had no choice but to allow him his sabre.

For he was Nadir only on his mother's side.

Through the line of his father he was the great-grandson of Regnak the Wanderer: the Earl of Bronze.

It was a problem for those who yearned to hate him.

How could they visit their hatred upon the descendant of the Drenai's greatest hero? It was not easy for them, but they managed it.

Goat's blood was daubed on his pillow, scorpions hidden in his boots. Saddle-straps were severed and finally a viper was placed in his bed.

It almost killed him as he rolled upon it, its fangs sinking into his thigh. Snatching a dagger from his bedside table, he killed the snake and then slashed a cross-cut by the fang marks, hoping the rush of blood would carry the venom clear. Then he lay very still, knowing any movement would accelerate the poison in his system. He heard footsteps in the corridor and knew it was Ananais, the officer of the guard, returning to his room after completing his shift.

He did not want to call out, for he knew Ananais disliked him. But neither did he want to die! He called Ananais' name, the door opened and the blond giant stood silhouetted in the doorway.

'I have been bitten by a viper,' said Tenaka.

Ananais ducked under the doorway and approached the bed, pushing at the dead snake with his boot. Then he looked at the wound in Tenaka's leg.

'How long ago?' he asked.

'Two, three minutes.'

Ananais nodded. 'The cuts aren't deep enough.'

Tenaka handed him the dagger.

'No. If they *were* deep enough you would sever the main muscles.'

Leaning forward, Ananais put his mouth over the wound and sucked the poison clear. Then he applied a tourniquet and left to get the surgeon.

Even with most of the poison flushed out, the young Nadir prince almost died. He sank into a coma that lasted four days and when he awoke Ananais was at his bedside.

'How are you feeling?'

'Good.'

'You don't look it. Still, I am glad you're alive.'

'Thank you for saving me,' said Tenaka, as the giant rose to leave.

'It was a pleasure. But I still wouldn't want you marrying my sister,' he said, grinning as he moved to the door. 'By the way, three young officers were dismissed from the service yesterday. I think you can sleep soundly from now on.'

'I shall never do that,' said Tenaka. 'For the Nadir, that is the way of death.'

'No wonder their eyes are slanted.' said Ananais.

Renya helped the old man to his feet, then heaped snow upon the small fire to kill the flames. The temperature plummeted as the storm-clouds bunched above them, grim and threatening. The girl was frightened, for the old man had ceased shivering and now stood by the ruined tree staring vacantly at the ground by his feet.

'Come, Aulin,' she said, slipping her arm around his waist. 'The old barracks are close by.'

'No!' he wailed, pulling back. 'They will find me there. I know they will.'

'The cold will kill you,' she hissed. 'Come on.'

Meekly he allowed her to lead him through the snow. She was a tall girl, and strong, but the going was tiring and she was breathing heavily as they pushed past the last screen of bushes before the Dragon Square.

'Only a few more minutes,' she said. 'Then you can rest.'

The old man seemed to gain strength from the promise of shelter and he shambled forward with greater speed. Twice he almost fell, but she caught him.

She kicked open the door of the nearest building and helped him inside, removing her white woollen burnoose and running a hand through her sweat-streaked, close-cropped black hair.

Away from the biting wind, she felt her skin burning as her body adjusted to the new conditions. She unbelted her white sheepskin cloak, pushing it back over her broad shoulders. Beneath it she wore a light blue woollen tunic and black leggings, partially hidden by thigh-length boots, sheepskin-lined. At her side was a slender dagger.

The old man leaned against a wall, shaking uncontrollably.

'They will find me. They *will*!' he whimpered. Renya ignored him and moved down the hallway.

A man came into sight at the far end and Renya started, her dagger leaping to her hand. The man was tall and dark and dressed in black. By his side was a longsword. He moved forward slowly, yet with a confidence Renya found daunting. As he approached she steadied herself for the attack, watching his eyes.

They were, she noticed, the most beautiful violet colour, and slanted like those of the Nadir tribesmen of the north. Yet his face was square-cut and almost handsome, save for the grim line of his mouth.

She wanted to stop him with words, to tell him that if he came any closer she would kill him. But she could not. There was about him an aura of power – an authority which left her no choice but to respond.

And then he was past her and bending over Aulin.

'Leave him alone!' she shouted. Tenaka turned to her.

'There is a fire in my room. Along there on the right,' he said calmly. 'I will take him there.' Smoothly he lifted the old man and carried him to his quarters, laying him on the narrow bed. He removed the man's cloak and boots, and began to rub gently at his calves where the skin was blue and mottled. Turning he threw a blanket to the girl. 'Warm this by the fire,' he said, returning to his work. After a while he checked the man's breathing – it was deep and even.

'He is asleep?' she asked.

'Yes.'

'Will he live?'

'Who can say?' said Tenaka, rising and stretching his back.

'Thank you for helping him.'

'Thank you for not killing me,' he answered.

'What are you doing here?'

'Sitting by my fire and waiting for the storm to pass. Would you like some food?'

They sat together by the blaze, sharing his dried meat and hardcake biscuits and saying little. Tenaka was not an inquisitive man and Renya intuitively knew he had no wish to talk. Yet the silence was far from uncomfortable. She felt calm and at peace for the first time in weeks, and even the threat of the assassins seemed less real, as if the barracks were a haven protected by magic – unseen but infinitely powerful.

Tenaka leaned back in his chair, watching the girl as she in turn gazed into the flames. Her face was striking, oval-shaped with high cheekbones and wide eyes so dark that the pupils merged with the iris. Overall the impression he gained was one of strength, undermined by vulnerability, as if she held a secret fear or was tormented by a hidden weakness. At another time he would have been attracted by her. But when he reached inside himself he could find no emotions, no desire . . . No life, he realised with surprise.

'We are being hunted,' she said at last.

'I know.'

'How would you know?'

He shrugged and added fuel to the fire. 'You are on a road to nowhere, with no horses or provisions, yet your clothes are expensive and your manner cultured. Therefore you are running away from something or someone, and it follows that they are pursuing you.'

'Does it bother you?' she asked him.

'Why should it?'

'If you are caught with us, you will die too.'

'Then I shall not be caught with you,' he said.

'Shall I tell you why we are hunted?' she enquired.

'No. That is of your life. Our paths have crossed here, but we will both go on to separate destinies. There is no need for us to learn of one another.'

'Why? Do you fear it would make you care?'

He considered the question carefully, noting the anger in her eyes. 'Perhaps. But mainly I fear the weakness that follows caring. I have a task to do and I do not need other problems in my mind. No, that is not true – I do not *want* other problems in my mind.'

'Is that not selfish?'

'Of course it is. But it aids survival.'

'And is that so important?' she snapped.

'It must be, otherwise you would not be running.'

'It is important to him,' she said, pointing at the man in the bed. 'Not to me.'

'He cannot run from death,' said Tenaka, softly. 'Anyway there are mystics who maintain there is a paradise after death.'

'He believes it,' she said, smiling. 'That is what he fears.'

Tenaka shook his head slowly, then rubbed his eyes.

'That is a little too much for me,' he said, forcing a smile. 'I think I will sleep now.' Taking his blanket, he spread it on the floor and stretched himself out, his head resting on his pack.

'You are Dragon, aren't you?' said Renya.

'How did you know?' he asked, propping himself on one elbow.

'It was the way you said "my room".'

'Very perceptive.' He lay down and closed his eyes.

'I am Renya.'

'Goodnight, Renya.'

'Will you tell me your name?'

He thought of refusing, considering all the reasons why he should not tell her.

'Tenaka Khan,' he said. And slept.

Life is a farce, thought Scaler, as he hung by his fingertips forty feet above the stone courtyard. Below him a huge Joining sniffed the air, its shaggy head swinging ponderously from side to side, its taloned fingers curled

525

around the hilt of the saw-edged sword. Snow swept in icy flurries, stinging Scaler's eyes.

'Thanks very much,' he whispered, transferring his gaze to the dark, pregnant storm-clouds above. Scaler was a religious man, who saw the gods as a group of Seniles – eternals playing endless jokes on humanity with cosmic bad taste.

Below him the Joining sheathed its sword and ambled away into the darkness. Taking a deep breath, Scaler hauled himself over the window-sill and parted the heavy velvet curtains beyond. He was in a small study furnished with a desk, three chairs of oak, several chests and a row of bookshelves and manuscript holders. The study was tidy – obsessively so, thought Scaler, noting the three quill pens placed exactly parallel at the centre of the desk. He would have expected nothing less of Silius the Magister.

A long silvered mirror, framed in mahogany, was fixed to the far wall, opposite the desk. Scaler advanced towards it, drawing himself up to his full height and pulling back his shoulders. The black face-mask, dark tunic and leggings gave him a forbidding look. He drew his dagger and dropped into a warrior's crouch. The effect was chilling.

Perfect, he told his reflection. I wouldn't want to meet you in a dark alley! Replacing the dagger, he moved to the study door and carefully lifted the iron latch, easing the door open.

Beyond was a narrow stone corridor and four doors – two on the left and two on the right. Scaler padded across to the furthest room on the left and slowly lifted the latch. The door opened without a sound and he moved inside, hugging the wall. The room was warm, though the log fire in the grate was burning low, a dull red glow illuminating the curtains around the large bed. Scaler moved forward to the bed, pausing to look down on fat Silius and his equally fat mistress. He lay on his stomach, she on her back; both were snoring.

Why am I creeping about? he asked himself. I could have come in here beating a drum. He stifled a chuckle, found the jewel box in its hidden niche below the window, opened it and poured the contents into a black canvas pouch tied to his belt. At full value they would keep him in luxury for five years. Sold, as they must be, to a shady dealer in the southern quarter, they would keep him for barely three months, or six if he didn't gamble. He thought of not gambling but it was inconceivable. Three months, he decided.

Re-tying his pouch, he backed out into the corridor and turned . . .

Only to come face to face with a servant, a tall, gaunt figure in a woollen nightshirt.

The man screamed and fled.

Scaler screamed and fled, hurtling down a circular stairway and cannon-ing into two sentries. Both men tumbled back, shouting as they fell. Scaler hit the floor in a tumbler's roll, came to his feet and sprinted left, the sentries close behind. Another set of steps appeared on his right and he took them three at a time, his long legs carrying him at a terrifying speed.

Twice he nearly lost his footing before reaching the next level. Before him was an iron gate – locked, but the key hung from a wooden peg. The stench from beyond the gate brought him to his senses and fear cut through his panic.

The Joinings' pit!

Behind him he could hear the sentries pounding down the stairs. He lifted the key, opened the gate and stepped inside, locking it behind him. Then he advanced into the darkness, praying to the Seniles to let him live for a few more of their jests.

As his eyes grew accustomed to the darkness of the corridor he saw several openings on either side; within, sleeping on straw, were the Joinings of Silius.

He moved on towards the gate at the far end, pulling off his mask as he did so.

He was almost there when the pounding began behind him and the muffled shouts of the sentries pierced the silence. A Joining stumbled from its lair, blood-red eyes fastening on Scaler; it was close to seven feet tall, with huge shoulders and heavily-muscled arms covered with black fur. Its face was elongated, sharp fangs lining its maw. The pounding grew louder and Scaler took a deep breath.

'Go and see what the noise is about,' he told the beast.

'Who you?' it hissed, the words mangled by the lolling tongue.

'Don't just stand there – go and see what they want,' ordered Scaler sharply.

The beast brushed past him and other Joinings came into the corridor and followed it, ignoring Scaler. He ran to the gate and slipped the key in the lock. As it turned and the gate swung open, a sudden bellowing roar blasted in the confines of the corridor. Scaler twisted round to see the Joinings running towards him, howling ferociously. With shaking fingers he dragged free the key and leapt through the opening, pulling the gate shut behind him and swiftly locking it.

The night air was crisp as he ran up the short steps to the western courtyard and on to the ornate wall, scaling it swiftly and dropping into the cobbled street beyond.

It was well after curfew, so he hugged the shadows all the way to the inn, then climbed the outer trellis to his room, rapping on the shutters.

Belder opened the window and helped him inside.

'Well?' asked the old soldier.

'I got the jewels,' stated Scaler.

'I despair of you,' said Belder. 'After all the years I spend on you, what do you become? A thief!'

'It's in the blood,' said Scaler, grinning. 'Remember the Earl of Bronze?'

'That's Legend,' replied Belder. 'And even if it's true, not one of his descendants has ever lived a less than honourable life. Even that Nadir-spawn Tenaka!'

'Don't speak ill of him, Belder,' said Scaler softly. 'He was my friend.'

2

Tenaka slept and the familiar dreams returned to haunt him.

The Steppes rolled away from him like a green, frozen ocean, all the way to the end of the world. His pony reared as he dragged the rawhide rein, then swung to the south with hooves drumming the hard-packed clay.

With the dry wind in his face Tenaka grinned.

Here, only here, was he his own man.

Half-Nadir, half-Drenai, wholly nothing – a product of war, a flesh-and-blood symbol of uneasy peace. He was accepted among the tribes with cool courtesy, as befitted one in whose veins ran the blood of Ulric. But there was little camaraderie. Twice the tribes had been turned back by the strength of the Drenai. Once, long before, the legendary Earl of Bronze had defended Dros Delnoch against Ulric's hordes. Twenty years ago the Dragon had decimated Jongir's army.

Now here was Tenaka, a living reminder of defeat.

So he rode alone and mastered all the tasks they set him. Sword, bow, spear, axe – with each of these he was skilled beyond his peers, for when they ceased practice to enjoy the games of childhood he worked on. He listened to the wise – seeing wars and battles on a different plane – and his sharp mind absorbed the lessons.

One day they would accept him. If he had patience.

But he had ridden home to the city of tents and seen his mother standing with Jongir. She was crying.

And he knew.

He leapt from the saddle and bowed to the Khan, ignoring his mother, as was fitting.

'It is time for you to go home,' said Jongir.

He said nothing, merely nodded.

'They have a place for you within the Dragon. It is your right as the son of an Earl.' The Khan seemed uncomfortable, and did not meet Tenaka's steady gaze. 'Well, say something,' he snapped.

'As you wish, Lord, so let it be.'

'You will not plead to stay?'

'If you desire me to.'

'I desire nothing of you.'

'Then when shall I leave?'

'Tomorrow. You will have an escort – twenty riders, as befits my grandson.'

'You honour me, Lord.'

The Khan nodded, glanced once at Shillat and then walked away. Shillat opened the tent-flap and Tenaka entered their home. She followed him and once inside he turned to her and took her in his arms.

'Oh, Tani,' she whispered through her tears. 'What more must you do?'

'Maybe at Dros Delnoch I shall truly be home,' he said. But hope died within him as he said it, for he was not a fool.

Tenaka awoke to hear the storm hissing and battering at the window. He stretched and glanced at the fire – it had faded to glowing coals. The girl slept in the chair, her breathing deep. He sat up and then moved to the fire, adding fresh wood and gently blowing the flames to life. He checked the old man; his colour was not good. Tenaka shrugged and left the room. The corridor was icy, the wooden boards creaking under his boots. He made his way to the old kitchen and the indoor well; it was hard to pump, but he enjoyed the exercise and was rewarded when water jetted to the wooden bucket. Stripping off his dark jerkin and grey woollen shirt, he washed his upper body, enjoying the near-pain of the ice-touched water on his sleep-warm skin.

Removing his remaining clothes, Tenaka moved out into the gym area beyond. There he twirled and leapt, landing lightly – first his right hand slicing the air, then his left. He rolled to the floor, then arched his back and sprang to his feet.

From the doorway Renya watched him, drawing back into the shadows of the corridor. She was fascinated. He moved like a dancer, yet there was something barbaric in the scene: some primordial element that was both lethal and yet beautiful. His feet and hands were weapons, flashing and killing invisible opponents, yet his face was serene and devoid of all passion.

She shivered, longing to withdraw to the sanctuary of his room but unable to move. His skin was the colour of gold under sunlight, soft and warm, but the muscles beneath strained and swelled like silver steel. She closed her eyes and stumbled back, wishing she had never seen him.

Tenaka washed the sweat from his body and then dressed swiftly, hunger eating at him. Back in his room he sensed the change in the atmosphere. Renya avoided meeting his eyes as she sat by the old man, stroking his white hair.

'The storm is breaking,' said Tenaka.

'Yes.'

'What is the matter?'

'Nothing . . . except that Aulin is not breathing well. Will he be all right, do you think?'

Tenaka joined her at the bedside. Taking the old man's frail wrist between his fingers he felt for the pulse. It was weak and irregular.

'How long since he has eaten?' he asked.

'Two days.'

Tenaka delved in his pack, producing a sack of dried meat and a smaller pack of oats. 'I wish I had sugar,' he said, 'but this will have to do. Go and fetch some water and a cooking pot.'

Without a word Renya left the room. Tenaka smiled. So that was it – she had seen him exercising and for some reason it had unsettled her. He shook his head.

She returned with an iron pot brimming with water.

'Throw half of it away,' he told her. She splashed it in the hallway and he took the pot to the fire, slicing the meat with his dagger. Then he carefully placed the pot on the flames.

'Why did you not speak this morning?' he asked, his back towards her.

'I don't know what you mean.'

'When you saw me exercising?'

'I did not see you.'

'Then how did you know where to fetch the pot and get the water? You did not go past me in the night.'

'Who are you to question me?' she snapped.

He turned to her. 'I am a stranger. You do not need to lie to me, or pretend. Only with friends do you need masks.'

She sat down by the fire, stretching her long legs to the flames.

'How sad,' she said, softly. 'Surely it is only with friends that one can be at peace?'

'It is easier with strangers, for they touch your life but for an instant. You will not disappoint them, for you owe them nothing, neither do they expect anything. Friends you can hurt, for they expect everything.'

'Strange friends you have had,' she said.

Tenaka stirred the broth with his dagger blade. He was uncomfortable suddenly, feeling that he had somehow lost control of the conversation.

'Where are you from?' he asked.

'I thought you did not care.'

'Why did you not speak?' Her eyes narrowed and she turned her head.

'I did not want to break your concentration.'

It was a lie and they both knew it, but the tension eased and the silence gathered, drawing them together. Outside the storm grew old and died, whimpering where once it had roared.

As the stew thickened Tenaka added oats to further swell the mixture, and finally salt from his small store.

'It smells good,' said Renya, leaning over the fire. 'What meat is it?'

'Mule, mostly,' he told her.

He went to fetch some old wooden platters from the kitchen and when he returned Renya had wakened the old man and was helping him to sit up.

'How are you feeling?' Tenaka enquired.

'You are a warrior?' asked Aulin, his eyes fearful.

'Yes. But you need not fear me.'

'Nadir?'

'Mercenary. I have prepared you some stew.'

'I am not hungry.'

'Eat it anyway,' ordered Tenaka. The old man stiffened at the authoritative tone, then averted his eyes and nodded. Renya fed him slowly as Tenaka sat by the fire. It was a waste of food, for the old man was dying. Still, he did not regret it and could not understand why.

With the meal over, Renya collected the platters and the pot. 'My grandfather wishes to speak with you,' she said and left the room.

Tenaka moved to the bedside, staring down at the dying man. Aulin's eyes were grey and bright with the beginnings of fever.

'I am not strong,' said Aulin. 'I never was. I have failed everyone who ever trusted me. Except Renya . . . I never failed her. Do you believe me?'

'Yes,' Tenaka answered. Why was it that weak men always felt the need for confession?

'Will you protect her?'

'No.'

'I can pay.' Aulin gripped Tenaka's arm. 'Just take her to Sousa. The city is only five, six days south.'

'You are nothing to me. I owe you nothing. And you cannot pay me enough.'

'Renya says you were Dragon. Where is your sense of honour?'

'Buried under desert sands. Lost in the swirling mists of time. I don't want to talk to you, old man. You have nothing to say.'

'Please listen!' Aulin begged. 'When I was a younger man I served the Council. I supported Ceska, worked for his victory. I believed in him. So I am, at least in part, responsible for the appalling terror he has visited on this land. I was a Source priest once. My life was in harmony. Now I am dying and I don't know anything any more. But I cannot die leaving Renya to be taken by the Joinings. I *cannot*. Don't you see? My whole life has been a failure – my death *must* achieve something.'

Tenaka pulled away the old man's hand and stood.

'Now you listen,' he said. 'I am here to kill Ceska. I do not expect to live beyond the deed, but I have neither the time nor the inclination to take on your responsibilities. You want to see the girl get to Sousa, then recover. Use your will.'

Suddenly the old man smiled, tension and fear falling from him. 'You want to kill Ceska?' he whispered. 'I can give you something better than that.'

'Better? What could be better?'

'Bring him down. End his reign?'

'Killing him should achieve that.'

'Yes, indeed, but one of his generals would only take over. I can give you the secret which would destroy his empire and free the Drenai.'

'If this is to be a tale of enchanted swords or mystic spells, do not waste your time. I have heard them all.'

'No. Promise me you will protect Renya as far as Sousa.'

'I will think about it,' said Tenaka. Once more the fire was dying and he fed the last of the wood to the flames before leaving the room in search of the girl. He found her sitting in the cold kitchen.

'I don't want your help,' she said, without looking up.

'I haven't offered it yet.'

'I don't care if they take me.'

'You are too young not to care,' he said, kneeling before her and lifting her chin. 'I will see that you get safely to Sousa.'

'Are you sure he can pay you enough?'

'He says that he can.'

'I don't like you very much, Tenaka Khan.'

'Welcome to the majority view!' he said.

Leaving her, he returned to his room and the old man. Then he laughed and moved to the window, throwing it wide to the winter air.

Before him the forest stretched on for a white eternity.

Behind him the old man was dead.

Hearing his laughter Renya entered the room. Aulin's arm had slid from the bed and his bony fingers now pointed at the wooden floor. His eyes were closed and his face peaceful.

She went to him and touched his cheek gently. 'No more running, Aulin. No more fear. May your Source bring you home!'

She covered his face with a blanket.

'Now your obligation is over,' Renya told the silent Tenaka.

'Not yet,' he said, pulling shut the window. 'He told me he knew of a way to end Ceska's reign. Do you know what he meant?'

'No.' She turned away from him and gathered her cloak, her heart suddenly empty. Then she stopped, her cloak falling from her hands as she stared at the dying fire and shook her head. Reality receded. What was there to live for?

Nothing.

What was there to care for?

Nothing.

She knelt by the fire, staring unblinking as a terrible ache filled the emptiness within. Aulin's life had been a steady tale of small kindnesses, tenderness and caring. Never had he been intentionally cruel or malicious; never greedy. But he had ended his life in a deserted barracks – hunted as a criminal, betrayed by his friends and lost to his god.

Tenaka watched her, no hint of emotion in his violet eyes. He was a man used to death. Quietly he stowed his gear in the canvas pack, then lifted her to her feet, fastened her cloak and pushed her gently through the doorway.

'Wait here,' he said. Returning to the bed, he pulled his blanket clear of the corpse. The old man's eyes had opened and he seemed to be staring at the warrior.

'Sleep truly,' whispered Tenaka. 'I will take care of her.' He closed the dead eyes and folded his blanket.

Outside the air was crisp. The wind had died and the sun shone weakly in a clear sky. Tenaka took a slow deep breath.

'Now it is over,' whispered Renya. Tenaka glanced round.

Four warriors had left the screen of trees and were walking forward with swords in hand.

'Leave me,' she said.

'Be silent.'

He loosed his pack, lowering it to the snow, then pushed back his cloak from his shoulders, revealing the scabbard sword and hunting-knife.

532

Walking forward ten paces he waited for the warriors, gauging each man in turn.

They wore the red and bronze breastplates of Delnoch.

'What do you seek?' asked Tenaka, as they drew near.

None of the soldiers spoke, which marked them as veterans, but they spread out slightly – ready for any aggressive action from the warrior.

'Speak, or the emperor will have your heads!' said Tenaka. That stopped them and their eyes flickered to a sharp-featured swordsman on the left; he stepped forward, his blue eyes cold and malevolent.

'Since when does a northern savage make promises on behalf of the emperor?' he hissed.

Tenaka smiled. They had all stopped and were waiting for an answer; they had lost their momentum.

'Perhaps I should explain,' he said, maintaining the smile and moving towards the man. 'It's like this . . .' His hand flashed out and up, fingers extended, smashing the man's nose. The thin cartilage sliced up into the brain and he dropped without a sound. Then Tenaka whirled and leapt, his booted foot hammering into the throat of a second man. Even as he leapt he drew the hunting-knife. Landing on the balls of his feet he spun, parried a thrust and buried his blade in his opponent's neck.

The fourth man was running towards Renya, sword raised. She stood still, watching him without interest.

Tenaka hurled the hunting-knife, which hit the man hilt-first at the base of the helm. Unbalanced, the warrior tumbled in the snow, losing his grip on his sword. Tenaka ran forward as he scrambled to rise, then threw himself on the man's back and he pitched forward once more, his helm tumbling from his head. Tenaka grabbed his hair, tugging the head back, then took hold of the man's chin and wrenched it to the left. His neck snapped like dry wood.

Recovering his knife, Tenaka wiped it clean and replaced it. He scanned the clearing. All was silent.

'Nadir we,' he whispered closing his eyes.

'Shall we go?' asked Renya.

Puzzled, he took her arm, gazing down into her eyes.

'What is the matter with you? Do you want to die?'

'No,' she said absently.

'Then why did you just stand there?'

'I don't know. Shall we go?'

Tears welled in her night-dark eyes, spilling to her cheek, but her pale face remained impassive. Reaching up, he smoothed a tear from her skin.

'Please don't touch me,' she whispered.

'Now you listen to me. The old man wanted you to live; he cared for you.'

'It doesn't matter.'

'It mattered to him!'

'Does it matter to *you*?' The question caught him cold, like a blow. He absorbed it and searched himself swiftly for the right answer.

'Yes, it does.' The lie came easily, and only when it was spoken did he realise it was not a lie.

She looked deeply into his eyes, then nodded.

'I will come with you,' she said. 'But know this: I am a curse to all who love me. Death haunts me, for I should never have tasted life.'

'Death haunts everyone, and never fails,' he said.

Together they walked to the south, stopping by the stone dragon. Icy rain had stung her flanks, giving her a diamond sheen. Tenaka's breath caught in his throat as he gazed upon her face – the water had run to the ruined fangs of her upper mouth, forming new teeth of sparkling ice, renewing her grandeur, restoring her power.

He nodded, as if hearing a silent message.

'She is beautiful,' said Renya.

'Better than that,' said Tenaka softly, 'she is alive.'

'Alive?'

'In here,' he answered, touching his heart. 'She is welcoming me home.'

Throughout the long day they pushed on towards the south. Tenaka said little, concentrating on the snow-hidden trails and keeping a wary eye for patrols. He had no way of knowing if the four soldiers were the full complement of hunters, or whether there were several groups pursuing the girl.

In a strange way he did not care. He forced the pace, rarely looking back to see if Renya was struggling. When he did pause, to check out skylines or scan stretches of open ground, she was always just behind him.

For her part Renya followed quietly, eyes fixed on the tall warrior, noting the sureness of his movements and the care with which he chose the route. Again and again two scenes played in her mind: the naked dance in the deserted gymnasium, and the dance of death with the soldiers in the snow. One scene overlaid the other . . . blending, merging. The same dance. The movements were so smooth, almost liquid, as he leapt and turned. The soldiers by comparison seemed ungainly, disjointed, like Lentrian puppets with knotted string.

And now they were dead. Did they have families? Probably. Did they love their children? Probably. They had walked into that clearing as confident men. And yet, in a matter of icy moments, they were gone.

Why?

Because they chose to dance with Tenaka Khan.

She shivered. The light was failing and long shadows crept from the trees.

Tenaka chose a site for his fire against a jutting of rock, sheltered from the wind. It was set in a hollow surrounded by gnarled oaks and the fire was well-screened. Renya joined him, gathering dead wood and stacking it carefully. A sense of unreality gripped her.

All the world should be like this, she thought, ice-covered and cleansed: all plants sleeping, waiting for the golden perfection of spring; all evil withering under the purifying ice.

Ceska and his demon-spawned legions would fade away like the nightmares of childhood and joy would return to the Drenai, like the gift of dawn.

Tenaka removed a pot from his pack and placed it on the fire, scooping handfuls of snow into the container until it was half-full with warming water. Then, from a small canvas sack he poured a generous mixture of oats into the liquid, adding salt. Renya watched him in silence, fixing her gaze on his slanted violet eyes. Once again, sitting with him by the fire, she felt at peace.

'Why are you here?' she asked.

'To kill Ceska,' he replied, stirring the porridge with a wooden spoon.

'*Why* are you here?' she repeated.

Moments passed, but she knew he was not ignoring her and waited, enjoying the warmth and the closeness.

'I have nowhere else to go. My friends are dead. My wife . . .'. I have nothing. The reality is that I have always had . . . nothing.'

'You had friends . . . a wife.'

'Yes. It's not easy to explain. There was a wise man once, in Ventria, near where I lived. I spoke with him often about life, and love, and friendship. He chided me, made me angry. He talked about clay diamonds.' Tenaka shook his head and lapsed into silence.

'Clay diamonds?' she asked.

'It doesn't matter. Tell me about Aulin.'

'I do not know what he planned to tell you.'

'I accept that,' he said. 'Just tell me of the man.' Using two sticks he lifted the pot from the flames and set it on the ground to cool. She leaned forward, adding fresh wood to the fire.

'He was a peaceful man, a Source priest. But he was also an Arcanist and liked nothing better than to scour the land for relics of the Elders. He gained a name for his abilities. He told me that when Ceska first came to power he supported him, believed all the promises about a better future. But then the terror began. And the Joinings . . .'

'Ceska always loved sorcery,' said Tenaka.

'You knew him?'

'Yes. Go on.'

'Aulin was one of the first to explore the Graven site. He found the hidden door below the forest and the machines that lay there. He told me his research proved the machines had been created to heal certain diseases suffered by the Elders. But instead of using them in this fashion, Ceska's adepts created the Joinings. At first they were used only in the arenas, tearing each other to pieces to thrill the crowds; but soon they began appearing on the streets of Drenan wearing armour and the markings of Ceska's guard.

'Aulin blamed himself and journeyed to Delnoch, ostensibly to examine the Chamber of Light beneath the Keep. From there he bribed a sentry and tried to escape through Sathuli lands. But the chase began and we were forced south instead.'

'Where do you come into the story?' he asked.

'You did not ask about me, but about Aulin.'

535

'I am asking now.'

'May I have some porridge?'

He nodded, tested the pot and handed it to her. She ate in silence and then passed the remains to Tenaka. Finishing the meal, the warrior leaned back against the cold rock.

'There is a mystery around you, lady. But I will leave it lie. The world would be a sad place without mysteries.'

'The world *is* a sad place,' she said, 'full of death and terror. Why is evil so much stronger than love?'

'Who says that it is?' he responded.

'You have not been living among the Drenai. Men like Aulin are hunted down like criminals; farmers are butchered for failing to reach absurd crop levels; the arenas are packed with baying crowds who laugh while animals rip and tear women and children. It is vile! All of it.'

'It will pass,' he said gently. 'And now it is time to sleep.' He held out his hand to her, but she shrank back, her dark eyes suddenly fearful. 'I will not harm you, but we must let the fire die. We will share warmth, but that is all we will share. Trust me.'

'I can sleep alone,' she said.

'Very well.' He untied the blanket and passed it to her, then wrapped himself in his cloak and leaned his head back to the rock, closing his eyes.

Renya stretched herself out on the cold ground, pillowing her head on her arm.

As the fire died so the night cold grew, seeping into her limbs. She awoke shivering uncontrollably and sat up, rubbing warmth into her numbed legs.

Tenaka opened his eyes and held out his hand. 'Come,' he said.

She moved to him and he opened his cloak, wrapping it around her and pulling her in to his chest before covering them both with the blanket. She nestled against him, still shivering.

'T-t-tell me about c-c-clay diamonds,' she asked.

He smiled. 'The wise man was called Kias. He said that too many people go through life without pausing to enjoy what they have and he told of a man who was given a clay jug by a friend. The friend said, "Examine it when you have the time." But it was just a simple clay jug and the man put it aside and forged on with his life, spending his time acquiring riches. One day, when he was old, he took the jug and opened it. Within was a huge diamond.'

'I do not understand.'

'Kias claimed that life was like that clay jug. Unless we examined it and understood it, we could not enjoy it.'

'Sometimes understanding robs you of joy,' she whispered.

He said nothing, transferring his gaze to the night sky and the distant stars. Renya fell into a dreamless sleep, her head tipping forward, dislodging the woollen burnoose that covered her close-cropped hair. Tenaka reached up to replace it, then stopped as his hand touched her head. The hair was not close-cropped – it had grown as long as it would grow. For it was not hair but dark fur, soft as sable. Gently he pulled the burnoose into place and closed his eyes.

The girl was a Joining, half-human, half-animal.

No wonder she did not care for life.

Were there diamonds in the clay for such as she? he wondered.

3

At the Dragon barracks a man pushed his way past the screen of bushes before the parade ground. He was a big man, broad shoulders tapering to lean hips and long legs, was dressed in black and carried an iron-tipped ebony quarterstaff. Hooded, his face was covered by a shaped mask in black leather. He moved easily – the rolling, fluid gait of the athlete – yet he was wary, his bright blue eyes flickering to every bush and shadow-haunted tree.

When he saw the bodies he circled them slowly, reading the brief battle in the tracks.

One man against four.

The first three had died almost instantly and that spoke of speed. The fourth had run past the lone warrior. The tall man followed the track and nodded.

So. Here was a mystery. The lone warrior was not alone – he had a companion who took no part in the fray. The footprints were small, yet the stride long. A woman?

Yes, a woman. A tall woman.

He glanced back at the bodies.

'That was well done,' he said aloud, the voice muffled by the mask. 'Damn well done.' One against four. Not many men could survive against such odds, yet this man had not only survived but won the day with skill to spare.

Ringar? He was a lightning killer with astonishing reflexes. Yet he barely chanced a neck cut, more often choosing the lower torso: the disembowelling cut.

Argonin? No, he was dead. Strange how a man could forget such a thing.

Who then? An unknown? No. In a world where skill with arms was of paramount importance, there were few unknowns of such bewildering talent.

He studied the tracks once more, picturing the battle, seeing at last the blurred print at the centre. The warrior had leapt and spun in the air like a dancer before hammering home the death blow.

Tenaka Khan!

Realisation struck the big man like a blow to the heart. His eyes glittered strangely and his breathing grew ragged.

Of all the men in the world he hated, Tenaka had pride of place.

Or was that still true? He relaxed and remembered, his thoughts tracing his memories like salt over a festering wound.

'I should have killed you then,' he said. 'None of this would have happened to me.'

He pictured Tenaka dying, his blood seeping into the snow. It gave him no joy, but still he hungered for the deed.

'I will make you pay,' he said.

And set off to the south.

Tenaka and Renya made good progress on the second day – seeing no one, nor any track made by man. The wind had died down and the clean air held the promise of spring. Tenaka was silent through most of the day and Renya did not press him.

Towards dusk as they clambered down a steep incline, she lost her footing and pitched forward, tumbling and rolling to the foot of the hill and striking her head on a gnarled tree-root. Tenaka ran to her side, pulling free her burnoose and examining the seeping gash on her temple. Her eyes flared open.

'Don't touch me,' she screamed, clawing at his hands.

He moved back, handing her the cotton burnoose.

'I don't like to be touched,' she said apologetically.

'Then I shall not touch you,' he answered. 'But you should bandage that wound.'

She tried to stand, but the world spun and she fell to the snow. Tenaka made no move to help her. Glancing around for a place to camp, he spotted a likely site some thirty paces away to the left: a natural screen of trees blocking the wind, with overhanging boughs to halt any storm snow. He made his way to it, collecting branches as he went. Renya watched him walk away and struggled to rise, but felt sick and began to tremble violently. Her head throbbed, the pain a rhythmic pounding which sent waves of nausea through her. She tried to crawl.

'I . . . don't need you,' she whispered.

Tenaka prepared the fire, blowing the tinder until tiny flames shivered above the snow. Then he added thicker twigs and finally branches. When the blaze was well set he returned to the girl, stooping to lift her unconscious body. He laid her by the fire, then climbed a nearby fir tree to hack away green boughs with his short sword. Gathering them he made a bed for her, lifted her on to it and then covered her with the blanket. He examined the wound – there was no fracture as far as he could tell, but an ugly bruise was forming around an egg-sized lump.

He stroked her face, admiring the softness of her skin and the sleekness of her neck.

'I will not harm you, Renya,' he said. 'Of all the things that I am, of all the deeds I have done that shamed me, I have never harmed a woman. Nor a child. You are safe with me . . . Your secrets are safe with me.

'I know what it is like, you see. I too am between worlds – half-Nadir, half-Drenai, wholly nothing. For you it is worse. But I am here. Believe in me.'

He returned to the fire, wishing he could say those words when her eyes were open but knowing he would not. In all his life he had opened his heart to only one woman: Illae.

Beautiful Illae, the bride he had purchased in a Ventrian market. He smiled at the memory. Two thousand pieces of silver and he had taken her home only to have her refuse to share his bed.

'Enough of this nonsense,' he had stormed. 'You are mine. Body and soul! I bought you!'

'What you bought was a carcass,' she retorted. 'Touch me and I will kill myself. And you too.'

'You will be disappointed if you try it in that order,' he said.

'Don't mock me, barbarian!'

'Very well. What would you have me do? Re-sell you to a Ventrian?'

'Marry me.'

'And then, I take it, you will love and adore me?'

'No. But I will sleep with you and try to be good company.'

'Now there is an offer that's hard to refuse. A slave girl who offers her master less than he paid for, at a much greater price. Why should I do it?'

'Why should you not?'

They had wed two weeks later and ten years of their life together had brought him joy. He knew she did not love him, but it didn't matter. He did not need to *be* loved, he needed to *love*. She had seen that in him from the first, and played on it mercilessly. He never let her know that he understood the game, he merely relaxed and enjoyed it. The wise man, Kias, had tried to warn him.

'You give too much of yourself to her, my friend. You fill her with your dreams and your hopes, and your soul. If she leaves or betrays you, what will you have left?'

'Nothing,' he had answered truthfully.

'You are a foolish man, Tenaka. I hope she stays by you.'

'She will.'

He had been so sure. But he had not bargained for death.

Tenaka shivered and drew his cloak about him as the wind picked up.

He would take the girl to Sousa and then head on for Drenan. It would not be hard to find Ceska, nor to kill him. No man is so well protected that he becomes safe. Not as long as the assassin is prepared to die. And Tenaka was more than prepared.

He desired death, longed for the bleak emptiness and the absence of pain.

By now Ceska would know Tenaka was on his way. The letter would have reached him within the month, travelling as it did by sea to Mashrapur and then north-east to Drenan.

'I hope you dream of me, Ceska. I hope I walk in your nightmares.'

'I don't know about him,' said a muffled voice, 'but you walk in mine.'

Tenaka spun to his feet, his sword flashing into the air.

Before him stood the giant in the black mask.

'I have come to kill you,' he said, drawing his longsword.

Tenaka edged away from the fire, watching the man, his mind clearing and his body easing into the smooth confident fluidity of combat.

The giant twirled his sword and spread his arms wide for balance. Tenaka blinked as recognition hit him.

'Ananais?' he said.

The giant's sword whistled for his neck, but Tenaka blocked the cut and jumped back.

'Ananais, *is* it you?' he said again.

The giant stood silently for a moment. 'Yes,' he said, at last. 'It is I. Now defend yourself!'

Tenaka sheathed his sword and walked forward. 'I could not fight you,' he said. 'And I know not why you should desire my death.'

Ananais leapt forward, hammering a fist to Tenaka's head and pitching him to the snow.

'Why?' he shouted. 'You don't know *why*? Look at me!'

He wrenched the leather mask from his face and in the flickering firelight Tenaka saw a living nightmare. There was no face, only the twisted, scarred ruin of features. The nose was gone, and the upper lip, jagged white and red scars criss-crossing the remaining skin. Only the blue eyes and the tightly-curled blond hair showed evidence of humanity.

'Sweet gods of light!' whispered Tenaka. 'I didn't do that . . . I never knew.'

Ananais moved forward slowly, lowering the point of his sword to touch Tenaka's neck.

'The pebble that caused the landslide,' said the giant cryptically. 'You know what I mean.'

Tenaka lifted his hand and slowly pushed aside the sword-blade.

'You will have to tell me, my friend,' he said, sitting up.

'Damn you!' shouted the giant, dropping his sword and hauling Tenaka to his feet, dragging him forward until their faces were inches apart. '*Look at me!*'

Tenaka gazed steadily into the ice-blue eyes, sensing the edge of madness lurking there. His life hung on a thread.

'Tell me what happened,' he said softly. 'I am not running away. If you desire to kill me, so be it. But tell me.'

Ananais released him and turned, seeking his mask, presenting his broad back to Tenaka. And in that moment Tenaka knew what was required of him. Sadness filled him.

'I cannot kill you,' he said.

The giant turned again, tears flowing from his eyes.

'Oh, Tani,' he said, his voice breaking, 'look what they did to me!' As he sank to his knees, hands covering the ruined face, Tenaka knelt beside him in the snow and embraced him. The giant began to weep, his chest heaving, his sobbing loud and painful. Tenaka patted his back as if he were a child and felt his pain as if it were his own.

Ananais had come not to kill him, but to die at his hand. And he knew why the giant blamed him. On the day the order to disband the Dragon had been served, Ananais had gathered the men ready to march on Drenan and depose Ceska. Tenaka and the Dragon Gan, Baris, had defused the situation, reminding the men that they had lived and fought for democracy. Thus the revolution was over before it had begun.

And now the Dragon was destroyed, the land in ruins and terror stalked the Drenai.

Ananais had been right.

Renya watched silently until the sobbing ceased, then she stood and walked to the two men, pausing to add fuel to the dying fire. Ananais glanced up and saw her, then scrabbled for his mask.

She moved to his side, kneeling by him, then gently touched the hands that held the mask in place. Curling her fingers around his hands, she pulled the mask clear, her dark eyes fixed only to the giant's own.

As the ruined face came into view Ananais closed his eyes and bowed his head. Renya leaned forward and kissed his brow, then his scarred cheek. His eyes opened.

'Why?' he whispered.

'We all have scars,' she said. 'Better by far for them to be worn on the outside.' She rose and returned to her bed.

'Who is she?' asked Ananais.

'She is hunted by Ceska,' Tenaka told him.

'Aren't we all?' commented the giant, replacing his mask.

'Yes, but we will surprise him,' said Tenaka.

'That would be nice.'

'Trust me, my friend. I mean to bring him down.'

'Alone?'

Tenaka grinned. 'Am I still alone?'

'No! Do you have a plan?'

'Not yet.'

'Good. I thought perhaps the two of us were going to surround Drenan!'

'It might come to that! How many of the Dragon still live?'

'Precious few. Most followed the call. I would have done so too, had it reached me in time. Decado still lives.'

'That is good news,' said Tenaka.

'Not really. He has become a monk.'

'A *monk*? Decado? He lived to kill.'

'Not any more. Are you thinking of gathering an army?'

'No, it would do no good against the Joinings. They are too strong, too fast – too everything.'

'They can be beaten,' said Ananais.

'Not by men.'

'I defeated one.'

'You?'

'Yes. After we disbanded I tried farming. It didn't work out. I had heavy debts and Ceska had opened the arenas for combat games, so I became a gladiator. I thought I would have maybe three fights and earn enough to settle my debts. But I enjoyed the life, you know? I fought under another name, but Ceska found out who I was. At least, that's what I assume. I was due to fight a man named Treus, but when the gates opened there stood a Joining. Gods – he must have been eight feet tall.

542

'But I beat him. By all the demons in Hell, I beat him!'

'How?'

'I had to let him come in close and think he had won. Then I gutted him with my knife.'

'That was an awful risk,' said Tenaka.

'Yes.'

'But you got away with it?'

'Not quite,' answered Ananais. 'He tore off my face.'

'I really thought I could kill you, you know?' said Ananais as they sat together by the fire. 'I really believed it. I hated you. The more I saw the nation suffer, the more you came into my mind. I felt cheated – as if all I had ever lived for had been ruined. And when the Joining . . . when I was injured . . . I lost my mind. My courage. Everything.'

Tenaka sat silently, his heart heavy. Ananais had been a vain man, but gifted with humour that was always self-mocking; it took the edge from his vanity. And he had been handsome, adored by the ladies. Tenaka did not interrupt him. He had the feeling that a long, long time had passed since Ananais had sat in company. The words flowed like a torrent, but always the giant returned to his hatred of the Nadir prince.

'I knew it was irrational, but I couldn't help it, and when I found the bodies at the barracks and knew it was you, I was blind with rage. Until I saw you sitting there. And then . . . then . . .'

'Then you thought to let me kill you,' said Tenaka softly.

'Yes. It seemed . . . fitting.'

'I am glad we found each other, my friend. I just wish some of the others were here.'

The morning was bright and fresh and the warmth of the promise of spring kissed the forest, lightening the hearts of the travellers.

Renya watched Tenaka with new eyes, remembering not only the love and understanding he had shown to his scarred friend, but the words he had said to her before the giant arrived: 'Believe in me.'

And Renya believed.

But more than this. Something in his words touched her heart and the pain in her soul eased.

He knew.

And yet he cared. Renya did not know what love was, for in all her life only one man had ever cared for her, and that was Aulin, the ancient Arcanist. Now there was another. He was not ancient.

Oh, no. Not ancient at all!

He would not leave her in Sousa. Or anywhere else. Where Tenaka Khan walked, there would be Renya. He was unaware of it as yet. But he would learn.

That afternoon Tenaka stalked a young deer – bringing it down with a dagger hurled twenty paces – and the companions ate well. They slept early, making up for the late night before, and the following morning sighted the spires of Sousa to the south-east.

'You'd best stay here,' Ananais advised. 'I should imagine your description has been circulated throughout Drenai by now. Why ever did you write that damned letter? It's not the sensible thing to let the victim know the assassin is on his way!'

'On the contrary, my friend. Paranoia will *eat* at him. It will keep him awake – on edge – he will not think clearly. And for every day that there is no news of me, his fears will grow. It will make him uncertain.'

'You think,' said Ananais. 'Anyway, I will take Renya into the city.'

'Very well. I shall wait here.'

'And does Renya have nothing to say about this arrangement?' said the girl sweetly.

'I did not think it would displease you,' answered Tenaka, nonplussed.

'Well it does!' she snapped. 'You do not own me; I go where I will.' She sat down on a fallen tree and folded her arms, staring into the trees.

'I thought you wanted to go to Sousa,' said Tenaka.

'No. Aulin wanted me there.'

'Well, where do you want to go?'

'I am not sure yet. I will let you know.'

Tenaka shook his head and turned to the giant, spreading his hands.

Ananais shrugged. 'Well, I will go in anyway. We need some food – and a little information would not go amiss. I shall see what I can find out.'

'Stay out of trouble,' warned Tenaka.

'Don't worry about me, I will blend in. I shall just find a large crowd of tall black-masked men and stick with them.'

'You know what I mean.'

'Yes. Don't worry! I will not risk fifty per cent of our new army on one reconnaissance.'

Tenaka watched him walk away and returned to the girl, sweeping the snow from the trunk and sitting down beside her.

'Why did you not go with him?'

'Did you want me to?' she countered, turning to look into his violet eyes.

'Want you to? What do you mean?'

She leaned into him. He caught the musky perfume of her skin and noticed again the sleekness of her neck and the dark beauty of her eyes.

'I want to stay with you,' she whispered.

He closed his eyes, shutting out the magic of her beauty. But the perfume lingered.

'This is insane,' he said, pushing himself to his feet.

'Why?'

'Because I am not going to live very long. Don't you understand? Killing Ceska is not a game. My chances of survival are one in a thousand.'

'It is a game,' she said. 'A man's game. You don't need to kill Ceska – it is not for you to take on the burden of the Drenai.'

'I know that,' he said. 'It is personal. But I will see it through and so will Ananais.'

'And so will I. I have as much reason to hate Ceska as both you and your friend. He hounded Aulin to death.'

544

'But you are a woman,' he said desperately.

She laughed at him, a rich, pealing sound which was full of humour. 'Oh, Tenaka, how I have longed for you to say something foolish. You are always so right. So clever. A woman, indeed! Yes, I *am*. And more than that. Had I wished, I could have slain those four soldiers myself. My strength is as great as yours, possibly greater, and I can move just as fast. You know what I am: a Joining! Aulin knew me in Drenan, where I was a cripple with a twisted back and a ruined leg. He took pity on me and brought me to Graven, where he used the machines as they were intended. He healed me, by blending me with one of Ceska's pets. You know what he used?'

'No,' whispered Tenaka.

In a blur of motion she sprang from the fallen trunk. His arms came up as she hit him and he fell to the snow, air exploding from his lungs. Within seconds she had pinned him to the ground. He struggled, but could not move. Holding his arms flat to the snow, she twisted her body until she was lying on top of him, her face inches from his own.

'He blended me with a panther,' she said.

'I would still have believed it if you had merely said it,' he told her. 'The demonstration was unnecessary.'

'Not for me,' said Renya. 'For now I have you at my mercy.'

He grinned . . . arched his back and twisted. With a scream of surprise Renya was hurled to the left. Tenaka swivelled and dived on her, pinning her arms beneath her.

'I am seldom at anyone's mercy, young lady,' he said.

'Well?' she asked him, raising an eyebrow. 'Now what will you do?'

His face reddened and he did not answer. Nor did he move. He could feel the warmth of her body, smell the perfume of her skin.

'I love you,' she said. 'Truly!'

'I have no time, I cannot. I have no future.'

'Neither do I. What is there for a Joining? Kiss me.'

'No.'

'Please?'

He did not answer. He could not. For their lips touched.

4

Scaler stood in the crowd and watched the girl as they tied her to the stake. She did not struggle or cry out, and only contempt showed in her eyes. She was tall and fair-haired – not beautiful, but striking. As the guards piled brushwood against her legs they did not look at her, and Scaler sensed their shame.

It matched his own.

The officer climbed to the wooden platform beside the girl and surveyed the crowd. He felt their sullen anger wash over him and rejoiced in it. They were powerless.

Malif adjusted his crimson cloak and removed his helm, tucking it neatly into the crook of his arm. The sunshine felt good and the day promised to be fine. Very fine.

He cleared his throat.

'This woman has been accused of sedition, witchcraft, dealing in poisons and theft. On all counts she has been righteously condemned. But if there be any to speak for her, let them do so now!'

His eyes flickered to the left, where a movement began among the watchers. An old man was being restrained by a younger. No sport there!

Malif swept his arms to the right, pointing at a Joining in the red and bronze livery of Silius the Magister.

'This servant of the law has been appointed to defend the decision of the court. If any should wish to champion the girl, Valtaya, let him first gaze upon his opponent.'

Scaler gripped Belder's arm. 'Don't be a fool!' he hissed. 'You will be killed; I will not allow it.'

'Better to die than see this,' said the old soldier. But he ceased to struggle and with a weary sigh turned away and pushed his way back through the crowd.

Scaler glanced up at the girl. Her grey eyes were looking into his and she was smiling. There was no hint of mockery in the smile.

'I am sorry,' he mouthed, but she had looked away.

'May I speak?' she asked, her voice clear and strong.

Malif turned to her. 'The law says that you may, but let there be nothing seditious in your words or I shall have you gagged.'

'My friends,' she began, 'I am sorry to see you here today. Death means nothing but the absence of joy is worse than death. Most of you I know. And I love you all. Please go from here and remember me as you knew me. Think of the laughter and put this evil moment from your minds.'

'No need for that, lady!' someone shouted. The crowd parted and a tall man dressed in black moved to the open space before the pyre.

Valtaya looked down into the man's bright blue eyes. His face was covered by a mask of shining black leather and she wondered if a man with such beautiful eyes could possibly be the executioner.

'Who are you?' demanded Malif. The man removed his leather cloak, carelessly tossing it into the crowd.

'You requested a champion, did you not?'

Malif smiled. The man was massively built, but even he was dwarfed by the Joining.

What a fine day, to be sure!

'Remove your mask, so that we may see you,' he ordered.

'That is not necessary, nor is it part of the law,' replied the man.

'Indeed it is not. Very well. The contest will be decided in hand-to-hand combat, without weapons.'

'No!' shouted Valtaya. 'Please sir, reconsider – it is madness! If I must die, then let it be alone. I am reconciled to it, but you only make it more difficult.'

The man ignored her as from his broad black belt he tugged a pair of leather gauntlets.

'Is it permitted for me to wear these?' he asked.

Malif nodded and the Joining ambled forward. It was almost seven feet tall, with a huge vulpine head. Its hands ended in wickedly curved talons. A low growl issued from its maw, and its lips curled back to show gleaming fangs.

'Are there any rules to this combat?' asked the man.

'None,' replied Malif.

'Fine,' said the man, hammering a fist into the beast's mouth. One fang snapped under the impact and blood sprayed into the air. Then he leapt forward, blows thundering to the beast's head.

But the Joining was strong, and after the initial shock it roared its defiance and sprang to the offensive. A fist snapped its head back, then its taloned claw flashed out. The man jumped back, his tunic slashed, blood seeping from shallow cuts in his chest. The two circled each other.

Now the Joining leapt and the man threw himself into the air feet first, his boots thundering into the beast's face. The Joining was hurled to the ground and the man rolled to his feet, running forward to aim a kick, but the Joining swept up an arm and knocked him to the ground. The beast reared up to its full height, then staggered, with eyes rolling and tongue lolling. The man jumped forward, hurling blow after blow to the creature's head, and the Joining toppled face-first into the dust of the market square. The man stood above it, chest heaving; then he turned to the stunned Malif.

'Cut the girl loose!' he said. 'It is over.'

'Sorcery!' shouted Malif. 'You are a warlock. You will burn with the girl. Take him!'

An angry roar rose from the crowd and they surged forward.

Ananais grinned and leapt to the platform as Malif stumbled back, scrabbling for his sword. Ananais hit him and he flew from the platform. The guards turned and ran and Scaler climbed to the stake, slicing his dagger through the ropes.

'Come on!' he yelled, taking Valtaya by the arm. 'We must get out of here. They will be back.'

'Who has my cloak?' bellowed Ananais.

'I have it, general,' shouted a bearded veteran. Ananais swirled the cloak around his shoulder, fixing the clasp, then lifted his hands for silence.

'When they ask who freed the girl, tell them it was the army of Tenaka Khan. Tell them the Dragon is back.'

'This way, quickly!' shouted Scaler, leading Valtaya to a narrow alley. Ananais leapt lightly from the platform and followed them, pausing to glance down at the lifeless Malif, his neck grotesquely twisted. He must have fallen badly, thought Ananais. But then if the fall had not killed him, the poison would have done so. Carefully he removed his gauntlets, pressing the hidden stud and sliding the needle covers in place over the knuckles. Tucking them into his belt, he raced after the man and the girl.

They ducked through a side door off a cobbled street and Ananais found himself in a darkened inn, the shutters closed and the chairs stacked on tables. The man and the girl were standing by the long bar.

The landlord – a short, balding fat man – was pouring wine into clay jugs. He glanced up as Ananais walked forward out of the shadows and the carafe fell from his trembling fingers.

Scaler spun round, his eyes fearful.

'Oh, it's you!' he said. 'You certainly move quietly for a big man. It's all right, Larcas; this is the man who rescued Valtaya.'

'Pleased to meet you,' said the landlord. 'Drink?'

'Thanks.'

'The world's gone mad,' said Larcas. 'You know, during the first five years that I ran this inn there was not one murder. Everyone had at least a little money. It was a joy in those days. The world's gone mad!'

He poured wine for Ananais, refilling his own glass which he drained at a single swallow. 'Mad! I hate violence. I came here for the quiet life. A corn city just off the Sentran Plain – no trouble. And look at us now. Animals that walk like men. Laws no one can understand, let alone obey. Informers, thieves, murderers. Break wind during the anthem and you are dubbed a traitor.'

Ananais pulled a chair from a table and sat down with his back to the trio. Gently he lifted his mask and sipped the wine. Valtaya joined him and he turned his head away, then finished the wine and replaced his mask. Her hand reached out and covered his own.

'Thank you for the gift of life,' she said.

'It was my pleasure, lady.'

'Your scars are bad?'

'I have not seen worse.'

'Have they healed?'

'Mostly. The one under my right eye opens now and then. I can live with it.'

'I will heal it for you.'

'It is not necessary.'

'It is a small thing. I would like to do it for you. Have no fear. I have seen scars before.'

'Not like these, lady. I have no face beneath this mask. But I was handsome once.'

'You are handsome still,' she said. His blue eyes blazed and he leaned forward, fist clenched.

'Do not make a fool of me, woman!'

'I merely meant . . .'

'I know what you meant – you meant to be kind. Well, I do not need kindness. Or understanding. I was handsome and I enjoyed it. Now I am a monster and I have learned to live with it.'

'Now *you* listen,' ordered Valtaya, leaning forward on her elbows. 'What I was going to say was that looks mean nothing to me. Deeds paint better pictures of a man than skin hanging from tendons and bones. What you did today was handsome.'

Ananais leaned back in his chair, folding his arms across his broad chest.

'I am sorry,' he said. 'Forgive me.'

She chuckled and reached forward, gripping his hand.

'There is nothing to forgive. We just know each other a little better.'

'Why did they seek to burn you?' he asked, laying his hand on hers and enjoying the warmth of her skin.

She shrugged: 'I deal in herbs and medicines. And I always speak the truth.'

'That accounts for witchcraft and sedition. What about theft?'

'I borrowed a horse. Tell me about you.'

'Little to tell. I am a warrior in search of a war.'

'Is that why you came back to Drenai?'

'Who knows?'

'Do you really have an army?'

'A force of two. But it's a beginning.'

'It's optimistic anyway. Does your friend fight as well as you?'

'Better. He's Tenaka Khan.'

'The Nadir prince. The Khan of Shadows.'

'You know your history.'

'I was raised at Dros Delnoch,' she said, sipping her wine. 'I thought he would be dead with the rest of the Dragon.'

'Men like Tenaka do not die easily.'

'Then you must be Ananais. The Golden One?'

'I once had that honour.'

'There are legends surrounding you both. The two of you routed twenty Vagrian raiders a hundred miles west of Sousa. And later you surrounded and destroyed a large group of slavers near Purdol in the east.'

'There were not twenty raiders, only seven – and one was sick with fever. And we outnumbered the slavers two to one.'

'And did you not rescue a Lentrian princess from Nadir tribesmen, travelling hundreds of leagues to the north?'

'No, but I often wondered how that story came about. All this happened before you were born – how do you know so much about it?'

'I listen to Scaler; he tells wonderful stories. Why did you save me today?'

'What kind of question is that? Am I not the man who travelled hundreds of leagues to rescue a Lentrian princess?'

'I am not a princess.'

'And I am no hero.'

'You took on a Joining.'

'Yes. But then from my first blow he was dying. I have poison spikes in my gauntlets.'

'Even so, not many men would have faced it.'

'Tenaka would have killed it without the gauntlets. He's the second fastest man I've ever known.'

'The *second*?'

'You mean you have never heard of Decado?'

Tenaka built up the fire and then knelt beside the sleeping Renya. She was breathing evenly. He touched her face gently with one finger, stroking the skin of her cheek. Then he left her and walked to the top of a nearby rise to stare out over the rolling hills and plains to the south as the dawn sun crested the Skeln mountains.

Forests, rivers and long meadows swept on into a distant blue haze, as if the sky had melted and linked with the land. To the south-west the defiant Skoda mountains pierced the clouds like dagger points, red as blood and shining proud.

Tenaka shivered and pulled his cloak about him. Void of human life, the land was beautiful.

His thoughts drifted aimlessly, but always Renya's face returned to his mind's eye.

Did he love her? Could love be born with such speed, or was it just the passion of a lonely man for a child of sorrow?

She needed him.

But did he need her?

Especially now, with all that lay before him?

You fool, he told himself, as he pictured life with Renya in his Ventrian palace – it is too late for that. You are the man who stepped off the mountain.

He sat down on a flat rock and rubbed his eyes.

What is the sense to this hopeless mission? he asked himself, an edge of bitterness washing over him. He could kill Ceska – of that there was no doubt. But what would be the point? Would the world change with the death of one despot?

Possibly not. But the course was set.

'What are you thinking about?' asked Renya, moving up to sit beside him and curling her arm around his waist. He opened his cloak, lifting it around her shoulders.

'I was just dawn-dreaming,' he said. 'And admiring the view.'

'It is beautiful here.'

'Yes. And now it is perfect.'

'When will your friend be back?'

'Soon.'

'Are you worried about him?'

'How did you know?'

'The way you told him to stay out of trouble.'

'I always worry about Ananais. He has an instinct for the dramatic and a sublime belief in his physical talents. He would tackle an army, convinced he could win. He probably could too – a small army anyway.'

'You like him a great deal, don't you?'

'I love him.'

'Not many men can say that,' said Renya. 'They feel the need to add "like a brother". It's nice. Have you known him long?'

'Since I was seventeen. I joined the Dragon as a cadet and we became friends soon after.'

'Why did he want to fight you?'

'He didn't really. But life has dealt harshly with him and he blamed me for it – at least in part. A long time ago, he wanted to depose Ceska. He could have done it. Instead I helped to stop him.'

'Not an easy thing to forgive,' she said.

'With hindsight, I agree.'

'Do you still mean to kill Ceska?'

'Yes.'

'Even if it means your own death?'

'Even then!'

'Then where do we go from here? To Drenan?'

He turned to her, lifting her chin with his hand.

'You still wish to travel with me?'

'Of course.'

'It's selfish, but I am glad,' he told her.

A man's scream broke the dawn silence and flocks of birds rose from the trees screeching in panic. Tenaka leapt to his feet.

'It came from over there,' shouted Renya, pointing north-east. Tenaka's sword flashed into the sunlight and he began to run, Renya only yards behind him.

A bestial howling mingled now with the screams and Tenaka slowed his run.

'It's a Joining,' he said, as Renya caught up.

'What shall we do?'

'Damn!' he said. 'Wait here.'

He ran forward, over a small rise and into a narrow clearing ringed by snow-covered oak. At the centre a man was crouching at the base of a tree, his tunic covered with blood and his leg hideously slashed. Before him stood a huge Joining.

Tenaka shouted as the creature lunged for the man and the beast twisted, its blood-red eyes turning on the warrior. He knew he was looking

551

into the eyes of Death, for no man could stand against this beast and live. Renya ran to his side, her dagger held before her.

'Get back!' order Tenaka.

She ignored him. 'What now?' she asked coolly.

The beast reared up to a full nine feet tall and spread its taloned paws wide. It was obviously part bear.

'Run!' shouted the wounded man. 'Please leave me!'

'Good advice,' said Renya.

Tenaka said nothing and the beast charged, sending a blood-chilling roar echoing through the trees. He crouched, his violet eyes fixed on the awesome creature bearing down upon him.

As its shadow fell across him he leapt forward, screaming a Nadir war-cry.

And the beast vanished.

Tenaka fell to the snow, dropping his sword. He rolled to his feet instantly to face the wounded man, who was standing now, and smiling. There was no trace of wounds upon his blue tunic or his body.

'What the devil is happening here?' demanded Tenaka.

The man shimmered and vanished. Tenaka swung to Renya, who was standing wide-eyed and staring at the tree.

'Someone played us for fools,' said Tenaka, brushing snow from his tunic.

'But why?' asked the girl.

'I don't know. Let us away – the forest has lost its magic.'

'They were so real,' said Renya. 'I thought we were finished. Were they ghosts, do you think?'

'Who knows? Whatever they were they left no tracks, and I have little time for such mysteries.'

'But there must have been a reason,' she persisted. 'Was it done just for us?'

He shrugged, then helped her up the steep incline back to their camp.

Forty miles away four men sat silently in a small room, their eyes closed and their minds open. Then one by one they opened their eyes, leaning back in their chairs and stretching as if awakening from deep sleep.

Their leader, the man who had appeared to be under attack in the clearing, stood and walked to the narrow stone window, gazing out over the meadow below.

'What do you think?' he asked, without looking round. The other three exchanged glances and then one, a short stocky man with a thick yellow beard, said, 'He is worthy at least. He did not hesitate to aid you.'

'Is that important?' asked the leader, still gazing from the window.

'I believe it is.'

'Tell my why, Acuas.'

'He is a man with a mission, yet he is a humanist. He was willing to risk his life – no, throw it away – rather than let a fellow human suffer alone. Light has touched him.'

'What do you say, Balan?'

'It is too early for judgements. The man may just be rash,' answered a taller, slimmer man with a shock of dark curly hair.

'Katan?'

The last man was slender, his face long and ascetic, his eyes large and sorrowful. He smiled.

'Were it my choice, I would say yes. He is worthy. He is a man of the Source, although he knows it not.'

'Then we are – in the main – agreed,' said the leader. 'I think it is time we spoke with Decado.'

'But should we not be more sure, Lord Abbot?' asked Balan.

'Nothing in life is sure, my son. Except the promise of death.'

5

It was an hour past curfew and the streets of Drenan were deserted, the vast white city silent. A three-quarter moon hung in a clear sky, its reflection glinting from a thousand rainwashed cobbles on the Street of Pillars.

From the shadows of a tall building came six men in black armour, dark helms covering their faces. They walked swiftly, purposefully towards the palace, looking neither to right nor left.

Two Joinings, armed with massive axes, barred their path and the men stopped. Six pairs of eyes fastened on the beasts and they howled in pain and fled.

The men walked on. From behind shutters and heavily curtained windows eyes watched their progress and the marchers felt the stares, sensing the curiosity turning to fear as they were recognised.

They moved on in silence until they reached the gates, where they waited. After several seconds they heard the grating movement of the bar beyond, and the gate opened. Two sentries bowed their heads as the black-armoured men marched forward across the courtyard and on into the main torchlit corridors lined with guards. All eyes avoided them. At the far end the double doors of oak and bronze slid open, the leader raised his hand and his five companions halted, turning on their heels to stand before the doors with black-gloved hands resting on ebony sword-hilts.

The leader lifted his helm and entered the room beyond.

As he had expected, Ceska's chief minister Eertik waited alone at his desk. He looked up as the warrior appeared, his dark, heavy-lidded eyes fixing on the knight.

'Welcome, Padaxes,' he said, his voice dry and faintly metallic.

'Greetings, counsellor,' answered Padaxes, smiling. He was a tall man, square-faced, with eyes the grey of a winter sky. His mouth was full-lipped and sensual, yet he was not handsome. There was about his features a strangeness – a taint hard to define.

'The emperor has need of your services,' said Eertik. As he stood and moved round the desk of oak, his dark velvet garments rustled. Padaxes registered the sounds, considering them not dissimilar to a snake moving through dry grass. He smiled again.

'I am always at the emperor's command.'

'He knows that, Padaxes, just as he knows you value his generosity. There is a man who seeks harm to the emperor. We have had word that he is in the north and the emperor wishes him taken or slain.'

'Tenaka Khan,' said Padaxes.

Eertik's eyes opened wide in surprise. 'You know of him?'

'Obviously.'

'May I ask how?'

'You may not.'

'He is a threat to the empire,' said Eertik, masking his annoyance.

'He is a walking corpse from the moment I leave this room. Did you know that Ananais was with him?'

'I did not,' said Eertik, 'although now you say it, I understand the mystery. Ananais was thought to be dead of his wounds. Does this intelligence pose a problem for your Order?'

'No. One, two, ten or one hundred. Nothing can stand against my Templars. We will ride in the morning.'

'Can I aid you in any way?'

'Yes. Send a child to the Temple in two hours. A girl child under ten years. There are certain religious rites which must be performed. I must commune with the power that holds the universe.'

'It shall be done.'

'Our temple buildings are in need of repair. I was considering a move to the country and the commissioning of a new temple – something larger,' said Padaxes.

'The emperor's thoughts exactly,' said Eertik. 'I will have some plans drawn up for your return.'

'Convey my thanks to the Lord Ceska.'

'I will indeed. May your journey be swift and your return joyful.'

'As the Spirit wills it,' answered Padaxes, replacing his black helm.

From his high tower window the Abbot gazed down into the upper garden where twenty-eight acolytes knelt before their trees. Despite the season the roses thrived, the perfume of their blooms filling the air.

The Abbot closed his eyes and soared, his spirit rising and flowing. Gently he descended to the garden, coming to rest beside the slender Katan.

Katan's mind opened to receive him and the Abbot joined the acolyte, flowing within the fragile stems and capillary systems of the plant.

The rose welcomed them. It was a red rose.

The Abbot withdrew and, one by one, joined each of the acolytes in turn. Only Balan's rose had failed to flower, but the buds were full and he was but a little way behind the rest.

The Abbot returned to his body in the high tower, opening his eyes and breathing deeply. He rubbed his eyes and moved to the southern window, looking down to the second level and the vegetable garden.

There, kneeling in the soil, was a priest in a dirty brown cassock. The Abbot walked from the room, descending the circular stair to push open the door to the lower level. He stepped out on to the well-scrubbed flagstones of the path and descended the stone steps to the garden.

'Greetings, brother,' he said.

The priest looked up, then bowed. 'Greetings, Lord Abbot.'

The Abbot seated himself on a stone bench nearby.

'Please continue,' he said. 'Do not let me disturb you.'

The man returned to his work, weeding the soil, his hands black with dirt and his fingernails cracked and broken.

The Abbot looked about him. The garden was well-tended, the tools sharp and cared-for, the pathways clean and clear of weeds.

He gazed fondly on the priest. The man had changed greatly since that day five years ago when he had walked into the monastery declaring his wish to become a priest. Then he had been dressed in garish armour, two shortswords strapped to his thighs and a baldric belt across his chest bearing three daggers.

'Why do you wish to serve the Source?' the Abbot had asked.

'I am tired of death,' he had replied.

'You live to kill,' said the Abbot, staring into the haunted eyes of the warrior.

'I want to change.'

'You want to hide?'

'No.'

'Why did you choose this monastery?'

'I . . . I prayed.'

'Did you receive an answer?'

'No. But I was heading west and after praying I changed my mind and came north. And you were here.'

'You think that is an answer?'

'I don't know,' answered the warrior. 'Is it?'

'Do you know what order this is?'

'No.'

'The acolytes here are gifted beyond other men and they have powers you could not comprehend. Their whole lives are given over to the Source. What do you offer?'

'Only myself. My life.'

'Very well. I will take you. But hear this and mark it well. You will not mix with the other acolytes. You will not walk to the upper level. You will live below in a crofter's hut. You will put aside your weapons and never touch them again. Your tasks will be menial and your obedience total. You will not speak to anyone at any time – only when I address you, may you answer.'

'I agree,' said the warrior without hesitation.

'I will instruct you each afternoon and I will gauge your progress. If you fail in any way, I will dismiss you from the monastery.'

'I agree.'

For five years the warrior had obeyed without question, and as the seasons passed the Abbot watched the haunted expression fade from his dark eyes. He had learned well, though never could he master the release of the spirit. But in all other things the Abbot was pleased.

'Are you happy, Decado?' the Abbot asked now. The priest leaned back and turned.

'Yes, Lord Abbot.'

'No regrets?'

'None.'

'I have news of the Dragon,' said the Abbot, watching him carefully. 'Would you care to hear it?'

The priest looked thoughtful. 'Yes, I would. Is that wrong?'

'No, Decado, it is not wrong. They were your friends.'

The priest remained silent, waiting for the Abbot to speak.

'They were wiped out in a terrible battle by the Joinings of Ceska. Although they fought valiantly and well, they could not stand against the power of the beasts.' Decado nodded and returned to his work.

'How do you feel?'

'Very sad, Lord Abbot.'

'Not all your friends perished. Tenaka Khan and Ananais have returned to the Drenai and they plan to kill Ceska – to end his terror.'

'May the Source be with them,' said Decado.

'Would you like to be with them?'

'No, Lord Abbot.'

The Abbot nodded. 'Show me your garden,' he said. The priest rose and the two men walked among the plants, coming at last to the tiny hut that housed Decado. The Abbot walked around the outside. 'You are comfortable here?'

'Yes, Lord Abbot.'

Behind the hut the Abbot stopped, staring down at a tiny bush and the single flower that grew there.

'And what is this?'

'It is mine, Lord Abbot. Have I done wrong?'

'How did you come by it?'

'I found a seedpod someone had thrown from the upper level and I planted it three years ago. It's a beautiful plant; it usually flowers much later.'

'Do you spend much time with it?'

'When I can, Lord Abbot. It helps me to relax.'

'We have many roses on the upper levels, Decado. But none of this colour.'

It was a white rose.

Two hours after dawn Ananais returned to the camp-site, bringing with him Valtaya, Scaler and Belder. Tenaka watched them approach. The older man, he could see, was a veteran who moved carefully, hand on sword-hilt. The woman was tall and well-made and she stayed close to the black-garbed Ananais. Tenaka grinned and shook his head. Still the Golden One, he thought. But the young man was interesting. There was about him something familiar, yet Tenaka was sure they had never met. Athletic and tall, clear-eyed and handsome, his long dark hair was held in place by a black metal circlet adorned with an opal at the centre. He wore a leaf-green cloak and calf-length brown walking boots. His tunic was of soft leather and he carried a shortsword in his hand. Tenaka sensed his fear.

He stepped from the trees to greet them.

Scaler looked up as he appeared. He wanted to rush forward and embrace him, but resisted the urge. Tenaka would never recognise him. The Nadir prince had changed little, he thought, save for the few grey hairs glinting in the sunlight. The violet eyes were still piercing, the stance still unconsciously arrogant.

'You cannot resist surprises, my friend,' said Tenaka.

'So true,' answered Ananais. 'But I have breakfast in the pack, and explanations can wait until I have eaten.'

'Introductions cannot,' said Tenaka softly.

'Scaler, Valtaya and Belder,' said Ananais, waving an arm at the trio. With that he strode past Tenaka and on towards the fire.

'Welcome!' said Tenaka lamely, spreading his hands.

Scaler walked forward. 'Our presence in your camp is temporary,' he said. 'Your friend helped Valtaya and it was vital that we left the city. Now that she is safe, we shall return.'

'I see. Join us for food first,' offered Tenaka.

The silence around the fire was uncomfortable, but Ananais ignored it, taking his food to the edge of the trees and sitting with his back to the group so that he could remove his mask and eat.

'I have heard much of you, Tenaka,' said Valtaya.

He turned to her. 'Much of what people say is untrue.'

'There is always a grain of truth at the centre of such sagas.'

'Perhaps. Where did you hear the stories?'

'From Scaler,' she replied. Tenaka nodded and turned to the young man, who was blushing furiously.

'And where did you hear them, my friend?'

'Here and there,' replied Scaler.

'I was a soldier. Nothing more. My ancestry gave me fame. I could name many better swordsmen, better riders, better men. But they had no name to carry before them like a banner.'

'You are too modest,' said Scaler.

'It is not a question of modesty. I am half-Nadir of the line of Ulric and half-Drenai. My great-grandfather was Regnak, the Earl of Bronze. And yet I am neither Earl nor Khan.'

'The Khan of Shadows,' said Scaler.

'How did such a thing come about?' asked Valtaya.

Tenaka grinned. 'It was the Second Nadir War and Regnak's son Orrin made a treaty with the Nadir. Part of the price was that his son, Hogun, should marry the Khan's daughter, Shillat. It was not a marriage of love. It was a grand ceremony, I am told, and the union was consummated near the Shrine of Druss on the northern plain before Delnoch. Hogun took his bride back to the fortress, where she dwelt unhappily for three years. I was born there. Hogun died in a riding accident when I was two and his father sent Shillat home. It was written into the marriage contract that no child of the union could inherit Dros Delnoch. And as for the Nadir, they desired no half-breed to lead them.'

'You must have been very unhappy,' said Valtaya.

'I have known great joys in my life. Do not feel pity for me, lady.'

'How did you come to be a Dragon general?'

'I was sixteen when the Khan, my grandfather, sent me to Delnoch. Again it was part of the marriage contract. My other grandfather was there to greet me. He told me he had arranged a commission in the Dragon. It is that simple!'

Scaler stared into the fire, his mind flowing back.

Simple? How could such a terrible moment be described as simple?

It was raining, he remembered, when the guard on the Eldibar tower sounded the trumpet. His grandfather Orrin had been in the keep, engaged in a war-game with their guest. Scaler was perched on a high chair, watching them roll the dice and move the tiny regiments, when the trumpet call echoed eerily in the storm winds.

'The Nadir spawn has arrived,' said Orrin. 'He picked the right day for it.'

They dressed Scaler in a cloak of oiled leather and a wide-brimmed leather hat, then began the long walk to Wall One.

Once there, Orrin gazed down on the twenty riders and the dark-haired youth on the white shaggy pony.

'Who seeks entry to Dros Delnoch?' called Orrin.

'The son of Shillat,' yelled the Nadir captain.

'He only may enter,' said Orrin.

The great gates creaked open and the Nadir troop wheeled their mounts, riding swiftly back to the north.

Tenaka did not turn to watch them go, and no word passed between them. The youth touched his heels to the pony and cantered into the gate tunnel and up on to the green field between Walls One and Two. There he slid from the saddle and waited for Orrin to approach.

'You are not welcome here,' said Orrin, 'but I will stand by my bargains. I have arranged a commission in the Dragon and you will leave in three months. Until then you will learn Drenai ways. I want no relative of mine eating with his fingers in the officers' mess.'

'Thank you, grandfather,' said Tenaka.

'Don't call me that,' snapped Orrin. 'Not ever! You will call me "My Lord" or in company "Sir". Do you understand?'

'I believe that I do, grandfather. And I shall obey you.' Tenaka's gaze flickered to the child.

'This is my true grandson,' said Orrin. 'All my children are dead. Only this little lad survives to continue my line. His name is Arvan.'

Tenaka nodded and turned to the dark-bearded man to Orrin's left.

'And this is a friend of the House of Regnak – the only counsellor worth his salt in the entire country. His name is Ceska.'

'Delighted to meet you,' said Ceska, reaching out his hand. Tenaka clasped it firmly, his gaze locking to the man's dark eyes.

'Now let us get inside and out of this damned rain,' muttered Orrin. Lifting the child to his broad shoulders, the white-bearded Earl strode away towards the distant keep. Tenaka gathered the reins of his pony and followed, Ceska beside him.

'Do not be upset by his manner, young prince,' said Ceska. 'He is old and set in his ways. But he is a fine man, truly. I hope you will be happy among the Drenai. If ever there is anything I can do for you, do not hesitate to tell me.'

'Why?' asked Tenaka.

'I like you,' said Ceska, clapping him on the shoulder. 'And who knows – you may be Earl some day.'

'That is unlikely.'

'True, my friend. But the House of Bronze has been unlucky of late. As Orrin said, all his children are gone. Arvan alone survives.'

'He looks a strong child.'

'Indeed he does. But looks can be so deceptive, can they not?'

Tenaka was not sure he understood the meaning of Ceska's words, but he knew there were undercurrents of dark promises. He said nothing.

Later Tenaka listened in silence as Valtaya talked of the rescue in the marketplace, and of their bribing a night sentry to let them pass through the northern postern gate of the city. Ananais had brought a huge pack of food, plus two bows and eighty shafts in doeskin quivers. Valtaya had extra blankets and a rolled canvas sheet for a small tent.

After they had eaten, Tenaka took Ananais into the trees. They found a secluded spot and cleared the snow from some rocks before sitting down to talk.

'There is an uprising in Skoda,' said Ananais. 'Two villages were sacked by Ceska's Legion. A local named Rayvan gathered a small army and destroyed the raiders. They say men are flocking to him, but I don't think he can last. He's a common man.'

'Not of the Blood, you mean,' said Tenaka dryly.

'I have nothing against common men. But he has not the training to plan a campaign.'

'What else?'

'Two risings in the west – both ruthlessly put down. All the men crucified, fields sown with salt. You know the system!'

'What about the south?'

'Difficult to say. News is scarce. But Ceska's there. On hand. I don't think they will rise. It is said that there is a secret society against Ceska, but that is likely to be no more than talk.'

'What do you suggest?' asked Tenaka.

'Let us go to Drenan, kill Ceska and then retire.'

'That simple?'

'The best plans are always simple, Tani.'

'What about the women?'

Ananais shrugged. 'What can we do? You say Renya wants to be with you? Let her come. We can leave her with friends in Drenan. I still know one or two people I think we can rely on.'

'And Valtaya?'

'She won't stay with us – there is nothing for her. We will leave her in the next town.'

Tenaka raised an eyebrow. 'Nothing for her?'

Ananais looked away. 'Not any more, Tani. Once, maybe.'

560

'All right. We will head for Drenan, but angle to the west. Skoda should be beautiful at this time of the year.'

Side by side they returned to the camp, where they found three strangers waiting. Tenaka spoke softly: 'Scout around, Ani. See how many other surprises are in the offing.' Then he walked forward. Two of the men were warriors, both about the same age as Tenaka himself. The third was an old man, blind and wearing the tattered blue robes of the Seekers.

The warriors approached him. They were uncannily alike, black-bearded and stern of eye, though one was fractionally taller than the other. It was the shorter man who spoke.

'I am Galand and this is my brother, Parsal. We have come to join you, general.'

'For what purpose?'

'To put down Ceska. Why else?'

'I need no help for that, Galand.'

'I don't know what game this is, general. The Golden One was in Sousa and he told the crowd the Dragon was back. Well, if that is so, then I reckon I am back too. You don't recognise me, do you?'

'In truth I do not,' said Tenaka.

'I was not bearded then. I was Bar Galand of the Third Wing under Elias. I was the Sword Master and I beat you in a tourney once.'

'I remember. The half-moon riposte! You would have ripped out my throat. As it was I had a ghastly bruise.'

'My brother is as good a man as I. We want to serve.'

'There is nothing to serve, my friend. I plan to kill Ceska. That is the work of an assassin – not an army.'

'Then we will stick by you until the deed is done! I was sick with fever when the call came and the Dragon re-formed. I have been sick with sorrow since. A lot of fine men were lured into that trap. It does not seem right.'

'How did you find us?'

'I followed the blind man. Strange, don't you think?'

Tenaka moved to the fire and sat down opposite the Seeker.

The mystic's head lifted. 'I seek the Torchbearer,' he said, his voice a dry whisper.

'Who is he?' asked Tenaka.

'The Dark Spirit is over the land, like a great shadow,' whispered the man. 'I seek the Torchbearer, from whom all shadows flee.'

'Who is this man you seek?' persisted Tenaka.

'I don't know. Is it you?'

'I doubt it,' answered Tenaka. 'Will you eat with us?'

'My dreams told me the Torchbearer would bring me food. Is it you?'

'No.'

'There are three,' said the man. 'Of Gold, and Ice, and Shadow. One is the Torchbearer. But which one? I have a message.'

Scaler moved forward to crouch at the man's side.

'I seek the truth,' he said.

'I have the truth,' replied the mystic, extending his hand. Scaler dropped a small silver coin into his palm.

'Of Bronze you sprang, haunted and hunted, drawn on your father's path. Kin to shadow, never resting, never silent. Dark spears hover, black wings to devour. You will stand when others flee. It is in the red you carry.'

'What does it mean?' asked Tenaka. Scaler shrugged and moved away.

'Death calls me. I must answer,' whispered the mystic. 'And yet the Torchbearer is not here.'

'Give me the message, old man. I will pass it on, I promise you.'

'Dark Templars ride against the Prince of Shadows. He cannot hide, for the torch is bright against the night. But thought is faster than arrows, and truth is sharper than blades. The beasts can fall, but only the King Beyond the Gate can bring them down.'

'Is that all?' asked Tenaka.

'You are the Torchbearer,' said the man. 'Now I see you clearly. You are chosen by the Source.'

'I am the Prince of Shadows,' said Tenaka. 'But I do not follow the Source, or any god. I believe in none of them.'

'The Source believes in you,' said the old man. 'I must go now. My rest is near.'

As Tenaka watched him hobble from the camp, his bare feet blue against the snow, Scaler joined him.

'What did he say to you?'

'I did not understand it.'

'Tell me the words,' said Scaler and Tenaka repeated them. Scaler nodded. 'Some of it is easy to decipher. The Dark Templars, for example. Have you heard of The Thirty?'

'Yes. Warrior priests who spend their lives becoming pure in the heart before riding off to die in a distant war. The Order died out years ago.'

'The Dark Templars are an obscene parody of The Thirty. They worship the Chaos Spirit and their powers are dark, yet deadly. Every form of vileness is pleasure to them, and they are formidable warriors.'

'And Ceska has sent them against me?'

'It would seem so. They are led by a man named Padaxes. There are sixty-six warriors in each temple, and ten temples. They have powers beyond those of normal men.'

'They will need them,' said Tenaka grimly. 'What of the rest of his words?'

'Thought is faster than arrows? That you must outthink your enemies. The King Beyond the Gate is a mystery. But you should know.'

'Why?'

'Because the message was for you. You must be part of it.'

'And what of your message?'

'What about it?'

'What did it mean?'

'It meant I must travel with you, though I do not desire it.'

'I don't understand,' said Tenaka. 'You have free will – you may go where you please.'

'I suppose so,' said Scaler, smiling. 'But it is time I found my path. You remember the old man's words to me? "Of Bronze you sprang"? My ancestor was also Regnak the Wanderer. "Kin to Shadow"? That is you, cousin. "Dark spears hover"? The Templars. The red I carry? The blood of the Earl of Bronze. I have run long enough.'

'Arvan?'

'Yes.'

Tenaka placed his hands on the young man's shoulders. 'I have often wondered what became of you.'

'Ceska ordered me slain and I ran away. I have spent a long time running away. Too damned long! I'm not much of a swordsman, you know.'

'No matter. It is good to see you again.'

'And you. I followed your career and I kept a diary of your exploits. It is probably still at Delnoch. By the way, there was something else the old man said, right at the beginning. He said that there were three. Of Gold, and Ice, and Shadow. Ananais is the Golden One. You are the Khan of Shadows. Who is Ice?'

Tenaka turned away, staring through the trees.

'There was a man once. He was known as the Ice Killer, since he lived only for death. His name is Decado.'

For three days the companions skirted the forest, moving south and west towards the Skoda mountains. The weather was growing warmer, the snow retreating before the spring sunshine. They moved warily and on the second day they found the body of the blind seeker, kneeling by a twisted oak. The ground was too hard to attempt a burial and they left him there.

Galand and his brother paused by the corpse.

'He doesn't seem too unhappy,' said Parsal, scratching his beard.

'It's hard to know whether he's smiling, or whether death has pulled his face into a grin,' said Galand. 'He won't look too happy in about a month.'

'Will *we*?' whispered Parsal. Galand shrugged and the brothers moved on to follow the others.

Galand had been luckier than most and considerably more astute than many Dragon warriors. When the order to disband was given he had moved south, keeping his background to himself. He bought a small farm near Delving forest, south-west of the capital. When the terror began, he was left alone. He married a village girl and started a family, but she had disappeared on a bright autumn day six years before. It was said that the Joinings stole women, but Galand knew she had never loved him . . . and a village lad named Carcas had disappeared on the same day.

Rumours came to Delving about the round-up of former Dragon officers, and it was said that Baris himself had been arrested. This did not surprise Galand – he had always suspected Ceska would prove a tyrant.

Man of the people! Since when did one of his stinking class care about the people?

The small farm had prospered and Galand bought an adjoining parcel of land from a widower. The man was leaving for Vagria – he had a brother in Drenan who had warned him about impending changes – and Galand had bought him out for what seemed a peppercorn price.

Then the soldiers arrived.

A new law meant that non-titled citizens could own only four acres of land. The state acquired the rest at a price that made peppercorn seem a king's ransom. Taxes were increased and crop levels set. These were impossible to meet after the first year, for the land was robbed of its goodness. Fallow fields were planted and the yields dropped.

Galand took it all, never voicing complaints.

Until the day his daughter died. She had run out to see the horsemen canter and a stallion had kicked out at her. Galand watched her fall and ran to her, cradling her to him.

The horseman dismounted. 'Is she dead?' he asked.

Galand nodded, unable to speak.

'Unfortunate,' said the rider. 'It will increase your tax level.'

The rider died with Galand's dagger buried in his heart. Then Galand dragged the man's sword clear of its scabbard and leapt at a second horseman, whose mount shied; the man toppled to the ground, where Galand killed him with a throat-cut. The other four wheeled their mounts and rode back some thirty paces. Galand turned to the dark stallion which had killed his daughter and hammered the sword two-handed across its neck. Then he ran to the second mount, vaulted into the saddle and rode for the north.

He had located his brother in Vagria, where he worked as a stonemason.

Now Parsal's voice cut through his thoughts, as they walked some thirty paces behind the others.

'What did you say?'

'I said I never thought I would ever follow a Nadir.'

'I know what you mean; it makes the blood run cold. Still, he wants the same as us.'

'Does he?' whispered Parsal.

'What does that mean?'

'They're all the same breed: the warrior elite. It's just a game to them – they don't *care*.'

'I don't like them, brother. But they are Dragon, and that means more than blood. I cannot explain it. Though we are worlds apart, they would die for me – and I for them.'

'I hope you're right!'

'There are few things in life I am sure about. That is one of them.'

Parsal was not convinced but he said nothing, staring ahead at the two warriors.

'What happens when we kill Ceska?' he asked suddenly.

'How do you mean?'

'I don't know really. I mean – what do we do?'

Galand shrugged. 'Ask me when his body lies bleeding at my feet.'

'Strikes me that nothing will change.'

'Maybe not, but I will have had my payment.'

'It doesn't bother you that you may die getting it?'

'No! Does it you?' asked Galand.

'Damn right!'

'You don't have to stay.'

''Course I do! I've always looked after you. Can't leave you with a Nadir, can I? Why does the other one wear that mask?'

'I think he has scars or something. He was an arena warrior.'

'We've all got scars. Bit vain, isn't it?'

'Nothing suits you at the moment, does it?' said Galand, grinning.

'Just a thought. Those other two seem an odd pair,' muttered Parsal, flicking a glance at Belder and Scaler as they walked beside the women.

'You can't have anything against them – you don't even know them.'

'The old boy looks handy.'

'But?'

'I don't think the young one could fight his way through a fog.'

'While we're at it, I don't suppose you would care to criticise the women?'

'No,' said Parsal, smiling. 'Nothing at all to criticise there. Which do you fancy?'

Galand shook his head and chuckled. 'I'm not getting into this,' he said.

'I like the dark one,' said Parsal, unabashed.

They made camp in a shallow cave. Renya ate sparingly and then walked out into the night to watch the stars. Tenaka joined her and they sat together, wrapped in his cloak.

He told her of Illae and Ventria and the beauty of the desert. And while he spoke he stroked her arm and her back, and kissed her hair.

'I cannot say if I love you,' he said suddenly.

She smiled. 'Then do not say it.'

'You don't mind?'

She shook her head and kissed him, curling her arm up and around his neck.

You are a fool, Tenaka Khan, she thought. A wonderful, loving fool!

6

The black man was enjoying himself. Two of the robbers were down and another five remained. He hefted the short iron bar and twirled the chain attached to it. A tall man with a quarterstaff leapt forward and the black man's hand flashed out, the chain whipping round the staff. As he tugged, his attacker stumbled – into a crunching left upper-cut. He slumped to the ground.

Two of the remaining four robbers dropped their clubs, pulling curved daggers from their belts. The other two ran back into the trees, fetching longbows.

This was getting serious. Up to now the black man had killed no one, but that would have to change. He discarded the mace and pulled two throwing knives from his boots.

'Do you really want to die?' he asked them, his voice deep and sonorous.

'No one is going to die,' said a voice from the left and he turned. Two more men stood at the edge of the trees; both had bows bent, aimed at the outlaws.

'A timely intervention!' commented the black man. 'They killed my horse.'

Tenaka gently released the pressure on the bowstring and came forward.

'Put it down to experience,' he told the man. Then he turned to the outlaws. 'I suggest you put away your weapons – the fight is over.'

'He was more trouble that he was worth, anyway,' said the leader, walking over to check the fallen.

'They are all alive,' said the black man, replacing his knives and collecting the mace chain.

A scream sounded from the woods and the outlaw leader jerked to his feet.

Galand, Parsal and Belder moved into view.

'You were right, general,' said Galand. 'There were two more of them creeping in.'

'Did you kill them?' asked Tenaka.

'No. Sore heads, though!'

Tenaka swung to the outlaw. 'Are we likely to have any more trouble with you?'

'You are not going to ask for my word, are you?' replied the man.

'Is it worth anything?'

'Sometimes!'

'No, I don't want your word. Do as you please. But the next time we meet, I will see you all dead. That is *my* word!'

'The word of a barbarian,' said the man. He hawked and spat.

Tenaka grinned. 'Exactly so.' Turning his back, he walked back to Ananais and then on into the trees. Valtaya had prepared a fire and was talking to Scaler. Renya, dagger in hand, returned to the clearing as Tenaka arrived; he smiled at her. The others followed, except Galand who was keeping an eye on the outlaws.

The black man arrived last, carrying two saddlebags across one broad shoulder. He was tall and very powerful, dressed in a tight-fitting tunic of blue silk under a sheepskin cloak. Valtaya had never seen anyone like him, though she had heard stories of dark races far to the east.

'Greetings to you, my friends,' he said, dumping his saddlebags to the ground. 'Many blessings be upon you all!'

'Will you eat with us?' asked Tenaka.

'That is kind, but I have my own provisions.'

'Where are you headed?' asked Ananais as the black man delved into his bags, pulling out two apples which he polished on his tunic.

'I am visiting your fine land. I have no set destination for the moment.'

'Where are you from?' asked Valtaya.

'A far way, my lady, many thousands of leagues east of Ventria.'

'You are on a pilgrimage?' enquired Scaler.

'You could say that. I have a small mission to perform and then I shall return home to my family.'

'How are you called?' asked Tenaka.

'I fear my name would be difficult to you to pronounce. However, one of the robbers called me something that touched a chord. You may call me Pagan.'

'I am Tenaka Khan.' Swiftly he introduced the others.

Ananais held out his hand; Pagan took it in a firm clasp and their eyes met. Tenaka leaned back, watching them. Both men were from the same mould, immensely powerful and inordinately proud. They were like two prize bulls, each gauging the other.

'Your mask is dramatic,' said Pagan.

'Yes. It makes us look like brothers, black man,' replied Ananais and Pagan chuckled, a deep rolling sound full of good humour.

'Then brothers we are, Ananais!' he said.

Galand appeared and moved to Tenaka. 'They've gone north. I don't think they will be back.'

'Good! That was fine work back there.' Galand nodded and moved to sit beside his brother. Renya signalled to Tenaka and the two of them moved away from the fire.

'What is it?' he asked.

'The black man.'

'What about him?'

'He carries more weapons than anyone I have ever seen. He has two knives in his boots; a sword and two bows that he left in the trees back there. And there's a broken axe under his horse. He's like a one-man army.'

'So?'

'Did we meet him by accident?'

'You think he might be hunting us?'

567

'I don't know. But he is a killer, I can sense it. His pilgrimage has to do with death. And Ananais doesn't like him.'

'Don't worry,' he said softly.

'I am not Nadir, Tenaka. I'm not a fatalist.'

'Is that all that's worrying you?'

'No. Now you mention it – the two brothers; they don't like us. We don't belong together and we are none of us close – just a group of strangers thrown together by events.'

'The brothers are strong men and good warriors. I know about these things. I also know they regard me with suspicion, but there's nothing I can do about that. It has always been the way. But we share a common goal. And they will come to trust me. Belder and Scaler? I don't know. But they will do us no harm. And as for Pagan – if he is hunting me, I will kill him.'

'If you can!'

He smiled. 'Yes. If I can.'

'You make it sound easy. I don't see it that way.'

'You worry too much. The Nadir way is better: tackle each problem as it arises and worry about nothing.'

'I shall never forgive you if you let yourself be killed,' she said.

'Then you watch out for me, Renya. I trust your instincts – I mean that, truly. You are right about Pagan. He is a killer and he may be hunting us. It will be interesting to see what action he now takes.'

'He will offer to travel with us,' she said.

'Yes, but that would make sense. He is a stranger in our land and has already been attacked once.'

'We should refuse him. We are conspicuous enough with your giant friend and his black mask. But to add a black man in blue silk?'

'Yes. The gods – if such there be – are in humorous mood today.'

'I am not laughing,' said Renya.

Tenaka awoke from a dreamless sleep, his eyes flaring open and fear touching him like a cold caress. He rose to his feet. The moon was unnaturally bright, glowing like an eldritch lantern, and the branches of trees rustled and swayed though there was no breath of wind.

He looked around him – his companions were all sleeping. Then he glanced down and shock hit him hard: his own body lay there, wrapped in its blankets. He began to shiver.

Was this death?

Of all the cruel jests fate could play . . .

A faint stirring, like the memory of yesterday's breeze, caused him to turn. At the edge of the trees stood six men in dark armour, their black swords in their hands. They advanced on him, spreading out in a half-circle. Tenaka reached for his own blade but could not touch it; his hand passed through the hilt as if it were mist.

'You are doomed,' said a hollow voice. 'The Chaos Spirit calls.'

'Who are you?' asked Tenaka, ashamed that his voice quavered.

Mocking laughter came from the dark knights.

'We are Death,' they said.

Tenaka backed away.

'You cannot run. You cannot move,' said the first knight. Tenaka froze. His legs would not obey him and still the knights came closer.

Suddenly a feeling of peace swept over the Nadir prince and the knights halted their slow advance. Tenaka glanced left and right. Beside him stood six warriors in silver armour and white cloaks.

'Come then, you dogs of darkness,' said the silver warrior nearest him.

'We will come,' replied a dark knight. 'But not when you call.' One by one they backed away into the trees.

Tenaka turned slowly, lost and frightened, and the silver warrior who had spoken placed his hand on the Nadir prince's shoulder.

'Sleep now. The Source will protect you.'

Darkness settled over him like a blanket.

On the morning of the sixth day they cleared the trees and entered the broad plains stretching from Skultik to Skoda. In the distance, to the south, was the city of Karnak, but only the tallest spires could be seen as white pinpoints against a green horizon. The snow lay in white patches now, the spring grass groping for the sunlight.

Tenaka held up his hand as he saw the smoke.

'It cannot be a grass fire,' said Ananais, shielding his eyes from the harsh sunlight.

'It's a village burning,' said Galand, walking alongside. 'Such sights are all too common these days.'

'Yours is a troubled land,' said Pagan, dumping his huge pack on the ground at his feet and laying his saddlebags upon it. Attached to the pack was a bronze-edged shield of stiffened buffalo hide, an antelope horn bow and calf-hide quiver.

'You carry more equipment than a Dragon platoon,' muttered Ananais.

'Sentimental reasons,' answered Pagan, grinning.

'We'd best avoid the village,' said Scaler. His long hair was greasy with sweat and his lack of fitness was telling on him. He sat down beside Pagan's pack.

The wind shifted and the sound of drumming hooves came to them.

'Spread out and lie low,' said Tenaka. The companions ran for cover, dropping to their bellies in the grass.

A woman crested the top of a small hill, running at top speed, her auburn hair flowing behind her. She was dressed in a skirt of green wool and wore a brown shawl. In her arms she carried a small babe whose piping screams carried to the travellers.

As the woman ran on, she cast occasional panic-stricken glances over her shoulder. The haven of the trees was an eternity away as the soldiers cantered into view, but still she ran, cutting towards the hidden Tenaka.

Ananais swore and stood up. The woman screamed and veered left – into the arms of Pagan.

The soldiers reined their mounts and the leader dismounted. He was a tall man, dressed in the red cloak of Delnoch, his bronze armour burnished to a sheen.

'Thank you for your help,' he said, 'though we did not need it.' The woman was quiet now and in her despair she buried her head against Pagan's broad chest.

Tenaka smiled. There were twelve soldiers, eleven of them still mounted. There was nothing to be done except to hand back the woman.

Then an arrow flashed into the neck of the nearest rider and he pitched from the saddle. Tenaka's eyes flared in shock. A second arrow buried itself in the chest of another soldier and he too fell back, his horse rearing and hurling him from the saddle. Tenaka drew his sword, plunging it into the officer's back, for the man had turned as the arrows struck home.

Pagan pushed the woman from him and dropped to his knee, drawing the throwing-knives from his boots. They flew from his hands and two more soldiers died as they tried to control their mounts. Tenaka ran forward, leaping into the saddle of a riderless horse, scooping up the reins and heeling the beast forward. The seven remaining soldiers had drawn their weapons and two charged at Pagan. Tenaka's mount crashed into the remaining five and one horse fell, the others rearing and whinnying madly. As Tenaka's sword sliced down, an arrow whipped by him, taking a rider through the left eye-socket.

Pagan drew his shortsword, then dived left as the horses thundered by him, rolling to his feet once more as the riders dragged their mounts to a halt. Running forward, he blocked a wild slashing cut and buried his blade in the rider's side. As the man screamed and fell from the saddle, Pagan vaulted to the beast's back; then he hurled himself at the second rider, carrying the man clear of his horse. They fell heavily and Pagan broke the man's neck with a single blow.

Renya hurled aside her bow and, dagger in hand, ran from cover to where Tenaka, joined by Ananais, was battling the remaining soldiers. She leapt to a horse's back behind its rider and hammered her dagger between his shoulder-blades. The man screamed and tried to twist round but Renya punched him behind the ear. His neck snapped and he tumbled clear.

The last two soldiers turned their mounts and spurred them clear of the fray, riding back towards the hill. But Parsal and Galand stepped out in their paths and the horses reared, throwing one man from the saddle. The other clung on grimly until Galand's sword opened his throat. Parsal pulled his blade clear of the downed rider.

'I'll say this,' he called, grinning broadly. 'It's not been dull since we came back.'

Galand grunted. 'We're damned lucky, is all I'll say.' Wiping his sword on the grass, he gathered the reins of the two horses and walked back to the main group.

Tenaka hid his anger and called out to Pagan, 'You fight well!'

'I think it must be all the practice I am getting,' answered the black man.

'What I want to know is, who fired that arrow?' shouted Ananais.

'Forget it – it's done,' said Tenaka. 'Now we had best move from here. I suggest we ride back to the forest until nightfall. Now that we have mounts, we can make up the time.'

'No!' said the woman with the babe. 'My family. My friends. They're being butchered back there!'

Tenaka went to her, placing his hands on her shoulders. 'Listen to me. Unless I am mistaken these soldiers were part of a half-century, which means there are almost forty men in your village. It is too many – we cannot help you.'

'We could try,' said Renya.

'Be silent!' snarled Tenaka and Renya's mouth dropped open, but she said no more. He turned back to the woman. 'You are welcome to stay with us and we will come to the village tomorrow. We will do what we can.'

'Tomorrow will be too late!'

'It is probably already too late,' said Tenaka and she pulled away from him.

'I would not expect help from a Nadir,' she said, tears flowing. 'But some of you are Drenai. Please help me!'

'Dying will not help anyone,' said Scaler. 'Come with us. You escaped – so may others. And anyway, there is nowhere else for you to go. Come on, I will help you to a horse.'

The companions mounted and headed for the forest. Behind them the crows circled and wheeled.

That night Tenaka called Renya to him and they went from the camp-site and into the trees. No word had passed between them all afternoon.

Tenaka's manner was cold and distant. He walked to a moonlit clearing, then turned on the girl.

'You loosed that arrow! Don't ever act again without my order.'

'Who are you to order me?' she snapped.

'I am Tenaka Khan, woman! Cross me again and I will leave you behind.'

'They would have killed that woman and baby.'

'Yes. But because of your action we might all be dead. What would that have achieved?'

'But we are *not* dead. And we saved her.'

'Through luck. A soldier may need luck on occasion, but we would rather not have to rely on it. I am not asking you, Renya, I am telling you: you will not do it again!'

'I do as I please,' she said. He struck her open-handed across the face. She hit the ground hard, but rolled to her feet with eyes blazing, fingers curled into talons. Then she saw the knife in his hand.

'You would kill me, wouldn't you?' she whispered.

'Without a thought!'

'I loved you! More than life. More than anything.'

'Will you obey me?'

'Oh, yes, Tenaka Khan, I will obey you. Until we reach Skoda. And

571

then I will leave your company.' She turned on her heel and strode back to the camp-site.

Tenaka sheathed his dagger and sat down on a boulder.

'Still the loner, eh, Tani?' said Ananais, stepping from the shadows of the trees.

'I don't want to talk.'

'You were hard on her, and quite right too. But you went a little far – you wouldn't have killed her.'

'No. I would not.'

'But she frightens you, doesn't she?'

'I said I didn't want to talk.'

'True, but this is Ananais – your crippled friend who knows you well. As well as any man. You think that because we risk death there is no place for love? Don't be a fool – enjoy it while it's there.'

'I cannot,' said Tenaka, head bowed. 'When I came here, I could see nothing but Ceska. But now I seem to spend more time thinking of . . . you know.'

'Of course I know. But what happened to your Nadir code? Let tomorrow look to itself.'

'I am only half-Nadir.'

'Go and talk to her.'

'No. It is better this way.'

Ananais stood up and stretched his back. 'I think I'll get some sleep.' He ambled away back to the camp, stopping where Renya sat staring miserably into the fire.

He squatted down beside her. 'It is a strange thing about some men,' he said to her. 'In matters of business or war, they can be giants; wise to a fault. In matters of the heart, they are like children. Now women are a different matter; they see the child in a man for what it is.'

'He would have killed me,' she whispered.

'Do you really think so?'

'Do you?'

'Renya, he loves you. He couldn't hurt you.'

'Then why? Why say it?'

'To make you believe it. To make you hate him. To make you go.'

'Well, it worked,' she said.

'That's a shame. Still . . . you shouldn't have loosed that arrow.'

'I know that!' she snapped. 'You don't need to tell me. I just . . . couldn't see them kill a baby.'

'No, I wasn't over-keen myself.' He glanced across the fire to where the woman lay sleeping. The black giant, Pagan, sat with his back to a tree, holding the babe against his chest. The child had reached a pudgy hand from its blanket and curled it around Pagan's finger, while he was speaking to it in low, gentle tones.

'Good with children, isn't he?' said Ananais.

'Yes. And with weapons.'

'A real man of mystery. Still, I am watching him.'

Renya glanced at the bright blue eyes beyond the black mask. 'I like you, Ananais. I really do.'

'Like me, like my friends,' he said, nodding towards the tall figure of Tenaka Khan as he made his way to his blankets.

She shook her head and returned her gaze to the fire.

'That's a shame,' he said again.

They rode into the village two hours after dawn. Galand had scouted ahead and reported that the soldiers were setting off towards the south and the distant spires of Karnak. The village was gutted, charred timbers oozing dark plumes of smoke. Bodies lay here and there, while around the edge of the burnt-out buildings ten crosses had been erected, from which hung the village council. They had been whipped and beaten before being nailed to the beams, finally their legs had been broken, causing their battered frames to slump and cut off the air supply to the lungs.

'We have become barbarians,' said Scaler, turning his mount away from the scene. Belder merely nodded, but he followed the young Drenai to the grass fields beyond.

Tenaka dismounted at the village square, where the mass of bodies lay – more than thirty women and children.

'There is no sense to it,' he said as Ananais joined him. 'Now who will work the fields? If this is happening all over the empire . . .'

'It is,' said Galand.

The woman with the babe lifted her shawl over her head and closed her eyes. Pagan glimpsed the movement and rode alongside her, taking the reins from her hands.

'We will wait for you outside the village,' he said.

Valtaya and Renya followed them.

'It is a strange thing,' said Ananais. 'For centuries the Drenai have turned back enemies who would have done this to our land. And now we do it ourselves. What breed of men are they recruiting now?'

'There are always those who love this kind of work,' answered Tenaka.

'Among your people, maybe,' said Parsal softly.

'What does that mean?' snarled Ananais, turning on the black-bearded warrior.

'Forget it!' ordered Tenaka. 'You are right Parsal; the Nadir are a vicious people. But the Nadir did not do this. Nor did the Vagrians. As Ananais has said, we are doing it to ourselves.'

'Forget I said it, general,' murmured Parsal. 'I am just angry. Let's get away from here.'

'Tell me something,' said Galand suddenly. 'Will killing Ceska change all this?'

'I don't know,' Tenaka replied.

'He needs to be smashed.'

'I don't think six men and two women can bring down his empire. Do you?'

'A few days ago,' said Ananais, 'there was only one man.'

'Parsal is right, let us get away from here,' said Tenaka.

At that moment a child began to cry and the four men ran to the bodies, hauling them aside. At last they reached an old fat woman, her dead arms curled protectively around a girl of five or six. The woman's back bore three terrible wounds and she had obviously crouched down over the child to shield her from the weapons. But a lance had ripped through her body and into that of the child beyond. Parsal lifted the girl clear, then blanched as he saw the blood that had soaked her clothing. He carried her out of the village to where the others had dismounted and Valtaya ran forward to relieve him of the slender burden.

As they laid her gently to the grass her eyes opened; they were blue and bright.

'I don't want to die,' she whispered. 'Please?' Her eyes closed and the woman from the village knelt by her, lifting her head and cradling the child in her lap.

'It's all right, Alaya; it's me, Parise. I have come back to look after you.'

The child smiled weakly, but then the smile froze and twisted into a grimace of pain. The companions watched life depart.

'Oh no! Please, no!' murmured Parise. 'Sweet gods of light, no!' Her own babe began to cry and Pagan lifted it from the ground to hold it against his chest.

Galand turned away and fell to his knees. Parsal moved to his side and Galand looked up at his brother, tears streaming from his eyes. He shook his head, for no words would come.

Parsal knelt beside him. 'I know, brother, I know,' he said gently. Galand took a deep breath and drew his sword.

'I swear by all that's holy and unholy, by all the beasts that crawl or fly, I will not rest until this land is clean again.' He lurched to his feet, waving his sword in the air. 'I'm coming for you, Ceska!' he bellowed. Hurling aside his blade, he stumbled away towards a small grove of trees.

Parsal turned apologetically to the others. 'His own daughter was killed. A lovely child . . . a child of laughter. But he meant what he said, you know. And . . . and I'm with him.' His voice was thick with emotion and he cleared his throat. 'We're not much, him and me. I wasn't even good enough for the Dragon. We're not officers or anything. But when we say a thing we mean it. I don't know what the rest of you want out of all this. But those people back there – they are my people, mine and Galand's. Not rich and noble. Just dead. That old fat woman died to protect that child. And she failed. But she tried . . . gave her life trying. Well, so will I!' His voice broke then and he swore. Turning he walked quickly to the grove.

'Well, general,' said Ananais, 'what are you going to do with your army of six?'

'Seven!' said Pagan.

'See, we are growing all the time,' said Ananais and Tenaka nodded.

'Why will you join us?' he asked the black man.

'That is my business, but our ends are the same. I came thousands of miles to see Ceska fall.'

'We will bury the child and head for Skoda,' said Tenaka.

They rode warily throughout the long afternoon, Galand and Parsal riding wide on the flanks. Towards dusk a sudden storm burst over the plains and the companions took refuge in a deserted stone tower on the banks of a fast-flowing stream. They picketed the horses in a nearby field, gathered what wood they could find near a cluster of trees and cleared an open space within the tower on the first level. The building was old and square, and had once housed twenty soldiers; it was a watchtower from the days of the First Nadir War. There were three levels, the top being open to the sky where sharp-eyed scouts would watch for Nadir or Sathuli raiders.

Around midnight, as the others slept, Tenaka called Scaler to him and led him up the winding stair to the turret.

The storm had moved on to the south and the stars were bright. Bats circled around the tower, dipping and wheeling, and the night wind was chill as it swept down from the snow-clad Delnoch range.

'How are you faring, Arvan?' Tenaka asked Scaler as they sat beneath the battlements away from the wind.

Scaler shrugged. 'A little out of place.'

'That will pass.'

'I am no warrior, Tenaka. When you tackled those soldiers, I just lay in the grass and watched. I froze!'

'No, you didn't. Everything happened at once and those of us standing just reacted more quickly. We are trained for it. Take the brothers: they moved to the only spot the soldiers would break for and stopped any survivors from escaping to bring help. I didn't tell them to do it, they're soldiers. Now, the whole skirmish lasted maybe two minutes. What could you have done?'

'I don't know. Drawn my sword. *Helped!*'

'There will be time for that. What is the situation at Delnoch?'

'I don't know. I left there five years ago and before that I had spent ten years in Drenan.'

'Who rules?'

'No one of the House of Bronze. Orrin was poisoned and Ceska put in his own man. His name is Matrax. Why do you ask?'

'My plans have changed.'

'In what way?'

'I was intending to assassinate Ceska.'

'And now?'

'Now I plan something even more foolish. I am going to raise an army and bring him down.'

'No army in the world can stand against the Joinings. Gods, man, even the Dragon failed – they didn't even come close!'

'Nothing in life is easy, Arvan. But it's what I am trained for. To lead an army. To bring death and destruction on my enemies. You heard Parsal and Galand; what they said was right. A man must stand against evil wherever he finds it and he must use all his talents. I'm not an assassin.'

'And where will you find this army?'

Tenaka smiled. 'I need your help. You must take Delnoch.'

'Are you serious?'

'Deadly!'

'You want me to take a fortress single-handed? A fortress that has withstood two Nadir hordes? It's insane!'

'You are of the House of Bronze. Use your head. There is a way.'

'If you have already thought of a plan, why don't *you* do it?'

'I cannot. I am of the House of Ulric.'

'Why so cryptic? Tell me what to do.'

'No. You are a man and I think you sell yourself short. We will stop in Skoda and see how the land lies. Then you and I will bring an army.'

Scaler's eyes widened and his mouth dropped open.

'A Nadir army?' he whispered, blood draining from his face. 'You would bring the *Nadir*?'

'Only if you can take Dros Delnoch!'

7

In the dark of the library the Abbot waited patiently, leaning forward on his desk, his fingers steepled and his eyes closed. His three companions sat opposite him, immobile, like living statues. The Abbot opened his eyes and regarded them all:

Acuas, the strong one, compassionate and loyal.

Balan, the sceptic.

Katan, the true mystic.

All were travelling, their spirits entwined as they sought the Dark Templars and threw a veil of mind mist over the movements of Tenaka Khan and his companions.

Acuas returned first. He opened his eyes, rubbing his hands over his yellow beard; he seemed tired, drained.

'This is not easy, my Lord,' he said. 'The Dark Templars have great power.'

'As have we,' said the Abbot. 'Go on.'

'There are twenty of them. They were attacked in Skultik by a band of outlaws but slew them with arrogant ease. They are truly formidable warriors.'

'Yes. How close are they to the Torchbearer?'

'Less than a day. We cannot deceive them for much longer.'

'No. A few more days will be invaluable,' said the Abbot. 'Have they tried another night attack?'

'No, my Lord, though I think it likely.'

'Rest now, Acuas. Fetch Toris and Lannad to relieve you.'

The Abbot left the room and the long corridor beyond, making his way slowly to the second level and the garden of Decado.

The dark-eyed priest welcomed him with a smile.

'Come with me, Decado. There is something for you to see.'

Without another word he turned on his heel and led the priest to the steps and the oak doors above. Decado hesitated in the doorway – during all his years in the monastery he had never ascended these steps.

The Abbot turned. 'Come!' he said and stepped into the shadows beyond. A strange sense of fear gripped the gardener, as if his world was slipping away from him. He swallowed and began to tremble. Then, taking a deep breath, he followed the Abbot.

He was led through a maze of corridors, but he looked neither to left nor right, focusing his gaze on the grey cassock of the man walking before him. The Abbot halted before a door shaped like a leaf; there was no handle.

'Open,' whispered the Abbot and the door slid silently into a recess. Inside was a long chamber containing thirty sets of silver armour, draped with cloaks of dazzling white. Before each set was a small table bearing scabbarded swords placed in front of helms crowned with plumes of white horse-hair.

'Do you know what these represent?' asked the Abbot.

'No.' Decado was sweating freely. He wiped his eyes and the Abbot noticed with concern that the haunted look had returned to the former warrior.

'This is the armour worn by The Delnoch Thirty, led by Serbitar – the men who fought and died during the First Nadir War. You have heard of them?'

'Of course.'

'Tell me what you have heard.'

'Where is this leading, my Lord Abbot? I have duties in the gardens.'

'Tell me of The Delnoch Thirty,' ordered the Abbot.

Decado cleared his throat. 'They were warrior priests. Not like us. They trained for years and then chose a distant war in which to die. Serbitar led The Thirty at Delnoch, where they advised the Earl of Bronze and Druss the Legend. Together they turned back the hordes of Ulric.'

'But why would priests take up weapons?'

'I don't know, Lord Abbot. It is incomprehensible.'

'Is it?'

'You have taught me that all life is sacred to the Source, and that to take life is a crime against God.'

'And yet evil must be opposed.'

'Not by using the weapons of evil,' answered Decado.

'A man stands above a child with spear poised. What would you do?'

'I would stop him – but not kill him.'

'You would stop him with a blow, perhaps?'

'Yes, perhaps.'

'He falls badly, strikes his head and dies. Have you sinned?'

'No . . . yes. I don't know.'

'He is the sinner, for his action ensured your reaction, and therefore it was his action that killed him. We strive for peace and harmony, my son – we long for it. But we are of the world and subject to its demands. This nation is no longer in harmony. Chaos controls and the suffering is terrible to behold.'

'What are you trying to say, my Lord?'

'It is not easy, my son, for my words will cause you great pain.' The Abbot moved forward, placing his hands on the priest's shoulders. 'This is a Temple of The Thirty. And we are preparing to ride against the darkness.'

Decado pulled back from the Abbot. 'No!'

'I want you to ride with us.'

'I believed in you. I *trusted* you!' Decado turned away and found himself facing one of the sets of armour. He twisted round. '*That* is what I came here to escape: death and slaughter. Sharp blades and torn flesh. I have been happy here. And now you have robbed me of it. Go ahead – play your soldier's games. I will have none of it.'

'You cannot hide for ever, my son.'

'Hide? I came here to change.'

'It is not hard to change when your biggest problem is whether the weeds prosper in a vegetable patch.'

'What does that mean?'

'It means that you were a psychopathic killer – a man in love with death. Now I offer you the chance to see if you have changed. Put on the armour and ride with us against the forces of Chaos.'

'And learn to kill again?'

'That we shall see.'

'I don't want to kill. I wish to live among my plants.'

'Do you think I want to fight? I am nearing sixty years of age. I love the Source and all things that grow or move. I believe life is the greatest gift in all the Universe. But there is real evil in the world, and it must be fought. Overcome. Then others will have the opportunity to see the joy of life.'

'Don't say any more,' snapped Decado. 'Not another damned word!' Years of suppressed emotion roared through him, filling his senses, and forgotten anger lashed him with whips of fire. What a fool he had been – hiding from the world, grubbing in the soil like a sweating peasant!

He moved to a set of armour placed to the right of the rest and his hand reached down to curl round the ivory hilt. With one smooth movement he swept the blade into the air, his muscles pulsing with the thrill of the weapon. Its blade was silver steel and razor-sharp, and the balance was perfection. He turned to the Abbot, and where he had once seen a Lord he now saw an old man with watery eyes.

'This quest of yours, does it involve Tenaka Khan?'

'Yes, my son.'

'Don't call me that, priest! Not ever again. I don't blame you – I was the fool for believing in you. All right, I will fight with your priests, but only because it will aid my friends. But do not seek to give me orders.'

'I will not be in a position to order you, Decado. Even now you have moved to your own armour.'

'*My* armour?'

'You recognise the rune on the helm?'

'It is the number One in the Elder script.'

'It was Serbitar's armour. You will wear it.'

'He was the leader, was he not?'

'As you will be.'

'So that is my lot,' said Decado, 'to lead a motley crew of priests as they play at war. Very well; I can take a joke as well as any man.'

Decado began to laugh. The Abbot closed his eyes and mouthed a silent prayer, for through the laughter he felt the cry of anguish from Decado's tortured soul. Despair swept through the priest and he left the room, the manic laughter echoing after him.

What have you done, Abaddon? he asked himself.

Tears were in his eyes as he reached his room and, once inside, he fell to his knees.

Decado stumbled from the chamber and returned to his garden, staring in disbelief at the tidy rows of vegetables, the neat hedges and the carefully pruned trees.

He walked on to his hut, kicking open the door.

Less than an hour before, this had been home – a home he loved. Contentment had been his.

Now the shack was a hovel and he left it and wandered to his flower garden. The white rose carried three new buds. Anger coursed through him and he grasped the plant, ready to rip it from the ground. Then he stopped and slowly released it, staring at his hand and then back at the plant. Not one thorn had ripped his flesh. Gently he smoothed out the crushed leaves and began to sob, meaningless sounds which became two words.

'I'm sorry,' he told his rose.

The Thirty assembled in the lower courtyard, saddling their mounts. The horses still bore their winter coats, but they were strong mountain-bred beasts and they could run like the wind. Decado chose a bay mare; he saddled it swiftly and then vaulted to its back, sweeping out his white cloak behind him and settling it over the saddle in Dragon fashion. Serbitar's armour fitted him as his own never had – it felt smooth, like a second skin.

The Abbot, Abaddon, stepped into the saddle of a chestnut gelding and moved alongside Decado.

Decado swung in the saddle, watching the warrior priests as they silently mounted – he had to admit that they moved well. Each adjusted his cloak precisely as Decado had done. Abaddon gazed wistfully at his erstwhile disciple; Decado had shaved his chin clean and bound his long dark hair at the nape of his neck. His eyes were bright and alive, and a half-mocking smile was on his lips.

The night before, Decado had been formally introduced to his lieutenants: Acuas, the Heart of The Thirty; Balan, the Eyes of The Thirty; and Katan, the Soul of The Thirty.

'If you want to be warriors,' he had told them, 'then do as I say, when I say it. The Abbot tells me that there is a force hunting Tenaka Khan. We are to intercept it. The men we shall fight are true warriors, so I am told. Let us hope your quest does not end at their hands.'

'It is your quest too, brother,' said Katan, with a gentle smile.

'There is no man alive who can slay me. And if you priests fall like wheat, I shall not stay.'

'Is not a leader obliged to stand by his men?' asked Balan, an edge of anger in his voice.

'Leader? This is all a priestly farce, but very well, I will play the game. But I will not die with you.'

'Will you join us in prayer?' said Acuas.

'No. You pray for me! I have spent too many years wasting my time in that fruitless exercise.'

'We have always prayed for you,' said Katan.

'Pray for yourselves! Pray that when you meet these Dark Templars your bowels do not turn to water.'

With that he had left them. Now he raised his arms and led the troop through the Temple gates and out over the Sentran Plain.

'Are you sure this choice is wise?' Katan mind-pulsed to Abaddon.

'It is not my choice, my son.'

'He is a man consumed by anger.'

'The Source knows our needs. Do you remember Estin?'

'Yes, poor man. So wise – he would have been a good leader,' said Katan.

'Indeed he would. Courageous, yet kind; strong, yet gentle; and possessed of intellect without arrogance. But he died. And on the day he died Decado appeared at our gates seeking sanctuary from the world.'

'But suppose, Lord Abbot, that it was not the Source that sent him?'

' "Lord Abbot" no longer, Katan. Merely "Abaddon".'

The older man severed the mind link and it was some moments before Katan realised his question had not been answered.

The years fled from Decado. Once more he was in the saddle, the wind in his hair. Once more the drumming of hooves sounded on the plain and the stirring in his blood brought his youth pounding back to his mind . . .

The Dragon sweeping down on the Nadir raiders. Chaos, confusion, blood and terror. Broken men and broken screams, and crows shrieking their joy in the dark skies above.

And then later, in one mercenary war after another in the most far-flung nations of the world. Always Decado walked away from the battle, not a wound upon his slender form, while his enemies journeyed to whatever hells they believed in, shadowed and forgotten.

The image of Tenaka Khan floated in Decado's mind.

Now there was a warrior! How many times had Decado fallen asleep dreaming of a battle with Tenaka Khan? Ice and Shadow in the dance of blades.

They had fought, many times. With wooden blades or tipped foils. Even with blunted sabres. Honours were even. But such contests were meaningless – only when death rested on the blades could a true victor emerge.

Decado's thoughts were interrupted as the yellow-bearded Acuas cantered alongside.

'It will be close, Decado. The Templars have found their trail at some devastated village. They will have made their move by morning.'

'How soon can we reach them?'

'Dawn at the earliest.'

'Back to your prayers, then, yellowbeard. And make them powerful.'

He spurred his horse to a gallop and The Thirty followed him.

It was close to dawn and the companions had ridden through most of the night, stopping only for an hour to rest the horses. The Skoda range loomed ahead and Tenaka was anxious to reach their sanctuary. The sun, hidden now beyond the eastern horizon, was stirring and the stars faded as a pink glow painted the sky.

The riders left a grove of trees and emerged on to a broad grassland, swirling in mist. Tenaka felt a sudden chill touch his bones; he shivered and drew his cloak about him. He was tired and discontented. He had not spoken to Renya since their fight in the forest, yet he thought of her constantly. Far from removing her from his mind by turning on her, he had succeeded only in bringing himself fresh misery. And yet he was incapable of crossing the gulf he had opened between them. He glanced back to where she rode alongside Ananais, laughing at some jest; then turned away.

Ahead, like dark demons out of the past, twenty riders waited in a line. They sat their horses immobile, black cloaks flapping in the breeze. Tenaka reined his mount some fifty paces from the centre of their line and his companions rode alongside.

'What in Hell's name are they?' asked Ananais.

'They are seeking me,' answered Tenaka. 'They came at me in a dream.'

'I don't wish to appear defeatist, but there are rather too many for us to handle. Do we run?'

'From these men you cannot run,' said Tenaka tonelessly as he dismounted.

The twenty riders followed course, walking forward slowly through the mist, and it seemed to Renya they moved like the shades of the dead on a ghostly sea. Their armour was jet, helms covered their faces, dark swords were in their hands. Tenaka went forward to meet them, hand on swordhilt.

Ananais shook his head. A strange trancelike state had come upon him, leaving him a powerless observer. He slid from the saddle, drew his own sword and joined Tenaka.

The Dark Templars halted and their leader stepped forward.

'We have no commission to kill you yet, Ananais,' he said.

'I don't die easily,' said Ananais. He was about to add an insult, but the words froze in his mouth as a terrible fear struck him like a blast of icy air. He began to tremble and the urge to run rose in him.

'You die as easily as any other mortal,' said the man. 'Go back! Ride away to whatever doom awaits you.'

Ananais said nothing; he swallowed hard and looked at Tenaka. His friend's face was bone-white, and it was obvious that the same fear washed over him.

Galand and Parsal moved alongside them, swords in hand.

'Do you think to stand against us?' said the leader. 'A hundred men could not stand against us. Listen to my words and hear the truth – feel it through your terror.'

The fear increased and the horses grew skittish, whinnying their alarm. Scaler and Belder leapt from the saddles, sensing the beasts were about to bolt. Pagan leaned forward, patting his horse's neck; the beast settled down, but its ears were flat against its skull and he knew it was close to panic. Valtaya and Renya jumped clear as their horses bolted, then helped the village woman, Parise, to dismount.

Shielding her baby who had begun to scream – Parise lay down on the ground, shaking uncontrollably.

Pagan dismounted and drew his sword, walking forward slowly to stand beside Tenaka and the others. Belder and Scaler followed.

'Draw your sword,' whispered Renya, but Scaler ignored her. It was all he could do to muster enough courage to stand alongside Tenaka Khan. Any thoughts of actually fighting beside him were buried under the weight of his terror.

'Foolish,' said the leader, contemptuously, 'like lambs to the slaughter!' The Dark Templars advanced.

Tenaka struggled to overcome his panic, but his limbs felt leaden as his confidence drained away. He knew dark magic was being used against him, but the knowledge was not enough. He felt like a child stalked by a leopard.

Fight it! he told himself. Where is your courage?

Suddenly, as in his dream, the terror passed and strength flowed to his limbs. He knew without turning that the white knights had returned, this time in the flesh.

The Templars halted their advance and Padaxes cursed softly as The Thirty moved into sight. Outnumbered now, he considered his options. Calling on the power of the Spirit, he probed his enemies, meeting a wall of force that resisted his efforts . . . Except around the warrior at the centre – this man was no mystic. Padaxes was no stranger to the legends of The Thirty – his own temples had been built to parody theirs – and he recognised the rune on the man's helm.

A non-mystic as leader? An idea formed in his mind.

'Much blood will be shed here today,' he called, 'unless we settle this as captains.'

Abaddon grasped Decado's arm as he moved forward. 'No, Decado, you do not understand his power.'

'He is a man, that is all,' answered the other.

'No, he is far more – he has the power of Chaos. If someone must fight him, let it be Acuas.'

'Am I not leader in this force of yours?'

'Yes, but . . .'

'There are no buts. Obey me!' Pulling himself free Decado moved on, halting a few feet away from the black-armoured Padaxes.

'What do you suggest, Templar?'

'A duel between captains, the loser's men leaving the field.'

'I want more,' said Decado coldly. 'Far more!'

'Name it.'

'I have studied much of the ways of mystics. It is . . . was . . . part of my former calling. It is said that in ancient wars champions carried the souls of their armies within them, and when they died their armies died.'

'That is so,' said Padaxes, disguising his joy.

'Then that is what I demand.'

'It shall be so. I swear it by the Spirit!'

'Swear nothing to me, warrior. Your oaths count for nothing. Prove it!'

'It will take a little time. I shall conduct the rites first and trust your word that you will follow,' said Padaxes. Decado nodded and walked back to the others.

'You cannot do this thing, Decado,' said Acuas. 'You doom us all!'

'Suddenly the game is not to your liking?' snapped Decado.

'It is not that. This man, your enemy, has powers you do not possess. He can read your mind, sense your every move before you make it. How on earth can you defeat him?'

Decado laughed. 'Am I still your leader?'

Acuas flicked a glance at the former Abbot. 'Yes,' he said, 'you are the leader.'

'Then when he has finished his ritual, you will align the life force of The Thirty to mine.'

'Tell me this before I die,' said Acuas gently. 'Why are you sacrificing yourself in this way? Why do you doom your friends?'

Decado shrugged. 'Who can say?'

The Dark Templars fell to their knees before Padaxes as he intoned the names of the lower demons, calling on the Chaos Spirit, his voice rising to a scream. The sun breasted the eastern horizon, yet strangely no light fell upon the plain.

'It is done,' whispered Abaddon. 'He has kept his word and the souls of his warriors are within him.'

'Then do likewise,' ordered Decado.

The Thirty knelt before their leader, heads bowed. Decado felt nothing, yet he knew they had obeyed him.

'Dec, is it you?' called Ananais. Decado waved him to silence and advanced to meet Padaxes.

The black sword hissed forward, to be parried instantly by the silver steel in Decado's hand. The battle had begun. Tenaka and his companions watched in awe as the warriors circled and struck, blades clashing and clanging.

Time wore on and desperation became apparent in every move Padaxes made. Fear crept into his heart. Though he anticipated his opponent's every move, such was the speed of the assault that it availed him nothing. He mind-pulsed a terror-thought but Decado laughed, for death held no terror for him. And then Padaxes knew his doom was sealed, and it irked him greatly that a mortal man could bring about his death. Launching a final savage assault, he experienced the horror of reading Decado's mind at the last moment, seeing the riposte in the fraction of a second before it was launched.

The silver steel whiplashed his own sword aside and buried itself in his groin. He sank to the ground, his lifeblood pumping to the grass . . . and the souls of his men died with him.

Sunlight blazed through the darkness and The Thirty rose to their feet, amazed that life still flowed in their veins.

Acuas walked forward.

'How?' he asked. 'How did you win?'

'There is no mystery, Acuas,' said Decado softly. 'He was only a man.'

'But so are you!'

'No. I am Decado. The Ice Killer! Follow me at your peril.'

Decado lifted his helm and sucked in a deep breath of cool dawn air. Tenaka shook his head to clear the webs of fear still clinging there.

'Dec!' he called. Decado smiled and walked to him; the men gripped wrists in the warrior's greeting. Ananais, Galand and Parsal joined them.

'By all the gods, Dec, you look fine. Very fine!' said Tenaka warmly.

'And you, general. I am glad we were in time.'

'Would you mind telling me,' said Ananais, 'just why all those warriors died?'

'Only if you will explain about that mask. It's ridiculous for someone as vain as you to hide such classical good looks.'

Ananais looked away while the others stood uneasily, the silence growing.

'Will no one introduce me to our rescuer?' said Valtaya, and the moment passed. The Thirty stood aloof as the conversation began, then split into groups of six and moved about collecting wood for camp-fires.

Acuas, Balan, Katan and Abaddon chose a position by a solitary elm. Katan started the fire and the four of them sat around it, seemingly silent and watching the dancing flames.

'Speak, Acuas,' pulsed Abaddon.

'I am saddened, Abaddon, for our leader is not one of us. I do not mean that arrogantly, but our Order is an ancient one and always we have sought high spiritual ideals. We do not go to war for the joy of killing, but to die in defence of the Light. Decado is purely a killer.'

'You are the Heart of The Thirty, Acuas. For you have always been emotionally charged. You are a fine man – you care . . . you love. But sometimes our emotions can blind us. Do not judge Decado yet.'

'How did he kill the Templar?' asked Balan. 'It was inconceivable.'

'The Eyes of The Thirty and yet you cannot see, Balan. But I will not explain it to you. In time you will tell me. I believe the Source sent Decado to us, and I accepted him. Will one of you tell me why he is the leader?'

Dark-eyed Katan smiled. 'Because he is the least among us.'

'But more than that,' said Abaddon.

'It is his only role,' said Acuas.

'Explain, brother,' asked Balan.

'As a knight he could not communicate with us, nor travel with us. Every move we made would have been a humiliation for him. Yet we go to a war that he understands. As our leader, his lack of talent is counterbalanced by his authority.'

'Very good, Acuas. Now let the Heart tell us where danger lies.'

Acuas closed his eyes and remained mind-silent for several minutes, focusing his concentration.

'The Templars will respond. They cannot suffer this defeat at our hands and allow the deed to go unavenged.'

'And?'

'And Ceska has sent a thousand men to crush the Skoda rebellion. They will arrive in less than a week.'

Some thirty paces from their fire Decado sat with Tenaka, Ananais, Pagan and Scaler.

'Come on, Dec,' said Ananais. 'How did you become the leader of a gang of warrior wizards? There must be a story to it.'

'How do you know I am not a wizard?' countered Decado.

'No, seriously,' whispered Ananais, glancing at the white-cloaked knights. 'I mean, they are an eerie bunch. None of them is saying anything.'

'On the contrary,' Decado told him. 'They are all talking – mind to mind.'

'Nonsense!' said Ananais, curling his fingers into the sign of the Protective Horn and holding his hand across his heart.

Decado smiled. 'I speak truly.' Turning, he called to Katan who joined them. 'Go on, Ani – ask something,' he ordered.

'I feel foolish,' muttered Ananais.

'Then I shall ask,' said Scaler. 'Tell me, my friend, is it true you knights can talk . . . without talking?'

'It is true,' said Katan softly.

'Would you give us a demonstration?'

'Of what nature?' asked Katan.

'The tall man over there,' said Scaler, pointing and lowering his voice. 'Could you ask him to remove his helm and put it on again?'

'If it would please you,' said Katan and all eyes turned to the warrior some forty paces distant. Obligingly he removed his helm, smiled and replaced it.

'That's uncanny,' said Scaler. 'How did you do it?'

'It is hard to explain,' said Katan. 'Please excuse me.' Bowing to Decado, he rejoined his companions.

'See what I mean?' said Ananais. 'Eerie, inhuman.'

'We have men in my land with similar talents,' said Pagan.

'What do they do there?' asked Scaler.

'Very little. We burn them alive,' said Pagan.

'Is that not a little excessive?'

'Perhaps,' answered the black man. 'But then I don't believe in interfering with tradition!'

Tenaka left them talking and moved across to where Renya sat with Valtaya, Parsal and the village woman. As Renya watched him approach, her heartbeat quickened.

'Will you walk with me awhile?' he asked. She nodded and they moved away from the fires. The sun was clear and strong and its light glinted on the silver streaks in his hair. She longed to reach out and touch him, but instinct made her wait.

'I am sorry, Renya,' he said, reaching out and taking her hand. She looked into the slanted violet eyes and read the anguish there.

'Did you speak the truth? Would you have used that dagger on me?'

He shook his head.

'Do you want me to stay with you?' she asked softly.

'Do you want to stay?'

'I desire nothing else.'

'Then forgive me for being a fool,' he said. 'I am not skilled in these things. I have always been clumsy around women.'

'I am damned glad to hear it,' she said, smiling.

Ananais watched them and his gaze slid to Valtaya. She was talking to Galand, and laughing.

I should have let the Joining kill me, he thought.

8

The journey to Skoda took three days, for the company travelled warily. Acuas told Decado that following the slaying of the soldiers, the Delnoch fortress commander had sent patrols throughout Skultik and the surrounding countryside, while to the south Legion riders scouted the lands for rebels.

Tenaka took time to speak with the leaders of The Thirty, for despite the many legends he knew little of their Order. According to the stories, The Thirty were semi-gods with awesome powers who chose to die in wars against evil. The last time they had appeared was at Dros Delnoch, when the albino Serbitar stood beside the Earl of Bronze and defied the hordes of Ulric, the greatest Nadir warlord of all time.

But though Tenaka questioned the leaders, he learned little.

They were courteous and polite – even distantly friendly – but their answers floated above his head like clouds beyond the grasp of common men. Decado was no different; he would merely smile and change the subject.

Tenaka was not a religious man, yet he felt ill-at-ease among these warrior priests and his mind constantly returned to the words of the Blind Seeker.

'Of Gold and Ice and Shadow . . .' The man had predicted the trio would come together. And they had. He had also foreseen the danger of the Templars.

On the first night of their journey, Tenaka approached the elderly Abaddon and the two walked away from the fire together.

'I saw you in Skultik,' said Tenaka. 'You were being attacked by a Joining.'

'Yes. I apologise for the deceit.'

'What was the reason for it?'

'It was a test, my son. But not merely of you – of ourselves.'

'I do not understand,' said Tenaka.

'It is not necessary that you should. Do not fear us, Tenaka. We are here to help you in whatever way we can.'

'Why?'

'Because it serves the Source.'

'Can you not answer me without religious riddles? You are men – what do you gain from this war?'

'Nothing in this world.'

'You know why I came here?'

'Yes, my son. To purge your mind of guilt and grief – to drown it in Ceska's blood.'

'And now?'

'Now you are caught up in the forces beyond your control. Your grief is assuaged by your love for Renya, but the guilt remains. You did not obey the call – you left your friends to be butchered by the Joinings of Ceska. You ask yourself if it would have been different, had you come. Could you have defeated the Joinings? You torment yourself thus.'

'Could I have defeated the Joinings?'

'No, my son.'

'Can I do it now?'

'No,' said Abaddon sadly.

'Then what are we doing here? What is the point?'

'That is for you to say, for you are the real leader.'

'I am not a torchbearer, priest! I am a man. I choose my own destiny.'

'Of course you do; I did not say otherwise. But you are a man of honour. When responsibility is thrust upon you, can you run from it? No – you never have and you never will. That is what makes you as you are. That is why men follow you, though they hate your blood. They trust you.'

'I am not a lover of lost causes, priest. You may have a desire to die, but I do not. I am not a hero – I am a soldier. When the battle is lost I retreat and regroup; when the war is over I lay down my sword. No last dashing charge, no futile last stand!'

'I understand that,' said Abaddon.

'Then know this: no matter how impossible this war, I shall fight to win. Whatever I have to do, I will do. Nothing could be worse than Ceska.'

'Now you are speaking of the Nadir. You want my blessing?'

'Don't read my mind, damn you!'

'I did not read your mind, only your words. You know the Nadir hate the Drenai – you will merely exchange one bloody tyrant for another.'

'Perhaps. But I shall attempt it.'

'Then we will help you.'

'As simply as that? No pleas, no urgings, no advice?'

'I have told you that your plan with the Nadir carries too many dangers. I shall not repeat myself. But you are the leader – it is your decision.'

'I have told only Arvan. The others would not understand.'

'I shall say nothing.'

Tenaka left him then and walked out into the night. Abaddon sat down with his back against a tree. He was tired and his soul felt heavy. He wondered then if the Abbots before him had known such doubts.

Did the poet Vintar carry such a burden when he rode with The Thirty into Delnoch? One day soon, he would know.

He sensed the approach of Decado. The warrior was troubled, but his anger was fading. Abaddon closed his eyes, resting his head against the rough bark of the tree.

'May we talk?' asked Decado.

'The Voice may speak to whomever he pleases,' answered Abaddon, without opening his eyes.

'May we talk as before, when I was your pupil?'

Abaddon sat up and smiled gently. 'Join me then, my pupil.'

'I am sorry for my anger and the harsh words I used.'

'Words are but noises, my son. I put you under great strain.'

'I fear I am not the leader the Source would prefer. I wish to stand down in favour of Acuas. Is that allowed?'

'Wait for a little while. Make no decision yet. Rather, tell me what changed your mind.'

Decado leaned back on his elbows, staring at the stars. His voice was low, barely above a whisper. 'It was when I challenged the Templar and I risked all your lives. It was not a worthy deed and it shamed me. But you obeyed. You put your souls in my hand. And I didn't care.'

'But you care now, Decado?'

'Yes. Very much.'

'I am glad, my boy.'

For a while they sat in silence and then Decado spoke. 'Tell me, Lord Abbot, how it was that the Templar fell so easily?'

'You expected to die?'

'I thought it a possibility.'

'The man you slew was one of the Six, the rulers of the Templars. His name was Padaxes. He was a vile man, a former Source priest, whose lusts overcame him.

'True, he had powers. They all have. Compared with ordinary men, they are invincible. Deadly! But you, my dear Decado, are no ordinary man. You also have powers, but they lie dormant. When you fight you release those powers and they make you a warrior beyond compare. But add to this the fact that you fought not just for yourself, but for others, and you became invincible. Evil is never truly strong, for it is born of fear. Why did he fall so easily? Because he tested your strength and saw the possibility of death. At that moment, had he possessed true courage, he would have fought back. Instead he froze – and died.

'But he will return, my son. In greater strength!'

'He is dead.'

'But the Templars are not. There are six hundred of them, and many more acolytes. The deaths of Padaxes and his group of twenty will have whiplashed through their Order. Even now they will be mustering, preparing for the hunt. And they have seen us.

'Throughout today I have felt the presence of evil. As we speak, they hover beyond the shield Acuas and Katan have placed over our camp.'

Decado shivered. 'Can we win against them?'

'No. But then we are not here to win.'

'Then why?'

'We are here to die,' said Abaddon.

Argonis was tired and not a little hung-over. The party had been fine and the girls . . . oh, the girls! Trust Egon to find the right women. Argonis reined in his black gelding as the scout galloped into view. He lifted his hand, halting the column.

The scout dragged back on his reins and his mount checked its run and reared, pawing the air. The man saluted.

'Riders, sir – about forty of them, heading into Skoda. They're well-armed and they seem military. Are they ours?'

'Let us find out,' said Argonis, lifting his arm and waving on the column. It was conceivable they were a scouting party from Delnoch, but in that case they would not head into the rebels' lair – not with only forty men. Argonis glanced back, seeking reassurance, and received it as his eyes wandered over the hundred Legion riders.

It would be a relief to see action and might even clear his head. Military men, the scout had said. That would make a change from witless villagers hacking about with hoes and axes.

Reaching the crest of a range of hills, Argonis gazed down over a rolling plain almost at the foot of the Skoda range. The scout rode alongside as Argonis shielded his eyes and studied the riders below.

'Ours, sir?' queried the scout.

'No. Delnoch issue red cloaks, or blue for officers – never white. I think they are Vagrian raiders.'

At that moment the column below broke into a canter heading for the sanctuary of the mountains.

'At the gallop!' yelled Argonis, drawing his sabre, and one hundred black-garbed horsemen set off in pursuit, hooves drumming on the hard-packed earth.

With the advantage of the slope, and the fact that they were cutting towards the enemy at an angle, the gap swiftly narrowed.

Excitement swept through Argonis as he bent low over his horse's neck, the morning breeze fanning his face, his sabre glinting in the sunlight.

'*No prisoners!*' he screamed. He was close enough now to see individual riders and to note that three were women. Then he saw the black man riding alongside one of them, obviously encouraging her – she was not sitting well in the saddle and appeared to be holding something in her arms. Her companion leaned over in the saddle and snatched the bundle from her; with both hands on the reins her mount picked up speed. Argonis grinned – what a futile gesture, for the Legion would be upon them before they reached the mountains.

Suddenly the white-cloaked riders wheeled their mounts. It was a spectacular example of discipline, for they made the move in perfect unison and before Argonis could react they had turned and were charging. Panic struck at Argonis' heart. Here he was, out in front leading the chase, and now thirty madmen were bearing down on him. He dragged on the reins and his men followed suit, confused and uncertain.

The Thirty hit them like a winter storm, silver blades flashing and slicing. Horses reared and men screamed as they fell from the saddle. Then the white-cloaked riders wheeled once more and galloped away.

Argonis was furious. 'After them!' he yelled, but wisely held back his own mount as his men thundered in pursuit. The mountains were nearer now and the enemy had begun the long climb to the first valley. A horse stumbled and fell, pitching a blonde woman to the grass; three riders spurred their horses at her. A tall man dressed in black, his face masked, swung his horse and raced to intercept. Argonis watched fascinated as the masked man ducked under a wild cut and disembowelled the first rider, swinging in the saddle to block an overhead cut from the second. Spurring his horse he cannoned into the third, downing horse and man.

The woman was up now and running. The masked man parried an attack from the second rider, and slashed the man's throat with a reverse cut. Then he was clear. Sheathing his sword, he galloped his horse towards the woman, leaning over in the saddle. His arm swept down to circle her waist and sweep her up in front of him, then they were gone into the Skoda range.

Argonis cantered back to the site of the battle. Thirty-one members of his force were down; eighteen dead, another six mortally wounded.

His men returned, dejected and demoralised. The scout, Lepus, approached Argonis and dismounted. Saluting swiftly, he held Argonis' mount as the officer slid from the saddle.

'Who in Hell's name were they?' asked Lepus.

'I don't know, but they made us look like children.'

'Is that what your report will say, sir?'

'Shut your mouth!'

'Yes, sir.'

'We will have a thousand Legion riders here in a few days. Then we will smoke them out – they cannot defend an entire range. We shall see those white-cloaked bastards again.'

'I'm not sure that I want to,' said Lepus.

Tenaka pulled his mount to a stop by a winding stream that trickled through a grove of elm on the western side of the valley. He swung in the saddle, seeking Ananais; he could see the warrior walking his horse, Valtaya sitting side-saddle behind him. They had made it without losing a single member of their party, thanks only to the spectacular skills of The Thirty.

Dismounting, Tenaka left his horse to graze; he loosened the saddle cinch and patted the beast's neck. Renya rode alongside and leapt from her saddle, her face flushed and her eyes bright with excitement.

'Are we safe now?' she asked.

'For the moment,' he answered.

Ananais lifted his leg over the pommel of his saddle and slid to the ground, turning to lift Valtaya clear. She smiled at him and draped her arms over his shoulders.

'Will you always be on hand to save my life?'

'Always is a long time, lady,' he answered, his hands on her waist.

'Did anyone ever tell you that you have beautiful eyes?'

'Not lately,' he said, releasing her and walking away.

Galand watched the scene and then moved to Valtaya.

'I should forget it, girl,' he said. 'The man is not for winning.'

'But you are, eh, Galand?'

'I am, lass! But take your time before saying yes. I'm not exactly a great catch.'

Valtaya laughed. 'You are better than you think.'

'But it's "No" just the same?'

'I don't think you are looking for a wife, are you?'

'If only we had the time,' answered Galand seriously and reaching out, he took her hand. 'You are a fine woman, Val, and I don't think a man could do better. I wish I had known you in better days.'

'Times are what we make them. There are other nations in the world where men like Ceska are shunned. Peaceful nations.'

'I don't want to be a foreigner, Val. I want to live in my own land among my own people. I want . . .' Galand's words tailed away and Valtaya saw the anguish in his eyes. She laid her hand on his arm and he looked away.

'What is it, Galand? What were you going to say?'

'It doesn't matter, lass.' He turned back to her, his eyes clear and his emotions masked. 'Tell me what you see in our scarred companion?'

'I don't know. That is a difficult question for a woman to answer. Come on, let us get some food.'

Decado, Acuas, Balan and Katan left the group at the camp-site and rode back to the mouth of the valley, pausing to gaze down on the green plain where the Legion were ministering to their wounded. The dead had been wrapped in blankets and tied across their saddles.

'You did well,' said Decado, lifting his helm and hooking it over his pommel.

'It was appalling,' said Katan.

Decado swung in the saddle. 'You chose to be a warrior. Accept it!'

'I know that, Decado,' answered the dark-eyed priest. He smiled ruefully and rubbed his face. 'But I cannot revel in it.'

'That's not what I meant. You have chosen to fight against evil and you have just won a small victory. The babe back there would now be dead, but for you and the others.'

'I know that, too. I am not a child. But it is hard.'

The four dismounted and sat on the grass, enjoying the sunshine. Decado removed his white cloak and folded it carefully. He closed his eyes, suddenly aware of a strange sensation like a cool breeze inside his head.

He tried to focus on it and became aware of subtle ebbs and flows within his mind, like the distant echo of rolling waves over shingle. He lay back, drifting and at peace, moving within himself towards the source of the sensation. He was not surprised when the whispering seas became faint voices, and he recognised that of Acuas.

'I still feel Abaddon could be wrong. Did you sense Decado's battle-lust as we struck the riders? The force was so powerful it almost infected me.'

'Abaddon says not to judge.' This from Katan.

'But he is the Abbot no longer.' Balan spoke.

'He will always be the Abbot of Swords. He must be respected.' Katan again.

'It makes me feel uncomfortable,' pulsed Acuas. 'Where is his Talent?

In all the long history of The Thirty there has never been a leader who could not Travel and Speak.'

'I think perhaps we should consider the alternatives,' pulsed Katan. 'If Abaddon was misled in his choice of the Voice, then that would mean Chaos has mastered the Source. In turn that would negate every other choice Abaddon has made and render us Outside the Destiny.'

'Not necessarily,' said Balan. 'We are all human. Abaddon could have made merely one mistake. He is Source-guided, but so much depends on interpretation. Estin's death and Decado's arrival could have been either coincidence or dark design.'

'Or Source-inspired?' pulsed Acuas.

'Indeed so.'

Decado opened his eyes and sat up. 'What are they planning?' he asked aloud, pointing to the Legion.

'They are waiting for the arrival of their army,' said Acuas. 'The leader there, a man named Argonis, is telling his men that we will be smoked out of these mountains and destroyed along with every other rebel in Skoda. He is trying to lift them.'

'But he is not succeeding,' put in Balan.

'Tell us of the Dragon, Decado,' asked Katan and Decado smiled.

'Days of long ago,' he said. 'It seems like another lifetime.'

'Did you enjoy the life?' enquired Acuas.

'Yes and no. More no than yes, I recall. The Dragon was strange. In some way I suppose it created a bond similar to yours except of course that we had no talent and could neither Travel nor Speak as you do. But we were a family. Brothers. And we held the nation together.'

'You must have been saddened when Ceska destroyed your friends,' said Balan.

'Yes. But I was a priest and my life had changed very much. I had my garden and my plants. The world had become a small place indeed.'

'It always amazed me that you produced so many varieties of vegetable in such a small section,' said Balan.

Decado chuckled. 'I grew tomatoes inside potatoes,' he said. 'I placed the seedlings in a potato, and while the tomatoes grew upwards the potatoes grew down. I was quite pleased with the results.'

'Do you miss your garden?' asked Acuas.

'No, I do not. And that makes me sad.'

'Did you enjoy your life as a priest?' said Katan.

Decado looked at the slender young man with the gentle face. 'Do you enjoy life as a warrior?' he countered.

'No. Not in the least.'

'In some ways I enjoyed my life. It was good to hide for a while.'

'From what were you hiding?' asked Balan.

'I think you know the answer to that. I deal in death, my friend – I always have. Some men can paint, others create beauty in stone or in words. I kill. But pride and shame do not match well and I found the disharmony daunting. In the moment of the kill there was bliss, but afterwards . . .'

'What happened afterwards?' asked Acuas.

'No man alive could match me with the blades, therefore all my enemies became defenceless. I was no longer a warrior, but a murderer. The thrill lessened, the doubts grew. When the Dragon was disbanded I travelled the world seeking opponents, but found none. Then I realised there was only one man who could test me, and I decided to challenge him. On the way to his home in Ventria I was trapped in a sandstorm for three days. It gave me time to think about what I was doing. You see, the man was my friend and yet, had it not been for the storm, I would have killed him. It was then that I returned home to the Drenai and tried to change my life.'

'And what became of your friend?' asked Katan.

Decado smiled. 'He became a Torchbearer.'

9

The council chamber had seen better days; now woodworm pockmarked the inlaid elm around the walls and the painted mosaic showing the white-bearded Druss the Legend had peeled away in ugly patches, exposing the grey of mould growing on the plaster.

Some thirty men and about a dozen women and children were seated on wooden benches, listening to the words of the woman sitting at the Senate chair. She was large, big-boned and broad of shoulder. Her dark hair swept out from her head like a lion's mane and her green eyes blazed with anger.

'Just listen to yourselves!' she roared, pushing herself to her feet and smoothing the folds in her heavy green skirt. 'Talk, talk, talk! And what does it all mean? Throw yourselves on Ceska's mercy? What in hell's name does that mean? Surrender, that's what! You, Petar – stand up!'

A man shuffled to his feet, head bowed and blushing furiously.

'Lift your arm!' bellowed the woman and he did so. The hand was missing and the stump showed evidence still of the tar that had closed the wound.

'*That* is Ceska's mercy! By all the gods, you cheered loud enough when my men of the mountains swept the soldiers from our lands. You couldn't do enough for us then, could you? But now they are coming back, you want to squeal and hide. Well, there *is* nowhere to hide. The Vagrians won't let us cross their borders, and for damn sure Ceska won't forgive and forget.'

A middle-aged man rose to his feet alongside the helpless Petar. 'It's no use shouting, Rayvan. What choices do we have? We cannot beat them. We shall all die.'

'Everybody dies, Vorak,' stormed the woman. 'Or had you not heard? I have six hundred fighting men who say we can defeat the Legion. And there are five hundred more who are waiting to join us when we can lay our hands on more weapons.'

'Suppose we do turn back the Legion,' said Vorak, 'what happens when Ceska sends in his Joinings? What use will your fighting men be then?'

'When the time comes, we shall see,' she promised.

'We shall see nothing. Go back where you came from and leave us to make peace with Ceska. We don't want you here!' shouted Vorak.

'Oh, speaking for everyone now, are we, Vorak?' Rayvan stepped from the dais and marched towards the man. He swallowed hard as she loomed over him, then her hand gripped his collar and propelled him towards the wall. 'Look up there and tell me what you see,' she commanded.

'It's a wall, Rayvan, with a picture on it. Now let me go!'

'That's not just a picture, you lump of dung! That's Druss! That's the man who stood against the hordes of Ulric. And he didn't bother to count them. You make me sick!'

Leaving him, she walked back to the dais and turned on the gathering. 'I could listen to Vorak. I could take my six hundred and vanish back into the mountains. But I know what would happen - you would all be killed. You have no choice but to fight.'

'We have families, Rayvan,' protested another man.

'Yes, and they will die too.'

'So you say,' said the man, 'but we are certain to be killed if we resist the Legion.'

'Do what you want, then,' she snapped. 'But get out of my sight – all of you! There used to be men in this land. Get out!'

Petar turned at the door, the last to leave. 'Don't judge us too harshly, Rayvan,' he called.

'Get *out*!' she bellowed. She wandered to the window and looked out at the city, white under the spring sun. Beautiful, but indefensible. There was no wall. Rayvan put together a string of oaths that rolled from her tongue with rare power. She felt better then . . . but not much.

Beyond the window in the winding streets and open squares people thronged, and although Rayvan could not hear their words she knew the subject of every conversation.

Surrender. The possibility of life. And beyond the words, the driving emotion – fear!

What was the matter with them? Had Ceska's terror eroded the strength of the people? She swung round and stared at the fading mosaic. Druss the Legend, squat and powerful with axe in hand, the mountains of Skoda behind him seeming to echo the qualities of the man – white-topped and indestructible.

Rayvan looked at her hands: short, stubby and still ingrained with the soil of her farms. Years of work, cripplingly hard work, had robbed them of beauty. She was glad there was no mirror. Once she had been the 'maid of the mountains', slim of waist and garlanded. But the years – such good years – had been less than kind. Her dark hair was now shot with silver and her face was hard as Skoda granite. Few men now looked on her with lust, which was just as well. After twenty years of marriage and nine children, she had somewhat lost interest in the beast with two backs.

Returning to the window, she looked out beyond the city to the ring of mountains. Whence would the enemy come? And how would she meet them? Her men were confident enough. Had they not defeated several hundred soldiers, losing only forty men in the process? Indeed they had – but the soldiers had been taken by surprise and they were a gutless bunch. This time would be different.

Rayvan thought long and hard about the coming battle.

Different?

They will cut us to pieces. She swore, picturing again the moment when the soldiers had swept into her lands and butchered her husband and two of their sons. The watching crowd had been subdued until Rayvan, armed with a curved meat cleaver, had run forward and hammered it into the officer's side.

Then it was pandemonium.

But now . . . Now was the time to pay for the dance.

She walked across the hall to stand with hands on hips below the mosaic.

'I have always boasted that I came from your line, Druss,' she said. 'It's not true – as far as I know. But I wish I had. My father used to talk of you. He was a soldier at Delnoch and he spent months studying the chronicles of the Earl of Bronze. He knew more about you than any man living. I wish you could come back . . . Step down from that wall! Joinings wouldn't stop you, would they? You would march to Drenan and rip the crown from Ceska's head. I cannot do it, Druss. I don't know the first thing about war. And, damn it, there is no time to learn.'

The far door creaked open. 'Rayvan?'

She turned to see her son, Lucas, bow in hand. 'What is it?'

'Riders – around fifty of them, heading for the city.'

'Damn! How did they get past the scouts?'

'I don't know. Lake is gathering what men he can find.'

'Why only fifty?'

'They obviously don't hold us in high account,' said Lucas, grinning. He was a handsome lad, dark-haired but grey-eyed; with Lake he was the pick of her litter, she knew.

'They will hold us in higher account when we've met them,' she said. 'Let's move.'

They left the chamber and made their way along the marbled corridor and down the wide stairs to the street. Already the news had spread and Vorak was waiting for them, backed by more than fifty traders.

'That's it, Rayvan!' he shouted as she came into the sunlight. 'Your war is over.'

'What does that mean?' she asked, holding her temper.

'You started all this – it's your fault. Now we're going to hand you over to them.'

'Let me kill him,' whispered Lucas, reaching for an arrow.

'No!' hissed Rayvan, her eyes sweeping the buildings opposite – in every window was an archer, bow bent. 'Go back into the chamber and get out through Bakers' Alley. Fetch Lake and do what you can to get away into Vagria. Sometime, when you can, avenge me.'

'I won't leave you, mother.'

'You will do as you're told!'

He swore, then backed away through the door. Rayvan walked slowly down the steps, her face set, her green eyes locked on Vorak. He backed away.

'Tie her!' he shouted, and several men rushed forward to pin Rayvan's arms behind her back.

'I shall come back, Vorak. From beyond the grave I shall return,' she promised. He hit her across the face with the flat of his hand. She made no sound, but blood trickled from a split in her lip. They dragged her through the crowd as they made their way to the outer city and the plain beyond where the riders had come into view. The leader was a tall man with a cruel face. He dismounted and Vorak ran forward.

'We have taken the traitress, sir. She led the rebellion, if such you can call it. We are innocent men, all of us.'

The man nodded and approached Rayvan. She stared into his slanted violet eyes.

'So,' she said softly, 'even the Nadir ride with Ceska, do they?'

'Your name, woman?' he said.

'Rayvan. Remember it, barbarian, for my sons will carve it on your heart.'

He turned to Vorak. 'What do you suggest we do with her?'

'Kill her! Make an example. Death to all traitors!'

'But you are loyal?'

'I am. I always have been. It was I who first reported the rebels in Skoda. You should know of me – I am Vorak.'

'And these men with you, they are also loyal?'

'None more so. Every one is pledged to Ceska.'

The man nodded, turning once more to Rayvan. 'And how did you come to be captured, woman?'

'We all make mistakes.'

The man lifted his hand and thirty white-cloaked riders moved out to surround the mob.

'What are you doing?' asked Vorak.

The man drew his sword, testing the edge with his thumb. He spun on his heel, the blade flashed out and Vorak's head tumbled from his neck, eyes wide with horror.

The head bounced at the man's feet as Vorak's body collapsed to the grass, blood pumping from his neck. The men in the crowd fell to their knees, begging for mercy.

'Silence!' bellowed a black-masked giant who sat a bay gelding. The noise subsided, though here and there the sound of sobbing could still be heard.

'I have no wish to kill you all,' said Tenaka Khan. 'So you will be taken to the valley and released to make your peace with the Legion. I wish you luck – I sincerely believe you will need it. Now get up and move out.'

Herded by The Thirty, the men began to walk to the east as Tenaka untied Rayvan's arms.

'Who are you?' she asked.

'Tenaka Khan, of the line of the Earl of Bronze,' he answered, bowing.

'I am Rayvan – of the line of Druss the Legend,' she told him, planting her hands on her hips.

Scaler wandered alone in the gardens of Gathere behind the city council hall. He had sat listening as Tenaka and Rayvan talked of the coming battle, but could find no sensible comments to add. So he had slipped out quietly, his heart heavy. He had been a fool to join them. What could he offer? He was no warrior.

He sat on a stone bench, staring into a rock pool and watching the

599

golden fish dart among the lilies. Scaler had been a lonely child. It had not been easy living with the irascible Orrin, knowing how the old man had pinned his hopes on Scaler becoming a worthy successor. The family had proved ill-fated and Scaler was the last of the line – if you discounted Tenaka Khan. And most people did.

But Arvan – as Scaler then was – had taken to the Nadir youngster, seeking his company at every opportunity, relishing the stories of life on the Steppes. His admiration had changed to hero worship on the night when the assassin climbed into his room.

The man, dressed all in black and hooded, had reached across his bed to clamp a gloved hand over his mouth. Arvan, a sensitive, frightened six-year-old, had fainted in fear, awaking only when the cold winter breeze touched his cheek. When his eyes opened he found himself staring down from the battlements to the cobbles far below. He twisted in the man's grip and felt his fingers loosen.

'If you value your life, don't do it!' said a voice.

The assassin cursed softly, but his hold strengthened.

'And if I let him live?' he asked, his voice muffled.

'Then you live,' said Tenaka Khan.

'You are just a boy. I could kill you too.'

'Then go on with your mission,' said Tenaka. 'And try your luck.'

For several seconds the assassin hesitated. Then he slowly pulled Arvan back over the battlements and placed him on the stone steps. The man backed away into the shadows and was gone. Arvan ran to Tenaka and the youth sheathed his sword and hugged him.

'He was going to kill me, Tani.'

'I know. But he's gone now.'

'Why did he want to kill me?'

Tenaka had not known the answer. Neither had Orrin, but thereafter a guard was placed at Arvan's door and his life continued with fear as a constant companion . . .

'Good afternoon.'

Scaler looked up to see, standing by the pool, a young woman dressed in a flowing gown of thin white wool. Her hair was dark and gently waved, and her green eyes were flecked with gold. Scaler stood and bowed.

'Why so gloomy?' she asked.

He shrugged. 'I would rather say melancholy. Who are you?'

'Ravenna, Rayvan's daughter. Why are you not in there with the others?'

He grinned. 'I know nothing about wars, campaigns or battles.'

'What do you know about?'

'Art, literature, poetry and all things of beauty.'

'You are out of your time, my friend.'

'Scaler. Call me Scaler.'

'A strange name, Scaler. Do you climb things?'

'Walls, mostly.' He gestured towards the seat. 'Will you join me?' he asked.

'For a little while only. I have errands to run.'

'I am sure they can wait. Tell me, how did a woman come to lead a rebellion?'

'To understand that, you have to know mother. She is of the line of Druss the Legend, you know, and will not be cowed by anyone or anything. She once drove off a mountain lion with a large stick.'

'A formidable lady,' said Scaler.

'Indeed she is. And she also knows nothing about wars, campaigns and battles. But she will learn. So should you.'

'I would sooner learn more about you, Ravenna,' he said, switching on his winning smile.

'I see there are some campaigns that you understand,' she said, rising from her seat. 'It was nice meeting you.'

'Wait! Could we meet again? Tonight, for instance?'

'Perhaps. If you live up to your name.'

That night, as Rayvan lay in her broad bed staring out at the stars, she felt more at peace than at any time during the last few hectic months. She had not realised just how irksome leadership could be. Nor had she ever intended to be a leader. All she had done was to slay the man who killed her husband – but from then on it had been like sliding down an icy mountain.

Within weeks of the campaign Rayvan's slender forces controlled most of Skoda. Those were the heady days of cheering crowds and cameraderie. Then word began to filter into the mountains of an army being gathered, and swiftly the mood changed. Rayvan had felt besieged in the city even before the enemy had arrived.

Now she felt light of heart.

Tenaka Khan was no ordinary man. She smiled and closed her eyes, summoning his image to her mind. He moved like a dancer in perfect control and he wore confidence like a cloak. The warrior born!

Ananais was more enigmatic but, by all the gods, he had the look of eagles about him. Here was a man who had been over the mountain. He it was who had offered to train her fledgling fighters and Lake had taken him back into the hills where they camped. The two brothers Galand and Parsal had travelled with them – solid men, with no give in them.

The black she was unsure of. He looked like a damned Joining, she thought. But for all that, he was a handsome devil. And there was little doubt he could handle himself.

Rayvan turned over, punching a little comfort into the thick pillow.

Send in your Legion, Ceska. We shall stove in their damned teeth!

Down the long corridor, in a room facing east, Tenaka and Renya lay side by side, an uncomfortable silence between them.

Tenaka rolled on to his elbow and looked down at her, but Renya did not return his gaze.

'What is the matter?' he asked.

'Nothing.'

'That is palpably untrue. Please, Renya, speak to me.'

'It was the man you killed.'

601

'You knew him?'

'No, I didn't. But he was unarmed – there was no need.'

'I see,' he said, swinging his long legs from the bed. He walked to the window, and she lay there staring at his naked form silhouetted against the moonlight.

'Why did you do it?'

'It was necessary.'

'Explain it to me.'

'He led the mob and he was obviously Ceska's man. By killing him suddenly, it cowed them. You saw them – all armed, many with bows. They could have turned on us, but his death stunned them.'

'It certainly stunned me – it was butchery!'

He turned to face her. 'This is not a game, Renya. Many men will die, even before this week is out.'

'It still was not right.'

'*Right?* This isn't a poem, woman! I am not some gold-armoured hero righting wrongs. I reasoned that his death would allow us to remove a cancer from the city without loss to ourselves. And anyway, he deserved to die.'

'It doesn't touch you, does it? Taking life? You don't care that he might have had a family, children, a mother.'

'You are right; I don't care. There are only two people in the world that I love – you are one and Ananais is the other. That man had made his decision. He chose sides and he died for it. I don't regret it and probably I would have forgotten it within the month.'

'That is a terrible thing to say!'

'You would prefer it if I lied to you?'

'No. I just thought you were . . . different.'

'Don't judge me. I am only a man doing my best. I know no other way to be.'

'Come back to bed.'

'Is the argument over?'

'If you want it to be,' she lied.

In the room above them Pagan grinned and moved away from the window.

Women were strange creatures. They fell in love with a man and then sought to change him. Mostly they succeeded – to spend the rest of their lives wondering how they could have married such boring conformists. It is the nature of the beast, Pagan told himself. He thought of his own wives, running their faces past his mind's eye, but he could picture only about thirty of them. You are getting old, he told himself. He often wondered how he had allowed the numbers to become so great. The palace was more crowded than a bazaar. Ego. That was it! There was no getting away from it. Just as there was no getting away from his forty-two children. He shuddered. Then he chuckled.

A faint shuffling noise disturbed his thoughts and he moved back to the window, peering out into the shadows.

602

A man was climbing the wall some twenty feet to the right – it was Scaler.

'What are you doing?' asked Pagan, keeping his voice low.

'I am planting corn,' hissed Scaler. 'What do you think I'm doing?'

Pagan glanced up to the darkened window above. 'Why didn't you just climb the stairs?'

'I was asked to arrive this way. It's a tryst.'

'Oh, I see. Well, goodnight!'

'And to you.'

Pagan ducked back his head through the window. Strange how much effort a man would make just to get himself into trouble.

'What's going on?' came the voice of Tenaka Khan.

'Will you keep your voice down?' snarled Scaler.

Pagan returned to the window, leaning out to see Tenaka staring upwards.

'He is on a tryst . . . or something,' said Pagan.

'If he falls he will break his neck.'

'He never falls,' said Belder, from a window to the left. 'He has a natural talent for not falling.'

'Will someone tell me why there is a man climbing the wall?' shouted Rayvan.

'He is on a tryst!' yelled Pagan.

'Why couldn't he climb the stairs?' she responded.

'We have been through all that. He was asked to come this way!'

'Oh. He must be seeing Ravenna then,' she said.

Scaler clung to the wall, engaged in his own private conversation with the Senile Eternals.

Meanwhile in the darkened room above, Ravenna bit her pillow to stop the laughter.

Without success.

For two days Ananais walked among the Skoda fighters, organising them into fighting units of twenty and pushing them hard. There were five hundred and eighty-two men, most of them tough and wolf-lean. Men to match the mountains. But they were undisciplined and unused to organised warfare. Given time, Ananais could have produced a fighting force to equal anything Ceska could send against them. But he did not have time.

On his first morning with the grey-eyed Lake, he had mustered the men and checked their weapons. There were not one hundred swords among them.

'It's not a farmer's weapon,' said Lake. 'But we have plenty of axes and bows.' Ananais nodded and moved on. Sweat trickled under his mask, burning against the scars that would not heal, and his irritation grew.

'Find me twenty men who could make leaders,' he said, then walked swiftly back to the crofter's cottage he had made his quarters. Galand and Parsal followed him.

'What's wrong?' asked Galand as the three men sat down in the cool of the main room.

'Wrong? There are nearly six hundred men out there who will be dead in a few days. That is what's wrong.'

'A little defeatist, aren't you?' said Parsal evenly.

'Not yet. But I am close,' admitted Ananais. 'They are tough and they are willing. But you cannot send a mob against the Legion. We don't even have a bugle. And if we did, there is not one man out there to understand a single call.'

'Then we shall have to cut and run – hit them hard and move away,' proposed Galand.

'You were never an officer, were you?' said Ananais.

'No. I didn't come from the right background,' snapped Galand.

'Whatever the reason, the simple fact is that you were not trained to lead. We cannot hit and run because that would mean splitting our force. Then the Legion would come after us piecemeal and we would have no way of knowing what was happening to the rest of the army. Equally, it would allow the Legion to enter Skoda and embark on a killing campaign against the cities and villages.'

'Then what do you suggest?' asked Parsal, pouring water from a stone jug and passing the clay goblets to the other two.

Ananais turned away and lifted his mask, noisily sipping the cool water. Then he turned back to them. 'To be truthful, I don't know yet. If we stay together they will cut us to pieces in a single day. If we split up, they will cut the villagers to pieces. The choices are not attractive. I have asked Lake to supply me with rough maps of the terrain. And we have maybe two days to drill the men so that they will respond to rudimentary calls – we will use hunting horns and work out simple systems. Galand, I want you to go among the men and find the best two hundred – I want men who will stand firm against horsemen. Parsal, you check the bowmen. Again I want the best brought together as one unit. I shall also want to know the finest runners. And send Lake to me.'

As the two men left, Ananais gently removed the black leather mask. Then he filled a bowl with water and dabbed the red, angry scars. The door opened and he swung round, turning his back on the newcomer. Having settled the mask in place, he offered Lake a chair. Rayvan's eldest son was a fine-looking man, strong and lean; his eyes were the colour of a winter sky and he moved with animal grace and the confidence of the man who knows he has limits, but has not yet reached them.

'You are not impressed with our army?' he said.

'I am impressed by their courage.'

'They are mountain men,' said Lake, leaning back in his chair and stretching out his long legs on to the table top. 'But you did not answer my question.'

'It was not a question,' replied Ananais. 'You knew the answer. I am not impressed. But then they are not an army.'

'Can we turn back the Legion?'

Ananais considered the question. With many another man he would have lied, but not with this one. Lake was too sharp.

'Probably not.'

'And will you still stay?'

'Yes.'

'Why?'

'A good question. But I cannot answer it.'

'It seemed simple enough.'

'Why will you stay?' countered Ananais.

'This is my land and they are my people. My family brought them to this.'

'Your mother, you mean?'

'If you like.'

'She is a fine woman.'

'Indeed she is. But I want to know why you will stay.'

'Because it is what I do, boy. I fight. I'm Dragon. Do you understand?' Lake nodded. 'So the war between good and evil does not concern you?'

'Yes, it does, but not greatly. Most wars are fought for greed but we are luckier here – we fight for our lives and the lives of the people we love.'

'And the land,' said Lake.

'Rubbish!' snapped Ananais. 'No man fights for dirt and grass. No, nor mountains. Those mountains were here before the Fall and they will be here when the world topples again.'

'I don't see it that way.'

'Of course not – you're young and full of fire. Me – I'm older than the sea. I have been over the mountain and looked into the eye of the Serpent. I have seen it all, young Lake. And I am not too impressed.'

'So! We understand one another, at least,' said Lake, grinning. 'What do you want me to do?'

'I want men sent now to the city. We have only seven thousand arrows and that is not enough. We have no armour – get some. I want the city scoured. We need food, oats, meal, dried beef, fruit. And I want horses – up to fifty. More if you can get them.'

'And how will we pay for all this?'

'Give them notes.'

'They will not accept promises from dead men.'

'Use your head, Lake. They will accept – because if they don't, you will take what you want. Any man who refuses will be branded a traitor and dealt with accordingly.'

'I am not going to kill a man because he won't let us rob him.'

'Then go back to your mother and send me a man who wants to win,' stormed Ananais . . .

The weapons and food began to arrive on the morning of the third day.

By the morning of the fourth day Galand, Parsal and Lake had chosen the two hundred men Ananais had requested to stand against the Legion.

605

Parsal had also organised the finest of the archers into a single group of just under one hundred.

As the sun cleared the eastern peaks, Ananais gathered the men together in an open meadow below the camp. Many of them now carried swords, by courtesy of the city armourer. All the archers carried two quivers of arrows, and even the occasional breastplate was to be seen among Ananais' new foot soldiers. With Parsal, Lake and Galand flanking him, Ananais climbed to the back of a cart and stood with hands on hips, eyes scanning the warriors seated around him.

'No fine speeches, lads,' he told them. 'We heard last night that the Legion is almost upon us. Tomorrow we will be in position to greet them. They are heading for the lower eastern valley, which I am told you call the Demon's Smile.

'There are about twelve hundred fighting men, all well-armed and well-horsed. Two hundred of them are archers – the rest lancers and swordsmen.' He paused to let the numbers sink in and watched men exchange glances, noting with pleasure the absence of fear in their faces.

'I have never believed in lying to the men under my command, and so I tell you this: our chances of victory are slim. Very slim! It is important we understand that.

'You know me by reputation. As yet you do not know me as a man. But I ask you to listen to what I say now, as if your own fathers were whispering in your ears. Battles are won in many cases by the actions of a single man. Each one of you could represent the difference between victory and defeat.

'Druss the Legend was such a man. He turned the battle for Skeln Pass into one of the greatest Drenai victories of all time. But he was just a man – a Skoda man.

'On the day one of you, or ten of you, or a hundred of you, will turn the battle. A moment's panic, or a single second of heroism.' He paused again and then lifted his hand, one finger pointing to the sky. 'One single second!'

'Now I am going to ask for the first act of courage from some of you. If there be any men here who believe they could fail their friends in tomorrow's fight, let them leave the camp before today's end.

'I swear by all I hold precious that I will look down on no man who does this. For tomorrow it is vital that the men who look into the eyes of death should not falter.

'Later today we will be joined by a warrior second to none on the face of this earth – the most skilful general I have ever known and the deadliest fighting man under the sun. He will have with him a group of soldiers having very special talents; these warriors will be split up among you and their orders are to be obeyed without hesitation. And I *mean* that!

'Lastly, I ask for something for myself. I was the Wing Gan of the finest army in the world – the Dragon. They were my family, my friends, my brothers. And they are dead, betrayed and lost to this nation. But the Dragon was more than an army, it was an ideal. A dream, if you like. It was a force to stand against Darkness, formed by men who would march into Hell with a bucket of water, knowing they would put out the fire.

'But you don't need glittering armour or a battle standard to be the Dragon. You just need to be willing.

'The forces of Darkness are marching against us, like storm winds against a lantern. They think to find us cowering in the mountains like sheep. But I want them to feel the Dragon's breath on their necks and the Dragon's teeth in their guts! I want those black-garbed, high-riding sons of sluts to burn in the Dragon's fire!' He was shouting now, his fists clenched and punching the air for emphasis. He took a deep breath, then another, and suddenly swung out his arm to encompass them all.

'I want you to *be* the Dragon. I want you to *think* Dragon. When they charge I want you to *fight* like Dragon!

'Can you do it? Well, CAN YOU?' he bellowed, pointing at a man in the front row.

'Damn right!' shouted the man.

'Can you?' said Ananais, pointing to a warrior several rows back. The man nodded. 'Use your voice!' stormed the general.

'I can!' the man called.

'And do you know the Dragon's roar?'

The man shook his head.

'The Dragon's roar is death. Death. DEATH! Let's hear you – you alone!'

The man cleared his throat and began to shout. He was blushing furiously.

'Give him some support, the rest of you!' cried Ananais, joining in with the man.

'Death, Death, DEATH . . .' and the sound grew, rolling across the meadow to echo in the white-capped mountains, growing in strength and confidence, hypnotic as it drew the men together.

Ananais stepped from the wagon, pulling Lake to him.

'Now you get up there, lad. And give them your fighting-for-the-land speech. They're ready for it now, by thunder!'

'No fine speeches, indeed,' said Lake, grinning.

'Get up there, Lake, and lift their blood!'

10

Pagan took the village woman Parise to an inn at the southern quarter of the city, where he passed three gold coins to the innkeeper. The man's eyes bulged at the sight of the small fortune glittering in his palm.

'I want the woman and the babe to receive your best,' said Pagan softly. 'I will leave more gold with friends, should this amount prove insufficient.'

'I will treat her like my own sister,' said the man.

'That is good,' said Pagan, smiling broadly and leaning over him. 'Because if you do not, I shall eat your heart.'

'There is no need to threaten me, black man,' said the stocky balding innkeeper, drawing back his shoulders and clenching his powerful fists. 'I require no instructions on how to treat a woman.'

Pagan nodded. 'These are not good times to rely on trust alone.'

'No, that's true enough. Will you join me for a drink?'

The two men sat together nursing their ale, while Parise fed the babe in the privacy of her new room. The innkeeper's name was Ilter and he had lived in the city for twenty-three years, ever since his farm failed during the great drought.

'You know you have given me too much money, don't you?' he said.

'I know,' answered Pagan. Ilter nodded and drained the rest of his ale.

'I have never seen a black man before.'

'In my land, beyond the dark jungles and the Mountains of the Moon, the people have never seen a white man, though there are legends that speak of such.'

'Strange world, isn't it?' said Ilter.

Pagan stared into the golden depths of his drink, suddenly homesick for the rolling veldt, the sunsets of scarlet and the coughing roar of the hunting lion.

He remembered the morning of the Day of Death. Would he ever forget it? The ships with black sails had beached in White Gold Bay and the raiders had swiftly made their way inland to his father's village. The old man had gathered his warriors swiftly, but there were not enough and they had been butchered at the last before the old king's kraal.

The raiders had come in search of gold, for legends were many concerning the people of the bay, but the old mines had been long worked out and the people had turned to the growing gold of maize and corn. In their fury the raiders took the women and tortured many, raping and murdering them at the last. In all four hundred souls passed over on that day – among them Pagan's father, mother, three sisters, a younger brother and four of his daughters.

One child escaped during the opening moments of the attack and ran like the wind, finding Pagan and his personal guard hunting in the High Hills.

With sixty men he raced barefoot over the veldt, his long-bladed spear resting on his shoulder. They reached the village soon after the raiders had left. Taking in the scene at a glance Pagan read the tracks. Three hundred men or more had attacked his father's kraal – too many for him to handle. Taking his spear, he snapped it across his knee, discarding the long shaft and hefting the stabbing blade like a short sword. His men followed suit.

'I want many dead – but one alive,' said Pagan. 'You, Bopa, will take the live one and bring him to me. For the rest, let us drink blood.'

'We hear and obey, Kataskicana,' they shouted, and he led them into the jungle and on to the bay.

Moving like black ghosts, they came upon the party singing and laughing as they made their way back to their ships. Pagan and his sixty fell upon them like demons of hell, hacking and stabbing. Then they were gone into the jungle.

Eighty raiders died in that one attack and one man was missing, presumed dead. For three days he wished that were so.

Pagan took the man to the ruined village and there he used all the barbarous skills of his people until at last the thing that had been a man gave up his soul to the void. Then Pagan had the carcass burned.

Returning to his palace, he called his counsellors to him and told them of the attack.

'My family blood calls to me for revenge,' he told them, 'yet our nation is too distant for war. The killers came from a land called Drenai, sent by their king to gather gold. I am a king and I carry the heart of my people in my hand. Therefore I alone shall carry this war to the enemy. I shall seek out their king and destroy him. My own son, Katasi, will sit on my throne until I return. If I am gone for longer than three years . . .' He turned to the warrior beside him. 'It is time for you to rule, Katasi. I was king at your age.'

'Let me go in your place, father,' pleaded the young man.

'No. You are the future. If I do not return, I do not wish my wives to burn. It is one thing for them to follow a king on the day of his death and at the place of his passing. But if I am to die it may be that it will happen soon. I cannot have my wives waiting three years only to be lost in the mists. Let them live.'

'To hear is to obey.'

'Good! I believe I have taught you well, Katasi. Once you hated me for sending you to Ventria to study – even as I hated my father. Now I think you will find those years to your benefit.'

'May the Lord Shem rest his soul upon your sword,' said Katasi, embracing his father.

It had taken Pagan more than a year to reach the lands of the Drenai, and cost him half the gold he carried. He had soon realised the enormity of his task. Now he knew the gods had given him his chance.

Tenaka Khan was the key.

But first they must defeat the Legion.

For the last forty hours Tenaka Khan had been camped in the Demon's Smile, riding and walking over the terrain, studying each curve and hollow, memorising details of cover and angles of possible attack.

Now he sat with Rayvan and her son Lucas at the highest point of the curving valley, staring out on to the plain beyond the mountains.

'Well?' said Rayvan, for the third time. 'Have you come up with anything?' Rubbing his tired eyes, Tenaka discarded the sketch he had been working on and turned to the warrior woman, smiling. Her ample frame was now hidden beneath a long mailshirt and her dark hair was braided beneath a round black helm.

'I hope you are not still intending to stand with the fighters, Rayvan,' he said.

'You cannot talk me out of it,' she replied. 'My mind is made up.'

'Don't argue, man,' advised Lucas. 'You will be wasting your breath.'

'I got them into this,' she said, 'and I will be damned if I let them die for me without being with them.'

'Make no mistake about it, Rayvan, there will be a deal of dying. We can achieve no cheap victory here; we shall be lucky if we don't lose two-thirds of our force.'

'That many?' she whispered.

'At least. There is too much killing ground.'

'Can't we just pepper them with arrows from the high ground as they enter the valley?' asked Lucas.

'Yes. But they would just leave half their force to keep us pinned down and then attack the city and the villages. The bloodshed would be terrible.'

'Then what do you suggest?' said Rayvan.

He told her and she blanched. Lucas said nothing. Tenaka folded the parchment notes and sketches and tied them with a strip of leather. The silence grew between them.

'Despite your tainted blood,' said Rayvan at last, 'I trust you, Tenaka. From any other man, I would say it was madness. Even from you . . .'

'There is no other way to win. But I accept it is fraught with dangers. I have marked out the ground where the work must be done, and I have made maps and charted distances for the archers to memorise. But it is up to you, Rayvan. You are the leader here.'

'What do you think, Lucas?' she asked her son.

He waved his hands. 'Don't ask me! I'm not a soldier.'

'You think *I* am?' snapped Rayvan. 'Give me an opinion.'

'I don't like it. But I cannot give you an alternative. As Tenaka says, if we cut and run we open Skoda to them. And we cannot win that way. But two-thirds . . .'

Rayvan pushed herself to her feet, grunting as her rheumatic knee half gave way beneath her. She walked away down the slope to sit beside a ribbon stream that rushed over white pebbles, glinting like pearls inches below the surface.

Burrowing in the pocket of her mailshirt she found a hard-cake biscuit. It had broken into three pieces against the iron rings.

She felt a fool.

What was she doing here? What did she know of war?

She had raised fine sons and her husband had been a prince among men, big and gentle and soft as goosedown. When the soldiers cut him down she had reacted in an instant. But from then on she had lived a lie – revelling in her new role as a warrior queen, making decisions and directing an army. But it was all a sham, just like her claim to Druss' line. Her head bowed and she bit the knuckle of her thumb to stop the tears flowing.

What are you, Rayvan? she asked herself.

A fat, middle-aged woman in a man's mailshirt.

Tomorrow, or at most the day after, four hundred young men would die for her . . . their blood on her hands. Among them would be her surviving sons. Dipping her hands into the stream, she washed her face.

'Oh, Druss, what should I do? What would you do?'

There was no answer. Nor did she expect one. The dead were dead – no golden shades in ghostly palaces gazing fondly down on their descendants. There was no one to hear her cry for help, no living thing. Unless the stream itself and the pearl-like stones beneath could hear her, or the soft spring grass and the purple heather. She was alone.

In a way this had always been so. Her husband, Laska, had been a great comfort and she had loved him well. But never with that all-consuming love she had dreamed about. He had been like a rock, a solid steadfast mountain of a man she could cling to when no others could see her. He had inner strength, and he didn't mind when she lorded it over him in public and appeared to be making all the family decisions. In reality she listened to his advice in the quiet of their room and, more often than not, acted upon it.

Now Laska was gone, and with him her other son, Geddis, and she sat alone in a ridiculous mailshirt. She gazed out at the mountains at the opening of the Demon's Smile, picturing the dark-cloaked Legion riders as they rode into the valley, remembering again the blow that had felled Laska. He had not expected an attack and was sitting by the well talking to Geddis. There must have been two hundred Skoda men in the area, waiting for the cattle auction. She had not heard what passed between the officer and her husband, for she was thirty feet away, chopping meat for the barbecue. But she had seen the sword flash into the air and watched the blade as it cut deep. Then she had been running, the meat cleaver in her hand . . .

Now the Legion were coming back for revenge – not just on her but on the innocents of Skoda. Anger flickered inside her – they thought to ride into her mountains and stain the grass with the blood of her people!

Pushing herself to her feet, she slowly made her way back towards Tenaka Khan. He sat motionless like a statue, watching her without emotion in those violet eyes. Then he rose. She blinked, for his movement was swift and fluid; one moment he was still, the next in motion. There was perfection in that movement and it gave her confidence, though she could not imagine why.

'You have made a decision?' he asked.

'Yes. We will do as you advise. But I stay with the men in the centre.'

'As you wish, Rayvan. I shall be at the mouth of the valley.'

'Is that wise?' she asked. 'Is that not very dangerous for our general?'

'Ananais will take the centre, Decado the right flank. I shall come back to cover the left. If I fall, Galand shall cover for me. Now I must seek Ananais, for I want his men working through the night.'

The leaders of The Thirty met together in a sheltered hollow on the eastern slopes of the Demon's Smile. Below in the bright moonlight four hundred men were toiling, stripping turf and digging channels into the soft black earth beneath.

The five priests sat in a tight circle, saying nothing as Acuas travelled, receiving reports from the ten warriors watching over the preparations. Acuas soared high into the night sky, revelling in the freedom of the air; there was no gravity here, no necessity for breath, no chains of muscle and bone. Here, above the world, his eyes could see for ever and his ears hear the sweet song of the solar winds. It was intoxicating and his soul swelled with the extravagance of the beauty of the universe.

It was an effort to return to his duties, but Acuas was a man of discipline. He thought-flew to the outer scouts holding the shield against the Templars, and felt the malice beyond the barrier.

'How goes it, Oward?' he pulsed.

'It is hard, Acuas. They are growing in strength all the time. We will not be able to hold them for much longer.'

'It is imperative the Templars do not see the preparations.'

'We are almost at our limits, Acuas. Much more and they will be through. Then the deaths will begin.'

'I know. Hold them!'

Acuas sped down and on past the mouth of the valley to where the Legion were camped. Hovering there was the warrior Astin.

'Greetings, Acuas!'

'Greetings. Any change?'

'I don't believe so, Acuas, but the Templars have now closed us off and I can no longer intercept the leader's thoughts. But he is confident. He does not expect serious opposition.'

'Have the Templars tried to get through to you?'

'Not as yet. The shield holds. How fare Oward and the others?'

'They are being pushed to the limit. Do not wait too long, Astin. I do not want to see you cut off.'

'Acuas,' pulsed Astin as the other made to leave.

'Yes?'

'The men we escorted from the city . . .'

'Yes?'

'They have all been slain by the Legion. It was ghastly.'

'I feared it would be so.'

'Are we responsible for their deaths?'

'I don't know, my friend; I fear so. Be careful.'

Acuas returned to his body and opened his eyes. He outlined the situation to the others and waited for Decado to speak.

'There is no more we can do,' said Decado, 'it is set. It will be dawn in less than three hours and the Legion will strike. As you know, Tenaka requires five of us to join his forces. The choice of men I will leave to you, Acuas. The rest of us will stand with Ananais at the centre. The woman, Rayvan, will be with us – Ananais wishes her protected at all costs.'

'No easy task,' said Balan.

'I didn't say it was easy,' answered Decado. 'Merely to try. Psychologically she is vital, for the Skoda men fight for her as well as for the land.'

'I understand that, Decado,' said Balan smoothly. 'But we can guarantee nothing. We will be on open ground with no horses and nowhere to run.'

'Do you imply criticism of Tenaka's plan?' asked Abaddon.

'No,' said Balan. 'We are all students of war here, and tactically his battle strategy is sound – technically brilliant, in fact. However, at best it has a thirty-per-cent chance of success.'

'Sixty,' said Decado.

Balan lifted an eyebrow. 'Really? Explain.'

'I accept you have skills beyond ordinary men. I accept also that your understanding of strategy is exceptional. But beware of pride, Balan.'

'In what way?' asked Balan, the hint of a sneer on his face.

'Because your training has been merely that – training. If we mapped out the battle as a game of chance, then thirty per cent is correct. But this is not a game. Down there you have Ananais, the Golden One. His strength is great and his skill greater. But more than this he has a power over men that comes close to your own psychic talents. Where he stands others will stand – he holds them with the power of his will. It is what makes him a leader. Any estimate of success in such a scheme will depend on the willingness of the line to hold, and the men to die. They may be beaten and slain, but they will not run.

'Add to this the speed of thought of Tenaka Khan. Like Ananais he has great skill and his understanding of strategy is beyond compare. But his timing is immaculate. He does not have Ananais' leadership qualities, but only because of his mixed blood. Men of the Drenai will think twice before following a Nadir.

'Lastly there is the woman, Rayvan. Her men will fight the stronger because she is with them. Revise your estimate, Balan.'

'I will reconsider, adjusting the points to incorporate your suggestions,' said the priest.

Decado nodded and then turned to Acuas. 'How far away are the Templars?'

'They will not arrive for tomorrow's battle, thank the Source! There are one hundred of them two days' ride from here. The rest are in Drenan while the leaders, the Six, meet with Ceska.'

'Then that is a problem for another day,' said Decado. 'I think I will rest now.'

Dark-eyed Katan spoke for the first time. 'Will you not lead us in prayer, Decado?'

Decado smiled gently. There was no hint of criticism from the young priest.

'No, Katan. You are closer to the Source than I and you are the Soul of The Thirty. You pray.'

Katan bowed and the group closed their eyes in silent communion. Decado relaxed his mind, listening for the faint sea roar. He drifted until the 'voice' of Katan grew and he floated towards it. The prayer was short and perfect in its sincerity, and Decado was touched to hear the young priest mention him by name, calling on the Lord of the Heavens to protect him.

Later, as Decado lay staring up at the stars, Abaddon came and sat beside him. The slim warrior sat up and stretched his back.

'Are you looking forward to tomorrow?' the Abbot asked.

'I am afraid that I am.'

The old man leaned back against a tree and closed his eyes. He looked tired, drained of all strength; the lines on his face – once as delicate as web threads – now seemed chiselled deep.

'I have compromised you, Decado,' whispered the Abbot. 'I have drawn you into a world you would not otherwise have seen. I have prayed about you constantly. It would be pleasant to know I was right. But that is not to be.'

'I cannot help you, Abaddon.'

'I know that. Every day I watched you in your garden and I wondered. In truth it was more hope than certainty. We are not a true Thirty – we never were. The Order was disbanded in my father's day but I felt – in my arrogance – that the world had need of us. So I scoured the continent, seeking out those children of special gifts. I did my best to teach them, praying the Source would guide me.'

'Perhaps you were right,' said Decado softly.

'I don't know any more. I have watched them all tonight, joined them in their thoughts. Where there should be tranquillity there is excitement, and even a lust for battle. It began when you killed Padaxes and they joyed in your victory.'

'What did you expect of them? There is not a man among them over twenty-five years of age! And they have never lived ordinary lives . . . been drunk . . . kissed a woman. Their humanity has been suppressed.'

'Think you so? I would prefer to think their humanity has been enhanced.'

'I am out of my depth in this conversation,' admitted Decado. 'I don't know what you expect from them. They will die for you – is that not enough?'

'No. Not by far. This grimy little war is meaningless against the vast scope of human endeavour. Don't you think these mountains have seen it all before? Does it matter that we may all die tomorrow? Will the world spin any less fast? Will the stars shine any more brightly? In a hundred years, not a man here today will still be alive. Will that matter? Many

614

years ago, Druss the Legend stood and died on the walls of Dros Delnoch to stop a Nadir invasion. Does that matter now?'

'It mattered to Druss. It matters to me.'

'But why?'

'Because I am a man, priest. Simply that. I don't know if the Source exists and I don't really care. All I have is myself, and my own self-respect.'

'There must be more. There must be the triumph of Light. Man is so beset by greed, lust and the pursuit of the ephemeral. But kindness, understanding and love are equally parts of humanity.'

'Are you now saying we should love the Legion?'

'Yes. And we must fight them.'

'That is too deep for me,' said Decado.

'I know. But I hope one day you will understand. I shall not be there to see it. Yet I pray for it.'

'Now you are getting morbid. That happens on the eve of a battle.'

'I am not morbid, Decado. Tomorrow is my last day on this earth. I know it. I have seen it. It doesn't matter . . . I just hoped that tonight you could convince me that I was right – at least with you.'

'What do you want me to say?'

'There is nothing you *can* say.'

'Then I cannot help you. You know what my life was before I met you. I was a killer and I revelled in death. I do not wish to sound weak, but I never asked to be that way – it was just me. I had neither the strength nor the inclination to change. You understand? But then I almost killed a man I loved. And I came to you. You gave me a place to hide and I was grateful. Now I am back where I belong, with a sword near to hand and an enemy close by.

'I don't deny the Source. I just don't know what game He is playing – why he allows the Ceskas of this world to survive. I don't want to know. While my arm is strong I shall oppose Ceska's evil, and at the end of all things if the Source says to me, "Decado, you do not deserve immortality," then I shall reply, "So be it." There will be no regrets.

'You could be right. You might die tomorrow. If the rest of us survive, I shall look after your young warriors. I shall try to keep them to your path. I think they will not let you down. But then you will be with your Source, and you must ask Him to lend a hand.'

'And what if I was wrong?' asked the Abbot, leaning forward and gripping Decado's arm. 'What if I resurrected The Thirty because of my own arrogance?'

'I don't know, Abaddon. But you acted in faith with no thought of gain. Even if you are wrong, your God should forgive you. If he does not, then he is not worth following. If one of your priests commits an indiscretion, do you not forgive him? Are you then more forgiving than your God?'

'I don't know. I'm not certain of anything any more.'

'You once told me that certainty and faith do not belong together. Have faith, Abaddon.'

'It is not easy, Decado, to be confident on the day of your death.'

'Why did you seek me out with this? I cannot help you to find faith. Why did you not speak to Katan, or Acuas?'

'I felt you would understand.'

'Well, I do not. You were always so sure – you radiated harmony, tranquillity. You had stars in your hair and your words were wisdom. Was it all a façade? Are these doubts so sudden?'

'I once accused you of hiding in your garden. Well, I also hid. It was easy to suppress doubts when the monastery walls were firm around us. I had my books and I had my pupils; it seemed then a grand project of the Light. But now men are dead and the reality is different. Those fifty men who sought to capture Rayvan: they were frightened and they wanted to live, but we marched them from the city and out on to the plain to be slaughtered. We did not let them say farewell to their wives and children. We just led them like cattle to the slaughterhouse.'

'Now I understand,' said Decado. 'You saw us as White Templars marching against evil, cheered by the crowds: a small band of heroes in silver armour and white cloaks. Well, it could never be like that, Abaddon. Evil lives in a pit. If you want to fight it – you must climb down in the slime to do so. White cloaks show the dirt more than black, and silver tarnishes. Now leave me and commune with your God – He has more answers than I.'

'Will you pray for me, Decado?' pleaded the Abbot.

'Why should the Source listen to me if he does not want to listen to you? Pray for yourself, man!'

'Please! Do this for me.'

'All right. But go and rest now.'

Decado watched the old man move away into the darkness. Then he lay back and gazed up at the lightening sky.

11

As the dawn sun rose in blood, Tenaka Khan stood on the high ground overlooking the plain. With him were one hundred men armed with bows, swords and axes. Only about thirty of them had shields, and these warriors Tenaka placed in the open ground facing the dip into the plain. Mountains towered on either side of the small force, while behind them the Demon's Smile widened on both sides, becoming wood-covered hills.

The men were becoming restless now and Tenaka had no words for them. They moved warily around the Nadir warrior, casting suspicious glances at him; they would fight alongside him, but only because Rayvan had asked it of them.

Tenaka raised a hand to shield his eyes and saw that the Legion were moving. He could make out the sunlight glittering on their spear-points and flashing from their polished breastplates.

After the Dragon, the Legion were the finest fighting men among the Drenai. Tenaka drew his sword and tested the edge with his thumb. Taking a small whetstone, he honed the blade once more.

Galand moved alongside him. 'Good luck, general!' he said.

Tenaka grinned and cast his eyes over his small force. Their faces were set, determined; there was no give in them. For countless centuries men like these had held the Drenai empire together, turning back the greatest armies in the world: the hordes of Ulric, the Immortals of Gorben and the ferocious raiders from Vagria in the Chaos Wars.

Now they stood again to face impossible odds.

The rolling thunder of hooves on the dry plain floated into the mountains, echoing like the drums of doom. To the left of the men with shields Rayvan's son, Lucas, notched an arrow to his bow. Swallowing hard, he wiped a sleeve across his brow; he was sweating heavily – strange how so much moisture could form on his face, while his mouth was so dry. He glanced back at the Nadir general to see him standing calmly with sword in hand, his violet eyes fixed on the charging horsemen. There was no trace of sweat on his brow.

Bastard, thought Lucas. Inhuman bastard!

The horsemen had reached the slope before the Smile and their charge slowed fractionally.

A single arrow soared out to meet them, falling short of the riders by thirty paces.

'Wait until you hear the order,' bellowed Galand, switching his gaze to the impassive Tenaka.

The riders thundered on, lances levelled.

'Now?' asked Galand, as the leading horsemen passed the mark made by the first arrow. Tenaka shook his head.

'Face front!' shouted Galand, as nervous archers craned their necks to see the command given.

The Legion were riding fifty abreast in twenty-five ranks. Tenaka gauged the gap between each rank as around six lengths. It was a well-disciplined charge.

'Now!' he said.

'Give them Hell!' screamed Galand and a hundred arrows flashed into the sunlight. The first line of horsemen disappeared as the shafts hammered home into their mounts. Men were hurled headlong on to the rocks as screaming horses reared and fell. The second line faltered, but the gap between ranks allowed the riders to adjust in time to leap the fallen. But they leapt into a second volley of arrows that killed, crippled or maimed their mounts. As the dazed riders rose to their feet, more shafts flashed death to them, slicing into exposed flesh. But still the charge continued and the horsemen were almost upon them.

With one shaft left, Lucas rose from his knees. A lancer broke the line and Lucas loosed the shaft without aiming. It bounced from the horse's skull, causing the beast to rear in pain, but the rider clung on. Lucas dropped his bow and ran forward, dragging his hunting knife into his hand. He leapt to the beast's back and struck the rider in the chest, but the man threw himself to the right and the combined weight of the two warriors toppled the horse. Lucas landed atop the rider, the fall combining with his weight to bury the blade to the hilt. The man groaned and died; Lucas strained to drag the knife clear, but it was buried too deep. Drawing his sword, he ran at a second lancer.

Tenaka ducked under a stabbing thrust and then leapt at the rider, dragging him from the saddle. A backhand cut to the throat left the man choking on his own blood.

Tenaka clambered into the saddle. The archers had dropped back from the mouth of the pass and were peppering the Legion as they breasted the rise. Men and horses jammed the mouth of the valley. All was chaos. Here and there riders had forced their way through and Skoda warriors armed with swords and axes hacked and hammered at them from the ground.

'Galand!' shouted Tenaka. The black-bearded warrior, fighting alongside his brother, despatched his opponent and turned to the call. Tenaka pointed forward at the mass and Galand waved his sword in acknowledgement.

'To me, Skoda!' he bellowed. 'To me!' With his brother and about twenty warriors, he charged the milling men. The riders dropped their lances, scrabbling for swords as the fighting wedge struck them. Tenaka heeled his horse and charged in to fight alongside them.

For several bloody minutes the battle continued, then a bugle sounded from the plain and the Legion wheeled their mounts and rode from the carnage.

Galand, scalp bleeding from a shallow cut, ran to Tenaka. 'They will turn immediately for another charge,' he said. 'We'll not hold them.' Tenaka sheathed his sword. He had lost almost half his force.

Lucas ran alongside. 'Let us get the wounded back,' he pleaded.

'No time!' said Tenaka. 'Take positions – but be ready to run when I give the word.' Kicking his horse forward, he rode to the rise. The Legion had turned at the foot of the slope and were re-forming into lines fifty abreast.

Behind him the Skoda archers were desperately gathering shafts, pulling them clear of bodies. Tenaka lifted his arm, calling them forward, and they obeyed without hesitation.

The bugle sounded once more and the black-cloaked riders surged forward. No lances this time, bright swords shone in their hands. Once more the thunder of charging hooves echoed in the mountains.

At thirty paces Tenaka lifted his arm. 'Now!' he yelled. Hundreds of shafts thudded home. 'Away!' he screamed.

The Skoda warriors turned and ran, sprinting for the transient security of the wooded hills.

Tenaka estimated the Legion had lost nearly three hundred men in the battle, and more horses. He turned his mount and galloped towards the hills. Galand and Parsal were ahead of him, helping Rayvan's injured son. Lucas had been dragging an arrow from the body of a rider, but the man was not dead and had struck out, lashing a cut to Lucas' left leg.

'Leave him to me!' shouted Tenaka as he rode alongside. Leaning over, he pulled Lucas across his saddle horn and glanced back. The Legion had breasted the rise and set off in pursuit of the fleeing warriors. Galand and Parsal sprinted off to the north.

Tenaka angled his run to the north-west and the Legion riders spurred their mounts after him.

Ahead was the first hill, beyond which Ananais waited with the full force. Tenaka urged his horse onward, but with double weight upon him the creature was labouring hard. Atop the hill Tenaka was no more than fifteen lengths clear of his pursuers, but ahead lay Ananais and four hundred men. Tenaka's tired mount galloped on. Ananais moved forward, waving Tenaka to the left. He dragged on the reins, steering the beast through the hazards he himself had organised throughout the long night.

Behind him a hundred Legion riders reined in, waiting for orders. Tenaka helped Lucas from the saddle and then dismounted.

'How did it go?' asked Ananais.

Tenaka lifted three fingers.

'It would have been nice had it been five,' he said.

'It was a disciplined charge, Ani, one rank at a time.'

'You have to give that to them – they were always well-disciplined. Still, the day is yet young.'

Rayvan pushed her way forward. 'Did we lose many?'

'Around forty men at the charge. But more will be caught in the woods,' answered Tenaka. Decado and Acuas made their way to the front.

'General,' said Acuas, 'the Legion leader has now been appraised of our position. He is calling in his outriders for a frontal charge.'

'Thank you. It is what we hoped for.'

'I hope he does it swiftly,' said Acuas, scratching his yellow beard. 'The

Templars have breached our defences and soon they will know of your preparations. Then they will convey them to the leader.'

'If that happens, we are dead,' muttered Ananais.

'With all your powers, can you not screen their leader?' asked Tenaka.

'We could,' answered Acuas stiffly, 'but it would be a grave risk to the men charged with the task.'

'It so happens,' snarled Ananais, 'that we are taking no small risk ourselves.'

'It will be done,' said Decado. 'See to it, Acuas.'

Acuas nodded and closed his eyes.

'Well, get to it, lad,' urged Ananais.

'He is doing it now,' said Decado softly. 'Leave him alone.'

The harsh shrieking blasts of the Legion bugles pierced the air and within seconds a line of black-garbed riders rimmed the hill opposite.

'Get back to the centre,' Ananais told Rayvan.

'Don't treat me like a milkmaid!'

'I am treating you like a leader, woman! If you fall in the first charge, then the battle is over.' Rayvan moved back and the men of Skoda readied their bows.

A single bugle blast heralded the charge and the horsemen swept down the low hill. Fear flickered through the ranks of defenders. Ananais sensed it rather than felt it. 'Steady, lads,' he called, his voice even.

Tenaka craned to see the formation: one hundred abreast, single lengths between ranks. He cursed softly. The leading rank reached the bottom of the hill and then continued up toward the defenders, slowing as the gradient increased. This brought the second rank even closer. Tenaka smiled. Thirty paces from the defenders, the first line of horsemen hit the hidden trenches, the soft turf laid upon thin branches. The line went down as if poleaxed by an invisible giant. The second line, too close in, went down with them in a milling mass of writhing horses.

'Charge!' shouted Ananais, and three hundred Skoda warriors dashed forward hacking and cleaving. The hundred that remained sent volleys of arrows over the heads of their comrades into the ranks of lancers beyond – these had pulled up their mounts and presented sitting targets to the archers. From the hill above, the Legion general, Karespa, cursed and swore. Swinging in his saddle he ordered his bugler to sound 'Recall'. The shrill notes drifted over the battling men and the Legion pulled back. Karespa waved his arm, signalling left, and the lancers wheeled their mounts for a flank attack. Ananais pulled back his force to the hilltop.

The Legion charged again – only for their horses to hit the hidden trip-wires in the long grass. Karespa ordered 'Recall' once more. Bereft of choices he ordered his men to dismount and advance on foot, archers to the rear. They moved forward slowly, the men in the front rank hesitant and fearful. They carried no shields and were loth to approach the bowmen among the Skoda defence.

Just out of bowshot the front rank stopped, readying themselves for the hectic race. At that moment Lake and his fifty men rose from the ground behind them, discarding their blankets interwoven with long grass and climbing from the well-hidden trenches beside granite boulders. From his vantage point on the hilltop, Karespa blinked in disbelief as the men appeared, seemingly from the earth itself.

Lake swiftly strung his bow, his men following suit. Their targets were the enemy archers. Fifty arrows screamed home, then fifty more. All was pandemonium. Ananais led his four hundred men in a sudden attack and the Legion wilted under the storm of slashing blades. Karespa swung in the saddle to order his bugler to sound 'Retreat', then his jaw dropped in amazement. His bugler had been dragged from the saddle by a black-bearded warrior, who now stood grinning beside Karespa's mount with a dagger in his hand. Other warriors stood close by, smiling mirthlessly.

Galand lifted the bugle to his lips and sent out the doleful call to surrender. Three times the bugle sounded before the last of the Legion warriors laid down their weapons.

'It is over, general,' said Galand. 'Be so good as to step down.'

'I'll be damned if I will!' snapped Karespa.

'Dead if you don't,' promised Galand.

Karespa dismounted.

In the trough below, six hundred Legion warriors sat on the grass as Skoda men moved among them, relieving them of weapons and breastplates.

Decado sheathed his sword and moved to where Acuas knelt beside the fallen Abaddon. There was no mark upon the Abbot.

'What happened?' asked Decado.

'His was the strongest mind among us. His talents were greater by far than any other's. He volunteered to screen Karespa from the Templars.'

'He knew he would die today,' said Decado.

'He will not die today,' snarled Acuas. 'Did I not say there were risks involved?'

'So a man has died. Many have died today.'

'I am not talking about death, Decado. Yes, his body is slain, but the Templars have taken his soul.'

Scaler sat on the high wall of the tower garden, watching the distant mountains for signs of the victorious Legion. He had been relieved when Tenaka had asked him to stay behind, but now he was unsure. Certainly he was no warrior and would have been of little help in a battle. Even so, at least he would have known the result.

Dark clouds bunched above the garden, blocking the sunlight; Scaler pulled his blue cloak around his shoulders and left the wall to wander among the sheltered blooms. Some sixty years before, an ageing senator had built the garden, his servants carrying more than three tons of topsoil to the tower. Now there were trees, bushes and flowers of every kind. In one corner laurel and elderflower grew alongside holly and elm, while elsewhere flowering cherry trees bloomed pink and white against the grey stone walls. Throughout the garden an ornate path wound its way among the flower-beds. Scaler wandered the path, enjoying the fragrance of the blooms.

Renya mounted the circular stairwell, entering the garden just as the sun cleared the clouds. She saw Scaler standing alone, his dark hair held in place by a black leather circlet on his brow. He was a handsome man, she thought . . . and lonely. He wore no sword and was studying a yellow flower at the edge of a rockery.

'Good morning,' she said and he glanced up. Renya was attired in a light-green woollen tunic and a rust-coloured silk scarf covered her hair. Her legs were bare and she wore no sandals.

'Good morning, lady. Did you sleep well?'

'No. And you?'

'I fear not. When do you think we will know?'

Renya shrugged. 'Soon enough.'

He nodded his agreement and together they strolled through the garden, drawn at last to the wall facing south towards the Demon's Smile.

'Why did you not go with them?' she asked.

'Tenaka asked me to stay.'

'Why?'

'He has a task for me and does not want me dead before I attempt it!'

'A dangerous task, then?'

'What makes you say so?'

'You said "Attempt it". That sounds as if you doubt your ability to succeed.'

He laughed grimly. 'Doubt? I don't doubt – I *know*. But it doesn't matter. No one lives for ever. Anyway, it may never come to that. First they must defeat the Legion.'

'They will,' said Renya, sitting on a stone bench and drawing up her long legs on to the seat.

'How can you be sure?'

'They are not the men to be beaten. Tenaka will find a way to win. And if he has asked you to help him, then he must be sure you have a chance.'

'How simply women view the world of men,' commented Scaler.

'Not at all. It takes men to make the simplest things sound complex.'

'A deadly riposte, lady. I am undone!'

'Are you defeated so easily, Scaler?'

He sat down beside her. 'I am easily defeated, Renya, because I don't care too much about winning. Just living! I run to survive. When I was young, assassins were all around me. My family all died at their hands. It was Ceska's doing – I see that now, but then he seemed a friend to my grandfather and myself. For years my rooms were guarded while I slept, my food tasted, my toys checked for hidden needles bearing poison. It was not what you would call a happy childhood.'

'But now you are a man,' she said.

'Not much of one. I frighten easily. Still, there is one consolation. If I was any tougher, I would be dead by now.'

'Or victorious.'

'Yes,' he admitted, 'perhaps victorious. But when they killed Orrin – my grandfather – I ran away. Gave up the earldom and went into hiding.

Belder came with me – the last retainer. I have been a great disappointment to him.'

'How did you survive?'

He grinned. 'I became a thief. Hence the name. I climbed into people's homes and stole their valuables. It is said that the Earl of Bronze began his career in this way, so I believe I am merely carrying on the family tradition.'

'Being a thief takes nerve. You could have been caught and hanged.'

'You have never seen me run – I move like the wind.'

Renya smiled and stood to glance over the wall to the south. Then she sat down once more.

'What does Tenaka require of you?'

'Nothing complex. He merely wants me to become an earl again and re-take Dros Delnoch, subduing ten thousand soldiers and opening the gates to allow a Nadir army through. That's all!'

'Seriously – what *does* he want you to do?'

Scaler leaned forward. 'I have told you.'

'I don't believe you. It's insane!'

'Nevertheless . . .'

'It's impossible.'

'True, Renya, true. However, there is a certain irony to the plan. Consider it: the descendant of the Earl of Bronze, who held the fortress against Ulric, is now commissioned to take the fortress and allow Ulric's descendant to pass through with his army.'

'Where will he get this army? He is hated by the Nadir, even as he is loathed by the Drenai.'

'Ah yes, but he is Tenaka Khan,' said Scaler drily.

'So how will you take the fortress?' she asked.

'I have no idea. I will probably march into the Keep, declare my identity and ask them all to surrender.'

'It's a good plan – simple and direct,' she said, straightfaced.

'All the best plans are,' he said. 'Tell me how you came to be mixed up in this business.'

'Just born lucky,' said Renya, standing once more. 'Damn it! Why don't they come?'

'As you said, we shall know soon enough. Will you join me for breakfast?'

'I don't think so. Valtaya is in the kitchens – she will cook you something.'

Sensing she wanted to be alone, Scaler made his way down the stairwell, following the delicious aroma of frying bacon.

He passed Valtaya on her way up and wandered on to the kitchen where Belder was ploughing his way through a heaped dish of bacon, eggs and long beans.

'A man of your age should have lost his appetite by now,' observed Scaler, slipping into place opposite the gnarled warrior.

Belder scowled at him. 'We should have been with them,' he said.

'Tenaka asked me to stay,' pointed out Scaler.

'I cannot think why,' snapped Belder, sarcasm heavy in his tone. 'Just think how handy we would have been.'

Scaler lost patience. 'I may not have said so before,' he remarked, 'but I am getting pretty sick of you, Belder. Either keep your mouth shut or keep out of my way!'

'The second option sounds like a pleasure,' said the old warrior, eyes blazing.

'Then do it! And forget the sanctimonious lectures. You have been on for years about my profligate ways, my fears and my failings. But you didn't stay with me out of loyalty – you stayed because you are a runner too. I just made it easy for you to hide. Tenaka asked me to stay, but he didn't ask you – you could have gone.'

Scaler pushed himself upright and left the room. The old man leaned forward on his elbows, pushing the plate away.

'I *did* stay out of loyalty,' he whispered.

In the aftermath of the battle Tenaka wandered off alone into the mountains, his heart heavy and a terrible melancholy settling over him.

Rayvan watched him walk away and moved to follow, but Ananais stopped her.

'It is his way,' said the giant. 'Leave him be.'

Rayvan shrugged and returned to the business of treating the wounded. Makeshift stretchers had been put together, using the Legion lances and cloaks. The Thirty, stripped of their armour, moved among the wounded using their awesome skills to remove pain while stitches were inserted.

On the open field the dead were laid side by side, Legion lancers alongside Skoda warriors. Six hundred and eleven lancers had died that day; two hundred and forty-six Skoda men lay alongside them.

Rayvan wandered through the ranks of the dead, staring down at the corpses, bringing the names of her warriors to mind and praying over each man. Many had farms and crofts, wives and children, sisters, mothers. Rayvan knew them all. She called Lake to her and told him to fetch paper and charcoal to list the dead.

Ananais washed the blood from his clothes and skin and then summoned the Legion general Karespa to him. The man was sullen and in no mood for conversation.

'I am going to have to kill you, Karespa,' said Ananais apologetically.

'I understand.'

'Good! Will you join me in a meal?'

'No, thank you. My appetite just left me.'

Ananais nodded his understanding. 'Do you have any preference?'

The man shrugged. 'What does it matter?'

'Then it will be a sword-thrust. Unless you would rather do it yourself?'

'Go to the devil!'

'Then I will do it. You have until dawn to prepare yourself.'

'I don't need until dawn. Do it now, while I am in the mood.'

'All right.' Ananais nodded once and pain like the fires of Hell exploded in Karespa's back. He tried to turn, but darkness blanketed his mind.

Galand pulled the sword clear and wiped it clean on the general's cloak. Moving forward, he sat beside Ananais.

'Shame about that,' said the black-bearded warrior.

'We couldn't let him go, knowing what he did.'

'I suppose not. Gods, general, but we won! Incredible, isn't it?'

'Not with Tenaka planning it.'

'Come now, anything could have happened. They didn't have to charge – they could have dismounted and sent in the archers to drive us back.'

'Could have. Might have. They did not. They went by the book. According to the Cavalry Manual, the obvious move for horsemen against irregular foot-soldiers is the charge. The Legion are disciplined men and therefore bound to operate by the Manual. You want me to quote chapter and verse?'

'It's not necessary,' muttered Galand. 'I expect you wrote it.'

'No. Tenaka Khan introduced the most recent alterations eighteen years ago.'

'But just suppose . . .'

'What's the point, Galand? He was right.'

'But he couldn't have known where Karespa would wait with his bugler. And yet he told Parsal and me to make for that hill.'

'Where else could Karespa watch the battle from?'

'He might have gone in with his men.'

'And left his bugler to make the decisions?'

'You make it sound so simple, but battles are not like that. Strategy is one thing, heart and skill another.'

'I don't deny it. The Legion didn't fight at their best. There are many good men among them and I don't suppose they relished their task. But that's in the past. For now I am going to ask the men of the Legion to join us.'

'And if they refuse?'

'I shall send them out of the valley – where you will be waiting with one hundred archers. No one man will leave alive.'

'You're a ruthless man, general!'

'I am alive, Galand. And I mean to stay alive.'

Galand heaved himself to his feet. 'I hope you do, general. And I hope Tenaka Khan can produce another miracle when the Joinings arrive.'

'That's tomorrow,' said Ananais. 'Let us enjoy today.'

12

Tenaka found the place of solitude he needed at a sheltered waterfall high in the mountains, where the air was cool and clean and the snow lay in patches on the slopes. Slowly, carefully, he built a fire in a ring of stones and sat watching the flames. He felt no elation at the victory, his emotions washed from him in the blood of the slain. After a while he moved to the stream, remembering the words of Asta Khan, the ancient shaman of the Wolfshead tribe.

'All things in the world are created for Man, yet all have two purposes. The waters run that we might drink of them, but they are also symbols of the futility of Man. They reflect our lives in rushing beauty, birthed in the purity of the mountains. As babes they babble and run, gushing and growing as they mature into strong young rivers. Then they widen and slow until at last they meander, like old men, to join with the sea. And like the souls of men in the Nethervoid, they mix and mingle until the sun lifts them again as raindrops to fall upon the mountains.'

Tenaka dipped his hand into the rushing water. He felt out of place, away from time. A bird hopped on to a rock nearby, ignoring him in its quest for food; it was tiny and brown. Suddenly it dived into the water and Tenaka jerked upright, leaning over the stream to see it flying beneath the surface: an eerie sight. It came to the surface, hopped to a rock and fluttered its feathers; then it returned to the stream. In a strange way Tenaka was soothed by the sight. He observed the bird for a while, then lay back on the grass watching the clouds bunch in the blue sky.

An eagle soared high on the thermals with wings spread, seemingly static as it rose on the warm air.

A ptarmigan fluttered into view, its feathers still mottled and part white – perfect camouflage, for the snow still patched the slopes. Tenaka considered the bird. In winter it was pure white against the snow. In spring it was part white, while in summer the mottling turned slate-grey and brown, allowing it to sit by the boulders – the image of a rock. Its feathers were its only defence.

The ptarmigan rose into the air and the eagle banked sharply, dropping like a stone. But it cut across the sun and its shadow fell athwart the ptarmigan, which swerved just as the talons flashed by. The little speckled bird fled back to the bushes.

The eagle settled on a tree branch close to Tenaka, its dignity ruffled. The Nadir warrior leaned back and closed his eyes.

The battle had been close and the strategy would not work again. They had gained a respite, but that was all. Ceska had sent his Legion to round up a few rebels – had they known Tenaka Khan was here, they would have adopted different tactics. Now they *would* know . . . Now all Ceska's skill would be pitted against Tenaka.

How many men would Ceska range against them now?

There was the rest of the Legion – four thousand men. The regulars numbering ten thousand. The Drenan Pikers, two thousand at the last count. But more terrifying than all the others were the Joinings. How many now had he created? Five thousand? Ten?

And how could they be rated against common men? One Joining to five? Even that would make them worth 25,000 soldiers.

Ceska would not make the mistake of underestimating the Skoda rebellion a second time.

Weariness settled on Tenaka like a shroud. His first plan had been so simple: kill Ceska and die. Now the complexities of his scheme swirled in his mind like mist.

So many dead, so many still to die.

He moved back to his fire and added fuel; then he lay down beside it, wrapping himself in his cloak. He thought of Illae and his Ventrian home. How good had been the years.

Then Renya's face formed in his thoughts and he smiled. All his life he had been lucky. Sad, lonely, but lucky. To have a mother as devoted as Shillat, that was luck. To find a man like Ananais to stand beside him. To be with the Dragon. To love Illae. To find Renya.

Such good fortune was a gift that more than made up for the loneliness and the pain of rejection. Tenaka began to shiver. Adding more wood, he lay back waiting for the nausea he knew would follow. The headache started first, with bright lights flickering in his eyes. He breathed deeply, calming himself for the onslaught. The pain grew, clawing at his brain with fingers of fire.

For four hours the pain tore at him until he almost wept. Then it receded and he slept . . .

He was in a dark corridor, sloping and cold. At his feet were the skeletons of several rats. He stepped over them and the skeletons moved, bones clicking in the silence. Then they ran into the darkness. Tenaka shook his head, trying to remember where he was. Ahead was a dead man hanging in chains, the flesh decomposed.

'Help me!' said the man.

'You are dead. I cannot help you.'

'Why won't you help me?'

'You are dead.'

'We are all dead. And no one will help us.'

Tenaka walked on, seeking a door, moving ever downward.

The corridor widened into a hall with dark pillars soaring into the void. Shadow-shrouded figures moved into sight, black swords in their hands.

'Now we have you, Torchbearer,' said a voice.

They wore no armour and the leader's face was familiar. Tenaka racked his brains for the man's name, but it remained elusive.

'Padaxes,' said the man. 'Even here I can read your frightened mind. Padaxes, who died under the sword of Decado. And yet am I dead? I am not! But you, Torchbearer – you will be dead, for you have entered the dominion of the Spirit. Where are your Templars? Where are the bastard Thirty?'

'This is a dream,' said Tenaka. 'You cannot touch me.'

'Think you so?' Fire leapt from the blade, scorching Tenaka's shoulders. He threw himself back, fear surging within him. Padaxes' laughter was shrill. 'Think you so *now*?'

Tenaka moved to his feet, drawing his own sword.

'Come, then,' he said. 'Let me see you die a second time.'

The Dark Templars moved forward, spreading in a semi-circle around him. Suddenly Tenaka was aware he was not alone. For a moment, as in his earlier dream, he believed The Thirty had come for him, but when he glanced to his left he saw a powerful, broad-shouldered Nadir warrior in a goatskin tunic. Others moved alongside him.

The Templars hesitated and the Nadir beside Tenaka lifted his sword. 'Drive these shadows away,' he told his warriors. Silently a hundred hollow-eyed tribesmen surged forward and the Templars fled before them.

The Nadir turned to Tenaka. His face was broad and flat, his eyes violet and piercing. There pulsed from him an aura of power and strength that Tenaka had not seen in any living man, and he knew him then. He fell to his knees before him and bent forward his body into a deep bow.

'You know me then, blood of my blood?'

'I do, my Lord Khan,' said Tenaka. 'Ulric, Lord of Hordes!'

'I have seen you, boy. Watched you grow, for my old shaman Nosta Khan is with me still. You have not displeased me . . . But then your blood is of the finest.'

'Not all have felt it so,' said Tenaka.

'The world is full of fools,' snapped Ulric. 'I fought against the Earl of Bronze and he was a mighty man. And rare. He was a man with doubts, who overcame them. He stood on the walls of Dros Delnoch and defied me with his pitiful force, and I loved him for it. He was a fighter and a dreamer. Rare. So very rare!'

'You met him, then?'

'There was another warrior with him – an old man, Druss. Deathwalker, we called him. When he fell I had his body carried to my camp and we built a funeral pyre. Imagine that. For an enemy! We were on the verge of victory. And that night the Earl of Bronze – my greatest enemy – walked into my camp with his generals and joined me at the funeral.'

'Insane!' said Tenaka. 'You could have taken him and the whole fortress.'

'Would you have taken him, Tenaka?'

Tenaka considered the question. 'No,' he said at last.

'Neither could I. So do not worry about your pedigree. Let lesser men sneer.'

'Am I not dead?' asked Tenaka.

'No.'

'Then how am I here?'

'You sleep. Those Templar maggots pulled your spirit here but I will help you return.'

628

'What hell is this, and how came you here?'

'My heart failed me during the war against Ventria. And then I was here. It is the Nethervoid, pitched between the worlds of Source and Spirit. It seems I am claimed by neither, so I exist here with my followers. I never worshipped anything but my sword and my wits – now I suffer for it. But I can take it, for am I not a man?'

'You are a legend.'

'It is not hard to become a legend, Tenaka. It is what follows when you have to live like one.'

'Can you see the future?'

'In part.'

'Will I . . . will my friends succeed?'

'Do not ask me. I cannot alter your fate, much as I might wish to. This is your path, Tenaka, and you must walk it like a man. You were born to walk it.'

'I understand, Lord. I should not have asked.'

'There is no harm in asking,' said Ulric, smiling. 'Come, close your eyes – you must return to the world of blood.'

Tenaka awoke. It was night, yet his fire still burned bright and warm and a blanket had been placed over his sleeping body. He groaned and rolled to his side, raising himself on his elbow. Ananais sat across from the fire, the light flickering on his mask.

'How are you feeling?' asked the giant.

'Good. I needed the rest.'

'Has the pain gone?'

'Yes. Did you bring food?'

'Of course. You had me worried for a while. You turned ghostly white and your pulse was slow as death.'

'I'm all right now.' Tenaka sat up and Ananais tossed him a canvas sack containing dried meat and fruit. They ate in silence. The waterfall glittered like diamonds on sable in the moonlight. Finally Ananais spoke.

'Four hundred of the Legion have joined us. Decado says they will fight true – claims his priests have read their minds. Only three did they turn away. Two hundred others chose to return to Ceska.'

Tenaka rubbed his eyes. 'And?'

'And what?'

'And what happened to those who chose to return?'

'I sent them out of the valley.'

'Ani, my friend, I am back now. I am all right. So tell me.'

'I had them slain in the valley. It was necessary, for they could have given information about our numbers.'

'This was known anyway, Ani – the Templars are watching over us.'

'All right. But even so – it is still two hundred fewer men that they will send against us in the days to come.'

Silence descended again and Ananais lifted his mask gently, probing at the angry scar tissue.

'Take the thing off,' said Tenaka. 'Let the air get to the skin.'

Ananais hesitated, then he sighed and removed the leather. In the red firelight he seemed like a demon, inhuman and terrible. His blue eyes were fixed on Tenaka in a piercing stare, as if he were trying to discern some evidence of revulsion.

'Give me your view of the battle,' said Tenaka.

'It went to plan. I was pleased with Rayvan's men, and her son Lake is an asset. The black man fought well. He is a fine warrior. Given a year, I could rebuild the Dragon around these Skoda men.'

'We don't have a year.'

'I know,' said Ananais. 'I reckon two months.'

'We cannot beat them like this, Ani.'

'You have a plan?'

'Yes. But you won't like it.'

'If it means our winning, I will like it,' promised Ananais. 'What is it?'

'I mean to bring the Nadir.'

'You are right – I *don't* like it. In fact it stinks like rotting meat. If Ceska is bad, the Nadir are worse. Gods, man, at least with Ceska we are still Drenai. Are you out of your mind?'

'It is all we have left, my friend. We have almost a thousand men. We cannot hold Skoda and would be hard-pressed to withstand a single charge.'

'Listen to me, Tani! You know I have never held your blood against you. Not personally. I love you better than a brother. But I hate the Nadir as I hate nothing else on this earth. And I am not alone. No man here will fight alongside them. And suppose you do bring an army? What the hell happens when we win? Do they just go home? They will have beaten the Drenai army; the land will be theirs and we shall have another bloody civil war.'

'I don't see it that way.'

'And how will you bring them? There are no secret ways through the mountains, not even through the Sathuli passes. No army can come from the north save through Delnoch, and even Ulric failed to pass those gates.'

'I have asked Scaler to take Dros Delnoch.'

'Oh, Tani, you have gone mad! He is a fop and a runner who has not joined in one battle so far. When we rescued the village girl, he just buried his head in his hands and lay in the grass. When we found Pagan, he remained with the women. When we were planning yesterday's sortie, he was shaking like grass in a breeze and you told him to stay behind. And *he* will take Delnoch?'

Tenaka added wood to the fire, discarding the blanket from his shoulders. 'I know all these things, Ani. But it can be done. Scaler is like his ancestor, the Earl of Bronze. He doubts himself and he has great fears. But beyond those fears, if he ever sees it, there waits a fine man – a man of courage and nobility. And he is bright and quick-thinking.'

'Our hopes then rest on him?' asked Ananais.

'No. They rest on my judgement of him.'

'Don't play with words. It is the same thing.'

'I need you with me, Ananais.'

Ananais nodded. 'Why not? We are only talking about death. I will stay with you, Tani. What is life if a man cannot count on his friends when he has gone mad?'

'Thank you, Ani. I mean that.'

'I know. And I am worn out. I shall sleep for a while.'

Ananais lay back, resting his head on his cloak. The night breeze felt good on his scarred face. He was tired – more tired than he could ever remember being. It was the weariness of disappointment. Tenaka's plan was a nightmare, yet there were no alternatives. Ceska held the land within the talons of his Joinings and maybe, just maybe, a Nadir conquest would cleanse the nation. But Ananais doubted it.

From tomorrow he would train his warriors as they had never been trained before. They would run until they fell, fight until their arms ached with weariness. He would drill them hard, preparing a force not only to withstand Ceska's legions, but hopefully one that would live on to battle the new enemy.

Tenaka Khan's Nadir.

At the centre of the valley the bodies of the fallen were placed in a hastily dug ditch and covered with earth and rocks. Rayvan said a prayer and the survivors knelt before the mass grave, whispering their own farewells to friends, brothers, fathers and kin.

After the ceremony The Thirty moved away to the hills, leaving Decado and Rayvan and her sons. It was some time before he noticed their absence.

Decado left the fire and went in search of them, but the valley was large and soon he realised the enormity of the task. The moon was high in the sky when he finally came to the conclusion that they had left him behind intentionally: they did not want to be found.

He sat down by a white marble boulder and relaxed his mind, floating down into the whispering realms of the subconscious.

Silence.

Anger nagged at him, dislodging his concentration, but he calmed himself and sought the sanctuary once more.

Then he heard the scream. It came at first as a soft, muted cry and grew into a soul-piercing expression of agony. Decado listened for a while, struggling to identify the source of the sound. Then it came to him. It was Abaddon.

And he knew where The Thirty had travelled: to rescue the Abbot of Swords and free him to die. He also knew that this was folly of the worst kind. He had promised Abaddon that he would look after his charges and now, within a day of the old man's death, they had left him in order to embark on a futile journey, travelling into the realms of the damned.

A terrible sadness assailed Decado, for he could not follow them. So he prayed, but no answer came to him and he expected none.

'What kind of a god are you?' he asked in his despair. 'What do you expect from your followers? You give them nothing and ask for everything. At least with the spirits of darkness there is some communion.

Abaddon died for you and still suffers. Now his acolytes will suffer in their turn. Why do you not answer me?'

Silence.

'You do not exist! There is no force for purity. All a man has is his will to do good. I reject you. I want no more to do with you!'

Decado relaxed then and probed deeper into his mind, seeking the mysteries Abaddon had promised him throughout his years of study. He had tried in the past, but never with this sense of desperation. He travelled yet deeper, tumbling and spinning through the roaring of his memories – seeing again the battles and skirmishes, the fears and the failures. On, on, through the bitter sadness of his childhood, back to his first stirrings in his mother's womb and beyond into separation: seed and egg, driving, waiting.

Darkness.

Movement. The snapping of chains, the soaring freedom.

Light.

Decado floated free, drawn to the pure silver light of the full moon. He halted his rise with an effort of will and gazed down on the curving beauty of the Demon's Smile, but a dark cloud drifted beneath him and obscured the view. He glanced down at his body, white and naked in the moonlight, and joy flooded his soul.

The scream froze him. He remembered his mission and his eyes blazed with cold fire. But he could not travel naked and unarmed. Closing his spirit eyes he pictured armour, the black and silver of the Dragon.

And it was there. But no sword hung at his side, no shield on his arm.

He tried again. Nothing.

The long-ago words of Abaddon drifted back over the years. 'In spirit travel a Source warrior carries the sword of his faith, and his shield is the strength of his belief.'

Decado had neither.

'Damn you!' he shouted into the cosmic night. 'Still you thwart me, even when I am on your business.' He closed his eyes once more. 'If it is faith I need, then I have faith. In myself. In Decado, the Ice Killer. I need no sword, for my hands are death.'

And he flew like a shaft of moonlight, drawn to the scream. He left the world of men with awesome speed, soaring over dark mountains and gloomy plains; two blue planets hovered over the land and the stars were dim and cold.

Below him an ebony castle squatted on a low hill. He halted in his flight, hovering above the stone ramparts. A dark shadow leapt at him and he swerved as a sword-blade flashed by his head. His hand lanced out, gripping the swordsman's wrist, spinning his enemy round. Decado's left hand chopped down at his opponent; the man's neck snapped and he vanished. Decado spun on his heel as a second attacker surged at him. The man wore the dark livery of the Templars. Decado leapt back as the sword cut a glittering semi-circle past his belly. As a back-hand slash hissed at his neck, Decado ducked and dived forward under the blade, ramming his skull under the man's chin. The Templar staggered.

Decado's hand stabbed out, the fingers burying themselves in the Templar's throat. Once more his opponent vanished.

Ahead was a half-open door leading to a deep stairwell. Decado ran forward but then stopped, his senses urging caution. Launching himself feet first, he smashed the door back on its hinges and a man groaned and slumped forward into view. Rolling to his feet, Decado hammered the blade of his foot into the man's chest, caving in the breastbone.

Running on, he took the stairs three at a time to emerge into a wide circular hall. At the centre The Thirty stood in a tight circle, surrounded on all sides by dark-cloaked Templars. Swords clashed silently and no sound issued from the battle. Outnumbered more than two to one, The Thirty were fighting for their lives.

And losing!

They had only one choice left. Flight. Even as he realised this Decado noticed for the first time that he could no longer soar into the air – as soon as he had touched these grim battlements his powers had left him. But why? In that instant he knew the answer; it lay in the words he had used to Abaddon: 'Evil lives in a pit. If you want to fight it, you have to climb down into the slime to do so.'

They were in the pit and the powers of light were lessened here, even as the powers of darkness failed against the hearts of strong men.

'To me!' yelled Decado. 'Thirty to me!'

For a moment the battle ceased as the Templars paused to check the source of the sound. Then six of them peeled off from the battle to charge him. Acuas cut his way into the gap and led the warrior priests towards the stairs.

The Thirty cut and slashed a path, their silver blades shining like torches in the gloom. No bodies lay on the cold stones – any pierced by swordblade in that bloodless battle merely vanished as if they had never been. Only nineteen priests still stood.

Decado watched death bear down upon him. His skill was great, but no man alive could tackle six men unarmed and survive. But he would try. A great calm settled upon him and he smiled at them.

Two swords of dazzling light appeared in his hands, and he attacked with blistering speed. A left cut, a parry and riposte, a right slash, a left thrust. Three down and gone like smoke in the breeze. The remaining three Templars fell back – into the eldritch blades of The Thirty.

'Follow me!' shouted Decado. Turning, he ran up the stairs ahead of them and out on to the battlements. Leaping to the wall, he gazed down on the jagged rocks so far below. The Thirty came out into the open.

'Fly!' ordered Decado.

'We shall fall!' shouted Balan.

'Not unless I tell you to, you son of a slut! Now move!'

Balan hurled himself from the battlements, swiftly followed by the other sixteen survivors. Last of all Decado leapt to join them.

At first they fell, but once clear of the pull of the castle they soared into the night, hurtling back to the realities of Skoda.

Decado returned to his body and opened his eyes. Slowly he walked towards the eastern woods, drawn by the pulsing mood of despair emanating from the young priests.

He found them in a clearing between two low hills. They had laid out the eleven bodies of the slain and now they prayed, heads bowed.

'Get up!' ordered Decado. 'On your feet!' Silently they obeyed him. 'My, how ridiculous you are! For all your talents you are but children. Tell me, how did the rescue go, children? Have we freed Abaddon? Are we going to have a celebration party? Look me in the eyes, damn you!'

He moved to Acuas. 'Well, yellowbeard, you have excelled yourself. You have achieved what neither the Templars nor the forces of Ceska could accomplish. You have destroyed eleven of your comrades.'

'That is not fair!' shouted Katan, tears in his eyes.

'Be silent!' thundered Decado. 'Fair? I am talking about reality. Did you find Abaddon?'

'No,' said Acuas softly.

'Have you worked out why?'

'No.'

'Because they never had his soul – that would be a feat beyond them. They lured you into their trap by deceit, which is something at which they excel. Now eleven of your brothers are slain. And you carry that burden.'

'And what about you?' said Katan, his normally serene face shaking with fury. 'Where were you when we needed you? What sort of a leader are you? You don't believe in our faith. You are just an assassin! There is no heart in you, Decado. You are the Ice Killer. Well, at least we fought for something we believed in, and travelled to die for a man we loved. All right, we were wrong – but we had no leader once Abaddon was dead.'

'You should have come to me,' replied Decado defensively.

'Why? You were the leader and you should have been there. We did seek you. Often. But even when you discovered your talents – talents we had prayed for – you hovered on the edge of our prayers. You never came forward. When do you eat with us, or talk with us? You sleep alone, away from the fire. You are an outsider. We are here to die for the Source. What are you here for?'

'I am here to win, Katan. If you want to die, just fall on your sword. Or ask me – I will do it for you, I will end your life in an instant. You are here to fight for the Source, to ensure that evil does not triumph in this land. But I will talk no more. I am the leader chosen and I require no oaths from you. No promises. Those who will obey me will come to me in the morning. We will eat together – aye, and pray together. Those who wish to follow their own road may do so. And now I leave you to bury the dead.'

Back in the city the populace cheered the victorious army from the fields a half-mile south, right through to the city centre and the makeshift barracks. But the cheers were muted, for the question remained on everyone's mind: What now? When will Ceska come with his Joinings?

Tenaka, Rayvan, Ananais, Decado and other leaders of the new army met together in the Senate Hall, while Rayvan's sons Lake and Lucas produced maps of the terrain to the east and south.

After an afternoon of heated discussion, it became obvious that much of Skoda was indefensible. The pass at the Demon's Smile could be walled and manned, but it would need a thousand men to hold it for any length of time, while to the north and south some six other passes gave entrance to the valleys and meadows of Skoda.

'It's like trying to defend a rabbit warren,' said Ananais. 'Ceska – even without his Joinings – can put into battle fifty times as many men. They could hit us on any of sixteen fronts. We simply cannot cover the ground.'

'The army will grow,' said Rayvan. 'Even now more men are coming down from the mountains. Word will spread outside Skoda and rebels will flock to join us.'

'Yes,' admitted Tenaka, 'but in that there is a problem. Ceska will send spies, agents, alarmists – they will all filter in.'

'The Thirty will help where they can and ferret out traitors,' said Decado. 'But if too many are allowed in, we will not be able to deal with them.'

'Then we must man the passes, spread The Thirty among the men,' said Tenaka.

And so it went on. Some men wanted to return to their farms to ready the fields for summer, others merely wished to return home with news of their victory. Lake complained that the food supplies were inadequate. Galand told of fights breaking out between Skoda men and the new Legion volunteers.

Throughout the long afternoon and into dusk, the leaders sought answers to the problems. It was agreed, finally, that half the men would be allowed home, so long as they promised to work on the farms of those who stayed behind. At the end of the month the first half would return, to be replaced at home by the others.

Ananais bristled with anger. 'And what of training?' he stormed. 'How in the devil's name do I get them ready for war?'

'They are not regular soldiers,' said Rayvan softly. 'They are working men, with wives and children to feed.'

'What about the city treasury?' asked Scaler.

'What about it?' queried Rayvan.

'How much is there?'

'I have no idea.'

'Then we should check. Since we rule Skoda, the money is ours. We could use it to buy food and stores from the Vagrians. They may not let us pass their borders, but they will not turn back our money.'

'Curse me for a fool!' said Rayvan. 'Of course we must. Lake, check the treasury now – if it has not been already bled dry.'

'We have had a guard on it, mother,' said Lake.

'Even so, get down there now and count it.'

'That will take all night!'

She flashed him an angry look and he sighed.

635

'All right, Rayvan,' he said. 'I'm going. But be warned – the moment I have finished I shall wake you with the total!'

Rayvan grinned at him and then turned to Scaler. 'You have a good brain in your head – will you go to Vagria and buy what we need?'

'He cannot,' said Tenaka. 'He has another mission.'

'Hasn't he just!' muttered Ananais.

'Well, I suggest,' interposed Rayvan, 'that we call a halt to tonight's meeting and break for supper. I could eat the best part of a horse. Can't we get together again tomorrow?'

'No,' said Tenaka. 'Tomorrow I leave Skoda.'

'Leave?' said Rayvan, astonished. 'But you are our general.'

'I must, lady – I have an army to find. But I shall return.'

'Where will you find an army?'

'Among my people.'

The silence in the Senate Hall was devastating. Men exchanged nervous glances and only Ananais seemed unmoved; he leaned back in his chair, placing his booted feet on the table top.

'Explain yourself,' murmured Rayvan.

'I think you know what I mean,' said Tenaka coolly. 'The one people with enough warriors to trouble Ceska are the Nadir. If I am lucky, I will raise an army.'

'You would bring those murderous savages into the Drenai? They are worse than Ceska's Joinings,' said Rayvan, pushing herself to her feet. 'I will not have it – I will die before those barbarians set foot on Skoda Land.'

All around men hammered their fists on the table in support. Then Tenaka stood up, raising his hands for silence.

'I appreciate the sentiments of everyone here. I was raised among the Nadir and I know their ways. But they do not eat babies, nor do they mate with demons. They are men, fighting men who live for war. It is their way. And they have honour. But I am not here to defend my people – I am here to give you a chance of staying alive through the summer.

'You think you have won a great victory? You won nothing but a skirmish. Ceska will throw fifty thousand men against you, come the summer. With what will you reply?

'And if you are defeated, what will happen to your families? Ceska will turn Skoda into a desert, and where there were trees there will be gibbets: a land of cadavers, desolate and tormented.

'There is no guarantee that I can raise an army among the Nadir. To them I am tainted by round-eye blood – accursed and less than a man. For they are no different from you. Nadir children are raised on stories of your debaucheries, and our legends are filled with tales of your genocides.

'I do not seek your permission for what I do. To be truthful, I don't give a damn! I leave tomorrow.'

He sat down to silence and Ananais leaned over to him.

'There was no need to beat about the bush,' he said. 'You should have given it to them straight.'

The comment produced an involuntary snort from Rayvan, which turned into a throaty chuckle.

Around the table the tension turned to laughter while Tenaka sat with arms folded, his face flushed and stern.

Finally Rayvan spoke. 'I do not like your plan, my friend. And I think I speak for everyone here. But you have played fair by us and without you we would now be crow's meat.' She sighed and leaned over the table, placing her hand on Tenaka's arm. 'You do give a damn, or else you would not be here, and if you are wrong – then so be it. I will stand by you. Bring your Nadir, if you can, and I will embrace the first goat-eating dog-soldier who rides in with you.'

Tenaka relaxed and looked long into her green eyes.

'You are quite a woman, Rayvan,' he whispered.

'You would be wise not to forget it, general!'

13

Ananais rode from the city at dusk, anxious to be free of its noisy confines. Once he had loved the city life, with its endless rounds of parties and hunts. There were beautiful women to be loved, men to be bested at wrestling or mock sword-play. There were falcons and tourneys and dances overlapping one another, as the most civilised western nation indulged in pleasure.

But then he had been the Golden One and the subject of legend.

He lifted the black mask from his torn face and felt the wind ease the angry scar. Riding to a nearby hilltop crowned with rowan trees, there he slid from the saddle and sat staring at the mountains. Tenaka was right – there had been no reason to kill the Legion men. It was proper that they wished to go back – it was their duty. But then hate was a potent force, and Ananais carried hate carved in his heart. He hated Ceska for what he had done to the land and its people and he hated the people for allowing it. He hated the flowers for their beauty and the air around him for granting him breath.

Most of all he hated himself, for not having the courage to end his misery.

What did these Skoda peasants know of his reasons for being among them? They had cheered him on the day of the battle, and again when he arrived in the city. 'Darkmask', they called him – a hero out of the past, built in the image of the immortal Druss.

What did they know of his grief?

He stared down at the mask. Even in this there was vanity, for the front was built out in the shape of a nose. He might just as well have cut two holes in it.

He was a man without a face and without a future. Only the past brought him pleasure – but with that came the pain. All he had now was his prodigious strength . . . and that was failing. He was forty-six years old and time was running out.

For the thousandth time he remembered the arena battle with the Joining. Had there been another way to kill the beast? Could he have saved himself this torment? He watched the battle once more through the eye of memory. There *was* no other way – the beast had been twice as strong and half again as swift as he. It was a miracle that he had slain it at all.

His horse whinnied, its ears flicking up, its head turning. Ananais replaced his mask and waited. Within seconds his keen hearing caught the soft clip-clopping of a walking horse.

'Ananais!' called Valtaya from the darkness. 'Are you there?' He cursed softly, for he was in no mood for company.

'Over here! On the lee of the hill.'

She rode to him and slipped from the saddle, dropping the reins over her mount's neck. The gold of her hair turned silver in the moonlight and her eyes reflected the stars.

'What do you want?' he asked, turning away and sitting down on the grass. She removed her cloak and spread it on the ground, seating herself upon it.

'Why did you ride here alone?'

'To be alone. I have much to think about.'

'Say the word and I shall ride back,' she said.

'I think you should,' he said, but she did not move, as he had known she would not.

'I, too, am lonely,' she murmured. 'But I do not want to be alone. I am alone and I have no place here.'

'I can offer you nothing, woman!' he snapped, his voice rough as the words ripped from him.

'You could let me have your company at least,' she said and the flood-gates opened. Tears welled from her eyes and her head dropped; then the sobs began.

'Whisht, woman, there's no call for tears. What have you to cry about? There is no need for you to be lonely. You are very attractive and Galand is well-smitten with you. He is a good man.' But as the sobs continued he moved to her side, curling a huge arm around her shoulder and pulling her to him.

She pushed her head against his chest and the sobbing died down into ragged crying. He patted her back and stroked her hair; her arm crept round his waist and she gently pushed him back to lie upon her cloak. A terrible desire seized Ananais and he wanted her then more than anything life could offer. Her body pressed down on his and he could feel the warmth of her breasts upon his chest.

Her hand moved to his mask, but he grasped her wrist with a swiftness that stunned her.

'*Don't!*' he pleaded, releasing her hand. But slowly she lifted the mask and he closed his eyes as the night air washed over his scars. Her lips touched his forehead, then his eyelids, then both ruined cheeks. He had no mouth to return her kisses and he wept; she held him close then until the crying passed.

'I swore,' he said at last, 'that I would die before a woman would see me this way.'

'A woman loves a man. A face is not a man, any more than a leg is a man, or a hand. I love you, Ananais! And your scars are a part of you. Do you see that?'

'There is a difference,' he said, 'between love and gratitude. I rescued you, but you don't owe me anything. You never will.'

'You are right – I am grateful. But I would not give myself to you out of gratitude. I am not a child. I know you do not love me. Why should you? You had your pick of all the beauties in Drenan and refused them. But I love you and I want you – even for the short time that we have.'

'You know, then?'

'Of course I know! We will not defeat Ceska – we never could. But that is not of consequence. He will die. All men die.'

'You think what we do is a nonsense?'

'No. There will always be those . . . must always be those . . . who will stand against the Ceskas of the world. So that in times to come, men will know that there have always been heroes to stand against the darkness. We need men like Druss and the Earl of Bronze, like Egel and Karnak, like Bild and Ironlatch. They give us pride and a sense of purpose. And we need men like Ananais and Tenaka Khan. It matters not that the Torchbearer cannot win – only that the light shines for a little while.'

'You are well-read, Val,' he said.

'I am not a fool, Ananais.' Leaning over him, she kissed his face once more. Gently she pressed her mouth to his. He groaned and his great arms encircled her.

Rayvan could not sleep; the air was oppressive and heavy with the threat of storms. Throwing aside her heavy blanket she left the bed, wrapping a woollen robe about her sturdy frame. Then she opened the window wide, but not a breath of wind travelled over the mountains.

The night was velvet dark and tiny bats skittered and flew around the tower and down into the fruit trees of the garden. A badger, caught in a shaft of moonlight, glared up at her window and then shuffled away into the undergrowth. She sighed – there was such beauty to the night. A flicker of movement caught her eye and from the window she could just make out the figure of a white-cloaked warrior kneeling by a rose bush. Then he stood, and in that fluid motion she recognised Decado.

Rayvan left the window and moved silently through the long corridors, down the winding stairway and out into the courtyard garden. Decado was leaning against a low wall, watching the moonlight on the mountains. He heard Rayvan's approach and turned to meet her, the ghost of a welcoming smile upon his thin lips.

'Engaged in solitude?' she asked him.

'Merely thinking.'

'This is a good place for it. Peaceful.'

'Yes.'

'I was born up there,' she said, pointing east. 'My father had a small farm beyond the timberline – cattle and ponies mostly. It was a good life.'

'We shall not hold any of this, Rayvan.'

'I know. When the time comes we will move further back into the high country, where the passes narrow.'

He nodded. 'I don't think Tenaka will come back.'

'Don't write him off, Decado. He is a canny man.'

'You don't need to tell me – I served under him for six years.'

'Do you like him?'

A sudden smile lit his face, burning the years from him. 'Of course I like him. He is the closest to a friend I have ever had.'

'What about your men, your Thirty?'

'What about them?' he asked guardedly.

640

'Do you see them as your friends?'

'No.'

'Then why do they follow you?'

'Who knows? They have a dream: a desire to die. It is all beyond me. Tell me about your farm – were you happy there?'

'Yes. A good husband, fine children, a nourished land beneath an open sky. What more can a woman ask on the journey between life and death?'

'Did you love your husband?'

'What kind of question is that?' she snapped.

'I did not mean to give offence. You never mention him by name.'

'That has nothing to do with lack of love. In fact the reverse is true. When I say his name, it brings home to me just what I have lost. But I hold his image in my heart – you understand that?'

'Yes.'

'Why did you never marry?'

'I never wanted to; never had the desire to share my life with a woman. I am not comfortable with people, save on my own terms.'

'Then you were wise,' said Rayvan.

'You think so?'

'I think so. You and your friends are very alike, you know. You are all incomplete men – terribly sad and very alone. No wonder you are drawn together! The rest of us can share our lives, swap jests and tall tales, laugh together, cry together. We live and love and grow. We offer each other small comforts daily and they help us to survive. But you have nothing like that to offer. Instead you offer your life – your death.'

'It is not that simple, Rayvan.'

'Life seldom is, Decado. But then I am but a simple mountain woman and I paint the pictures as I see them.'

'Come now, lady, there is nothing simple about you! But let us suppose – for a moment – that you are right. Do you think that Tenaka, or Ananais, or myself chose to be as we are? My grandfather had a dog. He desired that dog to hate the Nadir, so he hired an old tribesman to come into the farmyard every night and beat the puppy with a switch.

'The puppy grew to hate that old man and any other of his slant-eyed race. Would you blame the dog? Tenaka Khan was raised amid hatred and though he did not respond in kind, still the absence of love left its mark. He bought a wife and lavished all he had upon her. Now she is dead and he has nothing.

'Ananais? You only have to look upon him to know what pain he carries. But even so that is not the whole story. His father died insane after killing Ananais' mother before his eyes. Even before that, the father had bedded Ani's sister . . . she died in childbirth.

'And as for me, my story is even more sordid and sad. So spare me your mountain homilies, Rayvan. Had any of us grown to manhood on the slopes of your mountain, I don't doubt we would have been better men.'

She smiled then and heaved herself on to the wall, swinging round to look down on him. 'Foolish boy!' she said. 'I did not say you needed to be better men. You are the best of men, and I love all three of you. You are not like your grandfather's dog, Decado – you are a man. And a man can overcome his background, even as he can overcome a skilled opponent. Look around you more often: see the people as they touch and show their love. But don't watch coldly, like an observer. Don't hover outside life – take part in it. There are people out there waiting to love you. It is not something you should turn down lightly.'

'We are what we are, lady; do not ask for more. I am a swordsman. Ananais is a warrior. Tenaka is a general beyond compare. Our backgrounds have made us what we are. You need us as you see us.'

'Perhaps. But perhaps you could be even greater.'

'Now is not the time to experiment. Come – I will walk you back to your rooms.'

Scaler sat on the broad bed, staring at the dark-stained door. Tenaka was gone now, but he could still see the tall Nadir warrior and hear the softly-spoken commands.

It was a farce – he was trapped here, entangled in this web of heroes. Take Dros Delnoch?

Ananais could take Dros Delnoch, charging it single-handed with his silver sword flashing in the dawn sun. Tenaka could take it with some improvised plan, some subtle stroke of genius involving a length of twine and three small pebbles. These were men made for legend, created by the gods to fuel the sagas.

But where did Scaler fit in?

He moved to the long mirror by the window wall. A tall young man stared back at him, dark shoulder-length hair held in place by a black leather brow-circlet. The eyes were bright and intelligent, the chin square, giving the lie to the saga poets. The fringed buckskin jerkin hung well, drawn in to his lean waist by a thick sword-belt. A dagger hung at his left side. His leggings were of softest dark leather and his boots thigh-length after the fashion of the Legion. Reaching for his sword, he slotted it home in the leather scabbard and placed it at his side.

'You poor fool!' the mirror warrior told him. 'You should have stayed at home.'

He had tried to tell Tenaka how ill-equipped he felt, but the Nadir had smiled gently and ignored him.

'You are of the blood, Arvan. It will carry you through,' he had said. Words! Just words! Blood was merely dark liquid – it carried no secrets, no mysteries. Courage was a thing of the soul and not a gift that a man could bestow on his sons.

The door opened and Scaler glanced round as Pagan entered. The black man smiled a greeting and then eased himself into a broad leather chair. In the lantern light he loomed large, the immense sweep of his shoulders filling the chair. Just like the others, thought Scaler – a man to move mountains.

'Come to see me off?' he asked, breaking the silence.

The black man shook his head. 'I am coming with you.'

Relief struck Scaler with almost physical power, but he masked his emotions.

'Why?'

'Why not? I like riding.'

'You know my mission?'

'You are to take a fort and open the gates for Tenaka's warriors.'

'It is not quite so easy as you make it sound,' said Scaler, returning to the bed and sitting down. The sword twisted between his legs as he sat and he straightened it.

'Don't worry about it, you will think of something,' said Pagan, grinning. 'When do you want to leave?'

'In about two years.'

'Don't be hard on yourself, Scaler; it does no good. I know your mission is tough. Dros Delnoch is a city with six walls and a keep. More than seven thousand warriors are stationed there – and some fifty Joinings. But we will do what we can. Tenaka says you have a plan.'

Scaler chuckled. 'That is good of him. He thought of it days ago and waited for me to catch up!'

'So tell me.'

'The Sathuli – they are a mountain and desert people, fierce and independent. For centuries they fought the Drenai over the rights to the Delnoch ranges. During the First Nadir War they aided my ancestor, the Earl of Bronze. In return he gave them the land. I don't know how many there are – possibly ten thousand, maybe less. But Ceska has revoked the original treaty and border skirmishes have begun again.'

'So, you will seek aid from the tribesmen?'

'Yes.'

'But without great hope of success?'

'That's fair comment. The Sathuli have always hated the Drenai and there is no trust there. Worse than that, they loathe the Nadir. And even if they do help, how in Hell's name do I get them to leave the fortress?'

'One problem at a time, Scaler!'

Scaler stood up and the sword twisted again, half-tripping him; he pulled the scabbard from the belt and hurled it to the bed.

'One problem at a time? All right! Let us look at problems. I am no warrior, no swordsman. I have never been a soldier. I am frightened of battles and have never displayed much skill at tactics. I am not a leader and would be hard-pressed to get hungry men to follow me to a kitchen. Which of these problems shall we tackle first?'

'Sit down, boy,' said Pagan, leaning forward and resting his hands on the arms of the chair. Scaler sat, his anger ebbing from him. 'Now listen to me! In my own land, I am a king. I rose to the throne on blood and death, the first of my race to take the Opal. When I was a young man and full of pride, an old priest came to me telling me that I would burn in the fires of Hell for my crimes. I ordered a regiment to build a fire from many trees. It could not be approached closer than thirty paces and the flames beat against the vault of heaven. Then I ordered that regiment to put out the flames. Ten thousand men hurled themselves on the blaze and the fire died. "If I go to Hell," I told the priest, "my men will follow me and stamp out the flames." From the great Sea of Souls to the Mountains of the Moon, I ruled that kingdom. I survived poison in my wine-cup and daggers at my back, false friends and noble enemies, treacherous sons and summer plagues. And yet I will follow you, Scaler.'

Scaler swallowed as he watched the lantern light dance on the ebony features of the man in the chair.

'Why? Why will you follow me?'

'Because the thing must be done. And now I am going to tell you a great truth, and if you are wise you will take it to your heart. All men are stupid. They are full of fear and insecurity – it makes them weak. Always the other man seems stronger, more confident, more capable. It is a lie of the worst kind, for we lie to ourselves.

'Take yourself. When I came in here I was your black friend, Pagan – big, strong and friendly. But what am I now? Now am I not a savage king far above you? Do you not feel ashamed of having forced your tiny doubts upon me?'

Scaler nodded.

'And yet, *am* I a king? Did I truly command my regiment to stamp out a fire? How do you know? You do not! You listened to the voice of your inadequacy, and because you believed you are in my power. If I draw my sword, you are dead!

'And again, when I look at you I see a bright, courageous young man, well-built and in the prime of his manhood. You could be the prince of assassins, the deadliest warrior under the sun. You could be an emperor, a general, a poet . . .

'Not a leader, Scaler? Anyone can be a leader, because everyone wants to be led.'

'I am not a Tenaka Khan,' said Scaler. 'I am not of the same breed.'

'Tell me that in a month. But from now on, act the part. You will be amazed at the number of people you fool. Don't share your doubts! Life is a game, Scaler. Play it like that.'

Scaler grinned. 'Why not? But tell me – did you truly send your men into the fire?'

'You tell me,' said Pagan, his face hardening and his eyes glowing in the lamplight.

'No, you did not!'

Pagan grinned. 'No! I will have the horses ready at dawn – I'll see you then.'

'Make sure you pack plenty of honey-cakes – Belder has a fondness for them.'

Pagan shook his head. 'The old man is not coming. He is no good for you and his spirit is gone. He stays behind.'

'If you follow me, then you do as I damn well say,' snapped Scaler. 'Three horses and Belder travels with us!'

The black man's eyebrows rose and he spread his hands. 'Very well.' He opened the door.

'How was that?' asked Scaler.

'Not bad for a start. I'll see you in the morning.'

As Pagan returned to his room, his mood was sombre. Lifting his huge pack to the bed, he spread out the weapons he would carry tomorrow: two hunting-knives, sharp as razors; four throwing-knives to be worn in baldric sheaths; a short sword, double-edged, and a double-headed hand-axe he would strap to his saddle.

Stripping himself naked, he took a phial of oil from his pack and began to grease his body, rubbing hard at the bunched muscles of his shoulders. The damp western air was creeping into his bones.

His mind soared back over the years. He could still feel the heat of the blaze and hear the screams of his warriors as they raced into the flames . . .

Tenaka rode down from the mountain on to the slopes of the Vagrian plains. The sun rose over his left shoulder and the clouds bunched above his head. He felt at peace with the breeze in his hair; though mountainous problems reared ahead of him, he felt light and free of burdens.

He wondered if his Nadir heritage had made him uneasy among city dwellers, with their high walls and shuttered windows. The breeze picked up and Tenaka smiled.

Tomorrow death could flash towards him on an arrow point – but today . . . today was fine.

He pushed all thoughts of Skoda from his mind – those problems could be dealt with by Ananais and Rayvan. Scaler too was now his own man, riding for his own destiny. All Tenaka could do was fulfil his particular part in the tale.

His mind swam back to his childhood among the tribes. Spear, Wolfs-head, Green Monkey, Grave Mountain, Soul Stealers. So many camps, so many territories.

Ulric's tribe were acknowledged as the premier fighting men: the Lords of the Steppes, the Bringers of War. Wolfshead they were and their ferocity in war was legend. But who ruled the wolves now? Surely Jongir was dead.

Tenaka considered the contemporaries of his youth:

Knifespeaks, swift to anger and slow to forgive. Cunning, resourceful and ambitious.

Abadai Truthtaker, devious and devout in the ways of the shaman.

Tsuboy, known as Saddleskull after he killed a raider and mounted the man's skull on his saddle-horn.

All these were grandsons of Jongir. All descended from Ulric.

Tenaka's violet eyes grew bleak and cold as he brought the trio to mind. Each had showed his hatred of the half-breed.

Abadai had been the most vicious and had even resorted to poison during the Feast of the Long Knives. Only Shillat, Tenaka's vigilant mother, had observed the placing of the powder in her son's cup.

But none had challenged Tenaka directly, for even by the age of four-teen he had earned the name Bladedancer and was accomplished with every weapon of war.

645

And he sat for long night hours round the camp-fires, listening to the old men as they remembered wars past, picking up details of strategy and tactics. At fifteen he knew every battle and skirmish in Wolfshead history.

Tenaka drew on the reins and stared at the distant Delnoch mountains.

> Nadir we,
> Youth born,
> Axe wielders,
> Blood letters,
> Victors still.

He laughed and dug his heels into his gelding's flanks. The beast snorted and then broke into a full gallop across the plain, hooves drumming in the early morning silence.

Tenaka let the horse run for several minutes before slowing it to a canter and then a trot. They had many miles to go, and though the beast was game he did not wish to overtire it.

By all the gods, it was good to be free of people! Even Renya.

She was beautiful and he loved her, but he was a man who needed solitude – freedom for his plans to form.

She had listened in silence when he told her of his plan to travel alone. He had expected a bitter row, but she had offered none. Instead she embraced him and they had made love without passion, but with great tenderness.

If he survived this insane venture, he would take her to his heart and his home. If he survived? He calculated the odds against success at hundreds to one; perhaps thousands. A sudden thought struck him. Was he a fool? He had Renya and a fortune waiting in Ventria. Why risk everything?

Did he love the Drenai? He pondered the question, knowing that he did not but wondering just what his feelings were. The people had never accepted him, even as a Dragon general. And the land, though beautiful, had nothing of the savage splendour of the Steppes. So what were his feelings?

The death of Illae had unhinged him, coming so close to the destruction of the Dragon. The shame he felt for spurning his friends had merged with the agony of Illae's passing and in some strange way he saw her death as a punishment for his failure to fulfil his duty. Only Ceska's death – and his own – could wipe away the shame. But now it was different.

Ananais would stand alone if necessary, believing in Tenaka's promise that he would return. And friendship was something infinitely more solid and greatly more sustaining than love of the land. Tenaka Khan would ride across the deepest pit of Hell, endure the greatest hardships under the sun, to fulfil his promise to Ananais.

He glanced back at the Skoda mountains. There would the deaths begin in earnest. Rayvan's band stood upon the anvil of history, staring up defiantly at Ceska's hammer.

Ananais had ridden with him from the city just before dawn, and they had stopped on the brow of a hill.

'Look after yourself, you Nadir slop-swiller!'

'And you, Drenai. Look to your valleys!'

'Seriously, Tani, take care. Get your army and come back swiftly. We don't have long. I should think they will send a Delnoch force against us, to soften us up for the main thrust.'

Tenaka nodded. 'They will probe and cut – tire you out. Use The Thirty; they will be invaluable in the days to come. Have you anywhere in mind for a second base?'

'Yes, we are moving supplies to the high country south of the city. There are two narrow passes we could hold. But if they push us back there, we are finished. There is nowhere to run.'

The two men shook hands and then hugged one another warmly.

'I want you to know . . .' began Tenaka, but Ananais cut him short.

'I know, boy! You must hurry back. You can rely on old Darkmask to hold the fort.'

Tenaka grinned and rode for the Vagrian Plains.

14

For six days there was no sign of hostile activity on the eastern Skoda borders. Refugees poured in to the mountains, bringing tales of torture, starvation and terror. The Thirty screened the refugees as best they could, turning away those found to be lying or secretly sympathetic to Ceska.

But, day by day, the numbers swelled as the outer lands bled of people. Camps were set up in several valleys and the problems of food supply and sanitation plagued Ananais. Rayvan took it in her stride, organising the refugees into work parties to dig latrine trenches and build simple shelters for the elderly and infirm.

Young men came forward hourly to volunteer for the army and it was left to Galand, Parsal and Lake to sift them and find them duties among the Skoda militia.

But always they asked for Darkmask, the black-garbed giant. 'Ceska's Bane', they called him, and among the newcomers were saga poets whose songs floated out in the night from the valley camp-fires.

Ananais found it irksome but he hid it well, knowing how valuable the legends would be in the days to come.

Every morning he rode out into the mountains to study the valleys and the slopes, seeking the passes and gauging distances and angles of attack. He set men to work digging earth-walls and ditches, moving rocks to form cover. Caches of arrows and lances were hidden at various points, along with sacks of food hung high in the branches of trees, screened by thick foliage. Each section leader knew of at least three caches.

At dusk Ananais would call the section leaders to his fire and question them about the day's training, encouraging them to come forward with ideas, strategies and plans. He carefully noted those who did so, keeping them with him when others were dismissed. Lake, for all his idealistic fervour, was a sound thinker who responded intelligently. His knowledge of terrain was extensive and Ananais used him well. Galand too was a canny warrior and the men respected him; he was solid, dependable and loyal. His brother Parsal was no thinker, but his courage was beyond question. To these of the inner circle Ananais added two others; Turs and Thorn. Solitary men who said little, both were former raiders who had earned their living crossing Vagrian lands and stealing cattle and horses to trade in the eastern valleys. Turs was young and full of fire; his brother and two sisters had been killed in the raid that saw Rayvan rebel. Thorn was an older man, leather-tough and wolf-lean. The Skoda men respected them both and listened in silence when they spoke.

It was Thorn who brought news of the herald on the seventh day after Tenaka's departure.

Ananais was scouting the eastern slopes of the mountain Carduil, when Thorn found him and he rode east at speed. Thorn alongside him.

Their horses were well-lathered when Ananais finally reached the valley of the Dawn, where Decado and six of The Thirty waited to greet him. Around them were some two hundred Skoda men, dug into position overlooking the plain beyond.

Ananais walked forward to climb a craggy outcrop of rock. Below him were six hundred warriors wearing the red of Delnoch. At the centre on a white horse sat an elderly man in bright blue robes. His beard was white and long. Ananais recognised him and grinned sourly.

'Who is it?' asked Thorn.

'Breight. They call him the Survivor. I am not surprised – he has been a counsellor for over forty years.'

'He must be Ceska's man,' said Thorn.

'He is anybody's man, but a wise choice to send for he is a diplomat and a patrician. He could tell you that wolves lay eggs and you would believe him.'

'Should we fetch Rayvan?'

'No. I will talk to him.'

At that moment six men rode forward to flank the aged counsellor. Their cloaks and armour were black. As Ananais watched them look up and felt their eyes upon him, ice flowed into his veins.

'Decado!' he shouted as the fear hit him. Instantly the warmth of friendship blanketed him as Decado and his six warriors turned the power of their minds to protect him.

Angry now, Ananais bellowed for Breight to approach. The old man hesitated, but one of the Templars leaned in to him and he spurred his horse forward, riding awkwardly up the steep slope.

'That is far enough!' said Ananais, moving forward.

'Is it you, Golden One?' asked Breight, his voice deep and resonant. The eyes were brown and exceedingly friendly.

'It is I. Say what you have to say.'

'There is no need for harshness between us, Ananais. Was I not the first to cheer when you were honoured for your battle triumphs? Did I not secure your first commission with the Dragon? Was I not your mother's troth-holder?'

'All these things and more, old man! But now you are a lick-spittle lackey to a tyrant and the past is dead.'

'You misjudge my lord Ceska – he has only the good of the Drenai in his heart. These are hard times, Ananais. Bitter hard. Our enemies wage a silent war upon us, starving us of food. Not one kingdom around us wishes to see the enlightenment of the Drenai prosper, for it signals the end of their corruption.'

'Spare me this nonsense, Breight! I cannot be bothered to argue with you. What do you want?'

'I see your terrible wounds have made you bitter and I am sorry for that. I bring you a royal pardon! My lord is deeply offended by your actions against him, yet your past deeds have earned you a place in his heart. In your honour, he has pardoned every man who stands against

649

him in Skoda. Further, he promises to review personally every grievance you have, real or imagined. Can he be fairer than that?'

Breight had pitched his voice to carry to the listening defenders and his eyes scanned the line watching for their reactions.

'Ceska would not know "fair" if it burned his buttocks,' said Ananais. 'The man is a snake!'

'I understand your hatred, Ananais – look at you . . . scarred, deformed, unhuman. But surely there is a shred of humanity left in you? Why should your hatred carry thousands of innocent souls to terrible deaths? You cannot win! The Joinings are now assembling and there is no army on the face of the earth which can stand against them. Will you bring this devastation upon these people? Look into your heart, man!'

'I will not argue with you, old man. Down there your men wait, and among them are the Templars – they who feed on the flesh of children. Your semi-human beasts gather in Drenan, and daily thousands of inno-cents pour into this small bastion of freedom. All of this gives the lie to your words. I am not even angry with you, Breight the Survivor! You sold your soul for a silk-covered couch. But I understand you – you are a frightened old man who has never lived because you never dared to live.

'In these mountains there is life and the air tastes like wine. You are right when you say we may not stand against the Joinings. We know that for we are not fools. There is no glory here; but we are men and the sons of men, and we bend the knee to no one. Why don't you join us, and learn even now of the joys of freedom?'

'Freedom? You are in a cage, Ananais. The Vagrians will not let you move east into their lands, and we wait in the west. You delude yourself. What price your freedom? In a matter of days the armies of the emperor will gather here, filling the plain. You have seen the Joinings of Ceska – well, there are more to come. Huge beasts, blended from the apes of the east, from the great bears of the north, from the wolves of the south. They strike like lightning and they feed on human flesh. Your pitiful force will be swept aside like dust before a storm. Tell me then of freedom, Ananais. I desire not the freedom of the grave.'

'And yet it comes to you, Breight, in every white hair, every decaying wrinkle. Death will stalk you and lay his cold hands upon your eyes. You cannot escape! Begone, little man, your day is done.'

Breight looked up at the defenders and opened his arms.

'Don't let this man deceive you!' he shouted. 'My lord Ceska is a man of honour and he will abide by his promise.'

'Go home and die!' said Ananais, turning on his heels and striding back to his men.

'Death will come to you before me,' screamed Breight, 'and his coming will be terrible.' Then the old man wheeled his horse and cantered down-hill.

'I think the war will start tomorrow,' muttered Thorn.

Ananais nodded and waved Decado to him. 'What do you think?'

Decado shrugged. 'We could not pierce the screen the Templars mounted.'

'Did they pierce ours?'

'No.'

'Then we start even,' said Ananais. 'But they have tried to win us with words. Now it will be swords and they will try to demoralise us by a sudden attack. The question is where, and what are we going to do about it?'

'Well,' said Decado, 'the great Tertullian was once asked what he would do if he was attacked by a man stronger, faster and infinitely more skilful than he.'

'What did he say?'

'He said he would cut off his damned head for being a liar.'

'Sounds good,' put in Thorn, 'but words are not worth pigs' droppings now.'

'You are right there,' said Ananais, grinning. 'So what do you suggest, mountain man?'

'Let's cut off their damned heads!'

The hut was bathed in a soft red glow as the log fire burned low. Ananais lay on the bed, his head resting on his arm. Valtaya sat beside him rubbing oil into his shoulders and back – kneading the muscles, loosening the knots of tension around his spine. Her fingers were strong and the slow rhythmic movements of her hands soothing. He sighed and fell into a half-sleep, dreaming dreams of brighter days.

As her fingers began to burn with fatigue, she lifted them from his broad back, pushing pressure on to her palms for a while. His breathing deepened. She covered him with a blanket and then pulled a chair alongside the bed and sat staring at his ruined face. The angry scar below his eye seemed cooler now, and dry; she gently smoothed oil on the skin. His breath made a snuffling sound as it was sucked through the oval holes where his nose should have been. Valtaya leaned back, sadness a growing ache within her. He was a fine man and did not deserve his fate. It had taken all her considerable nerve just to kiss him, and even now she could not gaze on his features without feeling revulsion. Yet she loved him.

Life was cruel and infinitely sorrowful.

She had slept with many men in her life. Once it had been a vocation, once a profession. During the latter time many ugly men had come to her and with them she had learned to hide her feelings. She was glad now of the lessons, for when she had removed Ananais' mask two sensations had struck her simultaneously. One was the awful horror of his mutilated face. The other was the terrible anxiety in his eyes. Strong as he was, in that moment he was made of crystal. Now she transferred her gaze to his hair – tightly curled gold thread, laced with silver. The Golden One! How handsome he once must have been. Like a god. She pushed a hand through her own fair hair, sweeping it away from her eyes.

Tired, she stood and stretched her back. The window was part open and she pushed it wide. Outside the valley was silent beneath a scimitar moon.

'I wish I was young again,' she whispered. 'I would have married that poet.'

Katan soared above the mountains and wished that his body could fly as high as his spirit. He wanted to taste the air, feel the harsh winds upon his skin. Below him the mountains of Skoda reared like spear-points. He flew higher and now the mountains took on another image. Katan smiled.

Skoda had become a stone rose with jagged petals on a field of green. Rings of towering granite, interlinking to create a gargantuan bloom.

To the north-east Katan could just make out the fortress of Delnoch, while to the south-east were the glittering cities of the Drenai. It was all so beautiful. From here there was no cruelty, no torture, no terror. No room here for men with small minds and limitless ambition.

He turned again to the rose of Skoda. The outer petals concealed nine valleys through which an army could march. He scanned them all, gauging the contours and the gradients, picturing lines of fighting men, charging horsemen, fleeing infantry. Committing the facts to memory, he moved on to the second ring of mountains. Here there were only four main valleys, but three treacherous passes threaded their way through to the open pastures and woodlands beyond.

At the centre of the rose the mountains bunched with only two access points from the east – the valleys known as Tarsk and Magadon.

His mission completed, Katan returned to his body and reported to Decado. He could offer no hope.

'There are nine main valleys and a score of other narrow passes on the outer ring. Even on the inner ring around Carduil there are two lines of attack. Our force could not hold even one. It is impossible to plan a defence that stands a one-in-twenty chance of success. And by success I mean standing off one attack.'

'Say nothing to anyone,' ordered Decado. 'I will speak to Ananais.'

'As you wish,' said Katan coolly.

Decado smiled gently. 'I am sorry, Katan.'

'For what?'

'For what I am,' answered the warrior, moving away up the hill until he reached the high ground overlooking several spreading valleys. This was good country – sheltered, peaceful. The ground was not rich, like the Sentran Plain to the north-east, but treated with care the farms prospered and the cattle grew fat on the grass of the timberlands.

Decado's family had been farmers far to the east and he guessed that the love of growing things had been planted in him at the moment of conception. He crouched down, digging his strong fingers into the earth at his feet. There was clay here and the grass grew lush and thick.

'May I join you?' asked Katan.

'Please do.'

The two men sat in silence for a while, watching distant cattle grazing on fertile slopes.

'I miss Abaddon,' said Katan suddenly.

'Yes, he was a good man.'

'He was a man with a vision. But he had no patience and only limited belief.'

'How can you say that?' asked Decado. 'He believed enough to form The Thirty once more.'

'Precisely! He decided that evil should be met with raw force. And yet our faith claims that evil can only be conquered by love.'

'That is insane. How do you deal with your enemies?'

'How better to deal with them than to make them your friends?' countered Katan.

'The words are pretty, the argument specious. You do not make a friend of Ceska – you become a slave or die.'

Katan smiled. 'And what does it matter? The Source governs all things and eternity mocks human life.'

'You think it doesn't matter if we die?'

'Of course it does not. The Source takes us and we live for ever.'

'And if there is no Source?' asked Decado.

'Then death is even more welcome. I do not hate Ceska. I pity him. He has built an empire of terror. And what does he achieve? Each day brings him closer to the grave. Is he content? Does he gaze with love on any single thing? He surrounds himself with warriors to protect him from assassins, then has warriors watching the warriors to sniff out traitors. But who watches the watchers? What a miserable existence!'

'So,' said Decado, 'the Thirty are not Source warriors at all?'

'They are if they believe.'

'You cannot have it all ways, Katan.'

The young man chuckled. 'Perhaps. How did you become a warrior?'

'All men are warriors, for life is a battle. The farmer battles drought, flood, sickness and blight. The sailor battles the sea and the storm. I didn't have the strength for that, so I fought men.'

'And who does the priest fight?'

Decado turned to face the earnest young man. 'The priest fights himself. He cannot look at a woman with honest lust without guilt burning into him. He cannot get drunk and forget. He cannot take a day just to soak in the glory of the world's beauty, without wondering if he should be engaged on some worthy deed.'

'For a priest, you have a low opinion of your brothers.'

'On the contrary, I have a very high opinion of them,' said Decado.

'You were very hard on Acuas. He really believed he was rescuing Abaddon's soul.'

'I know that, Katan. I admire him for it – all of you, in fact. I was angry with myself. It was not easy for me, for I don't have your faith. For me the Source is a mystery I cannot solve. And yet I promised Abaddon I would see his mission fulfilled. You are fine young men and I am merely an old warrior in love with death.'

'Do not be too hard on yourself. You are chosen. It is a great honour.'

653

'Happenstance! I came to the Temple and Abaddon read more into it than he should.'

'No,' said Katan. 'Think on this: you came on the day when one of our brothers died. More than that – you are not just a warrior, you are possibly the greatest swordsman of the age. You defeated the Templars single-handed. Even more, you developed talents with which the rest of us were born. You came to our rescue in the Castle of the Void. How can you not be the natural leader? And if you are . . . what brought you to us?'

Decado leaned back, staring at the gathering clouds.

'I think we are in for rain,' he remarked.

'Have you tried praying, Decado?'

'It would still rain.'

'Have you tried?' persisted the priest.

Decado sat up and sighed deeply. 'Of course I have tried. But I get no answers. I tried on the night you journeyed into the Void . . . but He would not answer me.'

'How can you say that? Did you not learn to soar on that night? Did you not find us through the mists of non-time? You think you did that in your own strength?'

'Yes I do.'

'Then you answered your own prayers?'

'Yes.'

Katan smiled. 'Then keep praying. Who knows the heights to which it will carry you?'

Now it was Decado's turn to chuckle. 'You mock me, young Katan! I will not have it. Just for that you can lead the prayers this evening – I think Acuas needs a rest.'

'It will be my pleasure.'

Across the fields Ananais spurred his black gelding into a gallop. Bending low over the beast's neck he urged it on, hooves drumming on the dry ground. For those few seconds of speed he forgot his problems, revelling in the freedom of the race. Behind him Galand and Thorn were neck and neck, but their mounts were no match for the gelding and Ananais reached the stream twenty lengths ahead. He leapt to the ground and patted the horse, keeping him from the water and walking him round to cool down. The others dismounted.

'Unfair!' said Galand. 'Your mount is hands higher and bred for speed.'

'But I weigh more than both of you together,' said Ananais.

Thorn said nothing, merely grinned crookedly and shook his head. He liked Ananais and welcomed the change which had come over him since the fair-haired woman had moved into his hut. He seemed more alive – more in tune with the world.

Love was like that. Thorn had been in love many times, and even at sixty-two he hoped for at least another two or three romances. There was a widow woman who had a farm in the high, lonely country to the north; he stopped there often for breakfast. She hadn't warmed to him yet, but she would – Thorn knew women. There was no point in rushing in . . . Gentle talk, that was the answer. Ask them questions about themselves . . . Be interested. Most men travelled through life determined to rut as swiftly as the woman would allow. Senseless! Talk first. Learn. Then touch, gently, lovingly. Care. Then love and linger. Thorn had learned early, for he had always been ugly. Other men disliked him for his success, but they could never be bothered to learn from it. Fools!

'Another caravan from Vagria this morning,' said Galand, scratching his beard. 'But the treasury gold is running low. Those cursed Vagrians have doubled their prices.'

'It's a seller's market,' said Ananais. 'What did they bring?'

'Arrowheads, iron, some swords. Mostly flour and sugar. Oh yes – and a quantity of leather and hide. Lake ordered it. There should be enough food to last a month . . . but no more.'

Thorn's dry chuckle stopped Galand in full flow.

'What's so funny?'

'If we are still alive in a month I will be happy to go hungry!'

'Are the refugees still coming in?' asked Ananais.

'Yes,' said Galand, 'but the numbers are shrinking. I think we can handle it. The army now musters at two thousand, but we are being stretched thin. I don't like sitting around waiting to react. The Dragon operated on the premise that the first blow was vital.'

'We have no choice,' answered Ananais, 'since we must hold as wide a line as possible during the next few weeks. If we draw back they will simply ride in. At the moment they are undecided what to do.'

'The men are getting edgy,' said Thorn. 'It's not easy just to sit – it makes them think, wonder, imagine. Rayvan's performing miracles, travelling from valley to valley, fuelling their courage and calling them heroes. But it may not be enough.

'The victory was heady stuff, Ananais, but those who missed the battle now outnumber the men who fought in it. They are untried. And they're nervous.'

'What do you suggest?'

Thorn grinned his crooked grin. 'I'm not a general, Darkmask. You tell *me*!'

15

Caphas moved away from the tents and spread his black cloak on the dry earth as a blanket. He removed his dark helm and settled himself down. The stars were bright, but Caphas had no eyes for them. The night was cool and clean, but he hated the emptiness. He longed for the sanctuary of the Temple and the drug-induced orgies. The music of the torture room, the sweet sound of a victim's plea. Joy was what he missed here in this barren land. Laughter.

A special relationship came into being between the torturer and his victim. First there was defiance and hatred. Then tears and screams. Then begging. And finally, after the spirit was broken, there was a kind of love. Caphas cursed loudly and stood up, arousal creating anger within him. He opened the small leather pouch on his hip and removed a long Lorassium leaf. Rolling it into a ball, he placed it in his mouth and began to chew slowly. As the juices took hold and his mind swam, he became aware of the dreams of the sleeping soldiers and the slow, hungry thoughts of a badger in the undergrowth to his right. He screened them out, forcing his memory to replay a scene from the recent past when they had brought a girl-child to the torture room . . .

Uneasiness flooded him and he jerked his mind to the present, eyes flickering to the dark shadows in the trees.

A bright light grew before him, shimmering and coalescing into the shape of a warrior in silver armour. A white cloak was draped across his shoulders, the edges fluttering in the winds of Spirit.

Caphas closed his eyes and leapt from his body, black soul-sword in hand, dark shield upon his arm. The warrior parried the blow and stepped back.

'Come here and die,' offered Caphas. 'Twelve of your party are dead already. Come and join them!'

The warrior said nothing and only his blue eyes could be seen through the slit in the silver face-helm. The eyes were calm and the quiet confidence emanating from them seeped into Caphas' heart. His shield shrank.

'You cannot touch me!' he screamed. 'The Spirit is stronger than the Source. You are powerless against me!'

The warrior shook his head.

'Damn you!' shouted Caphas as his shield disappeared. He charged forward, slashing wildly.

Acuas parried the blow with ease and then slid his own blade deep into the Templar's chest. The man gasped as the icy sword cloved his spirit flesh. Then his soul guttered and died and, beyond it, his body toppled to the earth.

Acuas vanished. Two hundred paces into the wood he opened the eyes of his body and sagged into the supporting arms of Decado and Katan.

'All the Templar guards are dead,' he said.

'Good work!' praised Decado.

'I feel strained by their evil. Even to touch them is to be as one accursed.'

Decado moved back silently to where Ananais waited with one hundred warriors. Thorn crouched to his left, Galand to his right. Fifty of the warriors were legion men of whom Ananais was unsure. Though he trusted Decado's instincts, the talents of The Thirty left him sceptical still. Tonight he would see whether these men were with him. He was uncomfortably aware of their swords around him.

Ananais led the force to the edge of the trees. Beyond lay the tents of the Delnoch army – one hundred of them – each giving shelter to six men. Beyond the tents were the picket ropes where the horses were tethered.

'I want Breight alive and I want those horses,' whispered Ananais. 'Galand, take fifty men and lead the mounts clear. The rest can follow me.' He moved forward, crouching low, his dark-armoured warriors spreading out behind him.

As they reached the tents the force split up, armed men silently lifting the front flaps and stepping stealthily inside. Daggers were drawn across sleeping throats and men died without a sound. At the edge of the camp, a sleeping soldier was awakened by the pressure of a full bladder; he rolled from his blanket and stepped out into the night air. The first thing he saw was a black-masked giant bearing down on him, followed by twenty swordsmen. He screamed once . . . and died.

Suddenly all was chaos as men surged from the tents with swords in hand. Ananais cut two warriors from his path and cursed loudly. Breight's tent was just ahead, blue silk bearing the White Horse emblem of the Drenai herald.

'To me, Legion!' he bellowed and ran forward. A soldier ran at him with a spear but Ananais side-stepped the weapon, his own sword sweeping viciously in a tight arc that smashed the man's ribs to shards. Ananais ran on, wrenching open the tent-flap and stepping inside. Breight was hiding below his bed, but Ananais dragged him out by his hair and hurled him into the night.

Old Thorn ran to Ananais as he emerged. 'We are in a little trouble, Darkmask,' he said.

The Legion fifty had closed ranks by Breight's tent, but all around them the Delnoch warriors stood ready, waiting the order to move in. Ananais dragged Breight to his feet and pushed his way to the front of the line.

'Order your men to lay down their weapons or I will cut your miserable throat,' he hissed.

'Yes, yes,' whimpered the greybeard, holding up his hands. 'Men of Ceska, lay aside your weapons. My life is too valuable to be thrown away in such a fashion. Let them go, I command you!'

A Dark Templar stepped from the line. 'You are worth nothing, old man! You had one mission – to talk these dogs from the hills. You failed.' His arm swept back, then down, and a black dagger hammered into Breight's throat. The old man staggered and fell to his knees. 'Now take

657

them!' yelled the Templar and the Delnoch men surged forward. Ananais cut and thrust as the forces met, drawing the enemy to him like moths to a candle. His swords flickered among them faster than the eye could follow. Around him the Legion fought hard and well, and old Thorn ducked and cut cunningly.

Suddenly the thunder of hooves overrode the sounds of clashing steel and the Delnoch line wavered as men glanced back to see a fresh force racing into the fray.

Galand's group hit the rear of the Delnoch force like a hammer-blow, scattering the enemy. As Ananais ran forward, yelling for the men to follow him, a sword lanced into his side. He grunted and back-handed a cut that swept the attacker from his feet. Decado spurred his horse towards Ananais, holding out his left arm. Ananais grasped it and vaulted to the saddle behind the priest. Other Legion men followed suit and the Skoda warriors galloped from the camp. Ananais glanced back, seeking Thorn, and spotted him clinging to Galand.

'He's certainly a tough old man!' said Ananais.

Decado said nothing. He had just received a report from Balan, whose task had been to scout the land over Drenan in order to study the marshalling of Ceska's main force. The news was not good.

Ceska had wasted no time.

The Joinings were already on the march and there was no way Tenaka Khan could bring a Nadir force to intercept them.

According to Balan the army would be camped by the Skoda valleys in four days.

All Tenaka could do was avenge them, for no force on earth was going to hold the werebeasts of Ceska.

Ananais rode into the city, holding himself straight in the saddle though weariness sat upon him like a boulder. He had spent a day and two nights with his lieutenants and their section leaders, informing them of Ceska's lightning march. Many leaders would have disguised the threat, fearing desertions and loss of morale, but Ananais had never subscribed to that theory. Men waiting to die had every right to know what lay in store.

But now he was tired.

The city was quiet, for dawn was only two hours old, but even so children gathered to play in the street, halting their game to watch Dark-mask ride by. His horse almost lost its footing on the shiny cobbles and Ananais pulled up its head and patted its neck.

'Almost as tired as me – eh, boy?'

An old man, thickset and balding, stepped from a garden to the right. His face was flushed and angry.

'You!' he shouted, pointing at the rider. Ananais halted his mount and the man came forward, some twenty children bunching behind him.

'You want to talk to me, friend?'

'I am no friend to you, butcher! I just wanted you to see these children.'

'Well, I have seen them. They are a fine bunch.'

'Fine, are they? Their parents were fine, but now they're rotting in the Demon's Smile. And for what? So that you can play with a shiny sword!'

'Have you finished?'

'Not by a damn sight! What is going to happen to these children when the Joinings arrive? I was a soldier once and I know you can't hold those hell-beasts – they will come into this city and destroy every living thing. What will happen to these children then?'

Ananais touched his heels to his mount and the horse moved away.

'That's right!' yelled the man. 'Ride away from the problem. But remember their faces – you hear me?'

Ananais rode on through the winding streets until he reached the Council building. A young man came forward to take his horse and Ananais mounted the marble steps.

Rayvan sat alone in the hall staring – as she often did – at the faded mural. She had lost weight in the last few days. Once more she was wearing the chain-mail shirt and broad belt, her dark hair swept back and tied at her neck.

She smiled as she saw Ananais and gestured him to a chair beside her. 'Welcome, Darkmask,' she said. 'If you have bad news, hold on to it for a little while. I have enough of my own.'

'What happened?' asked Ananais.

She waved her hand and closed her eyes, unable to speak. Then she took a deep breath, exhaling slowly. 'Is the sun shining?' she asked.

'It is, lady.'

'Good! I like to see the sun on the mountains. It carries a promise of life. Have you eaten?'

'No.'

'Then let us go to the kitchen and find something. We will eat in the tower garden.'

They sat in the shade of a thick flowering shrub. Rayvan had picked up a black loaf and some cheese, but neither of them ate. The silence itself was comforting.

'I hear you were lucky to escape with your life,' said Rayvan at last. 'How is your side?'

'I heal fast, lady. The wound was not deep and the stitches will hold.'

'My son, Lucas – he died last night. We had to remove his leg . . . gangrene.'

'I'm so sorry,' said Ananais lamely.

'He was very brave. Now there is only Lake and Ravenna. Soon there will be no one. How did we come to this, Darkmask, tell me?'

'I don't know. We let a crazy man come to power.'

'Did we truly? It seems to me that a man has only as much power as we allow him. Can Ceska move mountains? Can he put out the stars? Can he tell rain to fall? He is only a man and if everyone disobeyed him he would fall. But they don't, do they? It is said that he has an army of forty thousand men. MEN! Drenai men, ready to march on other Drenai men. At least in the Nadir Wars we were sure of our enemy. Now there is no enemy. Only failed friends.'

'What can I say?' asked Ananais. 'I have no answers. You should have asked Tenaka. I am just a warrior. I remember a tutor who told me that all of the world's hunters had eyes that faced front: lions, hawks, wolves, men. And all the world's prey had eyes on either side to give them a greater chance of spotting the hunter. He said Man was no different from the tiger. We are nature's killers and we have great appetites for it. Even the heroes we remember show our love of war. Druss, the greatest killing machine of all time – it is his image you stare upon in the council chamber.'

'True enough,' said Rayvan. 'But there is a difference between Druss and Ceska. The legend fought always for others to be free.'

'Don't fool yourself, Rayvan. Druss fought because he loved to fight – it was what he did well. Study his history. He went east and battled for the tyrant Gorben; his army razed cities, villages, nations. Druss was part of it, and he would have offered no excuses. Neither should you.'

'Are you saying there never were true heroes?'

'I wouldn't know a hero if he bit my buttocks! Listen Rayvan, the beast is in all of us. We do our best in life, but often we are mean, or petty, or needlessly cruel. We don't mean to be, but that's the way we *are*. Most of the heroes we remember – we remember because they won. To win you must be ruthless. Single-minded. Druss was like that, which was why he had no friends – just admirers.'

'Can we win, Ananais?'

'No. But what we can do is to make Ceska suffer so greatly that someone else might win. We shall not live to see Tenaka return. Ceska is already on the march; but we must tie him down, give him losses – crack the aura of invincibility he has built around his Joinings.'

'But even the Dragon could not stand against the beasts.'

'The Dragon was betrayed, caught on open ground. And many of them were old men. Fifteen years is a long time. They were not the real Dragon. We are the real Dragon – and by the Gods, we'll make them suffer!'

'Lake has devised some weapons he wants you to see.'

'Where is he?'

'In the old stables at the southern quarter. But take some rest first – you look exhausted.'

'I will.' He pushed himself to his feet, staggered slightly and then laughed. 'I'm getting old, Rayvan.' He moved away several paces, then returned and placed his huge right hand on her shoulder. 'I am not good at sharing, lady. But I'm sorry about Lucas. He was a good man – a credit to you.'

'Go and get some rest. The days are growing shorter and you will need your strength. I'm relying on you – we are all relying on you.'

After he had gone she wandered to the wall and gazed out over the mountains.

Death felt very close.

And she didn't care.

Tenaka Khan was sick with fury. His hands were tied tightly with rawhide thongs and his body was lashed to the trunk of a slender elm. Before him five men sat around a camp-fire searching through his saddlebags. His small cache of gold had been discovered and now lay next to the leader – a one-eyed rogue, thickset and surly. Tenaka blinked away the thin stream of blood that trickled into his right eye and closed his mind to the pain of his bruises.

He had been too preoccupied as he rode into the forest and a stone from a sling had hammered into his temple, toppling him from his horse semi-conscious. Even then, as the outlaws rushed him he had drawn his sword and killed one before they bore him down, hitting him with clubs and sticks. The last words he heard before darkness fell were, 'He killed my brother. Don't kill him – I want him alive.'

And here he was, less than four days out of Skoda, tied to a tree and moments away from a gruesome death. Frustration tore at him and he wrenched at the ropes, but they were expertly tied. His legs ached and his back burned.

The one-eyed outlaw stood up and walked to the tree, his face a mask of bitterness.

'You pig-rutting barbarian – you killed my brother!'

Tenaka said nothing.

'Well, you will pay for it. I shall cut you into tiny pieces, then cook your flesh on that fire and force you to eat it. How do you like that?'

Tenaka ignored him and the man's fist lashed out. Tenaka tensed the muscles of his stomach just as the blow struck, but the pain was terrible. As his head sagged the man hit him in the side of the face.

'Speak to me, Nadir dung!' hissed the outlaw.

Tenaka spat blood to the ground and licked his swollen lip.

'You will talk to me; before dawn I will have you singing a sweet song.'

'Cut out his eyes, Baldur!' said one of the outlaws.

'No. I want him to see everything.'

'Just one, then,' urged the man.

'Yes,' said Baldur. 'Maybe just one.' He drew his dagger and moved forward. 'How would you like that, Nadir? One of your eyes dangling from your cheek?'

A ghostly cry echoed into the night, high-pitched and eerie.

'What in the seven Hells was that?' said Baldur, spinning round. The others made the sign of the Protective Horn and reached for their weapons.

'It sounded close,' said one, a short man with a sandy beard.

'Cat, maybe. Sounded like it could be a cat,' said Baldur. 'Build up the fire.' Two men scurried forward, gathering up dry wood as Baldur turned back to Tenaka. 'You ever heard that sound before, Nadir?'

Tenaka nodded.

'Well, what is it?'

'Forest demon,' said Tenaka.

'Don't tell me that! I've lived in forests all my life.'

Tenaka shrugged.

'Whatever it is, I don't like it,' said Baldur. 'So you don't die so slow.

I'll just open up your belly and you can bleed to death. Or maybe the forest demon will get you!'

His arm drew back . . .

A black feathered arrow appeared in his throat and for a moment he just stood there, as if stunned. Then he dropped his knife and slowly reached up to feel the shaft. His eyes widened, then his knees gave way and he pitched to the earth. A second arrow flashed across the clearing, taking the sandy-haired outlaw in the right eye. He fell screaming. The remaining three raced for the sanctuary of the forest, their weapons forgotten. For a while there was silence, then a little figure stepped from the trees with bow in hand.

She was wearing a tunic and troos in light brown leather, and a green burnoose covered her hair. A short, slender sword hung at her side.

'How are you, Tenaka?' asked Renya sweetly.

'I am certainly happy to see you,' he answered. 'Loose me.'

'Loose you?' she said, squatting by the fire. 'A big strong man like you. Come, now! Surely you don't need a woman's help?'

'Now is the wrong time for this conversation, Renya. Untie me.'

'And then do I come with you?'

'Of course,' he said, knowing he had no choice.

'You're sure I won't be a hindrance?'

Tenaka gritted his teeth, struggling to control his anger as Renya walked round the tree and slashed the rawhide with her shortsword. Tenaka stumbled and fell as the ropes gave way and she helped him to the fire.

'How did you find me?'

'It wasn't hard,' she hedged. 'How are you feeling?'

'Alive. Just! I shall have to be more careful once we cross the mountains.'

Renya's head came up, nostrils flaring. 'They're coming back,' she said.

'Damn! Get me my sword.' He glanced round but she had gone, vanished into the trees. He cursed and staggered to his feet, scooping up his sword from the far side of the fire. He felt in no condition to fight.

The terrible howling began again and his blood froze. Then Renya walked back into the clearing with a broad smile on her face.

'They're running so fast now, I don't think they will stop until they reach the sea,' she said. 'Why don't you get some sleep?'

'How do you do that?'

'It is a talent I have,' said Renya.

'I underestimated you, woman,' said Tenaka, stretching himself out beside the fire.

'The cry of men down the ages,' muttered Renya.

Night was falling once more when Renya and Tenaka sighted the deserted fortress of Dros Corteswain, nestling in the shadows of the Delnoch mountains. Built as a defence against Vagrian invasion during the days of Egel, the first Earl of Bronze, the fortress had been disused for more than forty years. The town that had sprung up around it was also deserted.

662

'Eerie isn't it?' said Renya as she guided her grey mare close in to Tenaka.

'Corteswain was always folly,' answered Tenaka, gazing up at the bleak battlements. 'Egel's only mistake. It is the one fortress in the Drenai that has never seen a battle.'

Their horses' hooves echoed in the night as they walked towards the main gates. The wood had been removed and the stone opening beckoned to them like a toothless mouth.

'Couldn't we camp in the open?' asked Renya.

'Too many forest demons,' said Tenaka, ducking as she swiped a blow at his head.

'Halt!' called a quavering voice and Tenaka's eyes narrowed.

In the open gateway stood an old man in rusty mailshirt. In his hands was a spear with a broken point. Tenaka reined in his mount.

'Give your name, rider!' called the old man.

'I am Bladedancer. This is my wife.'

'Are you friendly?'

'We are no threat to any man who does not threaten us.'

'Then you can come in,' said the old man. 'The Gan says it's all right.'

'Are you the Gan of Dros Corteswain?' asked Tenaka.

'No. This is the Gan,' said the old man, pointing to the space beside him. 'Can't you see?'

'Of course, forgive me! My compliments to your commanding officer.'

Tenaka rode in to the gateway and dismounted. The old man limped towards him. He looked as if he must be over eighty and his hair was wispy and thin, clinging to his yellow skull like mountain mist. His face was sunken and blue shadows spread beneath his watery eyes.

'Make no false move,' he warned. 'Look you to the battlements. There are archers covering your every step.' Tenaka glanced up – the ramparts were deserted, save for sleeping pigeons.

'Very efficient,' he said. 'Is there food here?'

'Oh yes. For those that's welcome.'

'Are we welcome?'

'The Gan says you look like a Nadir.'

'I am indeed, but I have the honour to serve in the army of the Drenai. I am Tenaka Khan of the Dragon. Will you introduce me to the Gan?'

'There are two Gans,' said the old man. 'This is Gan Orrin – he is the first Gan. Hogun is our scout.'

Tenaka bowed deeply. 'I have heard of Gan Orrin. My compliments on your defence of Dros Delnoch.'

'The Gan says you are welcome and may join him in his quarters. I am his aide. My name is Ciall – Dun Ciall.'

The old man put down his broken spear and wandered away to the darkened keep. Tenaka loosened the saddle-cinch and left his horse to wander in search of grass. Renya followed suit and they set off after Dun Ciall.

'He's mad!' said Renya. 'There's no one else here.'

'He seems harmless enough. And he must have food. I'd as soon save

663

as many of our supplies as I can. Listen – the men he is referring to are the original Gans of Dros Delnoch when my ancestor fought Ulric. Orrin and Hogun were the commanders before Rek became the Earl of Bronze. Humour him – it will be a kindness.'

In the Gan's quarters Ciall had set out a table for three. A jug of red wine was placed at the centre and a stew was bubbling in a pot over the fire. With trembling hands the old man filled their plates, said a prayer to the Source and set to with a wooden spoon. Tenaka tried the stew; it was bitter, but not unpleasant.

'They're all dead,' said Ciall. 'I am not mad – I know they're dead but they're here just the same.'

'If you see them, then they are here,' said Renya.

'Don't humour me, woman! I see them and they tell me stories . . . Wonderful stories. They forgave me. People didn't, but ghosts are better than people. They know more. They know a man can't be strong all the time. They know there are some times when he can't help running away. They forgave me – said I could be a soldier. They trust me to look after the fortress.'

Ciall winced suddenly and gripped his side. Renya looked down and saw blood flowing into the rust and dripping to the bench seat.

'You are hurt,' she said.

'It's nothing. I don't feel it. I am a good soldier now – they tell me that.'

'Remove your mailshirt,' said Tenaka softly.

'No. I am on duty.'

'Remove it, I say!' thundered Tenaka. 'Am I not a Gan? There will be no lack of discipline while I am here.'

'Yes sir,' said Ciall, fumbling with the ancient strap. Renya stepped forward to help him and slowly the mailshirt came away. The old man made no sound. His back was raw with the marks of a whip. Renya searched the drawers and cupboards, finding an old shirt. 'I'll get some water,' she said.

'Who did this to you, Ciall?' asked Tenaka.

'Riders . . . yesterday. They were looking for someone.' The old man's eyes glittered. 'They were looking for you, Nadir prince.'

'I expect they were.'

Renya returned carrying a copper bowl brimming with water. Gently she washed the old man's back, then tore the shirt into strips to place over the worst of the wounds.

'Why did they whip you?' Did they think you knew of my whereabouts?'

'No,' said Ciall sadly. 'I think they just enjoyed it. The ghosts could do nothing. But they were sorry for me – they said I bore it bravely.'

'Why do you stay here, Ciall?' asked Renya.

'I ran away, lady. When the Nadir were attacking I ran away. There was nowhere else to go.'

'How long have you been here?'

'A long, long time. Years probably. It's very nice here, with lots of people to talk to. They forgave me, you see. And what I do here is important.'

'What is it you do?' asked Tenaka.

'I guard the stone of Egel. It is placed by the gate and it says that the Drenai empire will fall when Corteswain is manned no more. Egel knew things. He's been here, you know, but I wasn't allowed to see him when he came; I hadn't been here long then and the ghosts didn't trust me yet.'

'Go to sleep, Ciall,' said Tenaka. 'You need your rest.'

'First I must hide your horses,' said Ciall. 'The riders will be coming back.'

'I will do that,' promised Tenaka. 'Renya, help him into bed.'

'I can't sleep here – it's the Gan's bed.'

'Orrin says that you can – he's going to meet Hogun and will share his quarters tonight.'

'He's a good man,' said Ciall. 'I'm proud to serve under him. They're all good men – even though they're dead.'

'Rest, Ciall. We will talk in the morning.'

'Are you the Nadir prince who led the charge on the Ventrian raiders near Purdol?'

'I am.'

'Do you forgive me?'

'I forgive you,' said Tenaka Khan. 'Now sleep.'

Tenaka awoke to the sound of galloping hooves on the cold stone of the courtyard. Kicking aside his blanket, he woke Renya and together they crawled to the window. Below some twenty riders were grouped together; they wore the red capes of Delnoch and shining helms of bronze topped with black horse-hair plumes. The leader was a tall man with a trident beard and beside him was one of the outlaws who had captured Tenaka.

Ciall limped out into the courtyard, broken spear in hand.

'Halt!' he said. His arrival broke the tension and the riders began to laugh.

The leader raised his hand for silence and then leaned forward over his horse's neck.

'We seek two riders, old man. Are they here?'

'You are not welcome at the fortress. The Gan commands you to leave.'

'Did you not learn your lesson yesterday, fool?'

'Must we force you to go?' countered Ciall.

The outlaw leaned over to whisper something and the leader nodded. He turned in the saddle. 'The tracker says that they are here. Take the old man and get him to talk.'

Two riders began to dismount. Ciall screamed a battle cry and ran forward; the officer was still half turned when the broken spear rammed into his side. He screamed and half-fell. Ciall dragged the spear loose and hacked at him once more, but a rider to the left dipped his lance and spurred his mount forward and Ciall was lifted from his feet as the iron tip plunged into him. The lance snapped and the old man fell to the stones.

The officer hauled himself upright in the saddle. 'Get me away from here; I'm bleeding to death!' he said.

'What about the riders?' asked the tracker.

'Damn them! We have men spread out from here to Delnoch and they can't escape. Get me away from here!' The tracker took the officer's reins and the troop cantered back through the gates. Tenaka raced out to the courtyard, kneeling beside the mortally wounded Ciall.

'You did well, Dun Ciall,' he said, lifting the man's head.

Ciall smiled. 'They've done it now,' he said. 'The stone.'

'You will still be here. With the Gan and the rest.'

'Yes. The Gan has a message for you, but I don't understand it.'

'What does he say?'

'He says to seek the King Beyond the Gate. You understand?'

'Yes I do.'

'I had a wife once . . .' whispered Ciall. And died.

Tenaka closed the old man's eyes; then lifted the frail body and carried it to the shade of the gate tower, laying it to rest beneath the stone of Egel. He placed the broken spear in the dead man's hand.

'Last night,' he said, 'he prayed to the Source. I don't know enough to believe in any god, but if you are there then I pray you will take his soul into your service. He was not an evil man.'

Renya was waiting in the courtyard when he returned.

'Poor man,' she said. He took her in his arms and kissed her brow.

'Time to go,' he told her.

'You heard what they said – there are riders everywhere.'

'First they must see us. Secondly they must catch us. We are only an hour's ride from the mountains, and where I go they will not follow.'

Throughout the long morning they rode, hugging the tree-line and moving carefully out on to open ground, avoiding the sky-lines. Twice they saw riders in the distance. By midday they had reached the base of the Delnoch peaks and Tenaka led them up into the high country. By dusk the horses were exhausted and the riders dismounted, seeking a place to camp.

'Are you sure we can cross here?' asked Renya, wrapping her cloak tightly about her.

'Yes. But we may not be able to take the horses.'

'It's cold.'

'It will get colder. We have maybe another three thousand feet to climb yet.'

Throughout the night they huddled together beneath their blankets. Tenaka slept fitfully. The task he had set himself was awesome. Why should the Nadir follow him? They hated him more than the Drenai did. The two-worlds warrior! He opened his violet eyes and watched the stars, waiting for the dawn.

It arrived in garish splendour, bathing the sky in crimson – a giant wound that seeped from the east. After a hurried breakfast they set off once more, moving ever higher into the peaks.

Three times during the morning they dismounted to rest the horses, leading them on over the patchy snow. Far below them Renya glimpsed the red cloaks of the Delnoch riders.

'They've found us!' she shouted.

Tenaka turned. 'They're too far back. Don't worry about them.'

An hour before dusk they breasted a rise. Before them the ground dropped away alarmingly. To the left a narrow trail hugged a sheer wall of icy rock; nowhere was the trail wider than six feet.

'We're not going to cross that?' asked Renya.

'Yes.'

Tenaka touched his heels to his mount and moved out. Almost at once the horse slipped, then righted itself. Tenaka kept up its head and began talking to the beast in a low soothing voice. His left leg was touching the rock wall, his right over the awesome drop; he did not dare swing his weight to see if Renya was following. The horse moved on slowly, its ears flat against its skull and its eyes wide in fear. Unlike the Nadir or Sathuli ponies, it had not been bred for mountain work.

The trail wound round the mountains, widening in some places and narrowing sickeningly in others, until at last they came to a slanting sheet of ice across their path. Tenaka had just enough room to slide from the saddle and he moved forward slowly, kneeling to examine the ice. The surface was powdery with fresh-fallen snow, but beneath it was glossy and sheer.

'Can we go back?' called Renya.

'No, there is nowhere to turn the horses. And the Delnoch riders will have reached the trail. We must go on.'

'Across that?'

'We must lead the horses,' said Tenaka. 'But if it starts to go, don't hold on. You understand?'

'This is stupid,' she said, staring down at the rocks hundreds of feet below.

'I couldn't agree more,' he answered with a wry grimace. 'Keep to the cliff face and don't curl the reins around your hand – hold them loosely. Ready?'

Tenaka stepped out on to the sloping ice, placing his foot carefully on the powdery snow.

He tugged on the reins, but the horse refused to budge; its eyes were wide with fear and it was close to panic. Tenaka stepped back, curling his arm over the beast's neck and whispering in its ear.

'There is no problem for you, noble heart,' he whispered. 'You have courage in your soul. It is merely a difficult path. I will be here with you.' For some minutes he spoke thus, patting and stroking the sleek neck. 'Trust me, great one. Walk with me for a little while.'

He stepped out on to the slope and pulled the reins and the horse moved forward. Slowly, and with great care, they left the safety of the trail.

Renya's horse slipped, but recovered its footing. Tenaka heard the commotion but could not look back. Solid rock was only inches away, but as Tenaka stepped on to it his horse slithered suddenly, whinnying in

667

terror. Tenaka grabbed the reins tightly with his right hand, his left snaking out to the cliff face and hooking round a jutting edge of rock.

As the horse slid back towards the drop, Tenaka felt the muscles across his back tighten and tear. It seemed his arms were being torn from their sockets. He wanted to let go of the reins, but could not; instinctively he had curled the leather round his wrist and if the horse fell, he would be drawn with it.

As suddenly as it had lost its footing the beast found a solid section of rock, and with Tenaka's help struggled back to the trail. Tenaka sagged against the cliff face. The horse nuzzled him and he patted it. His wrist was bleeding where the leather had burned through the skin.

'Stupid!' said Renya, leading her horse to the safety of the trail.

'I cannot deny it,' he said, 'but we made it. From here on the trail widens and there are few natural dangers now. And I do not think the Drenai will follow us over this path.'

'I think you were born lucky, Tenaka Khan. But don't use up all your luck before we reach the Nadir.'

They made camp in a shallow cave and fed the horses before lighting a fire with brushwood they had strapped to their saddles. Tenaka stripped off his leather jerkin and lay down on a blanket by the fire while Renya massaged his bruised back. The struggle to keep the horse from falling had taken its toll and the Nadir prince could hardly move his right arm. Renya gently probed the shoulder-blade and the swollen muscles around it.

'You are a mess,' she said. 'Your body is a patchwork of bruises.'

'You should feel them from this side.'

'You are getting too old for this,' she said mischievously.

'A man is as old as he feels, woman!' he snapped.

'And how old do you feel?'

'About ninety,' he admitted. She covered him with a blanket and sat staring out at the night. It was peaceful here, away from war and the talk of war. Truthfully she did not care about overthrowing Ceska – she did care about being with Tenaka Khan. Men were so stupid; they didn't understand the reality of life at all.

Love was what mattered. Love of one for one. The touching of hands, the touching of hearts. The warmth of belonging, the joy of sharing. There would always be tyrants. Man seemed incapable of existing without them. For without tyrants there would be no heroes. And Man could not live without heroes.

Renya wrapped herself in her cloak and added the last of the wood to the fire. Tenaka lay asleep, his head resting on his saddle.

'Where would you be without Ceska, my love?' she asked him, knowing he could not hear her. 'I think you need him more than you need me.'

His violet eyes opened and he smiled sleepily.

'Not true,' he said. Then his eyes closed once more.

'Liar,' she whispered, curling up beside him.

16

Scaler, Belder and Pagan lay on their bellies overlooking the Drenai camp. There were twenty soldiers sitting around five camp-fires. The prisoners sat back-to-back at the centre of the camp and sentries patrolled near them.

'Are you sure this is necessary?' asked Belder.

'It is,' Scaler told him. 'If we rescue two Sathuli warriors, it will give us a great advantage in seeking aid from the tribesmen.'

'They look too well-guarded to me,' muttered the older man.

'I agree,' said Pagan. 'There is one guard within ten paces of the prisoners. Two others patrol the edge of the trees and a fourth has positioned himself in the forest.'

'Could you find him?'

Pagan grinned. 'Of course. But what of the other three?'

'Find the one in the forest and bring me his armour,' said Scaler.

Pagan slipped away and Belder slithered across to lie beside Scaler. 'You're not going down there?'

'Of course. It's a deception – that's something I am good at.'

'You won't be able to pull it off. We shall be taken.'

'Please, Belder, no morale-boosting speeches – you will make me conceited.'

'Well, I'm not going down there.'

'I don't recall asking you.'

It was almost half an hour before Pagan returned. He was carrying the sentry's clothes wrapped in the man's red cloak.

'I hid the body as best I could,' he said. 'How soon will they change the guards?'

'An hour – maybe a little less,' said Belder. 'There's not enough time.'

Scaler opened the bundle, examined the contents and then buckled on the breastplate. It was a poor fit but better too large than too small, he thought.

'How do I look?' he asked, placing the plumed helm upon his head.

'Ridiculous,' said Belder. 'You won't fool them for a minute.'

'Old man,' hissed Pagan, 'you are a pain in the ears! We have only been together three days and already I am sick of you. Now close your mouth.'

Belder was about to whisper a cutting reply, but the look in the black man's eyes stopped him dead. The man was ready to kill him! His blood froze and he turned away.

'What is your plan?' asked Pagan.

'There are three guards, but only one near the prisoners. I intend to relieve him.'

'And the other two?'

'That's as far as I have worked it out.'

'It is a beginning,' said Pagan. 'If the first part works, and the man takes to his blankets, move across to the other two. Keep your knife handy and make your move when I make mine.'

Scaler licked his lips. Keep your knife handy? He wasn't sure he would have the nerve to plunge the blade into someone's body.

Together the two men crept through the undergrowth towards the camp. The moon was bright, but the occasional cloud masked it, plunging the clearing into darkness. The fires had burned low and the warriors were sleeping soundly.

Pagan put his mouth close to Scaler's ear and whispered: 'It's about ten paces to the first sleeping soldier. The next time a cloud passes the moon, move forward and lie down. When the clouds clear, sit up and stretch. Make sure the sentry sees you.' Scaler nodded.

Minutes passed in silent tension until at last darkness fell once more. Immediately Scaler was up and moving, hitting the ground just as the moon shone clear again.

He sat up and stretched his arms wide, waving to the sentry. Then he stood, looked around and gathered up a lance from beside a sleeping warrior. Taking a deep breath he walked across the clearing, yawning.

'Couldn't sleep,' he told the man. 'Ground is damp.'

'You should try standing here for a while,' grumbled the sentry.

'Why not?' offered Scaler. 'Go on – get some sleep. I'll take the watch.'

'Mighty large of you,' said the man. 'I'm due to be relieved soon.'

'Your choice,' said Scaler, yawning once more.

'I haven't seen you before,' said the man. 'Who are you with?'

Scaler grinned. 'Picture a man with the face of a pig with warts, and the brain of a retarded pigeon.'

'Dun Gideus,' said the man. 'Bad luck!'

'I've known worse,' commented Scaler.

'I've not,' said the man. 'I think there's a special place where they breed the fools. I mean – why attack the Sathuli? As if there are not enough pox-ridden problems in the Skoda. Baffles me!'

'Me too,' said Scaler. 'Still, as long as the pay comes through . . .'

'You had yours then? I've been waiting four months,' said the man, outraged.

'It was a joke,' said Scaler. 'Of course I haven't!'

'Don't joke about that, man. There's enough trouble brewing as it is.'

A second sentry joined them. 'Cal, is that the relief?'

'No, he just couldn't sleep.'

'Well, I'm going to wake them up. I've had enough of standing around,' said the second soldier.

'Don't be a fool,' advised the first. 'You wake up Gideus and we'll be for a flogging!'

'Why don't you go off and get some rest?' offered Scaler. 'I can stand watch – I'm wide awake.'

'Damn it, I think I will,' said the first man. 'I'm dead on my feet.

670

Thanks, friend,' he said, clapping Scaler on the shoulder before wandering away to lie down with the others.

'If you want to put your head down in the forest, I'll wake you when I see the relief getting ready,' suggested Scaler.

'No, thanks anyway. The last time a watchman was found asleep, Gideus had him hanged. Bastard! I won't take that risk.'

'Whatever you like,' said Scaler indifferently, his heart hammering.

'Bastards have cancelled leave again,' said the sentry. 'I haven't seen my wife and youngsters in four months.' Scaler eased his knife into his hand. 'Farm's not doing too well. Bastard taxes! Still, at least I'm alive, I suppose.'

'Yes, that's something,' agreed Scaler.

'Life's a pig, isn't it? Any time now they're going to send us into the Skoda, killing a few more of our own. Life's a pig and no mistake!'

'Yes.' Holding the knife behind his back, Scaler adjusted his grip, ready to hammer the blade into the man's throat.

Suddenly the man swore. 'I will take you up on that offer,' he said. 'This is the third night they've put me on watch. But promise you'll wake me?'

'I promise,' said Scaler, relief washing over him.

But then Pagan moved from the shadow, whipping his knife across the other sentry's throat. Scaler reacted instantly – his own blade slashing upwards, entering the man's neck under the jaw-line and plunging on into the brain. He sank without a sound, but Scaler caught the look in his eyes as he died, and looked away.

Pagan ran across to him. 'Good work. Let's free the prisoners and get away from here.'

'He was a good man,' whispered Scaler.

Pagan gripped him by the shoulders. 'There are a lot of good men dead in Skoda. Get a hold . . . Let's move.'

The two prisoners had watched the killings in silence. Both wore the robes of Sathuli tribesmen and had their faces part hidden by flowing burnooses. Pagan moved to them, his knife slashing through their bonds; Scaler joined them, kneeling by the first warrior as the man pulled the burnoose sash from his face and took a deep breath. His face was strong and dark, a curved nose above a full black beard; his eyes were deep-set and seemingly black in the moonlight.

'Why?' he said.

'We'll talk later,' said Scaler. 'Our horses are over there. Move quietly.'

The two Sathuli followed as they moved into the darkness of the forest. Minutes later they found Belder and the mounts.

'Now tell me why,' repeated the Sathuli.

'I want you to take me to your camp. I need to speak to the Sathuli.'

'You have nothing to say to which we would listen.'

'You cannot know that,' said Scaler.

'I know that you are Drenai and that is enough.'

'You know nothing,' said Scaler, lifting the helm from his head and hurling it into the undergrowth. 'But I will not argue with you now. Get on a horse and take me to your people.'

'Why should I?'

'Because of who I am. You owe me a debt.'

'I owe you nothing. I did not ask to be freed.'

'Not that debt. Listen to me, child of man! I have returned from the Mountains of the Dead, across the mists of the centuries. Look in my eyes. Can you see the horrors of Sheol? I dined there with Joachim, the greatest of Sathuli princes. You will take me into the mountains and let your leader decide. By the soul of Joachim, you owe me that much!'

'It is easy to speak of the great Joachim,' said the man uneasily, 'since he has been dead more than one hundred years.'

'He is not dead,' said Scaler. 'His spirit lives and it is sickened by Sathuli cowardice. He asked me to give you a chance to redeem yourselves – but it is up to you.'

'And who do you say you are?'

'You will find my likeness in your burial chambers, standing beside Joachim. Look at my face, man, and tell me who I am.'

The Sathuli licked his lips, uncertain and yet filled with superstitious fear.

'You are the Earl of Bronze?'

'I am Regnak, the Earl of Bronze. *Now* take me into the mountains!'

They rode through the night, cutting left into the Delnoch range and up through many passes, winding into the heart of the mountains. Four times they were intercepted by Sathuli scouts, but always they were allowed on. At last, as the morning sun reached the heights of midday, they rode into the inner city – a thousand white stone buildings filling the bowl of a hidden valley. Only one building stood higher than a single storey and this was the palace of Sathuli.

Scaler had never been here. Few Drenai had. Children gathered to watch them pass and as they approached the palace some fifty white-robed warriors carrying curved tulwars joined them, lining up on either side. At the palace gates a man waited, arms folded across his chest. He was tall and broad-shouldered and his face was proud.

Scaler halted his horse before the gates and waited. The man unfolded his arms and walked forward, dark brown eyes fixed firmly on Scaler's.

'You say you are a dead man?' asked the Sathuli. Scaler waited, saying nothing. 'If that is so, you will not mind if I pass my sword through your body?'

'I can die like any man,' said Scaler. 'I did it once before. But you will not kill me, so let us stop playing these games. Obey your own laws of hospitality and offer us food.'

'You play your part well, Earl of Bronze. Dismount and follow me.'

He led them to the west wing of the palace and left them to bathe in a huge marble bath, attended by male servants who sprinkled perfumes into the water. Belder said nothing.

'We cannot tarry here too long, Lord Earl,' said Pagan. 'How much time will you give them?'

'I have not decided yet.'

Pagan eased back his giant frame into the warm water, ducking his head below the surface. Scaler summoned a servant and asked for soap. The man bowed and backed away, returning with a crystal jar. Scaler poured the contents on his head and washed his hair; then he called for a razor and a glass and shaved his chin. He was tired, but he felt more human for the bath. As he mounted the marble steps, a servant ran forward with a towelling robe which he placed over Scaler's shoulders. Then he led him to a bedchamber, where Scaler found his clothes had been brushed clean. Taking a fresh shirt from his saddlebag, he dressed swiftly, combing his hair and placing his headband carefully over his brow. Then on impulse he removed the leather band and searched his saddlebag to find the silver circlet with the opal centrepiece. He settled it into place and another servant brought him a mirror. He thanked the man, noting with satisfaction the awe in the tribesman's eyes.

Lifting the mirror, he gazed at himself.

Could he pass himself off as Rek, the Warrior Earl?

Pagan had given him the idea when he said that men were always willing to believe that other men were stronger, faster, more capable than themselves. It was all a matter of portrayal. He had said that Scaler could appear to be a prince, an assassin, a general.

Then why not a dead hero?

After all, who could prove otherwise?

Scaler left the room; a tribesman carrying a spear bowed and requested him to follow. The man led him to a wide chamber in which sat the young man from the gates, the two Sathuli he had rescued and an old man in robes of faded brown.

'Welcome,' said the Sathuli leader. 'I have someone here who is anxious to meet you.' He pointed to the old man. 'This is Raffir, a holy man. He is of the line of Joachim Sathuli, and a great student of history. He has many questions concerning the siege of Dros Delnoch.'

'I will be happy to answer his questions.'

'I am sure you will. He also has another talent we find of use – he speaks with the spirits of the dead. Tonight he will enter into a trance and you will be delighted, I am sure, to attend.'

'Of course.'

'For myself,' said the Sathuli, 'I am looking forward to it. I have listened to Raffir's spirit voice many times and often questioned him. But to have the privilege of bringing together such friends . . . well, I feel great pride.'

'Speak plainly, Sathuli!' said Scaler. 'I am in no mood for children's games.'

'A thousand apologies, noble guest. I was merely trying to tell you that Raffir's spirit guide is none other than your friend, the great Joachim. I shall be fascinated to listen to your conversation.'

'Stop panicking!' said Pagan as Scaler paced the room. The servants had been dismissed and Belder, dismayed at the news, was strolling in the rose garden below.

673

'There is a time for panic,' said Scaler, 'when all else fails. Well, it has
– so I'm panicking.'

'Are you sure the old man is genuine?'

'What difference does it make? If he is a fake, he will have been
schooled by the prince to deny me. If he is genuine, the spirit of Joachim
will deny me. There is no way round it!'

'You could denounce the old man as a fake,' offered Pagan, without
conviction.

'Denounce their holy man in their own temple? I don't think so. It
stretches the laws of hospitality to breaking point.'

'I hate to sound like Belder, but this was your idea. You really should
have thought it through.'

'I hate you sounding like Belder.'

'Will you stop that pacing? Here, have some fruit.' Pagan tossed an
apple across the room but Scaler dropped it.

The door opened and Belder entered. 'It's a real mess and no mistake,'
he said glumly.

Scaler sank into a wide leather chair. 'It should be quite a night.'

'Are we allowed to go armed?' asked Pagan.

'If you like,' said Belder, 'though I cannot see even you fighting your
way through a thousand Sathuli!'

'I don't want to die without a weapon in my hand.'

'Bravely spoken!' said Scaler. 'I will take this apple. I don't want to die
without a piece of fruit in my hand. Will you put a stop to this talk of
dying? It's extremely unsettling!'

The conversation struggled on pointlessly until a servant tapped on the
door, entered and requested them to follow him. Scaler asked the man
to wait while he moved to the full-length mirror on the far wall and gazed
at his reflection; he was surprised to find himself smiling. He swung his
cloak over his shoulder dramatically and adjusted the opal headband on
his brow.

'Stay with me, Rek,' he said. 'I shall need all the help there is.'

The trio followed the servant through the palace until they reached the
porch to the temple, where the man bowed and backed away. Scaler
walked on into the cool shadows and out into the temple proper. Seats
on all sides were filled with silent tribesmen, while the prince and Raffir
sat side by side on a raised dais. A third chair was placed at Raffir's right.
Scaler drew himself upright and marched down the aisle, removing his
cloak and settling it carefully over the back of his chair.

The prince stood and bowed to Scaler. There was, Scaler thought, a
malevolent gleam in his dark eyes.

'I welcome our noble guest here this evening. No Drenai has ever stood
in this temple. But this man claims to be the Nadir Bane, the living spirit
of the Earl of Bronze, brother in blood to the great Joachim. Therefore
it is fitting that he should meet Joachim again in this holy place.

'Peace be on your souls, brothers, and let your hearts open to the music
of the Void. Let Raffir commune with the darkness . . .'

Scaler shivered as the vast congregation bowed their heads. Raffir leaned back in his seat; his eyes opened wide and then rolled back under the sockets. Scaler began to feel sick.

'I call upon you, spirit friend!' shouted Raffir, his voice high-pitched and quavering. 'Come to us from the holy place. Give us of your wisdom.'

The candles in the temple guttered suddenly, as if a breeze had sprung up in the midst of the building.

'Come to us, spirit friend! Lead us.'

Once more the candle-flames danced – and this time many went out. Scaler licked his lips; Raffir was no fake.

'Who calls Joachim Sathuli?' boomed a voice, deep and resonant. Scaler started in his seat, for the voice came from the scrawny throat of Raffir.

'Blood of your blood calls upon you, great Joachim,' said the prince. 'I have here a man who claims to be your friend.'

'Let him speak then,' said the spirit, 'for I have heard too often your whining voice.'

'Speak!' ordered the prince, turning on Scaler. 'You heard the command.'

'You do not command *me*, wretch!' snapped Scaler. 'I am Rek, the Earl of Bronze, and I lived in a day when the Sathuli were men. Joachim was a man – and my brother. Tell me, Joachim, how do you like these sons of your sons?'

'Rek? I cannot see. Is it you?'

'It is I, brother. Here among these shadows of you. Why could you not be here with me?'

'I cannot tell . . . So much time. Rek! Our first meeting. You remember your words?'

'I do. "And what is your life worth, Joachim?" And you answered, "A broken sword." '

'Yes, yes, I remember. But at the last, the words of importance. The words that brought me to Dros Delnoch.'

'I was riding towards death at the fortress and I told you so. Then I said, "Before me I have nothing but enemies and war. I would like to think I have left at least a few friends behind me." I asked you to take my hand as a friend.'

'Rek, it is you! My brother! How is it you enjoy the life of blood once more?'

'The world has not changed, Joachim. Still evil rises like pus in a boil. I fight a war without allies and with few friends. I came to the Sathuli, as I did in the past.'

'What do you need, my brother?'

'I need men.'

'The Sathuli will not follow you. Nor should they. I loved you, Rek, for you were a great man. But it would be an obscenity for a Drenai to lead the chosen tribe. You must be desperate even to ask. But in your great need I offer you the Cheiam to use as you will. Oh Rek, my brother, would that I could walk beside you once more, tulwar in hand! I can still see the Nadir breasting the last wall, hear their cries of hatred. We were men, were we not?'

675

'We were men,' said Scaler. 'Even with the wound in your side, you were mighty.'

'My people fare badly now, Rek. Sheep led by goats. Use the Cheiam well. And may the Lord of All Things bless you.'

Scaler swallowed hard. 'Has he blessed you, my friend?'

'I have what I deserve. Goodbye, my brother.'

A terrible sadness overcame Scaler and he sank to his knees, tears coursing his cheeks. He tried to stifle the sobs but they forced their way through as Pagan ran to him, pulling him to his feet.

'So much sorrow in his voice,' said Scaler. 'Take me away from here.'

'Wait!' ordered the prince. 'The ceremony is not yet over.'

But Pagan ignored him and half-carried the weeping Scaler from the temple. Not one Sathuli barred his path as the trio returned to their rooms. There Pagan helped Scaler to a wide satin-covered bed and fetched him water from a stone jug; it was cool and sweet.

'Have you ever heard such sadness?' Scaler asked him.

'No,' admitted Pagan. 'It made me value life. How did you do it? By all the gods, it was a performance unparalleled.'

'It was merely another deception. And it made me sick! What skill is there in deceiving a tormented, blind spirit? Gods, Pagan, he's been dead for over a hundred years. He and Rek met very rarely after the battle – they were of two different cultures.'

'But you knew all the words . . .'

'The Earl's diaries. No more, no less. I am a student of history. They met when the Sathuli ambushed my ancestor and Rek took on Joachim in single combat. They fought for an age and then Joachim's sword snapped. But Rek spared him and it was the start of their friendship.'

'You have chosen a difficult part to play. You are no swordsman.'

'No, I don't need to be. The act is enough. I think I will sleep now. Gods, I'm tired . . . and so damned ashamed.'

'You have no reason to feel shame. But tell me, what are the Cheiam?'

'The sons of Joachim. It is a cult, I think; I'm not sure. Let me sleep now.'

'Rest well, Rek, you have earned it.'

'There is no need to use the name in private.'

'There is every reason – we must all live the part from now on. I don't know anything about your ancestor, but I think he would have been proud of you. It took iron nerve to go through that.'

But Scaler missed the compliment, for he had fallen asleep.

Pagan returned to the outer room.

'How is he?' asked Belder.

'He is all right. But a word of advice for you, old man: no more cutting remarks! From now on he is the Earl of Bronze and will be treated as such.'

'How little you know, black man!' snapped Belder. 'He is not playing a role, he *is* the Earl of Bronze. By right and by blood. He thinks he is playing a part. Well, let him. What you see now is the reality. It was always there – I knew it. That was what made me so bitter. Cutting remarks? I am proud of the boy – so proud I could sing!'

'Well, don't,' said Pagan, grinning. 'You have the voice of a sick hyena!'

Scaler was wakened by a rough hand clamping over his mouth. It was not a pleasant awakening. The moonlight made a silver beam through the open window and the breeze billowed the curtain of lace. But the man leaning over his bed was in silhouette.

'Do not make a sound,' warned a voice. 'You are in great danger!' He removed his hand and sat down on the bed.

Scaler sat up slowly. 'Danger?' he whispered.

'The prince has ordered your death.'

'Nice!'

'I am here to help you.'

'I am glad to hear it.'

'This is no jest, Lord Earl. I am Magir, leader of the Cheiam, and if you do not move you will find yourself in the Halls of the Dead once more.'

'Move where?'

'Out of the city. Tonight. We have a camp higher in the range where you will be safe.' A slight scratching noise came from beyond the window, like a rope rubbing on stone. 'Too late!' whispered Magir. 'They are here. Get your sword!'

Scaler scrambled across the bed, dragging his blade from its scabbard. A dark shadow leapt through the window but Magir intercepted it, his curved dagger flashing upwards. A terrible scream rent the silence of the night. As two more assassins clambered into the room, Scaler screamed at the top of his voice and leapt forward, swinging the sword. It hammered into flesh and the man fell without a sound. Scaler tripped over the body just as a dagger flashed over his head, but rolled on to his back, thrusting his blade into the man's belly. With a grunt of pain he staggered back and pitched out of the window.

'Magnificent!' said Magir. 'Never have I seen the tumbler's roll so brilliantly executed. You could be of the Cheiam yourself.'

Scaler sat back against the wall, sword dropping from nerveless fingers.

Pagan crashed open the door. 'Are you all right, Rek?' he said. Scaler turned to see the giant black man filling the doorway like an ebony statue, while the door itself sagged on broken hinges.

'You could have merely opened it,' said Scaler. 'Gods, the drama around here is killing me!'

'Speaking of which,' said Pagan, 'I have just killed two men in my room. Belder is dead – they cut his throat.'

Scaler pushed himself to his feet. 'They killed *him*? Why?'

'You shamed the prince,' said Magir. 'He must kill you – he has no choice.'

'And what of the spirit of Joachim? What was the point of bringing him back?'

'I cannot answer that, Lord Earl. But you must leave now.'

'Leave? He killed my friend – probably the only friend I ever had. He was like a father to me. Get out and leave me alone – both of you!'

'Don't do anything foolish,' warned Pagan.

'Foolish! It's all foolish. Life is a farce – a stupid, sickening farce played out by fools. Well, this is one fool who has had enough. So get out!'

Scaler dressed swiftly, buckling on his sword-belt and taking his blade in his hand. Moving to the window, he leaned out. A rope swung in the night breeze and Scaler took hold of it, leaping from the window and sliding hand-over-hand to the courtyard below.

Four guards watched him in silence as he landed lightly on the marble flagstones. He walked out into the centre of the courtyard and stared up at the windows of the prince's chamber.

'Prince of cowards, come forth!' he shouted. 'Prince of lies and deceit, show yourself. Joachim said you were a sheep. Come out!'

The sentries exchanged glances but did not move.

'I am alive, prince. The Earl of Bronze is alive! All your assassins are dead and you are about to join them. Come out – or I will shrivel your soul where you hide. *Come out!*'

The curtains of the window moved and there stood the prince, his face flushed and angry. He leaned on the carved stone sill and shouted to the sentries.

'Kill him!'

'Come and do it yourself, you jackal!' yelled Scaler. 'Joachim called me his friend and so I am. In your own temple you heard him, yet you send assassins to my room. You spineless pig! You defile your ancestor and break your own laws of hospitality. Offal! Get down here!'

'You heard me – kill him!' screamed the prince. The sentries moved forward, lances levelled.

Scaler lowered his sword, his bright blue eyes fixed on the leading warrior.

'I will not fight you,' he said. 'But what will you have me tell Joachim when next I meet him? And what will you tell him when you walk the road to Sheol?' The man hesitated as behind Scaler Pagan ran across the courtyard, two swords in his hands. Magir was beside him.

The sentries braced themselves for the charge.

'Leave him be!' yelled Magir. 'He is the Earl and his challenge is laid down.'

'Come down, prince of cowards,' shouted Scaler. 'Your time is come!'

The prince clambered over the sill and leapt the ten feet to the flag-stones, his white robes flaring out in the breeze. Walking to a sentry he took the man's tulwar, testing it for balance.

'Now you will die,' said the prince. 'I know you are a liar. You are not the long-dead Earl – you are a deceiver.'

'Prove it!' snapped Scaler. 'Step forward. I am the greatest swordsman ever to walk the earth. I turned back the hordes of the Nadir. I broke the blade of Joachim Sathuli. Step forward and die!'

The prince licked his lips and stared into the blazing eyes. Sweat trickled down his cheeks and in that moment he knew he was doomed. Life was

678

suddenly very precious and he was far too important a man to allow some demon from the deep to trick him into combat. His hand began to shake.

He felt the stares of his men upon him and glanced up to see the courtyard ringed with Sathuli warriors. And yet he was alone; not one of them would come to his aid. He had to attack, but to do so meant death. With a wild scream he threw himself forward, tulwar raised. Scaler buried his sword in the prince's heart, then dragged it clear and the body sagged to the flagstones.

Magir stepped to Scaler's side. 'Now you must leave. They will allow you to pass from the mountains, then they will follow to avenge this killing.'

'That's of no importance to me,' said Scaler. 'I came here to win them. Without them we are lost anyway.'

'You have the Cheiam, my friend. We will follow you back into Hell itself.'

Scaler looked down at the dead prince. 'He didn't even try to fight – he just ran forward to die.'

'He was a dog and the son of a dog. I spit on him!' said Magir. 'He was not worthy of you, Lord Earl, though he was the greatest swordsman in all of Sathuli.'

'He *was*?' said Scaler, astonished.

'He was. But he knew you were a greater man and the knowledge destroyed him before your sword could do so.'

'The man was a fool. If he only . . .'

'Rek,' said Pagan, 'it is time to leave. I will fetch the horses.'

'No. I want to see Belder buried before we leave this place.'

'My men will see to it,' said Magir. 'But your friend speaks wisely and I will have horses brought to the courtyard. It is only an hour to our camp, where we can rest and speak of your plans.'

'Magir!'

'Yes, my Lord.'

'I thank you.'

'It was my duty, Lord Earl. I thought I would hate this duty, for the Cheiam bear no love for Drenai warriors. But you are a man.'

'Tell me, what are the Cheiam?'

'We are the Drinkers of Blood, the sons of Joachim. We worship only one god: Shalli, the spirit of Death.'

'How many of you are there?'

'One hundred only, Lord Earl. But judge us not by our number. Rather, watch the numbers of dead we leave behind us.'

17

The man was buried up to his neck, the dry earth packed tightly around him. Ants crawled on his face and the sun beat down on his shaven head. He heard the sound of approaching horses, but could not turn.

'A pox on you and all your family!' he shouted.

Then he heard someone dismount and a merciful shadow fell across him. Glancing up, he saw standing before him a tall figure in black leather tunic and riding boots; he could not see his face. A woman led the horses round to the front and the man squatted down.

'We are seeking the tents of the Wolves,' he said.

The buried man spat an ant from his mouth. 'Good for you!' he said. 'Why tell me? You think I have been left here as a signpost?'

'I was contemplating digging you out.'

'I shouldn't bother. The hills behind you are full of Pack-rats. They would not take kindly to your intrusion.'

'Pack-rats' was the name given to members of the Green Monkey tribe following a battle some two hundred years before, when they had been deprived of their ponies and forced to carry their possessions on their backs. The other tribes never forgot the humiliation, nor allowed the Monkeys to forget.

'How many are there?' asked Tenaka.

'Who knows? They all look alike to me.'

Tenaka held a leather canteen of water to the man's lips and he drank greedily.

'What tribe are you?' asked Tenaka.

'I'm glad you asked that after offering me water,' said the man. 'I am Subodai of the Spears.'

Tenaka nodded. The Spears were hated by the Wolfshead on the ample grounds that their warriors were equally as vicious and efficient as their own.

For the Nadir there was seldom respect for an enemy. Weaker foes were treated with contempt, stronger regarded with hatred. The Spears, though not exactly stronger, fell into the latter category.

'How did a Spear fall to the Pack-rats?' asked Tenaka.

'Luck,' answered Subodai, spitting more ants from his mouth. 'Pony broke a leg and then four of them jumped me.'

'Only four?'

'I have not been well!'

'I think I will dig you free.'

'Not a wise move, Wolfshead! I may be forced to kill you.'

'I am not concerned by any man who is captured by a mere four Pack-rats. Renya, dig him out.'

Tenaka moved back to sit down cross-legged on the ground, staring at the hills. There was no sign of movement, but he knew they were watching him. He stretched his injured back – over the last five days it had eased greatly.

Renya scraped away the hard-packed earth, freeing the man's arms which were bound behind him. Once free, he pushed her away and struggled until he had pulled himself clear. Without a word to Renya he walked to Tenaka and squatted down.

'I have decided not to kill you,' said Subodai.

'You have great wisdom for a Spear,' said Tenaka, without taking his gaze from the hills.

'This is true. I see your woman is a Drenai. Soft!'

'I like soft women.'

'There is something to be said for them,' agreed Subodai. 'Will you sell me a sword?'

'With what will you pay me?'

'I will give you a Pack-rat pony.'

'Your generosity is matched only by your confidence,' observed Tenaka.

'You are Bladedancer, the Drenai half-blood,' observed Subodai, removing his belted fur jacket and brushing more ants from his squat, powerful body.

Tenaka did not bother to reply; he was watching the dust swirl up in the hills as men took to their horses.

'More than four,' said Subodai. 'About that sword . . . ?'

'They are leaving,' said Tenaka. 'They will return in greater numbers.' Rising to his feet, he walked to his horse and vaulted to the saddle. 'Goodbye, Subodai!'

'Wait!' called the Nadir. 'The sword?'

'You have not paid me the pony.'

'I will – given time.'

'I have not time. What else can you offer?'

Subodai was trapped. Left here without a weapon, he would be dead within the hour. He contemplated leaping at Tenaka, but dismissed the idea – the violet eyes were disconcerting in their confidence.

'I have nothing else,' he said. 'But you have a thought, I can tell.'

'Be my bondsman for ten days and lead me to the Wolves,' suggested Tenaka.

Subodai hawked and spat. 'That sounds marginally more appealing than dying here. Ten days, you say?'

'Ten days.'

'With today counting as one?'

'Yes.'

'Then I agree.' Subodai raised his hand and Tenaka took it, hauling him into the saddle behind him. 'I'm glad my father is no longer alive to see this day,' muttered the Nadir.

As they cantered off to the north Subodai thought about his father. A strong man and a fine rider – but such a temper.

It was his temper that killed him. After a horse-race, which Subodai won, his father had accused him of loosening the saddle-cinch on his own mare. The argument had blown up into a full-scale fight with fists and knives.

Subodai still remembered the look of surprise on his father's face as his son's knife rammed home in his chest. A man should always know when to control his temper.

The Nadir twisted in the saddle, his black eyes resting on Renya. Now there was a good woman! Not good for the Steppes, maybe – but good for plenty else.

For nine days more he would serve Bladedancer. After that he would kill him and take his woman.

He turned his gaze to the mounts. They were fine beasts. He grinned suddenly as the full joy of life settled over him once more.

The woman he would take.

The horses he would keep.

For they would be worth riding more than once.

Lake was sweating heavily as he cranked the thick wooden handle, dragging the bow-arm and the twined leather back to the hook. A young man in a leather apron passed him a loosely tied bundle of fifty arrows, which Lake placed in the bowl of the device. Thirty feet down the room, two assistants lifted a thick wooden door into place against the far wall.

Ananais sat in a corner with his back against the cool grey stone wall of the old stable. The machine had so far taken more than ten minutes to load. He lifted his mask and scratched his chin. Ten minutes for fifty arrows! One archer could let fly twice that number in half the time. But Lake was trying hard and Ananais could see no reason to demoralise him.

'Ready?' Lake asked his assistants at the far end of the room. Both men nodded and hurried away behind large sacks of oats and grain.

Lake glanced at Ananais for approval and then tugged the release cord. The massive arm flashed forward and fifty arrows hammered into the oak door, some passing through and striking sparks from the wall beyond. Ananais strode forward, impressed by the killing power. The door was a mess, having given way at the centre where more than a third of the shafts had struck home.

'What do you think?' asked Lake anxiously.

'It needs to spread more,' said Ananais. 'If this had been loosed at a charging mass of Joinings, fully half the shafts would have hit only two beasts. But it needs to spread laterally – can you do that?'

'I think so. But do you like it?'

'Do you have any slingshot?'

'Yes.'

'Load that in the bowl.'

'It will ruin the cap,' protested Lake. 'It's designed to shoot arrows.'

Ananais put his hand on the young man's shoulder. 'It's designed to kill, Lake. Try the shot.'

An assistant brought a sack of shot and poured several hundred pebble-sized rounds of lead into the copper bowl. Ananais took over the cranking of the device and they hooked the leather into place within four minutes.

Then Ananais moved to one side, taking the release thong in his hand. 'Stand clear,' he ordered. 'And forget about the sacks. Get outside the door.' The assistants scurried to safety and Ananais tugged the release. The giant bow-arm leapt forward and the slingshot thundered into the oak door. The sound was deafening and the wood split with a groan, falling to the floor in several pieces. Ananais gazed down at the leather cap on the bow – it was twisted and torn.

'Better than arrows, young Lake,' he said as the young man ran to his machine, checking the cap and the leather drawstring.

'I will make a cap in brass,' he said, 'and increase the spread. We shall need two cranks, one on either side. And I'll have the slingshot filed to give points on four sides.'

'How soon can you have one ready?' asked Ananais.

'One? I already have three ready. The adjustments will take only a day and then we shall have four.'

'Good work, lad!'

'It's getting them up to the valleys that concerns me.'

'Don't worry about that – we don't want them in the first line of defence. Take them back into the mountains; Galand will tell you where to place them.'

'But they could help us to hold the line,' argued Lake, his voice rising. Ananais took him by the arm, leading him out from the stable, and into the clear night air.

'Understand this, lad: *nothing* will help us hold the first line. We don't have the men. There are too many passes and trails. If we wait too long we shall be cut off, surrounded. The weapons are good and we will use them – but further back.'

Lake's anger subsided, to be replaced by a dull, tired sense of resignation. He had been pushing himself hard for days without rest: seeking something, anything, that could turn the tide. But he was not a fool and secretly he had known.

'We cannot protect the city,' he said.

'Cities can be rebuilt,' answered Ananais.

'But many people will refuse to move. The majority, I wouldn't wonder.'

'Then they will die, Lake.'

The young man removed his leather work apron and sat back on a barrel top. He screwed the apron into a tight ball and dropped it at his feet. Ananais felt for him then, for Lake was staring down at his own crumpled dreams.

'Damn it, Lake, I wish there was something I could say to lift you. I know how you feel . . . I feel it myself. It offends a man's sense of natural justice when the enemy has all the advantages. I remember an old teacher of mine once saying that behind every dark cloud the sun was just waiting to boil you to death.'

Lake grinned. 'I had a teacher like that once. A strange old boy who lived in a hovel near the west hill. He said there were three kinds of people in life: winners, losers and fighters. Winners made him sick with their arrogance, losers made him sick with their whining and fighters made him sick with their stupidity.'

'In which category did he put himself?'

'He said he had tried all three and nothing suited him.'

'Well, at least he tried. That's all a man can do, Lake. And we shall try. We will hit them and hurt them. We will bog them down in a running war. Knuckle and skull, steel and fire. And with luck, when Tenaka gets back, he will mop them up with his Nadir riders.'

'We don't seem to be exactly overflowing with luck,' Lake pointed out.

'You make your own. I put no faith in gods, Lake. Never have. If they exist, they care very little – if at all – about ordinary mortals. I put my faith in me – and you know why? Because I have never lost! I've been speared, stabbed and poisoned. I've been dragged by a wild horse, gored by a bull and bitten by a bear. But I have never lost. I've even had my face ripped away by a Joining, but I'm still here. And winning is a habit.'

'You are a hard act to follow, Darkmask. I won a foot-race once, and was third in the Open Wrestling at the Games. Oh . . . and a bee stung me once when I was a child and I cried for days.'

'You'll do, Lake! Once I have taught you how to be a good liar! Now, let's get back in there and work on the weapons you have devised.'

From dawn to dusk for three days, Rayvan and scores of helpers toured the city preparing the people for evacuation into the depths of the mountains. The task was thankless. Many were those who refused to consider moving and some even scoffed at the threat Rayvan outlined. Why should Ceska attack the city, they asked? That's why it was built without walls – there was no need to sack it. Arguments developed and doors were slammed. Rayvan endured insults and humiliation, yet still she tramped the streets.

On the morning of the fourth day the refugees gathered in the meadows to the east of the city; their possessions were piled on carts – some drawn by mules, others by ponies or even oxen. The less fortunate carried their belongings on their backs in canvas bundles. In all there were fewer than two thousand people – twice that number had elected to stay.

Galand and Lake led them out on the long hard trek to the highlands, where already three hundred men were building crude shelters in hidden valleys.

Lake's weapons of war, covered in oiled leather, had been placed on six wagons which headed the column.

Rayvan, Decado and Ananais watched the refugees set out. Then Rayvan shook her head, cursed and marched back to the council chamber without another word. The two men followed her. Once inside, her anger burst into the open.

'What in the name of Chaos is going on in their heads?' she raged. 'Have they not seen enough of Ceska's terror? Some of those people have been friends of mine for years. They are solid, intelligent, reasoning people. Do they want to die?'

'It is not that easy, Rayvan,' said Decado softly. 'They are not used to the ways of evil and they cannot conceive why Ceska would want to butcher the city's population. It makes no sense to them. And you ask us if they have not seen enough of Ceska's terror. In short, they have not! They have seen men with their arms lopped off, but the spectators can ask: Did he deserve it? They have heard of starvation and plague in other areas, but Ceska has always had an answer for that. He slides the blame from himself with rare skill. And truly they do not *want* to know. For most men life is their home and their families, watching the children grow, hoping next year will be better than this.

'In southern Ventria an entire community lives on a volcanic island. Every ten years or so it spews ash, dust and burning rock, killing hundreds. Yet they stay, always convincing themselves that the worst is over.

'But do not torment yourself, Rayvan. You have done all that you could. More than could have been asked for.'

She sagged back in her seat and shook her head. 'I could have succeeded. About four thousand people are going to die down there. Horribly! And all because I started a war I could not win.'

'Nonsense!' said Ananais. 'Why are you doing this to yourself, woman? The war began because Ceska's men poured into the mountains and massacred innocent people. You merely defended your own. Where the Hell would we be if we just allowed such atrocities to occur? I don't like the situation; it smells worse than a ten-day-dead pig in summer, but it's not my doing. Nor is it yours. You want blame? Blame the people who voted him into power. Blame the soldiers who follow him still. Blame the Dragon for not putting him down when they could. Blame his mother for giving birth to him. Now, enough of this! Every man and woman down there had a choice, given to them freely. Their fate is in their hands. You are not responsible.'

'I don't want to argue with you, Darkmask. But somewhere along this dreadful line someone must claim responsibility. The war is not of my making, as you say. But I elected myself to lead these people and every one of them that dies will be on my head. I would have it no other way. Because I care. Can you understand that?'

'No,' said Ananais bluntly. 'But I accept it.'

'I understand it,' said Decado. 'But your care must now be for those people who have trusted you and moved to the mountains. What with refugees from outside Skoda, and the city folk, we will have over seven thousand people up there. There will be problems with food, sanitation, sickness. Lines of communication must be set up. Stores, supplies and medicines. That all takes organisation and manpower. And every man we lose to that side of the war is one fewer warrior standing against Ceska.'

'I shall be there to organise that,' said Rayvan. 'There are maybe twenty women I can call on.'

'With respect,' said Ananais, 'you will also need men. Penned up like that, tempers can flare and some people will become convinced they are getting less than their ration. Many of the men among the refugees are cowards – and often that makes them bullies. There will be thieves, and among so many women there will be men who seek to take advantage.'

Rayvan's green eyes blazed. 'All that I can handle, Darkmask. Believe it! No one will question my authority.'

Beneath his mask Ananais grinned. Rayvan's voice had an edge of thunder and her square chin jutted pugnaciously. She was probably right, he thought. It would be a brave man who went against her. And all the brave men would be facing a more formidable foe.

During the days that followed Ananais divided his time between the small army manning the outer mountain ring, and the setting-up of a passable fortress on the inner ring. Minor trails into the valleys were blocked and the main entrances – the valleys of Tarsk and Magadon – hastily walled with boulders. Throughout the long hours of daylight the mountain-hardened men of Skoda added to the fortifications, rolling huge boulders from the hills and wedging them into place across the mouths of the valleys. Slowly the walls increased in size. Pulleys and wooden towers were erected by skilled builders and larger rocks were lifted by ropes and swung into place, cemented by a mix of clay and rock-dust.

The main builder – and wall architect – was a Vagrian immigrant named Leppoe. He was tall, dark, balding and indefatigable. Men walked warily around him, for he had an unnerving habit of looking through a man, ignoring him totally as his mind wrestled with some problem of stress or structure. And then, with the problem solved, he would smile suddenly and become warm and friendly. Few workers could keep up with his pace and often he would work long into the night, planning refinements or taking over as foreman of a work party and pushing his men hard under the moonlight.

As the walls neared completion, Leppoe added yet another refinement. Planks were laid and cunningly fitted to create ramparts, while the outer walls were smeared with mortar and smoothed, making it more difficult for an enemy to scale them.

Leppoe had two of Lake's giant bows placed near the centre of each wall; these were tested for range and spread by Lake himself and the twelve men he had trained to handle them. Sacks of lead shot for slings were placed by the weapons, along with several thousand arrows.

'It all looks strong enough,' Thorn told Ananais. 'But Dros Delnoch it is not!'

Ananais strode along the ramparts of Madagon, gauging the possible lines of attack. The walls negated Ceska's cavalry, but the Joinings would have no trouble in scaling them. Leppoe had worked miracles getting them up to fifteen feet in height, but it was not enough. Lake's weapons would create havoc to within thirty feet of the walls, but nearer than that they would be useless.

Ananais sent Thorn to ride the two miles across the valley to Tarsk. Then he despatched two other men to run the same distance. It took Thorn less than five minutes to make the journey, while the runners took almost twelve.

The general's problem was a tough one. Ceska was likely to strike at both valleys simultaneously and if one was overrun, the second was doomed. Therefore a third force had to be held in check somewhere between the two, ready to move the instant a breach looked likely. But walls could be breached in seconds and they didn't have many minutes. Signal fires were useless, since the Skoda range loomed between the valley mouths.

However, Leppoe solved the problem by suggesting a triangular system of communication. By day, mirrors or lanterns could be used to send a message back into the valley, where a group of men would be constantly on the lookout. Once the message was received, the group would relay it back to the second valley in the same way. A force of five hundred men would camp between the valleys and once a signal was received, they would ride like the devil. The system was practised many times, both in daylight and in darkness, until Ananais was convinced it had reached its peak of efficiency. A call for help could be transmitted and a relief force arrive within four minutes. Ananais would have liked to halve the time, but he was content.

Valtaya had moved back into the mountains with Rayvan and taken control of the medical supplies. Ananais missed her terribly; he had a strange feeling of doom which he could not shake off. He was never a man to give a great deal of thought to death; now it plagued him. When Valtaya had said goodbye the previous night, he had felt more wretched than at any time in his life. Taking her in his arms, he had fought to say the words he felt, desperate to let her know the depth of his love for her.

'I . . . I will miss you.'

'It won't be for long,' she said, kissing his scarred cheek and averting her eyes from the ruined mouth.

'You . . . er . . . look after yourself.'

'And you.'

As he helped her to her horse, several other travellers cantered towards the hut and he scrambled to replace his mask. And then she was gone. He watched her until the night swallowed her.

'I love you,' he said at last, too late. He tore the mask from his face and bellowed at the top of his voice.

'I LOVE YOU!' The words echoed in the mountains as he sank to his knees and hammered the ground with his fist. 'Damn, damn, damn! I love you!'

18

Tenaka, Subodai and Renya had an hour's start on the tribesmen, but this was gradually whittled back for, despite the strength of the Drenai mounts, Tenaka's horse now carried double. At the top of a dusty hill Tenaka shaded his eyes with his hand and tried to count the riders giving chase, but it was not easy for a swirling dust-cloud rose up around them.

'I would say a dozen, no more,' said Tenaka at last.

Subodai shrugged. 'Could be a lot less,' he said.

Tenaka remounted, casting about for a likely ambush site. He led them up into the hills to a low outcropping of rock which jutted over the trail like an outstretched fist. Here the trail curved to the left. Tenaka stood up in the saddle and leapt to the rock. Startled, Subodai slid forward and took up the reins.

'Ride forward to that dark hill, then slowly circle until you come back here,' Tenaka told him.

'What are you going to do?' asked Renya.

'I'm going to get a pony for my bondsman,' said Tenaka, grinning.

'Come woman!' snapped Subodai and cantered off in the lead. Renya and Tenaka exchanged glances.

'I don't think I shall enjoy being the docile woman of the Steppes,' she whispered.

'I said as much,' he reminded her with a smile.

She nodded and heeled her horse after Subodai.

Tenaka lay flat on the rock, watching the horsemen approach; they were some eight minutes behind Subodai. At close range Tenaka studied the riders; there were nine of them, wearing the goatskin-hide jerkins of the Steppes rider and rounded leather helms fringed with fur. Their faces were flat and sallow, their eyes black as night and coldly cruel. Each carried a lance, and swords and knives were strapped to their belts. Tenaka watched them come, waiting for the back marker.

They thundered up the narrow trail, slowing as they came to the curve by the rock. As they passed Tenaka slid out, drawing up his legs under him; then, as the last rider cantered below him, he dropped like a stone to hammer his booted feet into the man's face. He catapulted from the saddle. Tenaka hit the ground, rolled, came upright and lunged for the pony's rein. The beast stood still, nostrils quivering with shock. Tenaka patted him gently and then led him to the fallen warrior. The man was dead and Tenaka stripped off his jerkin, pulling it over his own. Then he took the man's helm and lance and, vaulting to the saddle, set off after the others.

The trail wound on, veering left and right, and the riders became less bunched. Tenaka cantered close to the man in front, just before another bend.

'Hola!' he called. 'Wait!' The man drew back on the reins as his comrades moved out of sight.

'What is it?' enquired the rider. Tenaka drew up alongside him, pointing up in the air. As the man glanced up, so Tenaka's fist thudded into his neck and without a sound he fell from the saddle. Up ahead came the sound of triumphant yells. Tenaka cursed and heeled his mount into a gallop, rounding the bend to see Subodai and Renya facing the seven riders, swords in hand.

Tenaka hit their line like a thunderbolt, his lance punching a rider from the saddle. Then his sword was out and a second man fell screaming.

Subodai bellowed a war-cry and kicked his mount forward; blocking a wild cut, he swept down his sword, cleaving his opponent's collar-bone. The man grunted, but he was game and attacked once more. Subodai ducked as the tribesman's sword slashed through the air, then gutted the man expertly.

Two of the riders now charged at Renya, determined to gain some spoils. However, they were met by a feral snarl as she leapt from the saddle at the first, bearing man and pony to the ground. Her dagger sliced his throat so fast that he felt no pain and could not understand his growing weakness. Renya came up quickly, letting forth the blood-curdling shriek that had terrified the outlaws back in Drenai. The ponies reared in terror and her nearest opponent dropped his lance and grabbed the reins with both hands. Renya leapt, hammering a fist to his temple; he flew from the saddle, struggling to rise, then slumped to the ground unconscious.

The remaining two tribesmen disengaged and raced from the battleground as Subodai cantered to Tenaka.

'Your woman . . .' he whispered, tapping his temple. 'She is crazy as a moon-dog!'

'I like them crazy,' said Tenaka.

'You move well, Bladedancer! You are more Nadir than Drenai, I think.'

'There are those who would not see that as a compliment.'

'Fools! I have no time for fools. How many of these horses do I keep?' asked the Nadir, scanning the six ponies.

'All of them,' said Tenaka.

'Why so generous?'

'It stops me having to kill you,' Tenaka told him. The words moved through Subodai like ice knives but he forced a grin and returned the cool stare of Tenaka's violet eyes. In them Subodai saw knowledge, and it frightened him. Tenaka knew of his plan to rob and kill him – as sure as goats grew horns, he knew.

Subodai shrugged. 'I would have waited until after my bond was completed,' he said.

'I know that. Come, let us ride.'

Subodai shuddered; the man was not human. He gazed at the ponies – still, human or not, he was growing rich in Tenaka's presence.

For four days they moved north, skirting villages and communities, but on the fifth day their food ran out and they rode into a village of tents

689

nestling by a mountain river. The community was a small one, no more than forty men. Originally they had been of the Doublehair tribe far to the north-east, but a split had developed and now they were Notas – 'No Tribe' – and fair game for all. They greeted the travellers with care, not knowing if they were part of a larger group. Tenaka could see their minds working – the Nadir law of hospitality meant that no harm could come to visitors while they stayed in your camp. But once out on the Steppes . . .

'Are you far from your people?' asked the Notas leader, a burly warrior with a scarred face.

'I am never far from my people,' Tenaka answered him, accepting a bowl of raisins and some dried fruit.

'Your man is a Spear,' said the leader.

'We were pursued by Pack-rats,' answered Tenaka. 'We slew them and took their ponies. It is a sad thing for Nadir to kill Nadir.'

'But it is the way of the world,' commented the leader.

'Not in Ulric's day.'

'Ulric is long dead.'

'Some say he will rise again,' observed Tenaka.

'Men will always say that about kings of greatness. Ulric is forgotten meat and dusty bones.'

'Who leads the Wolves?' asked Tenaka.

'Are you Wolfshead then?'

'I am what I am. Who leads the Wolves?'

'You are Bladedancer.'

'Indeed I am.'

'Why have you come back to the Steppes?'

'Why does the salmon swim upstream?'

'To die,' said the leader, smiling for the first time.

'All things die,' observed Tenaka. 'Once the desert in which we sit was an ocean. Even the ocean died when the world fell. Who leads the Wolves?'

'Saddleskull is the Khan. So he says. But Knifespeaks has an army of eight thousand. The tribe has split.'

'So, now it is not only Nadir who kills Nadir, but Wolf who rends Wolf?'

'The way of the world,' said the leader once more.

'Which is the nearest?'

'Saddleskull. Two days north-east.'

'I will rest here with you tonight. Tomorrow I will go to him.'

'He will kill you, Bladedancer!'

'I am a hard man to kill. Tell that to your young men.'

'I hear you.' The leader rose to leave the tent but stopped at the flap. 'Have you come home to rule?'

'I have come home.'

'I am tired of being Notas,' said the man.

'My journey is perilous,' Tenaka told him. 'As you say, Saddleskull would desire my death. You have few men.'

'In the coming war we will be destroyed by one or other faction,' said the man. 'But you – you have the look of eagles about you. I will follow you, if you desire it.'

A sense of calm settled over Tenaka. An inner peace seemed to pulse from the very earth at his feet, from the distant blue mountains, to whisper in the long grass of the Steppes. He closed his eyes and opened his ears to the music of silence. Every nerve in his body seemed on edge as the land cried out to him.

Home!

After forty years Tenaka Khan had learned the meaning of the word.

His eyes opened. The leader stood very still, watching him; he had seen men in a state of trance many times, and always it brought a sense of awe, and a feeling of sadness that he could never experience this himself.

Tenaka smiled. 'Follow me,' he told the man, 'and I will give you the world.'

'Are we to be Wolves?'

'No. We are the Nadir Rising. We are the Dragon.'

At dawn the forty men of the Notas, less the three outriding sentries, sat in two lines outside Tenaka's tent. Behind them were the children: eighteen boys and three girls. Lastly sat the women, fifty-two of them.

Subodai stood apart from the group, baffled by this new turn of events. There was no point to it. Who would wish to start a new tribe at the dawn of a civil war? And what could Tenaka possibly gain from this shoddy band of goat-breeders? It was all beyond the Spear warrior; he wandered into an empty tent and helped himself to some soft cheese and a loaf of gritty black bread.

What did it matter?

When the sun was high he would ask Tenaka to release him from his bond, take his six ponies and ride home. Four ponies would buy him a fine wife and he would relax for a while in the western hills. He scratched his chin, wondering what would happen to Tenaka Khan.

Subodai felt strangely uncomfortable at the thought of riding away. Few were the moments of original interest in the harsh world of the Steppes. Fight, love, breed, eat. There was a limit to the amount of excitement these four activities could generate. Subodai was thirty-four years old and he had left the Spears for a reason none of his peers could understand:

He was bored!

He moved out into the sunlight. Goats were milling at the edge of the camp-site near the pony picket line, and high above a sparrowhawk circled and dived.

Tenaka Khan stepped out into the sunlight and stood before the Notas – arms folded across his chest, face impassive.

The leader walked towards him, dropped to his knees, bent low and kissed Tenaka's feet. One by one every member of the Notas followed him.

Renya watched the scene from within the tent. The whole ceremony disturbed her, as did the subtle change she sensed in her lover.

The previous night, as they lay together under fur rugs, Tenaka had made love to her. It was then that the first tiny sparks of fear had flashed in her subconscious. The passion remained, the thrill of the touch and the breathless excitement. But Renya sensed a newness in Tenaka which she could not read. Somewhere inside him one gate had opened and another closed. Love had been locked away. But what had replaced it?

Now she gazed at the man she loved as the ceremony continued. She could not see his face, but she could see the faces of his new followers: they shone.

When the last of the women backed away, Tenaka Khan turned without a word and re-entered the tent. Then the sparks within Renya became a fire, for his face reflected what he had become. He was no longer the warrior of two worlds. His Drenai blood had been sucked from him by the Steppes and what was left was pure Nadir.

Renya looked away.

By midday the tribesmen had seen their women dismantle the tents and pack them on wagons. The goats were rounded up and the new tribe headed north-east. Subodai had not requested to be free of his bond and he rode beside Tenaka and the Notas leader, Gitasi.

That night they camped on the southern slopes of a range of wooded hills. Towards midnight as Gitasi and Tenaka talked by a camp-fire, the pounding of hooves sent tribesmen rolling from their blankets to grab at swords and bows. Tenaka remained where he was, seated cross-legged by the fire. He whispered something to Gitasi and the scarred leader ran to his men, calming them. The hoofbeats grew louder and more than a hundred warriors rode into the camp, bearing down on the fire. Tenaka ignored them, calmly chewing on a strip of dried meat.

The horsemen dragged on their reins. 'You are in the land of the Wolfshead,' said the lead warrior, sliding from the saddle. He wore a helm of bronze, rimmed with fur, and a lacquered black breastplate edged with gold.

Tenaka Khan looked up at him. The man was close to fifty years old and his massive arms were criss-crossed with scars. Tenaka gestured to a place by the fire.

'Welcome to my camp,' he said softly. 'Sit and eat.'

'I do not eat with Notas,' said the man. 'You are on Wolfshead land.'

'Sit down and eat,' said Tenaka, 'or I shall kill you where you stand.'

'Are you a madman?' asked the warrior, taking a firmer grip on the sword in his hand. Tenaka Khan ignored him and, furious, the man swung the sword. But Tenaka's leg shot out, hooking his feet from under him, and he fell with a crash as Tenaka rolled to his right with his knife flashing in his hand. The point rested gently on the warrior's throat.

An angry roar went up from the riders.

'Be silent among your betters!' bellowed Tenaka. 'Now, Ingis, will you sit and eat?'

Ingis blinked as the knife was withdrawn. He sat up and recovered his sword.

'Bladedancer?'

692

'Tell your men to dismount and relax,' said Tenaka. 'There will be no bloodshed tonight.'

'Why are you here, man? It is insane.'

'Where else should I be?'

Ingis shook his head and ordered his men to dismount, then turned back to Tenaka.

'Saddleskull will be confused. He will not know whether to kill you or make you a general.'

'Saddleskull was always confused,' said Tenaka. 'It surprises me that you follow him.'

Ingis shrugged. 'He is a warrior, at least. Then you have not come back to follow him?'

'No.'

'I will have to kill you, Bladedancer. You are too powerful a man to have for an enemy.'

'I have not come to serve Knifespeaks.'

'Then why?'

'You tell me, Ingis.'

The warrior looked into Tenaka's eyes. 'Now I know you are insane. How can you hope to rule? Saddleskull has eighty thousand warriors. Knifespeaks is weak, with only six thousand. How many do you have?'

'All that you see.'

'How many is that? Fifty? Sixty?'

'Forty.'

'And you think to take the tribe?'

'Do I look insane? You knew me, Ingis; you watched me grow. Did I seem insane then?'

'No. You could have been . . .' Ingis cursed and spat into the fire. 'But you went away. Became a Lord of the Drenai.'

'Have the shamen met yet?' asked Tenaka.

'No. Asta Khan has called a council for tomorrow at dusk.'

'Where?'

'At the tomb of Ulric.'

'I shall be there.'

Ingis leaned in closer. 'You don't seem to understand,' he whispered. 'It is my duty to kill you.'

'Why?' asked Tenaka calmly.

'Why? Because I serve Saddleskull. Even sitting here talking to you is an act of betrayal.'

'As you pointed out, Ingis, my force is very small. You betray no one. But think on this: you are pledged to follow the Khan of Wolves, yet he is not chosen until tomorrow.'

'I will not play with words, Tenaka. I pledged my support to Saddleskull against Knifespeaks. I will not go back on it.'

'Nor should you,' said Tenaka. 'You would be less a man. But I also am against Knifespeaks, which makes us allies.'

'No, no, no! You are against them both, which makes us enemies.'

'I am a man with a dream, Ingis – the dream of Ulric. These men with me were once Doublehair. Now they are mine. The burly one by the far tent is a Spear. Now he is mine. These forty represent three tribes. United, the world is ours. I am an enemy to no one. Not yet.'

'You always had a good brain and a fine sword-arm. Had I known you were coming, I might have waited before pledging my force.'

'You will see tomorrow. For tonight – eat and rest.'

'I cannot eat with you,' said Ingis, rising. 'But I will not kill you. Not tonight.' He strode to his pony and climbed into the saddle. His men ran to their mounts and with a wave Ingis led them out into the darkness.

Subodai and Gitasi ran to the fire, where Tenaka Khan was quietly finishing his supper.

'Why?' asked Subodai. 'Why did they not kill us?'

Tenaka grinned, then yawned theatrically. 'I am tired. I will sleep now.'

Out in the valley beyond, Ingis was being asked the same question by his son, Sember.

'I cannot explain it,' said Ingis. 'You would not understand.'

'Make me understand! He is a half-blood with a rag-tag following of Notas scum. And he did not even ask you to follow him.'

'Congratulations, Sember! Most of the time you cannot grasp the simplest subtlety, but on this occasion you surpass yourself.'

'What does that mean?'

'It is simple. You have stumbled on the very reasons why I did not kill him. Here is a man with no chance of success, faced by a warlord with twenty thousand warriors under his banner. Yet he did *not* ask for my help. Ask yourself why.'

'Because he is a fool.'

'There are times, Sember, when I could believe your mother had a secret lover. Looking at you makes me wonder if it was one of my goats.'

19

Tenaka waited in darkness and silence as the sounds of movement in the small camp ceased. Then he lifted the flap of his tent and watched the sentries. Their eyes were scanning the trees around the camp and they were not interested in what went on within. Tenaka slid from the tent, hugging the moon shadows from the twisted trees as he silently edged into the deeper darkness of the woods.

Walking cautiously, he made his way for several miles, as the ground dipped and rose towards the distant hills. He cleared the edge of the wood some three hours before dawn and slowly began to climb. Far below, and to the right, lay the marble-covered tomb of Ulric – and the armies of Knifespeaks and Saddleskull.

Civil war was inevitable and Tenaka had hoped to convince whoever was the Khan that it would be profitable to aid the Drenai rebels. Gold was a scarce commodity on the Steppes. Now things would have to be different.

He continued to climb until he saw a cliff face, pock-marked by caves. He had been here once before, many years ago when Jongir Khan had attended a shamen council. Then Tenaka had sat with Jongir's children and grandchildren outside the caves while the Khan journeyed into the darkness. It was said that hideous rites were performed in these ancient places, and that no man could enter uninvited. The caves were, the shamen promised, the very gates of Hell where demons lurked at every corner.

Tenaka reached the mouth of the largest cave, where he hesitated, calming his mind.

There is no other way, he told himself.

And entered.

The darkness was total. Tenaka stumbled. He pushed on, hands stretched out before him.

As the caves wound on – twisting and turning, splitting and rejoining – Tenaka quelled the panic rising in him. It was like being in a honeycomb. He could wander lost in this blind gloom until he died of hunger and thirst.

He moved on, feeling his way along a cold wall. Suddenly the wall ended, cutting away at right-angles to his hand. Tenaka walked on, hands outstretched. Cool air touched his face. He stopped and listened. He had the impression of space all around him, but more than that he felt the presence of people.

'I seek Asta Khan,' he said, his voice booming in the cavern.

Silence.

A shuffling sound came from left and right of him and he stood still, folding his arms across his chest. Hands touched him, scores of hands. He felt his sword being drawn from its scabbard, his knife from its sheath. Then the hands withdrew.

'Speak your name!' commanded a voice as dry and hostile as a desert wind.

'Tenaka Khan.'

'You have been gone from us for many years.'

'I have returned.'

'Obviously.'

'I did not leave willingly. I was sent from the Nadir.'

'For your own protection. You would have been slain.'

'Perhaps.'

'Why have you returned?'

'That is not a simple question to answer.'

'Then take your time.'

'I came to aid a friend. I came to gather an army.'

'A Drenai friend?'

'Yes.'

'And then?'

'Then the land spoke to me.'

'What were its words?'

'There were no words. It spoke in silence, heart to soul. It welcomed me as a son.'

'To come here unsummoned is death.'

'Who decides what is a summons?' asked Tenaka.

'I do.'

'Then you tell me, Asta Khan – was I summoned?'

Darkness fell away from Tenaka's eyes and he found himself in a great hall. Torches shone on every side. The walls were smooth, embedded with crystals of every hue, while stalactites hung like shining spears from the vast dome of the roof. The cavern was packed with people, shamen from every tribe.

Tenaka blinked as his eyes grew accustomed to the light. The torches had not sprung up instantly. They had been alight all the time – only he had been blind.

'Let me show you something, Tenaka,' said Asta Khan, leading him from the cavern. 'This is the path you took to reach me.'

Directly ahead was a yawning chasm, crossed by a slender stone bridge.

'You walked that bridge in blindness. And so, yes, you were summoned. Follow me!'

The ancient shaman took him back over the bridge to a small room close to the main cave entrance. There the two men sat on a goatskin rug.

'What would you have me do?' asked Asta Khan.

'Initiate the Shamen Quest.'

'Saddleskull has no need of the Quest. He outnumbers his enemy and can win it by battle alone.'

'Thousands of brothers will die.'

'That is the Nadir way, Tenaka.'

'The Shamen Quest would mean the deaths of only two,' said Tenaka.

'Speak plainly, young man! Without the Quest you have no chance to rule. With it your chances rise to one in three. Do you truly care about a civil war?'

'I do. I have the dream of Ulric. I want to build the nation.'

'And what of your Drenai friends?'

'They are still my friends.'

'I am no fool, Tenaka Khan. I have lived many, many years and I can read the hearts of men. Give me your hand and let me read your heart. But know this – if there is deceit in you, I shall kill you.'

Tenaka held out his hand and the old man took it.

For several minutes they remained thus, then Asta Khan released him.

'The power of the shamen is maintained in many ways. There is generally very little direct manipulation of tribal directions. You understand?'

'I do.'

'On this occasion I will grant your request. But when Saddleskull hears he will send his executioner. There will be a challenge – it is all he can do.'

'I understand.'

'Do you wish to know of him?'

'No. It is immaterial.'

'You are confident.'

'I am Tenaka Khan.'

The Valley of the Tomb stretched between two ranges of iron-grey mountains; these were known as the Ranks of Giants and Ulric himself had named this place as his burial ground. It amused the great warlord to think of these ageless sentries standing guard over his mortal remains. The tomb itself was built of sandstone, covered with marble. Forty thousand slaves had died building this monolith, shaped like the crown Ulric never wore. Six pointed towers ringed the white dome and giant runes were carved upon every surface, telling the world and all succeeding generations that here lay Ulric the Conqueror, the greatest Nadir warlord of them all.

And yet, typically, Ulric's humour came through even this corpse-white colossus. The only carving to show the Khan depicted him riding his pony and wearing the crown of kings. Set sixty feet above the ground and back beyond a curving gateway, the statue was meant to depict Ulric waiting beyond the walls of Dros Delnoch, his only defeat. On his head was the crown, placed there by Ventrian sculptors who did not realise that a man could command an army of millions without being a king. This was a subtle jest, but one which Ulric would have enjoyed.

To the east and west of the tomb camped the armies of the two enemy kinsmen: Shirrat Knifespeaks and Tsuboy Saddleskull. More than 150,000 men waited for the outcome of the Shamen Quest.

Tenaka led his people down into the valley. Ramrod-straight on his Drenai stallion he rode, and beside him Gitasi felt a surge of pride. He was Notas no longer – he was a man again.

697

Tenaka Khan rode to a point south of the tomb and dismounted. Word of his coming had spread to both camps and hundreds of warriors began to drift towards his camp-site.

The women of Gitasi busied themselves erecting the tents while the men attended to their ponies and settled themselves down around Tenaka Khan. He sat cross-legged on the ground, staring at the great tomb, his eyes distant and his mind closed to the drifters.

A shadow fell across him. He waited for long seconds, letting the insult build, then he smoothly rose to his feet. This moment had to come – it was the opening move in a none-too-subtle game.

'You are the half-blood?' asked the man. He was young, in his middle twenties, and tall for a Nadir. Tenaka Khan looked at him coolly, noting the balanced stance, the slim hips and the wide shoulders, the powerful arms and the depth of chest. The man was a swordsman and confidence blazed from him. He would be the executioner.

'And who would you be, child?' said Tenaka Khan.

'I am a true-born Nadir warrior, the son of a Nadir warrior. It galls me that a mongrel should stand before the tomb of Ulric.'

'Then move away and continue your yapping elsewhere,' said Tenaka Khan. The man smiled.

'Let us cease this nonsense,' he said smoothly. 'I am here to kill you. It is obvious. Let us begin.'

'You are very young to wish for death,' said Tenaka. 'And I am not old enough to refuse you. What is your name?'

'Purtsai. Why do you wish to know it?'

'If I have to kill a brother, I like to know his name. It means that someone will remember him. Draw your sword, child.'

The crowd drew back, forming a giant circle around the combatants. Purtsai drew a curved sabre and a dagger. Tenaka Khan drew his own shortsword, and deftly caught the knife Subodai tossed to him.

And so the duel began.

Purtsai was good, skilled beyond the vast majority of tribesmen. His footwork was extraordinary and he had a suppleness unseen among the squat, bulky warriors of the Nadir. His speed was dazzling and his nerve cool.

He was dead within two minutes.

Subodai swaggered forward and stood with hands on hips, staring down at the body. He kicked it savagely, then spat upon it. Then he grinned at the watching warriors and spat again. Tucking his toe under the body, he flipped the corpse on to its back.

'This was the best of you?' he asked the crowd. He shook his head in mock sorrow. 'Whatever will become of you?'

Tenaka Khan walked to his tent and ducked under the flap. Inside Ingis was waiting, seated cross-legged on a fur rug and drinking a goblet of Nyis, a spirit distilled from goats' milk. Tenaka seated himself opposite the warlord.

'That did not take you long,' said Ingis.

'He was young, with much to learn.'

698

Ingis nodded. 'I advised Saddleskull against sending him.'

'He had no choice.'

'No. So . . . you are here.'

'Did you doubt it?'

Ingis shook his head. He removed his bronze helm and scratched at the skin beneath his thinning, iron-grey hair. 'The question is, Bladedancer, what am I to do about you?'

'Does it trouble you?'

'Yes.'

'Why?'

'Because I am trapped. I want to support you, for I believe you are the future. Yet I cannot, for I have sworn to uphold Saddleskull.'

'A thorny problem,' agreed Tenaka Khan, helping himself to a goblet of Nyis.

'What shall I do?' asked Ingis and Tenaka Khan stared at his strong honest face. He had only to ask and the man was his – he would break his oath to Saddleskull and pledge his warriors to Tenaka instead. Tenaka was tempted, but he resisted with ease. Ingis would not be the same man if he broke his oath for it would haunt him for the rest of his life.

'Tonight,' said Tenaka, 'the Shamen Quest begins. Those who stand for leadership will be tested and Asta Khan will name the Warlord. That is the man you are pledged to follow. Until that time you are bound to Saddleskull.'

'And what if he commands that I kill you?'

'Then you must kill me, Ingis.'

'We are all fools,' said the Nadir general bitterly. 'Honour? What does Saddleskull know of honour? I curse the day I swore to serve him!'

'Go now. Put these thoughts from your mind,' ordered Tenaka Khan. 'A man makes mistakes, but he lives by them. Foolish it may be, on occasion. But in the main it is the only way to live. We are what we say, only so long as our words are iron.'

Ingis rose and bowed. After he had gone Tenaka refilled his goblet and leaned back on the thick cushions scattered round the rug.

'Come out, Renya!' he called. She stepped from the shadows of the sleeping section and sat beside him, taking his hand.

'I feared for you when the warrior made his challenge.'

'My time is not yet.'

'He would have answered the same,' she pointed out.

'Yes, but he was wrong.'

'And have you so changed? Are you now infallible?'

'I am home, Renya. I feel different. I cannot explain it, and I have not yet tried to rationalise it. But it is wonderful. Before I came here I was incomplete. Lonely. Here I am whole.'

'I see.'

'No, I do not think that you do. You think I criticise you; you hear me talking of loneliness and you wonder. Do not misunderstand me. I love you and you have been a source of constant joy. But my purpose was not clear, and therefore I was what the shamen called me as a child: the

Prince of Shadows. I was a shadow in the world of stone reality. Now I am a shadow no longer. I have a purpose.'

'You want to be a king,' she said sadly.

'Yes.'

'You want to conquer the world.'

He did not answer.

'You have seen Ceska's terror and the folly of ambition. You have seen the horror that war brings. Now you will bring a greater horror than Ceska could ever dream of.'

'It does not have to be horror.'

'Do not fool yourself, Tenaka Khan. You have merely to look beyond this tent. They are savages – they live to fight . . . to kill. I don't know why I'm talking like this. You are beyond my words. After all, I am just a woman.'

'You are my woman.'

'I was. Not any longer. You have another woman now. Her breasts are mountains, and her seed waits out there to spill across the world. What a hero you are, great Khan! Your friend is waiting for you. In the blindness of his loyalty, he expects to see you riding on a white horse at the head of your Nadir. Then the evil will fall and the Drenai will be free. Imagine his surprise when you rape his nation!'

'You have said enough, Renya. I will not betray Ananais. I will not invade the Drenai.'

'Not now, maybe. But one day you will have no choice. There won't be anywhere else.'

'I am not yet the Khan.'

'Do you believe in prayer, Tenaka?' she asked suddenly, tears in her eyes.

'Sometimes.'

'Then think on this: I pray that you lose tonight, even if it means your death.'

'If I lose, it will,' said Tenaka Khan.

But she had already moved away from him.

The ancient shaman squatted in the dust, staring intently into a brazier of coals on an iron stand. Around him sat the chieftains of the Nadir, the warlords, the masters of the Horde.

Away from the crowd, within a circle of stones, sat the three kinsmen: Tsuboy Saddleskull, Shirrat Knifespeaks and Tenaka Khan.

The warlords studied each other with rare interest. Saddleskull was a blocky, powerful figure, with a braided top-knot and a wispy forked beard. He was stripped to the waist and his body gleamed with oil.

Knifespeaks was slimmer and his long hair, streaked with silver, was tied at the nape of the neck. His face was oblong accentuated by the drooping moustache, and mournful. But his eyes were sharp and alert.

Tenaka Khan sat quietly with them, staring up at the tomb which was shining silver in the moonlight. Saddleskull cracked his fingers noisily and tensed the muscles of his back. He was nervous. He had planned for years to take control of the Wolves. And now – with his army stronger than his brother's – he was forced to gamble his future on a single throw. Such was the power of the shamen. He had tried to ignore Asta Khan, but even his own warlords – respected warriors like Ingis – had urged him to seek their wisdom. No one wanted to see wolf rend wolf. But what a time for Tenaka the Mongrel to come home. Saddleskull cursed inwardly.

Asta Khan pushed himself to his feet. The shaman was old, older than any man living among the tribes, and his wisdom was legend. He moved slowly round to stand before the trio; he knew them well – as he had known their fathers and grandfathers – and he could see the resemblance between them.

He lifted his right arm. 'Nadir we!' he shouted, and his voice belied his age; resonant and powerful it floated above the massed ranks and the men echoed the shout solemnly.

'There is no going back from this quest,' said the shaman, addressing the trio. 'You are all kinsmen. Each of you claims blood link to the great Khan. Can you not agree amongst you who should lead?'

He waited for several seconds, but all three remained silent.

'Then hear the wisdom of Asta Khan. You expect to fight one another – I see that your bodies and your weapons are sharp. But there will be no battle of the blood. Instead I shall send you to a place that is not of this world. He that returns will be the Khan, for he will find the helm of Ulric. Death will be closer to you, for you will be walking within his realm. You will see terrible sights, you will hear the screams of the damned. Do you still wish this quest?'

'Let us begin!' snapped Saddleskull. 'Get ready to die, mongrel,' he whispered to Tenaka.

The shaman stepped forward, placing his hand on Saddleskull's head. The warlord's eyes closed and his head dropped. Knifespeaks followed . . . then Tenaka Khan.

Asta Khan squatted down before the sleeping trio, then he closed his eyes.

'Stand!' he ordered.

The three men opened their eyes and stood, blinking in surprise. They were still before the tomb of Ulric, only now they were alone. Gone were the warriors, and the tents, and the camp-fires.

'What is the meaning of this?' asked Knifespeaks.

'There is the tomb of Ulric,' answered Asta Khan. 'All you must do is fetch the helm from the sleeping Khan.'

Knifespeaks and Saddleskull loped off towards the tomb. There were no entrances visible – no doors, only smooth white marble.

Tenaka sat down and the shaman squatted beside him.

'Why do you not search with your cousins?' he asked.

'I know where to look.'

Asta Khan nodded. 'I knew you would come back.'

'How?'

'It was written.'

Tenaka watched his kinsmen circling the tomb, waiting for the moment when both of them were out of sight. Then he rose slowly and sped to the dome. The climb was not difficult, for the marble fascia had been pinned to the sandstone and this left hand-holds where the blocks joined. He was half-way to the statue of Ulric before the others spotted him. Then he heard Saddleskull curse, and knew they were following.

He reached the arch. It was seven feet deep and the statue of Ulric nestled at the rear.

The King Beyond the Gate!

Tenaka Khan moved forward carefully. The door was hidden behind the archway. He pushed at it and it creaked open.

Saddleskull and Knifespeaks arrived almost together, their enmity forgotten in their fear that Tenaka was ahead. Seeing the open door they pushed forward, but Saddleskull pulled back just as Knifespeaks entered. As Knifespeaks' foot crossed the threshold there was a loud crack and three spears hammered through his chest, punching through his lungs and jutting from his back. He sagged forward. Saddleskull moved round the body, seeing that the spears had been attached to a board, and the board to a series of ropes. He held his breath and listened carefully; he could hear the whispering fall of sand trickling on the stone. He dropped to his knees – there inside the doorway was a broken glass. Sand trickled from it.

As soon as Knifespeaks had broken the glass, the balance was lost and the death-trap released. But how had Tenaka avoided death? Saddleskull cursed and carefully moved into the doorway. Where the half-blood walked, he could surely follow? Immediately he disappeared, Tenaka stepped out from behind the ghostly statue of the Khan. He paused to study the trap which had killed Knifespeaks and then silently moved into the tomb.

The corridor beyond should have been in total darkness, but a strange green light glowed from the walls. Tenaka dropped to his hands and knees and crawled forward, scanning the walls on either side. There must be more traps. But where?

The corridor ended at a circular stair, dipping down into the bowels of the tomb. Tenaka studied the first few steps – they seemed solid. The wall alongside was panelled with cedar. Tenaka sat on the top stair. Why panel a stairwell?

He ripped a section of cedar from the wall and moved on down the stairs, testing each step. Halfway down he felt a slight movement beneath his right foot and withdrew it. Taking the cedar plank, he laid it flat against the edges of the steps and then lay back upon it and lifted his feet. The plank began to slide. It hit the rigged steps at speed and Tenaka felt the 'whoosh' of a steel blade slice above his head. The plank increased speed, hurtling down the stairs. Thrice more it triggered death-traps, but such was the speed of the makeshift sled that Tenaka was untouched. He thrust his booted feet against the walls to slow himself down, his arms and legs being battered and bruised as the journey continued.

The plank hit the ground at the foot of the stairs, pitching Tenaka through the air. Instantly, he relaxed, curling his body into a ball. The air was punched from him as he hit the far wall. He grunted and rolled to his knees. Gingerly he touched his ribs; at least one felt broken. He glanced round the chamber. Where was Saddleskull? The answer came seconds later: hearing the clatter on the stairs, Tenaka grinned and moved away from the stairwell. Saddleskull hurtled by him – his plank smashing to shards, his body cartwheeling into the far wall. Tenaka winced at the impact.

Saddleskull groaned and staggered to his feet; spying Tenaka, he drew himself upright.

'It didn't take me long to work out your plan, half-blood!'

'You surprise me. How did you get behind me?'

'I hid by the body.'

'Well, we are here,' said Tenaka, pointing to the sarcophagus on the raised dais at the centre of the chamber. 'All that remains is to claim the helm.'

'Yes,' said Saddleskull warily.

'Open the coffin,' said Tenaka smiling.

'You open it.'

'Come now, cousin. We cannot spend the rest of our lives here. We will open it together.'

Saddleskull's eyes narrowed. The coffin would almost certainly be rigged and he did not want to die. But if he allowed Tenaka to open the coffin, he would gain not only the helm but, more importantly, Ulric's sword.

Saddleskull grinned. 'Very well,' he said. 'Together!'

They moved to the coffin and heaved at the marble lid, which creaked open. The two men gave a final push and the lid fell to the floor, breaking into three pieces. Saddleskull lunged for the sword that lay on the chest of the skeleton within. Tenaka seized the helm and leapt to the far side of the coffin. Saddleskull chuckled.

'Well, cousin. Now what will you do?'

'I have the helm,' said Tenaka.

Saddleskull leapt forward, slashing wildly, but Tenaka jumped clear, keeping the coffin between them.

'We could do this for ever,' said Tenaka. 'We could spend eternity running round and round this coffin.'

His opponent hawked and spat. There was truth in what Tenaka said – the sword was useless unless he could get within range.

'Give me the helm,' said Saddleskull. 'Then we can both live. Agree to serve me and I will make you my Warmaster.'

'No, I will not serve you,' said Tenaka. 'But you can have the helm if you agree to one condition.'

'Name it!'

'That you let me lead thirty thousand riders into the Drenai.'

'What? Why?'

'We can discuss that later. Do you swear?'

'I do. Give me the helm.'

As Tenaka tossed the helm across the coffin, Saddleskull caught it deftly and pushed it on his head, wincing as a sharp edge of metal pricked his scalp.

'You are a fool, Tenaka. Did Asta not say that only one would return? Now I have it all.'

'You have nothing, numbskull. You are dead!' said Tenaka.

'Empty threats,' sneered Saddleskull.

Tenaka laughed. 'Ulric's last jest! No one can wear his helm. Did you feel the sharpness, cousin, when the poison needle pierced your skin?'

The sword fell from Saddleskull's hand and his legs gave way. He struggled to rise, but death pulled him down into the pit. Tenaka recovered the helm and replaced the sword in the coffin.

Slowly he climbed the stairs, squeezing past the blades jutting from the panels. Once into the open air he sat back, cradling the helm in his lap. It was bronze, edged with white fur and decorated with silver thread.

Far below Asta Khan sat watching the moon and Tenaka climbed down to him. The old man did not look round as he approached.

'Welcome, Tenaka Khan, Lord of Hosts!' he said.

'Take me home,' ordered Tenaka.

'Not yet.'

'Why?'

'There is someone you must meet.' A white mist billowed from the ground, swirling around them; from its depths strode a powerful figure.

'You did well,' said Ulric.

'Thank you, my Lord.'

'Do you mean to keep your word to your friends?'

'I do.'

'So the Nadir will ride to the aid of the Drenai?'

'They will.'

'It is as it should be. A man must stand by his friends. But you know that the Drenai must fall before you? As long as they survive, the Nadir cannot prosper.'

'I know this.'

'And you are prepared to conquer them . . . end their empire?'

'I am.'

'Good. Follow me into the mist.'

Tenaka did as he was bid and the Khan led him to the banks of a dark river. There sat an old man who turned as Tenaka approached. It was Aulin, the former Source priest who had died in the Dragon barracks.

'Were you true to your word?' he asked. 'Did you look after Renya?'

'I did.'

'Then sit beside me, and I shall be true to my word.'

Tenaka sat and the old man leaned back, watching the dark water bubble and flow.

'I discovered many machines of the Elders. I scanned their books and notes. I experimented. I learned much of their secrets. They knew the Fall was imminent and they left many clues for future generations. The world is a ball, did you know that?'

'No,' said Tenaka.

'Well, it is. At the top of the ball is a world of ice. And at the base, another. Round the centre it is hellishly hot. And the ball spins around the sun. Did you know that?'

'Aulin, I have no time for this. What do you wish to tell me?'

'Please, warrior, listen to me. I so wanted this knowledge shared – it is important to me.'

'Go on, then.'

'The world spins and the ice at the poles of the world grows daily: millions of tons of ice, every day for thousands of years. At last the ball begins to wobble as it spins, and then it tips. And as it tips, the oceans rise up and cover the land. And the ice spreads to cover whole continents. That is the Fall. That is what happened to the Elders. Do you see? It makes the dreams of men a nonsense.'

'I see. Now what can you tell me?'

'The machines of the Elders – they do not operate as Ceska thinks. There is no physical joining of beasts and men. Rather is it a harnessing of vital forces, held in delicate balance. The Elders knew it was important – vital – to allow the spirit of man to remain in the ascendant. The horror of the Joinings is the result of allowing the beast to emerge.'

'How does this help me?' asked Tenaka.

'I saw a joining revert once; it became a man again and died.'

'How?'

'When it saw something which jolted it.'

'What did it see?'

'The woman who had been its wife.'

'Is that it?'

'Yes. Is that helpful?'

'I don't know,' said Tenaka. 'It may be.'

'Then I shall leave you,' said Aulin. 'I shall return to the Grey.'

Tenaka watched him shuffle away into the mist. Then he stood and turned as Ulric stepped forward.

'The war has already begun,' said the Khan. 'You will not arrive in time to save your friends.'

'Then I shall be in time to avenge them,' answered Tenaka.

'What was the old man trying to tell you about the Fall?'

'I don't know – something about ice spinning. It wasn't important,' said Tenaka.

The old shaman bade Tenaka sit down and the new Khan obeyed. His eyes closed. When he opened them, he was sitting before the tomb as before, watched by the massed ranks of Nadir generals. To his left lay Shirrat Knifespeaks – his chest ripped apart, blood staining the dust. To his right was Saddleskull, a small trickle of blood on his temple. Before him was the helm of Ulric.

Asta Khan stood and turned to the generals.

'It is over and it has begun. Tenaka Khan rules the Wolves.'

The old man took the helm, returned to the brazier, swept up his cloak of ragged skins and walked from the camp. Tenaka remained where he was, scanning the faces before him and sensing the hostility. These were men prepared for war, supporters of Knifespeaks or Saddleskull. Not one man among them had considered Tenaka as Khan. Now they had a new leader and from this moment on Tenaka would need to walk with extreme care. His food would have to be tasted . . . his tent guarded. Among the men before him would be many who would desire his death.

And swiftly!

It was easy to become a Khan. The real trick lay in staying alive thereafter.

A movement in the ranks caught his eye and Ingis rose and walked towards him. Taking his sword from its scabbard and reversing the blade, he handed it hilt-first to Tenaka.

'I become your man,' said Ingis kneeling.

'Welcome, warrior. How many brothers do you bring?'

'Twenty thousand.'

'It is good,' said the Khan.

And one by one the generals trooped forward. It was dawn before the last backed away and Ingis approached once more.

'The families of Saddleskull and Knifespeaks have been taken. They are being held near your camp-site.'

Tenaka rose and stretched. He was cold, and very tired. With Ingis beside him, he walked from the tomb.

A great crowd had assembled to watch the deaths of the prisoners. Tenaka looked at the captives as they knelt in silent ranks, their arms tied behind them. There were twenty-two women, six men and a dozen boy-children.

Subodai came forward. 'You wish to kill them yourself?'

'No.'

'Gitasi and I will do it then,' he said with relish.

'No.' Tenaka walked on, leaving Subodai baffled and surprised.

The new Khan halted before the women, the wives of the dead warlords.

'I did not kill your husbands,' he told them. 'There was no blood feud between us. Yet I inherit their property. So be it! You were part of that property and I name you as wives of Tenaka Khan. Release them!' he ordered.

Muttering under his breath, Subodai moved along the line. A young woman ran forward as he freed her and threw herself at Tenaka's feet.

'If I am truly your wife, then what of my son?'

'Release the children also,' said Tenaka.

Only the six men remained now, close relatives of the dead warlords.

'This is a new day,' Tenaka told them. 'I give you this choice. Promise you serve me and you live. Refuse and you die!'

'I spit on you, half-blood,' shouted one man. Tenaka stepped forward, held out his hand for Subodai's sword and with one sweep severed the man's neck.

Not one of the five remaining prisoners spoke, and Tenaka moved along the line, killing them all. He called Ingis to him and the two men sat quietly in the shadows of the tent.

There they stayed for three hours while the Khan outlined his plans. Then Tenaka slept.

And while he slept twenty men ringed his tent, swords in hand.

20

Parsal continued to crawl, dragging himself through the long grass. The pain from his mutilated leg had faded from the searing agony of the previous afternoon to a throbbing ache which occasionally flared, causing him to lose consciousness. The night was cool, but Parsal was sweating freely. He no longer knew where he was going, only that he had to put as great a distance between himself and the horror as he could.

He crawled over an area of earth pitted with pebbles, and a sharp stone dug into his leg. Groaning, he rolled over.

Ananais had told them to hold on for as long as they could, then to draw back and make for Magadon. He had then gone to another valley with Galand. The events of the afternoon kept flooding Parsal's mind and he could not push them away . . . With four hundred men he had waited in a tiny pass. The cavalry had come first, thundering up the incline with lances levelled. Parsal's archers had cut them to pieces. The infantry were harder to repel, well-armoured and with their round bronze shields held high. Parsal had never been the swordsman his brother was but, by all the gods, he had given a good account of himself!

The Skoda men had fought like tigers and Ceska's infantry were forced back. That was the point when he should have ordered his men to withdraw.

Foolish, foolish man!

But he had been so uplifted. So proud! Never in his life had he led a fighting force. He had been turned down for the Dragon, while his brother had been accepted. Now he had repelled a mighty enemy.

And he waited for one more attack.

The Joinings had surged forward like demons of the pit. If he lived to be a hundred, he would never forget that charge. The beasts sent up a terrifying wall of sound, howling their blood-lust as they ran. Giant monsters with slavering maws and blood-red eyes, sharp talons and bright, bright swords.

Arrows scarce pierced their flesh and they swept aside the fighting men of Skoda as a grown man scatters unruly children.

Parsal gave no order to run – it was unnecessary. The Skoda courage vanished like water on sand and the force scattered. In his anguish Parsal ran at a Joining, aiming a mighty blow for the beast's head, but his sword bounced from the thick skull and the creature turned on him. Parsal was thrown back and the Joining dived, its great jaws closing on Parsal's left leg and ripping the flesh from the bone. A gallant Skoda fighter leapt to the beast's back, driving a long dagger into its neck; it turned away from Parsal to rip the throat from the warrior. Parsal rolled clear over a rise and tumbled down and down into the valley. And so his long crawl began.

He knew now that there was no victory for the Skoda men. Their dreams were folly. Nothing could stand against the Joining. He wished he had stayed on his farm in Vagria, far away from this insane war.

Something seized his leg and he sat up, waving a dagger. A taloned arm smashed it from his grip and three Joinings squatted around him – their eyes gleaming, saliva dripping from open maws.

Mercifully he blacked out.

And the feeding began.

Pagan edged forward until he was less than one hundred yards from the western quarter of the city. His horse was hidden in the woods behind him. Smoke from the burning buildings was swirling like mist and it was hard to see for any distance. Bodies were being dragged from the city by groups of Joinings, and the feast started in the meadows beyond. Pagan had never seen the beasts before and he watched them in grim fascination. Most were over seven feet tall and mightily muscled.

Pagan was at a loss. He had a message for Ananais from Scaler – but where would he now deliver it? Was the dark-masked warrior still alive? Was the war over? If it was, then Pagan must change his plan. He had sworn to kill Ceska and he was not a man to take an oath lightly. Somewhere among this army was the tent of the emperor – all he had to do was find it and gut the son of a whore.

That was all!

The deaths of Pagan's people weighed heavily on him and he was determined to avenge them. Once he killed Ceska, the emperor's shade would be consigned to the Land of Shadow to serve the slain. A fitting punishment.

Pagan watched the beasts feed for a while, noting their movements, and learning all he could against the day when he must fight them. He was under no illusion – the day would come. Man against beast, head to head. The beast might be strong, swift and deadly. But then Kataskicana the King had earned the title Lord of War. For he too was strong, swift and deadly. But added to this, he was cunning.

Pagan eased his way back into the woods. Once there he froze, his wide nostrils flaring. His eyes narrowed and he slid his axe into his hand.

His horse was standing where he had left it, but the beast was quivering in fear, its ears flat against its skull and its eyes wide.

Pagan delved into his leather tunic, pulling clear a short, heavy throwing-knife. Licking his lips, he scanned the undergrowth. Hiding places close by were few; he was in one such, which left three other obvious places. So, he reasoned, he was facing a maximum of three opponents. Did they have bows? Unlikely, for they would have to stand, draw and loose at a swiftly moving target. Were they human? Unlikely, for the horse was terrified and mere men would not create such fear.

So then – a possible three Joinings crouched in the bushes ahead of him.

His decision made, Pagan stood up and walked towards his horse.

A Joining leapt from the bushes to his right and another rose from the left. They moved with incredible speed. Pagan spun on his heel, his right arm flashing down; the knife plunged into the right eye-socket of the first beast. The second was almost upon him when the black man dropped to his knees and dived forward, crashing into the creature's legs. The Joining pitched over him and Pagan rolled, lashing the axe-blade deep into the beast's thigh. Then he was up and running. He tore the reins clear of the branches and vaulted to the saddle as the Joining ran at him. As Pagan leaned back in the saddle, tugging on the reins, the horse reared in terror, its hooves lashing at the beast and catching it full in the face. The Joining went down and Pagan heeled away his horse through the woods, ducking under overhanging branches. Once clear, he galloped to the west.

The gods had been with him, for he had seriously miscalculated. Had there been three Joinings he would have been dead. He had aimed the knife for the beast's throat, but so swift had been its charge that he had almost missed the target altogether.

Pagan slowed his horse as the burning city fell away behind him.

All over the lowlands would be the scouts of Ceska. He had no wish to gallop into a greater danger than that from which he fled. He patted the horse's neck.

He had left Scaler with the Cheiam. The new Earl of Bronze had grown in stature and his plans for taking the fortress were well-advanced. Whether or not they would work was another matter, but at least Scaler was tackling them with confidence. Pagan chuckled. The young Drenai was more than convincing in his new role and Pagan could almost believe that he really was the legendary Earl.

Almost. Pagan chuckled again.

Towards dusk he moved into a section of trees near a stream. He had seen no sign of the enemy and he scouted the area carefully. But a surprise lay in wait for him as he rode into a small hollow.

Some twenty children were seated around the body of a man.

Pagan dismounted and tethered his horse. A tall boy stepped forward, a dagger in his hand.

'Touch him and I will kill you!' said the boy.

'I will not touch him,' said Pagan. 'Put up the knife.'

'Are you a Joining?'

'No, I am merely a man.'

'You don't look like a man – you're black.'

Pagan nodded solemnly. 'Indeed I am. You, on the other hand are white and very small. I don't doubt your bravery, but do you really think you can stand against me?'

The boy licked his lips, but stood his ground.

'If I was your enemy, boy, I would have killed you by now. Stand aside.' He walked forward, ignoring the lad as he knelt by the body. The dead man was thickset and balding, his large hands locked on his jerkin.

'What happened?' Pagan asked a little girl sitting closest to the body. She looked away and the boy with the knife spoke.

'He brought us here yesterday. He said we could hide until the beasts went away. But this morning, as he was playing with Melissa, he clutched his chest and fell.'

'It wasn't me,' said Melissa. 'I didn't do anything!'

Pagan ruffled the child's mousey-blonde hair. 'Of course you didn't. Did you bring food with you?'

'Yes,' answered the boy. 'It's over there in the cave.'

'My name is Pagan and I am a friend of Darkmask.'

'Will you look after us?' asked Melissa. Pagan smiled at her, then stood and stretched. The Joinings would be on the loose now and he had no chance of avoiding them on foot with twenty children in tow. He strode to the top of a nearby hill, shading his eyes to view the mountains. It would take them at least two days to walk that distance – two days out in the open. He turned to see the boy with the knife sitting on a rock behind him. He was tall and about eleven years of age.

'You didn't answer Melissa's question,' said the boy.

'What is your name, lad?'

'Ceorl. Will you help us?'

'I don't know that I can,' answered Pagan.

'I cannot do it all by myself,' said Ceorl, his grey eyes locked on Pagan's face.

Pagan sat down on the grass. 'Try to understand, Ceorl. There is virtually no way that we can make it to the mountains. The Joinings are like beasts of the jungle; they track by scent, they move fast and range wide. I have a message to deliver to Darkmask; I am involved in the war. I have my own mission and have sworn to see it through.'

'Excuses!' said Ceorl. 'Always excuses. Well, I will get them there – trust me.'

'I will stay with you for a little while,' said Pagan. 'But be warned: I don't much like children chattering around me – it makes me irritable.'

'You can't stop Melissa chattering. She is very young and very frightened.'

'And you are not frightened?'

'I am a man,' said Ceorl. 'I gave up crying years ago.'

Pagan nodded and smoothly rose to his feet. 'Let's get the food and be on our way.'

Together they gathered together the children. Each child carried a small rucksack of food and a canteen of water. Pagan lifted Melissa and two other toddlers to the horse's back and led them out on to the plain. The wind was at their backs, which was good . . . unless there were Joinings ahead of them. Ceorl was right about Melissa; she chattered on and on, telling Pagan stories he could scarcely follow. Towards the evening she began to sway in the saddle and Pagan lifted her clear and held her to his chest.

They had covered maybe three miles when Ceorl ran alongside Pagan and tugged his sleeve.

'What is it?'

'They are very tired. I just saw Ariane sit down beside the trail back there – I think she's gone to sleep.'

'All right. Go back and get her – we will camp here.'

The children huddled in together around Pagan as he laid Melissa down on the grass. The night was cool, but not cold.

'Will you tell us a story?' asked the girl.

Keeping his voice soft, he told them of the Moon Goddess who came down to earth on silver steps to live the life of a mortal. There she met the handsome warrior prince Anidigo. He loved her as no man has loved a woman since, but she was coy and fled from him. Up into the sky she rose in a silver chariot, perfectly round. He could not follow and went to see a wise wizard who made him a chariot of pure gold. Anidigo swore that until he had won the heart of the Moon Goddess he would never return. His golden chariot, also perfectly round, soared into the sky like a gleaming ball of fire. Round and round the earth he went, but always she was ahead of him. Even to this day.

'Look up!' said Pagan. 'There she rides – and soon Anidigo will send her fleeing from the sky.'

The last child fell into a dreamless sleep and Pagan eased himself through them, seeking Ceorl. Together they walked some paces away.

'You tell a good story.'

'I have many children,' replied Pagan.

'If they irritate you, why have so many?' the boy asked.

'That's not easy to explain,' said Pagan, grinning.

'Oh, I understand,' snapped Ceorl. 'I am not so young.'

Pagan tried to explain.

'A man can love his children, yet be annoyed by them. I was delighted with the births of all my children. One of them stands now in my place at home, ruling my people. But I am a man who has always needed solitude. Children do not understand that.'

'Why are you black?'

'So much for the philosophical conversation! I am black because my country is very hot. A dark skin is a protection against the sunlight. Does your skin not darken during summer?'

'And your hair – why is it so tightly curled?'

'I don't know, young man. No more do I know why my nose is wide and my lips thicker than yours. It is just the way it is.'

'Does everybody look like you where you come from?'

'Not to me.'

'Can you fight?'

'You are full of questions, Ceorl!'

'I like to know things. Can you fight?'

'Like a tiger.'

'That's a kind of cat, isn't it?'

'Yes. A very *large* cat and distinctly unfriendly.'

'I can fight,' said Ceorl. 'I am a good fighter.'

'I'm sure that you are. But let us hope that we don't have to prove it. Go and sleep now.'

'I am not tired. I'll stand watch.'

'Do as I tell you, Ceorl. You can stand watch tomorrow.'

712

The boy nodded and went back to the children. Within minutes he was fast asleep. Pagan sat for a while thinking of his homeland. Then he too moved to where the children lay. Melissa was still sleeping soundly, cuddling a rag doll. The doll was ancient; it had no eyes and only two thin strands of yellow thread for hair.

Scaler had told him of his own strange religious belief. The gods, said Scaler, were all so old that they had grown senile. Their vast power was now employed in senseless japes upon humans, misdirecting their lives and leaving them in appalling situations.

Pagan was fast becoming a believer.

A distant howl echoed in the night. Then a second and a third added to the noise. Pagan cursed softly and drew his sword. Taking a small whetstone from his leather pouch, he spat upon it and honed the sword-blade; then he unstrapped the axe from his saddlebag and sharpened that also.

The wind shifted, carrying their scent to the east. Pagan waited, counting slowly. He had reached eight hundred and seven when the howling increased in intensity. Considering variations in the wind speed, that put the Joinings between eight and twelve miles behind them – it was not enough.

The kindest action would be to creep forward and cut all the children's throats as they slept, saving them the horror that ran behind. But Pagan knew he could take three of the smallest on his horse.

He drew his dagger and crept among them.

But which three?

With a soft curse he rammed his dagger home in its scabbard and woke Ceorl.

'The Joinings are close,' he said. 'Wake the children – we're moving out.'

'How close?' asked Ceorl, eyes wide in fear.

'An hour behind – if we're lucky.'

Ceorl rolled to his feet and moved among the youngsters. Pagan lifted Melissa to his shoulder. She dropped the doll and he retrieved it, tucking it into his tunic. The children huddled around him.

'See that peak yonder?' he said to Ceorl. 'Make for it! I shall be back.'

'You promise?'

'I promise.' Pagan climbed into the saddle. 'Put two of the smaller children behind me.' Ceorl did as he was bid. 'Now hold on tight, little ones – we're going for a ride.'

Pagan dug his heels into the stallion and he leapt forward into the night, eating the distance between the mountains. Melissa woke up and began to cry, so Pagan pulled out the doll and pushed it into her arms. After riding for some minutes at a fast run, he saw an outcropping of rock away to the right. Hauling on the reins, he directed the stallion up and into the boulders. The pathway was narrow, less than five feet, widening at the top into a shallow bowl. There was no exit but by the path.

Pagan helped the children down. 'Wait here for me,' he said and rode down into the plain once more. Five times he made the journey, and by the last Ceorl and the remaining four older boys had almost reached the rocks as he rode out. Jumping from the saddle, he handed the reins to the boy.

'Take the horse up into the bowl and wait there for me.'

'What are you going to do?'

'Do as I say, child!'

Ceorl stepped back a pace. 'I just wanted to help.'

'I'm sorry, boy! Keep your dagger handy – I intend to hold them here, but if they come through use your dagger on the youngest children. You understand?'

'I don't think that I can,' Ceorl faltered.

'Then do as your heart bids you. Good luck, Ceorl!'

'I . . . I don't really want to die.'

'I know. Now get up there and comfort them.' Pagan pulled his axe clear of the saddle and untied his bow and a quiver of arrows. The bow was of Vagrian horn and only a very strong man could draw it. Pagan settled himself down on the trail, watching the east.

It was said that the Kings of the Opal Throne always knew when their day was done.

Pagan knew.

He strung his bow and removed his tunic, letting the night air cool his body.

In a deep voice he began to sing the Song of the Dead.

At a prearranged meeting place Ananais and his captains sat together discussing the day's action. Once thrown back from the first ring of mountains, the Skoda force had split into seven, moving to high ground and ambushing the invading force as they swarmed into the heights. Hit-and-run raids harassed Ceska's troops, slowing the advance, and Skoda casualties had been remarkably light – with the exception of Parsal's force, of which not one man had escaped.

'They are moving faster than we had estimated,' said Katan. 'And their numbers have been swelled by Delnoch troops.'

'I'd say there were as many as fifty thousand in the invading force,' said Thorn. 'We can forget about holding anywhere but Tarsk and Magadon.'

'We shall keep hitting them,' maintained Ananais. 'How long can you hold the power of those damned Templars, Katan?'

'I think even now they are finding ways through.'

'Once they do, our raids could become suicidal.'

'I know that well, Darkmask. But we are not dealing here with an exact science. The battle in the Void is unceasing, but we are being pushed back.'

'Do your best, boy,' said Ananais. 'All right – we shall hit them for one more day, then pull everyone back to the walls.'

'Do you get the feeling we are spitting into the eye of a hurricane?' asked Thorn.

Ananais grinned. 'Maybe, but we've not lost yet! Katan, is it safe to ride?'

The priest closed his eyes and the men waited for several minutes. Then Katan jerked suddenly, his eyes flaring open.

'To the north,' he said. 'We must go now!'

The priest lurched to his feet, half-fell, recovered and ran to his horse. Ananais followed him.

'Thorn!' he shouted. 'Take your men back to the group. The rest of you follow me!'

Katan led them in a headlong gallop to the north, followed by Ananais and twenty warriors. It was almost dawn and the tips of the mountains to their right were bathed in red.

The priest lashed his mount and Ananais, close behind, bellowed, 'You'll kill the beast, you fool!' Katan ignored him, bending low over the horse's neck. Ahead was an outcropping of rock; Katan dragged on the reins and leapt from the saddle, racing into a narrow cleft. Ananais drew his sword and followed him.

Inside the cleft lay two dead Joinings, black-feathered arrows jutting from their throats. Ananais ran on. Another dead beast, shot through the heart. He rounded a bend and heard the sound of bestial growling and the clash of steel on steel. Hurdling three more bodies, he turned a corner with sword raised. Two dead Joinings lay before him, a third live beast was attacking Katan, and two others were engaged in a grim struggle with a man Ananais could not see.

'To me, Dragon!' yelled Ananais. One of the two Joinings turned on him, but he blocked a savage cut and plunged his sword into the beast's belly. Its talons lashed out and he threw himself back as his men raced in, hacking and cutting. The beast went down under a score of blows. Katan despatched his opponent with consummate ease and ran forward to assist the warrior, but it wasn't necessary. Pagan hammered his axe through the beast's neck and sagged back to the path.

Ananais ran to him, to find Pagan's body was a mass of wounds: his chest was ripped open, flesh hanging in bloody strips.

His left arm was almost severed and his face had been mauled.

The black man's breathing was ragged, but his eyes were bright and he tried to smile as Ananais cradled his head in his lap.

'There are children above,' whispered Pagan.

'We will fetch them. Lie still!'

'For what, my friend?'

'Just lie still.'

'How many did I get?'

'Nine.'

'That's good. I am glad you came – the other two would have been . . . difficult.'

Katan knelt beside Pagan, laying his hand on the bloody head. All pain vanished from the dying warrior.

'I failed in my mission,' said Pagan. 'I should have gone after Ceska back at the city.'

'I will get him for you,' Ananais promised.

'Are the children all right?'

'Yes,' Katan assured him. 'We are bringing them out now.'

'Don't let them see me. It will frighten them.'

'Have no fear,' said Katan.

'Make sure you have Melissa's rag doll . . . she would be lost without it.'

'We will make sure.'

'When I was young I ordered men into the fire! I should not have done it. It is a lasting regret. Well, Darkmask, now we will never know, will we?'

'I already know,' said Ananais. 'I could not have felled nine Joinings. I would not have thought it possible.'

'All things are possible,' said Pagan, his voice sinking to a whisper. 'Except the passing of regret.' He paused. 'Scaler has a plan.'

'Can it work?' asked Ananais.

Pagan grinned. 'All things are possible. He gave me a message for you, but it is useless now. He wanted you to know that ten thousand Delnoch men were on the march. But they arrived before I could.'

Ceorl pushed his way through to Pagan, kneeling by his side with tears in his eyes.

'Why?' he said. 'Why did you do this for us?'

But Pagan was dead.

Ananais took the lad by the arm. 'He did it because he was a man – a very great man.'

'He didn't even like children.'

'I think you are wrong there, boy.'

'He said so himself. We irritated him, he told me. Why did he let himself get killed for us?'

Ananais had no answer but Katan stepped forward.

'Because he was a hero. And that is what heroes do. You understand?'

Ceorl nodded. 'I didn't know he was a hero – he didn't say.'

'Maybe he didn't know,' said Katan.

Galand took the death of his brother hard. He withdrew into himself, suppressing his emotions, his dark eyes giving no hint of the agony he felt. He led his men on several raids against Drenai cavalry, hitting them fast and withdrawing at speed. Despite his desire to wreak vengeance upon them he remained a disciplined warrior – not for Galand the reckless charge, only the calculated risk. Among his three hundred men, losses were light and they cantered to the walls of Magadon having left only thirty-seven of their comrades buried back in the hills.

There was no gate at Magadon and the men released their horses and scaled rope ladders let down by the defenders. Galand was the last to climb the ramparts and at the top he turned, gazing back to the east. Somewhere there the body of Parsal was rotting on the grassland. No grave, no marker.

The war had claimed Galand's daughter and now his brother.

Soon it would claim him, he mused.

Strange how the thought struck no terror in him.

Among his men were another forty who had suffered wounds. He went down with them to the timber hospital where Valtaya and a dozen women tended them. Galand waved to the blonde woman and she smiled, then returned to her work stitching a shallow cut in a warrior's thigh.

He wandered out into the sunlight where one of his men brought him a loaf of bread and a jug of wine. Galand thanked him and sat down with his back to a tree. The bread was fresh, the wine young. One of his section leaders, a young farmer named Oranda, joined him. He had a thick bandage on his upper arm.

'They said the wound was clean – only six stitches. I should still be able to hold a shield.'

'Good,' said Galand absently. 'Have some wine?'

Oranda took a mouthful. 'It is a little young,' he said.

'Maybe we should lay it down for a month or two!'

'Point taken,' said Oranda, tilting the jug once more.

For a while they sat in silence, and the tension grew in Galand as he waited for the inevitable comment.

'I'm sorry about your brother,' said Oranda at last.

'All men die,' answered Galand.

'Yes. I lost friends in his force. The walls look strong, don't they? It's strange to see walls across this valley. I used to play here as a child and watch the wild horses run.'

Galand said nothing. Oranda handed him the wine-jug, wishing he could just get up and walk away, but he didn't want to be rude. When Valtaya joined them, Oranda greeted her with a grateful smile and slipped away.

Galand glanced up and smiled.

'You are looking lovely, lady. A vision.' She had removed the blood-drenched leather apron and now wore a dress of light blue cotton which moulded to her figure beautifully.

'Your eyes must be tired, blackbeard. My hair is greasy and there are purple rings under my eyes. I feel wretched.'

'In the eye of the beholder,' he said. She sat beside him, laying her hand on his arm.

'I am truly sorry about Parsal.'

'All men die,' he said, tired of the repetition.

'But I am glad you are alive.'

'Are you?' he asked, his eyes cold. 'Why?'

'What a strange question for a friend to ask!'

'I am not your friend, Val. I am the man who loves you. There is a difference.'

'I am sorry, Galand. There is nothing I can say – you know that I am with Ananais.'

'And are you happy?'

'Of course I am – as happy as anyone can be in the middle of a war.'

'Why? Why do you love him?'

'I cannot answer that question. No woman could. Why do you love me?'

He tilted the wine-jug, ignoring the logic.

'What hurts is that there is no future for any of us,' he said, 'even if we should survive this battle. Ananais will never settle down to married life. He's no farmer, no merchant . . . He will leave you in some lonely city. And I shall return to my farm. None of us will be happy.'

'Don't drink any more, Galand. It is making you melancholy.'

'My daughter was a joyous creature and a real rascal. Many's the smack I laid on her leg and many the tear I wiped away. Had I known how short her life was to be . . . And now Parsal . . . I hope he died swiftly. I feel it in a very selfish way,' he said suddenly. 'My blood runs in not a single living being, bar me. When I am gone, it will be as if I never was.'

'Your friends will care,' she said.

He pulled his arm from her comforting touch and glared at her through angry eyes.

'I *have* no friends! I never had.'

21

The emperor sat within his tent of silk surrounded by his captains. His warmaster, Darik, was beside him. The tent was huge, split into four sections: the largest, where the warriors now sat, had room for fifty men though only twenty were present.

Ceska had grown fat over the years and his skin was pasty and blotched. His dark eyes glittered with feral intelligence and it was said that he had learned the ways of the Dark Templars and could read minds. His captains lived in a state of cold dread around him, for often he would suddenly point at a man and scream 'Traitor!' That man would die horribly.

Darik was his most trusted warrior, a general of great guile, second only to the legendary Baris of the Dragon. A tall man in his early fifties, slender and wiry, Darik was clean-shaven and looked younger than his years.

Having heard the reports, and the numbers of the slain, Darik spoke: 'The raids seem casual, haphazard, yet I sense unity of thought behind them. What do you say, Maymon?'

The Dark Templar nodded. 'We are almost through their defences, but already we can see a great deal. They have walled the two passes known as Tarsk and Magadon. And they expect aid from the north, though without great confidence. The leader, as you expected, is Ananais, though it is the woman Rayvan who binds them together.'

'Where is she?' asked the emperor.

'Back in the mountains.'

'Can you get to her?'

'Not from the Void. She is protected.'

'They cannot protect all her friends?' suggested Ceska.

'No, my lord,' agreed Maymon.

'Then soul-take someone close to her. I want the woman dead.'

'Yes, my lord. But first we must break through the Void wall of The Thirty.'

'What of Tenaka Khan?' snapped Ceska.

'He escaped to the north. His grandfather, Jongir, died two months ago and there is civil war brewing.'

'Send a message to the Delnoch commander, ordering him to watch closely for any Nadir army.'

'Yes, my lord.'

'Leave me now,' said the emperor. 'All except Darik.'

The captains gratefully obeyed, walking out into the night. Around the tent stood fifty Joinings, the largest and most ferocious beasts in Ceska's army. The captains did not look at them as they passed.

Inside the tent Ceska sat silently for several minutes.

'They all hate me,' he said. 'Small men with small minds. What are they without me?'

'They are nothing, sire,' said Darik.

'Exactly. And what of you, general?'

'Sire, you can read men like an open book. You can see into their hearts. I am loyal, but the day you doubt me I shall take my life the instant you order it.'

'You are the only loyal man in the empire. I want them all dead. I want Skoda to be a charnel-house that will be remembered for eternity.'

'It shall be as you command, sire. They cannot hold against us.'

'The Spirit of Chaos rides with my forces, Darik. But it needs blood. Much blood. Oceans of blood! It is never satisfied.'

Ceska's eyes took on a haunted look and he lapsed into silence. Darik sat very still. The fact that his emperor was mad worried him not at all, but Ceska's deterioration was another matter. Darik was a strange man. Almost totally single-minded, he cared only for war and strategy and what he had told the emperor was the literal truth. When the day came – as come it must – that Ceska's madness turned on him, he would kill himself. For life would have nothing more to offer. Darik had never loved a single human being, nor been entranced by things of beauty. He cared not for paintings, poetry, literature, mountains nor storm-tossed seas.

War and death were his concerns. But even these he did not love – they merely maintained his interest.

Suddenly Ceska giggled. 'I was one of the last to see his face,' he said.

'Who, my lord?'

'Ananais, the Golden One. He became an arena warrior and a great favourite with the crowds. One day as he stood there acknowledging their cheers, I sent in one of my Joinings. It was a giant beast, a three-way breed of wolf, bear and man. He killed it. All that work and he killed it.' Ceska giggled again. 'But he lost face with the crowd.'

'How so, sire? Did they like the beast?'

'Oh no. He just *lost face*. It's a jest!'

Darik chuckled dutifully.

'I hate him. He was the first to sow seeds of doubt. He wanted to lead the Dragon against me, but Baris and Tenaka Khan stopped him. Noble Baris! He was better than you, you know.'

'Yes, sire. You have mentioned it before.'

'But not as loyal. You will stay loyal, won't you, Darik?'

'I will, sire.'

'You wouldn't want to become like Baris, would you?'

'No, sire.'

'Isn't it strange how certain qualities remain?' mused Ceska.

'Sire?'

'I mean – he is still a leader, isn't he? The others still look to him – I wonder why?'

'I don't know, sire. You look cold – can I fetch you some wine?'

'You wouldn't poison me, would you?'

'No, sire, but you are right – I ought to taste it first.'

'Yes. Taste it.'

Darik poured wine into a golden goblet and drank a little. His eyes widened.

'What is it, general?' asked Ceska, leaning forward.

'There is something in it, sire. It is salty.'

'Oceans of blood!' said Ceska, giggling.

Tenaka Khan awoke in the hour before dawn and reached for Renya, but the bed was empty. Then he remembered and sat up rubbing the sleep from his eyes. He seemed to recall someone saying his name, but it must have been a dream.

The voice called again and Tenaka swung his legs from the bed and gazed around the tent.

'Close your eyes, my friend and relax,' said the voice.

Tenaka lay back. In his mind's eye he could see the slender, ascetic face of Decado.

'How long before you reach us?'

'Five days. If Scaler opens the gates.'

'We will be dead by then.'

'I can move no more swiftly.'

'How many men do you bring?'

'Forty thousand.'

'You seem changed, Tani.'

'I am the same. How fares it with Ananais?'

'He trusts you.'

'And the others?'

'Pagan and Parsal are dead. We have been forced back to the last valleys. We can hold for maybe three days – no more. The Joinings are everything we feared.'

Tenaka told him of his ghostly meeting with Aulin and the words of the old man. Decado listened in silence.

'So you are the Khan,' he said at last.

'Yes.'

'Farewell, Tenaka.'

Back at Tarsk, Decado opened his eyes. Acuas and The Thirty sat in a circle around him, linking their powers.

Each of them had heard the words of Tenaka Khan, but more importantly each had entered his mind, sharing his thoughts.

Decado took a deep breath. 'Well?' he asked Acuas.

'We are betrayed,' answered the warrior priest.

'Not yet,' said Decado. 'He will come.'

'That is not what I meant.'

'I know what you meant. But let tomorrow look after itself. Our purpose here is to aid the people of Skoda. None of us will live to see the events thereafter.'

'But what is the point?' asked Balan. 'Some good should come of our deaths. Are we merely helping them to exchange tyrants?'

'And what if we are?' said Decado softly. 'The Source knows best. If we do not believe that, then it is all for nothing.'

'So you are now a believer?' said Balan sceptically.

'Yes, Balan, I am a believer. I think I always was. For even in my despair I railed at the Source. That itself was an admission of belief, though I could not see it. But tonight has convinced me.'

'Betrayal by a friend has convinced you?' asked Acuas, astonished.

'No, not betrayal. Hope. A glimmer of light. A sign of love. But we will talk of this tomorrow. Tonight there are farewells to be said.'

'Farewells?' said Acuas.

'We are The Thirty,' said Decado. 'Our mission is near completion. As the Voice of The Thirty I am the Abbot of Swords. But I am to die here. Yet The Thirty must live on. We have seen tonight that a new threat is growing and that in the days to come the Drenai will have need of us again. As in the past, so shall it be now. One of us must leave, take on the mantle of Abbot and raise a new group of Source warriors. That man is Katan, the Soul of The Thirty.'

'It cannot be me,' said Katan. 'I do not believe in death and killing.'

'Exactly so,' said Decado. 'Yet you are chosen. It seems to me that the Source always chooses us to perform tasks against our natures. Why, I do not know . . . but He knows.

'I am a poor man to be a leader. And yet the Source has allowed me to see His power. I am content. The rest of us will obey his will. Now, Katan, lead us in prayer for the last time.'

There were tears in Katan's eyes as he prayed and a great sadness rested upon him. At the end he embraced them all and walked away into the night. How would he manage? Where would he find a new Thirty? He mounted his horse and rode into the high country towards Vagria.

On a ridge overlooking the refugee settlement he saw the boy Ceorl sitting by the path. He reined in his horse and stepped down.

'Why are you here, Ceorl?'

'A man came to me and told me to be here – to wait for you.'

'What man?'

'A dream man.'

Katan settled down beside the boy. 'Is this the first time the man has come to you?'

'This man, you mean?'

'Yes.'

'Yes, it is. But often I see others – they talk to me.'

'Can you do magical things, Ceorl?'

'Yes.'

'Such as?'

'Sometimes when I touch things I know where they came from. I see pictures. And sometimes, when people are angry with me I hear what they are thinking.'

'Tell me of the man who came to you.'

'His name is Abaddon. He said he was the Abbot of Swords.'

Katan bowed his head and covered his face with his hands.

'Why are you sad?' asked Ceorl.

Katan took a deep breath and smiled. 'I am not sad . . . Not any more. You are the First, Ceorl. But there will be others. You are to ride with me and I will teach you many things.'

'Are we to be heroes, like the black man?'

'Yes,' said Katan. 'We are to be heroes.'

The armies of Ceska arrived with the dawn, marching in ranks ten deep and led by the Legion riders. The long column wound across the plain, splitting into two as it breasted the valley pass of Magadon. Ananais had ridden in with Thorn, Lake and a dozen men only an hour before. Now he leaned on the ramparts watching the force spread out and pitch their tents. Half the army rode on towards Tarsk.

Twenty thousand battle-hardened veterans remained. But there was no sign as yet of the emperor or his Joinings.

Ananais squinted against the rising sun. 'I think that's Darik – there in the centre. Now that's a compliment!'

'I don't think I would be comfortable with too many of his compliments,' muttered Thorn. 'He's a butcher!'

'More than that, my friend,' said Ananais, 'he is a warmaster. And that makes him a master butcher.'

For a while the defenders watched the preparations in grim, silent fascination. Wagons followed the army, piled high with crudely-made ladders, iron grappling-hooks, vine ropes and provisions.

An hour later, as Ananais was sleeping on the grass, the Joinings of Ceska marched into the plain. A young warrior woke the sleeping general and he rubbed his eyes and sat up.

'The beasts are here,' whispered the man. Seeing his fear, Ananais clapped him on the shoulder.

'Don't worry, lad! Keep a stick in your belt.'

'A stick, sir?'

'Yes. If they get too close to the wall, hurl the stick and shout "Fetch!" '

The joke didn't help, but it cheered Ananais who was still chuckling as he mounted the rampart steps.

Decado was leaning on the wooden shaft of the giant bow when Ananais joined him. The leader of The Thirty looked haggard and drawn; his eyes were distant.

'How are you feeling, Dec? You look tired.'

'Just old, Darkmask.'

'Don't you start with the Darkmask nonsense. I like my name.'

'The other suits you better,' said Decado, grinning.

The Joinings had settled down beyond the tents, creating a vast circle around a single black tent of silk.

'That will be Ceska,' said Ananais. 'He's taking no chances.'

'It seems we are to keep all the Joinings to ourselves,' concluded Decado. 'I see no sign of them splitting the force.'

'Lucky us!' said Ananais. 'It makes sense from their viewpoint, though. It doesn't matter which wall they take – just one and we are finished.'

'Tenaka will be here in five days,' Decado reminded him.

'We shall not be here to see him.'

'Perhaps. Ananais . . . ?'

'Yes?'

'It doesn't matter. When do you think they will attack?'

'I hate people who do that – what *were* you going to say?'

'It was nothing. Forget it!'

'What the hell is the matter with you? You look sadder than a sick cow!'

Decado forced a laugh. 'Yes – as I grow older so I become more serious. It's not as if there's anything to worry about after all – a mere twenty thousand warriors and a pack of hell-beasts.'

'I suppose you're right,' agreed Ananais. 'But I'll bet Tenaka mops them up in a damned hurry.'

'I would like to be here to see it,' said Decado.

'If wishes were oceans, we would all be fish,' said Ananais.

The huge warrior wandered away to the grass once more, settling down to finish his nap. Decado sat on the ramparts and watched him.

Was it wise to withhold from Ananais that Tenaka was now the Khan of the Drenai's greatest enemy? But what would it achieve to tell him? He trusted Tenaka, and when a man like Ananais gave his trust it was forged stronger than silver steel. It would be inconceivable to Ananais that Tenaka could betray him.

It was a kindness to let him die with his belief intact.

Or was it?

Did a man not have a right to know the truth?

'Decado!' called a voice in his mind. It was Acuas and Decado closed his eyes, concentrating on the voice.

'Yes?'

'The enemy has arrived at Tarsk. There is no sign of the Joinings.'

'They are all here!'

'Then we will travel to you. Yes?'

'Yes,' answered Decado. He had kept eight priests with him at Magadon and sent the other nine to Tarsk.

'We did as you suggested and entered the mind of one of the beasts, but I don't think you will like what we found.'

'Tell me.'

'They are Dragon! Ceska began rounding them up fifteen years ago. Some of the more recent came from amongst men captured when the Dragon re-formed.'

'I see.'

'Does it make a difference?'

'No,' said Decado. 'It only increases the sorrow.'

'I am sorry. Does the plan go ahead?'

'Yes. Are you sure we must be close?'

'I am,' said Acuas. 'The closer the better.'

'The Templars?'

'They have breached the Void Wall. We almost lost Balan.'

724

'How is he?'

'Recovering. Have you told Ananais about Tenaka Khan?'

'No.'

'You know best.'

'I hope so. Get here as soon as you can.'

On the grass below, Ananais slept dreamlessly. Valtaya saw him there and prepared a meal of roasted beef and hot bread. She carried it to him after about an hour and together they walked into the shade of some trees where he lifted his mask and ate.

She couldn't watch him eat and moved away to gather flowers. When he had finished she returned to him.

'Put on your mask,' she said. 'Someone might come by.'

His bright blue eyes burned into hers, then he looked away and pulled on the mask.

'Someone just did,' he said sadly.

22

Towards the middle of the morning bugles sounded in the enemy camp and some ten thousand warriors began to move purposefully around the wagons – pulling ladders clear, tying ropes to grappling hooks, hitching shields in place.

Ananais ran to the wall where Lake was bent over the giant bow, checking the ropes and ties.

The army lined up across the valley, sunlight flashing from swords and spears. A drum-beat began and the force moved forward.

On the wall, defenders licked dry lips with dry tongues and wiped sweating palms on their tunics.

The slow drum-beat echoed in the mountains.

Terror hit the defenders like a tidal wave. Men screamed and jumped from the wall, rolling on to the grass below.

'The Templars!' screamed Decado. 'It's only an illusion.'

But panic continued to well up in the Skoda ranks. Ananais tried to rally them, but his own voice was shaking with fear. More men leapt from the walls as the drums grew closer.

Hundreds of men now streamed back, skidding to a halt as they saw the woman standing before them in her rusty mailshirt.

'We don't run!' bellowed Rayvan. 'We are Skoda! We are the sons of Druss the Legend. *We don't run!*'

Drawing a shortsword, she walked through them towards the walls. Only a handful of men remained by the ramparts, and these were ghost-faced and trembling. Rayvan mounted the steps, fear growing as she reached the battlements.

Ananais staggered towards her, holding out his hand which she accepted gratefully.

'They can't beat us!' she said through gritted teeth, her eyes wide.

The Skoda men turned and saw her standing defiantly at the centre. Gathering their swords they moved forward again, pushing against the wall of fear before them.

Decado and The Thirty fought back against the force, holding a shield around Rayvan.

And then the fear vanished!

The Skoda warriors surged back to the walls, angry now. Shamed by the courage of the warrior woman who led them, they stood their ground, determination on every face.

The drum-beat stopped. A bugle sounded.

With a savage roar ten thousand warriors surged forward.

Lake and his workers hauled back the bowstrings on the two weapons, filling their bowls with filed lead shot. At fifty paces Lake lifted his arm.

At forty he dropped it and tugged the release. The arm whipped forward. The second machine let fly a moment later.

The first ranks of the enemy were scythed down and a great cheer rose from the defenders. Taking up their bows, the Skoda men sent volley after volley of arrows into the charging warriors. But they were heavily armoured and they held their shields before them.

Ladders thudded against the wall and grappling-hooks sailed over the ramparts.

'Now it begins!' said Ananais.

The first warrior to reach the ramparts died with Ananais' sword in his throat. As he fell, he dislodged the man below him.

And then they were over and the battle became hand-to-hand.

Decado and The Thirty fought together as a unit to the right of Ananais. Not one warrior gained the ramparts there.

But to the left the invaders forged an opening. Ananais charged among them, cutting and slashing, hacking and slaying. Like a lion among wolves he hammered his way through their ranks, and the Skoda men gathered behind him roaring their defiance. Slowly they pushed back the soldiers. At the centre Rayvan plunged her blade into a warrior's chest, but as he fell he lashed out, his sword slicing her cheek. She stumbled as another man ran at her and Lake, seeing his mother's danger, hurled his dagger to hit the assailant hilt-first, behind the ear. He half-fell and dropped his sword, whereupon Rayvan finished him with a two-handed cut to the neck.

'Get away from here, mother!' yelled Lake.

Decado, hearing the cry, left The Thirty and ran to Rayvan, helping her to her feet.

'Lake is right,' he said. 'You are far too important to risk yourself here!'

'Behind you!' she yelled, as a warrior leapt over the wall with axe raised. Decado spun on his heel and lunged. His sword skewered the man's chest – and snapped. Two more warriors climbed into view and Decado dived forward, scooping up the fallen axe and rolling to his feet. He blocked an overhead cut, then back-handed the warrior from the wall. The second man lanced his blade into Decado's shoulder but Lake, running in behind, hammered his sword through the attacker's skull.

The attackers drew back.

'Get the wounded from the wall,' shouted Ananais. 'They'll return at any moment.'

Ananais moved along the wall, hastily checking the wounded and dead. At least a hundred men would fight no more. Ten more attacks like this and they were finished.

Galand made his way from the far left, meeting Ananais at the centre.

'We could do with a thousand more men and a higher wall,' said Galand sourly.

'They did well. Losses will be fewer next time. The weakest of our men fell during this assault.'

'Is that all they are to you?' snapped Galand. 'Units with swords. Some good, some bad?'

'There is no time for this, Galand.'

'You make me sick!'

'I know Parsal's death . . .'

'Leave me alone!' said Galand, pushing past him.

'What was that about?' asked Thorn, climbing the rampart steps. A bandage had been wrapped around a shallow cut to his head.

'I don't know.'

'I brought some food,' said Thorn, handing Ananais a loaf filled with creamed cheese. Ananais had taken one bite when the drums began beating once more.

Five attacks were launched and repulsed before dusk, and one night attack was turned back with heavy losses among the Drenai.

Ananais remained on the wall until two hours before dawn, but Decado assured him no further attacks were planned and the general finally staggered away from the ramparts. Valtaya had a room in the hospital, but he resisted the impulse to go to her; instead he moved into the trees and fell asleep on a grassy knoll.

Four hundred men had been removed from the battle; the wounded overflowed the hospital and had been laid on blankets on the grass around the building. Ananais had sent for reinforcements, two hundred and fifty men of the reserve force.

At Tarsk, he learned from Acuas, the losses had been fewer, but then only three attacks had been launched. Turs, the young warrior who led the Tarsk troops, had done well by all accounts.

It was now obvious that the main thrust would be aimed at Magadon. Ananais hoped the Joinings would not be sent in tomorrow, but in his heart he knew that they would be.

Across from the hospital buildings a young warrior tossed in his sleep as the nightmare grew. Suddenly he stiffened and a strangled scream died in his throat. His eyes opened and he sat up, reaching for his knife. Reversing the blade, he slowly pushed it into his chest between the ribs until it sliced into his heart. Then he withdrew it and stood up. No blood ran from the wound . . .

Slowly he walked to the hospital building, staring through the open window. Inside Valtaya was working into the night, fighting to save the worst of the wounded.

He moved away from the window to the woods beyond, where some two hundred refugees had pitched their makeshift tents. By a camp-fire sat Rayvan, cradling a babe and talking to three women.

The dead man walked towards them.

Rayvan looked up and saw him – she knew him well.

'Can you not sleep, Oranda?'

He did not reply.

Then Rayvan saw the knife and her eyes narrowed. When the man knelt beside her, she looked into his eyes. Blank and dead, they stared back unseeing.

The knife flashed up and Rayvan twisted and dived, turning her body to protect the sleeping babe as the blade raked her hip. Letting the child roll clear, she blocked the next blow with her forearm and smashed a right cross to the man's chin. He fell, but rose again. Rayvan pushed herself to her feet. The other women were screaming now and the babe had begun to wail. As the corpse approached, Rayvan backed away; she could feel the blood oozing down her leg. Then a man ran forward, holding a blacksmith's hammer which he brought down savagely on the dead man's head. The skull cracked, but still no expression crossed his face.

An arrow flashed into the dead man's chest; he merely gazed down at it and then slowly pulled it clear. Galand ran forward just as the corpse reached Rayvan. As the knife came up, Galand lashed out and the knife-arm sailed from the body. The corpse staggered . . . And fell.

'They want you dead pretty badly,' said Galand.

'They want us all dead,' replied Rayvan.

'Tomorrow they will get their wish,' he observed.

Valtaya finished stitching the nine-inch cut on Rayvan's hip and then smeared a thick ointment along the wound.

'It will help to prevent an ugly scar,' said Valtaya, covering the wound with gauze.

'A matter of indifference to me,' said Rayvan. 'When you get to my age, no one is going to notice a scar on the hip – if you take my meaning?'

'Nonsense, you are a handsome woman.'

'Exactly. It is a rare man who notices a handsome woman. You are Darkmask's lover, are you not?'

'Yes.'

'Known him long?'

'No, not long. He saved my life.'

'I see.'

'What do you see?'

'You are a nice girl, but maybe you take debts too seriously.'

Valtaya sat down beside the bed, rubbing her eyes. She was tired, too tired for sleep.

'Do you always make snap judgements of people you meet?'

'No,' said Rayvan, sitting up carefully and feeling the pull of the stitches. 'But love is in the eyes and one woman knows when another woman is in love. When I asked you about Darkmask you showed your sadness. And then you said he had saved your life. It was not difficult to reach the obvious conclusion.'

'Is it so wrong to want to repay someone?'

'No, it isn't wrong – especially now. Anyway, he is a fine man.'

'I have hurt him,' said Valtaya. 'I didn't mean to, I was tired. Most times I try to ignore his face, but I told him to put on his mask.'

'Lake caught a glimpse of him once without his mask. He told me Ananais' face was hideously scarred.'

'There is no face,' said Valtaya. 'The nose and upper lip have been ripped away and the cheeks are a mass of scar tissue. One scar will not heal and oozes pus. It is a horror! He looks like a dead man. I have tried . . . I can't . . .' Tears fell and the words died.

'Don't think badly of yourself, my girl,' said Rayvan softly, leaning forward and patting her back. 'You *tried* – most women would not even have done that.'

'I am ashamed of myself. I told him once that a face was not a man. It was the man I tried to love, but the face keeps coming back to haunt me.'

'You were not wrong. The answer lies in your words – the man you *tried* to love. You took on too much.'

'But he's so noble and so tragic. He was the Golden One . . . He had everything.'

'I know. And he was vain.'

'How can you know that?'

'It's not hard. Consider his story: the rich young patrician who became a Dragon general. But what happened then? He entered himself in the arena games, and there he killed people to thrill the crowds. Many of the men he fought were prisoners, forced to fight and die. They had no choice, he did. But he couldn't stay away from the applause. There is nothing noble in that. Men! What do they know? They never grow up.'

'You are being very hard on him – he is willing to die for you!'

'Not for me. For himself. He is after revenge.'

'That's unfair!'

'Life is unfair,' said Rayvan. 'Don't misunderstand me, I like him. I like him a great deal. He is a fine man. But men don't come in just two groups, one of gold and the other of lead. They are a mix of both.'

'And what about women?' asked Valtaya.

'Pure gold, my girl,' answered Rayvan with a chuckle.

Valtaya smiled.

'That's better!' said Rayvan.

'How do you do it? How do you stay so strong?'

'I fake it.'

'That can't be true. You turned the tide today – you were magnificent.'

'That was easy. They killed my husband and my sons and they have nothing left to make me suffer. My father used to say that you can't stop a man who knows he is right. At first I thought it was a nonsense. An arrow through the gizzard stops anyone. But now I know what he meant. Ceska is unnatural, like a snowstorm in July. He cannot succeed just so long as enough people stand up to oppose him. All over the empire word of the Skoda rebellion will be spreading and other groups will rise up. Regiments will mutiny, honest men will take up their swords. He cannot win.'

'He can win here.'

'It will be shortlived.'

'Ananais believes that Tenaka Khan will return with a Nadir army.'

'I know,' said Rayvan. 'I don't feel too comfortable about that.'

In the next room Decado lay awake, his wounded shoulder throbbing. He smiled as he heard Rayvan's words. You can't fool a woman like her, he thought.

He stared at the wooden ceiling, ignoring the pain from his wound. He was at peace. Katan had come to him, telling him of the boy Ceorl, and Decado had been close to tears. All things were falling into place. Death was no longer a living fear.

Decado eased himself into a sitting position. His armour lay on a table to his right. Serbitar's armour. The Delnoch Thirty.

Serbitar was said to have been filled with doubts and Decado hoped that at the end these had been resolved. It was so good to *know*. He wondered how he could have been so blind to the truth when the facts shone before him with such crystal simplicity.

Ananais and Tenaka, drawn together near the Dragon barracks. Scaler and Pagan. Decado and The Thirty. Rayvan.

Every one a link in a web of mystery and magic. And who knew how many other links there were of equal importance?

Valtaya, Renya, Galand, Lake, Parsal, Thorn, Turs?

Pagan had been drawn from a far country to save one special child. But who would the child save?

Webs within webs within webs . . .

Perhaps the events themselves were merely links. The legendary battle for Dros Delnoch conspired after two generations to create Tenaka Khan. And Scaler. And the Dragon.

It was all too vast for Decado.

The pain in his shoulder flared once more and he grunted as it washed over him.

Tomorrow the pain would end.

Three more attacks began with the dawn. On the last the line almost gave way but Ananais, wielding two swords, hurled himself at the invaders in a berserk charge, cutting and cleaving his way through them. As they were thrown back a single bugle sounded in the enemy camp and the Joinings assembled, five thousand of them.

The beasts loped forward and the men of the Legion moved back through their ranks, leaving the way clear for the Joinings to advance.

Ananais swallowed hard and gazed left and right along the wall. This was the moment of dread. But there was no give in these Skoda men and he felt a surge of pride.

'There will be a warm fur rug for every man tonight!' he bellowed.

Grim laughter greeted the jest.

The beasts waited as the Dark Templars gathered among them – pulsing visions of blood and carnage, inflaming their bestial natures.

The howling began.

On the wall Decado called Balan to him. The dark-eyed priest approached and bowed formally.

'It is near the time,' said Decado.

'Yes.'

'You will remain behind.'

'What?' said Balan, stunned. 'Why?'

'Because they will need you. To link with Tarsk.'

'I don't want to be alone, Decado!'

'You will not be alone. We will all be with you.'

'No. You are punishing me!'

'It is not so. Stay close to Ananais and protect him as best you can. Also the woman Rayvan.'

'Let someone else stay. I am the worst of you – the weakest. I need you all. You cannot leave me alone.'

'Have faith, Balan. And obey me.'

The priest stumbled back from the ramparts, running headlong into the shadows of the trees beyond.

On the plain the howling grew to a terrible crescendo.

'Now!' cried Decado.

The seventeen warrior priests slid over the ramparts and dropped to the ground below, walking towards the beasts now some hundred paces distant.

'What in thunder?' said Ananais. 'Decado!' he bellowed.

The Thirty advanced in a wide line, their white cloaks flapping in the breeze, their swords in their hands.

The beasts charged, the Templars running behind them and spurring them on with mind-blasts of fearful power.

The Thirty dropped to their knees.

The leading Joining, a giant beast almost eight feet tall, staggered as the vision hit him. Stone. Cold stone. Shaped.

Blood, fresh blood, dripping from salty meat.

The beast ran on.

Stone. Cold stone. Wings.

Blood.

Stone.

Wings. Shaped wings.

Thirty paces separated the beasts from The Thirty. Ananais could watch no longer and turned his back upon the scene.

The Joining leader bore down on the silver-garbed warriors kneeling before it.

Stone. Shaped stone. Wings. Marching men. Stone . . .

The beast screamed.

Dragon. Stone Dragon. MY DRAGON!

All along the line the Joinings slowed. The howling faded. The image grew in strength. Long-lost memories struggled to surface. Pain, terrible pain burned in the awesome bodies.

The Templars pushed hard, sending searing mind-bolts at the beasts. One Joining turned and lashed out, his talons ripping a Templar's head from his shoulders.

The massive Joining leading the others halted before Decado, its great head hanging down, its tongue lolling. Decado looked up. Holding the image in the beast's mind, he saw the sorrow in its eyes. It *knew*. Its taloned arm came up and tapped its chest. The long tongue rolled around a single word that Decado could only just make out:

'Baris. Me Baris!'

The beast turned and ran back screaming towards the Templars. Other Joinings followed it and the Templars stood rooted to the spot, unable to comprehend what was happening. And then the beasts were upon them. But not all the Joinings were former Dragon and scores of them milled in confusion until one focused on the silver-garbed warriors.

It ran forward, followed by a dozen of its fellows.

In their trance state The Thirty were defenceless. Only Decado had the power to move . . . And he did not. The Joinings fell upon them, snarling and lashing out.

Decado closed his eyes and his pain ended.

The Templars fell in their hundreds as the beasts rampaged through the camp. The giant Joining that had been Baris, the Lord of the Dragon, leapt upon Maymon as he tried to run. With one bite he tore the man's arm from his shoulder. Maymon screamed, but a lashing blow from a taloned paw tore away his face, drowning the scream in blood.

Baris lunged to his feet and ran at the tent of Ceska.

Darik hurled a spear that took him in the chest, but it did not penetrate deeply and the Joining pulled the weapon clear and charged on.

'Legion, to me!' yelled Darik. Archers peppered the beast with arrows, but still it came on.

All over the field Joinings were collapsing, screaming in their death throes.

Still Baris pushed on. Darik watched in amazement as the giant Joining seemed to shrink before his eyes. An arrow pierced the beast's chest and it stumbled, then Darik ran forward to plunge his sword into the Joining's back. It tried to roll over . . . And died. Darik turned it with his foot. The beast quivered and he stabbed once more. Then he noticed that the movement had nought to do with life – it was reverting to human form. He turned away.

All over the plain the beasts were dying – all but the small group ripping at the silver-garbed warriors who had brought this chaos upon them.

Ceska sat within his tent. Darik entered and bowed.

'The beasts are dead, sire.'

'I can make more,' said Ceska. 'Take the wall!'

Scaler gazed down at the dead Templar. Two Sathuli warriors ran ahead to catch the dead man's horse, while Magir ripped the arrow from the man's throat and stuffed a cloth into the wound, staunching the blood.

Hastily they unbuckled the man's black breastplate, pulling it clear. Scaler wiped spots of blood from the straps. Two warriors carried on stripping the Templar as Scaler opened the leather pouch hidden inside the breastplate. Within it was a scroll, sealed with the sign of the Wolf. Scaler pushed it back into the pouch.

'Hide the body,' he said, and ran back into the haven of the trees.

For three days they had waited for a messenger on the lonely road through Skultik. Magir had downed him with a single arrow – it was fine marksmanship.

Back at the camp Scaler examined the seal. The wax was green and

733

marbled; there was nothing like it among the Sathuli. He toyed with the idea of opening it, then thrust it back in the pouch.

Sathuli outriders had brought news of Tenaka Khan. He was less than a day from the fortress and Scaler's plan had to be put into effect immediately.

Moving to the armour, Scaler tried on the breastplate. It was a little large. Removing it, he pierced the leather strap with his dagger point, tightening the buckle. Better.

The helm was a good fit, but Scaler would have been happier had the man not been a Templar. It was said they could communicate mind to mind. He hoped there were no Templars at Delnoch.

'When do you go in?' asked Magir.

'Tonight. After midnight.'

'Why so late?'

'With luck the commander will be sleeping. He will be drowsy and less inclined to question me.'

'This is a great risk, Lord Earl.'

'Don't remind me.'

'I wish we could have descended on the fortress with ten thousand tulwars.'

'Yes,' agreed Scaler uneasily. 'That would have been nice. Still, never mind!'

'You are a strange man, my Lord. Always the jest.'

'Life is sad enough, Magir. Laughter is a thing to be treasured.'

'Like friendship,' said the Sathuli.

'Indeed.'

'Was it hard being dead?'

'Not as hard as it is to be alive without hope.'

Magir nodded solemnly. 'I hope this venture is not in vain.'

'Why should it be?'

'I do not trust the Nadir.'

'You are a suspicious man, Magir. I trust Tenaka Khan. When I was a child, he saved my life.'

'Then he too is reborn?'

'No.'

'I do not understand.'

'I did not rise full-grown from the grave, Magir. I grew like any other child.'

'There is much I do not understand. But we shall leave it for another day. Now it is time to prepare.'

Scaler nodded, amazed at his own stupidity. How easily could a man betray himself.

Magir watched Scaler don the black armour, and he wondered. He was not a stupid man and he sensed the unease in the Earl, knowing in that moment that all was not as he had believed. And yet the spirit of Joachim had trusted him.

It was enough.

Scaler tightened the saddle-cinch on the black gelding and swung to the saddle, hooking the helm over the pommel.

'Farewell, my friend,' he said.

'May the god of fortune rest with you,' answered Magir.

Scaler heeled the gelding away through the trees. He rode for over an hour until at last the southern gates of Delnoch appeared before him, the great wall spanning the pass. It was so long since he had been home.

Two sentries saluted as he rode under the portcullis gate, turning left to the doors of the keep. A soldier came forward and took the reins as he dismounted.

Scaler marched forward and another sentry approached.

'Take me to the Gan,' ordered Scaler.

'Gan Paldin is asleep, sir.'

'Then wake him!' snapped Scaler, keeping his voice bleak and cold.

'Yes, sir. Follow me, sir,' said the man.

He led Scaler down the long torch-lit corridor, through the Hall of Heroes lined with statues and on up the marble staircase to Paldin's quarters. Once they had belonged to Scaler's grandfather. The sentry rapped on the door several times before a sleepy voice answered; the door swung open. Gan Paldin had pulled on a woollen robe. He was a short man of middle years, with large, protruding dark eyes. Scaler disliked him instantly.

'Could this not have waited?' asked Paldin testily.

Scaler handed over the scroll and Paldin ripped it open and read it swiftly.

'Well,' he said, 'is that it? Or is there a personal message?'

'I have another message, my Lord. From the emperor himself. He is expecting aid from the north and you are to allow the Nadir general through the gates. You understand?'

'How strange,' murmured Paldin. 'Let them through, you say?'

'That is correct.'

Paldin swung round, seizing a dagger from his bedside table. The blade swung up, resting on Scaler's throat.

'Then perhaps you would explain the meaning of this message?' he said, holding up the scroll for Scaler to read.

'*Watch out for Nadir army. Hold at all costs. Ceska.*'

'I do not intend to stand here for much longer with a knife at my throat,' said Scaler stonily. 'I do not wish to kill a general. Remove it this instant – or face the fury of the Templars.'

Paldin blanched but he removed the knife. The sentry had drawn his sword and was standing behind Scaler.

'Good,' said Scaler. 'Now read the message again. You will note that it says, "Watch out for Nadir army." Hence my message to you. "Hold at all costs" refers to the rebels and the damned Sathuli. What the emperor required of you is that you obey him. He needs the Nadir – you understand?'

'It is not clear.'

'It is clear enough to me,' snapped Scaler. 'The emperor has arranged a treaty with the Nadir. They are sending a force to help him stamp out the rebels, there and elsewhere.'

'I must have confirmation,' argued Paldin.

'Indeed? Then you refuse the emperor's orders?'

'Not at all. I am loyal, always have been. It is just that this is so unexpected.'

'I see. You criticise the emperor for not bringing you into all his plans?'

'Don't put words in my mouth. That is not what I said.'

'Do I look like a fool to you, Paldin?'

'No, that's . . .'

'What kind of a fool would I be, coming here with a letter that proved me a liar?'

'Yes, I see that . . .'

'Well, there are only two possibilities. I am a fool or . . . ?'

'I understand,' mumbled Paldin.

'However,' said Scaler, his voice taking on a more kindly tone, 'your caution is not without reason. I could have been a traitor.'

'Exactly.'

'Therefore I will allow you to send a message to confirm.'

'Thank you.'

'It is nothing. You have fine quarters here?'

'Yes.'

'Have you checked them thoroughly?'

'For what?'

'Hidden places where spies can lurk and listen.'

'There are no such places here.'

Scaler smiled and closed his eyes. 'I will search for you,' he said.

Gan Paldin and the sentry stood in silence as Scaler slowly turned on his heel. His finger stabbed out. 'There!' he said and Paldin jumped.

'Where?'

Scaler opened his eyes. 'There, by the panel. A secret passage!' He walked to the carved oak panelling and pressed a switch. The panel slid open to reveal a narrow walkway and a flight of stairs.

'You really should be more careful,' said Scaler. 'I think I will sleep now and travel back with your message tomorrow. Or would you prefer another messenger to go tonight?'

'Er . . . no!' said Paldin, peering into the web-shrouded chamber. 'How did you do that?'

'Question not the power of the Spirit!' said Scaler.

736

23

Ananais stepped down from the wall and joined Thorn, Lake and Galand on the grass below. Jugs of wine and plates of meat had been set out and the group ate in weary silence. Ananais had not watched as his old friend was torn apart, but he had turned back in time to see the power of the Templars ripped asunder by the awful ferocity of the dying beasts.

After that the Legion had attacked again, but half-heartedly. They were repulsed with ease. Darik called a halt while the bodies were cleared away: five thousand Joinings, three hundred Templars and another thousand soldiers had died in those terrifying minutes.

Ananais saw Balan sitting alone near the trees; taking a jug of wine, he joined him. Balan was a picture of misery, sitting with head bent staring at the ground. Ananais sat beside him.

'Tell me!' he ordered.

'What is to tell?' answered the priest. 'They gave their lives for you.'

'What did they do?'

'I cannot describe it to you, Darkmask. But simply they projected a picture into the minds of the beasts. The picture awakened that within them which was still human – it tore them apart.'

'Couldn't they have done it from the safety of the walls?'

'Perhaps. But the closer you are to a man, the stronger is your power. They had to get close in order to be sure.'

'And now only you are left.'

'Yes. Only Balan!'

'What is happening at Tarsk?'

'I shall find out for you,' said Balan, closing his eyes. Moments later he opened them again. 'All is well. The wall holds.'

'How many men did they lose?'

'Three hundred will not fight again. Only one hundred and forty have died.'

'*Only*,' muttered Ananais. 'Thank you.'

'Don't thank me,' said Balan. 'I loathe everything to do with this insane venture.'

Ananais left him and wandered back into the trees, pulling off his mask and allowing the cool night air to soothe his burning skin. Stopping by a stream he dunked his head, then he drank deeply. Rayvan saw him there and called out, giving him time to replace his mask.

'How goes it?' she asked.

'Better than we expected. But more than four hundred men are dead at both walls. At least another four hundred will not fight again.'

'How many does that leave us?'

'Around three hundred here. Five hundred at Tarsk.'

'Can we hold?'

'Who the Hell knows? Maybe one more day. Maybe two.'

'Still a day short,' said Rayvan.

'Yes. Tantalising, isn't it?'

'You look weary. Get some rest.'

'I will, lady. How are your wounds?'

'The scar on my face will enhance my looks. The hip is sore.'

'You have done well.'

'Tell that to the dead.'

'I don't need to,' said Ananais. 'They died for you.'

'What will you do if we win, Darkmask?'

'A strange question in the circumstances.'

'Not at all. What will you do?'

'Stay a soldier, I suppose. Re-form the Dragon.'

'What about marriage?'

'No one would have me. I am not exactly pretty under this mask.'

'Show me!' she said.

'Why not?' He pulled the mask clear.

'Yes,' she said, 'that is ghastly. I am surprised you survived. The fang-marks are almost at your throat.'

'Do you mind if I put this on again? I feel uncomfortable.'

'Not at all. It is said that you were once the most handsome man in the empire.'

'True, lady. In those days I would have swept you from your feet.'

'That's not saying much. I always had trouble saying no . . . And that was with ugly men. I even slept with Thorn once, though I daresay he wouldn't remember. It was thirty years ago – before I married, I might point out.'

'You must have been very young.'

'How gallant! But yes, I was. We are in the mountains, Darkmask, and there is precious little entertainment. But tell me, do you love Valtaya?'

'It's no business of yours,' he snapped.

'Indeed it is not. But answer me anyway.'

'Yes, I do.'

'This is going to sound hurtful, Ananais . . .'

'I wondered what we were leading up to.'

'Well, it is this: if you love her, leave her alone.'

'Did she ask you to come to me?'

'No. But she is confused, uncertain. I don't think she loves you. I think she is grateful and trying to prove it.'

'I take what I can get these days,' he said bitterly.

'I don't think that's true.'

'Leave me alone, Rayvan. Please!'

When she had gone Ananais sat alone for some hours, unable to sleep. His mind relived his triumphs, but strangely there was no longer any satisfaction in his memories. Cheering crowds, pliant women, envious men – he wondered if he had genuinely enjoyed any of it.

Where were the sons he should have bred?

Where was the woman of his heart?

Valtaya?

Be honest with yourself, man. Was it ever Valtaya? If you were still the Golden One, would you give her a second look? Dawn tinted the eastern sky and Ananais chuckled, then laughed aloud.

What the hell? He had lived as hard as a man could.

No use in morbid regret. The past was a dead beast anyway, and the future was a bloody sword in a Skoda valley.

You are nearing fifty years of age, he told himself, and you are still strong. Men follow you. The Drenai people depend on you. Your face may be gone, but you know who you are.

Ananais, the Golden One.

Darkmask, the Ceska Bane.

A bugle sounded. Ananais heaved himself to his feet and walked back to the ramparts.

Renya lay awake for the third night, angry and uncertain. The walls of her small tent crowded in on her and the heat was oppressive. For two days now the Nadir had been preparing for war; gathering provisions, choosing their ponies with care. Tenaka had selected two warlords to accompany him, Ingis and Murapi. Renya had learned this from Subodai, for not one word had passed between Tenaka and herself since the night before the Shamen Quest.

She sat up, hurling the sheepskin blanket across the floor. She was tired, yet tense as a bowstring. She knew why, yet knowledge was useless. She was in limbo, caught between her love of the man and her hatred of his mission. And she was lost, for her mind dwelt on him ceaselessly.

Renya's childhood had been built on rejection, for she was deformed and could not take part in children's games. They mocked her lame leg and twisted back and she withdrew into her room . . . and into her mind. Aulin had taken pity on her, giving her the gift of beauty through the machines of terror. But though outwardly she had changed, the inner Renya remained the same – fearful of affection lest it turned on her, afraid of love because it meant opening the heart and removing the defences. Yet love had taken her like an assassin's blade and she felt tricked. Tenaka had been a hero, a man she could trust. And she had welcomed the blade. Now she found it was tipped with poison.

She could not live with him.

She could not live without him.

The drab tent depressed her and she walked out into the night. The camp sprawled over almost half a mile, with Tenaka's tent at the centre. Subodai groaned and rolled over as she passed him. 'Sleep, woman!' he muttered.

'I cannot.'

He cursed and sat up, scratching his head. 'What's wrong with you?'

'None of your business.'

'His wives bother you,' decided Subodai. 'Natural for a Drenai woman. Greedy.'

'It has nothing to do with his wives,' snapped Renya.

739

'So you say! How come he put you out of his tent, eh?'

'I put myself out.'

'Mm. You're a good-looking woman, I will say that.'

'Is that why you sleep outside my tent? Waiting to be invited in?'

'Shhh, don't even whisper it!' said Subodai, his voice rising. 'A man could lose his head – or worse. I don't want you, woman. You are strange, crazy even. I heard you howl like an animal, watched you leap on those dumb Pack-rats. I wouldn't want you in my bed – I would never sleep for worrying!'

'Then why are you here?'

'The Khan ordered it.'

'So now you are his dog. Sit, stay, sleep outside the tent!'

'Yes, I am his dog. I am proud to be his dog. Better the hound of a king than a king among jackals.'

'Why?' asked Renya.

'What do you mean, why? Is it not obvious? What is life but a betrayal? We start out young, full of hope. The sun is good, the world awaits us. But every passing year shows how small you are, how insignificant against the power of the seasons. Then you age. Your strength fails and the world laughs at you through the jeers of younger men. And you die. Alone. Unfulfilled. But sometimes . . . sometimes there will come a man who is not insignificant. He can change the world, rob the seasons of their power. He is the sun.'

'And you think Tenaka is such a man?'

'Think?' said Subodai. 'What do I know of think? A few days ago he was Bladedancer. Alone. Then he took me. A Spear. Then Gitasi. Then Ingis. Then the nation. You understand? There is nothing he cannot do. Nothing!'

'He cannot save his friends.'

'Foolish woman. Still you do not see.'

Renya ignored him and walked away towards the centre of the camp. He followed her discreetly, keeping some ten paces behind. This was no hardship, for it allowed him to gaze at her with undisguised pleasure. His dark eyes lingered on her long legs and the subtle swing of her hips. Gods, what a woman! So young and strong. Such animal grace.

He began to whistle, but the sound died in an instant as he saw the tent of the Khan. There were no guards. He ran forward to Renya, pulling her to stop.

'Don't touch me,' she hissed.

'Something is wrong,' he said.

Her head came up, her nostrils catching the scents of the night. But the stench of the Nadir was all around her and she could detect nothing.

Dark shadows moved towards the tent.

'Assassins!' yelled Subodai, dragging clear his sword and running forward; the dark shapes converged on him. Tenaka Khan opened the flap of his tent, sword in hand, to see Subodai hacking and slashing his way forward. Tenaka watched him stumble and go down under the swinging blades.

740

He stepped out to meet the killers.

An eerie howl echoed through the camp and the assassins slowed in their advance.

Then the demon was upon them. A back-handed blow sent a man ten feet through the air. A second fell as her taloned hand opened his throat. Her speed was awesome. Tenaka ran forward, parried a thrust from a squat warrior, and slid his own blade between the man's ribs.

Ingis raced in with forty warriors and the assassins lowered their weapons, standing sullen-eyed before the Khan.

Tenaka cleaned his sword and then sheathed it.

'Find out who sent them,' he told Ingis, then strode to where Subodai lay. The man's left arm was gushing blood and there was a deep wound in his side above the hip.

Tenaka bound the arm. 'You'll live!' he said. 'But I am surprised at you, allowing yourself to be overcome by a few night-stalkers.'

'Slipped on some mud,' muttered Subodai defensively.

Two men came forward to carry the injured warrior to Tenaka's tent. The Khan stood up and looked for Renya, but she was nowhere to be seen. He questioned the warriors nearby and two of them claimed to have seen her running towards the west. Tenaka called for his horse.

Ingis approached him. 'It is not safe to go after her alone.'

'No. Yet I must do it.'

He climbed into the saddle and galloped through the camp. It was too dark to see a trail, but he rode on and out on to the Steppes. There was no sign of her.

Several times he slowed his horse and called out, but there was no response. Finally he stopped his mount and sat quietly staring at the land around him. Ahead to the left was a small grove of trees, screened by thick bushes. He turned his horse's head and cantered towards them, but suddenly the horse pulled up, whinnying in fear. Tenaka calmed the beast, stroking its neck and whispering soft words into its ear, but he could not make it move forward. He dismounted and drew his sword.

Logic told him that whatever was in the bushes could not be Renya, for the horse knew her. Yet something other than logic prevailed in his mind.

'Renya!' he called. The sound that greeted his call was like nothing he had ever heard: a keening, sibilant wail. He sheathed his sword and walked slowly forward.

'Renya! It is Tenaka.'

The bushes exploded outwards and her body hit him with immense force, hurling him from his feet to land on his back. One of her hands was locked about his throat; the other hovered above his eyes, the fingers curved into talons. He lay still, staring into her tawny eyes. The pupils had become slits, long and oval. Slowly he lifted his hand to hers. The feral gleam died in her eyes and the grip on his throat loosened. Then her eyes closed and she slumped forward into his arms. Gently he rolled her on to her back.

The sound of hooves on the Steppes caused him to push himself upright.

Ingis galloped into sight, his forty warriors behind him, and leapt from the saddle. 'Is she dead?'

'No, sleeping. What news?'

'The dogs would say nothing. I killed all but one and he is being questioned now.'

'Good! And Subodai?'

'A lucky man. He will heal swiftly.'

'Then all is well,' said Tenaka. 'Now help me get my woman home.'

'All is well?' echoed Ingis. 'There is a traitor at large and we must find him.'

'He failed, Ingis. He will be dead by morning.'

'How can you be sure?'

'Wait and see.'

Tenaka saw Renya safely installed in his tent before accompanying Ingis to the place where the assassin was being questioned. The man had been tied to a tree and his fingers had been broken, one at a time. Now a fire was being prepared beneath his feet. Tenaka walked forward and stopped the torturers.

'Your master is dead,' he told the man. 'There is no further need of this. How do you wish to die?'

'I don't care.'

'Do you have family?'

'They know nothing of this,' said the man, fear in his eyes.

'Look in my eyes, man, and believe me. I shall not harm your family. Your master is dead and you have failed. It is punishment enough. All I want to know is: why?'

'I am pledged to obey,' said the man.

'You were pledged to me.'

'Not so. Only my warlord – *he* was pledged to you, but I broke no oath. How did he die?'

Tenaka shrugged. 'Would you like to see the body?'

'I would like to die beside it,' said the man. 'I will follow him even in death, for he was good to me.'

'Very well.' Tenaka cut the man loose. 'Do you need to be carried?'

'I can walk, damn you!' spat the man. Followed by Tenaka, Ingis and the forty warriors, he led them through the camp until he reached the tent of Murapi where two guards stood at the entrance.

'I have come to see the body,' said the man. The guards gazed at him nonplussed and realisation hit him like a blow.

He spun to face Tenaka. 'What have you done to me?' he shouted.

The tent-flap opened and Murapi stood forth. He was past middle age and stockily built. He smiled thinly.

'Of all men,' he said calmly, 'I did not think you could break this one. Life is full of such surprises!'

The man fell to his knees. 'I was tricked, Lord,' he sobbed.

'It doesn't matter, Nagati. We will speak of it on the journey.'

Tenaka stepped forward. 'You broke a life-oath, Murapi. Why?'

'It was a gamble, Tenaka,' replied the man evenly. 'If you are right the gates of Dros Delnoch will be open to us, and the entire Drenai empire with it. But you merely wish to rescue your Drenai friends. It was just a gamble.'

'You know the price of failure?'

'Indeed I do. Will I be allowed to kill myself?'

'Yes.'

'Then you will not harm my family?'

'No.'

'You are generous.'

'Had you stayed with me, you would have found out how generous.'

'Is it too late?'

'Indeed it is. You have one hour.'

As Tenaka turned to walk back to his tent, Ingis fell into step beside him. 'You are a subtle man, Tenaka Khan.'

'Did you think otherwise, Ingis?'

'Not at all, my lord. May I give my son, Sember, command of Murapi's wolves?'

'No, I will command them.'

'Very well, my lord.'

'Tomorrow they will guard my tent.'

'You like living dangerously?'

'Goodnight, Ingis.'

Tenaka stepped inside the tent and made his way to Subodai's bed. The warrior was sleeping soundly and his colour was good. Then he moved on into the rear section of the tent where Renya lay. He touched her brow and she woke, her eyes returned to normal.

'Did you find me?' she whispered.

'I found you.'

'Then you know?'

'I know.'

'Mostly I control it. But tonight there were so many of them and I thought you would die. I lost control.'

'You saved me.'

'How is Subodai? Did he live?'

'Yes.'

'He adores you.'

'Yes.'

'So . . . tired,' she said. Her eyes closed and, leaning forward, he kissed her lips.

Her eyes opened. 'You are trying to save Ananais, aren't you?' Her lids drooped once more. He lifted the blanket around her and returned to the centre of the tent.

There he sat down and poured himself a goblet of Nyis, sipping it slowly.

Was he trying to save Ananais?

Truly?

Or was he glad that the decision had been taken from him?

743

If Ananais were to die, what would stop him from continuing his war deep into the Drenai lands?

True he was not hurrying, but then what was the point? Decado had told him they could not hold. What purpose would it serve, driving his men day and night to arrive exhausted at the battlefield?

What purpose?

He pictured Ananais standing defiantly before Ceska's hordes, sword in hand, blue eyes blazing.

He cursed softly.

And sent for Ingis.

24

The Legion swept forward and Lake's giant bows let fly with the last of the lead shot. Scores of men went down, mostly with leg injuries, for the infantry were more wary now and advanced with their shields held high. Archers sent a black cloud of arrows into their advancing ranks, then the ladders crashed against the walls.

The men of Skoda had moved beyond weariness and they fought like automatons. Their swords were blunted, their arms aching. Yet still they held.

Lake swept up a battle-axe, cleaving the blade through a helm that appeared over the battlements. The axe lodged in the skull and was torn from his grip as the man fell. Another soldier heaved his way over the wall, but Ananais ran forward to pitch the invader head-first to the ground below. He handed one of his two swords to Lake, then ran to the right where the line was bending back.

Balan joined him. And Galand. The defenders steadied, and rallied. To the left three Legion warriors broke through, leaping from the ramparts to the grass below and sprinting towards the hospital building. The first fell, an arrow piercing his back. The second stumbled as another shaft glanced from his helm, stunning him. Then Rayvan stepped from the building with sword in hand.

The men grinned as they ran at her.

With surprising speed she blocked the first blow and then dived into them, her great weight hurling them to the ground. Her sword snaked out, slicing the throat of the first.

The second man rolled clear. 'You fat sow!' he yelled.

Rayvan heaved herself upright as the man charged forward. Then Thorn loosed an arrow that thudded into the soldier's thigh; he shouted in pain and swung round. Rayvan's sword plunged into his back. She watched the battle on the wall for several moments . . . The line would not hold for much longer.

Galand fought beside Ananais now, moving where the battle was most deadly. The Legion, sensing victory close at hand, did not fall back but milled below the wall, pushing their ladders high. More and more Legion men gained the ramparts.

Ananais could feel the battle ebbing from them and a cold fury settled over him. Despite the odds against them, and his certain knowledge that they could not win, it still galled him terribly. He had done little with his life, save never to lose. Now even this small comfort was being stripped from him at the death.

He blocked a lunge, spun his blade and plunged it up and under a black helm. The man fell back, dropping his sword which Ananais swept up as he advanced into the mass, two swords now whirling and killing. He was bleeding from a score of minor cuts, but his strength was unimpaired.

A tremendous roar went up from behind the wall. Ananais could not turn, but he saw the consternation in the eyes of the invaders. Suddenly Rayvan was beside him, a shield on her arm and a sword in her hand. The Legion were pushed back.

The women of Skoda had arrived!

Lacking skill with weapons, they threw themselves forward lashing out blindly, bearing the invaders before them by sheer weight of numbers.

The last Legion warrior was hurled from the wall and the Skoda men took up their bows, sending the invaders running back out of range.

'Clear the dead from the ramparts!' shouted Ananais.

For several moments there was no movement as men hugged their wives and daughters, sisters and mothers. Others knelt by still bodies, weeping openly.

'There is no time for this,' said Ananais, but Rayvan caught his arm.

'There is always time for this, Darkmask – it is what makes us human. Leave them be.'

Ananais nodded and sagged to the ramparts, pushing his aching back against the wall.

'You amaze me, woman!'

'You are easily amazed,' she said, sliding in beside him.

He glanced at her and grinned. 'I'll bet you were a beauty in your youth?'

'I've heard you were, too!'

He chuckled and closed his eyes.

'Why don't we get married?' he suggested.

'We shall be dead by tomorrow.'

'Then we should forget about a long engagement.'

'You are too old for me, Darkmask.'

'How old are you?'

'Forty-six,' said Rayvan.

'Perfect!'

'You must be desperate. And you are bleeding – get off and have those wounds seen to.'

'One proposal and already you are starting to nag.'

'Women are like that. Go on with you!'

She watched him walk to the hospital, then pulled herself to her feet and transferred her gaze to the Legion. They were forming up again.

Rayvan turned to the defenders. 'Clear the dead from the walls, you numbskulls!' she shouted. 'Come on now. Move yourselves. You women, grab some swords. And find yourselves some helmets,' she yelled as an afterthought. A dead Legion soldier lay close to her and she tugged loose his helm before rolling the body from the ramparts. The helm was bronze with a black horse-hair plume. It fitted well, she thought, as she buckled the chin-strap.

'You looked damned fetching, Rayvan,' said Thorn, moving alongside her.

746

'Fancy people in helmets, do you, you old stag?'

'I have always fancied you, woman! Ever since that day in the north meadow.'

'Ah, you *do* remember? That is a compliment.'

Thorn laughed. 'I don't think any man would forget you.'

'Only you would talk about sex in the middle of a battle. You are a goat, old man! At least Ananais had the courtesy to ask me to marry him.'

'Did he now? Don't accept – he has a roving eye.'

'It won't rove far in a day,' she said.

The Legion charged again.

For an hour they fought to gain a toehold on the ramparts, but the defenders had found fresh strength and courage. Lake had gathered sacks of small stones which he poured into the bowls of his giant bows. Three times the missiles whistled and slashed into the Legion before one of the bows snapped under the strain.

The invaders fell back.

As the sun fell on the third day the wall still held.

Ananais called Balan to him. 'What news of Tarsk?'

'It is strange,' said Balan. 'There was one attack this morning, but since then nothing. The army merely sits.'

'I wish to Heaven they would do that here,' said Ananais.

'Tell me, Darkmask, are you a believer?'

'In what?'

'You mentioned Heaven.'

'I don't know enough to believe,' said Ananais.

'Decado promised me that I would not be alone. And yet I am. The others have gone. Either they are dead and I am a fool, or they have been taken to the Source and I am refused.'

'Why should you be refused?'

Balan shrugged. 'I never had faith, I had talents. My faith was part of a corporate faith. You understand? The others believed and I felt their belief. With them gone . . . I don't know any more.'

'I cannot help you, Balan.'

'No. No one can.'

'I think maybe it is better to believe than not to believe. But I couldn't tell you why,' said Ananais.

'It creates hope against the evil of the world,' said Balan.

'Something like that. Tell me, do husbands and wives stay together in your heaven?'

'I don't know. That has been a debating point for centuries,' said the priest.

'But there is a chance?'

'I suppose so.'

'Then come with me,' said Ananais, pulling the man to his feet. They walked across the grass to the tents of the refugees where Rayvan sat with her friends.

She watched them approach, then Ananais halted before her and bowed.

'Woman, I have a priest with me. Do you wish to wed again?'

'You fool!' she said, chuckling.

'Not at all. I have always wanted to find a woman with whom I would like to spend the rest of my life. But I never have. Now it looks as though I am going to spend the rest of my life with you. So I thought I would make an honest woman of you.'

'This is all well and good, Darkmask,' she said, pushing herself to her feet, 'except that I don't love you.'

'Nor I you. But once you appreciate my great qualities, I am sure you will come round.'

'Very well,' said Rayvan with a broad smile. 'But there will be no consummation until the third night. Mountain custom!'

'Agreed,' said Ananais. 'Anyway, I have a headache.'

'This is a nonsense,' snapped Balan. 'I will have no part in it – it makes a mockery of a sacred bond.'

Ananais laid his hand on Balan's shoulder. 'No, it does not, priest,' he said softly. 'It is a light-hearted moment in the midst of horror. Look around you at the smiles.'

Balan sighed. 'Very well. Both of you approach.'

Refugees poured from the tents as the word spread and several women gathered flowers which they turned into garlands. Wine was brought forth. Word even reached the hospital, where Valtaya had just finished working; she wandered out into the night, unsure of her feelings.

Ananais and Rayvan walked back to the ramparts hand in hand, and the men there cheered themselves hoarse. As they reached the steps he swept her to his shoulder and carried her up to the wall.

'Put me down, you lummox!' she yelled.

'Just carrying you over the threshold,' he explained.

Men swarmed around them and the noise of their laughter drifted to the Legion camp.

Ceska called Darik to him.

'What is happening?' he demanded.

'I don't know, sire.'

'They are laughing at me! Why have your men not taken the wall?'

'They will, sire. At dawn, I promise you!'

'If they do not, you will suffer, Darik. I am tired of this pestilential place. I want to go home.'

For three bloody hours the battle continued on the morning of the fourth day, but the Legion could not gain the wall. Ananais could scarce contain his joy, for even through his weariness he could sense the battle had swung. Without the Joinings the Legion fought mechanically, reluctant to risk their lives, while the men of Skoda battled with fresh heart and confidence. The heady wine of victory pounded in Ananais' veins and he laughed and joked with the men, hurling curses at the fleeing enemy soldiers.

But just before noon a marching column was seen to the east, and the laughter died.

Twenty officers rode into Ceska's camp, bringing with them five hundred arena Joinings from Drenan, specially-bred beasts standing eight feet tall – blended from the souls of men, bears of the north, apes of the east, lions, tigers and the grey timber-wolves of the west.

Ananais stood very still, his blue eyes scanning the horizon.

'Come on, Tani,' he whispered. 'By all that's holy, don't let it end like this.'

Rayvan joined him with Balan, Lake and Galand.

'There is no justice,' spat Rayvan. Silence greeted her comment, a silence that spread the length of the wall.

The giant Joinings did not hesitate in the camp but advanced in a wide line, their officers behind them.

Thorn tugged Ananais' sleeve. 'Got a plan, general?' he asked. Ananais glanced down at the old man, biting back the bitter reply as he saw the fear etched into Thorn's face. The man was grey and tight-lipped.

'No plans, my friend.'

The beasts did not charge but ambled forward bearing huge clubs, saw-edged swords, maces and axes. Their eyes were red as blood and their tongues lolled from gaping maws. They advanced in silence, a soul-sapping silence which ate away at the courage of the defenders. Men began to stir along the line.

'You must think of something to say, general,' urged Rayvan.

Ananais shook his head, his eyes bleak and empty. Once more he felt himself standing in the arena, tasting the bitterness of unaccustomed fear . . . watching the portcullis gate slowly lift . . . hearing the crowd fall strangely silent. Yesterday he could have faced these awesome beasts. But to have been in sight of victory – to have it so close that he could feel its sweet breath upon his brow . . .

One soldier leapt from the wall and Rayvan swung round.

'Olar! This is no time to leave!'

The man stopped and hung his head.

'Come back and stand with us, lad. We will all go down together – that's what makes us what we are. We're Skoda. We're family. We love you.'

Olar looked up at her, tears falling, and drew his sword.

'I wasn't running away, Rayvan. I was going to stand with my wife and son.'

'I know, Olar. But we must try at least to hold the wall.'

Lake nudged Ananais. 'Draw your sword, man!' But the giant did not move. He was no longer with them, but was fighting once more in a stone arena in another time.

Rayvan pulled herself up to stand on the battlements.

'Stand steady, my boys! Think on this: help is on the way. Turn back these creatures and we have a chance!'

But her voice was drowned in the terrifying blood-roar of the Joinings as they finally broke into a run. Behind them came the Legion.

Rayvan scrambled back as the beasts reached the wall. They needed no ropes and ladders – at full run they leapt, scrambling over the fifteen-foot rampart.

Shining steel met snarling fangs and ripping talons, but the first of the defenders were swept away. Rayvan thrust her sword into a gaping mouth and the Joining fell back, its teeth snapping the blade. Ananais blinked, dragging himself back to the present. Both his swords flashed in the bright sunshine. A beast towered over him but, stepping inside the first vicious sweep of an axe, Ananais plunged his right-hand sword into the creature's belly, twisting as the blade rammed home. A ghastly howl came from the Joining and it slumped forward, blood drenching the black-garbed warrior. Ananais pushed the beast clear, wrenching his blade from its body as another came to him, swinging a mace. He dropped his right-hand sword, took a double-handed grip on the left and sliced the blade through the creature's arm. Its taloned hand flew into the air, still clutching the mace as, screaming in pain and fury, it leapt at Ananais. The warrior ducked and drove his sword two-handed into the beast's belly as it went over him; it tore the sword from his hands.

Balan leapt from the battlements and ran back some twenty paces. Turning, he knelt on the grass and closed his eyes. Somewhere in all this pain and horror there had to be a purpose and a triumph. Yesterday the combined force of The Thirty had turned the Joinings back into men. Now there was only Balan.

He emptied his mind of all thought, reaching for the serenity of the Void, building his lack of thought into a channel to the beasts. He reached out . . .

And recoiled from the blood-lust and fury. Steeling himself he reached out once more.

Hate! Terrible, burning, all-consuming hate. He felt it and burned with it, hating the Joinings, their masters, Ananais, Rayvan and the world of untainted flesh.

No. Not hate. No hate. The horror washed over and past him. He was untouched, unsullied. He would not hate a man-made monster, nor even the man who had made them so.

The wall of hatred was all around him, but he pushed back.

He could not find a single memory to jolt the beasts, for they were not ex-Dragon, but he used the only emotion he could be sure they had known as men.

Love.

Love of a mother in a cold frightening night; love of a wife when all around you prove false; love of a daughter given so freely in a swift hug, in the first smile of a babe; love of a friend.

Growing in power, he sent out his feelings like a wave upon sand.

On the walls the carnage was terrible.

Ananais, bleeding from a dozen cuts and slashes, watched in horror as a Joining leapt at Rayvan and bore her from the battlements. He jumped after them. She twisted in the air and the Joining landed on its back with Rayvan above it. Her weight hammered the air from its lungs and, seeing

750

her chance, she rammed her dagger into its neck, rolling clear as the beast lashed out with its talon. It reared drunkenly to its feet and Ananais plunged his blade into the creature's back.

Above them the line broke and the beasts swept on over the battlements. The Skoda survivors broke and ran, but the Joinings surged after them, hacking them down.

Suddenly the beast closest to Balan staggered, dropping its sword and holding its head. A howl of despair filled the air and everywhere the Joinings fell back as the Skoda warriors watched in disbelief.

'Kill them!' shouted Galand, running forward and hacking his sword through a furry neck. The spell broke and the Skoda men fell upon the dazed beasts, cutting them down in scores.

'No,' whispered Balan. 'You fools!'

Two Joinings turned on the kneeling priest. A mace thundered down, smashing him from his feet, then talons ripped away his chest and his soul was torn screaming from his flesh.

The fury of the beasts returned and their murderous roaring rose above the sound of clashing steel. Galand, Rayvan and Lake sprinted with a score of warriors to the timber-built hospital. As Ananais cut his way through to them, a talon raked across his back, ripping his leather jerkin and snapping a rib. He twisted and stabbed out and the beast fell back. Hands pulled him inside and the wooden door was slammed shut.

A hairy fist smashed the wooden shutters of the window and Galand ran forward, spearing his sword through the creature's neck. A taloned hand grabbed his jerkin and hauled him against the wooden frame. He screamed once as giant jaws closed around his face, then fangs fastened upon his skull and it burst like a melon. His body was dragged though the window.

An axe splintered the upper door, narrowly missing Ananais' head. Valtaya stepped from the ward within, her face bone-white with fear. In her hand was a needle and thread and a bloody swab, which dropped from her fingers as she saw the werebeasts climbing through the open window.

'Ananais!' she screamed and he jumped back as the door burst open and a huge Joining with an axe leapt forward. Ananais lashed out savagely, opening a terrible wound across its belly which spilled its entrails to the wooden floor. The creature tripped and fell, dropping the axe which Ananais swept up.

Rayvan saw two Joinings running towards Valtaya and valiantly she leapt into their path, swinging her sword. A back-handed blow sent her reeling. Ananais beheaded a creature with the face of a lion and turned to aid Valtaya.

He hammered his axe into the back of the first Joining, tearing the weapon loose as swiftly as he could, but the second beast was towering over Valtaya.

'Here, you hellhound!' bellowed Ananais and the creature swung its great head, focusing on the puny black-masked figure. It backhanded the axe aside, ignoring the wound gashed in its forearm. Then its talons

snaked out, ripping Ananais' mask from his face and hurling him from
his feet. He hit the floor hard, losing hold of the axe. The creature leapt
towards him and he rolled to a standing position to launch himself feet-
first at the monster. Fangs snapped as his booted feet crunched home and
the beast was thrown back into the wall. Ananais swept up the axe and
whirled it in a murderous arc, caving in the creature's side.

'Behind you!' shouted Rayvan, but it was too late.

The spear entered Ananais' back, plunging through the lower chest.

He grunted, and twisted his powerful frame, tearing the weapon from
the Joining's talons. The creatures leapt forward and he tried to back
away, but the spear jammed against a wall. Ananais ducked his head and
grabbed the beast, pulling it into him in a bear-hug.

Fangs tore at Ananais' face and neck, but his mighty arms continued
to pull the creature forward on to the spear-point jutting from his own
chest. The Joining howled in pain and fury.

Rayvan watched it all and time appeared to freeze.

A man against a monster.

A dying man against a creature of darkness. Her heart went out to him
in that moment as she watched the muscles of his arms bunch and strain
against the power of the beast. She lurched to her feet, ramming her
dagger into the Joining's back. It was all the aid she could give . . . But
it was enough. With one convulsive heave Ananais dragged back the beast
and the spear-point plunged home.

Outside the rolling thunder of hooves echoed in the mountains. Men
of the Legion turned to the east, narrowing their eyes, trying to make out
the riders in the dust-cloud.

At the tent of Ceska, Darik ran forward, screening his eyes. What the
Hell was happening? Were they Delnoch cavalry? His mouth dropped as
the first line of riders appeared from the dust-storm.

Nadir!

Screaming for his men to form a shield ring about the emperor, he
dragged his sword from its sheath. It was impossible. How could they
have taken Delnoch so swiftly?

Legion men raced into place, forming their shields as a wall against the
riders. But there were too few, and none of them carried spears. The lead
horsemen leapt over the shield wall, swinging their mounts to attack from
the rear.

And then the wall collapsed, men running in all directions as the Nadir
swept over them. Darik fell in the doorway of the emperor's tent with a
lance through his chest.

Tenaka Khan leapt from the saddle and entered the tent with sword in
hand.

Ceska was sitting on his silk-covered bed.

'I always liked you, Tenaka,' he said.

The Khan advanced, his violet eyes gleaming.

'You were to be the Earl of Bronze. You know that? I could have had
you hunted down and killed in Ventria, but I did not.' Ceska wriggled his

fat frame back on the bed and knelt before Tenaka, wringing his hands. 'Don't kill me! Let me go away – I will never trouble you.'

The sword lanced out, sliding between Ceska's ribs.

The emperor fell back.

'See?' he said. 'You cannot kill me. The power of the Chaos Spirit is in me and I cannot die.' He began to laugh, high-pitched and shrill. 'I cannot die – I am immortal – I am a god.' He staggered to his feet. 'You see?' He blinked once, then sank to his knees.

'*No!*' he screamed and fell forward on his face. With one blow Tenaka severed the head. Gripping it by the hair, he walked out into the open and mounted his horse. Kicking the steed into a gallop, he rode to the wall where the Legion waited. On the plain every Legion soldier had been slain and the Nadir massed behind the Khan waiting for the order to attack.

Tenaka lifted the bloody head.

'This is your emperor! Lay down your arms and not one man will be slain.'

A burly officer leaned on the wall. 'Why should we trust your word, Nadir?'

'Because it is the word of Tenaka Khan. If there are any Joinings alive beyond that wall, kill them. Do it now if you want to live.'

Within the hospital building Rayvan, Lake and Valtaya struggled to break the lance pinning Ananais to the dead Joining. Thorn limped into the room, bleeding from a wound in the side.

'Get out of the way,' he said, taking up a fallen axe. With one blow he smashed the shaft. 'Now pull him off it.' With great care they eased Ananais from the spear and carried him to a bed where Valtaya plugged the wounds in his chest and back.

'Live, Ananais,' said Rayvan. 'Please *live*!'

Lake exchanged glances with Thorn.

Valtaya sat down beside Ananais and held his hand. The warrior's eyes opened and he whispered something, but no one could make out the words. Tears formed in Ananais' eyes, and he seemed to be staring beyond them. He made an effort to sit, but sagged back. Rayvan turned.

Tenaka Khan stood in the doorway. He came to the bed and leaned over the warrior, placing the mask carefully over his face. Rayvan moved aside as Ananais tried to speak and Tenaka leaned in close.

'Knew . . . you . . . would . . . come.'

'Yes, my brother. I came.'

'All . . . finished . . . now.'

'Ceska is dead. The land is free. You won, Ani! You held. As I knew you would hold. In the spring I will take you to visit the Steppes. I will show you some sights: Ulric's tomb, the Valley of Angels. Anything you would like.'

'No. No . . . lies.'

'No,' said Tenaka helplessly. 'No lies. Why, Ani? Why do you have to die on me?'

753

'Better . . . dead. No bitterness. No anger. Not much . . . of a hero now.'

Tenaka's throat seemed to swell and tears fell freely, splashing on the ruined leather mask. Ananais closed his eyes.

'*Ani!*'

Valtaya lifted his arm, feeling for a pulse. She shook her head. Tenaka stood, his face a mask of fury.

'You!' he stormed, pointing at Rayvan, his arm sweeping to take in the others. 'You miserable scum! He was worth a thousand of you.'

'Maybe he was, general,' agreed Rayvan. 'And where does that leave you?'

'In control,' he said, striding from the room.

Outside Gitasi, Subodai and Ingis waited with more than a thousand Nadir warriors. The Legion had been disarmed.

Suddenly a bugle sounded from the west and all heads turned. The warrior Turs and five hundred Skoda men came marching into the valley, followed by ten thousand Legion warriors, heavily armed and marching in fighting formation. Rayvan pushed past the Khan and ran to Turs.

'What happened?' she asked.

Turs grinned. 'The Legion mutinied and joined us. We came as fast as we could.' The young warrior looked around at the bodies littering the ramparts and the ground beyond.

'I see Tenaka was true to his word.'

'I hope so,' said Rayvan. Drawing herself upright, she walked back to Tenaka.

'My thanks, general, for your assistance,' she said formally. 'I want you to know that the entire Drenai nation will echo my words. I would like to offer you the hospitality of Dros Delnoch for a little while. While you are there, I shall journey to Drenan to gather a token of our appreciation. How many men did you bring?'

'Forty thousand, Rayvan,' he answered, smiling bleakly.

'Would ten gold Raq a head be acceptable as a token of our thanks?'

'It would indeed!'

'Walk with me a little way,' she said, and led him into the woods beyond the walls.

'Can I still trust you, Tenaka?' she asked.

He gazed about him. 'What is to stop me taking this land?'

'Ananais,' she said simply.

He nodded solemnly. 'You are right – it would be a betrayal at this time. Send the gold to Delnoch and I will leave for the north. But I will be back, Rayvan. The Nadir also have a destiny to fulfil.'

He turned to leave.

'Tenaka?'

'Yes?'

'Thank you for all you have done. I mean that.'

He smiled and a flash of the old Tenaka returned. 'Go back to your farm, Rayvan. Enjoy life – you have earned it.'

'You don't think politics would suit me?'

'It would suit you too well – I just don't want you for an enemy.'
'Time will tell,' she said.
She watched him return to his men.
Alone now, Rayvan bowed her head.
And wept for the dead.

Epilogue

Rayvan's rule was a popular one and the Drenai soon forgot the years of Ceska's terror. The machines at Graven were destroyed. Lake re-formed the Dragon, proving himself a skilled and charismatic general. Scaler married Ravenna, Rayvan's daughter, and took up his position as Earl of Dros Delnoch, Warden of the North.

Tenaka Khan fought many civil wars, absorbing each defeated tribe into his own army. Renya bore him three sons.

Ten years to the month after Ceska's defeat, Renya died in childbirth. Tenaka Khan gathered his army around him and rode south to Dros Delnoch.

Scaler, Lake and Rayvan were waiting for him.

And the gates were closed.